LANGUAGE
Its Structure and Use

Third Edition

Edward Finegan
University of Southern California

Harcourt Brace College Publishers

Fort Worth   Philadelphia   San Diego   New York   Orlando   Austin   San Antonio
Toronto   Montreal   London   Sydney   Tokyo

Publisher	Earl McPeek
Acquisitions Editor	J. Claire Brantley
Market Strategist	John Meyers
Project Editor	Elaine Richards
Art Director	Vicki Whistler
Production Manager	James McDonald

Cover credit: Kevin Tolman, Bare Bones Graphics

ISBN: 0-15-507827-5
Library of Congress Catalog Card Number: 98-71177

Address for Orders
Harcourt Brace College Publishers, 6277 Sea Harbor Drive, Orlando, FL 32887-6777
1-800-782-4479

Address for Editorial Correspondence
Harcourt Brace College Publishers, 301 Commerce Street, Suite 3700, Fort Worth, TX 76102

Web site Address
http://www.hbcollege.com

Harcourt Brace College Publishers will provide complimentary supplements or supplement packages to those adopters qualified under our adoption policy. Please contact your sales representative to learn how you qualify. If as an adopter or potential user you receive supplements you do not need, please return them to your sales representative or send them to: Attn: Returns Department, Troy Warehouse, 465 South Lincoln Drive, Troy, MO 63379.

Printed in the United States of America

8 9 0 1 2 3 4 5 6 7   0 1 6   9 8 7 6 5 4 3 2 1

Harcourt Brace College Publishers

PREFACE

For more than two millennia, philosophers, rhetoricians, and grammarians have analyzed and described the structures of human languages and the uses to which those structures can be put in particular contexts. In the twentieth century, linguists and cognitive scientists have broadened and deepened our understanding of language, including knowledge of its mental representation and its use in the high and low affairs of women and men. In recent decades, as space explorers have revised our images of the satellites of Uranus and microbiologists have traveled further into the recesses of DNA, so linguists have contributed a burst of new insight into the nature of language. In *Language: Its Structure and Use,* you will uncover a glimpse of language as linguists understand it at the beginning of the twenty-first century.

Despite the impressive pace at which investigators have gained insight into the nature and behavior of human language, many arenas are underexplored and many questions remain unanswered. As today's insights replace those of yesterday, we are reminded that tomorrow's will replace today's. There is far more yet to be discovered about language than is now known, and plenty of intellectually exciting and socially useful work remains for future generations—including student readers of this book. You are invited to participate in advancing knowledge of language, which is the single most powerful tool of human endeavor and one, remarkably, that is available to all human beings equally.

A WORD TO STUDENTS

Throughout this book you will find words in boldface type. When an important concept is first discussed (not necessarily when it is first mentioned), the term for it is set in boldface, thus highlighting its significance and indicating that it is defined in the Glossary (which begins on page 585 and is tabbed at the edge of the pages to make finding it easy). In the Glossary you can find terms defined or characterized whenever you need to refresh your memory. On the inside front cover you will find tables of English vowel and consonant symbols and on the inside back cover the consonant symbols used throughout the book. To learn more about a topic than you can find in this book, the Suggestions for Further Reading at the end of each chapter will steer you in useful directions. At the end of each chapter you'll also find a list of Internet and Other Resources—interesting and helpful videos and Internet addresses. Be sure to visit Harcourt Brace's Web site at http://english.harbrace.com/ling/ for additional support materials.

A WORD TO INSTRUCTORS

This book includes more topics than can normally be covered in a one-semester course. Typically, instructors cover the first six chapters and select from among the others according to their interests and the needs of their students. Students benefit from regular use of the Glossary, and you may wish to remind them of its availability from time to time. (I started reminding students about the Glossary after several told me at term's end that they hadn't realized the book contained one.)

The current edition differs from the previous one in several respects. Most apparent is the organization into three parts and the reordering of chapters, including the treatment of morphology before phonetics and phonology. This new organization accommodates most students because they find words more accessible to analysis than sounds and because morphology can be discussed without appeal to a phonetic alphabet, which can be daunting to students at the beginning of the term. The revised sequence invites instructors to teach morphology before phonology, but instructors who prefer the traditional order can still do that with this edition. To make the alternative orderings possible, the phonetics chapter and all but the morphophonology section of the phonology chapter are written in such a way that they can be studied without prior knowledge of morphology. To teach phonetics and phonology before morphology, instructors need only delay the section on "The Interaction of Morphology and Phonology" (pp. 125–131) until after they have taught the morphology chapter.

At the end of each chapter, you'll note some new features: a section on computers and language, a list of Internet and Other Resources, a division of references into Suggested Readings and Advanced Reading, and, for most chapters, separate sets of exercises for English and for other languages. Each chapter now opens with a section called What Do You Think?, which is designed to engage students prospectively in the contents of the chapter and to identify possible real world situations where the subject matter of the chapter may play a role. This edition also contains sidebars to supplement the text with points related to chapter topics.

A WORD ABOUT PHONETIC TRANSCRIPTION

Settling on a particular phonetic transcription is tricky business because custom in the United States strongly favors a modified version of the International Phonetic Alphabet, at least for transcribing English. But throughout the world, many linguists strictly favor the IPA. In this edition, I have increased the number of IPA symbols used in the transcription of English but have kept a very few of the preferred American symbols for some sounds. In this fashion, the purposes for which phonetic transcription is introduced in an introductory textbook can be adequately met without burdening students with the entire IPA. And for instructors who prefer using the IPA especially for consonants, those symbols are given in tables and referenced throughout the book.

WORKBOOK AND ANSWER KEYS

Like the second edition of LISU, this edition has an accompanying workbook (*Looking at Languages,* Second Edition by Paul Frommer and Edward Finegan), which is useful in helping students review, apply, and even extend basic concepts.

The textbook and workbook have answer keys, which contain a few suggestions for presenting the material to students.

I welcome comments and suggestions from instructors and students. Letters may be sent through the publisher or directly to me via the following e-mail address: finegan@usc.edu.

ACKNOWLEDGMENTS

I have drawn on the work of many scholars whose analysis and writing provided a footing from which to address the issues taken up here. References at the end of chapters only hint at the range of scholarship I've relied on, and I am no less indebted to scholars whose work has influenced me but who are not cited. Many colleagues and not a few student readers have offered helpful comments about the third edition. To each of them (and to anyone whose name I may have inadvertently omitted) goes an expression of special appreciation. I am also grateful to the editors of Linguist List, which has proven a useful source of information and inquiry and whose readership offered many of the suggestions that have been incorporated into this revision. For helpful suggestions on particular matters, I am indebted to Dwight Atkinson, Robin Belvin, Betty Birner, Steve Chandler, Paul Fallon, Andreas Fischer, John Dienhart, William A. Kretzschmar, John Hedgcock, Peter Lazar, Gregory C. Richter, Deborah Schmidt, Robert Seward, and Gunnel Tottie.

I remain indebted to those who contributed to earlier editions, including John Algeo, Joseph Aoun, Doug Biber, Dede Boden, Larry Bouton, Leger Brosnahan, William Brown, Paul Bruthiaux, Allan Casson, Bernard Comrie, Jeff Connor-Linton, Marianne Cooley, Carlo Coppola, David Dineen, Sandro Duranti, Paul Frommer, Kaoru Horie, José Hualde, Larry Hyman, Yamuna Kachru, Audrey Li, Ronald Macaulay and his students, Erica McClure, Joseph L. Malone, James Nattinger, John Oller, Doug Pulleyblank, La Vergne Rosow, Harold F. Schiffman, Trevor Shanklin, Robert R. van Oirsouw, Rebecca Wheeler, Roger Woodard, and Anthony Woodbury. The second edition benefited from data contributed by Zeina el-Imad Aoun, Liou Hsien-Chin, Yeon-Hee Choi, Du Tsai-Chwun, Eric Du, Jin Hong Gang, José Hualde, Yong-Jin Kim, Won-Pyo Lee, Mohammed Mohammed, Phil Morrow, Masagara Ndinzi, Charles Paus, Minako Seki, Don Stilo, and Bob Wu.

Thanks go, too, to the instructors who offered very useful feedback and revision suggestions in reviews of this third edition: Anthony Aristar, Texas A & M University; Janet Cowal, Portland State University; John Hagge, Iowa State University; Christine Kakava, Mary Washington College; Juliet Langman, Mary Washington College; Chad Thompson, Indiana–Purdue University; Edward Vajda, Western

Washington University; Heidi Waltz, University of California at Riverside; Thomas E. Young, Purdue University.

To Elaine Richards, Project Editor; Vicki Whistler, Art Director; and James Mc-Donald, Production Manager at Harcourt Brace go my thanks for intelligent editorial supervision and attentive production. A special word of appreciation must go to Leslie Taggart, who worked with me on the revisions for this edition and from the start contributed thoughtfully to making it more accessible and interesting. To Min Ju, I am indebted for her thorough indexing. Finally, I owe a special word of thanks to Julian Smalley, not only for his assistance with word processing and computer tutelage, but for a bounty of good cheer during the process of revision.

—Edward Finegan

CONTENTS IN BRIEF

CONTENTS IN DETAIL

CHAPTER 1

LANGUAGES AND

LINGUISTICS

◄►

WHAT DO YOU THINK?

Like you, two of your roommates are studying a foreign language. In a conversation among the three of you, one of them asks whether there is an ideal language and the other wonders what an ideal language would be like. What's your reply to them?

Suppose your fourth-grade daughter is looking at the newspaper and asks you what the word trial *means. Almost automatically, you ask her to read the whole sentence aloud. Then you tell her what* trial *means. Later she asks why you needed the whole sentence before answering her question. What do you tell her?*

At a family picnic, a fourteen-year-old boy is teasing his six-year-old cousin. He asks "Do you know when your birthday is?" When the cousin answers "September seventh," the fourteen-year-old retorts, "I didn't ask you when *your birthday is! I asked whether you* know *when your birthday is." What does the six-year-old know about language use that the older cousin teasingly pretends not to know?*

You and two friends are discussing what makes for good English. One friend reports that she and her family members almost always speak good English even at home among themselves but that she's heard some African-American classmates speaking Ebonics. She says Ebonics is just ungrammatical English. Your other friend disagrees. He claims that Ebonics is as grammatical as any other form of spoken English. They turn to you to resolve the issue. What do you say?

HUMAN LANGUAGE—THE WONDER OF IT

The daily newspaper of a major metropolitan area represents an impressive achievement of art and science, of business and technology. Each day's issue is crafted by reporters, editors, photographers, layout designers, advertising executives, accountants, secretaries, and printers, among others. Foresters grow the trees that lumberjacks fell to yield the pulp that produces the newsprint that carries the inks engineered by industrial chemists. People behind the scenes include the architects, engineers, bricklayers, and steamfitters who designed and built the structures; the maintenance and cafeteria staff who keep the buildings and people fueled and operating efficiently; and the designers, manufacturers, and software engineers whose achievements are the computers and printing presses. That pool of talent, skill, effort, and ingenuity comes together in a newspaper that, in the case of, say, the *Los Angeles Times*, appears in more than a million copies 365 days a year.

In the *Los Angeles Times* and other papers around the world you can find information about political success and failure, about poverty and plagues, about racial conflict here and religious harmony there, about political achievement and social anarchy, about medicine and health care, about entertainment, art exhibits, and music concerts, to name only a few. You can read editorials urging civic mindedness and tax reform, letters to the editor, advice from Dear Abby, film reviews and scheduled show times, stock market and weather reports, and information and comment about nearly countless other subjects. Several sections of the Sunday paper contain classified advertisements offering cars and pets for sale and apartments and commercial property for rent, along with a plethora of personal ads, some extending birthday greetings to relatives and friends dead and alive, others announcing religious ceremonies of more kinds on a single weekend than most people experience in a lifetime. The diversity of information, expression, and rhetorical forms in such a newspaper is breathtaking. The technology and wide-ranging know-how that make it possible, the army of reporters, critics, editors, publishers, typesetters, graphic artists, telephone operators, and others is daunting. It's easy to imagine tens of thousands of women and men, young and old, involved directly and indirectly in the creation, production, and delivery of just a single day's newspaper. Today's major metropolitan daily is an awesome phenomenon, a modern-day wonder, a twenty-first-century pyramid.

Of considerable human interest, tucked away in the "Life & Style" section of the *Los Angeles Times*, as in similar sections of newspapers and magazines elsewhere, readers can find personal ads like the one below. "Desperate," claims its brassy caption.

> SWF, 44, looks older, fatter, tall, opinionated, bossy, possibly senile, hates
> most things, tolerates music, dancing, movies, loves intelligence, laughing,
> broccoli. Seeks M.

With an obvious sense of humor, this SWF broadcast the sentences of her message through the 1,361,988 copies of the paper that were in circulation the day it appeared. In a mere 25 words she speaks volumes about herself and invites the companionship of male readers taken with her candor and whimsy.

Elsewhere in its pages, the paper displays punny headlines like "Graf Cut Down by Knee Surgery" (about Steffi Graf missing the Wimbledon and U.S Open tennis tournaments) and playful ones like "The Meter is Running" (about poet laureate Robert Pinsky, who wants "iambics on the Internet, verse on video and a poem on every tongue"). One also finds provocative headlines like "The Pastor and the Porn King"—an eye-catching and ear-fetching caption about Jerry Falwell (an American televangelist) meeting Larry Flynt (publisher of controversial magazines). The opening paragraph of the piece reads:

> They acted like long-lost pen pals. They said all the vitriol was behind them.
> They promised next time, they'd do lunch—or dinner, even—and since they
> were meeting at Larry's office in Los Angeles, next time they'd do it near
> Jerry's church in Lynchburg, Va.

Three sentences well calculated to keep readers reading. Falwell is quoted as saying about Flynt, "He is a warmhearted, very talented and very generous person. . . . And I'd like to be his pastor and his friend for the rest of my days." Nothing but a few words here. Just simple talk in simple sentences, but they offer a verbal glimpse of a sometimes topsy-turvy world.

In reading the book now in your hands you will come to see that in Desperate's ad, in the story about Falwell and Flynt, and in all the headlines, letters, editorials, reviews, and reports, the manifest language competence represents an achievement of immensely greater complexity and subtlety than the production and distribution of the newspaper itself. You will see that language constitutes an achievement far more wondrous than the publication of a major metropolitan newspaper. If publishing a newspaper is impressive, knowing and using language is an achievement of staggering proportions, diminished only by its familiarity and routine mastery by every ordinary child throughout the world. Knowledge of language is so taken for granted that its achievement seems small, but language is so complex in structure and so varied in use that it remains incompletely understood even after decades of continuing insight into its mysteries and after centuries of speculation about it.

In this book you will come to understand something of the complexity of human language and of what enables such complexity to be so easily mastered by every healthy child. You will analyze how language expresses meaning and how it is interpreted in context. You will find chapters treating dialects and the historical development of languages, the origins of English and its subsequent travels, writing and conversation, first language acquisition and foreign language learning, and differences and similarities among languages around the globe.

Language is the most central and powerful tool in achieving your educational goals, and it is the heart and substance of your social interaction, your sense of humor, and your intellectual maturity. It is a uniquely human phenomenon and a uniquely important one in understanding what it means to be human.

IDEAL LANGUAGES AND REAL LANGUAGES

Students sometimes ask whether there are any ideal languages. One answer might be that all languages are ideal. They have evolved to meet the needs of the particular social group and particular culture in which they function. Alternatively, one could say that no language is ideal. Languages are constantly changing, and that fact suggests continuing need for adaptation. In this section, we take a different approach to ideal languages.

TWO IDEAL LANGUAGES: UNEEKISH AND QUIKISH

One kind of ideal language system would organize a one-to-one correspondence between what you wanted to say and how you said it—between *content* and *expression*. Each thought would have an expression all its own, and each expression would represent just one thought. We can call this ideal language Uneekish and picture it as represented in the schema that follows:

UNEEKISH

A UNIQUE EXPRESSION FOR EVERY CONTENT

Content A ⟷	Expression "A"
Content B ⟷	Expression "B"
Content C ⟷	Expression "C"

In a language that organized such a one-to-one mapping between content and expression, no ambiguity would exist (even the word *it* would refer to the same thing no matter when or where it was used). Words like *him* and *her* would not exist in Uneekish because, as we now use them, they are shorthand devices to refer to any male or any female whose identity is made clear by the context. In an ideal language system like Uneekish there would be no synonymy because different expressions would never be used for the same content. If the expression *Steffi Graf* were used to refer to Steffi Graf, then Steffi Graf could never be referred to by any other expression, such as *she*. The phrase *in other words* would disappear from use because for any content there would be only a single expression; "other words" for it simply wouldn't exist. In Uneekish, communication would be consistently accurate and reliable for all speakers.

In some respects, the one-to-one matching between content and expression in Uneekish would be an ideal communication system. There would be no misunderstanding, no need to rely on context. But there would also be a downside: Uneekish would make the artful use of ambiguity and synonymy impossible—in jokes and poetry, for example. All wordplay, including puns and double entendres, would vanish from speech (and be sorely missed by many of us). Even simple abbreviations such as contractions and ordinary shorthand devices like pronouns would be impossible.

Rather than having a separate expression for each thought, a radically different kind of ideal language system would have the *same expression* for *every* thought—the same expression irrespective of the particular content you intended to convey. The sole expression needed in this kind of ideal language might be a simple "duh," and by uttering "duh" the content of your intended communication would be directly conveyed to your addressee. We can call this language Quikish and picture it as represented in the schema below:

QUIKISH

THE SAME EXPRESSION FOR ANY CONTENT

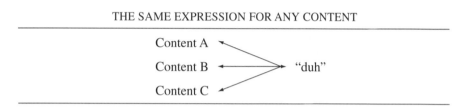

As with Uneekish, no communicative misfire could occur in Quikish. Whatever you wanted to convey would be unambiguously communicated simply by saying "duh." For example, your linguistics instructor would be refreshingly brief each day, walking into the classroom, perhaps raising a hand, and with due solemnity saying simply "duh." You and your classmates would then leave the lecture hall, knowing exactly what your instructor had intended to convey by the "lecture."

Now Uneekish, the first of our ideal languages, may appear initially to be within human reach. But in fact no natural language could achieve its one-to-one correspondence between content and expression because it could take hours or even days to utter moderately complicated thoughts in a one-to-one system, and it would take forever to learn such a language. Quikish, by contrast, would constitute an extraordinarily *efficient* language and be extremely easy to learn ("duh"), but it too would be an impossible language because it would require a degree of mental telepathy that lies beyond human ability—much to the frustration of infants who cannot yet express their needs verbally and much to the chagrin of adults stranded in a foreign culture whose language is unfamiliar to them. So much, then, for Uneekish and Quikish. At both ends of the expressive spectrum, such ideal languages lie beyond human capacities. In the real world all languages fall somewhere between our two ideal languages.

WHAT IS HUMAN LANGUAGE?

Like other inquiries central to human experience, questions about language and its functioning were not new to the twentieth century. As old as speculation on any subject, inquiry into the nature of language occupied Plato and Aristotle, as well as other

Greek and Indian philosophers. In some areas of grammatical analysis, the ancients made contributions that have remained useful for two thousand years, and some modern linguists regard Pāṇini, who lived near Kashmir in the fourth century B.C., as the greatest grammarian of all time. In the nineteenth and twentieth centuries the field of linguistics emerged to address certain questions, among them these:

- What is the nature of the relationship between signs and what they signify?
- What are the elements of language, and how are they structured into words, sentences, and discourse?
- What enables speakers to produce and understand sentences they have never heard before?
- How does language achieve its communicative function?
- In what ways do languages change and develop?
- In what ways are languages related to one another?
- What is the origin of language?
- What enables a child to learn a language so efficiently?
- What makes learning a foreign language so challenging for adults?
- What is the relationship between a language and a dialect?
- Are there right and wrong ways to say and write things, and, if so, who determines which is which?

This book provides a modern context for asking and addressing those questions. Here it is useful to make some general observations about the nature of language and offer a framework for understanding aspects of its structure, development, and use.

THREE FACES OF A LANGUAGE SYSTEM

Language seems to face in two directions, for the fundamental function of every language system is to link expression to content—to provide verbal expression for thought and feeling. A grammar can be viewed as a coin whose two sides are expression and meaning and whose task is to provide a systematic link between them. But there is more to the successful use of language than expression and meaning. Languages have a third face that is critically important for communicating and interpreting meaning, and that face is *context*. It is only in a particular context that the meaning of an expression can convey a speaker's intended content.

Imagine a holiday dinner conversation in which a guest asks the question, "Is there a state income tax in Connecticut?" Among the replies that this question is likely to elicit are "Yes," "No," and "I don't know." In other words, the question would ordinarily be taken as a request for information. Now consider an equally straightforward inquiry made by the same guest: "Is there any salt on the table?" In this instance, a host who earnestly replied "Yes," "No," or "I don't know," and let the matter rest there would seem dense.

Is there a state income tax in Connecticut?
Is there any salt on the table?

The form of the salt question resembles the form of the income tax question, but the point of the questions—their intended *content*—and the kinds of response expected could scarcely be more different. In the context of a dinner, a guest inquiring about salt would have every reason to expect a host to recognize that it isn't information about salt that's wanted but salt itself! And a host who ignored the *context* of the question and took it as a request for information would be regarded as dull indeed—or perhaps a tease. By contrast, in a related context—say, with the host standing in the kitchen, pepper mill in hand, and asking a guest who's just come from the dining room, "Is there any salt on the table?"—the host is likely to be understood as seeking information even though *the form of the question* and the meanings of its words are identical to those asked by the guest at the table. In the dining room, a reply of "Yes" or "No" would be bizarre. In the kitchen, "Yes" or "No" would be altogether appropriate.

You can see from these examples that conversationalists cannot always grasp the *content* of an utterance from expression alone. The meaning of the *expression* ("Is there any salt on the table?") is clear enough and remains stable from context to context, but the intended content of the message is *not* apparent from the expression alone. To grasp the intended content of an expression hearers must examine it *in light of its context*. In fact, in uttering expressions speakers routinely rely on a cooperative hearer's ability to recognize their intentions. In other words, effective language use is partly a guessing game (or an inferential calculus) in which a hearer must calculate what a speaker intended by uttering a particular expression in a particular context, and speakers plan their utterances on the assumption that hearers will rely on the context to help figure out the content.

Besides meaning and expression, then, there is a third aspect to language, and it is the *context* in which expression and meaning are linked. As represented in the triangle below, language is better viewed as a three-sided figure: expression, meaning, and context.

THREE FACES OF LANGUAGE

CONTEXT

In the case of the question "Is there any salt on the table?" the meanings of its words (*salt*, *table*) and phrases (for example, *on the table*) are the same in the dining room and the kitchen. But the intended use of the utterance—what we are calling its content—differs, and speakers expect hearers to interpret utterances in context.

Interpretation of expression requires knowledge of context. **Expression** encompasses words, phrases, sentences, and such pronunciation matters as intonation and stress. **Meaning** refers to the senses and referents of these elements of expression. **Context** refers to the social situation in which expression is uttered, and it includes whatever has been said earlier in that situation. **Content** refers to the intended message of an expression uttered in a particular context.

What links expression and meaning is grammar. What links grammar and interpretation is context, and grammar used in context is language. Without attention to both grammar and context, we cannot understand how language works.

LANGUAGE: MENTAL AND SOCIAL

Traditionally, language has been viewed as a vehicle of thought, a system of expression that mediates the transfer of thought from one person to another, and this is certainly one of its tasks. To view language solely this way, however, is to take a narrow perspective. In everyday life language serves social and emotional functions as well as intellectual ones, and these too are important.

Linguistics addresses language in two foundational arenas of human experience: the mental and the social. Linguists are interested in models of how language is organized in the mind and in how the social structures of human communities shape language, reflecting those structures in linguistic expression and interpretation. While knowledge of how languages are organized and put to use can be helpful in your interactions with members of your own and other societies, the main goal of this book is to provide an understanding of how human languages are structured and of how they function in social interaction.

SIGNS: ARBITRARY AND NONARBITRARY

⟶

We often use the word *sign* in everyday conversation. We talk about *signs* of trouble with the economy, no *sign* of a train coming into a railway station, someone's vital *signs* at the scene of an accident, and so forth. **Signs** are indicators of something else. In the examples we've just mentioned, the indicator is inherently related to the thing indicated—it is a nonarbitrary sign. That is to say, there is a direct, usually causal relationship between the indicator and the thing indicated. Smoke is a nonarbitrary sign of fire, clouds a nonarbitrary sign of impending rain.

ARBITRARY SIGNS

Nonarbitrary signs like clouds and smoke differ crucially from signs that are partly or wholly arbitrary. Arbitrary signs include traffic lights, railroad crossing indicators, flashing red or blue lights on police vehicles, wedding rings, national flags—and most notably *language*. There is no inherent connection between arbitrary signs and what they signify or indicate. For example, no property of the color red is inherently associated with stopping, but red lights are *conventionally* used to indicate that traffic must stop. Arbitrary indicators can be present even when the thing indicated is absent (as with a wedding band worn by a bachelor or a skull and crossbones on an empty poison bottle). There is nothing causal in the relationship between an arbitrary sign and what it signifies. Nor does anything in the nature of an arbitrary sign make it inherently better (or worse) than other potential representations for the same thing. If, for example, a national transportation department decided to use the color blue as a signal to stop traffic, nothing would prevent that from happening. Because they are only conventional representations, arbitrary signs can be changed. By contrast, it is impossible to change the relationship between smoke and fire or clouds and rain. Between words and what they represent the relationship is generally arbitrary. Language is a system of *arbitrary* signs.

REPRESENTATIONAL SIGNS

To make matters interesting, some essentially arbitrary signs are not entirely arbitrary. Sometimes an arbitrary sign can suggest its meaning to some degree. A skull and crossbones can indicate poison, ☀ can signify the sun, and the Roman numerals II and III refer respectively to the numbers two and three. These signs are not entirely arbitrary; they are partly iconic. But even in these cases there is no inherent connection between the sign and the thing signified. The sign can be present without the signified, and the signified can be present without the sign. Such basically arbitrary but partly iconic signs are called **representational signs**. Linguistic examples of representational signs might include *meow* and *trickle*, for it is commonly supposed that these words directly suggest what they signify.

Besides the kind of iconicity that words occasionally capture—as when the sound of *meow* echoes the sound of a kitten—iconic expression can appear spontaneously in ordinary speech. I once telephoned the home of a friend and had a brief conversation with her four-year-old son. I was trying to reach the boy's mother, but he reported that she was showering just then. I told him I'd call back in a few minutes, but he indicated that calling back soon would do no good. His explanation was this:

My mother is taking a *long, loong, looong* shower.

By repeating the word *long* and by stretching out his pronunciation of its vowel, the boy's expression directly captured his intended meaning—and demonstrated the potential for iconicity in human language. Representational (or iconic) language is linguistic expression that in any fashion mimics or directly suggests its content. The boy was iconically emphasizing the salient part of his meaning.

Similarly, certain aspects of grammar may show iconic influence. English, for example, has two ways of expressing conditional sentences:

If you behave, I'll bring you some candy. (condition + consequence)
I'll bring you some candy if you behave. (consequence + condition)

You have a choice between placing the condition (*if you behave*) before or after the consequence (*I'll bring you some candy*). Though contextual factors can influence the choice of alternative orders, speakers and writers show a strong preference for the first pattern (condition first, consequence second). This preference, also found in many other languages, is most apparent in speech. Why might the first pattern be preferred to the second? The answer has to do with the order of occurrence of real-world events described by conditional sentences. In this example, the hearer (the addressee) must first behave, and then the speaker will bring some candy. So the real-world events described by the sentences are ordered in time with condition first and consequence second. This real-world order is then reflected in the preferred linguistic order. There is thus an iconic explanation for preferring the condition-consequence order over the reverse order: With the condition-consequence order, the expression side iconically reflects or mimics the sequencing of events on the content side. Some languages allow *only* the condition-consequence pattern; others permit both patterns; but no language appears to limit conditional sentences to the non-iconic order of consequence before condition.

LANGUAGE—A SYSTEM OF ARBITRARY SIGNS

Despite occasional iconic characteristics, such as in the expression "a long, loong, looong shower," human language is *not* fundamentally representational. It is basically and essentially arbitrary. The form of an expression is generally independent of its meaning except for the associations that have been established by social convention. The fundamental arbitrariness of human language is unaltered by the fact that certain signs come to be so closely associated with what they signify that reaction to the sign may be as strong as reaction to what it signifies. Hence, the use of certain "four-letter" words can provoke strong reactions, and the burning of a national flag may be seen as the equivalent of treason.

We can illustrate the arbitrary nature of linguistic signs with a simple example. Imagine a parent trying to catch a few minutes of the televised evening news while cooking dinner. Suddenly a strong aroma of burning rice wafts into the TV room. This unmistakable *nonarbitrary sign* that the rice is burning will send the parent scurrying to salvage dinner. Contrast this nonarbitrary sign with the words of a youngster in the kitchen who sees the smoke and shouts, "The rice is burning!" As with the aroma, the youngster's utterance is likely to send the parent scurrying, but there is a world of difference between the signs. The aroma is *caused* by the burning rice and will convey its message to speakers of any language. There is nothing conventionalized about it; it is *nonarbitrary*. By contrast, the youngster's words are arbitrary. It is a set of facts about *English*—agreed to conventionally by generations of speakers—and not a set of facts about burning rice that enables the utterance to alert the parent. The utterance is thus an arbitrary sign.

Other languages would express the same meaning differently: Korean by the utterance *pap tʰanda*, Swahili by *wali inaunguwu*, Arabic by *yaḥtaqiru alruzzu*, and so on. The forms of these utterances have nothing to do with rice or its chemistry, or with the manner in which it is cooking, or with anything inherent in the situation; they are not iconic. Instead, they have to do solely with the nature of the systems of arbitrary expression that we call Korean, Swahili, and Arabic. Because the relationship between linguistic signs and what they represent is arbitrary, the meaning of a given sign can differ from culture to culture, and different cultures typically evolve different signs to represent the same thing. Even words that mimic natural noises are cross-linguistically distinct. Cats don't *meow* in all languages (compare Korean *yaong*, for instance).

A central fact about language is that the connection between the things signified and the words used to signify them—between signified and signifier—is arbitrary. In English, bakers make bread. The French call it *pain*, the Russians *xleb*. In Chinese, the word is *miànbāo*, in Fijian *madrai*. Not only can a given thing be signified differently in different languages, but even in a single language several signs can represent the same entity or notion. We purchase *a dozen* or *twelve* bagels for the same price. We can write 12 or XII for the same concept, as well as TWELVE, twelve, or Twelve. Thus, to represent even a straightforward numerical concept, English permits several alternative signs. For more complex content, the variety of possible expressions in phrases and sentences seems limitless.

LANGUAGES AS PATTERNED STRUCTURES

Precisely because the relationship between linguistic signs and what they represent is arbitrary, languages must be highly organized systems if they are to function as reliable vehicles of communication. If there were no pattern to the way we voiced our thoughts and feelings, listeners would face an insurmountable task in trying to unravel arbitrary signs for the meanings they encode.

To repeat: Language follows observable patterns that obey "rules." Language rules are not imposed from the outside and do not specify how something *should* be done. Instead, they merely capture the regularities that can be observed when people use language. In other words, the "rules" described in this book are based on the observed regularities of language behavior and of the underlying linguistic systems that we can infer from such language behavior. They are the "rules" that even children have mastered when as nine- or ten-year-olds they display extraordinary mastery of English—or Spanish or Mandarin or Japanese or Tok Pisin or Swahili. Language rules are more like the patterns describing how the digestive tract and the circulatory system work rather than traffic regulations or rules of protocol prescribing behavior with a visiting dignitary. Language rules are unconscious, not open to direct inspection, acquired without explicit teaching, and automatic.

A language is a set of elements and a system for combining them into patterned sentences that can be used to accomplish specific tasks in specific contexts. Utterances report news, greet relatives, invite friends to lunch, request the time of day, make wisecracks, poke fun, argue for a course of action, make inquiries, express admiration, propose marriage, create lost worlds—and so on, in an endless list. And languages accomplish their work with a finite system that a child masters in a few short years. The mental capacity that enables speakers to form grammatical sentences such as *My mother is taking a long shower* rather than "A taking long my shower is mother" (or literally thousands of other conceivable ill-formed strings of exactly the same words) is called **grammatical competence**. It enables speakers to produce an infinite number of sentences they've not generally heard before and to understand countless sentences they've never imagined.

SPEECH AS PATTERNED LANGUAGE USE

Of course there's more to the ability to speak than grammatical competence. Knowing the elements of a language and the patterns for putting them together into well-formed sentences falls short of knowing how to accomplish the work that speakers accomplish with language—it falls short of fluency. To be fluent in a language requires not only mastery of its grammatical rules but also competence in the appropriate use of the sentences that are structured by those rules. For example, fluency requires knowledge of how to put sentences together in conversations and of how to rely on linguistic and nonlinguistic context in shaping utterances appropriately, as well as interpreting them. Fluency presumes two kinds of competence: knowledge of how to form sentences (that's grammar) and knowledge of what those sentences do in various circumstances and of when and how to use them appropriately.

The capacity that enables us to use language appropriately is called **communicative competence**. It enables speakers (and writers) to weave utterances together into conversations, apologies, requests, directions, recipes, sermons, scoldings, or jokes and to do all the things that people do with language. When asked the whereabouts of the campus bookstore, a university student who replied "There's a great show about California condors on Channel 4 tonight" would certainly cause raised eyebrows, though you couldn't point to ungrammatical English as the culprit. The student's grammatical competence would appear to be fine, but his or her communicative competence would seem not up to snuff. Being a fluent speaker presumes both communicative competence and grammatical competence. Alone, neither one is sufficient to constitute fluency, which encompasses mastery of language structure and language use.

We can summarize by saying this: *Grammatical competence* is the language user's implicit knowledge of vocabulary, pronunciation, sentence structure, and meaning. *Communicative competence* is the implicit knowledge that underlies the appropriate use of grammatical competence in communicative situations. Because the patterns that govern the appropriate use of language differ from one speech community to the next, even a shared grammatical competence may not be adequate to make you a fluent speaker in another community, at least in some situations. For example, members of one culture may find jokes about other people's misadventures funny, whereas members of another culture may find them offensive. In fact, the very concept of telling jokes (*Did you hear the one about . . . ?*) as distinct from telling "funny stories" seems not to exist in certain societies. Likewise, even within the English-speaking world, what is considered impolite in one place might be routine interaction elsewhere. Differences in interactional customs explain why some visitors to the Big Apple think New Yorkers brusque or impolite when giving directions, though the same directions that provoke an unfavorable judgment in an outsider may be interpreted by a New Yorker as routinely polite.

THE ORIGIN OF LANGUAGES: BABEL TO BABBLE

A good many people in all parts of the world share a belief that the origin of language can be traced to the Garden of Eden, where the first woman and the first man spoke the language originally bestowed upon them by their creator. Even among people who may give little credence to that story, many are persuaded that language originated in a paradise where its pristine form was perfectly logical and grammatical. The belief is widespread that once-pure languages are becoming contaminated with illogicalities, ungrammaticalities, and impurities. English speakers and French speakers seem particularly inclined to worry over linguistic pollution, but they are not alone.

As examples of *impurities*, subscribers to this worried view cite borrowed words such as American *okay* and French *disco*, which have spread into many other languages, making them less "pure." Alleged *illogicalities* come in many shapes, with double negatives being a commonly cited English example. Here's the claim: Just as two negatives yield a positive in algebra or logic (*It is* **not un**true does mean 'It **is** true'), so *I do***n't** want **none** should logically mean 'I **do** want some' and *He* **never** *did* **nothing** should mean 'He **did** do something.' Of course they don't. Commonly cited among alleged ungrammaticalities is the use of the personal pronoun *I* in an expression like *just between you and I*, or the use of *him and me* as subjects (*Him and me were friends in the army*). The argument is offered that objects of a preposition must be in the objective case (thus, *just between you and me*) and that subjects of a sentence must be in the common (or subject) case (*He and I were friends in the army*). Of course, millions of speakers all around the globe use such allegedly impure, illogical, and ungrammatical expressions—and the sun continues to rise over them each morning and set each evening, and the moon continues to orbit around the earth, just as they do with those who deem their language use pure, logical, and grammatical. More to the point, no greater or more frequent misunderstanding arises among people using these disfavored expressions than among those using expressions alleged to be more pure, more logical, or more grammatical. The "laws" of language and the "laws" of logic are not the same, and linguistic signs are arbitrary.

As to why languages differ from one another and why they change, people have different ways of explaining the facts. The Old Testament relates that before the Tower of Babel all men and women spoke the same language and could understand one another. Eventually human pride provoked God into punishing people by confounding their communication with mutually unintelligible tongues. Given this story, language differences among people can be seen as a penalty for sinful behavior. Similarly, Moslems believe that God spoke to Mohammed in pure and perfect Arabic, which the Koran embodies. By contrast, the varieties of present-day Arabic spoken in the Gulf, North Africa, and elsewhere are seen as deriving from the subsequent weakness and culpability of their speakers.

Professional linguists take a different approach. They see the multiplicity of languages as resulting from natural historical change, the inevitable product of shaping and reshaping speech to meet people's changing social and intellectual needs and as reflecting contact with people speaking still other languages. When groups of people move to new places and mix with speakers of different tongues or settle areas with unfamiliar flora and fauna, their language must adapt to new circumstances. Meeting people with strange artifacts and different views of the world and confronting unfamiliar aspects of nature invite linguistic accommodation and adaptation. As a result, languages have evolved quite differently around the globe.

As increasing numbers of languages have been examined and as the tools of linguistic analysis have been sharpened, what is even more striking than the differences among the world's languages is the remarkable extent of their similarities. But this fact should not be surprising. Given that all languages must conform to the constraints imposed by the structure of the human brain, limited variation is possible. Of the many conceivable kinds of language and language structure, only a relatively narrow band can in fact be found among the world's languages (as discussed in Chapter 7).

As you recognized the first time you heard a foreign tongue, there are marked differences across languages. Not only do Japanese and French sound distinct, but French differs from its close relatives Spanish, Italian, Rumanian, and Portuguese. Different social groups speak even the same language differently, and every social group controls a range of language varieties for use in different situations: the language of conversation differs from that of sermons and political speeches. Whatever the ultimate explanation of the origins of language and whatever one's faith, language is inherently variable. Speakers show a powerful tendency toward linguistic diversification, with some language varieties marking groups of *users* (Burmese and Brooklynese, for example) and others marking situations of *use* (legalese and computerese). Each language variety marks something of the social identity of those who speak it and of the situation in which it is used.

LANGUAGES AND DIALECTS

⟶

Everyone knows that people of different nations tend to use different languages. Along with physical appearance and cultural characteristics, language contributes to defining nationality. Even within one nation's borders, people often speak different languages. In Canada, for example, ethnic French-Canadians in Montreal and Quebec maintain allegiance to the French language, while ethnic Anglos maintain loyalty to

English. In Switzerland, French, German, Italian, and Romansch are spoken. In India, scores of languages are spoken, some confined to villages, others used regionally or nationally. Papua New Guinea has hundreds of languages, and an English-based language called Tok Pisin is used for communication across groups.

Wherever speakers of a language have geographical or social distances between them, considerable linguistic variation is likely. Striking differences can be heard between the varieties of French spoken in Quebec and Paris and the varieties of Spanish spoken in Madrid and Mexico City. English speakers from Sydney, London, Delhi, Dublin, and Chicago speak notably different varieties. Even within essentially monolingual countries like Germany, France, and England, there is linguistic variation from group to group, and Americans recognize regional variation when they speak of a "Boston accent" or a "Southern drawl." When Lyndon Johnson succeeded to the presidency after John F. Kennedy's assassination, the pronunciation of the chief resident of the White House changed dramatically, as it did when Bill Clinton succeeded George Bush.

Some people seem to believe that *other* people speak a dialect, whereas *they themselves* don't: they think they speak a language or even *the* language. The truth is that everyone speaks a dialect. Native-born American speakers of English speak American English, and that's a dialect. Native-born Australian speakers of English speak Australian English, and that's a dialect. American English, Australian English, and British English are national dialects. Since a language can be thought of as a collection of dialects, anyone who speaks a dialect of English speaks the English language, and anyone who speaks the English language does so by using one of its dialects.

WHAT ARE SOCIAL DIALECTS?

Language varieties differ not only across borders and from region to region within a nation but also across age, ethnic, gender, and socioeconomic boundaries. Speakers of American English know that white Americans and black Americans may speak differently even when they live in the same city. Similarly, middle-class speakers can often be distinguished from working-class speakers by the language variety they use. You know too that women and men may differ in how they use language and that your grandparents and your friends speak differently. The characteristic linguistic practices of ethnic groups, socioeconomic groups, and gender and age groups also constitute dialects. The simple fact is that most African American and white residents of the United States speak the same language, though they may speak it somewhat differently. Middle-class and working-class speakers of American English share the same language, though each group has distinctive ways of speaking. And though mainstream American women and men speak the same language, their speech differs in patterned ways—they speak different dialects (or "genderlects," as some call them). Throughout the world, in addition to geographical dialects, there are ethnic, social, gender, and age dialects.

DIFFERENT DIALECTS OR DIFFERENT LANGUAGES?

The Romance languages arose from the regional varieties of Latin spoken in different parts of the Roman Empire. Those dialects of Latin eventually gave rise to Italian, French, Spanish, Portuguese, and Rumanian, now the distinct languages of different nations. Though these tongues share some structural features of grammar, pronunciation, and vocabulary, the nationalistic pride taken by the Italians, French, Spaniards, Portuguese, and Rumanians contributes to viewing their language varieties as separate languages rather than as dialects of a single language. The opposite situation characterizes Chinese. Although not all Chinese dialects are mutually intelligible (for example, speakers of Cantonese and Mandarin cannot understand one another), speakers regard themselves as sharing a single language, and they highlight that unity by using a single writing system.

Whether two varieties are regarded as dialects of one language or as distinct languages is as much a social as a linguistic question, and the call is strongly influenced by nationalistic and religious attitudes. The Hindus of northern India speak Hindi, while the Moslems there and in neighboring Pakistan speak Urdu. Opinions differ as to how well they understand one another. Until relatively recently, however, these varieties constituted a single linguistic unit called Hindustani, and the fact that linguists now write grammars of "Hindi-Urdu" reflects a professional judgment that the two varieties require only a single grammatical description. Naturally, with the passage of time, these varieties—whose different names proclaim that their speakers belong to different social, political, and religious groups—will become increasingly differentiated, as Spanish and Portuguese have done over the centuries.

WHAT IS A STANDARD VARIETY?

No single variety of English can be called *the* standard. To begin with, there are different national standards: standard British English, standard American English, standard Australian English, standard Canadian English, and so on. But there are several varieties of standard British English and several of standard American English and so on. Suffice it to note that many varieties of standard English can be identified.

What then is a **standard variety?** There are two useful ways to address that question. First, we could identify as standard the variety used by a group of people in their public discourse—in newspapers, radio broadcasts, schools, and so on. In other words, we could identify a standard variety as the one used for certain activities or in certain situations. In this case, there would be many standard varieties depending on where you were. Alternatively, we could identify as standard the variety that has undergone a process of standardization whereby it is organized for description in grammars and dictionaries and encoded in such reference works. This alternative way is the more familiar one.

The selection of a particular variety to be standardized is usually a matter of historical accident—sometimes merely of who got there first. A standardized variety does not differ in character from other varieties. It is not more logical or more grammatical. Nor is there any linguistic sense in which it could be said to be better, even if for some purposes it may be more useful. For example, this book is written in a variety of English that has been standardized, and that fact makes it possible to read it in many parts of the world. Instead of using spellings that reflect my own pronunciation (or that of anyone else), I have used spellings that have been standardized for American English and that differ from British spellings in only a few familiar ways.

Typically, varieties that become standardized are the local dialects spoken in centers of commerce and government. In such centers the need arises for a language variety that will serve more than local needs—for example, in the distribution of technical and medical information, the proclamation of laws, and the publication of books. These centers are also where dictionary makers and publishers are likely to be located. Samuel Johnson lived in London while he wrote his dictionary, and Noah Webster lived in New England. Had history been a bit different, the varieties represented in their dictionaries might well represent the dialects of other groups. Dictionaries serve to describe—even enshrine—a variety of the language that can be used for public discourse across regions and even countries. Not all situations are typical, of course. In standardizing the Basque language and Somali, the authorities combined forms from the various regions into a single standardized variety so as to be socially and regionally inclusive.

IS THERE A RIGHT AND A WRONG IN ENGLISH USAGE?

Is there a right way and a wrong way of saying and writing things? For example, of the two spellings *honor* and *honour*, which is correct, or at least *more* correct? Of the pronunciations for the word *schedule*—Canadian "shedule" or American "skedule"—which is right? Should the break between theater acts be called an *intermission* (as in the United States) or an *interval* (as in the United Kingdom). Should *theater* be spelled *theatre?* Americans, Canadians, and Britons may prefer their own expressions, but all these alternatives are correct, depending on who and where you are and what you want to accomplish. If you say "shedule" in the United States, you identify yourself as Canadian. If you say "skedule" in Canada, you may identify yourself as a Yankee. Well, you may say, that's fine for spelling and pronunciation from country to country. But what about within a country? And what about grammar—isn't grammar a different matter? For example, shouldn't road signs that say *Drive Slow* really say *Drive Slowly?* Aren't some things just plain ungrammatical? Aren't some structures right and others wrong?

To answer that question, it helps to think of grammar as a *description* of how language is organized and how it behaves. In that case, ungrammatical sentences of English would include these:

> Experience different something allergy season this.
> Season experience something different allergy this.
> Somerience diffthing seaserenton thallergyis exper.

The three strings of words above are *ungrammatical* variants of *Experience something different this allergy season*, which is a grammatical sentence that appeared in a print ad promoting an allergy medicine. No one who speaks English would normally say or write any of the three ungrammatical strings, and in that sense they *are* ungrammatical.

Another view would count as ungrammatical any violation of a relatively small set of prescriptive "rules" like these:

- Never end a sentence with a preposition.
- Never split an infinitive.
- Never begin a sentence with *and* or *but*.
- *It's me* is ungrammatical; *it is I* is grammatical.

Such prescriptions arose in the eighteenth century, and even then they did not accurately describe the language that people used. Commentators in this prescriptive tradition have formulated rules for what they regard as the "proper" use of *shall* and *will*, and they have condemned phrases like *between you and I* and completely banned the use of the word *ain't*.

Partly from this prescriptive tradition arose sympathy for judgments that some common expressions are unacceptable or ungrammatical, as with *Me and him would sit and talk all day* and *He don't like to cook* or *It don't matter*. These sentences are not standard English, but they are perfectly grammatical in some varieties. They are completely rule governed. One way in which varieties of English differ from one another is in their rules, and different rules lead to different grammatical structures. It is unreasonable to judge as ungrammatical the sentences permitted by the rules of one variety simply because they don't follow the rules of another variety. That logic would allow us to judge as ungrammatical any expression that is permitted in standard American English but not in British English. Standard English is not the only variety with a grammar and grammatical rules.

All functioning varieties are fully grammatical. Not all have been standardized, and not all are standard. In early 1997 when Ebonics was a hot topic in newspapers throughout the United States, many commentators judged its sentences to be ungrammatical. Of course, the sentences of Ebonics might well be ungrammatical if judged by the rules of another variety. But by that standard, all varieties of English except Ebonics would be ungrammatical if judged by the rules of African American English (as most linguists call Ebonics). African American English, like all other varieties of English, is perfectly regular and perfectly grammatical.

Because language relies essentially on arbitrary signs to accomplish its work, there is no justification for believing that there is only one right way of saying something. If you can accept that Japanese and French are both grammatical and that American English and British English are both grammatical, then it is logical to accept that Brooklynese and Washingtonese and African American English are grammatical. Different from one another, of course. But ungrammatical? No way. From a linguistic point of view, there is no basis for preferring the structure of one language variety over another. Judgments like "illogical" and "impure" are imported from outside the realm of language and represent attitudes to varieties or to forms of expression within particular varieties. Often they represent judgments of speakers rather than of speech.

Throughout this book we use the notion "ungrammatical" only to characterize utterances that *cannot* be said by native speakers of a language. We limit the term "ungrammatical" to an utterance like *Book the reading am I right now* (compare *I am reading the book right now*) because it does not occur in the speech of those who know English (except as an example of an ill-formed sentence made up for use in textbooks like this one). We do not call an expression like *just between you and I* "ungrammatical."

MODES OF LINGUISTIC COMMUNICATION

People have different ways of communicating. You can communicate feelings and moods with gestures, as dancers do, or through music or painting. You can draw sequences of figures, as on a treasure map. Channels of artistic communication like these fall outside the realm of linguistic communication and lie beyond the scope of this book. In linguistic communication, by contrast, meaning is conveyed chiefly through the channels of language. There are three basic **modes** of linguistic communication, corresponding to different modes of perception: oral communication, which relies on the use of speech and hearing organs; writing, a visual representation; and signing, also a visual (or tactile) representation.

SPEAKING

The most common vehicle of linguistic communication is the voice, and speech is a primary mode of human language and has some advantages over other modes. Because it does not need to be seen, speech can do its work effectively in darkness and in light, as well as around corners and in other visually inaccessible spots. Although in its natural state speech cannot span time, its physical reach is longer than arm's length. During the development of the human species, when hands and eyes were occupied in hunting, fishing, and food gathering—the manual activities of work and play—speech was free to do other work: to report, ask for and give directions, explain, promise, bargain, warn, and flirt.

Speaking has still other advantages. For one thing, the human voice is complex and has many channels. It has variable volume, pitch, rhythm, and speed: it is capable of wide-ranging modulation. Besides a set of sounds, speech takes advantage of the organization of those sounds—of their sequencing into words and sentences. Like writing and signing, speech can take advantage of word choice and word order.

WRITING

Long before the invention of writing, people had painted stories on cave walls and exploited other visual signs to record events. Such *pictograms* were independent of language—a kind of cartoon world, in which anyone with knowledge of the lives of people but without specific linguistic knowledge could reconstruct the depicted story. Pictograms (✳, for example) are language independent. When shown to adult speakers, depicted stories can be told in Japanese, Arabic, English, Swahili, Indonesian, or any other language. Pictograms can be understood in any language because they are a direct, nonlinguistic symbolization, like a silent film or the road signs used internationally to indicate a curved roadway or the availability of food and lodging.

If such drawings come to be associated not with the objects they represent but with the words that refer to the objects, we have a much more sophisticated system. Written representation becomes *linguistic* when it relies on language for its organization and communicative success. For example, while it is very difficult to use pictograms to express a message about abstractions (hunger or danger, for instance), the task becomes manageable if the graphic signs represent existing words. The moment some imaginative and inventive soul first recognized that the written sign ✳ could represent not only the sun itself but also the word *sun*, the initial step was taken toward the development of writing. Writing was invented about five thousand years ago by ingenious souls who chanced upon an occasion to use pictograms to represent spoken words instead of the objects they customarily represented.

Speech and writing are related in different ways to the world they symbolize. Speech directly represents entities in the world—things like sun, moon, fish, grain, light, and height. Writing, on the other hand, only indirectly represents the physical world. A written sentence like *Chris caught a fish* is a secondary symbolization in which the written signs represent the spoken words, not the entities themselves.

Writing has certain advantages over speech. For one thing, though it generally takes longer to produce than speech, it can be read much faster. Leaving aside recorded speech, writing—whether in letters or books, or on cave walls—endures longer than speech. For related reasons, writing has a greater reach geographically and chronologically. A message can be left on a blackboard for someone to read after its author has left the room. The same cannot be said for a spoken utterance.

SIGNING

The third mode of linguistic communication is signing, the use of gestures to communicate messages. All speakers use gestures and facial expressions to convey some meaning, but such gestures differ from signing in that they only support oral communication and would not be adequate by themselves for communication. By contrast, signing (also accompanied by facial expression and other gestures) can be used as the sole means of conveying messages and accomplishing the work of language.

Two kinds of signing are popular. One consists of spelling out words by "drawing" with the hands the shape of written signs (such as letters) that are used in writing to represent sounds. This method depends on the prior existence of a spoken language and requires a form of written representation. Thus, any signing system that relies on the modeling of letters (such as the one used by the deaf and blind Helen Keller) is two steps removed from the linguistic system that hearing and seeing children acquire.

A more common kind of signing is independent of the written and spoken word and can be used cross-linguistically, provided users understand the code. In this type of signing, particular gestures stand for particular words. The fact that these words may be pronounced differently from one language to another does not matter because the gesture does not make reference to the words of any language. Such a system was traditionally in use among certain American Indian nations in the western United States and among certain Australian Aborigine nations. It is also what underlies certain signing systems in use today. Signing differs from writing in that signers must be in full sight of one another to communicate successfully.

In this book we focus on language as represented in spoken and written communication. It is important to keep in mind that historically and developmentally writing is a secondary mode of linguistic communication. Speaking is the primary mode. This priority can be a challenge to students, whose principal focus and context for discussing language has been writing.

WHAT IS LINGUISTICS?

Linguistics can be defined as the systematic or scientific inquiry into human language—into its structures and uses and the relationship between them, as well as into the development and acquisition of language. The scope of linguistics includes both language structure (and the grammatical competence underlying it) and language use (and its underlying communicative competence).

Language is often defined as an arbitrary vocal system used by human beings to communicate with one another. This definition is useful as far as it goes, but it downplays not only writing and signing but an important fact that philosophers have emphasized about language. Language is more than communication. It is social action and has work to perform. It is a system that speakers, writers, and signers exploit purposefully. Language is used to *do* things, not merely to *report* them or *discuss* them: "That color looks terrific on you!" is not likely to be a mere report (whereas "Halloween falls on a Tuesday next year" might well be). More likely, it is a compliment. "Out!" is a mere opinion or conjecture when shouted by fans at a baseball game, but uttered by the umpire, "Out!" is a call—and it can end an inning or the game.

As mentioned earlier, people have been interested in language structure and language use for millennia. Plato and Aristotle discussed language in the fourth and third centuries B.C., and we have inherited several categories of grammatical analysis from them. More than a century earlier, Pāṇini wrote a description of Sanskrit that is one of the finest grammars ever produced for any language. Today, the empirical study of language has taken on additional importance in an age where communication is critical to social, intellectual, political, economic, and ethical concerns. Now augmented by insights from neurology, computer science, psychology, sociology, anthropology, philosophy, and rhetoric as well as from communications engineering and other sciences, linguistics has become a prominent academic discipline throughout the world.

WHAT ARE THE BRANCHES OF LINGUISTICS?

There are several branches of linguistics. Historically, the central branch has been *grammar*, and many linguists study grammatical systems—sentence formation, speech sounds, word structure, and meaning. Some are interested in the description of particular languages, others in uncovering universal patterns across languages and explaining them in cognitive or social terms.

Other linguists focus on *language variation*: across speech communities and within a single community, across time, across different situations of use—in conversation and sports announcer talk, for example. Like grammarians, linguists interested in variation seek two kinds of explanation—cognitive ones having to do with constraints on our human language-processing capacities and social ones having to do with the organization of societies and of social interaction.

A third group of linguists applies the findings of the discipline to real-world problems: In *educational* matters, to the acquisition of literacy (reading and writing) and of second languages and foreign languages. In *clinical* matters, to understanding aspects of Alzheimer's disease and aphasia. In *forensic* settings, to analysis of conversation for evidence of conspiracy, threats, defamation, and other possible illegalities; to interpretation of contracts (from rental agreements and insurance policies to agreements for manufacturing airplanes); to clarification of public safety instructions (like medical labels and dosage directions); and to identification of voices or the authors of documents. Other applied linguists address problems in *language policy* at national and local levels: what languages to designate for use in schools, courts, voting booths, and so on; what kind of writing system to aim for in a culturally diverse modern nation; what regulation of existing language is needed, as in the Plain English movement in the United States or in the development and production of the tools of standardization, such as dictionaries and grammars. As the world shrinks and cultures mix together, linguists are also applying the tools of their trade to the challenges of cross-cultural communication.

COMPUTERS AND LANGUAGE

 Each chapter in this book contains a section that discusses pertinent aspects of computers and language. You don't have to be a computer whiz or even computer literate to benefit from them. Even if your instructor does not assign these sections, you will probably find them helpful to read because they offer a different perspective on the chapter.

WHAT IS COMPUTATIONAL LINGUISTICS?

Computational linguistics has two principal objectives: to test theories of language and to apply linguistic knowledge to real-world problems by using computers. To understand something about using computers to test theories of language, it is helpful to view linguistics as a field of inquiry that attempts to make explicit what native speakers know implicitly about their language. Imagine trying to build a model of what a child must know in order to use its language. The model would have a list of elements—words, for example—and a set of rules for combining them into strings that would resemble the sentences of the child's language. To the extent that the implicit linguistic knowledge possessed by a fluent speaker can be made explicit in a model, investigators can use computers to test the accuracy of the model. In other words, a program incorporating the elements and rules of the model produces strings of words that can be checked to see whether they are in fact possible sentences. It is extremely challenging to make explicit what even a child must know in order to be a fluent speaker, and computers can assist in evaluating models by obediently and efficiently producing the strings that the model predicts to be sentences of the language. If you write a program that uses words and rules for combining them into strings, and that program generates strings like "a Chris caught fish" or "caught Chris fish a," you can be sure your rules are wrong because they produce strings that native speakers reject as *not* English.

As to applications, we mention two. Linguists and speech scientists would like to write programs that could synthesize speech from written text. You could then feed a printed page into a synthesizer that would read it aloud in a reasonably efficient and natural fashion. You are already familiar with synthesized music. Well, synthesized speech is related, even though producing modulations of the human voice has proven more challenging. You may know that machines for "text to speech" synthesis already exist, but linguists and speech scientists are far from satisfied with their success thus far. (If you want, you can have a computer synthesize speech from your written sentences at the Internet Web sites identified at the end of Chapter 4.)

The flip side of speech synthesis is speech recognition. Linguists would like to know enough about interpreting speech to enable computers to turn speech into writing and even to carry out spoken commands. A successful speech recognition program would allow physicians to make oral reports of their findings during a physical examination of a patient and to have the oral reports automatically converted to written ones. But this task, which is relatively straightforward for a human transcriber, is still so little understood that decades of research have not yet succeeded in enabling machines to do it as well as we wish. When computer programs are able to analyze speech and turn it into writing, applications will be plentiful and extremely valuable. At present, certain speech recognition and speech synthesis tasks can be accomplished in rudimentary ways, but a great deal remains to be achieved. In later chapters you'll see some of what has been achieved so far.

COMPUTERS AND MACHINE-READABLE TEXTS

In the middle of the eighteenth century when Samuel Johnson wrote his dictionary he chose illustrative sentences (called "citations") from books in order to exemplify how words were used by English authors. During his own reading, Johnson marked sentences whose particular context made a word's meaning or use especially clear. His assistants then transcribed the marked passages onto sheets of paper, and Johnson organized them to compile and illustrate the entries in his famous dictionary. In the nineteenth century essentially the same process was used to compile the *Oxford English Dictionary*. Under the supervision of Sir James A. H. Murray, that project required thousands of readers and ultimately consumed half a century to complete. In the twentieth century, *Webster's Third New International Dictionary* also relied on a collection of several million citations to discover different senses of words and to illustrate their uses. Today, dictionary making is changing dramatically, owing to advances in computers and the availability of computerized bodies of texts known as *corpora*.

The singular of *corpora* is *corpus*, which means 'body.' **Corpus linguistics** is the term used for the activities involved in compiling collections of texts and using them to help answer questions about language use. In this context a **corpus** is a systematically collected and representative body of texts. While nothing in the nature of corpus linguistics requires computers, as a practical matter reliance on computers makes it possible to manipulate the large body of texts in a modern corpus. You are already familiar with the kinds of machine-readable texts that are created by word processors, and at supermarket or department store checkout counters you have seen scanning devices that read barcodes from products in order to report prices and keep track of inventory. Machine-readable texts can be manipulated far more easily and rapidly than slips of paper. Computerized texts are simply machine-readable passages (ranging in size from a personal letter to a novel). Linguists compiled the first collections of computerized texts in the 1960s. The first computerized corpus—the Brown Corpus—included five hundred texts from American books, newspapers, and magazines that had been published in 1961. The texts were selected to represent 15 genres, including

science fiction, romance fiction, press reportage, scholarly and scientific writing, and popular lore. Each text in the Brown Corpus is 2000 words long, and the total collection contains a million words (500 texts of 2000 words each). Subsequently, researchers at universities in Europe collaborated to compile a parallel million-word corpus of British English called the London–Oslo/Bergen Corpus, or LOB for short. The two earliest major corpora are thus parallel collections of American and British writing that appeared in print in 1961. The Brown Corpus and LOB remain useful, and numerous studies of English have been based on them. Some data in this chapter and some of the exercises rely on findings from the Brown Corpus.

In the decades since these corpora were compiled, computers have become much cheaper and far more powerful; in addition, inexpensive, reliable scanners have been developed so that it is no longer necessary to keyboard texts into a computer. Those developments have made it easier to compile a corpus, and some recent corpora contain more than 100 million words. Corpora of languages other than English are also being compiled, and the field of corpus linguistics has important applications inside and outside the field of linguistics. With the widespread availability of personal computers nowadays, some universities offer courses in methods of compiling corpora and exploiting them for real-world applications. Corpora are proving useful, even essential, not only in dictionary making but in many other ways, including speech recognition and artificial intelligence.

SUMMARY

- Human language is an enormously complex system that is easily mastered by children in a remarkably short time.

- A linguistic system with maximally simple expression would have to rely on telepathy for conveying thought.

- Speakers of a language that made everything explicit would not need to rely on context but would have to expend enormous amounts of time learning their language and expressing things in it.

- Natural processes of linguistic change affect all languages over time, and linguistic change is not linguistic decay.

- All languages are equally logical (or equally illogical).

- Human language is a system primarily of arbitrary signs, but some linguistic signs are representational.

- Grammar is a system of elements and patterns that organizes linguistic expression.

- Linguistic communication can operate in three modes: speaking, writing, and signing.

- Computers can be used to test models of language as it is hypothesized to exist in the brain.

- In the developing field of corpus linguistics, large bodies of computerized texts called corpora are used to explore natural language use in all its contexts.

EXERCISES

1-1. With respect to an ideal language like Quikish, with only a single expression for everything you might want to say, what form would your final exam questions take? What about your answers and those of your classmates? Would everyone receive the same grade? Would all instructors be equally clear and equally appreciated as lecturers? How would you know what a grade of "duh" represented?

1-2. From a tape-recorded radio or television program list examples of various kinds (representing length, loudness, speed, repetition, ordering, etc.) in which the expression used is representational (i.e., iconic). (*Hint*: It may be easier to find examples in sitcoms or in programs for children or featuring children.)

1-3. Below is a list of characteristics that describe linguistic communication through speaking, writing, and signing. Decide which modes of linguistic communication the characteristic applies to, and provide examples to illustrate your claim. Pay particular attention to the different types of spoken, written, and signed communication, for some of these characteristics might apply to some but not others. Also note the impact of modern communication technology on these characteristics.

(1) A linguistic message is ephemeral—that is, it cannot be made to endure.
(2) A linguistic message can be revised once it has been produced.
(3) A linguistic message has the potential of reaching large audiences.
(4) A linguistic message can be transmitted over great distances.
(5) A linguistic message can rely on the context in which it is produced; the producer can refer to the time and place in which the message is produced without fearing misunderstanding.

(6) A linguistic message relies on the senses of hearing, touching, and seeing.

(7) The ability to produce linguistic messages is innate; it does not have to be learned consciously.

(8) A linguistic message must be planned carefully before it is produced.

(9) The production of a linguistic message can be accomplished simultaneously with another activity.

1-4. Consider the following quotation from a mid-twentieth-century dictionary (*A Pronouncing Dictionary of American English* by John S. Kenyon and Thomas A. Knott, Springfield, MA: Merriam, 1953, p. vi).

> As in all trustworthy dictionaries, the editors have endeavored to base the pronunciations on actual cultivated usage. No other standard has, in point of fact, ever finally settled pronunciation. This book can be taken as a safe guide to pronunciation only insofar as we have succeeded in doing this. According to this standard, no words are, as often said, "almost universally mispronounced," for that is self-contradictory. For an editor the temptation is often strong to prefer what he thinks "ought to be" the right pronunciation; but it has to be resisted.

  a. Provide two arguments to support the view that editors should resist the temptation to record their own personal pronunciation preferences in a dictionary. Do your arguments also apply to an editor's expressing his or her personal preferences for other aspects of language, such as spelling or usage? Explain your view.

  b. In what sense is it accurate to say that the phrase "almost universally mispronounced" is self-contradictory?

  c. What do you understand by the phrase "cultivated usage"? How would a dictionary editor determine whose usage is "cultivated"? Whose usage do you think a dictionary should set out to describe? Explain your view.

1-5. In writing papers and exams comparing natural conversation with written varieties of English, students sometimes claim that conversation is filled with errors and ungrammaticalities. The examples they point to include utterances like those given below. Offer an alternative explanation to the claim that they are errors.

> I was like, "Hi," and she goes, "Hi."
> I said, "Hi Pat," I went, she goes, "Hi Chris."

1-6. Consider the following quotation from John Simon's *Paradigms Lost* (New York: Penguin, 1980, pp. 58–59) concerning Edwin Newman's book *A Civil Tongue*:

> With demonic acumen, Newman adduces 196 pages' worth of grammatical errors. Clichés, jargon, malapropisms, mixed metaphors, monstrous neologisms, unholy ambiguities, and parasitic redundancies, interspersed with his own mocking comments . . . and exhortations to do better. The examples are mostly true horrors, very funny and even more distressing. . . .

Worse than a nation of shop-keepers, we have become a nation of word-mongers or word-butchers, and abuse of language whether from ignorance or obfuscation, leads, as Newman persuasively argues, to a deterioration of moral values and standards of living.

a. Simon seems to equate "grammatical errors" with clichés, jargon, malapro-prisms, and so on. Which of these can legitimately be called errors of grammar in the linguistic sense? What would be a more appropriate way to characterize the others?

b. Cite three ungrammatical structures that you have heard from nonnative speakers of English. Have you heard similar errors of grammar from native speakers? What do you judge to be the reason for your findings about native speaker errors and nonnative speaker errors?

c. The point that Newman and Simon make about "abuse of language" leading to a deterioration of moral values and standards of living is a common claim of language guardians. What kinds of abuse does Simon seem to have in mind when he makes that claim? Are he and Newman correct in claiming that such abuses lead to a deterioration of moral values? Could it be the other way around? What stake could anyone have in advancing the Newman/Simon claim? (Who are the winners and who are the losers if their view prevails?)

d. Do you think that genuine grammatical errors (like those nonnative speakers make) could lead to a deterioration of moral values? Explain your position.

1-7. Writing and gesture are visual modes of linguistic communication. What is the relationship between writing and Braille (the writing system used for blind readers)? Is Braille a mode of linguistic communication? How many modes of linguistic communication are there?

1-8. When there is a choice between linguistic modes, as in telephoning a distant friend or sending a letter, what are the advantages and disadvantages of each mode? List some of the circumstances in which each mode of linguistic communication would be preferred over the others.

INTERNET AND OTHER RESOURCES

Internet

A good deal of information and considerable laboratory experience are available on the Internet. In this section of every chapter you will find addresses that may help you understand the material in this book and provide you a laboratory unlike any previously available to beginning students of linguistics at even the best equipped universities. A word of caution: Internet addresses can change unexpectedly, so the ones given below may have relocated between the time of writing and the time you want to try them. If they have moved, there is sometimes an automatic connection possible to the new address from the old one. Updated addresses can also be found at the Harcourt Brace Web site—the first one given below—where you can also find new addresses that may interest you.

- **Harcourt Brace: http://english.harbrace.com/ling/**
  The Web site for users of this textbook. Provides updated Internet addresses as well as supplemental material for students and instructors.
- **The Field of Linguistics: http://www.lsadc.org**
  For general information go to the Web site of the Linguistic Society of America and click on "The Field of Linguistics." You will find brief treatments of language and thought, computers and language, endangered languages, prescriptivism, writing, slips of the tongue, language and the brain, linguistics and literature, and more than a dozen others.
- **A Basic Dictionary of ASL Terms:**
  http://www.masterstech-home.com/ASLDict.html
  Here you can find a large dictionary of American Sign Language signs, including schematics and definitions.
- **An Animated ASL Dictionary: http://dww.deafworldweb.org/asl/**
  At this Web site you can see animated representations for a substantial dictionary of ASL signs.

Videos
- **The Human Language Series**
  An award-winning set of videos, originally broadcast on PBS in 1995: *Discovering the Human Language*: *"Colorless Green Ideas," Acquiring the Human Language*: *"Playing the Language Game,"* and *The Human Language Evolves*: *"With and without Words."* The 55-minute videos are informative and entertaining. Available from Transit Media, 22 Hollywood Avenue, Ho-Ho-Kus, NJ 07423.

SUGGESTIONS FOR FURTHER READING

- **Jean Aitchison. 1996.** *The Seeds of Speech*: *Language Origin and Evolution* (Cambridge: Cambridge UP). A basic treatment of language beginnings.

- **Douglas Biber, Susan Conrad, and Randi Reppen. 1998.** *Corpus Linguistics*: *Investigating Language Structure and Use* (Cambridge: Cambridge UP). A basic introduction to corpus linguistics, accessible and useful.

- **David Crystal. 1997.** *Cambridge Encyclopedia of Language*. **2nd ed**. (Cambridge: Cambridge UP). Highly recommended; treats topics in a couple of pages each and usually offers interesting illustrations or photographs.

- **Ray Jackendoff. 1994.** *Patterns in the Mind*: *Language and Human Nature* (New York: Basic Books). Accessible, fascinating discussion of the cognitive aspects of language structure and language acquisition.

- **Edward Sapir. 1921.** *Language*: *An Introduction to the Study of Speech* (New York: Harcourt). A classic that remains in print because it continues to hold interest and yield insight; accessible even to novices.

Advanced Reading

Crystal's (1997) *Dictionary of Linguistics and Phonetics* is a useful reference work for a wide set of terms and concepts. Certain topics covered in this chapter are treated clearly and concisely in Slobin (1979). For discussion of the relationship between arbitrary and nonarbitrary signs consult de Saussure (1959). The papers in Haiman (1985) touch on the still little understood iconic elements in syntax and intonation. For sources on speaking and writing, refer to the "Suggestions for Further Reading" in Chapter 12. On standard varieties and attitudes to usage, see Finegan (1980) and Milroy and Milroy (1991). For information on American Sign Language and other sign languages, see Stokoe (1970), and for a survey of sign languages among Native Americans and Australian Aborigines, see Umiker-Sebeok and Sebeok (1978). On the origins of language, see Lieberman (1991). For various approaches to linguistics, see Sampson (1980). For corpus linguistics, see McEnery and Wilson (1996); for computers and language, Barnbrook (1996).

REFERENCES

- Barnbrook, Geoff. 1996. *Language and Computers* (Edinburgh: Edinburgh UP).

- Crystal, David. 1997. *A Dictionary of Linguistics and Phonetics,* 4th ed. (Oxford: Blackwell).

- de Saussure, Ferdinand. 1959. *Course in General Linguistics*, trans. from French by Wade Baskin (New York: Philosophic Library).

- Finegan, Edward. 1980. *Attitudes toward English Usage: The History of a War of Words* (New York: Teachers College P).

- Haiman, John, ed. 1985. *Iconicity in Syntax* (Amsterdam: Benjamins).

- Lieberman, Philip. 1991. *Uniquely Human*: *The Evolution of Speech*, *Thought, and Selfless Behavior* (Cambridge, MA: Harvard UP).

- McEnery, Tony, and Andrew Wilson. 1996. *Corpus Linguistics* (Edinburgh: Edinburgh UP).

- Milroy, James, and Lesley Milroy. 1991. *Authority in Language: Investigating Language Prescription and Standardisation,* 2nd ed. (London: Routledge).

- Sampson, Geoffrey. 1980. *Schools of Linguistics* (Stanford: Stanford UP).

- Slobin, Dan I. 1979. *Psycholinguistics,* 2nd ed. (Glenview, IL: Scott Foresman).

- Stokoe, William C., Jr. 1970. *Semiotics and Human Sign Languages* (The Hague: Mouton).

- Umiker-Sebeok, Jean D., and Thomas A. Sebeok, eds. 1978. *Aboriginal Sign Languages of the Americas and Australia,* 2 vols. (New York: Plenum).

PART ONE

LANGUAGE STRUCTURES

⌒

WORDS are the centerpiece of language, and when people think about languages they typically think of words. In examining language in this book, words are a focal point, and we begin our investigation of language structures by looking at words from four perspectives:

> their meaningful parts
> the sounds and syllables that make them up
> the principles that organize them into phrases and sentences
> the semantic relationships that link them in sets

In the first part of this book, you'll see how a small number of elements combine into speech sounds, how a few speech sounds combine to form a larger number of syllables, how syllables combine to produce word parts that carry meaning, and how languages package these word parts and a finite vocabulary into an infinite number of sentences. You'll also see how the systematic principles of language structure help you understand utterances even when you haven't heard or read them before. Finally, you'll examine the semantic relationships that organize sets of words.

CHAPTER 2

WORDS AND THEIR PARTS:

LEXICON AND MORPHOLOGY

WHAT DO YOU THINK?

These English-language signs were spotted in shops or hotels around the world. What do they indicate to you about how English words are formed or used?

- *Here speeching American.*
- *Take one of our horse-driven city tours. We guarantee no miscarriages.*
- *Please leave your values at the front desk.*
- *The lift is being fixed for the next day. During that time we regret that you will be unbearable.*

Suppose you are the parent of a three-year-old daughter who asks if you "maked" a cake and "speaked" with your friends and "telled" them about it. How would you describe the pattern your daughter uses to mark past time on these verbs?

Assume you teach English as a Second Language in a junior high school. You are teaching your students to change verbs into their "opposites," for example appear *into* disappear. *How many examples of such pairs can you think of?*

You have agreed to make a list of foods that volunteers could contribute to a fundraiser for a college athletic team about to undertake an international tour. All the items must have a name that English borrowed from another language. What foods, dishes, and drinks would be on your list? (If there are too many, limit yourself to one continent or one region!)

Suppose a nephew is having trouble learning the parts of speech for his junior high school English class. How would you teach him to figure out the part of speech of newer, boys, played, surprise? *After reading this chapter, come back to your answer and see if it has changed.*

If you were to guess the "top ten" words used in printed English, what would they be? Why did you choose these?

INTRODUCTION: WORDS ARE TANGIBLE

⟶

The most tangible elements of a language are its words. You've heard people say "There's no such word" or "What does the word *fledgling* mean?" Someone doing a crossword puzzle may have asked you a question like, "What's a three-letter word for 'excessively'?" We say that one person likes to use "two-bit" words while another has a preference for "four-letter" words. In all these instances people seem to have clear intuitions of what a word is.

On the other hand, when it comes to meaningful parts smaller than a word, our intuitions are less confident. Though we readily intuit that *car*, *sing*, and *tall* have a single meaningful part each and that *bookstore*, *laptop*, and *headset* have two each, our intuitions may be less certain about words like *bookkeeper*, *sneakers*, *women's*, *sang*, *presumption*, and *impracticality*. This chapter examines words and their meaningful parts, as well as the principles that govern the composition of words and their functions in sentences. You will see what it means to know a word and how languages expand their stock of words.

WHAT DOES IT MEAN TO KNOW A WORD?

⟶

Consider what a child must know in order to use a word. The child who asks "Can you take off my shoes?" knows a good deal more about the word *shoes* than what it refers to. Obviously, she knows the sounds in *shoes* and the sequence in which they occur. She knows that the word can be used in the plural (as distinct from nouns like *milk*) and that the plural is not irregular like *teeth* or *children* but is formed regularly. She also knows how to use the word in a sentence—for example, that it is a common noun and can be preceded by the word *my*.

Using a word requires four kinds of information:

- Its sounds and their sequencing (this is called *phonological* information and is discussed in Chapters 3 and 4)
- Its meanings (*semantic* information, discussed in Chapter 6)
- How related words such as the plural (for nouns) or past tense (for verbs) are formed (*morphological* information, treated in this chapter)

- Its category (e.g., noun or verb) and how to use it in a sentence (*syntactic information*, discussed here and in Chapter 5)

Using any word requires information about sounds, meanings, related words, and use in sentences, and that information must be stored in the brain's dictionary (called the *lexicon* or the *mental lexicon*) For every word he uses, a child relies on the four kinds of information stored in his lexicon as part of that word's entry.

There are some parallels between the kinds of information stored in the mental lexicon and the kinds that can be found in a desk dictionary. A desk dictionary contains information about pronunciation, meaning, related words, and sentence use. But it also contains information that is not needed for speaking—including information about a word's spelling and historical development (called its *etymology*). Good dictionaries also provide illustrations of how a word has been used by respected authors or speakers. Obviously a child's lexicon will not normally contain etymological, illustrative, or spelling information.

LEXICAL CATEGORIES (PARTS OF SPEECH)

The ability to use any word in a sentence requires knowledge of its *lexical category*. That means that even young children know the category of every word they use—they know which ones are verbs and which are nouns or adjectives, for example. Of course the child's knowledge is implicit, and even a grammarian's child wouldn't ordinarily know the *names* of the categories.

How To Identify Lexical Categories

There are several ways to help identify the lexical category of a word, and to some extent they rely on principles similar to those that children must use in figuring out the same information. One way focuses on the word itself and involves noting its closely related forms. In this respect, *fork* and *forks*, *book* and *books*, and *truck* and *trucks* show parallel patterns of related forms, and words with parallel forms belong to the same category—in this case, the one that grammarians call nouns. Words like *old*, *tall*, and *bright* have a different pattern. Unlike the nouns just examined, *old*, *tall*, and *bright* don't have related forms with -*s* ("olds," "talls," and "brights" are not English words). Instead, their related forms have -*er* and -*est* endings: *older/oldest*, *taller/tallest*, and *brighter/brightest*. *Old*, *tall*, and *bright* are thus members of a different category—in this case, the one called adjectives. Finally, words like *jump* and *kick* can appear with parallel endings, including -*ed* in *jumped* and *kicked*, -*ing* in *jumping* and *kicking*, and -*s* in *jumps* and *kicks*. Other words that share this pattern would include *laugh*, *play*, and *return*—all of which belong to the category of verbs.

Another way of identifying categories focuses on which words and categories can occur together in phrases. For example, the nouns above can be preceded by *the* and *a* (or *an*): *a fork/the fork*, *a/the book*, *a/the truck*, and the plural forms in -*s* can be preceded by *the* (though not by *a* or *an*). Basic adjectives like *old*, *tall*, and *bright* can be preceded by *very* or *too*, as in *very old*, *very tall*, and *too bright.* Basic verbs can follow the words *can* or *will*: *can kick, will laugh*, and so on.

Below are examples of these patterns for the three lexical categories of noun, adjective, and verb.

NOUNS

bike	bikes		a bike	the bike(s)
aunt	aunts		an aunt	the aunt(s)
camp	camps		a camp	the camp(s)

ADJECTIVES

old	older	oldest		very old	too old
new	newer	newest		very new	too new
red	redder	reddest		very red	too red

VERBS

look	looks	looked	looking		can look	will look
play	plays	played	playing		can play	will play
camp	camps	camped	camping		can camp	will camp

As a result of knowing the typical related forms in each lexical category, English speakers can readily gauge that *sharper* is related to the adjective *sharp* (compare *too sharp, very sharp*), *jackets* to the noun *jacket*, and *missed* to the verb *miss* (*missing/misses, can miss, will miss*). Dictionary users know that to locate a word requires seeking its base form because dictionaries do not have separate entries for words with endings like *sharper, jackets,* or *missed.* To generalize, we can say that from an early age English speakers recognize that words belonging to different categories have characteristic endings or forms and characteristic distributions in phrases. In more technical terms, different categories have different patterns of inflection and co-occurrence of categories.

A third way of identifying lexical categories relies not on properties of form or co-occurrence but on meaning. Relying on meaning is less trustworthy, however, and should be used principally to form an initial hypothesis if a word's related forms are not already apparent. From the perspective of meaning, nouns are said to name (or refer to) persons, places, or things: Thus, *swimmer, Cleveland,* and *trees* would all be nouns. Adjectives are said to name qualities or properties of nouns, as with *tall* and *impressive* in the phrases *the tall trees* or *an impressive swimmer.* Note that related forms of *tall* could be identified in *taller* and *tallest,* but related forms of *impressive* do not occur, although both *tall* and *impressive* can be preceded by *very* and *too,* thus making them adjectives. Verbs are said to describe actions, as with *jumped* and *missed.*

VERBS

English-speaking children know that **verbs** have a set of related forms: *talk*, *talks*, *talked*, and *talking*. They also know that the basic verb form—the one without an ending—can be preceded by *can* and *will*. This knowledge remains implicit, of course.

Subcategories of Verbs   For every verb, a child must also know the kinds of sentence structures it allows. Because a child must store this knowledge in its mental lexicon, it is convenient to treat it here. Consider sentences 1 through 6. An asterisk indicates an ill-formed sentence.

1. Sarah told the joke.
2. *Sarah laughed the joke.
3. *Sarah told at the joke.
4. Sarah laughed at the joke.
5. *Sarah told.
6. Sarah laughed.

Note that the verbs *told* and *laughed* do not permit the same complements. Sentences with forms of *tell* require a noun phrase complement (here, noun phrase means *the* plus noun) after the verb, as the ill-formedness of 5 demonstrates. Not all verbs require a noun phrase as complement, as 6 shows. In fact, *laugh* doesn't permit a noun phrase complement, as 2 illustrates, but it does permit the phrase *at the joke*, which is a prepositional phrase as we'll see in Chapter 5. Other verbs like *play* permit a following noun phrase but don't require one, as 7 and 8 demonstrate:

7. The diva played.
8. The diva played the piano.

Sentences 1 through 8 illustrate an important point about words like *tell*, *laugh*, and *play*. All belong to the *category* verb, but they permit different sentence structures. In other words, they belong to different *subcategories*. And information about **subcategorization** must be noted in a child's lexicon if the child is to avoid sentences like 2, 3, and 5. Verbs that take a noun phrase after them are called **transitive** while those that do not require a noun phrase are called **intransitive.** Each verb in a speaker's lexicon is categorized as a verb and subcategorized as transitive or intransitive.

NOUNS

Nouns constitute another class of words. We have already seen that English nouns share certain properties of form. They have a shared set of endings, or inflections. The inflection we examined above (*fork/forks*) represents information about *number*. **Number** is the term used to cover *singular* and *plural*, and many languages besides

English mark nouns for number. In English nearly all nouns have distinct singular and plural forms, as with the regular *cat/cats* and *dish/dishes* and the irregular *tooth/teeth* and *child/children*. A very few exceptions like *deer* and *sheep* have the same singular and plural form. Not all languages mark number on nouns. Chinese, for example, does not mark number on any nouns, just as English does not mark it on a few of its nouns. (In many languages, nouns occur in several categories called genders, and later in the chapter we examine gender and other inflectional categories besides number.)

ADJECTIVES

We saw above that many **adjectives** can be recognized by the pattern of their related forms, namely, the endings *-er* and *-est*, as in *larger* and *largest*. But many other adjectives, especially those of more than two syllables, do not permit these endings. Thus, **beautifuller* and **beautifullest* are not well-formed English words (and hence are starred). But *beautiful* is nevertheless an adjective, as demonstrated by its having similar co-occurrence patterns to adjectives like *large*. In particular, it can be preceded by *very* or *too*: *too/very beautiful*. Another feature of adjectives is their ability to precede nouns, as in *beautiful flowers*.

PRONOUNS

Pronouns constitute a relatively small category but with several different kinds or subcategories. Besides personal pronouns, there are demonstrative pronouns, interrogative pronouns, relative pronouns, and indefinite pronouns.

Personal Pronouns   The most familiar pronouns are personal pronouns—such as *I*, *me*, *she*, *him*, *they*, and *theirs*. Primarily, personal pronouns are distinguished from one another by representing different parties to a conversation or discussion, whether spoken or written. This aspect of pronouns is called *person* and is an easy notion to understand: the speaker or speakers are called the first person; the person or persons spoken *to* are called the second person; and the person(s) or thing(s) spoken *about* are called the third person. In other words, the first person is the speaker, the second person the addressee, and the third person anyone or anything else.

> First person—speaker: *I/me/mine, we/us/ours*
> Second person—addressee: *you/yours*
> Third person—spoken about: *she/her/hers, he/him/his, it/its, they/them/theirs*

Demonstrative Pronouns   Demonstrative pronouns refer to definite things relatively near (*this, these*) or, by contrast, relatively far away (*that, those*) when the referent can be identified by pointing or from the context of a discussion. Demonstrative pronouns do not occur in different persons. Examples of demonstrative pronouns include *that* in *That really bothers Pat* and *those* in *Those are Pat's*.

Interrogative Pronouns   Interrogative pronouns are used to ask questions. *Who* in *Who played Emma?* and *what* in *You told Jack what?* and *What did you tell Jack?* are interrogative pronouns. In the sentence *Whose are those?*, *whose* is an interrogative pronoun (*those* is a demonstrative pronoun).

Relative Pronouns   Although relative pronouns have the same forms as other kinds of pronouns, they are used differently. In the sentences that follow, examples include *who* in 1 and *that* in 2 and 3. Other relative pronouns include *which*, *whose*, and *whom*. Notice that a relative pronoun is related to a preceding noun phrase. In the examples, the relative pronoun and the related noun phrase are italicized, with the relative pronoun underlined.

1. Ellen's *a doctor <u>who</u>* specializes in gerontology.
2. *The show <u>that</u>* won most awards is "60 Minutes."
3. It produced *an atmosphere <u>that</u>* prompted sheriffs to cover the windows.

Indefinite Pronouns   Indefinite is the name used for a set of pronouns including: *someone, anyone, everyone, no one, somebody, anybody, everybody, nobody, something, anything, everything, nothing*.

It is important when identifying pronouns to recognize that they are used independently and not as modifiers of other words. That is clear enough for words like *I* and *something*, but some word forms can be pronouns (in *Whose is this?*, both *whose* and *this* are pronouns) or another category (in *Whose book is this red one? whose* and *this* are determiners, as explained in the following section).

DETERMINERS

Determiners constitute another small category. Determiners can precede nouns (*a book, an orchestra, the players, this problem, those guys, which film, whose ball*), although words belonging to other lexical categories can intervene (*a great book, an acclaimed orchestra, the very best players*). Determiners do not have endings like adjectives or verbs. They fall into several subcategories:

> Definite and indefinite articles: *the, a, an*
> Demonstratives: *this, that, these, those*
> Possessives: *my, our, your, her, his, its, their*
> Interrogatives: *which, what, whose*

Unlike nouns, adjectives, and verbs, determiners can be fully enumerated, and for the named subcategories this is the full list of English determiners.

PREPOSITIONS AND POSTPOSITIONS

Prepositions constitute a class with few members, and the prepositions of English could be enumerated. **Prepositions** are invariant in form: they do not have endings or other variations. They typically precede a noun phrase that complements them, as in *at home* and *on Tuesday.* They indicate a semantic relationship between other entities. The prepositions in *The book is on/under/near the table* indicate *location* of one thing (the book) with respect to another (the table). *Sarah rode to/from Athens* (indicate *direction* with respect to Athens) *with/without Fred* (indicate *accompaniment*) *at/near/by her side* (indicate *location* of Fred with respect to Sarah).

Instead of prepositions, some languages have postpositions. **Postpositions** function just like prepositions except that they follow their noun phrase complement instead of preceding it. Japanese has postpositions, as the Japanese-English pairs below illustrate:

JAPANESE POSTPOSITIONS	**ENGLISH PREPOSITIONS**
Taroo *no*	*of* Taro
hasi *de*	*with* chopsticks
Tookyoo *e*	*to* Tokyo

The placement of "pre"positions, which seems so natural to speakers of English (and French, Spanish, Russian, and many other languages), would seem unnatural to speakers of Japanese, Turkish, Hindi, and the many other languages that postpose instead of prepose this lexical category. To refer to prepositions and postpositions as a single category, the term **adposition** can be used.

ADVERBS

Most adverbs cannot be identified from form alone and rarely have related forms. While many adverbs are derived from adjectives by adding *-ly*, as with *swiftly* (from *swift*), *usually* (from *usual*), and *possibly* (from *possible*), many other adverbs carry no distinctive marker (and some words ending in *-ly* are not adverbs, as with the adjectives *manly* and *heavenly*, in which the *-ly* has been added to a noun, not an adjective). The common adverbs *then, now, here, soon,* and *away* can be identified as adverbs only by their distribution in sentences—that is, by where they occur and which lexical categories they co-occur with. (As with other lexical categories, the meaning of an adverb can also hint at its likely category—adverbs often tell how, when, or where.)

As the name suggests, adverbs can have a connection with verbs, as in the following examples, where the italicized adverbs modify verbs. (By way of contrast, sentences with comparable adjectives are provided in parentheses.)

✳ADVERBS MODIFYING VERBS ✳

He talked *loudly.* (He was a *loud* talker.)
She slept *soundly.* (She was a *sound* sleeper.)
She thought *quickly.* (She was a *quick* thinker.)
They studied *diligently.* (They were *diligent* students.)

Not all adverbs are derived from adjectives, as demonstrated in the examples that follow, where ill-formed sentences with adjectives are shown in parentheses.

ADVERBS MODIFYING VERBS

She spoke *often*. (*She was an often speaker.)
She studied *here*. (*She was a here student.)
They'll arrive *soon*. (*They'll have a soon arrival.)
She believes it *now*. (*She has a now belief.)

Adverbs can modify adjectives or other adverbs, as in these examples:

ADVERBS MODIFYING ADJECTIVES	ADVERBS MODIFYING ADVERBS
a *very* tall$_{Adj}$ tree	*very* soon$_{Adv}$
a *bitterly* cold$_{Adj}$ winter	*unbelievably* quickly$_{Adv}$
a *truly* splendid$_{Adj}$ evening	*truly* unbelievably $_{Adv}$ fast

Semantically, **adverbs** indicate when (*often*, *now*, *then*), where (*here*, *there*), manner (*quickly*, *suddenly*), or to what degree (*very*, *too*). Grammatically, they can play a range of functions, including modifying verbs, adjectives, or adverbs.

CONJUNCTIONS

School House Rock -

There are two principal kinds of **conjunctions**. One includes such words as *and*, *but*, and *or*. These are **coordinating conjunctions**, which serve to conjoin expressions of the same status or category—for example, noun phrase with noun phrase (*Dungeons and Dragons*, *Joe or I*), verb with verb (*trip and fall*, *break and enter*), adjective with adjective (*slow and painful*, *hot and cold*), and sentence with sentence (*She sang and he danced*; for more examples see Chapter 5).

Subordinating conjunctions are words like *that*, *whenever*, *while*, and *because*, which serve to link clauses to one another in a noncoordinate (that is, a subordinate) role, as in *She visited Montreal while she attended Bates College* or *He said that she was ill*. Subordinate clauses are discussed further in Chapter 5.

Subordinating conjunctions are usually referred to simply as *subordinators* and coordinating conjunctions simply as *conjunctions*.

MORPHEMES ARE WORD PARTS THAT CARRY MEANING

⟶

English speakers are aware that words like *girl*, *ask*, *tall*, *uncle*, and *orange* cannot be divided into smaller meaningful units. *Orange*, for example, is not made up of *o + range* or *or + ange* or *ora + nge*. Nor is *uncle* made up of, say, *un* and *cle*. But many words do have more than one meaningful part. *Oranges, uncles, grandmother, asks, asked, asking, homemade, taller,* and *tallest* have two elements each. Other words with more than one element contributing to their overall meaning include *beautiful, supermarkets,* and *bookstores.* A set of words can be built up by adding certain elements to a core element. For example, the following set of words is built up around the core element *true*:

truer	untrue	truthfully
truest	truth	untruthfully
truly	truthful	untruthfulness

Speakers of English recognize that these words share a stem whose meaning or lexical category has been modified by the addition of other elements. The meaningful elements of a word are called **morphemes.** Thus, *true* is a single morpheme; *untrue* and *truly* contain two morphemes each; and *untruthfulness* contains five (UN- + TRUE + -TH + -FUL + -NESS). *Truer,* with the two elements TRUE and -ER ('more'), means 'more true.' The morphemes in *truest* are TRUE and -EST ('most'); in *truly,* TRUE and -LY; in *untrue,* TRUE and UN-; in *truthful,* TRUE + -TH + -FUL.

We have been using the word *meaningful* loosely, for it is only by stretching things somewhat that we call *-er* in *truer* or *taller* and *-ed* in *looked* or *-s* in *kites* meaningful elements. Most morphemes have lexical meaning, as with *look, kites,* and *tall,* but some morphemes represent a grammatical category or semantic notion such as the past tense of verbs (the *-ed* in *looked*) or the plural of nouns (the *-s* in *kites*) or the comparative degree in adjectives (the *-er* in *taller*).

Morphemes cannot be equated with syllables. On the one hand, a single morpheme can have more than one syllable, as in *harvest, grammar, river, gorilla, hippopotamus,* and *Connecticut.* On the other hand, there are sometimes two or more morphemes in a single syllable, as in *kissed* (KISS + 'PAST TENSE'), *dogs* (DOG + 'PLURAL'), and *feet* (FOOT + 'PLURAL'), with two morphemes each, and *men's,* with three morphemes (MAN + 'PLURAL' + 'POSSESSIVE').

SOME MORPHEMES ARE FREE, SOME BOUND

Some morphemes like TRUE, MOTHER, and ORANGE can stand alone as words. Others like UN-, TELE-, -NESS, and -ER cannot stand alone and function only as parts of words. Morphemes that can stand alone as words are called **free morphemes.** Those that function only as parts of words are called **bound morphemes.**

MORPHEMES THAT DERIVE OTHER WORDS

Certain bound morphemes (like the underscored parts of the following words) have the effect of changing the lexical category of the word to which they are attached: *doubtful, establishment, darken, frighten,* and *teacher.* When added to the noun *doubt,* -FUL derives the adjective *doubtful;* -MENT added to the verb *establish* derives the noun *establishment. Dark* is an adjective, *darken* a verb; *fright* a noun, *frighten* a verb; *teach* a verb, *teacher* a noun. In English (though not in all languages) such derivational morphemes tend to be added to the ends of words as suffixes. We can represent these relationships as in the following rules of derivation:

Suffix

Noun + -FUL	→	Adjective (*doubtful, beautiful*)
Adjective + -LY	→	Adverb (*beautifully, truly*)
Verb + -MENT	→	Noun (*establishment, amazement*)
Verb + -ER	→	Noun (*teacher, rider, thriller*)
Adjective + -EN	→	Verb (*sweeten, brighten, harden*)
Noun + -EN	→	Verb (*frighten, hasten, christen*)

A similar process uses prefixes instead of suffixes. In English, prefixes typically change the meaning of a word but do not alter its lexical category.

Prefix

MIS- + Verb	→	Verb (*misspell, misstep, misdeal, misfire, misclassify*)
UN- + Adjective	→	Adjective (*unkind, uncool, unfair, unfaithful, untrue*)
UN- + Verb	→	Verb (*undo, unchain, uncover, unfurl, undress*)
UNDER- + Verb	→	Verb (*underbid, undercount, undercut, underrate, underscore*)
RE- + Verb	→	Verb (*reestablish, rephrase, rewrite, reassess*)
EX- + Noun	→	Noun (*ex-cop, ex-nun, ex-husband, ex-convict*)

✷ Processes of **derivation**—whereby one word is transformed into a word with a related meaning but belonging to a different lexical category—are common in the languages of the world. Here's an example from Persian. (*Note*: æ is pronounced like the *a* in English *hat*, and x like the *ch* in German *Bach*.)

dærd 'pain'	dærdnak 'painful'
næm 'dampness'	næmnak 'damp'
xætær 'danger'	xætærnak 'dangerous'

The suffix *-nak* can be added to certain nouns to derive adjectives. Thus Persian has the following rule of derivational morphology:

Noun A + -NAK → Noun 'the quality of being or having A'

Another derivational suffix of Persian creates abstract nouns from adjectives, as illustrated in these word pairs:

gærm 'warm'	gærma 'heat'
pæhn 'wide'	pæhna 'width'

This process of derivational morphology can be expressed by this rule:

$$\text{Adjective} + \text{-}_\text{A} \qquad \rightarrow \qquad \text{Noun}$$

Not every word belonging to the lexical category can undergo a given derivational process. In English, the nouns *doubt* and *beauty* can take the suffix *-ful*, but the nouns *trust* and *book* cannot. Unless words are marked in the mental lexicon for particular derivational processes, the ungrammatical forms **trustful* and **bookful* would result instead of the grammatical *trusting* and *bookish*, which are derived by other rules.

In Fijian *vaka-*, meaning 'in the manner of,' is a derivational morpheme that can be prefixed to adjectives and nouns to derive adverbs according to these two rules:

$$\text{VAKA-} + \text{Adjective} \qquad \rightarrow \qquad \text{Adverb}$$
$$\text{VAKA-} + \text{Noun} \qquad \rightarrow \qquad \text{Adverb}$$

The following adverbs exhibit the morpheme VAKA-: *vaka-Viti* 'in the Fijian fashion' (from *Viti* 'Fijian'), *vakatotolo* 'in a rapid manner, rapidly' (from *totolo* 'fast, rapid'); to illustrate the derivation from a noun, consider *vakamaarama* 'ladylike' (formed by prefixing *vaka-* to *maarama* 'lady').

Not all bound morphemes serve to change the lexical category of words. Adding other bound morphemes like English DIS-, RE-, and UN- (*disappear, repaint, unfavorable*) to a word changes its meaning but not its lexical category. For example, *appear* and *disappear* are both verbs, as are *paint* and *repaint*; *favorable* and *unfavorable* are both adjectives. There is a notable tendency in English for morphemes that change meaning without altering lexical category to be added to the front of words as prefixes, though this is not universal across all languages (and in fact some languages lack prefixes altogether, as Turkish does).

The two types of morpheme we have just examined are called **derivational morphemes**. They produce new words from existing words in two ways. First, they can change the meaning of a word: *true* versus *untrue*; *paint* versus *repaint*. Second, they can change the lexical category of a word: *true* is an adjective, *truly* an adverb, *truth* a noun.

INFLECTIONAL MORPHEMES

Another type of bound morpheme is illustrated in the underscored parts of the words *cats, collected, sleeps,* and *louder*. These morphemes differ from derivational morphemes: they change the form of a word but not its lexical category or its central meaning. These **inflectional morphemes** create variant forms of a word to conform to different roles in a sentence or in discourse. On nouns and pronouns, inflectional morphemes serve to mark semantic notions like *number* and grammatical categories like *gender* and *case*. On verbs, they can mark such things as *tense* or *number*, while on adjectives they serve to indicate *degree*. They shape the so-called "related forms" we used earlier in the chapter to help identify lexical categories. We return to inflectional morphology in detail later in the chapter.

HOW ARE MORPHEMES ORGANIZED WITHIN WORDS?

MORPHEMES ARE ORDERED IN SEQUENCE

Within a word, morphemes are not arranged randomly but have a strict and systematic linear sequence.

Affixes   Some morphemes, called **suffixes**, always follow the stems they attach to, like 'PLURAL' in *girls* and -MENT in *commitment*: both **sgirl* and **mentcommit* are ill formed. Languages can also have **prefixes**, which attach to the front of a stem, as in the words *untrue*, *disappear*, and *repaint*. (Compare **trueun*, **appeardis*, and **paintre*; and, of course, English does not permit **nessfultruthun* or any arrangement other than *untruthfulness*.)

Derivational morphemes can be either prefixes (*unhappy*, *disappear*) or suffixes (*happiness*, *appearance*). Generally, inflectional morphemes are added to the outermost parts of words: they precede derivational prefixes or follow derivational suffixes. Taken together, prefixes and suffixes are called **affixes.**

Infixes   Besides affixes, some languages have infixes. An **infix** is a morpheme that is inserted within another morpheme. If English had morphemes TTH meaning 'tooth' and GSE meaning 'goose' (which it doesn't), then we could say that -*oo*- was an infix meaning 'singular' and -*ee*- an infix meaning 'plural.' English speakers find any interpretation calling for singular and plural infixes in words like *tooth/teeth* and *goose/geese* to be counterintuitive, but other languages do exploit this morphological possibility. Tagalog (the most widely spoken language of the Philippines) has infixing. For example, the word *gulay* meaning 'greenish vegetables' can take the infix -*in*-, creating the word *ginulay*, meaning 'greenish blue.' Compared to prefixes and suffixes, infixes are relatively rare in the languages of the world.

MORPHEMES CAN BE DISCONTINUOUS

Not all morphological processes can be viewed as joining or concatenating morphemes to one another by adding a continuous sequence of sounds (or letters) to a stem. In other words, not all morphological processes add prefixes, suffixes, or even infixes. The technical term for discontinuous morphology is *nonconcatenative.*

Circumfixes   Some languages combine a prefix and a suffix in a single morpheme called a **circumfix**—a morpheme that occurs in two parts, on both sides of a stem. Samoan, for example, has a morpheme FE-/-AʔI, meaning 'reciprocal': the verb 'to quarrel' is *finau*, and the verb meaning 'to quarrel with each other' is *fefinauaʔi*—FE + FINAU + AʔI.

Interweaving Morphemes   An interesting morphological phenomenon that involves interweaving morphemes can be found in the system that marks categories in Semitic languages, such as Arabic and Hebrew. We illustrate with Arabic.

Arabic nouns and verbs generally have a root consisting of three consonants, such as KTB. For example, the Arabic word for 'book' is *kitaab.* By interweaving **k-t-b** and various other morphemes, Arabic creates a great many nouns, verbs, and adjectives with this single root. The nouns and verbs in Table 2-1 all contain the same KTB root, with other morphemes interwoven.

Table 2-1

DERIVATIONAL MORPHOLOGY IN ARABIC

kitaaba	'writing'	kataba	'he wrote'
kaatib	'writer'	kaataba	'he corresponded with'
maktab	'office'	ʔaktaba	'he dictated'
maktaba	'library'	ʔiktataba	'he was registered'
maktuub	'letter'	takaataba	'he exchanged letters with'
miktaab	'typewriter'	inkataba	'he subscribed'
kutubii	'bookseller'	iktataba	'he had a copy made'

(Incidentally, the English words *Moslem, Islam,* and *salaam,* which have been borrowed from Arabic, all contain the root SLM, with its core meaning of 'peace, submission.')

PORTMANTEAU WORDS CONTAIN MERGED MORPHEMES

Another morphological phenomenon joins two or more morphemes in such a way that the sounds in the word cannot be assigned tidily to each of its morphemes. The classic example is the French word *du,* which represents the two morphemes *de* 'of' and *le* 'the.' You can see the difficulty of assigning the sounds to one morpheme or the other. Some analysts include blends like *smog* (from *smoke* and *fog*) among portmanteau words.

MORPHEMES ARE ORGANIZED IN HIERARCHIES

As with all other aspects of language, morphemes are organized in patterned ways. Besides their linear order, the morphemes in a word also have a layered, or hierarchical, structure. *Untrue,* for example, is *true* with *un-* prefixed to it (not *un* with *true* added). *Truthful* is composed of a stem *truth* with *-ful* suffixed to it (and *truth* is itself *true* with *-th* added). Examining more complex words, it is easy to see that *untruthful* would be incorrectly analyzed if we claimed that it was composed of *untrue* with *-thful* suffixed. Instead it is *truthful* with *un-* prefixed.

Consider the word *uncontrollably*. Is it *controllably* with *un-* prefixed? Or *un-control* with *-ably* suffixed? Or still another possibility? It's helpful to picture the sequence of morpheme layering as built up from the root *control* and a set of widely applicable derivational rules:

Verb + -ABLE → Adjective

UN- + Adjective → Adjective

Adjective + -LY → Adverb

control (Verb)

controllable (Adjective)

uncontrollable (Adjective)

uncontrollably (Adverb)

In looking at this sequence, it is clear that the root of *uncontrollably* is *control*, which functions as the stem for *-able*; that *controllable* functions as the stem for *uncontrollable*; and that *uncontrollable* functions as the stem for *uncontrollably*.

The structure can be represented using a tree diagram like the one in Figure 2-1.

Figure 2-1

HIERARCHICAL STRUCTURE OF *UNCONTROLLABLY*

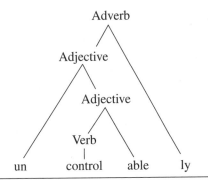

A representation using labeled brackets would be as follows:

[[un [[control$_{Verb}$] + [able]$_{Adj}$]$_{Adj}$] ly$_{Adv}$]

HOW DO LANGUAGES INCREASE THEIR VOCABULARY?

Languages have three principal ways of extending their vocabulary. Sometimes entirely new words are created, although this is not very common. Alternatively, words that exist in another language are borrowed. Most often new words in a language are formed from already existing words and word parts.

SOME WORD CLASSES ARE OPEN, SOME CLOSED

In some cultures, the need for new nouns, adjectives, and verbs arises frequently, and additions to these lexical categories occur freely. For this reason the lexical categories of noun, adjective, and verb are called *open classes.* Compared with these open classes, other categories are relatively closed, and additions are rarely made. Prepositions, pronouns, and determiners are *closed classes,* and new words are seldom added in these categories. Century after century, English has added thousands of new words, many borrowed from other languages and many more constructed from elements already present in the English word stock.

HOW TO DERIVE NEW WORDS

Affixes   Adding morphemes to an existing word is a very common way of creating new words. As an example, English has added the agentive suffix -ER to the prepositions *up* and *down* to create the nouns *upper* and *downer*, which refer to things that lift or dampen one's spirits. More commonly, -ER is added to verbs (V) to create a word with the sense 'one who Vs' as in *runner* 'one who runs,' *campaigner* 'one who campaigns,' and *designer* 'one who designs.'

English adds morphemes in two principal ways: prefixing and suffixing. Prefixes like UN-, PRE-, and DIS- serve to change the meaning of words, though not usually their lexical category. For example, the prefix UN- added to the adjectives *true, popular, successful,* and *favorable* creates new adjectives with the opposite meanings: *untrue, unpopular, unsuccessful, unfavorable.* Added to a verb, UN- creates a new verb with the opposite meaning: *unplug, unbutton, unlatch, untie, unscrew, undo.* The prefix DIS- added to a verb creates a verb with the opposite meaning, as in *disobey, disapprove, disappear, displease,* and *dishonor.* PRE- serves as a prefix to several categories of words. It can be prefixed to verbs (*preplan, prewash, premix, preaffirm,* and *preallot*), adjectives (*pre-Copernican, precollegiate, precultural, prenatal, presurgical*), or nouns (*preantiquity, preaffirmation, preplacement*). The prefix PRE- has roughly the same sense in each of these words, and from an existing word it creates a new word in the same lexical category. A very productive prefix in the 1990s is CYBER- as in *cyberspace* and *cyberpal,* which are nouns, maintaining the lexical category of *space* and *pal.*

English derivational suffixes are added to the tail end and typically have a different effect from prefixes. Usually they change a word's lexical category—say, from a verb to a noun. For example, adding the suffix -MENT to a verb makes a noun of the verb: *arrangement, agreement,* and *consignment.* The suffix -ATION does the same thing: *resignation, organization, implementation, observation,* and *reformation.* (*Discrimination* and *alienation,* which appear to have the same affix, actually derive from the verbs *discriminate* and *alienate.*)

Suffixes are widely exploited in other languages as well. The Indonesian suffix -KAN changes a noun to a verb, and among the various meanings it can produce are these: 'to cause to become X' (*rajakan* 'to crown' from *raja* 'king') and 'to put in X' (as in *penjarakan* 'imprison' from *penjara* 'prison' + -KAN).

Reduplication   Reduplication is the morphological process by which a morpheme or part of a morpheme is repeated, thereby creating a word with a different meaning or a different lexical category. For example, the Mandarin Chinese word *sànsànbu* 'to take a leisurely walk' is formed by reduplicating the first syllable of *sànbu* 'to walk' (itself a compound of *sàn* 'to tread' and *bù* 'a step'), and *hónghón* 'bright red' is formed by reduplicating *hóng* 'red.' There is partial reduplication, which repeats only part of the morpheme, or full reduplication, in which the entire morpheme is reduplicated. In the Papua New Guinea language Motu, *mahuta* 'to sleep' reduplicates fully as *mahutamahuta* 'to sleep constantly' and reduplicates partially as *mamahuta* 'to sleep' (when agreeing with a plural subject). In Turkish, adjectives like *açik* 'open,' *ayri* 'separate,' and *uzun* 'long' are reduplicated (by prefixing the initial vowel followed by a consonant) as *apaçik* 'wide open,' *apayri* 'entirely separate' and *upuzun* 'very long.' Reduplication is not to be confused with repetition, which does not create new words but simply reiterates the same word, as in English *very, very* (*tired*) and *night-night*. English does not have a productive process similar to the reduplication of Chinese, Motu, or Turkish.

Reduplication can have different functions in languages. It can moderate or intensify the meaning of a word, as illustrated by the Chinese, Motu, and Turkish examples just given. It can mark grammatical categories, as in Indonesian, where certain kinds of noun plurals are formed by reduplication: *babibabi* 'an assortment of pigs' is a reduplicated form of *babi* 'pig.'

COMPOUNDS

English speakers show a disposition for putting existing words together to create new words using a process called compounding. Recent compounds include *moon shot, waterbed, upfront, color code, computerlike,* and *radiopharmaceutical.* Even more recent ones include *V-chip, e-mail, online, Web page, Web site,* and *download.* To gauge the popularity of compounding in English, consider that a single relatively short piece in an issue of the *Los Angeles Times* contained the following examples.

NOUNS			ADJECTIVES
petroleum engineer	whistle-blower	pay phone	whistle-blowing
government documents	troublemaker	phone call	baby-faced
government witness	debt ceiling	storerooms	highranking
subcommittee hearing	brain cancer	cover-up	overzealous
aircraft carrier	reserve account	kickbacks	born-again
training course	sea power	breakup	middle-aged

Compounding occurs in many languages. Mandarin, for example, has numerous compounds, such as *fàn-wăn* 'rice bowl,' *diàn-năo* ('electric' + 'brain') 'computer,' *tái-bù* 'tablecloth,' *fēi-jī* ('fly' + 'machine') 'airplane,' and *hēi-băn* ('black' + 'board') 'blackboard.' German is famous for its compounding tendencies. The word *Fernsprecher* (literally 'far speaker') was for a long time the preferred word for what is today usually called *Telefon*. A ballpoint pen is called *Kugelschreiber* ('ball' + 'writer'); a glove *Handschuh* ('hand' + 'shoe'); mayor is *Bürgermeister* ('citizen' + 'master'). Indonesian has exploited compounding in a word made familiar to Westerners from its use as the assumed name of a well-known World War I socialite and spy: *matahari*, meaning 'sun,' comes from *mata* 'eye' and *hari* 'day.' The word for 'eyeglasses' is *kacamata*, a compound of *kaca* 'glass' and *mata* 'eye' (similar to the English compound *eyeglasses* but with a different order of elements).

SHORTENINGS

Shortenings of various sorts are a popular means of multiplying the words of a language. Regular shortenings like *radial* (*radial tire*), *jet* (*jet airplane*), *narc* (*narcotics agent*), *feds* (*federal agents*), *obits* (*obituaries*), *poli-sci* (*political science*) and *app* or *apps* (referring to computer application programs) are common enough.

Acronyms Acronyms are a familiar form of shortening. In an acronym the initials of an expression are joined together and pronounced as a word: *UNESCO*, *NATO*, *NASA*, *WASP*, *radar* (radio detecting and ranging), *yuppy* (young urban professional + -Y), *dink* (*double income no kids*), *ASCII* (pronounced "ask-ee" and derived from *American standard code for information interchange*) and *DOS* (*disk operating system*). Some shortened forms resemble acronyms but are *not* acronyms because they are pronounced as a sequence of letters rather than as a word. For example, the University of Southern California can be referred to as *U-S-C* and New York University as *N-Y-U*. A grade point average may be called a *G-P-A*, and customers of the Internet provider America Online refer to it as *A-O-L*. The shortening *PC* has become popular in recent years in two distinct meanings—'politically correct' and 'personal computer.' Given its pronunciation, *PC* is not an acronym, but an *initialism*.

Blends English speakers are also fond of *blends*, words created by combining parts of existing words. Among the better-known blends are *smog* (from *smoke* and *fog*) and *motel* (*motor* and *hotel*); others like *glasphalt* (*glass* and *asphalt*) and *infomercial* are less frequently used, though the elements are familiar. *Modem* is well known, though its elements are less familiar (*modulator* and *demodulator*). *Netizens* and *netiquette* are recent creations blending *net* (a shortened form of *Internet*) with *citizens* and *etiquette*. A recent example combines the existing blend *smog* with the tail end of *metropolis* to form *smogopolis*. One group of blends captures the fact that certain languages have borrowed intensely from each other: *Spanglish*, *Franglais*, *Yinglish*. Probably best considered a blend is the recent noun *wannabes* (or *wannabees*), which refers to people who want to be something other than what they are. It combines *want* + *to* + *be*, the first two elements already commonly shortened to *wanna*. Trade names like *Amtrak* and *Amway* also are blends.

BACK FORMATION

A special type of shortening is suggested by some words derived from *computer*. The word *computer* was originally formed by adding the suffix *-er* to the verb *compute*. A *computer* was a machine that computed (in the mathematical sense). Now from the word *computer*, a new verb *compute* has been "back formed" and carries the meaning 'to use a computer' (for computation or any other task). Other back formations are the verbs *typewrite*, *baby-sit*, and *edit*, which were invented after their noun forms *typewriter*, *baby-sitter*, and *editor*.

CONVERSION OR FUNCTIONAL SHIFT

English and some other languages permit a word belonging to one lexical category to be converted to another lexical category without any overt marking on the word itself. Transferring a word of one lexical category for use in another without altering its form is called *functional shift*. In English we request someone to *update* (verb) a report and then refer to the revised report as an *update* (noun). We can ask a fellow employee to *e-mail* or *fax* the report, both of which are verbs converted from shortened forms of nouns (*electronic mail, facsimile*). Companies *hire* (verb) a group of employees and refer to them as the new *hires* (where *hires* is a noun). Conversion of this type commonly leads to noun/verb and noun/adjective pairs. As Table 2-2 illustrates,

Table 2-2

SOME ENGLISH FORMS BELONGING TO MORE THAN ONE LEXICAL CATEGORY

NOUN	VERB	ADJECTIVE
e-mail	e-mail	
bookmark	bookmark	
bust	bust	
outrage	outrage	
homer	homer	
delay	delay	
plot	plot	
play	play	
local		local
inaugural		inaugural
illegal		illegal
average	average	average
model	model	model
surprise	surprise	surprise
ghost	ghost	ghost
prime	prime	prime

sometimes the same form can be used for all three categories—as noun, verb, and adjective. Once a form has been shifted to a new lexical category, it conforms to the inflectional morphology of that category: an *update*, two recent *updates*, she is *updating* the report now, and he *updated* it last month.

SEMANTIC SHIFT

Existing words can take on new meanings by shrinking or extending the domain of their reference. During the Vietnam War, the word *hawk* came to be used for supporters of the war while *dove* referred to supporters of peace, extending the meaning of these words from the combative nature of hawks and the symbolically peaceful role assigned to doves. Today, computer users often utilize a *mouse* and *bookmark* Internet addresses. These new meanings did not replace the earlier ones but yielded new uses for the words by extending their range of application. Called *semantic shift* or *metaphorical extension*, this phenomenon creates *metaphors*. The metaphorical use of words often leads to new meanings that come to seem perfectly natural and whose metaphorical content is all but lost. Consider the meanings of the underscored parts of the following phrases: *to derail congressional legislation, a buoyant spokesman, an abrasive chief of staff, to sweeten the farm bill with several billion dollars to skirt a veto fight.* Such originally metaphorical uses have become an integral part of the language.

BORROWING WORDS

"Neither a borrower nor a lender be," Shakespeare advised, but speakers pay little heed when it comes to language, and English has been extraordinarily receptive to borrowed words. It has accepted words from nearly a hundred languages just in the last hundred years. As in most of its history, English has borrowed more words from French during the twentieth century than from any other language. For recent borrowings, following French at some distance are Japanese and Spanish, Italian and Latin and Greek, German, and Yiddish. In smaller numbers, English is now host to words borrowed from Russian, Chinese, Arabic, Portuguese, and Hindi, as well as from numerous languages of Africa and some Native American languages.

In turn, many languages have welcomed English words into their stock, although some languages have been less receptive. The Japanese have drafted the words *beesubooru* 'baseball,' *futtobooru* 'football' and *booringu* 'bowling' along with the sports they name, trading them (to use a sports analogy) for *judo, jujitsu*, and *karate*, which have joined the English-language team. Officially at least, the French are not open to borrowings, especially from English, and have banned the use of words like *weekend, drugstore, brainstorming*, and *countdown*, as well as the popular term *jumbo jet*. In fact, for using *jumbo jet* Air France was fined by the French government, which had insisted that *gros porteur* was the proper French name for, well, for the jumbo jet. The Americanism *OK* is now in use virtually everywhere, as

JEANS AND DISCOS

The *jean* in your favorite blue jeans is a Middle English form of the word *Genoa*. *Jeans* is a shortening of *jean fustian* 'Genoa fustian,' referring to a coarse cloth once produced in Genoa, Italy. The word *denim*, for the cloth from which jeans are made, evolved from *serge de Nîmes*, a cloth product from the French city of Nîmes. You might wear your favorite *jeans* to a *disco*. The French word *discothèque* 'record library,' is a compound of two French morphemes, *disque* meaning '*disk*' or '*record*' and the suffix *-thèque* as in *bibliothèque* 'library.' *Discothèque* was first recorded in English in 1954, and as an abbreviation, *disco*, ten years later. *Disco*, the noun, has also undergone functional shift to *disco*, the verb, meaning 'dance to disco music.' Music buffs may note that *disco*, the verb version, was first recorded in 1979. Both noun and verb can be heard around the world in many cities whose inhabitants speak neither English nor French.

are terms such as *jeans* and *discos*, which accompanied the items they name as they spread around the globe.

As is true of other languages, most borrowings into English have been nouns, but some adjectives have been borrowed, as have a few verbs and interjections. Among the nouns borrowed into English and having to do with food and drink are *hummus* (from Arabic), *aioli* (from Provençal), *mai tai* (from Tahitian), and *burrito, enchilada, fajita,* and *taco* (from Spanish). Yiddish has given us the more general term *nosh*. Other popular borrowings include Italian *ciao*, Spanish *macho*, Chinese (Cantonese) *wok*, German *glitch*, and Yiddish *chutzpah, klutz, nebbish, schlep* and *schlepper*.

Despite their sometimes unusual spellings, borrowed words come sooner or later to conform to the pronunciation and grammatical rules of the language that borrows them. In time, borrowed words undergo the same processes that affect other words. *Nosh*, for example, was borrowed as a verb that could not take an object (*I feel like noshing*) but has since taken on new use as a verb that can take an object (*Let's nosh some hot dogs*). The verb *nosh* has also taken on the suffix *-er* to become the noun *nosher*, which means 'one who noshes,' and *nosh* itself has come to be used as a noun meaning 'a snack.' In British usage *nosh* has been compounded into the noun *nosh-up*, meaning 'a large or elaborate meal.'

INVENTING WORDS

Inventing new words from scratch is relatively rare. The advantages of using familiar elements in forming new words and the ease of borrowing words from other languages are sufficiently strong that languages do not often create new words. In recent years, invention has contributed such words as *granola, zap, quark,* and *lollapalooza* to the English word stock. Dr. Seuss invented the word *nerd*.

WHAT ARE THE TYPES
OF MORPHOLOGICAL SYSTEMS?

We have now seen examples of derivational morphology in several languages and of inflectional morphology in a few. Not all languages have inflectional morphology, and some have little or no morphology at all. Still other languages have relatively complex words with distinct parts, each representing a morpheme. Traditionally, these three types of languages have been identified as isolating, agglutinating, or inflectional.

ISOLATING MORPHOLOGY

Chinese is an oft-cited example of a language with isolating morphology—in which each word tends to be a single isolated morpheme. An isolating language lacks both derivational and inflectional morphology. By the use of separate words, Chinese expresses certain content that an inflecting language can express by using inflectional affixes. For example, whereas English permits both an inflectional possessive (*the boy's hat*) and what is called an analytical possessive (*hat of the boy*), Chinese permits only the equivalent of *hat of the boy.* Chinese also lacks tense markers and does not mark gender, number, or case distinctions on pronouns. Where English has six different words—*he*, *she*, *him*, *her*, *they*, and *them*—Chinese uses only a single word (though of course it can indicate plurality with a separate word). The sentence below illustrates the one-morpheme-per-word pattern typical of Chinese:

> wǒ gāng yào gěi nǐ nà yì bēi chá
> I   just will give you that one cup tea
> 'I am about to bring you a cup of tea.'

Vietnamese, even more than Chinese, approximates the one-morpheme-per-word model that characterizes isolating languages. Each word in the sentence below has only one form, and you can see that the word *tôi* is translated as *I*, *my*, and *we*, the last based upon a coupling of the words for 'I' and 'plural.' Like Chinese, Vietnamese lacks tense markers on verbs and case markers on nouns and pronouns, as well as number distinctions (though it can indicate plurality with a separate word).

> khi tôi đến nhà   bạn   tôi, chúng tôi bắt đầu làm bài
> when I   come house friend I   Plural I begin   do lesson
> 'When I came to my friend's house, we began to do lessons.'

Some languages that tend to minimize inflectional morphology nevertheless exploit derivational morphology to extend their word stocks in economical ways.

Indonesian, for example, has only two inflectional affixes, but it utilizes about two dozen derivational morphemes, some of which we've seen earlier in the chapter.

AGGLUTINATING MORPHOLOGY

A second type of morphology is called agglutinating. In agglutinating languages, words can have several prefixes and suffixes, but characteristically they are distinct and readily segmented into their parts—like English *announce-ment-s* or *under-score-s* but unlike *sang* (SING + 'PAST') or *men* (MAN + 'PLURAL'). Greenlandic Eskimo is an example of such a language, as illustrated by the following sentence, in which hyphens represent morpheme boundaries within a word:

> qajar-taa-va   asirur-sima-vuq
> kayak-new-his break-done-it
> 'His new kayak has been destroyed.'

INFLECTIONAL MORPHOLOGY

Many languages have large inventories of inflectional morphemes. Russian and German have maintained elaborate inflectional systems over the centuries, while English has shed most of its inflections, until today it has only eight remaining ones—two on nouns, four on verbs, and two on adjectives, as shown in Table 2-3. The eight inflectional morphemes of English are fully productive. When new nouns, verbs, and adjectives are added to the language or when a child learns new words, they are extremely likely to be inflected like the examples listed.

Table 2-3

INFLECTIONAL MORPHEMES OF ENGLISH

LEXICAL CATEGORY	GRAMMATICAL CATEGORY	EXAMPLES
Noun	Plural	cars, churches
	Possessive	car's, children's
Verb	Third person	(she) swims, (it) seems
	Past tense	wanted, showed
	Past participle	wanted, shown (or showed)
	Present participle	wanting, showing
Adjective	Comparative	taller, sweeter
	Superlative	tallest, sweetest

Compare this inflectional system of English with the examples from the Russian noun *žena* 'wife' and verb *pisat'* 'to write' in Tables 2-4 and 2-5.

Grammatical Functions of Inflections   Consider the English sentences below. Though they contain exactly the same words, they do not express the same meaning.

1. The farmer saw the wolf.
2. The wolf saw the farmer.

These sentences illustrate how English uses word order to express meaning: different orders can communicate different scenarios about *who* did what to *whom*. When semantic facts like who did what to whom are expressed by word order rather than inflection, it is not a morphological matter but a syntactic one, and is the subject of Chapter 5.

A comparison with Latin is enlightening because Latin had relatively free word order. If F represents 'the farmer' and W 'the wolf,' speakers of Latin could have arranged sentence 1 ('The farmer saw the wolf') in these two ways (among others):

F vīdit W.
W vīdit F.

Table 2-4

RUSSIAN NOUN INFLECTIONS: *ŽENA* 'WIFE'

CASE	*SINGULAR*	*PLURAL*
NOMINATIVE	žena	žëny
ACCUSATIVE	ženu	žën
GENITIVE	ženu	žën
DATIVE	žene	žënam
INSTRUMENTAL	ženoy	žënami
AFTER SOME PREPOSITIONS	žene	žënax

Table 2-5

RUSSIAN PRESENT-TENSE VERB INFLECTIONS: *PISAT'* 'WRITE'

PERSON	SINGULAR	PLURAL
FIRST PERSON	pišu	pišem
SECOND PERSON	pišeš	pišete
THIRD PERSON	pišet	pišut

The word order has no effect on the meaning. Sentence 2 ('The wolf saw the farmer') could be expressed in Latin using the same word orders. Obviously, Latin speakers did not rely on word order to communicate who saw whom. Instead, they relied on inflections on the nouns. Thus, the three Latin sentences below all mean the same thing, irrespective of word order.

> Agricola vīdit lupum.
> Lupum vīdit agricola.   } 'The farmer saw the wolf.'
> Agricola lupum vīdit.

To express the 'opposite' meaning different inflections were required:

> Agricolam vīdit lupus.
> Lupus vīdit agricolam.   } 'The wolf saw the farmer.'
> Agricolam lupus vīdit.

The inflectional suffixes -*a* on *agricola* and -*us* on *lupus* in the first set above identified them as subjects, whereas *agricolam* and *lupum* were identified by their -*am* and -*um* inflections as direct objects.

A loose parallel to Latin noun inflections can be seen in English in certain pronoun uses, in which the form of the pronouns and the word order reinforce one another:

> She praised him. (*She* is the subject, *him* the object.)
> He praised her. (*He* is the subject, *her* the object.)

In both English and Latin, nouns have inflections for number and case. English nouns exhibit only two cases, called possessive and common. Common case is unmarked—as with *cat* or *student*—and is used for all grammatical functions except possession; an unmarked noun can serve as subject of a sentence, direct and indirect object, and object of a preposition. The possessive case, sometimes called "genitive," is marked (*cat's*, *student's*).

Besides a genitive case, Latin exhibited inflections for several other cases, notably nominative (used principally for subjects), dative (for indirect objects), accusative (for direct objects and the objects of some prepositions), and ablative (for the objects of still other prepositions). Latin generally had five or six case inflections in the singular and in the plural, although some inflectional forms were pronounced alike, as can be seen in Table 2-6. The set of forms constituting the inflectional variants of a word is known as a **paradigm**, and paradigms for nouns are called **declensions.** Latin had several declensions, such as the two given for *agricola* and *hortus* in Table 2-6. The declensions for the equivalent English words *farmer* and *garden* are given in Table 2-7.

Notice that the four written forms in the English paradigms represent only two distinct pronunciations because *farmers*, *farmer's*, and *farmers'* are pronounced

Table 2-6

PARADIGMS FOR TWO LATIN NOUNS

SINGULAR	'FARMER'	'GARDEN'
NOMINATIVE	agricola	hortus
ACCUSATIVE	agricolam	hortum
GENITIVE	agricolae	hortī
DATIVE	agricolae	hortō
ABLATIVE/INSTRUMENTAL	agricolā	hortō

PLURAL	'FARMERS'	'GARDENS'
NOMINATIVE	agricolae	hortī
ACCUSATIVE	agricolās	hortōs
GENITIVE	agricolārum	hortōrum
DATIVE	agricolīs	hortīs
ABLATIVE/INSTRUMENTAL	agricolīs	hortīs

alike, as are *gardens*, *garden's,* and *gardens'*. Spoken English usually has only two forms of a regular noun, but most irregularly formed plurals have four spoken and four written forms: *man*, *man's*, *men*, *men's*; *child*, *child's*, *children*, *children's*.

With some English pronouns a third case form exists—the objective case. It is roughly comparable to the dative, accusative, and ablative/instrumental cases of Latin. In Table 2-8, compare the paradigms for first- and third-person pronouns in English. First-person pronouns exhibit distinct forms for three cases in the singular and three in the plural. Third-person pronouns have distinct masculine, feminine, and neuter forms in the singular, although no distinction for gender is made in the plural. The neuter singular *it* does not have distinct forms for common and objective cases.

Table 2-7

PARADIGMS FOR TWO ENGLISH NOUNS

SINGULAR

COMMON	farmer	garden
POSSESSIVE	farmer's	garden's

PLURAL

COMMON	farmers	gardens
POSSESSIVE	farmers'	gardens'

Table 2-8

PARADIGMS FOR FIRST- AND THIRD-PERSON PRONOUNS IN ENGLISH

	FIRST PERSON	THIRD PERSON		
		MASCULINE	FEMININE	NEUTER
SINGULAR				
COMMON	I	he	she	it
POSSESSIVE	my, mine	his	her, hers	its
OBJECTIVE	me	him	her	it
PLURAL				
COMMON	we	they		
POSSESSIVE	our, ours	their, theirs		
OBJECTIVE	us	them		

Second-person pronouns and third-person singular neuter pronouns do not have distinct objective forms, as can be seen in Table 2-9; like regular nouns, they have only two forms.

In English, gender distinctions in pronouns are based on biological sex. Things that are neither male nor female are referred to by the neuter pronoun *it*. In some languages, including Latin, German, and Old English, nouns have grammatical (not biological) gender, and certain categories of words, such as determiners and adjectives that are part of a noun phrase, carry inflections that agree with those of the noun in gender, number, and case.

Table 2-9

SECOND- AND THIRD-PERSON PRONOUNS COMPARED TO NOUNS IN ENGLISH

	PRONOUNS		NOUNS
	SECOND	THIRD	
SINGULAR			
COMMON	you	it	farmer
POSSESSIVE	your, yours	its	farmer's
PLURAL			
COMMON	you		farmers
POSSESSIVE	your, yours		farmers'

Table 2-10

PARADIGM FOR GERMAN DEFINITE ARTICLE

	SINGULAR			PLURAL
	MASCULINE	FEMININE	NEUTER	ALL GENDERS
NOMINATIVE	der	die	das	die
ACCUSATIVE	den	die	das	die
GENITIVE	des	der	des	der
DATIVE	dem	der	dem	den

In contrast to the English definite article *the* (with a single written form representing two pronunciations "thuh" and "thee"), the German definite article has forms for three genders and four cases in the singular, though there are no distinct gender markers in the plural, as Table 2-10 illustrates.

French and Spanish also exhibit variant forms of the definite article, though neither is as varied as German. French distinguishes only two genders in nouns; it marks masculine nouns with the definite article *le* (indefinite *un*), feminine ones with *la* (indefinite *une*); *les* is the plural form of the definite article for both genders. Spanish is similar in having two genders, but it marks them in the plural as well as the singular. Table 2-11 gives examples in French and Spanish.

Although there is not always a strict demarcation between agglutinating and inflectional languages and some languages are difficult to classify, the distinction among the three types of morphology—inflectional, isolating, and agglutinating—is nevertheless useful in characterizing languages with respect to their morphological systems.

Table 2-11

FRENCH AND SPANISH DEFINITE ARTICLES WITH NOUNS

	FRENCH	SPANISH	
MASCULINE	le chat	el gato	'the cat'
	les chats	los gatos	'the cats'
FEMININE	la maison	la casa	'the house'
	les maisons	las casas	'the houses'

USING COMPUTERS TO STUDY WORDS

A good deal of information can be derived from a corpus like the Brown Corpus. (The Brown Corpus is described on page 24 of Chapter 1). For example, word frequencies are easily compiled, and the most frequent and least frequent word forms can be identified in the corpus as a whole or in any of its genres, such as science fiction, press editorials, learned writing. You won't be surprised to learn that three of the four most frequent words in the corpus are *the*, *of*, and *and*. By contrast, words like *oblong*, *obstinate*, *radionic*, *narcosis*, and *mystification* occur only once.

Besides word frequencies, information about how general or specialized a word is can also be gauged. As you would guess, *the*, *and*, and *of* occur in all 500 texts of the corpus, whereas a proper name might occur often in a single text but nowhere else in the corpus. For example, the name *Mussorgsky* occurs seven times in the corpus, but all of them are in a single 2,000–word text. And such narrow distributions are not limited to proper names.

The noun *dialysis* occurs twelve times, all of them in a single text; *radiosterilization* occurs six times, and they too are all in a single text.

Contrast such extremely specialized ranges of use with a word like *moreover*, which occurs 88 times in 63 different texts and in 13 of the 15 genres represented in the corpus. You can see that the word *moreover* is not exceptionally frequent but is widely distributed, occurring in nearly all the genres of published English represented in the Brown Corpus and in nearly as many texts as the number of occurrences.

Table 2-12 contains examples of the simplest kinds of information that you can derive from the Brown Corpus. Next to each listed word is the total number of times it occurs, as well as the number of genres (out of 15) and number of texts (out of 500) in which it occurs. The four words occur fewer than 65 times each in the million-word corpus, and those occurrences are spread across at least 12 genres. This distribution across genres suggests that they are not specialized vocabulary items.

Table 2-12

FREQUENCY OF FOUR WIDELY DISTRIBUTED WORDS IN THE BROWN CORPUS

WORD	OCCURRENCES	GENRES	TEXTS
establishment	52	12	43
careful	62	14	56
powerful	63	14	54
unusual	63	15	52

You can compare these widely occurring words with others whose distribution is narrower. The words listed in Table 2-13 occur in fewer than half the genres of the corpus. That relatively narrow distribution identifies more specialized words that appear in few contexts despite their frequency in the corpus as a whole. Consider the word *anode*, which appears 75 times in the corpus—more frequently than *establishment*, *careful*, *powerful*, and *unusual*, the words listed in Table 2-12. Despite its greater frequency, *anode* occurs in only two texts, both in the same genre. This illustrates that a specialized word like *anode* does not occur widely but that when it is on topic, it may be used frequently. This is particularly true of more technical or scientific writing, as we discuss in Chapter 10. (As a further example, consider how often the words *corpus* and *corpora* have been used in this section but how seldom they are used in other contexts.) In Table 2-13 *budget* and *fiscal* are also specialized and occur in fewer than half the genres. Think about which words you would choose to include in the vocabulary of a textbook for international students learning basic English and about how you could best determine what those words would be.

Table 2-13

FREQUENCY OF FIVE NARROWLY DISTRIBUTED WORDS IN THE BROWN CORPUS

WORD	OCCURRENCES	GENRES	TEXTS
artery	51	3	5
budget	53	7	23
dictionary	55	3	5
anode	75	1	2
fiscal	115	5	26

In addition to providing word frequencies for the kinds of texts it represents, having a corpus makes it easy for investigators to determine which words typically occur near one another. These co-occurrence patterns are called **collocations** and are useful for several purposes, one of which is in preparing naturalistic teaching materials for nonnative speakers; they are also very helpful in distinguishing among the senses of words, as we shall see in Chapter 7.

For the most part, the information reported above relies on simple counts of word forms and not on information about lexical category. In actual practice, the words in a corpus are often "tagged" with additional information such as lexical category. In a tagged corpus nouns carry a tag of noun, verbs a tag of verb, and so on. Among other things, such tagging makes it possible to study group characteristics of words carrying a particular tag. Tagging a large corpus by hand (that is, by inspecting each word and keyboarding the tag into the corpus) would be enormously time consuming. (Imagine adding the lexical category to the words in this paragraph, to say nothing about a million or a hundred million words.) Consequently, researchers have devised ways to tag a corpus automatically. One relatively straightforward way is simply to have a computerized reference dictionary that lists the lexical category for the most common words, or for as many words as possible. Then each word in an untagged corpus can be automatically assigned the tag of the corresponding word in the tagged dictionary. In that way, if the word forms *information* and *distribution* appeared in the corpus and in the tagged dictionary, the tag "noun" that accompanied them in the dictionary would automatically be transferred to them in the corpus. Likewise, such forms as *lexical* and *frequent* would automatically be tagged as adjectives (because they are always members of that category), *the* and *a* would be tagged as determiners, *identify* and *see* as verbs, and so on.

As you may have already recognized, this process of matching forms in the corpus to forms in the tagged dictionary won't succeed at identifying the category of all forms because some forms can be members of more than a single category (as illustrated in Table 2-2 on page 51). In the present paragraph, you can note several words whose form does not uniquely identify them as belonging to a particular category. For example, *words*, *forms*, *can*, *use*, *present*, and *process* can all be nouns or verbs. Because English has so many word forms that belong to more than one category, accurate tagging must rely on more complicated procedures than can be provided by automatic matching with a tagged dictionary. Of course, in context (that is, in actual use) a word form will typically belong to only one category. Consequently, achieving accurate tagging of an English corpus can be helped by identifying the lexical category of the words immediately preceding (or following) a form whose category is ambiguous.

We can take *deal* as an example. As a word form, it could be a noun or a verb. Suppose the corpus contained the phrase *a good deal of trouble*, and suppose that the automatic matching to the tagged dictionary had already tagged *good* "adjective." Given a choice between an adjective preceding a noun or a verb, it is a much safer bet to assign noun because in English adjectives typically precede nouns and do not typically precede verbs; thus, *deal* in *a good deal of trouble* can reasonably be judged a noun. In other words, since *good* is unambiguously an adjective, it would have been tagged "adjective" on an initial round of tagging that matched forms in the corpus to the tagged dictionary. As you can see, if you begin a tagging routine by tagging only the words that belong uniquely to a single category and then use that information to help clarify ambiguous cases, many of the unclear cases can be resolved. What typically happens in actual practice is that words are tagged initially for all parts of speech to which they may belong, and then adjacent word categories are used to decide the category of words that carry several tags.

Once a corpus has been tagged, other useful information can be produced. For example, more useful than knowing how often a particular form occurs in a corpus is knowing how often it occurs as a noun or a verb (if it could be either). In fact, to know anything about the noun *list*, you would need to group all its forms together (*list*, *lists*, *list's*, *lists'*), and likewise about the verb you'd need to know about all its forms (*list*, *lists*, *listed*, *listing*). For reasons that will become clearer later in this book, researchers are also interested in determining whether some genres (press reportage or scientific writing or financial news, for example) have frequent adjectives or nouns or verbs or prepositions or pronouns as compared with other genres. This kind of information about the distribution of lexical categories (rather than of particular words) can be helpful in designing teaching materials and in creating speech recognition systems.

SUMMARY

- A morpheme is a minimal unit of meaning or grammatical function.

- Words can contain a single morpheme (*house, swim*) or several (*houses, repatriation, monomaniacal*).

- In the mental lexicon, each morpheme contains abstract information about sounds, related words, phrasal co-occurrence patterns, and meaning.

- Free morphemes can occur as independent words: CAR, HOUSE, FOR.

- Bound morphemes cannot occur as independent words but must be attached to another morpheme: CAR + **-S**, LOOK + **-ED**, ESTABLISH + **-MENT**.

- Bound morphemes can mark nouns for information like number (e.g. 'PLURAL') and case (e.g. 'POSSESSIVE') or verbs for information like tense (e.g. 'PAST') and person (e.g. 'THIRD PERSON').

- Bound morphemes serve to derive different words from existing morphemes; e.g. UN- (*untrue*), DIS- (*displease*), and -MENT (*commitment*).

- Bound morphemes can be affixes (prefixes or suffixes), infixes, or circumfixes.

- Within words morphemes have a significant linear and hierarchical structure.

- Languages have an array of morphological processes for increasing their word stock, including compounding, reduplication, affixation, and shortening.

- Languages borrow words from other languages, sooner or later submitting the borrowings to the pronunciation patterns and morphological processes, both inflectional and derivational, of the borrower language.

- Among the types of morphological systems are inflectional, isolating, and agglutinating systems.

- Isolating systems tend to have one morpheme per word.

- Agglutinating systems tend to have distinct prefixes and suffixes.

- Corpus study is valuable in showing the distribution of categories of words and morphemes as well as particular words and morphemes in different genres.

- Co-occurrences of a word with other words are called collocations.

- Words in a corpus can be automatically tagged with their lexical category, although several rounds of tagging may be necessary to tag all words.

EXERCISES

Based on English

2-1. Identify the category of the italicized words in the sentences below. Use the abbreviations N for noun, V for verb, Adj for adjective, Adv for adverb, Prep for preposition, Pro for pronoun.

a. *People who rarely read in bedrooms* can *feel abnormal.*
b. *Nobody really knows* what *normal reading* is.
c. *The market for audiobooks* is *very large.*

2-2. For the five words in Table 2-2 (page 51) that belong to three lexical categories, provide a sentence illustrating their use in each category. Examples are provided for *average.*

Is there a difference between an *average* and a median? (noun)
A guide can *average* $75 a day in tips. (verb)
He worked hard but earned only *average* grades. (adjective)

2-3. a. For each word listed below, identify its lexical category.
   b. List all the morphemes (each word here contains more than one) and indicate whether they are free or bound.
   c. Indicate for each affix whether it is derivational or inflectional.

heard ✓	tinier	unproductive
toys	saw	bookshops
listened ✓	reassessment	children's
fixer-upper	fatherly	improbable
improbability	repayment	unamusing
tidiest	realignments	calculating
disarms	unremarkable	forewarned
untidiness	realigned	unpretentiousness

2-4. a. The three sentences below contain capitalized DEMONSTRATIVE PRONOUNS and italicized *demonstrative determiners*. Characterize the difference in how they are used. (*Hint*: What are the lexical categories of the words they precede?)
   1) THIS is the last time I'm doing THAT.
   2) *This* time I'm not going to make one of *those* fancy pizzas.
   3) I've had enough of THESE; give me one of *those* red ones.
   b. List each pronoun in the passage below and identify its kind (personal, demonstrative, interrogative, relative). For personal pronouns, also indicate the person (first, second, third).

   What about those books? Whose are they? They look like they come from the library, so they should be returned. If you want, you can put them into a shopping bag and I'll return them for you if I can get Pat to take me in her car. It's been in the shop for a few days. I hope it's ready now.

2-5. The popular compounds *convenience food* and *natural food* are not structured in the same way. *Convenience food* 'food that is convenient to buy, cook, or eat' is a noun-noun compound. *Natural food* 'food made with natural ingredients, free of chemical preservatives and pesticides' is an adjective-noun compound. Both compounds function as nouns. List six compound nouns that contain a noun-noun combination and six that are unmistakably adjective-noun combinations.

2-6. From a passage of about 500 words in a weekly newsmagazine like *Time*, *Newsweek*, or *The Economist* make a list of 20 compounds, marking the lexical category of each constituent word of the compound and of the compound as a whole. Thus, given *telephone tag* you would identify *telephone* as noun (or N), *tag* as noun (or N) and the compound *telephone tag* as noun (or N).

CATEGORY OF:	1ST ELEMENT	2ND ELEMENT	COMPOUND
telephone tag	N	N	N
software	Adj	N	N
bozo filter	N	N	N

2-7. *Cyber-* has become a popular prefix during the 1990s. It has been attached principally to nouns to form new nouns, as in *cyberlove, cyberland, cyberspace,* and *cybercowboy*. List ten words that use the prefix *cyber-*, identifying any examples of *cyber-* being prefixed to a lexical category other than noun.

2-8. Draw trees similar to that on page 47 for these English words:

revaccinations	recapitalization	unlikelihood	reassuringly
disenchantment	unreasonableness	unshockability	updated

2-9. Consider the two analyses of *untruthful* given below. Give arguments for preferring one analysis over the other.

a. [[[un + [true$_{Adj}$] $_{Adj}$] + th $_N$] + ful$_{Adj}$] *we can have Untrueth in* ← *explains more like why*
   our language.

b. [un [[[true$_{Adj}$] + th $_N$] + ful$_{Adj}$] $_{Adj}$]

2-10. The following terms are associated with computer or Internet use. For each one, identify the kind of formation (compound, shortening, acronym, conversion, and so on) and its lexical category. If you are familiar with the term, provide a brief definition or a sentence in which you use it in its customary way. (Just in case you are unfamiliar with some of the shortenings, *FAQ* stands for "frequently asked questions," *IMHO* for "in my honest opinion," and *WYSIWYG* for "what you see is what you get."

Example: *Chatgroup*—compound, noun, 'a group of people "talking" together via the Internet'

client-server	cyberizing	FAQ	source code
cyberenthusiast	cyberspace	domain name	programming language
a flame	to flame out	IMHO	to download
info pike	info superpike	to e-mail	code writer
Internetter	I-way	to lurk	Mac
a lurker	netiquette	netter	PC
newbee or newbie	a remailer	smileys	browser
spamming	a sysop	a thread	mouse
a twit filter	WYSIWYG	software	to keyboard

2-11. Graduates of the University of California at Los Angeles usually call their alma mater U-C-L-A, but it is sometimes lightly referred to as "youkla" or "ookla." Which of these three pronunciations would count as acronyms? List six other shortenings that constitute acronyms and six that could be acronyms but are not. (As an example, the University of Southern California is often called U-S-C but never "usk.")

2-12. a. As determined by their frequency in a million-word corpus of texts (the Brown Corpus), the twenty-six most common words in printed American English are listed below. The category of a few of these words has already been specified. For each of the others, specify its category and then answer the questions below. Choose your categories from this list: N (noun), V (verb), Adj (adjective), Prep (preposition), Det (determiners, including articles), Pro (pronoun).

the	_____	they	_____
be	_____	with	_____
of	_____	not	adverb
and	_____	that	conjunction
a	_____	on	_____
in	_____	she	_____
he	_____	as	conjunction
to	infinitive marker	at	_____
have	_____	by	_____
to	_____	this	_____
it	_____	we	_____
for	_____	you	_____
I	_____	from	_____

(1) List the pronouns that fall among the twenty-six most frequent words of written English: _____

_____

(2) List the prepositions: _____

(3) List the determiners: _____

(4) List the verbs: _____

(5) List the adjectives: _____

(6) List the nouns: _____.

b. The words listed in the two columns are so common in print that one of every four words in the Brown Corpus ranks among the first eight words on the list (*the* through the infinitive marker *to*). To put it another way, over 250,000 of the million words in the Corpus are the same eight words used over and over. With that in mind, answer the following questions.

(1) Which two lexical categories are strikingly absent from the list? What explanation can you offer for their infrequency?

(2) What explanation can you offer for the frequency of prepositions in the Brown Corpus? (*Hint*: It may help to think about what prepositions do.)

(3) What explanation can you offer for the frequency of pronouns as compared to nouns?

(4) The verbs *be* and *have* appear on the list. If you knew that the twenty-seventh word on the list was a verb, which verb would you guess it to be? Why?

(5) Of the twenty-one words whose lexical category you were asked to identify in part a, how many belong to closed classes of words and how many to open classes?

2-13. The words or phrases below come from an article discussing electronic commerce (*Newsweek*, July 7, 1997, p. 80). Next to each word (or italicized word) write the name of the process by which that word has come to have its use in this discussion, drawing the names from this list: compounding, affixation, invention, shortening, conversion, derivation, semantic shift, borrowing, blend.

a. cluelessness   D

b. Information *Highway*   C

c. into *hyperdrive*

d. the digital world   C

e. the *wonky* title   Invention

f. a *cutting-edge* blueprint   C

g. a cutting-edge *blueprint*

h. a virtual *storefront*

i. cyberspace

j. that will *grease* commerce   SS

k. *zipless* electronic commerce   D

l. CDA 'Communications Decency Act'   *shooting*

Based on Languages Other Than English

2-14. a. Analyze the Turkish nouns below and provide a list of their constituent morphemes, along with a gloss for each. (*Note*: In writing Turkish, i represents a vowel similar to u.)

kitap	'book'	elmalar	'apples'	saplar	'stalks'
at	'horse'	masa	'table'	kiz	'girl'
oda	'room'	odalar	'rooms'	masalar	'tables'
sap	'stalk'	atlar	'horses'	sonlar	'ends'
elma	'apple'	adamlar	'men'	meyvar	'fruit (sg.)'

   b. On the basis of your analysis, provide the Turkish words for the following
      English glosses: 'books,' 'man,' 'girls,' 'end,' 'fruit (pl.).'

   c. Given Turkish *odalarda* 'in the rooms' and *masalarda* 'on the tables,' pro-
      vide the Turkish words meaning 'in the books' and 'on the horse.'

2-15. Consider the following pairs of singular and plural nouns for human beings in
Persian. How does Persian form these noun plurals? (*Note*: æ represents a
vowel sound like the one in English *hat* and x represents a sound like the final
consonant of German *Bach.*)

zæn	'woman'	zænan	'women'
mærd	'man'	mærdan	'men'
bæradær	'brother'	bæradæran	'brothers'
pesær	'boy'	pesæran	'boys'
xahær	'sister'	xahæran	'sisters'
doxtær	'daughter'	doxtæran	'daughters'

2-16. Consider the following Persian word pairs with their English glosses. Note the
lexical category of the words in column I, and give the complete rule for forming the words of column II from those in column I. (In these words, š represents a sound like the *sh* in English *ship*; for the pronunciation of x, see
Exercise 2-15.)

I		II	
dana	'wise'	danai	'wisdom'
xub	'good'	xubi	'goodness'
darošt	'thick'	darošti	'thickness'
bozorg	'big'	bozorgi	'size'
širin	'sweet'	širini	'sweetness'

2-17. In the Niutao dialect of the Polynesian language Tuvaluan, some verbs and
adjectives have different forms with singular and plural subjects, as in these
examples:

SINGULAR	PLURAL	
kai	kakai	'eat'
mafuli	mafufuli	'turned around'
fepaki	fepapaki	'collide'
apulu	apupulu	'capsize'
nofo	nonofo	'stay'
maasei	maasesei	'bad'
takato	takakato	'lie down'
valea	valelea	'stupid'

   a. Describe the rule of morphology that derives the plural forms of these
      verbs and adjectives from the singular forms.

   b. In the Funaafuti dialect of the same language the process is slightly differ-
      ent, as the following plural forms of the same verbs and adjectives show.

(Double consonants indicate that the sound is held for a longer period of time.) How are plurals formed from singular forms in this dialect? How does that process differ from the process of plural formation in the Niutao dialect described in part a of this exercise?

kkai	nnofo
maffuli	maassei
feppaki	takkato
appulu	vallea

2-18. On the basis of the examples given below, determine whether the following languages have an isolating, inflectional, or agglutinating morphology, and justify your answer.

SAMOAN
ʔua   maalamalama aʔu i   le mataaʔupu
Present understand   I   Object the lesson
'I understand the lesson.'

TURKISH
herkes   ben üniversite-ye bašla-yacağ-im san-iyor
everyone I   university-to start-Future-I believe-Present
'Everyone believes that I will start university.'

FINNISH
tyttö   silitti   paidat
girl-Subject-Sing. iron-Past-Sing. shirt-Object-Plural
'The girl ironed the shirts.'

JAPANESE
akiko ga   haruko ni mainiti   tegami o   kaku
Akiko Subject Haruko to everyday letter   Object write
'Akiko writes a letter to Haruko every day.'

MOHAWK
t-en-s-hon-te-rist-a-wenrat-eʔ
Dual-Future-Repetitive-Plural-Reflexive-metal-cross-Punctual
'They will cross over the railroad track.'

THAI
kʰruu   hây sàmùt   nákrian săam lêm
teacher give notebook student three Article
'The teacher gave the students three notebooks.'

2-19. The following are sentences of Tok Pisin (New Guinea Pidgin English):

manmeri ol   wokabaut long rot
people   they stroll   on   road
'People are strolling on the road.'

mi harim toktok bilong yupela
I   listen speech of   you-Plural
'I listen to your (plural) speech.'

mi harim toktok bilong yu
I   listen speech of   you-Sing.
'I listen to your (sing.) speech.'

em no brata   bilong em ol   harim toktok bilong mi
he and brother of   he they listen speech of   me
'He and his brother listen to my speech.'

mi laikim dispela manmeri long rot
I   like   these people   on   road
'I like these people (who are) on the road.'

dispela man no prend bilong mi ol   laikim dispela toktok
this   man and friend of   me they like   this   speech
'This man and my friend like this speech.'

Relying on the meaning of the morphemes that you can identify in the previous sentences translate the following sentences into Tok Pisin:

(1) These people like my speech.
(2) I am strolling on the road.
(3) I like my friend's speech.
(4) I like my brother and these people.
(5) These people on the road and my friend like his speech.
(6) You (sing.) and my brother like the speech of these people.
(7) These people listen to my friend's and my brother's speech.

INTERNET RESOURCES

A good deal of valuable information is available on the Internet. The addresses listed in this section may be helpful in understanding this chapter or in exploring related aspects of language on your own. Internet addresses often change, so the ones given below may go out of date. If you try an out-of-date address, an automatic connection to the new address is often possible. The Web site for this textbook (Harcourt Brace) will also post updates to Internet addresses as well as new addresses that become available after publication.

- **Harcourt Brace: http://english.harbrace.com/ling/**
  The Web site for *Language*: *Its Structure and Use*, 3rd ed., provides updated Internet addresses as well as supplemental materials for students and instructors using this textbook.
- **Merriam-Webster OnLine: http://www.m-w.com**
  Entry to the world of dictionaries produced by the Merriam-Webster Company. Well worth bookmarking for its definitions, which are available online.

- **Merriam-Webster New Book of Word Histories:**
  http://www.m-w.com/whist/etyterm.htm
  A Web page for *The Meriam-Webster New Book of Word Histories*. You'll find a
  couple dozen fascinating examples of word histories, as well as definitions and illustrations of some terms used in this chapter, including blends, clipping, and
  shortened forms.
- **Tutorial on Corpus Linguistics:**
  http://www.georgetown.edu/cball/corpora/tutorial.html
  Catherine Ball of Georgetown University maintains a three-hour on-line tutorial
  for corpus linguistics. If you're interested in corpus linguistics, a good place to
  begin your exploration.
- **Corpus Linguistics: http://www.ruf.rice.edu/~barlow/corpus.html.**
  Maintained by Michael Barlow, this Web site (with a four-star rating by Magellan)
  is a goldmine of references to corpora in many languages, as well as to software for
  exploring corpora and information about many other aspects of corpus linguistics.
- **LTG Helpdesk**: **http://www.ltg.ed.ac.uk/helpdesk/faq/index.html**
  Provides a set of frequently asked questions (FAQ) and answers, as well as a
  large number of links to a wide variety of language technology projects. Among
  the FAQs to which answers are provided you'll find these: "I'm looking for a
  tagged corpus of English." "Are there any part-of-speech taggers available for
  Spanish?" "I'm looking for a list of the most frequent words of English, French,
  Italian, Russian, Polish." You can also find links here to on-line taggers that will
  assign part-of-speech labels for texts you submit.

SUGGESTIONS FOR FURTHER READING

- **Jean Aitchison. 1994.** *Words in the Mind*: *An Introduction to the Mental Lexicon*,
  2nd ed. (New York: Blackwell). The Rupert Murdoch Professor of Communications
  at Oxford University provides an entertaining and accessible treatment of the mental
  lexicon.

- **Laurie Bauer. 1983.** *English Word-Formation* (Cambridge: Cambridge UP). A solid,
  accessible introduction to English word formation.

- **Leonard Bloomfield. 1933.** *Language* (New York: Holt). A founder of American
  structural linguistics, Bloomfield gave considerable attention to morphology, and his
  classic treatment of the topic makes informative reading to this day.

- **Ronald W. Langacker. 1972.** *Fundamentals of Linguistic Analysis* (New York:
  Harcourt). An excellent introduction to linguistic analysis, based largely on problem
  solving. Chapter 2 is a particularly good discussion of morphological analysis, with
  illustrations from many languages, including Native American languages. Helpful
  model solutions provided to some problems.

- *12,000 Words*: *A Supplement to Webster's Third New International Dictionary*.
  1987. (Springfield, MA: Merriam). A list of 12,000 new words added to English in
  the twenty-five years after the publication of *Webster's Third New International
  Dictionary* in 1961.

- **John and Adele Algeo. "Among the New Words."** *American Speech.* In each quarterly issue of the journal *American Speech*, the Algeos write a column that defines the most recent additions to the English word stock. You'll be surprised at how many words that are part of your everyday life are brand-new to English. Look up the most recent "Among the New Words" next time you're in the periodicals room of your library.

- *The Merriam-Webster New Book of Word Histories.* **1991.** (Springfield, MA: Merriam). This exciting book provides word histories for thousands of English words from A (i.e., *assassin*) to Z (i.e., *zombie*) and includes all sorts of interesting words in between such as *jeep* and *OK*. (See the Web page address in the previous section.)

Advanced Reading

A good general treatment of morphological processes can be found in Katamba (1993). Matthews (1991) is more advanced. Nida (1949) is a traditional descriptive text with more than two hundred problems from a variety of languages. Our examples of reduplication in Turkish come from Underhill (1976). Good treatments of morphology can be found in Shopen (1985), especially the chapters by Stephen R. Anderson on "Typological Distinctions in Word Formation" and "Inflectional Morphology," by Bernard Comrie on "Causative Verb Formation and Other Verb-Deriving Morphology," and by Comrie and Sandra A. Thompson on "Lexical Nominalization." Comrie (1987), from which a few of the examples in this chapter are taken, provides valuable descriptions of more than forty major languages, usually including discussion of morphology. The Vietnamese example is taken from Comrie (1989).

REFERENCES

Comrie, Bernard, 1989. *Language Universals and Linguistic Typology*, 2nd ed. (Chicago: U of Chicago P).

Comrie, Bernard, ed. 1987. *The World's Major Languages* (New York: Oxford UP).

Katamba, Francis. 1993. *Morphology* (New York: St. Martin's).

Matthews, Peter H. 1991. *Morphology*, 2nd ed. (Cambridge: Cambridge UP).

Nida, Eugene A. 1949. *Morphology: The Descriptive Analysis of Words*, 2nd ed. (Ann Arbor: U of Michigan P).

Shopen, Timothy, ed. 1985. *Grammatical Categories and the Lexicon*, vol. 3 of *Language Typology and Syntactic Description* (Cambridge: Cambridge UP).

Underhill, Robert, 1976. *Turkish Grammar* (Cambridge: MIT P).

CHAPTER 3

THE SOUNDS OF LANGUAGES:

PHONETICS

❧

WHAT DO YOU THINK?

A whiz at reading, your third-grade daughter reports one day that she has discovered that English has five vowels—a, e, i, o, u. You recall reading that it has about three times that many! How would you go about figuring out with your daughter just how many vowel sounds English has?

A friend tells you that George Bernard Shaw claimed that English spelling is so chaotic that "ghoti" could be pronounced "fish," and she challenges you to identify examples of words whose pronunciation and spelling could have led Shaw to his seemingly preposterous conclusion. What words do you give—for example, a word in which <gh> is pronounced "f"?

Suppose you are a fifth-grade teacher and your class complains that English spelling is chaotic. They firmly believe that spelling should reflect pronunciation. As an example they claim that if electricity were spelled <elektrisity> and electrical <elektrikal>, learning to read English would be much easier. What arguments can you offer them for keeping traditional spellings in these and similar cases?

Because you're studying linguistics, one of your roommates asks you whether English has twenty-six sounds to match the twenty-six letters of the alphabet. You reply that English has more than twenty-six sounds, and, thinking quickly, point out that English doesn't have a letter to represent the initial sound in chill and so must use two letters to represent it. You're then asked for other examples where two letters are often required to represent a single English sound. What's your reply?

Imagine that your ESL class notices that you pronounce later, fatter, and metal as though they were spelled with a <d>—as in lady,

> ladder, *and* medal. *They ask why you don't pronounce those words with the <t> sound that appears in the spelling. What's your explanation?*

SOUNDS AND SPELLINGS: NOT THE SAME THING

As a reader of English, you are accustomed to seeing language written down as a series of words set off by spaces, with each word consisting of a sequence of separate letters that are also separated by spaces. You readily recognize that words exist as separate entities made up of a relatively small number of discrete sounds. The words *spat* and *post*, for example, are readily judged by English speakers to have four sounds each, while *adult* has five and *set* has three. Somewhat less obvious is the number of sounds in the words *speakers*, *series*, *letters*, and *sequence*, which do not have the same number of letters and sounds. This lack of correspondence is common in English. *Cough* has three sounds but is spelled with five letters; *freight* has only four sounds despite its seven letters.

Through with seven letters and *thru* with four are alternative spellings for a word with three sounds. *Phone* and *laugh* have three sounds each, represented by five letters. *Delicacy*, with an equal number of sounds and letters, uses the letter <c> to represent two different sounds, a *k*-like sound and an *s*-like sound.

Because of the close association between writing and speaking in the minds of most literate people, it is important to stress that in this chapter we are interested in the sounds of spoken language, not in the letters of the alphabet that are used to represent those sounds in writing.

SAME SPELLING, DIFFERENT PRONUNCIATIONS

Observe the variety of pronunciations represented by the same letter or series of letters in different words. Consider the pronunciations of the following words, all of which are represented in part by the letters <ough>:

cough	"k<u>off</u>"
tough	"t<u>uff</u>"
bough	"b<u>ow</u>"
through	"thr<u>u</u>"
though	"th<u>o</u>"
thoroughfare	"thurr<u>a</u>fare"

Though the precise sounds of these words may vary somewhat among English speakers, still the lesson of the distant relationship between sounds and letters will

Figure 3-1

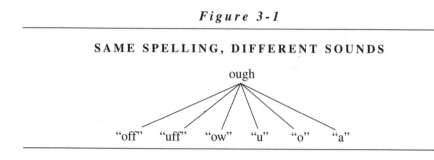

SAME SPELLING, DIFFERENT SOUNDS

ough

"off"   "uff"   "ow"   "u"   "o"   "a"

not be lost on any of them. The spelling <ough> represents at least six different pronunciations in English, as indicated in Figure 3-1.

SAME PRONUNCIATION, DIFFERENT SPELLINGS

Other sets of English words are pronounced alike but spelled differently, as school children learn when they are taught sets of homophones (or homonyms) like *led/lead*, *bear/bare*, and *to/two/too*.

Consider the set of words in Figure 3-2, where nine different spellings represent a single sound, as in the word *see*. Still other spellings for the sound of the word *see* could be cited, including *situ* and *cee* (the name of the letter). Notice that the letter <x>, as in *sexy*, stands for the two sounds [k] and [s] (as in <folksy>).

If you compare the sound and spelling of the words *woman* and *women*, you will note that the difference in the written vowels <a> and <e> does not represent a difference in pronunciation: the second syllables of these words are pronounced alike. On the other hand, <o>—the vowel letter that does not change—represents two different sounds (the sound represented by the <oo> of *wood* in *woman* and by the <i> of *win* in *women*). The pair *Satan* (the devil) and *satin* (the cloth) illustrates the same point: the <a> of the first syllable represents different sounds, while the <a> and <i> of the second syllables represent the same sound.

Playwright George Bernard Shaw, a keen advocate of spelling reform, pointed up the problems in establishing correspondences between sounds and spelling in English when he alleged that *fish* could be spelled <ghoti>: the <gh> as in *cough*, the <o> as in *women*, and the <ti> as in *nation*. Despite the efforts of Shaw and other reformers, English spelling has remained relatively fixed. You can see some very modest success at simplification in such isolated spellings as *thru*, *nite*, and *foto*—though not even these few examples have been widely adopted to replace the more traditional *through*, *night*, and *photo*.

WHYS AND WHEREFORES OF SOUND/SPELLING DISCREPANCIES

There are five principal reasons for the discrepancy between the written representations of many English words and their actual pronunciation.

Figure 3-2

DIFFERENT SPELLINGS, SAME SOUND

see/senile/sea/seize/scenic/siege/ceiling/cedar/cease/juicy/glossy/sexy

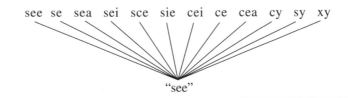

---

1. Written English has diverse origins with different spelling conventions:
   (a) The system that had evolved in Wessex before the Norman Invasion of 1066 gave us such spellings as *ee* for the sound in words like *deed* and *seen.*
   (b) The system that was overlaid on the Old English system by the Normans, with their French writing customs, gave us such spellings as *queen* (for the earlier *cwene*) and *thief* (for earlier *theef*).
   (c) A Dutch influence from Caxton, the first English printer, who was born in England but lived in Holland for thirty years, gave us such spellings as *ghost* (which replaced *gost*) and *ghastly* (which replaced *gastlic*).
   (d) During the Renaissance, an attempt to reform spelling along etymological (that is, historically earlier) lines gave us *debt* for earlier *det* or *dette* and *salmon* for earlier *samon.*
2. A spelling system established several hundred years ago is still used for a language that continues to change its spoken form. Thus the initial <k> in words like *knock, knot, know,* and *knee* was once pronounced, as was the <gh> in *knight* and *thought.* As to vowels, pronunciation change in progress when the writing system was developing and further change in pronunciation afterwards have led to such discrepancies as those represented in *beat/great* and *food/foot,* where different vowel pronunciations are represented by the same spellings.
3. English is spoken differently throughout the world (and in different regions within a country), despite a relatively uniform standard for spellings. Though this spelling uniformity facilitates international communication, it also increases the disparity between the way English is written and spoken in any given place.
4. Word parts alter their pronunciation depending on the adjacent sounds and stress patterns. For example, in *electric* the second <c> represents the sound [k] as in *kiss,* but in *electricity* it represents [s] as in *silly.* Compare also the pronunciations of <i> in *senile* (like the <I> of *I'll*) and *senility* (like the <i> of *ill*).

5. Spoken forms differ from one set of circumstances to another—for example, in formal and informal situations. While some degree of variation is incorporated into the written system (*do not/don't*; *it was/'twas*), there is relatively little tolerance for spellings like *gonna* ('going to'), *wanna* ('want to'), *gotcha* ('got you'), and *j'eat?* ('did you eat?'). Such variable spellings would force readers to determine the pronunciation of the represented speech before arriving at meaning instead of reading directly for meaning, as adult readers normally do.

Advantages of Fixed Spellings   The disadvantages of an irregular set of sound-spelling correspondences are obvious, but there are some advantages too. Consider Chinese, in which many written characters have little or no reference to sounds but instead symbolize meanings directly—much as numerals such as <3> and <7> and miscellaneous other symbols like <+> and <%> do for European languages. With such characters, groups of people whose spoken languages are so dissimilar that mutual intelligibility is difficult can nevertheless communicate well in writing, as is the case between speakers of Cantonese and Mandarin Chinese. Thus the symbol <7> has a uniform meaning across the various European languages, even though the word for the concept for which it stands is pronounced and spelled differently in different speech communities: *seven* in English, *sept* in French, *sette* in Italian, *sieben* in German, and so on. Similarly, then, the fact that English spelling is somewhat removed from pronunciation is not altogether unfavorable for a language that has exceptionally varied dialects, from New Zealand to Jamaica to India—as well as in hundreds of places where English is used in official capacities alongside indigenous native tongues or as a second language for scientific and other international enterprises. Despite diverse pronunciations around the globe, a uniform written word symbol is associated with a single meaning in English. Moreover, in a language with different pronunciations for the same element of meaning, stable spellings can contribute to reading comprehensibility—as in *musical/musician*, *electrical/electricity*, and even the <s> of *cats* and *dogs* (which is pronounced [s] and [z], respectively).

Independence of Script and Speech   The untidy relationship between sound and spelling is not limited to English; it is found in other languages whose writing systems are centuries old but whose speech continuously renews itself in everyday use. It is therefore important to distinguish between the sounds of a language and the way those sounds are customarily represented in writing.

To underscore the independence of sounds and spellings, bear in mind that some languages are represented by different writing systems. For instance, Hindi-Urdu is written by Hindus living in India in Devanāgarī, an Indic script that derives from Sanskrit. The same language is written with Arabic script by Moslems living in Pakistan and parts of India. Sometimes, too, people adopt a new writing system. (The technical term for a writing system is "orthography.") In the early part of this century, the government of Turkey switched from Arabic script to the Roman alphabet to represent Turkish.

Sometimes languages have different scripts for different purposes. Imagine sending an international telegram in a language that uses a script other than the Roman alphabet—in Japanese, Korean, Greek, Russian, Persian, Thai, or Arabic, for example. Rather than using their customary writing systems, speakers of these languages use the Roman alphabet for sending telegrams internationally. Even within a country, an alternative to the customary writing system may be needed: In China, a numeric system is used for sending telegrams. Each Chinese character has a four-digit numeral assigned to it and these numerals are sent telegraphically and then "translated" back into Chinese characters. Sometimes a language uses more than one writing system for different aspects of writing. Written Japanese draws upon three different kinds of writing: *kanji*, based on the Chinese character system, in which a symbol represents a word independent of its pronunciation, and two syllabaries. (A *syllabary* is a writing system in which each symbol represents a spoken syllable.) Thus, throughout the world there are discrepancies between sounds as they are spoken and as they are represented in writing.

In Chapter 12 we return to the relationship between sound and written representation. Now, we focus on the sounds of spoken language and not the letters of the alphabet. The rest of this chapter examines the human vocal apparatus and the sounds it can produce; Chapter 4 examines the nature of the sound systems of human language.

PHONETICS: THE STUDY OF SOUNDS

～

Phonetics is the study of the sounds made in the production of human languages. It has three principal branches.

1. *Articulatory phonetics* focuses on the human vocal apparatus and describes sounds in terms of their articulation in the vocal tract; it has been central to the discipline of linguistics.
2. *Acoustic phonetics* uses the tools of physics to study the nature of sound waves produced in human language; it is playing an increasingly larger role in linguistics as attempts are made to use machines for interpreting speech patterns in voice identification and automatic voice-initiated mechanical operations.
3. *Auditory phonetics* studies the perception of sounds by the brain through the human ear; it has played only a minor role in linguistics to date, but it too can be expected to play a larger role in the future.

Our discussion will be limited almost exclusively to articulatory phonetics—to the nature of human sounds as they are produced by the vocal apparatus.

PHONETIC ALPHABETS

In discussing the sounds of human language from the point of view of their articulation, phoneticians have evolved descriptive techniques to allow comparison across languages and to avoid the difficulties inherent in describing sounds in terms of ordinary written language. You now know that it is not possible to use customary written representations to analyze sound structure: Even within one language, some sounds correspond to more than one letter while some letters correspond to more than one sound. And, of course, a single letter can be used to represent different sounds in different languages. As a result, we need a completely separate system to represent the actual sounds of human languages.

In scientific discussion, the requisite characteristics of symbols for representing sounds are clarity and consistency. The best tool is a phonetic alphabet, and the one most widely used is the International Phonetic Alphabet (IPA), which is created and updated by the International Phonetic Association. The IPA attempts to provide a unique written representation of every sound in all the languages of the world. In keeping with customary practice in American textbooks, we use a very slightly modified

Table 3-1

ENGLISH CONSONANTS ARRANGED BY POSITION IN WORD (ALTERNATIVE PHONETIC SYMBOLS IN PARENTHESES)

PHONETIC SYMBOL	INITIAL	MEDIAL	FINAL
p	pill	caper	tap
b	bill	labor	tab
t	till	petunia	bat
d	dill	seduce	pad
k	kill	sicker	lick
g	gill	dagger	bag
f	fill	beefy	chief
v	villa	saving	grave
θ	thin	author	breath
ð	then	leather	breathe
s	silly	mason	kiss
z	zebra	deposit	shoes
š (ʃ)	shell	rashes	rush
ž (ʒ)	—	measure	rouge
č (tʃ)	chill	kitchen	pitch
ǰ (dʒ)	jelly	bludgeon	fudge
m	mill	dummy	broom
n	nill	sunny	spoon
ŋ	—	singer	sing
h	hill	ahoy	—
y (j)	yes	beyond	toy
r (ɹ)	rent	berry	deer
l	lily	silly	mill
w	will	away	cow

version of the latest IPA by substituting more familiar symbols (sometimes with diacritics such as ˘) for a few of the IPA symbols.

A list of the symbols used to represent the consonant sounds of English is given in Table 3-1. The table shows the phonetic symbol for each sound, alongside representative words that have the relevant parts emphasized. In the six instances where our symbols differ from those of the IPA, the IPA symbol is shown in parentheses. The words illustrate word-initial, word-medial, and word-final occurrences of the sounds.

THE VOCAL TRACT

The processes that the vocal tract uses in creating a multitude of sounds are similar to those of wind instruments and organ pipes, which produce different musical sounds by varying the shape, size, and acoustic character of the cavities through which air passes. Every speech sound sounds different from every other speech sound because of some unique combination of features in the way that you shape your mouth and tongue and move parts of the vocal apparatus when you make the speech sound. Examine the simplified drawing of the vocal tract in Figure 3-3. In this section we will look at the different parts of the human vocal tract and show how these parts work together to produce different sounds.

How are speech sounds made? First, air coming from the lungs passes through the vocal tract, which shapes it into different speech sounds. The air then exits the vocal tract through the mouth or nose or both.

Despite the fact that speakers of all languages have the same vocal apparatus, no language takes advantage of all the possibilities for forming different sounds, and

Figure 3-3

THE VOCAL TRACT

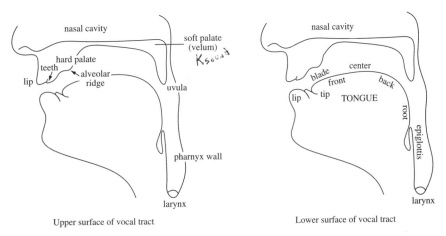

Upper surface of vocal tract   Lower surface of vocal tract

Adapted from Ladefoged 1993

there are striking differences in the sounds that occur in different languages. For example, Japanese and Thai lack the [v] sound of English *van*, and Japanese lacks the [f] sound of *fan*. Thai lacks the sounds represented by <g> in *gill*, <z> in *zebra*, <sh> in *shell*, <s> in *measure*, and <j> and <dg> in *judge*. French, Japanese, and Thai lack the quite different <th> sounds in *either* and *ether*.

Just as some languages lack sounds that English has, other languages have sounds that English does not have. You are probably aware that English lacks the rolled *r* that exists in Spanish and Italian and that German has a sound at the end of words like *Bach* 'stream' and *hoch* 'high' that does not occur among the inventory of English sounds. Arabic has a sound similar to the German <ch> of *Bach*, but in Arabic it can occur word initially. A similar (but not identical) sound occurring word finally in the German word *ich* occurs in English (for those dialects that pronounce the <h>) in the initial sound of *human* and *huge*. Still, it can be tough for English speakers learning German to pronounce the sound in a word like *ich* because English doesn't permit that sound to occur at the end of a word.

DESCRIBING SOUNDS

—

As we explore the inventory of sounds, use your vocal tract to produce the sounds that are described. Pronounce them aloud, noting the shape of your mouth and the position of your tongue as each sound is produced. Such firsthand experience will familiarize you with the reference points of phonetics, make the discussion easier to follow, and give you confidence in your ability to master articulatory phonetics.

In our early discussion, we will continue to use square brackets to enclose the symbols representing sounds. Thus [t] will symbolize the initial and final sounds in *tot*, [d] the initial and final sounds in *did*, and [z] the initial sound in *zebra*, the medial consonant in *busy*, and the final sound of *buzz* and *dogs*.

Different speech sounds can be identified in terms of their *articulatory* properties—that is, by *where* in the mouth and *how* they are produced. All consonants can be described in terms of three properties.

> **Voicing** (whether the vocal cords are together and vibrating or open and not vibrating)
> **Place of articulation** (where the airstream is most obstructed)
> **Manner of articulation** (the particular way the airstream is obstructed)

VOICING

Begin by distinguishing between [s] (as in *bus* or *sip*) and [z] (as in *buzz* or *zip*). When you pronounce a long, continuous [zzzzz] and alternate it with a long, continuous [sssss], you will notice that the position of your lips and the position of your tongue within your mouth remain the same for [s] and [z], even though these sounds are noticeably different. You can feel this difference by touching your **larynx** (Adam's apple) while saying [zzzzz sssss zzzzz sssss]. The vibration that you feel

THE VOCAL CORDS AND VOICING

Human beings have no organs that are used only for speech. The organs that produce speech sounds have evolved principally to serve the life-sustaining processes of breathing and eating. Speech is a secondary function of the human "vocal apparatus" and in that sense is sometimes said to be parasitic on these organs. The vocal cords offer an illustration of the "parasitic" nature of speech: the primary function of these two muscle flaps is to keep food from going down the wrong tube and entering the lungs.

With respect to speech, the vocal cords are used to distinguish voiced and voiceless sounds. You can perceive the difference between voiced and voiceless consonants by alternating between the pronunciations of [f] and [v] or [s] and [z] while holding your hands clapped over your ears. You may also find it helpful to see whether you can tell from pronouncing the words *tall*, *talent*, *bid*, *dead*, and *dilemma* whether [t] or [d] is voiced; take care not to confuse the voicing that is part of the pronunciation of the vowels following the consonants in question. In English, vowels are always voiced. Check your conclusions against Table 3-7 on page 98.

from your larynx when you utter [zzzzz] but not [sssss] is called *voicing*; it is the result of air being forced through a narrow aperture (called the **glottis**) between two folds of muscle (the vocal cords) in the larynx, much like the leaf with a slit in it that children use to make a vibrating noise by blowing air through it. When the vocal cords are held together, the air forced through them from the lungs causes them to vibrate. It is precisely this vibration, or "voicing," that distinguishes [z] from [s] and enables speakers to differentiate between two otherwise identical sounds.

Using these very similar but distinct sounds enables us to create words that differ by only a single feature of voicing on a single sound but carry quite different meanings, as in *bus* and *buzz*, *sip* and *zip*, *peace* and *peas*, *sane* and *Zane*.

Not only [s] and [z] but other sounds in English and many other languages are characterized by a voiced versus voiceless contrast. Consider [f] and [v], as in *fine* and *vine*: both sounds are produced with air being forced through a narrow aperture between the upper teeth and the lower lip; [f] being voiceless, [v] voiced. Other voiceless/voiced pairs include [p] and [b] as in *pet* and *bet* and [t] and [d] as in *ten* and *den*. Most, perhaps all, languages have some pairs of sounds that are phonetically different only in that one is voiced and the other voiceless—though this difference is not necessarily significant in all languages, as you will see in the case of Korean.

MANNER OF ARTICULATION

Besides having a voicing feature, [s] and [z] can be further characterized as to their *manner of articulation*. In pronouncing them, air is continuously forced through a narrow opening at a place behind the upper teeth. Compare the pronunciation of [s] and [z] with the sounds [t] and [d]. Unlike [s] and [z], [t] and [d] are not pronounced by making a continuous stream of air pass through the mouth. Instead, the air is completely stopped behind and above the upper teeth and then released (or exploded) in a small burst of air. For this reason, [t] and [d] are called stops; because the air is released through the mouth (and not the nose), they can also be called oral stops. Sounds like [s] and [z] that are made by a continuous stream of air passing through a narrowed passage in the vocal tract are called fricatives. *Task*: Pronounce the sounds [p], [b], [f], and [v] to determine which are stops and which are fricatives.

PLACE OF ARTICULATION

Of the sounds we have analyzed so far, [s] and [t] are voiceless, while [z] and [d] are voiced. All four of them are pronounced with the point of greatest closure immediately behind the upper teeth. Pronounce *ten* and *den* aloud, feeling where the tip of your tongue touches the top of your mouth for the consonants. Both words start (and finish) at the alveolar ridge. Because [t], [d], and [n] are all articulated at the alveolar ridge, they are called **alveolars**. [s] and [z] are also articulated at the alveolar ridge, as you will notice by pronouncing the words *sin* and *zen*. (Of course, as to manner of articulation, [s] and [z] are fricatives, whereas [t] and [d] are stops.)

There are three major *places of articulation* for English stops: the alveolar ridge, the lips, and the soft palate (or velum). If you say the words *pin* and *bin*, you will notice that for the initial sound in each word air is built up behind the two lips and then released. Thus the point of greatest closure is at the lips, and [p] and [b] are therefore called **bilabial** stops ("bilabial" means 'two lips'). If you compare your pronunciations of [p] and [t], you will see that both are voiceless and that the only difference between them is in the place of articulation.

If you attend to the pronunciation of the first sound of *kin*, you will notice that [k], like [p] in *pill* and [t] in *till*, is a voiceless stop, but it differs from them in its place of articulation: [k] is pronounced with the tongue touching the roof of the mouth at the velum (the soft palate) and is therefore called a **velar**; [k] is thus a voiceless velar stop.

Corresponding to the three voiceless stops [p], [t], and [k], English has three voiced stops: [b] as in *bib* is a voiced bilabial stop; [d] as in *did* is a voiced alveolar stop; and [g] as in *gig* is a voiced velar stop. Altogether, then, English has six stops, three pairs with each pair pronounced at the same place of articulation but one with a voiceless and the other a voiced sound. *Task*: Identify the pair of stops pronounced at the lips, at the alveolar ridge, and at the velum.

Besides lips, alveolar ridge, and velum, English takes advantage of other articulators to produce some sounds. The <th> of *thin* is a fricative pronounced with the tongue between the teeth. It is described as a voiceless **interdental** fricative and has the Greek letter theta [θ] as its phonetic symbol. [š] (the sound represented by <sh> in *shoot* and *wish*) and [ž] (the final sound in *beige* and the middle consonant in *measure*) are pronounced between the alveolar ridge and the velum (or palate); sounds produced there are called **alveo-palatals**. [š] (IPA [ʃ]) is a voiceless alveo-palatal fricative; [ž] (IPA [ʒ]) is a voiced alveo-palatal fricative.

CONSONANT SOUNDS

Consonants are sounds produced by partially or completely blocking air in its passage from the lungs through the vocal tract. If you review the inventory of English consonants given in Table 3-1 and pronounce the sounds aloud while concentrating on the place and manner of articulation, you will perceive how the rest of the table represents the distribution of English consonants according to their voicing, their place of articulation, and their *manner of articulation*. We now describe these consonants, grouped here according to their manner of articulation and described in terms of their voicing and their place of articulation. While concentrating on the consonant sounds of English, we also mention selected consonants from other languages.

STOPS

The principal stops of English are [p], [b], [t], [d], [k], [g]. By pronouncing words with these sounds in them (see Table 3-1), you can recognize that [p] and [b] are bilabial stops, [t] and [d] alveolar stops, and [k] and [g] velar stops. **Stops** are formed when air is built up in the vocal tract and suddenly released through the mouth.

ENGLISH STOPS

PLACE OF ARTICULATION

	BILABIAL	ALVEOLAR	VELAR	GLOTTAL
VOICELESS	p	t	k	ʔ
VOICED	b	d	g	

In addition, many languages have a glottal stop, pronounced by briefly and completely blocking air from passing in the throat with the glottis (and therefore voiceless by definition). The glottal stop is represented in the IPA by [ʔ]. In English, the glottal stop occurs only as a marginal sound—between the two parts of the exclamation *Uh-oh!* in American English and in Cockney English as the medial consonant of words like *butter* and *bottle.* In languages like Hawaiian, the glottal stop is a full-fledged consonant that can distinguish two different words: *paʔu* 'smudge' and *pau* 'finished.'

FRICATIVES

To pronounce the alveolar fricatives [s] and [z], air is forced through a narrow opening between the tip of the tongue and the alveolar ridge. English has a large inventory of fricatives, some of them articulated in front of [s] and [z], others behind them. **Fricatives** are characterized by a forcing of air in a continuous stream through a narrow opening. In pronouncing the first sound in the words *thin, three,* and *theta* and the final sound in *teeth* and *bath*, notice that the tongue tip is placed between the upper and lower teeth, where the airstream is most constricted and makes its articulation. Represented by the phonetic symbol [θ], the sound in these words is a voiceless interdental fricative. The voiced counterpart is the initial sound in the words *there* and *then* and the middle consonant sound in *either.* Notice that in English the spelling <th> is used for two distinct sounds: [θ] as in *ether* and [ð] as in *either* or *feather.*

If you pronounce the following words, you will discover other fricatives and become aware of their common properties as well as their different places of articulation:

fine/vine	[f] [v] labio-dental fricatives
thigh/thy; *ether/either*	[θ] [ð] interdental fricatives
sink/zinc	[s] [z] alveolar fricatives
rush/rouge; *fishin'/vision*	[š] [ž] alveo-palatal fricatives (IPA [ʃ] [ʒ])
here/ahoy	[h] glottal fricative

ENGLISH FRICATIVES

PLACE OF ARTICULATION

	LABIO-DENTAL	INTER-DENTAL	ALVEOLAR	ALVEO-PALATAL	GLOTTAL
VOICELESS	f	θ	s	š (ʃ)	h
VOICED	v	ð	z	ž (ʒ)	

Some languages have other fricatives articulated in different parts of the vocal tract. Spanish, for example, has a voiced bilabial fricative (represented by the phonetic symbol [β]), as in *cabo* 'end.' Japanese has a voiceless bilabial fricative represented by the phonetic symbol [ɸ] and pronounced somewhat like [f] but by bringing together both lips instead of the lower lip and the upper front teeth. The West African language Ewe has both a voiced [β] and a voiceless [ɸ]. Spanish has a voiceless velar fricative [x], which also exists in many other languages, and a voiced velar fricative [ɣ], which is less common. Pronounce [x] as if you were gently clearing your throat. The sound occurs in the Spanish word *jova* 'jewel' and the personal name *José* (which, when borrowed into English, are pronounced with an [h], the closest sound to [x] that English has). [ɣ] is represented by <g> in Spanish *lago* 'lake.' German, Irish, and Mandarin Chinese have a voiceless palatal fricative [ç], as in the German word *Reich* 'empire.'

Notice that in English the physical distance in the mouth between the places of articulation for the fricatives is not as great as the distance for the different stops. The bilabial, alveolar, and velar places of articulation for the stop consonants are spaced farther apart than are the labio-dental, interdental, alveolar, and alveo-palatal articulations of the fricatives. The tighter packing of the fricatives in the mouth can cause difficulty in perceiving them as distinct, especially when any interference is present. If you ask a friend to identify the fricative sounds either over the telephone or when you pronounce them while facing away, you'll discover that they're tougher to distinguish from one another than you might have thought. The acoustic differences may be especially difficult to perceive for speakers of languages that have fewer fricatives than English does or that have them better spaced. Because French does not have the interdental fricatives [θ] and [ð], some French speakers tend to perceive (and pronounce) English words like *thin* and *this* as though they were "sin" and "zis". One fricative that does not occur in English but is familiar to English speakers is the French voiced uvular *r* (as in *Paris* or *rue* 'street'), which is made farther back in the mouth and is represented by the phonetic symbol [ʁ].

AFFRICATES

Two consonant sounds in English are a little more complex to describe than stops and fricatives but are closely related to them. These are the sounds that occur initially in the words *chin* and *gin* and finally in the words *batch* and *badge.* If you pronounce these sounds slowly enough, you can recognize that they are stop-fricatives. We refer to stop-fricatives as affricates. In the pronunciation of an **affricate**, air is built up by a complete closure of the oral tract at some place of articulation, then released (something like a stop) and continued (like a fricative). The sound in *chin*, for example, is a combination of the stop [t] and the fricative [š] (IPA [ʃ]); we represent it as [č] or IPA [tʃ]. The sound at the beginning and end of *judge* is a combination of the stop [d] and the fricative [ž] (IPA [ʒ]); we represent it as [ǰ] or IPA [dʒ]. English has just these two affricates, both of which are alveo-palatal affricates.

Other affricates occur in other languages. The most common are the alveolar affricates [ts] and [dz], which occur at the beginning of the Italian words *zucchero* 'sugar' and *zona* 'zone' respectively.

ENGLISH AFFRICATES

PLACE OF ARTICULATION

	ALVEO-PALATAL
VOICELESS	č (tʃ)
VOICED	ǰ (dʒ)

OBSTRUENTS

Because they share the phonetic property of constricting the airflow through the vocal tract, fricatives, stops, and affricates are together referred to as **obstruents.**

ENGLISH APPROXIMANTS

PLACE OF ARTICULATION

	BILABIAL	ALVEOLAR	PALATAL
VOICED (CENTRAL)	w	ɾ	y
VOICED (LATERAL)		l	

APPROXIMANTS

English has four sounds that are known as **approximants** because they are produced by two articulators approaching one another almost like fricatives but not coming close enough to produce audible friction. The English approximants are [y], [r], [l], and [w]. [y] is a palatal approximant as in *you*; the word *cute* begins with the consonant cluster [ky]. As to [r] and [l], among the languages of the world it is not so common as English speakers might expect for them to be distinctive sounds as in English *rid/lid* or *fear/feel*. Because [r] is pronounced by channeling air through the central part of the mouth, it is called a central approximant. To pronounce [l] air is channeled on each side of the tongue and [l] is therefore called a lateral approximant. To distinguish them from the other approximants, [r] and [l] are sometimes called liquids. The difference between [r] and [l] is not always easy to master. (In some Asian languages, [r] and [l] are not distinct sounds, so native speakers of these languages find it challenging to distinguish them when speaking English.)

In pronouncing the approximant [w], the lips are rounded, as in *wild*. For certain dialects, in some words [h] precedes [w] as in *which* or *whether*. When [w] is the second element of a consonant cluster (as in *twine* or *quick*), the initial sound ([t] or [k]) is rounded in anticipation of the [w].

NASALS

Nasal consonants are pronounced by lowering the velum, thus allowing the stream of air to pass out through the nasal cavity instead of through the oral cavity. English has three nasal stops: [m] as in *mad, cram, drummer*; [n] as in *new, ten, sinner*; and a third, symbolized by [ŋ] and pronounced as in the words *sing* and *singer*.

ENGLISH NASALS

PLACE OF ARTICULATION

BILABIAL	ALVEOLAR	VELAR
m	n	ŋ

[ŋ] does not occur word initially in English. Because of the way we spell it, English speakers sometimes think of [ŋ] as a combination of [n] and [g], but it is actually a single sound, as you can see by comparing your pronunciation of the words *singer* and *finger.* Leaving aside the initial sounds [s] and [f], if your pronunciation of these words differs (for some speakers of English it does *not*), then you have [ŋ] in *singer* and [ŋg]—not [ng]—in *finger.* Most American English speakers have a three-way contrast among *simmer, sinner,* and *singer* solely according to whether the middle consonant is [m], [n], or [ŋ]. By noticing where the tongue touches the upper part of the mouth in the articulation of these nasal consonants (and by comparing their place of articulation with other sounds identified above), you will be able to determine that [m] is a bilabial nasal, [n] an alveolar nasal, and [ŋ] a velar nasal. If, while you are saying [mmmmm], you cut off the airstream passing through the nose by pinching it closed (as a clothespin would), the sound stops abruptly; this demonstrates that nasal stops are produced by passing air through the nose. Compare cutting off the air passing through your nose while saying [nnnnn] and [sssss], and you will get a clear sense of the use of the nasal and oral cavities in sound production. You will see that when you cut off the air passing through the nose there is virtually no difference in the quality of the sound for oral consonants, but when you cut off the air passing through the nose for a nasal consonant no sound at all is made.

If you have successfully identified the places of articulation for the nasals and understood why they fit in their particular slots in the consonant table, you will have noticed that English has three sets of consonants articulated in the same places though differing in their manner of articulation: the oral stops [p] and [b] and the nasal stop [m] are articulated at the two lips and are known as bilabials; the oral stops [t] and [d] and the nasal stop [n] are articulated at the alveolar ridge and are called alveolars; [k], [g], and [ŋ] are articulated at the velum and are called velars.

The nasal consonants of English are [m], [n], [ŋ]. Other languages have other nasals. French, Spanish, and Italian, for instance, all have a palatal nasal [ɲ]; examples include the French word *mignon* 'cute' (which English has borrowed in the phrase *filet mignon*), the Spanish words *señor* and *cañón* (*cañón* has been borrowed into English as *canyon*), and the Italian *bagno* 'bath' and *lasagna* (also borrowed into English).

CLICKS, FLAPS, TRILLS

Some languages have consonants that belong to the same classes we have discussed but are strikingly different from those in European languages. Several languages of southern Africa, for instance, have among their stop consonants certain **click** sounds that are an integral part of their sound system. One example is the lateral click made on the side of the tongue; it occurs in English when we urge a horse to move on, for example, but it is not part of the inventory of English speech sounds; it is represented with the IPA symbol [ǁ]. Another click sound that occurs in some of these languages can be represented in English writing by the reproach *tsk-tsk.* This last click is not a lateral but a dental (IPA [ǀ]) or a (post)alveolar (IPA [!]) made with the tip of the tongue at the teeth or the alveolar ridge.

A few consonant sounds are not stops, fricatives, affricates, approximants, or nasals. The middle consonant of the word *butter* is commonly pronounced in American English as an alveolar **flap**, produced by throwing the tongue against the alveolar ridge. We represent this flap (which will be discussed in Chapter 4) with the IPA symbol [ɾ]). Spanish, Italian, and Fijian have an alveolar **trill** *r*, as in Spanish *correr* 'to run,' represented by the symbol [r̃] (IPA [r]).

VOWEL SOUNDS

Vowel sounds differ from consonant sounds in that they are produced not by blocking air in its passage from the lungs but by passing air through different shapes of the mouth and different positions of the tongue and lips unobstructed by narrow passages (except at the glottis). Some languages have as few as three distinct vowels in their sound systems; others have more than a dozen. Many people think of English as having only five vowels; but this is a reflection of the writing system rather than the spoken language (and is a clear example of the influence of writing on our thinking about language). In pronouncing the following words, you will realize that English has many more than five vowels: *peat, pit, pet, pate, pat, put, putt, poke, pot, part,* and *port.*

VOWEL HEIGHT AND FRONTNESS

Unlike consonants, which are described by place and manner of articulation, vowels are characterized by the position of the tongue and the lips, in particular by the relative height and relative frontness or backness of the tongue and the relative rounding of the lips. We refer to vowels as being high or low and front or back; we also consider whether the lips are rounded (as for *pool*) or nonrounded (as for *pill*). You can get a feel for these descriptors by alternately saying *feed* and *food*, the first of which contains a front vowel, the second a back vowel. To get a feel for tongue height, alternate saying *feet* and *fat*. If you fail to feel the difference between high and low vowels with this pair of sounds, look at yourself in the mirror (or at a classmate saying them); you'll see that because the tongue is lower, the mouth is open much wider for the vowel of *fat* than for the vowel of *feet*.

Figure 3-4 indicates the relationship of the English vowels to one another and the approximate positions of the tongue during their articulation.

Here are English words for each of the vowel symbols shown in the figure:

i	Pete, beat			u	pool, boot
ɪ	pit, bit			ʊ	put, foot
e	late, bait	ə	about, sof<u>a</u>	o	poke, boat
ɛ	pet, bet	ʌ	putt, but	ɔ	port, bought
æ	pat, bat	a	park (in Boston)	ɑ	pot, father

The symbol [ə] (called *schwa*) and the symbol [ʌ] (called *caret* or *wedge*) represent very similar sounds. Both sounds occur in the word *above* [əbʌv]. In this book we use [ə] to represent a mid central vowel in unstressed syllables, as in the second

Figure 3-4

THE VOWELS OF ENGLISH

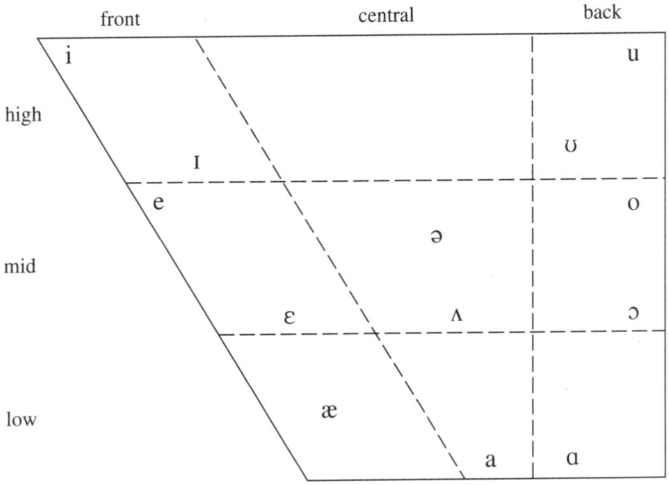

syllables of *buses* [bʌsəz] and the second and third syllables of *capable* [kepəbəl]. We also use it before [r] in the same syllable whether stressed, as in *person* [pərsən] and *sir* [sər], or unstressed, as in *pertain* [pərten] and *tender* [tɛndər]. We use [ʌ] to represent mid central vowels in other stressed syllables, such as *suds* [sʌdz] and the first syllable of *flooded* [flʌɾəd]. (*Note*: Some books use [ɜ] to represent a mid central vowel with *r* coloring. In systems using the [ɜ] notation, *person* would be transcribed [pɜsən], *sir* [sɜ], and *pertain* [pɜten].)

DIPHTHONGS

English also has **diphthongs**, represented by pairs of symbols to capture the fact that a diphthong is a vowel sound for which the tongue starts in one place in the mouth and moves to another: [ay] (as in *bite*); [aw] (as in *pout*, *bout*); [ɔy] (as in *boy*, *toy*). (*Note*: Some books transcribe these sounds as [aɪ], [aʊ], and [ɔɪ], respectively.) Diphthongs change in quality while being pronounced, as you can notice by pronouncing these words slowly: *buy*, *boy*, *bough*. Thus American English dialects have up to thirteen distinctive vowel sounds (plus three diphthongs), not the five vowels that are commonly said to exist when we fail to distinguish between sounds and letters. In England and certain parts of the United States, including metropolitan New York City, sixteen distinct vowels and diphthongs exist; in some parts of the United States, including Pittsburgh and surrounding areas, fewer distinct vowel and diphthong sounds exist, because no distinction is made between the vowels of *bought* and *pot*; thus *caught* and *cot* are homonyms.

OTHER ARTICULATORY FEATURES OF VOWELS

Languages have other possibilities besides tongue height and backness for creating differences among vowels. Five other features of vowel quality that languages can exploit to add to their inventory of distinctive vowels are tenseness, rounding, lengthening, nasalization, and tone.

Tenseness Many languages make a distinction between tense and lax vowels. Tense vowels are produced with greater overall muscular tension in the mouth; lax vowels are pronounced with less tension and tend to be shorter. In English the contrast between [i] of *peat* and [ɪ] of *pit* is in part a tense/lax contrast; likewise for *bait/bet* and *cooed/could.*

Rounding Whereas in English high front vowels tend automatically to be unrounded (and high back vowels to be rounded), some languages have both rounded and unrounded front vowels. To cite two examples, French and German have high front and mid front rounded vowels as well as unrounded ones. French has a high front unrounded [i] in words such as *dire* 'to say' and *dix* 'ten' and a high front rounded vowel [ü], as in *rue* 'street'; it also has a contrast between upper mid front unrounded [e] (as in *fée* 'fairy') and upper mid front rounded [ø] (*feu* 'fire'); and between lower mid front unrounded [ɛ] (*serre* 'hothouse') and lower mid front rounded [œ] (*soeur* 'sister'). German has similar contrasts.

Length German has two of each vowel type—one long, the other short. The pronunciation of long vowels is held longer than that of short vowels. Long vowels are commonly represented with a special colon after them in phonetic transcriptions or by the vowel symbol doubled. (In dictionaries and some writing systems, a macron (⁻) is sometimes used above the vowel symbol.) Thus, in addition to the short vowels [i] and [ü], as in *bitten* 'to request' and *müssen* 'must,' German has words with high front long vowels, such as unrounded [i:] in *bieten* 'to wish' and rounded [ü:] in *Mühle* 'mill.' These German examples illustrate how languages can multiply differences among vowels by exploiting long and short varieties of the same vowel. English, too, has vowels of differing length, although it does not exploit length to create different words (see Chapter 4). To sense differences in the duration of vowels, pronounce the English words *beat, bead, bit.* You should be able to hear that the vowel of *bead* is longer than that of *beat*, and that both are longer than that of *bit.*

Nasalization All vowel types can also be nasalized. This is done by pronouncing the vowel while passing air through the nose (as for nasal stops) as well as through the mouth. Nasal vowels are indicated by a tilde (˜) above the vowel symbol. As is well known, French has several nasal vowels paralleling the oral vowels. It has a contrast between *lin* [lɛ̃] 'flax' and *lait* [lɛ] 'milk,' between *ment* [mɑ̃] '(he) is lying' and *ma* [mɑ] 'my' (feminine), and between *honte* [ɔ̃t] 'shame' and *hotte* [ɔt] 'hutch.' Other languages with nasal vowels include Irish, Hindi, and the Native American languages Delaware, Mixtec, Navaho, and Seneca. English also has some nasal vowels; but they are not significant (see Chapter 4).

Tone In many languages of Asia, Africa, and North America, a vowel may be pronounced on several pitches and be perceived by the native speakers of these languages as different sounds. Typically, a vowel pronounced on a low pitch contrasts with the same vowel pronounced on a higher pitch. An example of such a two-tone language is Hausa, spoken in West Africa. In Hausa, the word *górà* 'bamboo,' in which the first vowel is pronounced with a high tone (´) and the second vowel with a low tone (`), contrasts with the word *gòrá* 'large gourd,' in which the sequence of tones is reversed. Other tone languages have more complex systems. The Beijing (Peking) dialect of Chinese has four tones: a high level tone (symbolized with ¯); a rising tone (´); a falling-rising tone (ˇ), in which the pitch begins to fall and then rises sharply; and a falling tone (`), in which the pitch falls sharply. Thus there is a four-way contrast among the following four vowels pronounced on different tones; these vowels happen to be words by themselves, with separate meanings.

ī (high level)	'one'
í (rising)	'proper'
ĭ (falling-rising)	'already'
ì (falling)	'thought'

(Note that a given accent mark can be used to represent different tones in different languages. Thus, ´ represents a high tone in Hausa but a rising tone in Chinese; ` represents a low tone in Hausa but a falling tone in Chinese.)

Table 3-2

FRENCH VOWELS WITH ILLUSTRATIVE WORDS

	FRONT UNROUNDED	FRONT ROUNDED	CENTRAL UNROUNDED	BACK ROUNDED
ORAL				
high	i	ü		u
upper mid	e	ø		o
mid			ə	
lower mid	ɛ	œ		ɔ
low			a	
NASAL				
lower mid	ɛ̃	œ̃		ɔ̃
low				ɑ̃
	i gr<u>i</u>s 'grey'	ü m<u>û</u>r 'ripe'	ə ch<u>e</u>min 'path'	u f<u>ou</u> 'crazy'
	e ferm<u>é</u> 'shut'	ø j<u>eû</u>ne 'fasts'	a p<u>a</u>r 'by'	o m<u>o</u>t 'word'
	ɛ fr<u>ais</u> 'fresh'	œ j<u>eu</u>ne 'young'		ɔ f<u>o</u>rt 'strong'
	ɛ̃ br<u>in</u> 'sprig'	œ̃ br<u>un</u> 'brown'		ɔ̃ f<u>on</u>d 'bottom'
				ɑ̃ f<u>aon</u> 'fawn'

Some languages have even more complex tone systems: Thai has five tones; the standard dialect of Vietnamese has six tones; and the Guangzhou (Canton) dialect of Chinese has nine different tones. Tone is thus not only a widespread phenomenon, but a diverse one.

Tables 3-2 through 3-5 are vowel charts illustrating the sound patterns of four of the world's major languages—French, Spanish, German, and Japanese.

Table 3-3

SPANISH VOWELS WITH ILLUSTRATIVE WORDS

	FRONT UNROUNDED	CENTRAL UNROUNDED	BACK ROUNDED
HIGH	i		u
MID	e		o
LOW		a	
	i chiste 'joke'	a mar 'sea'	u sur 'south'
	e fe 'faith'		o boca 'mouth'

Table 3-4

GERMAN VOWELS WITH ILLUSTRATIVE WORDS

	FRONT UNROUNDED	FRONT ROUNDED	CENTRAL UNROUNDED	BACK ROUNDED
HIGH				
long	iː	üː		uː
short	i	ü		u
UPPER MID				
long	eː	øː		oː
short	e			o
MID				
short			ə	
LOWER MID				
long	εː			
short		œ		
LOW				
long			aː	
short			a	
	iː bieten 'to wish'	üː Mühle 'mill'	ə liebe 'dear'	uː Huhn 'hen'
	i bitten 'to request'	ü müssen 'must'	aː Rabe 'raven'	u Mutter 'mother'
	eː wen 'whom'	øː ölig 'oily'	a Ratte 'rat'	oː Ofen 'oven'
	e wenn 'when'	œ Röntgen 'X-ray'		o Ochs 'ox'
	εː Käse 'cheese'			

Table 3-5

JAPANESE VOWELS WITH ILLUSTRATIVE WORDS

	FRONT UNROUNDED	CENTRAL UNROUNDED	BACK UNROUNDED	BACK ROUNDED
HIGH	i		ɯ	
MID	ɛ			ɔ
LOW	a	a		

i ima 'now'
ɛ sensei 'teacher'
a aki 'autumn'
ɯ buji 'safe'
ɔ yoru 'to approach'

Tables 3-6 and 3-7 summarize all the vowels and consonants introduced in this chapter.

COMPUTERS AND PHONETICS

From experience with your favorite compact disks (better known as CDs) you know that computers can "digitalize" sound. The process of digitalizing differs from the analog process that is represented on tape recordings, and the difference is akin to the difference between an analog clock (whose hands move continuously to represent hours, minutes, and seconds) and a digital clock (which records time at discrete points such as 12:21:58). The analog clock moves continuously while the digital clock moves in discrete units—for example from 12:21:58 to 12:21:59 to 12:22:00. By contrast, on an analog clock the second hand moves gradually so that, at least in principle, a countless number of points could occur between 12:21:58 and 12:22:00 in addition to the point represented as 12:21:59 on a digital clock.

In Chapter 4 we look more closely at the challenge of using computers to understand speech and to synthesize speech from written texts. Here it is useful simply to note that digitalization represents discrete or separate points. Over the centuries, it has proven useful to phoneticians to think of speech sounds as discrete, and alphabetic writing systems also rely on the notion of discrete sounds. But in reality—in conversation, for example—sounds are not discrete and do not occur separately. Instead each sound touches the next sound in a word (and in an utterance), and in fact sounds and words merge into another.

Imagine a machine that could create discrete sounds that seem quite natural when spoken in isolation—for example, a computer that could produce the sounds [ɪ], [n], [k], [l], [u], [d] and [ə]. If the computer put these sounds together (and added another [d]), it would produce the sequence [ɪnkludəd]. Now you might think that if your computer put these sounds together in sequence, it would produce a noise that sounded like the word *included*. But consider these complications. The word *included* as it is usually pronounced does not have the same [ɪ] sound that occurs in the word *sit*, and the [n] in *included* is often pronounced more like the [ŋ] of *sing* than the [n] of *tin*. So the production of words by computers could not rely on a simple sequence of sounds if even remotely natural-sounding words are to be produced.

Suppose instead that for the word *included* the computer put together the sounds [ɪ̃], [ŋ], [k], [l], [u], [d], [ə], and [d]. How would that combination sound? Well, it would sound more natural, but still very stilted. To understand why, consider that the first and second sounds represented by <d> in *included* differ from one another and that both of them differ from the sound represented by <d> in *dig*. So still further refinement would be needed to approximate a natural-sounding

word. Even that wouldn't go far enough, for the individual sounds would have to run into one another as in natural speech: they couldn't be separated from one another as they are in spelling or phonetic transcription. As a further complication, consider that a word like *photo* could be represented phonetically as [foɾo], but exactly the same standard spelling would be represented phonetically as [forəgræf] in *photograph* and as [fətɑgrəfər] in *photographer.* In other words, without some general principles of pronunciation, a computer could not simply combine the sounds represented in spelling and produce synthesized speech sounds that seemed like words. We return to this matter in the following chapter.

SUMMARY

- Sounds must be distinguished from letters and other visual representations of language.

- Phonetic alphabets represent sounds in a way that is consistent and comparable across different languages; each sound is assigned a distinct representation, independently of the customary writing system used to represent a particular language.

- The phonetic alphabet used in this book is a slightly modified version of the International Phonetic Alphabet (IPA).

- All languages contain consonants and vowels.

- Consonants are produced by obstructing the flow of air as it passes from the lungs through the vocal tract and out through the mouth or nose.

- To produce fricative consonants, air is forced through a narrow opening in the passage to form a continuous noise, as in the initial and final sounds of *says* [sɛz] and *five* [fayv].

- For stop consonants the air passage is completely blocked and then released, as in the initial and final sounds of the words *tap* and *cat.*

- Affricates are produced by combining a stop and a fricative, as in the final sound of the word *peach* or the initial and final sounds of *judge.*

- As a group, fricatives, stops, and affricates are called obstruents.

- An approximant is produced when one articulator approaches another but the vocal tract is not sufficiently narrowed to create the audible friction of a consonant. Examples are the initial sounds of *west* [wɛst], *yes* [yɛs], *rest* [rɛst], *lest* [lɛst].

- Liquid is a cover term for [r] and [l] sounds.

- Consonant sounds can be described as a combination of articulatory features: voicing, place of articulation, and manner of articulation. For example: [t] is a voiceless alveolar stop; [v] is a voiced labio-dental fricative.

- Vowels are produced by positioning the tongue and mouth to form differently shaped passages.

- Oral vowels are released through the mouth; nasal vowels are released through the nose and mouth.

- Vowels are described by citing the relative height and frontness of the tongue. For example: [æ] is a low front vowel; [u] is a high back vowel.

- Secondary features of vowel production—such as tenseness, nasality, lengthening, or rounding—are sometimes specified, as in "long vowel" or "nasal vowel."

- In many languages vowels can be pronounced on different pitches, or tones.

- Languages differ from one another in the number of speech sounds they have.

- Although phoneticians find it useful to conceptualize the sounds of speech as distinct from one another, the sounds are actually connected in real speech.

EXERCISES

Based on English

3-1. Give a phonetic description of the following sounds. For consonants, include voicing and place and manner of articulation. For vowels, include height, a

---

Table 3-6

VOWELS DISCUSSED IN CHAPTER 3

(ALL VOWELS CAN BE NASALIZED AND EITHER SHORT OR LONG.)

	FRONT UNROUNDED	FRONT ROUNDED	CENTRAL UNROUNDED	BACK UNROUNDED	BACK ROUNDED
high					
tense	i	ü		ɯ	u
lax	ɪ				ʊ
upper mid	e	ø			o
mid			ə		
lower mid	ɛ	œ	ʌ		ɔ
low	æ		a	ɑ	

Table 3-7

CONSONANTS DISCUSSED IN CHAPTER 3

PLACE OF ARTICULATION

MANNER OF ARTICULATION AND VOICING	BILABIAL	LABIO-DENTAL	INTER-DENTAL	ALVEOLAR	ALVEO-PALATAL	PALATAL	VELAR	UVULAR	GLOTTAL
Stops									
voiceless	p			t			k		ʔ
voiced	b			d			g		
Nasals	m			n		ɲ	ŋ		
Fricatives									
voiceless	ɸ	f	θ	s	š (ʃ)	ç	x		h
voiced	β	v	ð	z	ž (ʒ)		ɣ		
Affricates									
voiceless				ts	č (tʃ)				
voiced				dz	ǰ (dʒ)				
Approximants									
voiced central	w			r (ɹ)		y (j)		ʁ	
voiced lateral				l					
Others									
voiced trill				r̃ (r)					
voiced flap				ɾ					

frontness/backness dimension, and where needed a tense/lax distinction. *Examples*: [s]—voiceless alveolar fricative; [i]—high front tense vowel.

Consonants: [z] [t] [b] [n] [ŋ] [r] [y] [š] [θ] [ð]
Vowels: [ɛ] [æ] [ɔ] [ɪ] [ʊ] [o] [ə] [ɑ] [e] [ay]

3-2. A minimal pair is a set of two words that have the same sounds in the same order, except that one sound differs: *pit* [pɪt] / *bit* [bɪt]; *bell* [bɛl] / *bill* [bɪl]; and *either* [iðər] / *ether* [iθɛr].

    a. For each of the following pairs of English consonants, provide minimal pairs that illustrate their occurrence in initial, medial, and final position. (Examples are given for the first pair.)

		Initial	Medial	Final
[s]	[z]	sue/zoo	buses/buzzes	peace/peas
[k]	[b]	_____	_____	_____
[t]	[b]	_____	_____	_____
[s]	[t]	_____	_____	_____
[r]	[l]	_____	_____	_____
[m]	[n]	_____	_____	_____

    b. For each of these pairs of vowels, cite a minimal pair of words illustrating the contrast. *Example*: [u] [æ] *boot/bat*.

        [i] [ɪ]; [ɔy] [ay]; [u] [ʊ]; [æ] [e]

3-3. Write out in ordinary spelling the words represented by the following transcriptions. *Examples*: [pɛn] *pen*; [smok] *smoke*; [bənænə] *banana*

[læŋgwəǰ]	[træpt]	[spawts]
[θwɔrt]	[ðiz]	[ðɪs]
[lʌvd]	[plɛžər]	[kwɪkli]
[mənatənəs]	[frənɛtək]	[ɛntərprayzɪŋ]

3-4. The names below are phonetic transcriptions of the names of popular movies in the late 1990s. Write its name using ordinary English spellings.

    kɑn ɛːr
    fɑrgo
    ðə pipəl vərsəz læri flɪnt
    bʌɾi
    trayəl ənd ɛrər
    əvitə
    ðə lɔst wərld ǰəræsək pɑrk
    taytænək

3-5. Transcribe each of the following words as you say them in casual speech. (Don't be misled by the spelling.) *Examples*: *bed* [bɛd]; *rancid* [rænsəd]; *shnook* [šnʊk]

changes	mostly	very	friend	teacher
semantics	system	ready	more	musician
crackers	peanuts	palm	music	photographer
pneumonia	attitude	psalm	fuel	photograph

3-6. The transcription below represents one person's reading of a passage about the actor Will Smith (adapted from *Newsweek*, July 7, 1997). The transcription does not represent secondary features such as vowel length or consonant aspiration. Write out the passage using ordinary English spellings.

[wɪl smɪθ hæz ə dɑrk ferəl flɔ	1
ɪts ən əbsešən əv sɔrts	2
ðə kaynd əv θɪŋ ðæt kən drayv lʌvd wʌnz krezi	3
ən mayt ivən ɪf əlawd tə rʌn əmʌk	4
direl ən dəbɪlətet ən ʌðərwayz prɑməsɪŋ kərir	5
hi hets bæd græmər	6
prənʌnsiešən ɛrərz mɪsteks əv ɛni lɪŋgwɪstək sɔrt	7
ðe mek hɪm nʌts	8
hɪz gərlfrend ði æktrəs ǰedə pɪŋkət noz ət	9
əkežənəli ɪn ðer ǰentləst most kærɪŋ we	10
ðe tray tə košən hɪm əbawt ðə sɪriəsnəs əv hɪz əflɪkšən	11
sɪrɪŋ dawn ovər brekfəst wʌn mɔrnɪŋ	12
ɪn ðer spænɪš stayəl vɪlə awtsayd ɛle	13
pɪŋkət kæsts ə tentərəv glæns ɪn hɪz dərekšən	14
wɑt wər yə telɪŋ mi ði ʌðər de ši sɛz	15
ðæt pipəl se ðə wərd ɔfən layk ɔf fən wen ɪts rɪli prənawnst ɔf tən	16
smɪθ lʊkɪŋ spɔrti ən prɑpər ɪn ə wayt rælf lɔren polo šərt	17
wayt swetpænts ən nayki ɛr ʌp tempoz	18
sɛts dawn ə plærər əv bənænə pænkeks wɪθ ə dɪsəpruvɪŋ θʌd	19
no no hi sɛz	20
ðə rayt we ɪz ɔfən	21
pipəl hu prənawns ðə ti ɑr trayɪŋ tə sawn səfɪstəkerəd	22
bʌt ðe ǰəst sawn rɔŋ	23
pɪŋkət gɪgəlz ðen əfɛks ə supərmæn ton əv vɔys	24
ɪts ə nawn ɪts ə vərb	25
no ɪts kæptən kərekšən]	26

3-7. The following transcription represents one person's reading of a passage about love potions (adapted from *The Encyclopedia of Things That Never Were*, p. 159). Write out the passage using ordinary English spellings.

[æz ðə nem ɪndəkets 1
ðiz pošənz ɑr kɑmpawndəd spəsɪfəkli tu ətrækt ə sʌbǰekt 2
hu ɪz rilʌktənt tə sərendər tə wʌnz kɑrnəl dəzayərz 3
ðə pošən me bi hæd æɾə prays frəm ɛni ælkəmɪst 4
ər ʌðər pərsən skɪld ɪn ðə prepərešən əv mayn čenǰɪŋ kɑmpawnz 5
wɪčəz wɪzərdz ən sɔrsərərz 6
hu ɑr ǰenrəli nɑt ɪntrəstəd ɪn lʌv 7
ɑr sʌmtaymz ənwɪlɪŋ tə mænyəfækšər ðə pošənz 8
ðə pərčəsərz onli prɑbləm me bi ðæt əv pərswerɪŋ 9
ði abǰekt əv hɪz ɔr hər dəzayər 10
tə swɑlo ɛni əv ðə pošən 11
ə risənt resəpi fɔr ə lʌv pošən ɪŋkluɾəd 12
ǰɪnǰər sɪnəmən drayd ən grawnd grep sidz 13
ɔystərz ɛlk æntlər ən tel her frəm ə mel ænəməl 14
ænd ɛni suɾəbəl abǰekt frəm ðə pərsən 15
sʌč æz hɪz ər hər nel klɪpɪŋz] 16

3-8. Examine the following list of consonants as they are represented in four popular desk dictionaries, and compare the dictionary symbols with the phonetic symbols used in this book. (MWCD stands for *Merriam-Webster's Collegiate Dictionary*, tenth edition; WNWD for *Webster's New World Dictionary*, third college edition; AHD for *The American Heritage Dictionary of the English Language*, third edition; COD for *The Concise Oxford Dictionary of Current English*, eighth edition.)

Phonetic Symbol	MWCD	WNWD	AHD	COD
p	p	p	p	p
k	k	k	k	k
θ	th	th	th	θ
ð	<u>th</u>	*th*	*th*	ð
s	s	s	s	s
š (ʃ)	sh	sh	sh	ʃ
ž (ʒ)	zh	zh	zh	ʒ
č (tʃ)	ch	ch	ch	tʃ
ǰ (dʒ)	j	j	j	dʒ
ŋ	ŋ	ŋ	ng	ŋ
h	h	h	h	h
y (j)	y	y	y	j

Note that some of the symbols used by these dictionaries are the same as those used in this book, but not all. Choose three sounds for which one or more of the dictionaries use a different symbol than the one used in this book, and discuss why that different symbol might have been chosen.

3-9. Examine the following list of vowels as they are represented in three dictionaries; compare the dictionary symbols with the phonetic symbols used in this book. (See Exercise 3-8 for identification of the dictionaries.)

Phonetic Symbol	Words	MWCD	WNWD	AHD	COD
i	peat, feet	ē	ē	ē	iː
ɪ	pit, bit	i	i	ĭ	ɪ
ɛ	pet, bet	e	e	ĕ	e
e	wait, late	ā	ā	ā	eɪ
æ	pat, bat	a	a	ă	æ
ə	soda, item	ə	ə	ə	ə
ʌ	but, love	ə	u	ŭ	ʌ
u	pool, boot	ü	o͞o	o͞o	uː
ʊ	push, put	u̇	oo	o͝o	ʊ
o	boat, sold	ō	ō	ō	əʊ
ɔ	port, or	ȯ	ô	ô	ɔː
ɑ	pot, bottle	ä	ä	ŏ	ɒ
aw	cow, pout	au̇	ou	ou	aʊ
ay	buy, tight	ī	ī	ī	aɪ
ɔy	boy, toil	ȯi	oi	oi	ɔɪ

In contrast to their practice with consonants, the desk dictionaries differ from one another and from our representation in their transcription of vowels. Cite three instances of a difference from the transcription in this book; discuss the advantages and disadvantages of the dictionary's representation as compared to ours.

3-10. George Bernard Shaw's tongue-in-cheek claim that English spelling is so chaotic that *ghoti* could be pronounced [fɪš] "fish" has been called misleading. That judgment is based on observations like these: <gh> can occur word initially in only a few words (for example, *ghost* and *ghastly*), and then it is always pronounced [g]; only following a vowel in the same syllable (as in *cough* and *tough*) can <gh> be pronounced as [f]; thus, *ghoti* could not be pronounced with an initial [f]. What other generalizations about the English spelling patterns of <gh>, <o>, and <ti> can be used to argue that Shaw's claim is at least exaggerated?

INTERNET RESOURCES

- **International Phonetic Association:
  http://www.arts.gla.ac.uk/IPA/ipa.html**
  If you're interested in the International Phonetic Alphabet (IPA), visit this site, maintained for the International Phonetic Association. You'll find the

latest version of the IPA, including vowels, consonants, diacriti
suprasegmentals, tones, and word accents. You'll also find link
where you can download IPA fonts for your word processing p
well as information about recordings of the sounds of the IPA.

- **IPA Vowel Chart:**
  http://www.kayelemetrics.com/ipattfig.htm#Screen 2
  Here you'll find a 3-D-like view of the vowels of the International Phonetic
  Alphabet as provided in the software offered by Kay Elemetrics.
- **The Sounds of the IPA:**
  http://www.phon.ucl.ac.uk/home/wells/cassette.htm
  A cassette and CD of the sounds of the International Phonetic Alphabet are
  available. For ordering information, use the link at the IPA home page or
  go directly to this Web site.

SUGGESTIONS FOR FURTHER READING

- **David Crystal. 1997.** *A Dictionary of Linguistics and Phonetics*, **4th ed.** (Oxford: Blackwell). A rich source of information about the meanings of terms.

- **Peter B. Denes and Elliot N. Pinson. 1993.** *The Speech Chain*, **2nd ed.** (New York: W. H. Freeman). An accessible account of the physics and biology of spoken language; includes chapters on acoustic phonetics, digital processing of speech sounds, speech synthesis, and automatic speech recognition.

- **Peter Ladefoged. 1993.** *A Course in Phonetics*, **3rd ed.** (Fort Worth: Harcourt). An excellent introduction to the production mechanisms of speech and to the variety of sounds in the languages of the world.

- **Peter Ladefoged and Ian Maddieson. 1996.** *The Sounds of the World's Languages* (Oxford and Cambridge, MA: Blackwell). An advanced treatment of the articulatory and acoustic phonetics of the various sounds in the languages of the world.

- **Ian R. A. MacKay. 1987.** *Phonetics*: *The Science of Speech Production*, **2nd ed.** (Boston: Little Brown). The most complete elementary treatment of all aspects of phonetics; accessible and with excellent illustrations.

- **Ian Maddieson. 1984.** *Patterns of Sound* (Cambridge: Cambridge UP). An inventory of the sounds in a representative sample of the world's languages; the inventories vary from a low of 11 to a high of 141 sounds.

- **Geoffrey K. Pullum and William A. Ladusaw. 1996.** *Phonetic Symbol Guide*, **2nd ed.** (Chicago: U of Chicago P). Discusses the various symbols used in the International Phonetic Alphabet (IPA) and by other writers in their treatments of phonetics and phonology; arranged like a dictionary, with each symbol clearly illustrated.

- **Michael Stubbs. 1980.** *Language and Literacy*: *The Sociolinguistics of Reading and Writing* (London: Routledge). Contains an excellent discussion of the relationship between sounds and spelling in English and other languages; offers insights into the problems facing spelling reform.

CHAPTER 4

THE SOUND SYSTEMS

OF LANGUAGE: PHONOLOGY

WHAT DO YOU THINK?

Imagine you are a junior high school teacher of German and one of your students returns from a city where German is the predominant language. She tells the class that when she listened to the radio, she could not separate the stream of speech into distinct words—"It all seemed a blur; not like English, where all the words are distinct." She claims that English words are separated in speech almost as in writing but that German doesn't seem to be structured that way. She asks you what accounts for the difference between the two languages. Your reply?

Suppose you visited Paris with a cousin who had studied French for five years and prided herself on her mastery of the language. Your cousin is fluent enough to give complicated directions to a taxi driver taking you to the theater, and you are impressed. At the end of the ride, though, the driver asks your cousin which American city she comes from. Crestfallen that the driver recognized that she wasn't a native speaker of French and could even identify her home country, your cousin asks you which characteristics in her French identify her as an American and why she hasn't been able to eliminate them. What do you tell her?

You visit a seventh-grade class of international students studying English, and the students present you with a list of "English" names they have coined for games. You recognize that several could not be English words. From their list, which follows, which names do you judge to be impossible and how do you explain to the students why they could not be English names? skokey, skwinty, twint, stwink, plopeo, splopt, sprats, skretcht, spretched, skwickt, spwint, stwirl, tprash, stpop, frash, quirt, splast, plsats

> *You are working in an office and get a written message from the secretary that your friend Jewel Spiker called. The message reads: "Call Jules Biker." When you return the call, you tell Jewel about the misspelling and she reports that she pronounced her name clearly and wonders what accounts for the secretary's perception of* p *as* b. *What would you tell her?*
>
> *A friend of yours, a fan of synthesized music, tells you that machines can now synthesize speech so well that you can't tell the difference between a real person speaking and a synthesizer. You are a fan of the Internet and determine to explore its resources on this subject. After an hour on the Internet what do you report to your friend about the state of speech synthesis?*

INTRODUCTION: SOUNDS IN THE MIND

This chapter focuses on the systematic structuring of sounds in languages—on which phonetic distinctions are significant enough to signal differences in meaning; on the relationship between how sounds are pronounced and how they are stored in the mental lexicon; and on the ways sounds are organized within words.

It's useful to approach this task from the point of view of children acquiring their native language. Although children acquire different parts of their language at different stages, they all know a great deal about speaking before they learn even the most basic things about the visual representation of speech in writing. To repeat a point stressed earlier, we are interested in sound systems as such—independently of their representation in writing.

Imagine the task of an infant listening to utterances made by its parents, siblings, and others. From the barrage of utterances that it faces in its early life, a child must decipher the code of its language and learn to speak its mother tongue. It's true that caretakers in some cultures sometimes use the slow and careful speech of baby talk in addressing children, but they don't do so consistently; and the utterances that children hear are often incomplete, interrupted, or flawed in other ways.

In Chapter 3 you learned to distinguish between the number of letters in a written word and the number of sounds in the word's pronunciation. You know, for example, that *set* has an equal number of sounds and letters, while *white* does not. In our discussion, we have taken it for granted that words have a specific number of sounds. But children hearing language in their earliest months would seem to have no ready access to that simple fact. It would be instructive to listen to a conversation or a radio broadcast in a language you didn't know. If you attempt to count the number of words in a sample of even a few seconds' duration, you will discover how difficult that task is because most words are generally run together with no separation between them. This is true of all spoken languages and all dialects.

Ifthesentencesonthispagewereprintedwithoutspacesb
etweenwordsitwouldbeverydifficulttofigureoutwouldntit?

As you can recognize, it would be tough to sort out the individual words. Yet the task of sorting out the continuous noise of utterances into separate words is part of the challenge that you faced when as a child you began acquiring your first language.

Actually, the task is even more difficult than is suggested by the run-together words in the printed sentence above. The reason is simple: whereas the letters in the run-together sentence are distinct and separated from one another, the individual sounds in a spoken word are not separated but blend together into a continuous noise stream. To take our writing analogy a step farther, imagine attempting to spot the beginning and end points of each letter in a handwritten sample: this would more closely capture the challenge that infants face in deciphering the code of distinct sounds in their language. Consider the following:

In cursive writing, the letters of each word are joined.

Although anyone who knows English and is able to decipher this handwriting can count the letters in each word, there is no clear separation in their visual representation. Each word is written continuously, with the letters blending into one another. No beginning or end can be pinpointed (except for the initiation of the first letter and the termination of the last letter in each word). The same is true of the speech that infants hear; there is no separation between the individual sounds of a word, no beginning or end for the individual sounds in the speech stream. And for children the situation is even more difficult because the words themselves aren't separated. Children nevertheless learn the words of their language quickly and efficiently, a feat all the more remarkable considering how much else they have to learn in their earliest years.

If you examine a physical "picture" of a word as made by a sound spectrogram, you can see that there is no separation between the sounds. (The gap in the sound spectrogram of Figure 4-1 represents not a space between words but the complete closure of the vocal tract in the production of the stop consonant /b/.) One important reason for the continuity between sound segments is that a particular sound's phonetic features—for example, voicing and nasalization—do not all begin or end at the same time. In other words, when you speak the word *lint* you don't say [l] and then stop and then start [ɪ] and then when that's finished say [n] and so on. Instead the individual features of one sound can continue into the next sound, and the features of a following sound can be anticipated by a preceding sound. Thus, the nasalization of [n] in *lint* is anticipated in the vowel, which is partly nasalized. To take another example, the voicing of a particular sound may be discontinued in anticipation of a following voiceless sound—as in *imp*, in which the tail end of [m] is devoiced in anticipation of the following voiceless [p]. Figure 4-1 is a spectrogram that illustrates how the simple utter-

Figure 4-1

SOUND SPECTROGRAM OF A CASUAL UTTERANCE

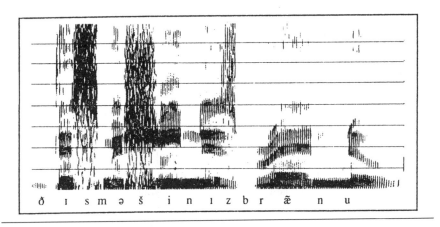

ð ɪ s m ə š i n ɪ z b r æ n u

ance *This machine is brand new* appears acoustically. There is not only no separation between one sound and another within words but no physical separation between one word and the next. In the same way, the acoustic signal that an infant's ears pick up is continuous, and part of the task of acquiring a language is to sort out words within sentences and sounds within words. The language system that every child acquires must eventually contain words as separate units and sounds as separate units within a word.

You may wonder, then: what must a child understand in order to know a word of its language? Well, it's clear that to know a word is to know its meaning and its sounds— that is, both content and expression. Children pass through several stages in learning the words of their language, and there is some disagreement about how they succeed at this task. Some children appear to take up the phrases and clauses of utterances as whole units and only later dissect them into their parts (this is called a gestalt approach). Others seem to manage a more analytic approach from the start—they take up words directly and construct phrases and clauses from them as necessary. All children eventually sort utterances into distinct units of meaning that are stored in the brain.

Focusing attention on one crucial ingredient in the acquisition of words, we can ask what kind of information a child must learn about the sounds of a word. What is required to be able merely to recognize a word? Well, one thing is that children must recognize pronunciations of a given word by different people as the same word, whether uttered by a woman or a man, a teenager or an octogenarian, a sniffler with a cold, or anyone else. To identify words—to understand language—it is essential to disregard certain voice characteristics and certain particularities of volume, speed, and pitch.

A child must observe a word's sounds and the order in which they occur. When learning the word *bad*, for example, a child must recognize that it contains the three sounds [b], [æ], and [d] and contains them in exactly that order. After all, *bad* and *dab* are not the same word even though they have the same sounds.

PHONEMES AND ALLOPHONES

Eventually every child also learns that sounds are pronounced differently in different contexts—in other words that the "same sound" can have more than one pronunciation. Two examples will help reconcile this seeming contradiction.

Although English speakers aren't generally aware of the fact, the words *cop* [kɑp] and *keep* [kip] begin with somewhat different [k] sounds. You can notice this if you alternately pronounce the two words. Don't just listen for the difference, which is difficult for English speakers to hear. Instead, notice where your tongue touches the roof of your mouth at the very beginning of each word. You will discover that your tongue touches the velum farther back for *cop* than for *keep*. The reason for this difference is easy enough to understand: [ɑ] is a back vowel and [i] is a front vowel, and in anticipation of pronouncing the back vowel in *cop* you pronounce the [k] farther back in the mouth than you do for the [k] that precedes the front vowel [i] in *keep*.

If pronouncing these words aloud while attending to the position of the back of your tongue as it touches the roof of your mouth fails to reveal the difference, try this: Position your tongue as if you were about to say *keep*. Then, when your tongue is in position for the initial sound of *keep*, say *cop* instead. You will discover that you must reposition your tongue in order to pronounce *cop*; if you say *cop* from the *keep* position, it will sound peculiar or foreign. The need to reposition the back of your tongue to achieve a natural pronunciation demonstrates that the two [k] sounds are not identical, though speakers of English think of them as the same.

For the second example, you should readily be able to identify differences in the sounds represented by <p> in the first and second words of the pairs *pot/spot* and *poke/spoke*. If you hold the back of your hand (or a small piece of paper) up to your mouth when saying these word pairs, you should feel (or see) a considerable difference in the puff of air that accompanies the sounds represented by <p>. The sound that <p> represents in *pot* and *poke* is strong enough to blow out a lighted match held in front of the mouth; it is an aspirated stop, represented as [pʰ]. The sound following <s> in *spot* and *spoke* is not aspirated (and will not blow out a match); we represent it as [p].

In discussing these two *p* sounds, we have noted that they occur in different positions within words. Examine the following list of words to identify the positions in which unaspirated [p] and aspirated [pʰ] occur.

pill	[pʰɪl]
poker	[pʰokər]
plate	[pʰlet]
sprint	[sprɪnt]
spine	[spayn]

Notice that aspirated [pʰ] occurs at the beginning of words (as in *pill*, *poker*, and *plate*), whereas unaspirated [p] occurs after [s] (as in *sprint* and *spine*). When different sounds do not occur in the same position in words but only in different positions, we say they occur in **complementary distribution.** Complementary distribution simply means that where one sound occurs, the other does not occur.

In the words just listed, aspirated [pʰ] occurs only word initially, whereas unaspirated [p] occurs only after [s]; thus, [pʰ] and [p] occur in complementary distribution. By definition, because they occur in complementary distribution they could never occur in the same position in a word and therefore could not serve to distinguish words from one another. Thus [pʰ] and [p] are not distinctive sounds in English words. Instead, they constitute a single unit of the English sound system and, as such, are called *allophones* of a single *phoneme*—in this case, allophones of the phoneme /p/. A **phoneme** is a distinctive structural element in the sound system of a language. **Allophones** are variants of a single structural element in the sound system of a language. Allophones of a given phoneme cannot serve to create different words; as a result, we say they are noncontrastive. To native speakers they seem to be the same sound despite their physical difference, and they function as a unit in the sound system of the language. Given that aspirated [pʰ] and unaspirated [p] are allophones of the phoneme /p/ in English, English could not have a pair of words such as [pʰit] and [pit] that would have different meaning—and of course it doesn't. Likewise the two [k] sounds of *cop* and *keep* are allophones of the phoneme /k/ in English and cannot serve to make contrasting words. Note that we have now started using slanted lines / / to enclose phonemes and square brackets [ ] to enclose allophones (different sounds of a single phoneme). We will continue this practice, though sometimes we will have to choose one representation or the other when either would serve as well. (Angled brackets enclose written letters.)

Besides the aspirated and unaspirated allophones of /p/, there is a third voiceless bilabial stop in English, also represented orthographically by <p>, as in the word *mop*. This allophone of /p/ occurs sometimes at the end of a word when that word occurs at the end of a sentence: *Where's the mop?* In this position, the lips can stay closed so that the sound represented by <p> is not released. We represent this allophone as [p˺]. But in this case we don't have complementary distribution because both unaspirated [p] and unreleased [p˺] occur in the same position in a word, namely word finally. When two sounds can occur in the same position in a word without contrasting—that is, without creating different words—those sounds are said to occur in **free variation**. At the end of an utterance, English speakers can pronounce the word lip as [lɪp] or as [lɪp˺]. Thus, both the unaspirated and unreleased voiceless bilabial stops are allophones of the phoneme /p/, and /p/ therefore has three allophones: aspirated [pʰ], unaspirated [p], and unreleased [p˺]. To repeat, the allophones of a phoneme occur in complementary distribution or in free variation; in neither case can a change of meaning be signaled by the different allophones.

DISTRIBUTION OF ALLOPHONES

One way to differentiate phonemes from allophones is to view a phoneme as an abstract structural element in the sound system of a language—a skeleton unit of sound that lacks a fully specified pronunciation but can be pronounced in a specific way depending on where in a word it occurs. For example, while the phoneme /p/ would have the skeletal features *voiceless bilabial stop*, one allophone might be aspirated,

Table 4-1

ALLOPHONES OF /p/ IN ENGLISH WORDS

A	B	C	D
[pʰ]	[pʰ]	[pʰ]	[p]
pédigree	petúnia	empórium	rápid
pérsonal	patérnal	compúter	émpathy
pérsecute	península	rapídograph	competítion
pílgrimage	pecúliar	compétitive	computátional

another unaspirated, and a third unreleased. The pronunciation of the phoneme /p/ cannot be fully specified unless its position in a word (or utterance) is known. Only then can its aspiration and release be determined.

We have just seen that particular allophones are determined by where they occur in a word. If you examine the sets of words in Table 4-1, you will see that the picture is a bit more complicated. In these words the accent mark (´) is used to indicate primary stress on the syllable (as in *rídicule* versus *ridículous*).

All the words have /p/ in syllable-initial position. The words in column A have primary stress on the first syllable, with [pʰ] as the initial sound. Those in column B also have aspirated [pʰ] word initially, though primary stress occurs on the second syllable. The words in columns A and B demonstrate that /p/ is aspirated word initially in stressed and unstressed syllables. In column C aspirated [pʰ] introduces the second syllable, which carries primary stress in each case. Thus aspirated [pʰ] occurs not only word initially but word internally, introducing a stressed syllable. The words in column D demonstrate that unaspirated [p] occurs word internally introducing unstressed syllables. In summary, the phoneme /p/ is aspirated word initially in stressed and unstressed syllables, but it is aspirated word internally only when it initiates a stressed syllable.

Given these observations, we must refine our description of the distribution of the allophones of /p/ to account for the stress patterns of a word. The distribution of these allophones of /p/ is described in Table 4-2.

Table 4-2

TWO ALLOPHONES OF ENGLISH /p/

PHONEME	ALLOPHONES	DISTRIBUTION
/p/	[pʰ]	In syllable-initial position in a stressed syllable and in word-initial position
	[p]	Elsewhere (as in a consonant cluster following /s/ and in word-final position)

Contrast these facts about [pʰ] and [p] with the facts about /p/ and /s/. If a child trying to say the word *sat* instead said *pat*, it would have failed to make one of the significant differences in English pronunciation: /p/ and /s/ are distinct phonemes and can serve to distinguish words, as in these word pairs.

A	B	C	D
[pɪt] pit	[pʌn] pun	[læpt] lapped	[sip] seep
[sɪt] sit	[sʌn] sun	[læst] last	[sis] cease

The words in each pair have different meanings and differ by only a single sound. Two words that differ by only a single sound constitute a **minimal pair**. (Note that the distinction depends on sounds, not spelling.) Minimal pairs are valuable in identifying the significant sounds—the phonemes—of a language. Each minimal pair above demonstrates that /s/ and /p/ are distinct phonemes of English and not allophones of the same phoneme. Articulatory descriptions of /s/ and /p/ show that these two phonemes differ in both place and manner of articulation.

	/s/	/p/
VOICING	voiceless	voiceless
PLACE OF ARTICULATION	alveolar	bilabial
MANNER OF ARTICULATION	fricative	stop

To take another example, /s/ and /b/ differ from one another not only in place and manner of articulation but also in voicing.

	/s/	/b/
VOICING	voiceless	voiced
PLACE OF ARTICULATION	alveolar	bilabial
MANNER OF ARTICULATION	fricative	stop

/s/ is a voiceless alveolar fricative, /b/ a voiced bilabial stop. The fact that /s/ and /b/ contrast (as in the minimal pair *sat/bat*) proves that they are significantly different sounds—that they belong to distinct phonemes.

Sounds (allophones) that belong to a single phoneme share certain phonetic features but differ in at least one other feature—such as voiced/voiceless, stop/fricative, dental/alveolar, or aspirated/unaspirated. When analyzing the sound system of a language, it is important to take particular note of the distributions of sounds that have similar phonetic descriptions. Consider this list of English words.

[pʰæt]	pat
[bæt]	bat
[tʰæp]	tap

[tʰæb]	tab
[spæt]	spat

[pʰ] and [b] are both bilabial stops; they share those two features. On the other hand, [pʰ] is voiceless and aspirated, while [b] is voiced and unaspirated. Are they distinct phonemes or are they allophones of a single phoneme? You cannot answer that question by examining the phonetic descriptions alone. But, because there is a minimal pair above, we know that [pʰ] and [b] contrast. That is, *pat/bat* demonstrates that [pʰ] and [b] are members of different phonemes. Since there are no examples in English in which aspirated [pʰ] and unaspirated [p] contrast (in fact, they occur in complementary distribution), [pʰ] and [p] are allophones of a single phoneme. From the minimal pair *tap/tab* above, we know that unaspirated [p] contrasts with [b]; thus aspirated [pʰ] and unaspirated [p]—both voiceless bilabial stops—contrast with the voiced bilabial stop [b].

The phonemes /p/ and /b/ contrast in both word-initial and word-final position, as we saw. Sometimes, however, two sounds contrast in some positions but not all. Nevertheless, two sounds remain distinctive if they contrast in any one position. Consider, for example, the position following /s/ as in the word s_at: there are no two words of English like *sbat* and *spat* that carry different meanings. Thus, even though /p/ and /b/ are different phonemes in English, the contrast between them is not exploited in the position following /s/.

Now consider the very different situation in Korean. Like English, Korean has the three bilabial stops [pʰ], [p], and [b], as in the following words.

[pʰul]	'grass'
[pul]	'fire'
[pəp]	'law'
[mubəp]	'lawlessness'

The minimal pair [pʰul] and [pul] demonstrates that [p] and [pʰ] contrast in Korean. On the other hand, even with a large sample of words you could not find a minimal pair in which [p] contrasts with [b]. The reason is that, in Korean, [p] and [b] are in complementary distribution: [b] occurs only between vowels and other voiced segments, as in [mubəp], but [p] never occurs in that environment. This demonstrates that while [p] and [pʰ] are distinct phonemes in Korean, [p] and [b] are allophones of a single phoneme.

The diagram in Table 4-3 represents the difference in the phonological systems of English and Korean with respect to these three sounds. Although the same three sounds occur in both languages, their systematic role in those languages is altogether different. In English, [pʰ] and [p] are noncontrastive allophones of a single phoneme and therefore cannot signal a difference of meaning. In Korean, [pʰ] and [p] are significantly different sounds; that is, they *are* separate phonemes and *can* distinguish one word from another (as in [pʰul] and [pul]). In terms of articulatory properties, voicing is phonemic in English; the *voiced* bilabial stop [b] is distinct

Table 4-3

THREE SOUNDS OF ENGLISH AND KOREAN COMPARED

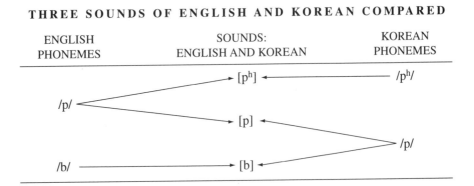

ENGLISH PHONEMES	SOUNDS: ENGLISH AND KOREAN	KOREAN PHONEMES

from the *voiceless* bilabial stop [p]. Aspiration, however, is not phonemic in English. That means that no two English phonemes differ solely in aspiration. In Korean, on the other hand, the voiced bilabial stop [b] is an allophone of /p/ occurring between voiced sounds; hence [b] and [p] cannot be used to distinguish Korean words.

We can summarize by saying that voicing is not contrastive in Korean but aspiration is, while aspiration is not contrastive in English but voicing is.

PHONOLOGICAL RULES AND THEIR STRUCTURE

You're probably aware that French has nasal vowels, and you may conclude that English lacks nasal vowels. In fact, however, English has nasal vowels, and it is instructive to look closely at them. In Table 4-4, the words in column B have nasalized vowels (vowels pronounced through the nose, in addition to the mouth), while those in column A have oral vowels (vowels pronounced through the mouth). To discover that the vowels in column B are nasalized, pinch your nose closed while saying the

Table 4-4

ORAL AND NASAL VOWELS IN ENGLISH

A	B
sit	sin
pet	pen
light	lime
brute	broom
sitter	singer

words in each column. For the words in column A, it will make no perceptible difference in the pronunciation; for those in column B, it will make a striking difference. This demonstrates that when you pronounce the words of column B, air from the lungs exits through the nasal passage; hence when that passage is blocked the sound of the vowel changes perceptibly.

If you search out nasal vowels in English words, you will discover that all of them precede one of the nasal consonants /m n ŋ/. The distribution of nasal vowels in English is regular and predictable: a vowel is nasalized before a nasal consonant. Since the distribution is predictable in English, the occurrence of nasal vowels cannot signal a meaning distinction (although it can in French and other languages where its distribution is not predictable). Two sounds whose distribution with respect to one another is predictable constitute allophones of a single phoneme; their distribution is describable by a general rule.

Regular **phonological rules** have this general form:

$$A \rightarrow B \ / \ C\_D$$

You can read such a rule as "A becomes B in the environment following C and preceding D." Often the phrase "in the environment" is omitted, thus "A becomes B following C and preceding D." A, B, C, and D are generally specified in terms of phonological features, although in this book rules will be presented in more informal terms. In cases where it is unnecessary to specify both C and D, one of them will be missing. For example, the phonological process of nasalization can be represented by the following rule statement:

NASALIZATION RULE
vowel → nasal / ___ nasal
(Vowels become nasalized preceding nasal sounds.)

As noted in the introduction to this chapter, in acquiring a word a child must learn the number of phonemes in the word, what those phonemes are, and in what order they occur. As the English *cop/keep* alternation shows for the allophones of /k/ and the *poke/spoke* alternation shows for the allophones of /p/, a child must also learn to pronounce particular allophones of a phoneme depending on the phoneme's position in a word and the character of nearby sounds. This is done not by memorizing the sounds in each individual word but by acquiring rules that apply to all words, as with the nasalization rule above.

The situation for a child acquiring Korean [p] and [b] is parallel to that of an English-speaking child acquiring nasal vowels. Since [p] and [b] never contrast, they are allophones of a single phoneme, and only one form is needed to represent them in the lexicon (along with a phonological rule that specifies the distribution of [b] between vowels and [p] elsewhere). The alternative to having a single representation in the lexicon for [p] and [b] in Korean would involve considerable inefficiency. It would require a specific differentiation between these sounds in every word that contains either of them. For example, *pəp* 'law' and *mubəp* 'lawlessness' would have different specifications for [p] and [b]. To speakers of English (which does not have a predictable distribution of [p] and [b] because they are distinct phonemes), this differentiation seems natural and necessary. But to have different forms for [p] and [b] in the lexicon of a Korean speaker would be equivalent to an English speaker's having different representations in the lexicon for the different /k/ sounds of *cop* and *keep*, for the different /p/ sounds of *poke* and *spoke*, or for the different /i/ sounds of *seat* and *seen*. Moreover, unless there were consistent different spellings assigned to each allophone, a reader coming across the preceding word pairs for the first time would be unable to know their pronunciations. However, each phoneme is represented in the lexicon by only a single underlying form. Native speakers internalize the phonological rules specifying the distribution of allophones and automatically apply these rules wherever the phoneme appears.

WHY ENGLISH SPEAKERS SPEAK FRENCH WITH A FOREIGN ACCENT

One indication that information such as the differences between allophones is not stored in the lexicon but is determined by the application of regular rules can be found in foreign accents. Consider a native speaker of English who knows no French and has been introduced by a French speaker to a neighbor named *Pierre*. As you recall, English speakers aspirate initial voiceless stops like /p/ (aspirated sounds are accompanied by a puff of air) but French does not aspirate them. That means that the French speaker introducing Pierre will pronounce his name without aspiration. Despite the fact that the English speaker has *not* heard aspiration in the pronunciation of *Pierre*, he or she will nevertheless tend to pronounce *Pierre* with an aspirated [pʰ] in conformity with the phonological rules of English (rather than French), and this indicates that English speakers have a rule that aspirates initial /p/ (even when attempting to pronounce

French names). The subconscious application of the phonological rules of your native tongue to a foreign language contributes to a foreign accent and marks you as a nonnative speaker.

On the other side of the coin, speakers may fail to make a distinction that is required in a foreign language. We saw that English distinguishes between the *k* sounds of *cop* and *keep* and that it does so by rule. In other words, English speakers don't have to learn separately for *cop* and *keep* which *k* sound to use. But in some languages—including Basque, Malay, and Vietnamese—these two sounds are distinctive; they are separate phonemes. The initial sound of *cop* is represented by IPA [k] and of *keep* by IPA [c]. In languages like Basque, Malay, and Vietnamese, it is critical to know which velar stop occurs in a word, much as English speakers must learn whether /p/ or /t/ occurs, because those sounds are not distributed by rule.

Since the distribution of the allophones of every phoneme is regular, a great deal of memory in the mental dictionary is saved by specifying only the phonemes in a word; a few general phonological rules can then specify the correct allophone for each occurrence of the phoneme. To see how this process works, imagine the brain as a computer with a very large but finite memory. Every redundant piece of information that is stored in a computer makes valuable memory space unavailable for other uses. A significant amount of "space" in the brain's "computer" is saved by specifying only the distinctive features of each phoneme (thus, "voiceless bilabial stop" for /p/) and leaving the specification of allophonic features (such as "aspiration") to a few general rules that apply to tens of thousands of words and to all new words as they enter a person's lexicon.

GENERALIZING PHONOLOGICAL RULES

Until now we have considered phonological rules as though they were formulated to apply to particular sounds; in fact, they are more general. Consider the aspiration that accompanies the production of initial /p/ in English words like *pillow* and *pot*; it can be represented by the following rule:

1. For /p/:
voiceless
bilabial   →   aspirated / word initially and initially in stressed syllables
stop

This rule says that a voiceless bilabial stop is aspirated in specific environments.

If you examine other English words with stop consonants, you will discover that it is not only /p/ that has aspiration when it is syllable initial but also /t/ and /k/. Since /p t k/ have parallel distributions of these allophones, English would appear to need two additional rules like the one in 1. These are given in 2 and 3.

2. For /t/:
voiceless
alveolar   →   aspirated / word initially and initially in stressed syllables
stop

3. For /k/:
voiceless
velar   →   aspirated / word initially and initially in stressed syllables
stop

Because these three rules exhaust the list of voiceless stops in English, they can be collapsed into a single rule of greater generality as follows:

4. For /p/, /t/, and /k/:
voiceless
stop   →   aspirated / word initially and initially in stressed syllables

Notice in 4 that the combination of the phonetic features "voiceless" and "stop" leaves the place of articulation unspecified. In the absence of any specification, a phonological rule like 4 will apply to all voiceless stops irrespective of place of articulation; it will apply to bilabial, alveolar, and velar voiceless stops—that is, to /p/, /t/, and /k/.

The more general a rule is, the simpler it is to state using phonetic feature notation, and there is evidence that the brain's lexicon seeks similar simplicity. It appears that internalized phonological rules are specified not in terms of allophones such as [p] and [pʰ], or in terms of phonemes such as /p/, /t/, and /k/, but in terms of classes of sounds specified by sets of phonetic features such as "voiceless" and "stop."

NATURAL CLASSES OF SOUNDS

A set of phonemes such as /p t k/ that can be described using fewer features than would be necessary to describe each sound individually is called a natural class of sounds. A **natural class** of sounds contains all the sounds that share one or more features. Thus /p t k/ constitute the natural class of voiceless stops in English. /p t k/ share the two features "voiceless" and "stop," and there are no other sounds in English that have both of those features.

Now consider the set /p t k b d g/. This is the natural class of stops. There are no other stops in English, and all the sounds in the set share the feature "stop."

The set of sounds /p t k b d/ would not constitute a natural class. To be sure, the five sounds share the feature "stop"—but so does /g/, which is not included. Whatever feature we use to describe this set would also describe /g/. Notice too that the set /p t k m/ does not constitute a natural class, because any feature we introduce to specify /m/ also belongs to other sounds. Adding the feature "nasal" to the description in order to accommodate /m/ would entail including /n/ and /ŋ/, because these too are nasals. Notice, however, that in order to specify the set /p t k m n ŋ/ we would need an either/or description: either "voiceless stop" or "nasal." There is no combination of features that would uniquely specify just those six sounds; therefore /p t k m n ŋ/ is not a natural class of sounds.

UNDERLYING FORMS

Thanks to internalized rules that yield the correct allophones for every phoneme in a given word, children eventually can produce entries in their lexicons like those in Table 4-5. Such forms are called **underlying forms**; we will represent them between slanted lines, using the same notation we have used for phonemes. The **surface form**, which characterizes a word's actual pronunciation, results from the application of the phonological rules of English to the underlying forms. In some cases the surface form is the same as the underlying form simply because there are no applicable phonological rules.

Table 4-5

UNDERLYING AND SURFACE FORMS
FOR SIX ENGLISH WORDS

UNDERLYING FORM	RULE	SURFACE FORM	WRITTEN FORM
/kʌlər/	aspiration	[kʰʌlər]	color
/bʊk/	none	[bʊk]	book
/bit/	none	[bit]	beat
/ʌp/	none	[ʌp]	up
/spɪn/	nasalization	[spĩn]	spin
/pɪn/	aspiration/nasalization	[pʰĩn]	pin

RULE ORDERING

One additional phonological rule will illustrate a point about the organization of phonological rules in the internalized grammar. Consider the following words:

A	B		A	B
write	ride		treat	treed
neat	need		cute	cued
rope	robe		root	rude
lop	lob		moat	mowed
lock	log		wrote	road
tap	tab		clout	cloud
pick	pig		boot	booed

If you listen carefully while pronouncing these words, you may notice that the vowels in column B have a longer duration than those in the corresponding words of column A. In phonetic symbols, we represent long vowels with a colon after them as in [aː]. Since in English there is no minimal pair such as [pit]/[piːt] or [bæt]/[bæːt], we know that vowel length is not contrastive, not phonemic. In English, vowel length is predictable and can be specified by a general phonological rule. What environment in the words in the list causes vowel lengthening? If you look past the spelling, you will see that all the words of column A end with a voiceless consonant, while the words of column B end in a voiced consonant. In fact, there is a general process of English phonology that lengthens vowels preceding voiced consonants. We can state the rule as follows (V stands for vowel, C for consonant):

LENGTHENING RULE

$$V \rightarrow Vː \quad / \_\_\_ \quad C$$
$$\text{voiced}$$

(Vowels are lengthened preceding voiced consonants.)

As a result of this rule, the following processes take place in English:

ε   →   εː   / __ /d/ (as in *bed* versus *bet*)

o   →   oː   / __ /g/ (as in *brogue* versus *broke*)

ay   →   aːy   / __ /d/ (as in *slide* versus *slight*)

(Note that this rule applies to diphthongs like /ay/.) Because vowel length is predictable in English, it can be specified by rule and need not be learned for every word individually. In many other languages, vowel length is not predictable, not specifiable by a rule and must be learned word by word. In Fijian, for example, there is a minimal pair *oya* 'he, she' and *oyaa* that means 'that (thing).' *Dredre* means 'to laugh'; *dreedree* means 'difficult.' *Vakariri* means 'to boil'; *vakaririi* means 'speedily.' Thus in Fijian, vowel length cannot be assigned by a phonological rule, and vowel length is therefore contrastive, significant, phonemic in that language.

Now consider the following pairs of words, paying particular attention to how the pronunciation of each word in column A differs from that of the corresponding word in column B. Notice that the difference is not the one represented by the spelling difference of <t> and <d>; instead, it is a difference of vowel length. For most dialects of American English, the first vowels in the words of column B are longer than those of column A.

A	B
writer	rider
liter	leader
seater	seeder
rooter	ruder

The reason the medial consonants do not differ in pronunciation is that Americans tend to flap (or "tap") /t/ and /d/ between vowels in these words. (Recall that a flap is a sound produced when one articulator rapidly touches another articulator a single time.) In the pronunciation of /t/ or /d/ in words like those above, the tip of the tongue rapidly taps the alveolar ridge. Because the flap allophones of /t/ and /d/ are identical (represented in some books by the symbol [D] but here and in IPA by [ɾ]), the difference of pronunciation that might have resulted from the *t/d* distinction is lost, or **neutralized**. Notice that the distinction is not lost in the words *write* [rayt]/*ride* [raːyd]. The flapping rule for American English is specified as follows, with V an abbreviation for any vowel:

FLAPPING RULE

alveolar
stop   →   flap   /   V __ V
                                           unstressed

(/t/, /d/ become [ɾ] between two vowels, the second of which is unstressed.)

Even though the *t/d* (voiceless/voiced) distinction is lost in this environment by the flapping rule, many Americans pronounce the column B words differently from those in column A. By combining the flapping rule and the lengthening rule, they pronounce the words in column B with a vowel of longer duration, despite the fact that there is no difference in the pronunciation of the medial consonant. It's useful to examine why.

We have now specified two rules of English that can operate on the same words, and we want to see how they interact in producing a pronounceable surface form. Consider the pair of words *writer* and *rider.* Assume that the underlying forms in the lexicon are /raytər/ for *writer* and /raydər/ for *rider.* We can then represent the derivation of the surface forms as in Table 4-6. (When the form of a word does not meet the requirements of a rule, that rule does not apply, and we write *DNA.*) From the underlying forms and the application of the two rules in the order shown (lengthening first, flapping second), the surface forms [rayɾər] and [raːyɾər] are produced. This is in fact the correct output—the correct pronunciations of these words for some speakers of English—let's call them speakers of dialect A.

If we apply the same two rules in the reverse order (flapping first, lengthening second), the results will be different because the flapped sound is voiced; therefore the vowel preceding it would be lengthened in both words. As Table 4-7 shows, this is precisely what happens for speakers of another variety of English—call it dialect B.

The two identical surface forms [raːyɾər] and [raːyɾər] that are derived by applying the flapping rule prior to the lengthening rule would not be correct for dialect A. In that dialect (the more common one), *writer* and *rider* are not pronounced alike; instead, *rider* has a longer vowel than *writer.* Thus, given the same underlying forms, we see that the same pair of phonological rules if applied in one order produces surface forms that are correct in a given dialect; if applied in the other order, however, the rules produce incorrect forms. Evidence such as this has led researchers to hypothesize that rule ordering is an essential part of the organization of phonological rules.

Table 4-6

DERIVATION OF *WRITER* AND *RIDER* IN DIALECT A

	WRITER	RIDER	
Underlying form	/raytər/	/raydər/	(input)
Lengthening rule	DNA		
Derived form	[raytər]	raːydər]	(output/input)
Flapping rule			
Surface form	[rayɾər]	[raːyɾər]	(output)

Table 4-7

DERIVATION OF *WRITER* AND *RIDER* IN DIALECT B

	WRITER	RIDER	
Underlying form	/raytər/	/raydər/	(input)
Flapping rule			
Derived form	[rayrər]	[rayrər]	(output/input)
Lengthening rule			
Surface from	[raːyrər]	[raːyrər]	(output)

Note that the forms resulting from the second derivation (Table 4-7), though incorrect in dialect A, are correct in dialect B. This illustrates how speakers of different dialects can share the same underlying forms and the same rules but apply them in different sequences to produce different surface forms. Dialects that apply the lengthening rule before the flapping rule will have distinct forms of *writer* and *rider.* Dialects that apply flapping before lengthening will produce identical forms, both with a long vowel. Different orderings of the same rules are thus one possible explanation of pronunciation differences between dialects.

SYLLABLES AND SYLLABLE STRUCTURE

We have said little so far about how sounds are organized sequentially within words (although our analyses have presumed a certain organization, as you will see). It may seem obvious that sounds occur in words as a simple sequence *abcdef,* but that isn't entirely correct. Instead, sounds are organized into syllables, and syllables are organized into words. Thus each word consists of one or more syllables, and each syllable consists of one or more sounds, as indicated below.

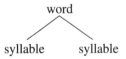

Syllable is not a tough notion for speakers to grasp intuitively, and there is considerable agreement in counting syllables. But technical definitions have proven challenging, especially in terms of articulatory or acoustic phonetics. Still, there is agreement that a **syllable** is a phonological unit consisting of one or more sounds and that syllables can be divided into two parts—a rhyme and an onset. The rhyme consists of a nucleus and any consonants following it. The nucleus is usually a vowel, although a class of consonants called sonorants can also function as a syllable nucleus. **Sonorants** include nasals like [n] and the class of liquids, like [r] and [l]. Consider the words *button*, *butter*, and *bottle*, whose second syllables we have represented in this book as [əC], containing the vowel [ə] and a consonant. These same words are represented in other books as [bʌtn̩], [bʌɾr̩], and [bɑɾl̩], where the diacritic [̩] under the final sonorant indicates that it is functioning as the nucleus of a syllable. Consonants that precede the rhyme in a syllable constitute the onset. Any consonants following the nucleus as part of the rhyme are called the coda.

The chart below represents the structure of a syllable as just described.

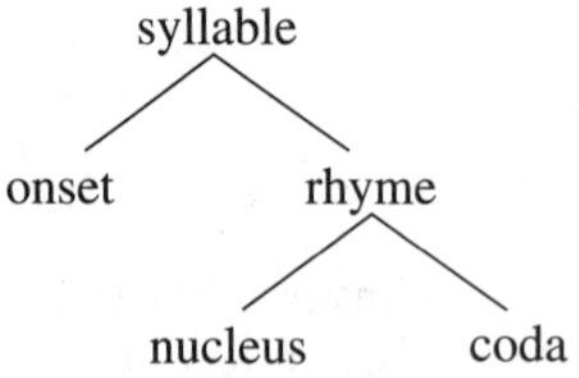

The only essential element of a syllable is the nucleus. Thus, not every syllable requires an onset nor every rhyme a coda. Consequently, a single sound can constitute a syllable, and a single syllable can constitute a word, both of which are illustrated in the phrase *a book*. Table 4-8 gives some English words with one, two, three, and four syllables.

Table 4-8

ENGLISH WORDS DIVIDED INTO SYLLABLES

1 SYLLABLE	2 SYLLABLES	3 SYLLABLES	4 SYLLABLES
ton [tʌn]	even [i-vən]	loveliest [lʌv-li-əst]	anybody [ɛ-ni-bɑ-ɾi]
spin [spɪn]	although [ɔl-ðo]	anyone [ɛ-ni-wən]	respectively [ri-spɛk-təv-li]
through [θru]	consists [kən-sɪsts]	computer [kəm-pyu-ɾər]	algebraic [æl-ǰə-bre-ək]
sail [sel]	writer [ray-ɾər]	syllable [sɪ-lə-bəl]	definition [dɛ-fə-nɪ-šən]

PHONOTACTIC CONSTRAINTS

The sequences of sounds that can make up a syllable differ from language to language and are strictly limited within each language. If you examine the four words of the following phrase, you will notice that English syllables allow several patterns of consonants (C) and vowels (V). (As in the transcriptions above, we use dashes to separate syllables within a word.)

in a pre-vi-ous chap-ter
/ɪn ə pri-vi-əs čæp-tər/
VC V CCV-CV-VC CVC-CVC

From this example, you can see that English permits the following syllable types: VC, V, CCV, CV, and CVC. Some other permissible syllable types can be seen in monosyllabic words like *past* [pæst] (CVCC), *queen* [kwin] (CCVC), *churned* [čərnd] (CVCCC), and *squirts* [skwərts] (CCCVCCC).

Not every language allows so wide a variety of syllable types as English does. In fact, the preferred syllable type among the world's languages is a single consonant followed by a single vowel: CV. Another very common type is CVC, and a third is simply V. (All three of these occur in the illustrative phrase above.) Polynesian languages such as Samoan, Tahitian, and Hawaiian have CV and V syllables only. Similarly, Japanese allows syllables basically of the forms CV, V, and (if the last consonant is a nasal) CVC. Korean permits V, CV, and CVC syllables. Mandarin permits syllables of the forms V, CV, and (if the second consonant is [n] or [ŋ]) CVC.

It is not very common in the languages of the world to have onset consonant clusters—CC—as in the English words *try*, *twin*, and *stop*, and it is very uncommon to have onset consonant clusters of more than two consonants—CCC—as in *scream*, *sprint*, and *stress*. Even in English there is a limited range of consonants that can occur in each of the positions C_1 and C_2 of a two-consonant onset cluster (C_1C_2) and an extremely narrow range of consonants in each of the positions $C_1C_2C_3$ of a three-consonant onset cluster. (It is no coincidence that all three illustrations of initial CCC begin with /s/.) Likewise, English three-consonant onset clusters have different constraints from those clusters that constitute the coda.

The rules that characterize permissible syllable structures in a language are called **phonotactic constraints**, and they determine what constitutes a possible syllable. As a result of such constraints, there are—besides the words that do exist in a language—thousands more that do not exist but could and thousands upon thousands that could not exist because their syllable structures are not permissible sequences of consonants and vowels in that language. The following would be impossible words in Hawaiian and Japanese because they violate the phonotactic constraints of those languages: "pat" (CVC), "pleat" (CCVC), and "spa" (CCV).

SNIGLETS

Comedian Rich Hall has compiled lists of "sniglets"—words that do not appear in a dictionary but should. Here are a few of Hall's sniglets and proposed definitions.

> *charp* 'the green mutant potato chip found in every bag'
> *elbonics* 'the actions of two people maneuvering for one arm in a movie theater'
> *glarpo* 'the juncture of the ear and skull where pencils are stored'
> *hozone* 'the place where one sock in every laundry disappears to'
> *spibble* 'the metal barrier on a rotary telephone that prevents you from dialing
> past O'

Notice that these sniglets conform to the phonotactic constraints of English. By contrast, the following violate the phonotactic constraints of English and therefore could not serve as sniglets: "ptlin," "brkow," "tsmtot," "ngang."

Facing foreign languages whose syllable structures differ from those of their native tongue, speakers tend to impose the phonotactic constraints of their native syllable structures on the foreign words. For example, neither Spanish nor Persian permits onset clusters such as /st/ and /sp/, so it is not uncommon for speakers of those languages to pronounce the English words *study* and *speech* as /ɛs-tʌdi/ and /ɛs-pič/, which conform to their native phonotactic constraints. Similarly, the words *baseball* and *strike* have been borrowed by Japanese speakers as *beesubooru* and *suturaiko*, in which forms they obey the phonotactic constraints of their language.

STRESS

A shopworn aphorism among American linguists points out that "Not every white house is the White House, and not every black bird is a blackbird." The point is simply that stress patterns on words can be significant. In pronouncing the phrase *every white house*, relatively strong stress is given to both *white* and *house*: *whíte hóuse*. In referring to the official residence of the American president, relatively strong stress is assigned to *White* but only secondary stress to *House*: *Whíte Hòuse*. The stress pattern assigned to the name of the president's residence matches that in the word *téachèr*: *Whíte Hòuse*. The stress pattern of the same words in the phrase (*every*) *whíte hóuse* does not. From the fact that stress can vary and that the meanings of the two expressions differ, it follows that stress can be contrastive in English. Below is a list of several other English word pairs. The pairs of column A are distinct words—they constitute noun phrases, comprising an adjective and a noun (as well as an article); the stress patterns of the pairs of column B match the pattern of *téachèr*—they constitute compound nouns.

A	B
a bláck bóard	a bláckbòard
a blúe bírd	a blúebìrd

A	B
a hígh cháir	a híghchàir
a réd néck	a rédnèck
a jét pláne	a jétstrèam
an íced téa	an íce crèam
a yéllow jácket (clothing)	a yéllow jàcket (a kind of wasp)

English thus has variable, rather than fixed, stress. The same is also true of German and some other languages, but many languages have fixed stress. In such languages, stress is assigned to a particular syllable in words. For example, Polish and Swahili words typically have stress on the next to last syllable (called the penultimate syllable), while Czech words carry stress on the first syllable and French words usually carry it on the last syllable. Obviously, in languages that have fixed word stress, contrastive stress cannot normally occur.

SYLLABLES AND STRESS IN PHONOLOGICAL PROCESSES

We saw earlier in this chapter that certain important phonological rules depend for their formulation on the syllable or on stress or on both. As we formulated it, the aspiration of voiceless stops (/p/, /t/, /k/) in English occurs "word initially and initially in stressed syllables" (page 116). Such a formulation assumes that words are organized into syllables. In turn, that means that children must have some grasp of how words are organized into syllables. Likewise, the flapping rule that produces [rayɾər] for *writer*, [mɛɾəl] for *metal*, and so on relies on stress, and you can probably guess now that our flapping rule could be reformulated in terms of syllables and their parts, instead of vowel segments, as we formulated it on page 119.

As the investigation of phonological systems has unfolded in recent decades, interest in the role of syllables in phonological processes has increased, along with interest in how words are structured phonologically. No longer viewing words as comprising only sound segments in sequence, current phonological models of words comprise multiple tiers to accommodate such phonologically significant levels as segments, syllables, and stress.

THE INTERACTION OF MORPHOLOGY AND PHONOLOGY

Before leaving the subject of phonology, let's examine the pronunciation of the most productive inflectional suffixes of English: We discuss the phonological processes that affect plural and possessive morphemes on nouns and the third-person singular and past-tense morphemes on verbs. Then we analyze variation in the surface forms of free morphemes in different lexical environments.

ENGLISH PLURAL, POSSESSIVE, AND THIRD-PERSON SINGULAR MORPHEMES

For regular nouns, there are several pronunciations of the plural morpheme, as in *lips* [lɪp + s], *seeds* [sid + z], and *fuses* [fyuz + əz]. The various surface forms underlying different pronunciations of a morpheme are called **allomorphs** of that morpheme. As the words in the following lists demonstrate, the allomorphs of the plural morpheme are determined by the last sound of the singular noun to which the morpheme is attached.

ALLOMORPHS
OF THE ENGLISH 'PLURAL' MORPHEME

[əz]	[s]	[z]
bushes	cats	pens
judges	tips	seeds
peaches	books	dogs
buses	whiffs	cars
fuses	paths	rays

Though far from complete, these lists indicate the pattern of distribution for the plural allomorphs of English.

1. [əz] occurs on nouns that end in /s, z, š, ž, č, ǰ/ (sounds constituting the natural class called *sibilants*).
2. [s] occurs following all other voiceless sounds.
3. [z] occurs following all other voiced sounds.

You may want to think of arguments for positing one of the three allomorphs as the abstract underlying form of the plural morpheme. We will assume that it is /z/. From this underlying form, all three allomorphs must be derivable by general rules that apply to all regular nouns (that is, nouns other than those that are specially marked as taking an irregular plural marker).

From an underlying /z/, a rule of the following sort would be needed in order to derive the [əz] allomorph following sibilants; note that + marks a morpheme boundary and # marks a word boundary.

SCHWA INSERTION RULE

/z/   →   [əz] / sibilant + _____#

(Schwa is inserted before a word-final /z/ that follows a morpheme ending in a sibilant.)

In order to derive the allomorph [s] from the underlying morpheme /z/ following voiceless sounds, a rule that partially assimilates the voiced /z/ to the unvoiced sound of the stem morpheme would be needed.

ASSIMILATION RULE

/z/ $\rightarrow$ voiceless / voiceless + _____#
(Word-final /z/ is devoiced following a morpheme ending in a voiceless sound.)

These two rules must have considerable generality because they must derive the correct forms of all regular plural nouns. Table 4-9 illustrates this for the nouns *coops*, *judges*, and *weeds*, which exemplify the three different allomorphs. (Recall that *DNA* means that a rule does not apply because the conditions necessary for its application are not present, slanted lines / / represent underlying forms, and square brackets [ ] represent forms derived by application of a phonological rule.)

Our rules for deriving the plural forms of regular nouns have much wider applicability. If you examine two other inflectional morphemes of English—namely, the possessive of nouns (*judge's*, *cat's*, and *dog's*) and the third-person singular marker on verbs (*teaches*, *laughs*, and *swims*)—you'll discover that the distribution of the allomorphs of these morphemes is parallel to the distribution for the plural morpheme.

Table 4-9

DERIVATION OF ENGLISH PLURAL NOUNS

	COOPS	JUDGES	WEEDS
Underlying forms	/kup+z/	/ǰʌǰ+z/	/wid+z/
Schwa insertion	DNA		DNA
Derived form		[ǰʌǰ+əz]	
Assimilation		DNA	DNA
Surface form	[kup+s]	[ǰʌǰ+əz]	[wid+z]

POSSESSIVE MORPHEME ON NOUNS

[s]	ship, cat, Jack
[z]	John, arm, dog
[əz]	church, judge, fish

THIRD-PERSON SINGULAR MORPHEME ON VERBS

[s]	leap, eat, kick, laugh
[z]	hurry, seem, lean, crave, see
[əz]	preach, tease, judge, buzz, rush

If we posit /z/ as the underlying phonological form of these morphemes, then the very same rules that derive the correct allomorphs of the plural morpheme will also derive the correct allomorphs of the possessive morpheme of nouns and the third-person singular morpheme of verbs. (Unlike plurals, many of which are irregular, all nouns are regular with respect to the possessive morpheme, and all verbs are regular with respect to the third-person singular morpheme except for *is*, *has*, *says*, and *does*.)

ENGLISH PAST-TENSE MORPHEME

The inflectional morpheme that marks the past tense of regular verbs in English has three allomorphs:

[t]	wish, kiss, talk, strip, preach
[d]	wave, bathe, play, lie, stir, tease, roam, ruin
[əd]	want, wade, wait, hoot, plant, seed

If we posit /d/ as the underlying phonological form of the past-tense morpheme, we need only two simple rules to derive the past-tense forms on all regular verbs.

SCHWA INSERTION RULE

/d/ → [əd] / alveolar stop + _____#
(Schwa is inserted preceding a word-final /d/ that follows a morpheme ending in an alveolar stop.)

ASSIMILATION RULE

/d/ → voiceless / voiceless + _____#
(Word-final /d/ is realized as [t] following a morpheme that ends in a voiceless sound.)

Derivations of the past-tense forms of the verbs *wish*, *want*, and *wave* are provided in Table 4-10 as examples.

Inspection of the last two sets of rules reveals striking similarities in both the schwa insertion processes and the assimilation processes required to generate the correct forms of four inflectional morphemes: the plural and possessive forms of nouns, the third-person singular forms of verbs, and the past-tense forms of verbs.

UNDERLYING PHONOLOGICAL FORM OF MORPHEMES
IN THE LEXICON

In this section we explore the phonological form of words as they exist in the mental lexicon of speakers. The form of a word in the lexicon is called its underlying form, and, as you'll see, the form in the lexicon is not necessarily the same as the form of a word as it is pronounced.

Table 4-10

DERIVATION OF ENGLISH PAST-TENSE VERBS

	WISHED	WANTED	WAVED
Underlying form	/wɪš+d/	/wɑnt+d/	/wev+d/
Schwa insertion	DNA		DNA
Derived form	[wɪš+d]	[wɑnt+əd]	[wev+d]
Assimilation		DNA	DNA
Surface form	[wɪš+t]	[wɑnt+əd]	[wev+d]

Consonants   The same kinds of phonological processes that operate between a stem and an inflectional suffix also operate between a stem and a derivational morpheme. Imagine, for example, that you are a child who knows the words *metal* and *medal*. For a speaker of North American English, the sound that occurs in the middle of both words is an alveolar flap, neither [t] nor [d] but [ɾ]. (Recall that an alveolar flap is the sound created when the tip of the tongue flaps quickly against the alveolar ridge, as in *later* and *ladder.* [ɾ], which is phonetically different from both [t] and [d], is the way most Americans usually say the middle consonant of *metal* and *medal*.)

As an American child hearing *metal* and *medal*, you would have entered exactly what you heard into your lexicon—/mɛɾəl/ in both cases. But consider what must happen after you have internalized /mɛɾəl/ for both and then subsequently hear someone say that her new car is painted *metallic* [mətʰæl+ək] *red*. If you failed to recognize that *metallic* and *metal* share an element of meaning, you would simply enter a new morpheme into your lexicon. That new morpheme would have the meaning 'metal-like' but would not be related to the morpheme METAL; the two entries would be completely independent of one another. However, once you recognized that *metallic* is made up of METAL with the derivational suffix -IC added, then the two pronunciations [mɛɾəl] and [mətʰæl+ək] must be reconciled. (This recognition will accompany the knowledge that -IC is a morpheme that also appears in such words as *atomic*, *Germanic*, *alcoholic*, and *demonic*.) The task of a language learner is to posit the simplest underlying form from which all surface forms for pronunciation can be correctly derived given the phonological rules of English.

Now consider the task you face when you subsequently hear someone report that the car's *medallion* is missing from the hood. For *medal* and *medallion*, you hear [mɛɾəl] and [mədælyən]. What underlying form must be posited in the lexicon once the morpheme MEDAL is recognized as occurring in both words?

Assume you recognized that METAL was a common element in both *metal* and *metallic* and that MEDAL was a common element in *medal* and *medallion*. The following pronunciations can be observed:

METAL		MEDAL	
[mɛɾəl]	[mətʰæl + ək]	[mɛɾəl]	[mədæl + yən]
metal	metallic	medal	medallion

You can account for the different pronunciations of the morpheme METAL by positing the form /mɛtæl/ in the lexicon and postulating phonological rules that change this abstract underlying form into the various surface forms that do occur. Ignoring the vowels for a moment, the underlying form /mɛtæl/ will require a process that changes /t/ into [ɾ] in the word *metal* [mɛɾəl]. (In the next section you'll see why æ is the vowel that's posited.)

This same process will be needed to change /d/ into [ɾ] in the word *medal* [mɛɾəl]. The flapping rule changes underlying /t/ and /d/ into [ɾ] when they occur between a stressed vowel and an unstressed vowel. Using a more formal notation, the rule would be:

$$\begin{matrix} \text{alveolar} \\ \text{stop} \end{matrix} \quad \rightarrow \text{flap} \quad \Big/ \quad \begin{matrix} \text{vowel} \underline{\quad} \text{vowel} \\ \text{stressed} \underline{\quad} \text{unstressed} \end{matrix}$$

You can see that phonological rules that must be postulated to account for one set of facts sometimes account for other facts. Phonological rules, after all, apply to all morphemes and words unless there is a specific marking in the lexical entry of a particular morpheme to block the application of some process. For instance, nouns with an irregular plural form, like *tooth*, are marked in the lexicon as not taking the regular plural morpheme. If the morpheme TOOTH were not so marked, then speakers would say *tooths* instead of *teeth*, exactly as children do before they learn to exempt TOOTH from these regular morphological and morphophonemic processes.

Thus the relationship between the phonological representation of morphemes in the lexicon and their actual pronunciation in speech is mediated by a set of phonological processes that can be represented in rules of significant generality. It is not only *metal* and *medal* that will be affected by the flapping rule but every word that meets the conditions specified in the rule. This includes single-morpheme words like *butter*, *bitter*, and *meter*; two-morpheme words like *writer*, *rider*, *raider*, *rooter*; and thousands of others.

Vowels Consider a youngster who knows the words *photograph* [forəgræf] and *photographer* [fətʰagrəf + ər]. At some point speakers of English posit a single entry in the lexicon to represent the core of these two words—that is, PHOTOGRAPH. When you think about what the underlying form must be, you will see that /fotagræf/ best represents the knowledge needed to produce the two pronunciations above. Given the underlying representation /fotagræf/ and the surface forms [forəgræf] and [fət^{h}agrəf + ər], a rule that changes unstressed vowels into [ə] will produce the correct vowels.

If instead we postulated /ə/ in the underlying form, it would be impossible to formulate a rule that would produce the correct surface forms. In order to produce the [ɑ] in [fət^{h}agrəf + ər] from an underlying form with schwas /fətəgrəf + ər/, we would need a rule that produced [ɑ] from underlying /ə/. For the word *photograph*, on the other hand, we would need a rule that produced [o] from underlying /ə/ in the first syllable and [æ] from underlying /ə/ in the third syllable. This would amount to knowing which vowels exist in the surface pronunciation and encoding that knowledge in the underlying form in the mental lexicon along with the /ə/, but that is exactly what we assume does not happen. Instead, if we postulate different vowels in the underlying forms, we can formulate a single rule that derives [ə] from any underlying vowel when it occurs in unstressed position; we can now derive the customary pronunciations for these words. We formulate the rule as follows:

$$\begin{matrix} \text{vowel} \\ \text{unstressed} \end{matrix} \quad \rightarrow \quad [\text{ə}]$$

(An unstressed vowel becomes schwa.)

This rule will not affect stressed vowels; underlying vowels that are unstressed become schwa [ə]. Of course, a rule that relies on information about stress requires prior assignment of stress. The rules for assigning stress in English are more complex than we can discuss in this chapter. If you wish to pursue the topic further, some of the references at the end of the chapter contain treatments of the stress placement rules of English.

COMPUTERS AND PHONOLOGY

Several decades ago researchers thought it would be a matter of only a few years before computers would be able to recognize speech and to synthesize it. (You can think of this simply as being able to turn spoken language into print and print into spoken language.) Although there has been some progress on both fronts, the process has taken longer than most researchers anticipated. The reasons do not lie in any absence of sophistication in computers but rather in the complexity of the phonological processes that characterize human languages and in our inability to model in a computer just what speakers do when they produce spoken utterances and understand the utterances of others. For example, as we saw earlier in this chapter, natural speech occurs in a continuous stream and is not readily segmented without knowledge of the particular language involved. Just how human beings segment a continuous stream of spoken language into distinct words and recognize the sound segments in those words remains unclear.

The synthesis of speech by machine has also proved challenging. To understand why, focus on a string of sounds such as would occur in a simple word like *sand*. It would seem to be a straightforward matter to put together a machine-generated form of /sænd/: just get the machine to produce first a voiceless alveolar fricative, then the vowel /æ/, then the alveolar nasal /n/, and finally the alveolar stop /d/. It seems simple enough, but notice that when you pronounce *sand*, its vowel quality differs markedly from the "same" vowel in a word like *hat*. If a speech synthesizer produced the vowel of *hat* in the word *sand*, it would sound highly artificial. Likewise, if it produced the vowel of *sand* in the word *hat*, that too would seem very unnatural. You already know that the vowel of *sand* gets nasalized before the nasal stop that follows it. (See the rule on p. 114.) What happens in articulatory terms is that in anticipation of the following nasal consonant and as the vocal tract starts to move toward that nasal consonant, the vowel itself takes on nasal characteristics. Therein lies one challenge for speech synthesis—how to blend sounds into one another in the way that people do. Just as there is no separation between words in ordinary human speech, so there is no separation between sounds.

But the situation is even more complex. We have seen that a sound is essentially a bundle of phonetic features. Thus we could think of the phonological form of *sand* as being not just the four segments /sænd/ but as the (partial list of) features given below each segment:

/s/	**/æ/**	**/n/**	**/d/**
voiceless	voiced	voiced	voiced
alveolar	low-front	alveolar	alveolar
fricative	unrounded	nasal	stop

The phonetic characteristics of the segments of *sand* are more complicated than we have indicated, but the representation above will serve for our purposes. Consider that the articulation of the phonetic features in each segment does not start and end at the same time as the others. In other words, the voicelessness of /s/ doesn't abruptly end and the voicing of /æ/ start at exactly the same time as the fricative character of the consonant stops and the vowel character of /æ/ begins. The mouth and the other features of the vocal tract move continuously in the production of even a simple word like *sand* (as you can feel by saying the word and concentrating on your tongue movement).

If the aim of speech synthesis is to make artificial speech sound as natural as possible, a good deal more about the nature of phonetic realizations of underlying phonological forms will have been achieved. (Below, in the section on Internet resources, you will find the addresses for Internet Web sites at which you can hear speech synthesized from your typewritten message.)

SUMMARY

- Phonology is the study of the sound systems of languages.

- A phoneme is a unit in the phonological system of a language. It is an abstract element, a set of phonological features having several possible manifestations (called allophones) in speech.

- Two words can differ minimally by virtue of having a single pair of different phonemes (as in *pin/bin*).

- Each phoneme comprises a set of allophones—each allophone being the particular realization of the phoneme in a particular linguistic environment.

- The allophones of a phoneme occur in complementary distribution or in free variation; they never contrast. Allophones of a single phoneme cannot be the sole difference in a minimal pair of words with different meanings.

- Different languages can have the same sounds and yet structure them differently in their sound systems. Both Korean and English have the three sounds [p], [pʰ], and [b] in their inventories. In English, unaspirated [p] and aspirated [pʰ] are allophones of one phoneme, while [b] belongs to a different phoneme. By contrast, in Korean, aspirated [pʰ] and unaspirated [p] are distinct phonemes (they contrast), while [b] is merely the allophone of the phoneme /p/ that occurs between voiced sounds.

- Each simple word in a speaker's internalized lexicon consists of a sequence of phonemes that constitutes the underlying phonological representation of the word. Underlying forms differ from pronunciations and cannot generally be observed in speech directly.

- From the underlying form of a word, the phonological rules of a language specify the allophonic features of its phonemes in accordance with their linguistic environments.

- One fundamental task of children in acquiring a language is to uncover its phonological rules and to infer efficient, economical underlying forms for word units. Given these underlying forms, the phonological rules of a language will specify the rule-governed features of the surface form.

- Phonological rules may be ordered with respect to one another, the first applicable rule applying to the underlying form to produce a derived form, the subsequent rules applying in turn to successive derived forms until the last applicable rule produces a surface form. The surface form is the basis of a word's pronunciation. Two dialects of a language may contain some of the same rules but apply them in a different order, thereby producing different surface forms for different pronunciations.

- Words are made up of groups of sounds called syllables, not of sounds themselves.

- Different languages have different phonotactic constraints on the structure of permissible syllable types and the occurrence of particular consonants and vowels within syllable types.

- CV is the most common syllable type in the world's languages. English has an unusually large range of syllable types, including clusters of two and three consonants, though which consonants can appear in each position is constrained.

- Stress is contrastive in English, as captured in the aphorism, "Not every white house is the White House."

- Phonological processes (for example, aspiration and flapping in English) can depend on syllable structure and stress, as well as on a sequence of sound segments.

EXERCISES

Based on English

4-1. Consider the following words of English with respect to how the sound represented by <t> is pronounced. For each column, specify the phonetic character of the allophone (how it is pronounced). For example, is it aspirated? flapped? Then, as was done in this chapter for the allophones of English /p/, describe the allophones of /t/ and specify their distribution.

A	B	C	D
tougher	standing	later	petunia
talker	still	data	potato
teller	story	petal	return

4-2. Using the monosyllabic English words below, provide a list of fifteen ordered pairs whose stress patterns indicate they constitute a compound. It will be helpful to mark the stress pattern on the vowel of each element, using ´ to represent primary stress and ` for secondary stress.

Examples: tímezòne, shówhòrse

ball	beam	court	face	fall	free	gear	hand	hat
heart	hold	horse	house	kick	lance	land	life	light
paint	port	rein	ride	road	show	style	table	throw
tide	time	way	weight	year	zone			

4-3. We think the following words do not exist in English. Some of them are candidates for "sniglets" (they could exist); others could not be sniglets because they violate the phonotactic constraints of English. Identify the potential sniglets, and explain why the others are not permitted. For the potential sniglets, provide an appropriate spelling in the standard orthography.

pɛtribɑr	twɪnč	rizənənt
læktomæŋgyulešən	pʌpkəss	blɪbyulə
pæŋgəkd	spret	spwənt

4-4. a. Make a list of as many words as you can, each of which represents a different initial three-consonant cluster. *Example: spr in spread; str in strike.*

   b. Examine the initial clusters you listed in part a and answer the following questions about English:

   Which consonants can occur first in an initial three-consonant cluster?

   Which consonants can occur second in an initial three-consonant cluster?

   Which consonants can occur third in an initial three-consonant cluster?

   Examine the three lists that you have made to decide whether they constitute natural classes or not, and provide the name for any that do.

4-5. Although English makes a contrast between /p/ and /b/ (*pill* versus *bill*), it doesn't exploit the contrast in the environment following /s/ (as in *spell* and *spin*). Hence, there is no pair of words such as /sbɪn/ and /spɪn/. When a language exploits a distinction in some environments but not all, there is a tendency for the potential contrast to be neutralized where it isn't exploited. As a consequence, the /p/ of *pill* differs more from the /b/ of *bill* than does the /p/ of *spin* (try distinguishing "spin" from "sbin"). For one thing, the /p/ of *spin* (but not the /p/ of *pill*) lacks aspiration, like the /b/ of *bill*. Thus at least one feature that distinguishes /p/ and /b/ elsewhere is not exploited following /s/.

Below are two sets of words containing a contrast that is exploited in the environment in column I but neutralized in the environment in column II.

	I	II
i.	bit beat	here, beer, peer (contrast *mill*/*meal*)
ii.	sit seat	sing, ring, king
iii.	hat hate	hang, sang, rang
iv.	tad dad	sting, star, study
v.	cad gad	skill, score, scam

a. Identify the segment that is likely to prompt different transcriptions and specify what those transcriptions would be.

b. Characterize the environment that supports the neutralization.

c. Based on your knowledge of English phonology (such as its phonotactic constraints), provide reasons for preferring one of the transcriptions over the other.

4-6. On page 125, we said you could probably guess that the English flapping rule could be reformulated in terms of syllables and their parts instead of in terms of vowel segments, as formulated on page 119. Formulate the flapping rule in terms of syllables and their parts.

Based on Languages Other Than English

4-7. Fijian has prenasalized stops among its inventory of phonemes. The prenasalized stop [^{n}d] consists of a nasal pronounced immediately before the stop, with which it forms a single sound unit. Consider the following Fijian words as pronounced in fast speech:

vi^{n}di	'to spring up'	dina	'true'
ke^{n}da	'we'	dalo	'taro plant'
tiko	'to stay'	vu^{n}di	'plantain banana'
tutu	'grandfather'	ma^{n}da	'first'
viti	'Fiji'	tina	'mother'
dovu	'sugarcane'	mata	'eye'

do^{n}do	'to stretch out one's hand'	mokiti	'round'
		veve^{n}du	(a type of plant)

On the basis of these data, determine whether [d], [^{n}d], and [t] are allophones of a single phoneme or constitute two or three distinct phonemes. If you find that two of them (or all of them) are allophones of a single phoneme, give the rule that describes the distribution of each allophone. If you analyze all three as distinct phonemes, justify your answer. (*Note*: In Fijian all syllables end in a vowel.)

4-8. Examine the following words of Tongan, a Polynesian language. (*Note*: In Tongan all syllables end in a vowel.)

tauhi	'to take care'	sino	'body'
sisi	'garland'	totonu	'correct'
motu	'island'	pasi	'to clap'
mosimosi	'to drizzle'	fata	'shelf'
motomoto	'unripe'	movete	'to come apart'
fesi	'to break'	misi	'to dream'

a. On the basis of these data, determine whether [s] and [t] are allophones of a single phoneme in Tongan or are distinct phonemes. If you find that they are allophones of the same phoneme, state the rule that describes where each allophone occurs. If you conclude that they are different phonemes, justify your answer.

b. In each of the following Tongan words, one sound has been replaced by a blank. This sound is either [s] or [t]. Without more knowledge of Tongan than you could figure out from the preceding question, is it possible to make an educated guess as to which of these two sounds fits in the blank? If so, provide the sound; if not, explain why.

___ili	'fishing net'	fe___e	'lump'
___uku	'to place'	lama___i	'to ambush'

c. In the course of this century, Tongan has borrowed many words from English and has adapted them to fit the phonological structure of its words.

kaasete	'gazette'	suu	'shoe'
tisi	'dish'	koniseti	'concert'
sosaieti	'society'	pata	'butter'
salati	'salad'	suka	'sugar'
maasolo	'marshall'	sikaa	'cigar'
sekoni	'second'	taimani	'diamond'

How does the phonemic status of [s] and [t] differ in borrowed words and in native Tongan words? In other words, is the situation the same in these borrowed words? Write an integrated statement about the status of [s] and [t] in Tongan. (*Hint*: Your statement will have to include information about which area of the Tongan vocabulary each part of the rule applies to.)

4-9. The distribution of the sounds [s] and [z] in colloquial Spanish is represented by the following examples in phonetic transcription:

izla	'island'	čiste	'joke'
fuersa	'force'	eski	'ski'
peskado	'fish'	riezgo	'risk'
muskulo	'muscle'	fiskal	'fiscal'
sin	'without'	rezvalar	'to slip'
rasko	'I scratch'	dezde	'since'
resto	'remainder'	razgo	'feature'
mizmo	'same'	beizbɔl	'baseball'
espalda	'back'	mas	'more'

Are [s] and [z] distinct phonemes of Spanish or allophones of a single phoneme? If they are distinct phonemes, support your answer; if they are allophones of the same phoneme, specify their distribution.

4-10. Consider the following Russian words. On the basis of this limited list, where does Russian appear to have a contrast between [t] and [d] and where does it appear not to have one? (*Note:* An apostrophe makes a patalized consonant.)

pərʌxot	'steamboat'	t'ɛlə	'body'
gʌz'etə	'newspaper'	pot	'perspiration'
zapət	'west'	dərʌgoy	'dear'
rat	'glad'	d'ɛlə	'business'
zdan'iyə	'building'	štat	'state'
most	'bridge'	pot	'under'

4-11. In Samoan, words may have two forms, one called "bad speech" (used in formal oratory when addressing peers or kin) and another called "good speech" (used with chiefs or strangers in literary and religious situations). The difference between the two forms can be described by phonological rules. (*Note:* The Samoan words for "good" and "bad" do not carry the same connotations in this case as the English words.)

"bad"	"good"	
taatou	kaakou	'us all'
teine	keiŋe	'girl'
taŋata	kaŋaka	'man'
ŋaŋana	ŋaŋana	'language'
totoŋi	kokoŋi	'price'
nofo	ŋofo	'to stay'
ŋaalue	ŋaalue	'to work'
fono	foŋo	'meeting'

a. Describe the phonological difference between the "bad" and "good" forms. Which form is more basic—the "good" form or the "bad" form?

(In other words, which one can serve as the underlying form for both forms?)

b. Wherever possible, fill in the blanks in the following table. If it is impossible to know the form of a missing word, say why.

"bad"	"good"	
manu	_____	'bird'
mate	_____	'dead'
_____	maŋoo	'shark'
_____	kili	'fishing net'
tonu	_____	'correct'
_____	kaɲi	'to cry'

4-12. In German, the sequence of letters <ch> can represent (among other things) either of two sounds: [ç] (a voiceless palatal fricative) or [x] (a voiceless velar fricative). On the basis of the following data, determine whether these two sounds are distinct phonemes in German or allophones of a single phoneme.

kɛlç	*Kelch*	'cup'
fɪçtə	*Fichte*	'fir tree'
knœçl	*Knöchel*	'knuckle'
kɔx	*Koch*	'cook'
tsurɛçt	*zurecht*	'in good order'
vʊxt	*Wucht*	'weight'
çɪrʊrk	*Chirurg*	'surgeon'
nüçtərn	*nüchtern*	'sober'
bux	*Buch*	'book'
bərayç	*Bereich*	'scope'
hɛkçən	*Häkchen*	'apostrophe'
bax	*Bach*	'brook'

If [ç] and [x] are distinct phonemes, justify your answer; if they are allophones of the same phoneme, specify their distribution.

4-13. In light of our discussions in this chapter and your experience with some of the preceding exercises, discuss the following quote from Halle and Clements (1983).

The perception of intelligible speech is . . . determined only in part by the physical signal that strikes our ears. Of equal significance . . . is the contribution made by the perceiver's knowledge of the language in which the utterance is framed. Acts of perception that heavily depend on active contributions from the perceiver's mind are often described as illusions, and the perception of intelligible speech seems . . . to qualify for this description. A central problem of phonetics and phonology is . . . to provide a scientific characterization of this illusion which is at the heart of all human existence.

INTERNET RESOURCES

- **Speech on the Web: http://www.tue.nl/ipo/hearing/webspeak.htm#On-line**
  If you're interested in hearing synthesized speech, several Web sites can provide examples. This site is a "jump station" providing links to speech synthesizers around the globe. Once you choose one, you can type in something you wish to hear synthesized. Then, assuming that your computer has multimedia capabilities, you can experience state-of-the-art text-to-speech synthesis.

- **Voices Demonstration Page: http://www.att.com/aspg/odemo.html**
  This demo illustrates the capabilities of the WATSON Flex Talk™ speech synthesizer. You can type in up to fifty words and receive an audio file of what you've typed that is compatible with your computer and can be played using your multimedia capabilities. You can choose from among several voices, including child, woman, man, raspy, or singer.

- **SpeechLinks: http://www.speech.cs.cmu.edu/comp.speech/SpeechLinks.html**
  This is a speech technology hyperlinks page containing hundreds of links to projects around the world. Besides the links to technical papers (most of which will be beyond the reach of beginning students), you will also find links to sites exploring speech recognition and speech synthesis.

SUGGESTIONS FOR FURTHER READING

- **Francis Katamba. 1989.** *Introduction to Phonology* (New York: St. Martin's). A thorough treatment, sensitive to theoretical, as well as descriptive, concerns.

- **Clarence Sloat, Sharon Henderson Taylor, and James E. Hoard. 1978.** *Introduction to Phonology* (Englewood Cliffs, NJ: Prentice-Hall). Unusually clear and accessible in both phonetics and phonology and in treating a range of languages.

- **Walt Wolfram and Robert Johnson. 1982.** *Phonological Analysis*: *Focus on American English* (Washington, DC: Center for Applied Linguistics/Harcourt). An excellent introduction to the phonological analysis of English, with many illustrations and examples.

Advanced Reading

Clark and Yallop (1990) and Carr (1993) are basic textbooks that will be largely accessible to readers who have mastered some phonetics and the phonology of this chapter. The "problem book" by Halle and Clements (1983) covers a broader range of languages than Wolfram and Johnson and has an excellent introductory chapter that goes beyond what we have covered; it also has separate chapters on complementary distribution, natural classes, phonological rules, and systems of rules. Chomsky and Halle (1968) is a classic book, now available in paperback. Kaye (1989) is a lively, provocative, and mostly accessible follow-up to this chapter. A more specialized treatment is available in Hogg and McCully (1987).

REFERENCES

- Carr, Philip. 1993. *Phonology* (New York: St. Martin's).

- Chomsky, Noam, and Morris Halle. 1968. *The Sound Pattern of English* (New York: Harper & Row).

- Clark, John, and Colin Yallop. 1995. *An Introduction to Phonetics and Phonology,* 2nd ed. (New York: Blackwell).

- Hall, Rich. 1984. *Sniglets* (New York: Collier).

- Halle, Morris, and G. N. Clements. 1983. *Problem Book in Phonology* (Cambridge, MA: MIT P).

- Hogg, Richard, and C. B. McCully. 1987. *Metrical Phonology: A Coursebook* (Cambridge: Cambridge UP).

- Kaye, Jonathan. 1989. *Phonology: A Cognitive View* (Hillsdale, NJ: Erlbaum).

CHAPTER 5

THE STRUCTURE OF PHRASES
AND SENTENCES: SYNTAX

WHAT DO YOU THINK?

In a high school English class one of your students says he understands that people know the meaning of expressions like "How are you?" and "What time is it?" because we say them frequently. But, he asks, how do people know the meaning of sentences they've never heard or read before? What do you tell the class?

At lunch, a friend of yours, an engineering major, reports that she's reading Steven Pinker's The Language Instinct *and has some questions about ambiguity. She understands how a word like* bank *can mean 'savings bank' or 'river bank' but asks you how a string of unambiguous words can produce an ambiguous sentence. As an example, she gives "Visiting relatives can be a disaster." What explanation can you offer?*

A college friend expresses annoyance that the grammar checker in his word processor objected to this sentence: "Each of the following English sentences has the same meaning." The checker suggested followings *instead of* following, *and your friend suspects that the checker took* following *to be a noun. He wants to know what you think of his analysis. What do you tell him?*

Your friend (the grammar checker critic) phones to say that his checker objected to the phrase "the common nouns books and justice" and suggested instead "the common nouns' books and justice" or "the common noun's books and justice." He's aware that checkers operate only on forms and know nothing of meanings, but he remains perplexed at the checker's stupid suggestion and wonders what it could be "thinking." Your analysis?

INTRODUCTION: REFERRING AND PREDICATING

This chapter explores how morphemes and words are organized within phrases and sentences. It examines the parts of a sentence and their relationships with one another, as well as the relationships between various kinds of sentences such as statements and questions. We explore how a finite grammar can generate an infinite number of sentences and how the "creative" aspects of language and the understanding of completely novel sentences are part of everyone's competence.

All languages have ways of referring to entities—to people, places, things, ideas, events, and so on. The expressions used to refer to entities are known as noun phrases. There are simple noun phrases like the proper nouns *Lauren* and *Paris*, the common nouns *books* and *justice*, and the personal pronouns *you* and *it*. There are also more complex noun phrases like *a magical book*, *his mother*, *the star of the film*, and *a judge he had known forty years earlier.*

Languages also have ways of saying something about the entities they make reference to. In other words, languages can make predications about the entities signaled by the referring expressions. All languages have ways of making statements, both affirmative ones and negative ones. They can also ask questions, issue directives, and so on.

Let's illustrate with affirmative statements. In the following sentences, reference is made to an entity and then a predication is made about it.

REFERRING EXPRESSION	PREDICATION
Judge Judy	has a daughter.
She	uses an answering machine.
The ghost	reappeared last night.

In the first example, reference is made to Judge Judy, and something is then predicated of her—namely, that she has a daughter. Likewise for the second and third examples.

Syntax governs the form of strings by which a language makes statements, asks questions, gives directives, and so on. The study of syntax treats the structure of sentences and their structural relationships to one another. In syntactic terms, referring expressions are noun phrases, and predicates are verb phrases. All languages, however much they differ from one another, have noun phrases and verb phrases.

SENTENCE TYPES

Traditional grammars distinguish three major sentence types. A **simple sentence** consists of a single clause that stands alone as a sentence. In a **coordinate sentence** (called "compound" in traditional grammars), two or more clauses are joined by a conjunction in a coordinate relationship like "X and Y." A **complex sentence** combines clauses in such a way that one clause functions as a grammatical part of another one, as in "X said Y."

Simple Sentences = Clauses

Simple sentences contain only one clause. Each **clause** contains a single verb group. The following are examples of simple sentences:

> Danny <u>fell</u>.
> Karen <u>assembled</u> the new grill.
> Joe <u>cooked</u> the hot dogs.
> A runner from Ohio <u>won</u> the marathon last year.
> Denise <u>will buy</u> a new raincoat this fall.
> Her uncle <u>had put</u> the gifts in the car.
> The psychiatrist <u>should have believed</u> in banshees.

Each contains only one verb group, but a verb group itself can consist of one word (as in *fell*, *assembled*, *cooked*, and *won*) or more than one word (as in *will buy*, *had put*, and *should have believed*). The central element in a clause is the verb; each clause—and therefore each simple sentence—contains just one verb group.

Coordinate Sentences

Two clauses can be conjoined to make a coordinate sentence, as in these examples:

> Karen assembled the new grill, <u>and</u> Joe cooked the hot dogs.
> Denise bought a new coat, <u>but</u> she didn't wear it often.

A coordinate sentence consists of two clauses joined by a coordinating conjunction such as *and*, *but*, or *or*.

The clauses in a coordinate sentence hold equal status. That means that neither clause is part of the other clause, and each clause could stand by itself as an independent sentence. Figure 5-1 represents the structure of a coordinate sentence and illustrates the equivalent status of the *coordinate clauses*. We use the label S for the whole sentence and for each coordinate clause in it; Conj stands for conjunction.

Complex Sentences

Embedded Clauses Besides being conjoined to another clause, a clause can be incorporated *into* another clause. The clause *Danny fell* can be incorporated into another clause to produce the sentence *Sue said Danny fell.* In each of the following examples, the underlined clause is incorporated (or embedded) into another clause.

Figure 5-1

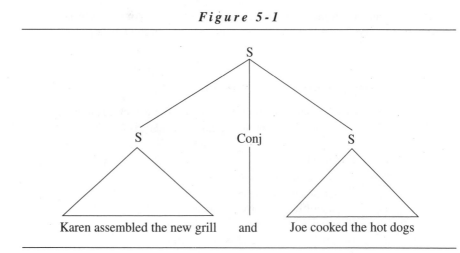

1. Sue said <u>Danny fell</u>.
2. <u>That the runner from Ohio won the marathon</u> surprised Sheila.
3. She suspected a party <u>when Pat put the gifts in the car</u>.
4. It was clear <u>that the patient should have received a refund</u>.

In sentence 1, the clause *Danny fell* is embedded into the clausal structure *Sue said* ————. The clause *Danny fell* thus corresponds structurally (though not semantically, of course) to the word *something* in the sentence *Sue said something.* In 2, the clause *That the runner from Ohio won the marathon* is embedded into the clausal structure ———— *surprised Sheila.* The embedded clause in 2 (*That the runner from Ohio won the marathon*) is grammatically equivalent to *It* in *It surprised Sheila* or to *The news* in *The news surprised Sheila.* In 3, the clause *when Pat put the gifts in the car* is embedded into the clause *She suspected a party* ————; it corresponds to the role of *then* in *She suspected a party then.*

Subordinators   In most of the examples just given, the embedded clause is introduced by a word that would not occur there if the clause were standing as an independent sentence: *that* in 2 and 4 and *when* in 3. When a clause is embedded into another clause, it is often introduced by a subordinating conjunction. Such subordinators mark the beginning of the embedded clause and help identify its function in the sentence. Not all embedded clauses must be introduced by a subordinator, although in English they usually can be. Compare these sentence pairs:

1. a. Sue said <u>that</u> Dan washed the dishes.
   b. Sue said Dan washed the dishes.
2. a. <u>That</u> she won surprised us.
   b. *She won surprised us.

Notice that 1-a and 1-b are well formed (that is, with or without the subordinator *that*). But in 2, only 2-a is well formed. (The asterisk, or star, preceding 2-b indicates a structure that is not well formed.)

Unlike coordinate sentences, which contain clauses of equal status, complex sentences contain clauses of unequal status. In the complex sentences we have been examining, one clause is subordinate to another and functions as a grammatical part of it. The subordinate clause is called an *embedded clause*, and the clause in which it is embedded is called a *matrix clause*. By definition, every subordinate clause is embedded in a matrix clause and serves a grammatical function in it. (Grammatical functions include subject and direct object, and we will discuss them further below.) For example, in the next sentences, where brackets enclose the embedded clauses, each embedded clause functions as a grammatical unit in its matrix clause. Each embedded clause has the same grammatical function in its matrix clause as the underlined word in the sentence directly below it (direct object in 1; subject in 2; adverbial in 3).

1. a. Sally said [she saw a ghost].
   b. Sally said <u>it</u>.
2. a. [That Jack feared mice] upset his wife.
   b. <u>It</u> upset his wife.
3. a. Joe cooked them [after Karen assembled the grill].
   b. Joe cooked them <u>then</u>.

CONSTITUENCY AND TREE DIAGRAMS

In analyzing sentences, one pivotal tool is the recognition that sentences consist not of words but of structural units called **constituents.** Consider the sentence *Sally said she saw a ghost.* It can be viewed in several ways. Obviously, it is made up of words, and each word contains at least one morpheme. Since morphemes have sounds associated with them, we could say that the sentence is made up of sounds (such as /g/, /o/, /s/, /t/ in *ghost* and /s/, /ɛ/, /d/ in *said*), or of morphemes (SAY and 'PAST TENSE'), or of words (*Sally* and *said*). Such an approach would be like describing a shopping mall as made up of cement and electrical wires—accurate, but beside the point. We want to say that a shopping center has shops, restaurants, parking areas, recreational facilities, and so on. We could then go further and describe the composition and relationship of these basic units. The point is to identify *structural units* that are relevant to some purpose or some level of organization.

TREE DIAGRAMS

We can represent syntactic relationships in tree diagrams. The tree in Figure 5-2 represents the fact that the sentence *Sue liked Casper* consists of two parts: the referring expression *Sue* and the predicate expression *liked Casper.* In tree diagrams, S stands for sentence (= clause), N stands for noun or pronoun, and V stands for verb.

Figure 5-2

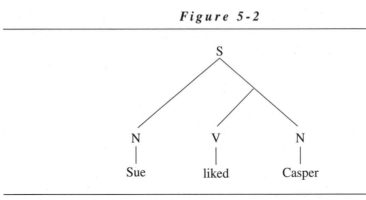

This tree diagram can also represent other clauses, such as *Sally said it*, as illustrated in Figure 5-3. Later we'll see that Figures 5-2 and 5-3 somewhat oversimplify the structures represented. Tree diagrams can also illustrate the relationship among the clauses of a sentence like *Sally said she saw a ghost*. In representing a complex sentence, we can substitute the clause *she saw a ghost* for the word *it*, as in Figure 5-4. This tree diagram captures the fact that the embedded clause S_2 (*she saw a ghost*) functions structurally as part of the matrix clause S_1 (*Sally said——*). The embedded clause fills the same slot in the matrix clause as the word *it* fills in *Sally said it*.

We saw earlier that coordinate sentences are made up of coordinate clauses. Figure 5-5 illustrates that a subordinate clause can be embedded within a coordinate sentence. The tree diagram in Figure 5-5 represents the fact that S_2 and S_3 are coordinate clauses of S_1, and that S_4 is embedded in the matrix clause S_2.

In the remainder of this chapter, we focus principally on clauses that are embedded in other clauses and make only incidental reference to sentences containing coordinate clauses.

Figure 5-3

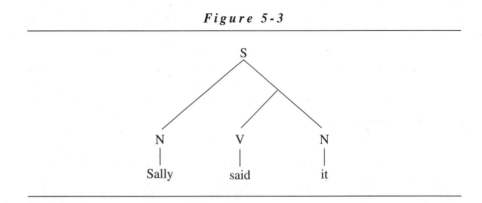

Figure 5-4

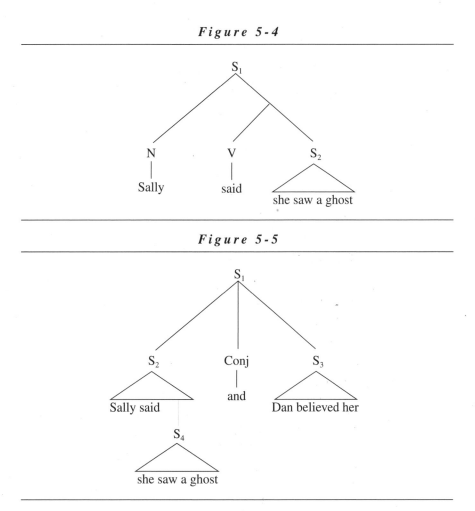

Figure 5-5

CONSTITUENCY

Linguists treat sentences as consisting, first, of their largest grammatical units. These units in turn can be broken into smaller units, which in turn can be analyzed further. From this point of view, the constituents of a coordinate sentence are its coordinate clauses and the conjunction joining them, as in this example:

$$\text{Sarah bought Sam a new coat} \quad \text{but} \quad \text{he doesn't wear it often.}$$
$$\text{clause 1 (S}_1\text{)} \qquad \text{conj} \qquad \text{clause 2 (S}_2\text{)}$$

This structure can be represented schematically as in Figure 5-6.

Figure 5-6

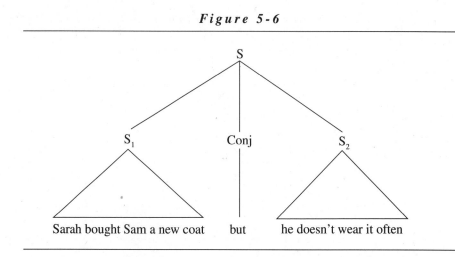

The immediate constituents of a complex sentence are its clauses, as in the next example:

That Jack feared mice   upset his wife.
clause 2 (S_2)   clause 1 (S_1)

This structure can be represented as in Figure 5-7.

Linear Order of Constituents   It is obvious that the words of a sentence must occur in some order, and it follows that constituents also have their elements in some

Figure 5-7

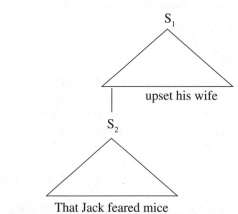

order. Sentences are thus expressed with an *ordered* sequence of words. Sentences such as those that follow, as well as all other clauses and sentences in every language, necessarily express words in a sequential order.

> An old plumber from Pasadena sat in the park.
> Jill touched the harpie.
> Helen claims to be from Xanadu.

Now we ask whether the order in which words are arranged is fixed or not. If it is fixed, is it equally fixed across different languages? We begin by examining the following sentences:

> The farmer saw the ghost.
> The ghost saw the farmer.

Both are well-formed sentences of English, and both contain exactly the same words. Clearly, however, they do not mean the same thing. Since the words are the same, the only thing that could signal the difference in meaning must be the word order. The word order signals *who* saw *whom.* Now consider the following:

> The farmer saw the ghost.
> *Farmer the ghost the saw.

The first string is well formed; the second is not. This demonstrates that word order is an essential part of English sentence structure. If we rearrange the words in an English sentence, we sometimes get other well-formed sentences with a different meaning, but we can also produce sentences that are ill formed (or "ungrammatical"). Sometimes a change of word order can produce a different well-formed sentence with the same meaning, as here:

> Yesterday I heard a poltergeist in the attic.
> I heard a poltergeist in the attic yesterday.

Thus word order is not absolutely fixed. But rearranging the order of words can sometimes change meaning and sometimes produce an ill-formed sentence, so the order of words in an English sentence is significant.

Not all languages exploit word order to the same extent that English does. As you saw in Chapter 2, Latin could express 'The farmer saw the ghost' by using any of the following word orders:

> Agricola   vīdit   umbram.
> farmer   saw   ghost   } 'The farmer saw the ghost.'
> Agricola umbram vīdit.
> Umbram agricola vīdit.

Who did what to *whom* is indicated in Latin not by word order, as it is in English, but by inflectional suffixes. The same is true of Russian, German, and many other languages. Thus, with constant inflections on the nouns, all the following Latin sentences have the same meaning:

Umbra	vīdit	agricolam.
ghost	saw	farmer
Umbra agricolam vīdit.		
Agricolam umbra vīdit.		

'The ghost saw the farmer.'

There are three other possible orders for arranging these three words in sequence, and all would indicate the same meaning. (Though all of them are well formed, not all are equally likely to occur in Latin speech.) Word order is a potential marker of meaning in all the world's languages, but not all languages exploit this potentiality, and very many languages do not exploit it to the same extent that English does.

Hierarchical Order of Constituents   Does a sentence have structure besides the linear order of its words? To answer this question, consider the phrase *gullible boys and girls*. It can mean either 'gullible boys and gullible girls' or 'gullible boys and (all) girls.' This ambiguity of interpretation reflects the fact that the phrase *gullible boys and girls* has two possible internal organizations for the same linear sequence of words. These internal organizations differ as to whether the adjective *gullible* modifies *boys and girls* or just *boys*. We call the internal organization of a linear string of words its constituent structure. **Constituent structure** refers to the grouping of words (and morphemes) into grammatical units. We represent constituent structure using tree diagrams. Figures 5-8 and 5-9 illustrate ways of representing the phrase *gullible boys and girls*. In the tree diagrams notice that at the highest level there are two constituents in Figure 5-8 but three in Figure 5-9. In other words, branching from the top mode there are two lines in Figure 5-8 but three in Figure 5-9.

From these trees you can see that a given string of words with a specified linear order can have more than one constituent structure. Both of these tree diagrams represent the same four words in the same linear order. But the constituent structures

Figure 5-8

gullible boys and girls

'gullible boys and gullible girls'

Figure 5-9

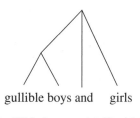

gullible boys and   girls

'gullible boys and (all) girls'

differ. In Figure 5-8, *gullible boys and girls* has two constituents: *gullible* and *boys and girls*. In Figure 5-9, there are three constituents: *gullible boys* and *and* and *girls*. The difference in meaning between these two identical sequences of words arises because they have different constituent structures.

Structural Ambiguity   Structural ambiguity of the sort we have just examined is not limited to phrases. It can occur in sentences as well. Consider sentence 1:

> 1. He sold the car to his brother in New York.

This string of words is ambiguous. That is, it has more than one possible interpretation. Sometimes ambiguity results from the fact that a word has two meanings, as in *He ate near the bank* (in which *bank* can be a financial institution or the edge of a river). In 1 the ambiguity arises not from the individual words (which are all unambiguous) but from the fact that the string of words has two possible constituent structures. We can bracket 1 in different ways to indicate the different constituent structures:

> 2. He sold the car [to [his brother in New York]].
> 3. He sold the car [to his brother] [in New York].

Sentence 2 can be paraphrased as 4 but not as 5 or 6; sentence 3 can be paraphrased as 5 or 6 but not as 4:

> 4. It was to his brother in New York that he sold the car.
> 5. It was in New York that he sold the car to his brother.
> 6. In New York he sold the car to his brother.

These examples illustrate that the words of a sentence are organized into units or *constituents* and that constituency is not available to inspection—it cannot be identified from the string of words itself. The linear order of words in a written English sentence—which word is first, which second, and so on—is available to inspection. (It is obvious and you don't even need to know English to identify which word comes first, which second, and so on.) But only a speaker of English can recognize constituent structure in English sentences and know that a given string of words may have more than one possible constituent structure.

MAJOR SENTENCE CONSTITUENTS

The words in a sentence have an obvious linear order and a constituent structure that is not obvious but is nevertheless understood by native speakers. The linear order of speech is automatically represented when we say or write a sentence. Consider the sentences in Figure 5-10, which have two constituents each. Even more elaborate sentences can be analyzed similarly.

NOUN PHRASE AND VERB PHRASE

In general, simple sentences (and therefore clauses) consist of two principal constituents. In the examples in Figure 5-11, the constituent on the left is called NP (for Noun Phrase), and the one on the right is called VP (for Verb Phrase). Each NP contains a noun (or pronoun) and each VP contains a verb. You can identify NPs and VPs sometimes by the slots they fill in a sentence and sometimes from their functions. Thus *Lou* and *The guy with the earring* function alike—as referring expressions about which the predication in the sentence is made. Similarly, *fell* and *spilled the potion* function alike, they make predications made about an NP.

NPs can also be identified by substitution procedures such as those implied in the list of alternatives to the basic two-part structure in Figure 5-11. Thus, for *Lou* we could substitute forms varying from *Alex* to *The guy with the earring*. Both *Alex* and the longer phrase are NPs because they can occur in the slot ___ *won a bicycle*.

Other slots in a sentence can also be filled by NP. In sentence 3 below, the VP is *spilled the potion*. Unlike the VP of 1, which consists of the single word *fell*, the VP of 3 contains two parts: the verb *spilled* and the NP *the potion*. Thus a VP can contain an NP.

Figure 5-10

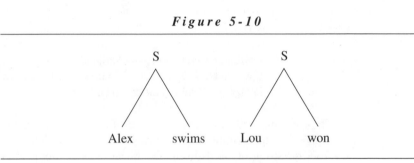

Figure 5-11

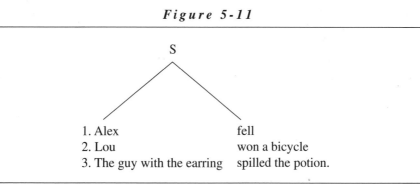

	NP	**VP**
1.	[Alex]	[fell].
2.	[The dog]	[is barking].
3.	[Bob]	[spilled *the potion*].
4.	[The guy with the earring]	[won *the bike* in *a contest*].
5.	[The witch]	[said *Bob* spilled *the potion*].

The potion, *the bike*, *a contest*, and *Bob* are NPs. In fact, anything you could insert in the slots below would be an NP:

> She enjoyed talking about ___ incessantly.
> Invariably, ___ upset her.

The following words and phrases could be inserted in either slot and are therefore NPs; we have underlined the <u>head noun</u> (or simply *head*) in each.

<u>you</u>	his <u>return</u> to his first wife
<u>animals</u>	the <u>fact</u> that her family is so poor
the <u>weather</u>	Peter's <u>winning</u> the race
her aged <u>instructor</u>	the <u>guy</u> with the earring
the <u>thief</u> who stole her purse	the little old <u>plumber</u> from Pasadena

Notice that instead of containing a noun, NP can be a pronoun. Pronouns are NPs in that they have the same distribution in clauses; they occur where NPs can occur.

Verb Phrases (VP) can be identified using similar substitution procedures. Consider the frame *Lou* ____. The following strings fit this frame and are thus VPs (the head verb in each VP is underlined):

> <u>fell</u>
> <u>won</u> the race
> <u>claimed</u> he won a prize

<u>claimed</u> he won a prize for his efforts in the tournament

<u>admitted</u> that he would not enter the contest in any case

To this point, we have seen two major constituents in a sentence: NP and VP. What is true of simple sentences applies equally to clauses embedded within other clauses: clauses have two principal constituents—NP and VP.

RELATING ACTIVE AND PASSIVE SENTENCES

An NP functions as a unified constituent in a sentence, regardless of how big or small it is. Even elaborate NPs like *the guy with the earring* and *what she wanted to receive for her twenty-fifth birthday* function structurally as units, exactly like simple NPs such as *lions*, *she*, and *Bob*. In this section we investigate passive sentences to illustrate the unity of NP constituents.

Consider these active/passive sentence pairs:

1. Zelda auctioned the famous wooden spoon. (Active)
2. The famous wooden spoon was auctioned by Zelda. (Passive)

3. The judge fined an old plumber from Pasadena. (Active)
4. An old plumber from Pasadena was fined by the judge. (Fassive)

5. The mail truck crushed the bike I gave Karen. (Active)
6. The bike I gave Karen was crushed by the mail truck. (Passive)

Even schoolchildren who have never heard of active and passive sentences can usually provide the passive version of an active sentence when given a few model pairs. They implicitly know how a passive sentence is related to an active one. Let's attempt to make explicit what that knowledge must be.

On the basis of sentences 1 and 2 above, one might hypothesize this operation: "To make a passive sentence from an active one, interchange the first word (*Zelda*) with the last four (*the famous wooden spoon*)." (For our present purposes, we can ignore the verb *was* and the preposition *by*, but in a complete statement of the operation all aspects of passivization would also have to be specified.) Our tentative hypothesis produces a well-formed string when applied to sentence 1. But if it is applied to 3 it produces the ill-formed 7, and if it is applied to 5 it produces the ill-formed 8:

3. The judge fined an old plumber from Pasadena.
7. *Old plumber from Pasadena judge was fined an by the.

5. The mail truck crushed the bike I gave Karen.
8. *Bike I gave Karen mail truck was crushed the by the.

Check for yourself to see that 7 and 8 would indeed result from interchanging the first word and the last four words of sentences 3 and 5 (and introducing *by* and the appropriate form of *be*). Clearly, what speakers of English know about the relationship between active and passive sentences depends *not* on counting words. Instead, it depends on knowledge of constituent structure. The operation that relates active and passive sentences is *structure dependent.*

Refer again to the constituents that are interchanged in the active/passive sentences 1 through 6. The strings of words in each of the following sets share a structural property in that they function similarly:

1. Zelda/The judge/The mail truck
2. the famous wooden spoon/an old plumber from Pasadena/the bike I gave Karen

Each NP in sets 1 and 2 contains at least one noun, a head, which is underlined. The NPs share an ability to function alike in sentences and in particular to be moved *as units* in the syntactic operation of passivization. In relating active and passive sentences, NPs function as syntactic units—as constituents—no matter how long they are.

PHRASE-STRUCTURE RULES
⌐

EXPANDING NOUN PHRASE

We can now characterize and exemplify certain types of NP:

Noun (N): *Karen, oracles, justice, swimming*
Determiner (Det) + N: *that amulet, a potion, some gnomes, my saucer*
Det + Adjective (Adj) + N: *an ancient oracle, these hellish precincts, the first omen, my flying saucer*
Det + Adj + N + Prepositional Phrase (PP): *the coldest weather of the year, the youngest woman on the moon, that loud clap of thunder*

One way of representing these various NP patterns is by the use of **phrase-structure rules** (or phrase-structure expansions) like the following:

1. NP	→	**N**	(NP consists of N)
2. NP	→	Det **N**	(NP consists of Det + N)
3. NP	→	Det Adj **N**	(NP consists of Det + Adj + N)
4. NP	→	Det Adj **N** PP	(NP consists of Det + Adj + N + PP)

These four expansions can be combined into one rule. To do that we place parentheses around optional elements (elements that need *not* be present). Notice that the *only* constituent required in all NP expansions is N; the other constituents—Det, Adj, and PP—are optional and are therefore placed in parentheses. The combined rule looks like this:

5. NP → (Det) (Adj) **N** (PP)

Rule 5 can be expanded into the four separate rules (1–4) that we intended to capture, but it also has several expansions that we did not anticipate. Because Det, Adj, and PP are optional, we can expand NP not only as in 1, 2, 3, and 4 but also in other ways, including 6 and 7:

6. NP → Adj **N**
7. NP → Det **N** PP

Rule 5 thus permits expansions that we did not intend to capture. If it happens that English has well-formed NP structures consisting of Adj N, as in 6, and of Det N PP, as in 7, as well as any other expansions 5 would permit, then rule 5 is valid. Otherwise, we would have to revise it to exclude any structures that are not well formed.

Well, of course, English does permit NPs that consist of Adj N, as in *extraterrestrial life* and *great books*, and it also permits NPs consisting of Det N PP, as in *those dishes on the table*, *the whale on the beach*, and *a cloud in the sky*. (One advantage of formalisms such as the combined rule 5 is that they sometimes entail unanticipated claims that can be checked against other data—and they thus provide a test of their own validity.)

EXPANDING PREPOSITIONAL PHRASE

The notation PP stands for prepositional phrase, of which previous examples include *in the car*, *from Xanadu*, *in New York*, *to his brother*, *with the earring*, and *by the judge*. Every PP consists of a preposition (Prep) and a noun phrase (NP), and the phrase-structure rule for PP is this:

PP → **Prep** NP

EXPANDING SENTENCE AND VERB PHRASE

To capture the fact that sentences and clauses have two basic constituent parts, we can formulate the following phrase-structure rule:

S → NP VP

Every phrase-structure rule can represent a tree diagram, and this one would represent the following tree:

Having already seen various expansions of NP, we turn now to the internal structure of VP. We explore its expansions and the phrase-structure rules necessary to represent them. The following expansions of our frame for identifying VPs reveal that the structures on the right (those following *Lou*) are VPs; the labels under constituents of the VP indicate their categories.

$$\_VP\_$$
1. Lou   won
              V

$$\_\_\_\_VP\_\_\_\_$$
2. Lou   won <u>a bicycle</u>
              V   NP

$$_____VP_____$$
3. Lou   won <u>the bike</u> <u>in May</u>
              V   NP   PP

Sentences 1, 2, and 3 indicate three ways to expand VP:

$$
\begin{array}{c}
\mathbf{V} \\
VP \;\rightarrow\; \mathbf{V}\ NP \\
\mathbf{V}\ NP\ PP
\end{array}
$$

V is the only constituent that occurs in all three expansions. NP and PP are both optional. Using parentheses to enclose optional elements, these three expansions can be combined into a single rule, which represents that VP must have V and may have NP or PP or both:

$$VP \;\rightarrow\; \mathbf{V}\ (NP)\ (PP)$$

Just as we discovered options that we had not anticipated when we combined four expansions of NP into one, so the combined expansion for VP permits the structure V PP, which is not represented among sentences 1, 2, and 3 (which formed the basis of the constituent structure rules for VP). Again we can check the validity of the expansion. V PP is a needed expansion for VP in order to represent sentences such as (*Jane*) *swims at noon*, (*Alex*) *raced around the track*, and (*Pat*) *flew to Balnibarbi*.

$$_____VP_____$$
Pat   flew <u>to Balnibarbi</u>
              V   PP

PHRASE STRUCTURE AND TREE DIAGRAMS

We have formulated four phrase-structure rules:

$$
\begin{array}{lcl}
S &\rightarrow& NP\ VP \\
NP &\rightarrow& (Det)\ (Adj)\ \mathbf{N}\ (PP)
\end{array}
$$

$$VP \rightarrow \mathbf{V} \, (NP) \, (PP)$$
$$PP \rightarrow \mathbf{Prep} \, NP$$

These represent the fact that sentences have an NP and a VP; that NP has an N; that VP has a V; and that PP has a Prep. According to these rules, other possibilities are optional.

The following tree diagram can be generated by our rules:

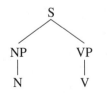

It would represent sentences like *Lou fished, He fell, Jane swims.* Now consider another structure generated by our rules. In the example shown in Figure 5-12, we have supplied one sample sentence for the structure. Thus, our four phrase-structure expansions can represent sentences that are simple in structure or more elaborate.

Figure 5-12

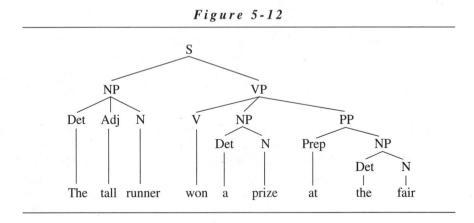

REFINING PHRASE-STRUCTURE RULES

Now we examine certain other sentences to see whether they can be represented by our four phrase-structure rules above. Consider this one:

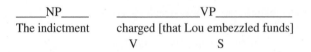

Because our expansion for VP does not permit V S, this sentence cannot be generated by our rules. But *The indictment charged that Lou embezzled funds* is a grammatical sentence of English, and its structure suggests the following as a necessary expansion of VP:

$$VP \quad \rightarrow \quad V\ S$$

Other English sentences indicate that VP can also consist of V NP PP S, as here:

```
_NP_    _____VP_____
Julia    warned [the cook] [on Monday] [that he must wash the celery]
          V       NP         PP                 S
```

To represent all these examples, a more adequate phrase-structure rule for VP would be this:

$$VP \quad \rightarrow \quad V\ (NP)\ (PP)\ (S)$$

This rule can be expanded into all the following, with examples given in parentheses:

	V	(won)
	V NP	(won the race)
	V NP S	(denied the fact [that he lied])
	V NP PP S	(told the cook on Monday [that he must wash the celery])
VP →		
	V S	(charged [that Lou embezzled funds])
	V PP	(flew to Balnibarbi)
	V NP PP	(won the bike in a contest)
	V PP S	(denied in court [that Pat flew to Balnibarbi])

(In addition, PP can be repeated, a fact that we do not account for here.)

We have now arrived at the following phrase-structure rules for English:

$$
\begin{array}{rcl}
S & \rightarrow & NP\ VP \\
NP & \rightarrow & (Det)\ (Adj)\ N\ (PP) \\
VP & \rightarrow & V\ (NP)\ (PP)\ (S) \\
PP & \rightarrow & Prep\ (NP)
\end{array}
$$

We begin with an initial symbol S. S is expanded into NP VP. In turn, both NP and VP can be expanded. NP can be expanded as Det N, for example. Some symbols (NP, VP, and PP) can be expanded as a sequence of symbols. Others (N or Prep, for example) cannot be expanded further. Finally one arrives at a string in which no symbol can be expanded except by attaching individual words.

SUBJECT, DIRECT OBJECT, AND OTHER
GRAMMATICAL RELATIONS

Earlier in this chapter in the course of discussing English clauses and sentences, we used the terms *subject* and *direct object*. Until now we've used these terms only incidentally, relying on your past acquaintance with them. Using phrase-structure expansion, it is now possible to define the terms subject and direct object precisely. In defining them, two expansions are important:

$$S \quad \rightarrow \quad NP\ VP$$
$$VP \quad \rightarrow \quad V\ (NP)\ (PP)\ (S)$$

IMMEDIATE DOMINANCE

We can represent the relevant parts of these expansions in a tree diagram. Looking at Figure 5-13, you see that the circled NP is immediately under the S node, that the boxed NP is immediately under the VP node, and that the VP node is immediately under the S node. When a node A is immediately under a node B, we say that node A is *immediately dominated* by node B. Thus in Figure 5-13, V is immediately dominated by VP; the circled NP is immediately dominated by S; the boxed NP is immediately dominated by VP; and both VP and the circled NP are immediately dominated by S.

SUBJECT AND DIRECT OBJECT

We can now define subject and direct object in terms of phrase-structures and tree diagrams. In English, **subject** is defined as the NP that is immediately dominated by S. In Figure 5-13, the circled NP is the subject of S. **Direct object** is defined as an NP that is immediately dominated by VP. In Figure 5-13 it is the boxed NP. Since NP is an optional element in the expansion of VP, it follows that not every sentence will have an NP immediately dominated by VP. In other words, not every sentence will have a direct object.

Figure 5-13

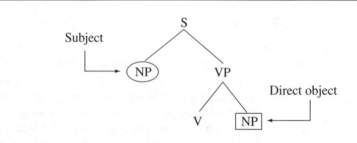

Transitive and Intransitive   A sentence that lacks a direct object has an *intransitive* verb, as we saw in Chapter 2. Examples would include *die*, *cough*, and *laugh*, as in *She died*, *He coughed*, and *They all laughed.* Verbs that take a direct object are called *transitive* verbs. Typical examples are *make*, *buy*, and *find*, as in *make a potion*, *buy a pencil*, and *find a penny.*

Some verbs can be either transitive or intransitive, as shown in these sentences:

INTRANSITIVE	TRANSITIVE
Casper won.	Casper won a prize.
Ed sings.	Ed sings lullabies.
Sue studied at Oxford.	Sue studied physics at Oxford.

GRAMMATICAL RELATIONS

Certain structural properties of subjects and direct objects cannot be equated with anything else, including meaning. Subject and direct object are categories known as grammatical relations. **Grammatical relation** is the term used to capture the syntactic relationship that exists in a clause between an NP and the predicate. In other words, grammatical relations indicate the syntactic role that an NP plays in its clause. Besides **subject** and **direct object**, sentences can have other grammatical relations, such as **indirect object**, **oblique**, and **possessor.** English has the grammatical relations *oblique* for NPs that are the object of a preposition (*The ghost spoke about **a toothache***) and *possessor* (***Joan's** car*). There is disagreement about the status of the indirect object as a grammatical relation in English.

PASSIVE SENTENCES AND STRUCTURE DEPENDENCE

Having defined subject and direct object in structural terms, we can now return to a syntactic relationship we examined earlier. The notions of subject and direct object allow us to reformulate the relationship between active and passive sentences as follows: "To convert an active sentence to a passive one, interchange the subject NP and the direct object NP." (As before, provision must be made for the preposition *by* and a form of the verb *be.*) The following will serve as an example:

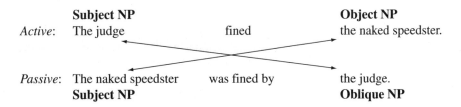

	Subject NP		**Object NP**
Active:	The judge	fined	the naked speedster.

Passive:	The naked speedster	was fined by	the judge.
	Subject NP		**Oblique NP**

From these sentences, you can see that in a passive sentence the direct object of the active sentence appears as subject (that is, it is the NP node dominated by S), and the subject of the active sentence appears as an oblique (preceded by the preposition *by*). This analysis again underscores the fact that syntactic operations like passivization are structure dependent.

SURFACE STRUCTURES AND DEEP STRUCTURES

We have seen that speakers understand more about the structure of a sentence than is apparent in the linear sequence of its words. For one thing, they have implicit knowledge of constituent structure. For another, they often understand more constituents in a sentence than are actually expressed. For example, knowledge of English syntactic operations is essential to understand the meaning of sentences such as the following:

Mary won a prize but Alex . . .

1. didn't.
2. didn't care.
3. didn't tell Sarah.
4. didn't celebrate with her.
5. didn't visit Paris to buy a tie.
6. didn't train tigers.
7. didn't win a prize.

Although the list of possible sentences following this pattern is endless, the only legitimate interpretation of 1 is sentence 7. Sentences 2 through 6 are well formed, but they are not possible interpretations of 1. You understand sentence 1 as having the implicit completion "win a prize."

To explain this fact about your understanding of unexpressed constituents, recall that in Chapter 4 we postulated underlying forms of sounds in our discussion of phonology and underlying forms of morphemes in our discussion of words. Well, we can accommodate implicit knowledge of sentence structure by positing underlying syntactic structures. For instance, we can represent the meaning of sentence 1 by positing an underlying structure something like *Mary won a prize but Alex didn't win a prize*. If we assumed such an underlying form, syntactic operations would have to delete the second occurrence of *win a prize* and generate the sentence *Mary won a prize but Alex didn't*. (We call such syntactic operations *transformations*, and we will discuss them shortly.)

EQUI-NP DELETION

With the aim of identifying an element in 2 that is understood as part of its meaning but is not expressed, consider the following sentences:

1. Fred wanted Sarah to win.
2. Fred wanted to win.

Given the ordinary interpretation of sentence 2, it would be reasonable to hypothesize that it has an underlying structure that parallels the structure of 1, something like this:

3. Fred wanted Fred to win.

We could represent this sentence by the figure below, in which the subscript $_j$ is an index indicating that *Fred* refers to the same person in both instances.

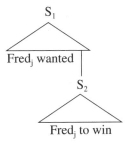

If this structure is taken as a rough approximation of the underlying structure of *Fred wanted to win*, then a syntactic process must be postulated that deletes *Fred* from the embedded clause S_2. Known as equi-NP deletion, this operation deletes the subject NP of an embedded clause when that NP is the same as the subject NP of the matrix clause and has the same index. If such a process were not postulated, then *Fred* would not be deleted from the underlying structure and the ill-formed string **Fred$_j$ wanted Fred$_j$ to win* would result. From these and other examples, we can conclude that the underlying structure of a sentence differs from its surface structure in systematic ways. From the underlying structure, the syntactic operations of a language generate surface structures.

To capture the facts just examined in sentences like *Fred wanted to win*, we postulate two levels of sentence structure. One level is represented by the linear string of words as uttered or written. It is called the **surface structure.** Surface structure encompasses both the linear order of the constituents (which is obvious from inspection) and their hierarchical order (which is not expressed explicitly but is understood). The other level of structure is an abstract level underlying the surface structure. It is called the **deep structure** or **underlying structure.**

From an underlying structure, a surface structure is generated by a series of syntactic operations. These operations change an underlying constituent structure into a surface constituent structure. We represent the situation schematically as follows:

In a widely adopted model of this type, phrase-structure rules generate deep structures. Then syntactic operations known as *transformations* systematically alter the deep structure to produce a surface structure. In turn, the phonological rules of the language (which we examined in Chapter 4) operate on the surface structure to produce a pronounceable utterance. The schema looks like this:

PHRASE-STRUCTURE RULES
|
Deep Structure
|
TRANSFORMATIONS
|
Surface Structure
|
PHONOLOGICAL RULES
|
Pronounceable Sentence

TRANSFORMATIONS

We have already seen several transformational operations of English, including passivization and equi-NP deletion. Now we analyze several other transformations.

SUBJECT-AUXILIARY INVERSION AND WH-MOVEMENT

In this section we explore two operations involved in forming questions. We'll also note certain implications of these operations for the underlying structure of all English sentences.

Two principal kinds of questions exist in English: yes/no questions and information questions.

Yes/No Questions   In the pairs of statements and questions below, the questions are called "yes/no questions" because they can be answered with a reply of *yes* or *no*.

1. Sue will earn a fair wage.
   Will Sue earn a fair wage?

2. John was winning the race when he stumbled.
   Was John winning the race when he stumbled?

If you compare the *form* of the statement with the *form* of the question above, you will see that a yes/no question requires inverting the subject NP with the auxiliary verb. (Verbs such as *will* in 1 above and *was* in 2—as well as *did* and *does* in 3 and 4 below—are called auxiliary verbs, as distinguished from main verbs like *earn* and *winning*. **Auxiliary verbs** are precisely those that can be inverted with the subject NP to form questions; they are also the constituent of the verb phrase that carries the negative element in contractions such as ***can't, shouldn't,*** and ***wasn't.***) In fact, a yes/no question has an auxiliary verb even when the corresponding statement does not, as 3 and 4 show:

> 3. Alvin *studied* alchemy in college.
>   *Did* Alvin *study* alchemy in college?

> 4. Inflation always *hurts* the poor.
>   *Does* inflation always *hurt* the poor?

Sentence pairs like 3 and 4 provide an argument for positing an auxiliary verb in the underlying structure of every sentence, even though not every sentence expresses an auxiliary in the surface structure. Notice, however, that in English an auxiliary verb must appear in the surface structure of negative sentences (*Alvin **didn't** study alchemy*) and questions (***Does** inflation hurt?*) and typically appears to express emphasis (*But she **does** exercise every day!*) and certain other semantic information such as time reference (*She **will** win*) and aspect (*They **are** walking home*). (Aspect and temporal deixis are discussed in Chapter 6).

Given that an auxiliary verb often appears in the surface structure (and for additional reasons that we do not discuss here), an auxiliary constituent is postulated in the underlying structure of sentences. Like all constituents in the underlying structure, the auxiliary can be generated by a phrase-structure rule. Instead of the earlier expansion of S as NP VP, the following expansion is assumed:

$$ S \rightarrow NP\ AUX\ VP $$

We can represent the structure of this expansion in a tree diagram:

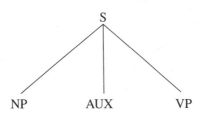

The operation that transforms the constituent structure of the statements in 1, 2, 3, and 4 above to the constituent structure of the yes/no questions does so by inverting NP and AUX. Thus, subject-auxiliary inversion does this:

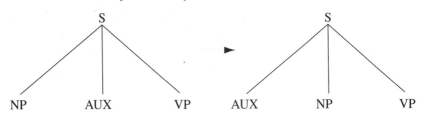

Figure 5-14

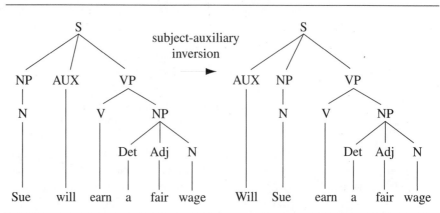

We represent the underlying form of the sentences of 1 on page 164 as in the tree on the left in Figure 5-14. The tree on the right is the constituent structure that results from application of subject-auxiliary inversion.

The transformation could be represented as follows:

$$NP\ AUX\ VP \quad \rightarrow \quad AUX\ NP\ VP$$

Notice once more that the syntactic operation relies not on knowledge of words but on knowledge of structures. Subject-auxiliary inversion is a structure–dependent operation.

Information Questions   Information questions require more than a simple yes-or-no reply. In an information question, the information that is sought—the questioned constituent—is represented by a WH-word (*who, why, when, where, which, what,* or *how*). Because information questions contain a WH-word, they are sometimes called WH-questions. (*Note*: In the example sentences in the remainder of this chapter, we use what seem to be the most common forms of *who* and *whom* in the context of a particular sentence; in so doing, we sometimes ignore the distinction drawn between these forms in traditional grammar and in much careful writing and speaking.)

Information questions occur in two forms. One is called an *echo question* because it "echoes" the form of a statement, as in these examples:

(He's boiling horsefeathers.)	He's boiling *what?*
(She was looking for Sigmund Freud today.)	She was looking for *who* today?

Echo questions are used when you have failed to hear something completely or cannot believe what you have heard. The linear form of an echo question is identical to that of the statement, except that in the echo question a WH-word occurs in place of the questioned constituent.

More common than echo questions are information questions that take the form illustrated below in which an operation called WH–movements has fronted the WH–word.

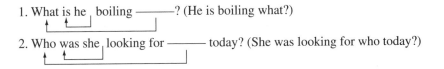

1. What is he ˌ boiling ———? (He is boiling what?)
2. Who was she ˌ looking for ——— today? (She was looking for who today?)

If you compare these ordinary information questions with the parenthesized echo questions, you can see that two changes have occurred:

- The WH-word appears at the front of its clause.
- The auxiliary verb appears in the position preceding the subject NP.

Notice that ordinary information questions leave a "gap" in the structure at the place vacated by the fronted WH-word (indicated here by a dash ———). By contrast, echo questions do not have a gap because the WH-word stays in its underlying position.

RELATIVE CLAUSE FORMATION

A **relative clause** is formed when one clause is embedded into an NP of another clause to produce structures like these, in which the relative clauses are underlined:

1. The board dismissed [the teacher <u>who flunked me</u>].
2. [The jewels <u>that he bought</u>] were fakes.
3. This is [the officer <u>that I talked to last night</u>].
4. Sally saw a new film by [the Taiwanese director <u>that Tom raves about</u>].
5. Sally saw a new film by [the Taiwanese director <u>Tom raves about</u>].

When clauses share a pair of NPs that have the same referent, a relative clause is formed by embedding one clause into the other, as in this illustration, in which identical indexes indicate coreferential NPs:

I sent your book to my aunt$_j$ my aunt$_j$ lives in Dublin

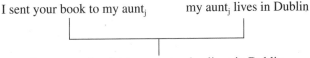

I sent your book to my aunt$_j$ who$_j$ lives in Dublin

English relative clauses contain (and are usually introduced by) a relative pronoun such as *who* (or *whom* or *whose*), *which*, or *that*. As in 5 above, the pronoun can be omitted from certain structures. Relative clauses modify nouns, and the noun that the relative clause modifies is called the *head noun*. In English, the head noun is

Figure 5-15

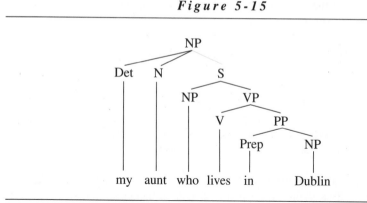

"repeated" in the embedded clause, where it is *relativized* (which means it takes the form of a relative pronoun). A relative clause is part of the same noun phrase as its head noun. The structure of the resulting noun phrase can be represented as in Figure 5-15 in which the head noun *aunt* is labeled N. Notice that in this instance the relativized NP *who* functions as the subject of its clause (the NP that is immediately dominated by S). In other clauses, the relativized NP may be another grammatical relation like direct object, as in this illustration:

The jewels *that he bought* were fakes.

Here the relative clause *that he bought* derives from the underlying clause *he bought the jewels.*

A relativized NP can also be an oblique as in 1 or a possessor as in 2:

1. This is the officer *whom I told you about.* (Compare *I told you about the officer.*)
2. This is the officer *whose car was vandalized.* (Compare *The officer's car was vandalized.*)

Thus in English a relativized NP can have these grammatical relations within its clause: subject, direct object, oblique, or possessor.

COMP Node Now let's analyze the syntactic operations associated with relative clause formation. Examine the following sentences, noting the gap in the structure (indicated by the dash ⸺):

1. There's the teacher that I warned you about ⸺ .

2. David Lodge wrote the novels that I recommend ⸺ .

3. The fans who ⸺ braved the weather paid a price.

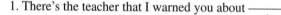

Figure 5-16

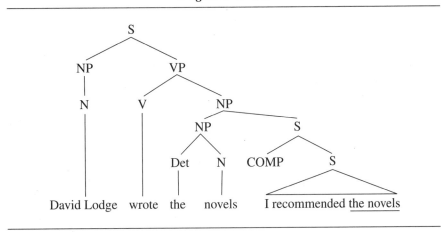

We can represent the underlying constituent structure of these sentences in a tree diagram, as Figure 5-16 illustrates for sentence 2.

In order to produce the relative clause structure of 2, the NP *the novels* (the underlined instance in Figure 5-16) is relativized (i.e., pronominalized) and moved to the front of its clause by WH-movement, which we described for information questions. In Figure 5-16 there is a node labeled COMP (for 'complementizer'), which we have not previously identified. It is possible to discuss WH-movement for relative clauses without utilizing the COMP node (as we did for information questions), but there is evidence for such a node. It serves as a "magnet" for WH-constituents, such as *that* and *who* (illustrated in sentences 1–3 above), and other relative pronouns, as well as the WH-constituents of information questions.

Since transformations systematically change one constituent structure into another, we can represent the output of WH-movement as applied to Figure 5-16 by the tree given in Figure 5-17. Thus, by WH-movement a WH-constituent is extracted from S and attached to the COMP node. We have examined WH-movement with respect to relative clauses, but the same operation could move any WH-constituent to the COMP node, including question words in information questions.

TYPES OF TRANSFORMATIONS

While it is not known for certain how many types of syntactic operations exist in human languages, recent theories of syntax reflect evidence that transformations are considerably more general than our detailed specifications of particular transformations might suggest. Movement operations are extremely common in the languages of the world, and in one theoretical model of syntax, all transformations are forms of movement rules.

Figure 5-17

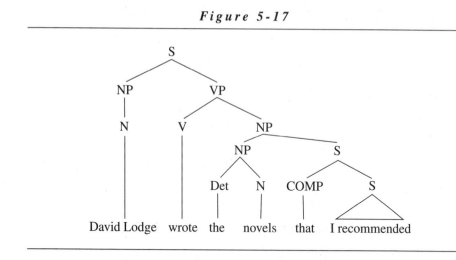

CONSTRAINTS ON TRANSFORMATIONS

One question that challenges grammarians is the extent to which limitations exist on the kinds of transformations that operate in human language. We can illustrate the kinds of constraints that may exist by analyzing movement transformations.

COORDINATE NP CONSTRAINT

In each of the two sets of sentences below, the (a) example is an echo question, the (b) example the corresponding information question, the (c) example an echo question in which the WH-word occurs in a coordinate noun phrase of the type "NP and NP," and the (d) example is the ill-formed structure that results if the WH-word is moved to the front of its clause. Examples 1-d and 2-d demonstrate that WH-movement cannot occur when the WH-word is part of a coordinate NP structure like *Grendel and who.*

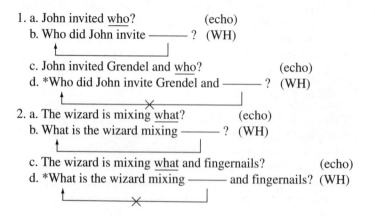

1. a. John invited <u>who</u>?　　　　(echo)
  b. Who did John invite ——— ?　(WH)

  c. John invited Grendel and <u>who</u>?　　　(echo)
  d. *Who did John invite Grendel and ——— ?　(WH)

2. a. The wizard is mixing <u>what</u>?　　　(echo)
  b. What is the wizard mixing ——— ?　(WH)

  c. The wizard is mixing <u>what</u> and fingernails?　　　(echo)
  d. *What is the wizard mixing ——— and fingernails?　(WH)

These sentences illustrate that WH-movement is blocked when the WH-constituent occurs in a coordinate noun phrase. The constraint that blocks the movement is called the *coordinate NP constraint.*

RELATIVE CLAUSE CONSTRAINT

The sentences below demonstrate that WH-words cannot be moved (or "extracted") from relative clauses. The first sentence in each set is an echo question, in which the WH-word is grammatical. But a WH-word extracted from its relative clause by WH-movement would produce an ungrammatical sentence. The relative clauses are bracketed.

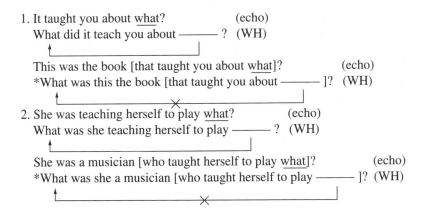

1. It taught you about <u>what</u>?   (echo)
   What did it teach you about ——— ?   (WH)

   This was the book [that taught you about <u>what</u>]?   (echo)
   *What was this the book [that taught you about ———]?   (WH)

2. She was teaching herself to play <u>what</u>?   (echo)
   What was she teaching herself to play ——— ?   (WH)

   She was a musician [who taught herself to play <u>what</u>]?   (echo)
   *What was she a musician [who taught herself to play ———]?   (WH)

Notice that the echo questions are completely grammatical and also make sense. So the difficulty with the ill-formed sentences is not semantic but purely syntactic. We can conclude that WH-movement from relative clauses is blocked. The ill-formed sentences are prohibited by a constraint on a syntactic operation.

CONSTRAINTS AND LANGUAGE LEARNING

An important observation can be made about such constraints. The ungrammatical sentences that would result from violating the constraints do not occur among the utterances of children or second-language learners. In other words, first- and second-language learners show no tendency to overgeneralize movement operations in a way that would violate the constraints. Whereas children and second-language learners do overgeneralize morphological rules (*tooth/tooths*; *go/goed*), they do not violate constraints in the application of movement rules. What could account for this?

Naturally, to the extent that such constraints may be built into the language faculty, perhaps from birth, a child would not need to figure out how particular operations work and what constraints exist. Clearly, the more that such constraints were built into syntactic operations, the easier it would be for a child to acquire its language because there would be less to learn. Otherwise, it would be a daunting task to figure out when WH-extraction is and is not possible. On the other hand, if certain types of extraction are impossible (because the relevant parts of the brain simply can't handle them, let's say), then the conditions blocking those extractions would not have to be learned at all. That would greatly simplify a child's task and help explain why children are so adept at language acquisition—and why they don't overgeneralize movement operations.

COMPUTERS AND THE STUDY OF SYNTAX

You saw in Chapter 2 that computer programs can tag the words in a sentence with their part of speech. Automatic taggers are good at identifying categories for many English words. But even a sentence whose words have been tagged with their part of speech is far from being syntactically analyzed. Programs that analyze strings of categories for their constituent structure are known as *parsers*, and some parsers achieve impressive success in assigning constituent structure. (You can judge for yourself just how good they are: at the end of this chapter you'll find Internet addresses that will parse sentences you submit.)

Tagging a sentence for part of speech does not identify its constituent structure. Just as certain strings of words can have more than one constituent structure, so can a particular string of categories. As we saw earlier (pp. 150–151), the noun phrase *gullible boys and girls* can have either of two constituent structures. It follows that the string of lexical categories for that phrase could likewise have either of two bracketings:

1. [Adj [N Conj N]]
2. [Adj N] [Conj] [N]

Some sophisticated computer programs can analyze tagged sentences and produce a labeled constituent structure or tree diagram. In the case of *gullible boys and girls*, a parser would produce two candidate constituent structures.

Researchers have faced substantial challenges in designing parsers that can analyze a wide range of English sentences. While many English sentences are straightforward and easy to parse, many others are not. Interestingly, made-up sentences are often easier to parse than the sentences that occur in ordinary conversation or the relatively straightforward writing that you can find in a textbook. Let's see how a parser operates.

First, given a sentence like *That rancher saw the wolves*, a tagger would assign part–of–speech tags as follows:

$$that_{Det} \ rancher_N \ saw_V \ the_{Det} \ wolves_N$$

In principle, *saw* could be a noun or a verb, and *that* could also have several possible tags; but even moderately good taggers will have no difficulty determining the correct tags in a sentence like this. Once part-of-speech tags have been assigned, a parser can produce a tree diagram or a constituent-structure bracketing using only a few phrase-structure expansions. You can envision the process as working from the bottom of a tree structure to the top. For example, the phrase-structure expansion NP → Det N will bracket *that rancher* and *the wolves* as NPs: they are both sequences of Det N. That would produce the sequence NP V NP. The phrase-structure rule VP → V NP will identify *saw the wolves* as VP, giving NP VP. That in turn will be recognized as an expansion of S.

Taken together then, the tagged string can be parsed as in 3 below. This labeled bracketing is entirely equivalent to the tree diagram below it.

3. [$_S$ [$_{NP}$ [that$_{Det}$] [rancher$_N$] $_{NP}$] [$_{VP}$saw$_v$ [$_{NP}$ [the $_{Det}$] [wolves $_N$]$_{NP}$]$_{VP}$]$_S$]

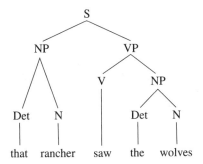

With more complicated strings (as most naturally occurring strings are), assigning the correct constituent structure will be less straightforward.

Grammar checkers in word processors contain relatively simple parsers. On the basis of those parsers, they sometimes suggest changes to your sentence structure in the in-terest of grammatical correctness or stylistic refinement. As you will see in the exercises, grammar checkers often suggest revisions that indicate they have parsed your sentence incorrectly. Even more often, they find actual sentences too long or too complicated to parse, and the most they can do is suggest that the sentence be shortened.

SUMMARY

- All languages have referring expressions and predication expressions.

- In syntactic terms, a referring expression is called NP (noun phrase) and a predication expression VP (verb phrase).

- Sentences consist of one or more clauses.

- A clause consists of a verb with the necessary set of NPs.

- Clauses can be conjoined with one another to form a coordinate sentence, or one clause can be embedded within another clause to form a complex sentence.

- Speakers of every language can generate an unlimited number of sentences from a finite number of operations for combining words and morphemes.

- Syntactic rules are of two types—phrase-structure expansions and transfor-mations.

- Phrase-structure expansions generate underlying constituent structures.

- All syntactic operations are structure dependent.

- Transformations change one constituent structure into another constituent structure.

- Underlying structures are posited to help explain certain elements of meaning and certain syntactic and semantic relationships that speakers understand between sentences.

- The most important and most general syntactic operations are movement transformations, such as WH-movement and subject-auxiliary inversion.

- Constraints limit the ways in which transformations can operate on constituents.

- In limiting the range of possible grammars of human languages, constraints on transformations may facilitate language acquisition in children.

EXERCISES

Based on English

5-1. a. List as many examples of these constituents as you can identify in sentences (1) and (2) below: NP, PP, VP.

   b. List as many examples of these lexical categories as you can identify in sentences (1) and (2) below: N, Prep, V.

    (1) A Guns 'N' Roses concert at an arena near St. Louis ended in disaster after some 2500 fans staged a full-fledged riot.

    (2) The trouble started when Axl Rose asked venue security to confiscate a camera he saw near the front of the stage.

5-2. For each of the expansions of VP given on page 159, provide an illustration.

   Example: V PP: *swims in the pond.*

5-3. a. Draw a labeled tree diagram for each of the phrases given below.

    (1) ancient inscriptions
    (2) in the dark night
    (3) concocted a potion
    (4) borrowed the book that the teacher recommended
    (5) the monstrous members of a terrible kingdom

   b. Provide a tree diagram for each of the sentences given below.

    (1) Witches <u>frighten him.</u>
    (2) The skies deluged the earth <u>with water.</u>
    (3) <u>A ghost has the spirit</u> of a dead person.
    (4) <u>Do ghosts exist in the physical world?</u>
    (5) <u>Does she</u> believe that ghosts exist?
    (6) The teacher <u>that I described to you</u> won the race.

c. For each underlined group of words in the sentences above, determine whether or not it is a constituent; if it is, give the name of the constituent.

5-4. What is the difference in the relationship between *Harry* and the verb *see* in (1) and (2)? Draw tree diagrams of the underlying structure of the two sentences that will reveal the difference in the structures.

(1) John advised Harry to see the doctor.
(2) John promised Harry to see the doctor.

5-5. English has an operation called dative movement that derives sentence (2) from the structure underlying sentence (1):

(1) I sent a letter to Hilda.
(2) I sent Hilda a letter.

The following also exemplify sentences derived by dative movement:

He sold *his brother* a sailboat.
Harold won't tell *me* Hilda's new phone number.
I'm giving *my cousin* a new pair of pajamas.

a. Give the basic sentences corresponding to the three derived sentences.
b. Dative movement applies to prepositional phrases that begin with the preposition *to* and cannot apply to prepositional phrases that begin with most other prepositions:

*I will finish you the homework. (*from* I will finish the homework with you.)
*My neighbor heard the radio the news. (*from* My neighbor heard the news on the radio.)

But dative movement does not apply to all phrases that begin with the preposition *to*. The sentences in (3) cannot undergo dative movement, as witnessed by the ungrammaticality of the corresponding sentences in (4).

(3) He's driving a truck to New Orleans.
    He'll take his complaint to the main office.
(4) *He's driving New Orleans a truck.
    *He'll take the main office his complaint.

Describe dative movement in detail.

c. Now observe the ungrammatical sentences in (5) below, which are derived through dative movement from the sentences underlying the corresponding basic sentences in (6). How must you modify your description of dative movement so that it does not generate the ungrammatical sentences of (5)?

(5) *I gave my new neighbor it.
    *I'm taking my little sister them.

*They will probably send him me.

(6) I gave it to my new neighbor.
I'm taking them to my little sister.
They will probably send me to him.

5-6. Although we have downplayed the distinction between *who* and *whom* in the examples of this chapter, writers who regularly make the distinction in relative clauses do so as follows:

(1) That's the goblin *who* visits me each year.
(2) Where is the author *whom* you were talking about?
(3) That's the wizard from *whom* I bought the potion.
(4) That's the witch *whom* I stole the bread crumbs from.
(5) That's the witch *who* married the wizard.
(6) Which is the demon to *whom* he sold his soul?
(7) That's the ghost of the man *whom* Grendel slew.

After examining these sentences, formulate a statement that will capture the facts about when such writers use *who* and *whom* in relative clauses. (*Hint*: Examine the grammatical relation of the relative pronoun in its clause.)

5-7. English has the grammatical relations of subject, direct object, oblique, and possessor. But it is debatable whether indirect object is a distinct grammatical relation and, if so, whether it occurs in sentences like *The witch offered the child a potion* or *The witch offered a potion to the child.* The syntactic properties of *the child* differ in the two sentences. What syntactic evidence can you offer for arguing that *the child* does not have the same grammatical relation in each sentence? (*Hint*: At least one transformation examined in this chapter does not produce grammatical strings for both sentences.)

5-8. English has two types of relative clauses. Type 1 (described in this chapter) leaves prepositions where they are in the underlying clause.

This is the man [who I talked *to* — last night]. (*Underlying clause*: I talked to the man last night)
In Type 2, the preposition moves with the WH-word to the beginning of the clause.

This is the man [*to* whom I talked last night].

Describe the relative-clause transformation that forms Type 2 relative clauses, focusing on how it differs from the transformation that forms Type 1 relative clauses. Identify which relative pronouns can occur in which type of relative clause, and in which cases the two types differ. Base your discussion on the following data:

This is the man [that left]. (Types 1 and 2)
*This is the man [left]. (Types 1 and 2)

This is the man [that I saw]. (Types 1 and 2)
This is the man [who I saw]. (Types 1 and 2)
This is the man [whom I saw]. (Types 1 and 2)
This is the man [I saw]. (Types 1 and 2)

This is the man [who I gave the book to]. (Type 1)
This is the man [whom I gave the book to]. (Type 1)
This is the man [that I gave the book to]. (Type 1)
This is the man [I gave the book to]. (Type 1)

*This is the man [to who I gave the book]. (Type 2)
This is the man [to whom I gave the book]. (Type 2)
*This is the man [to that I gave the book]. (Type 2)
*This is the man [to I gave the book]. (Type 2)

5-9. On p. 167 we noted that the relative pronoun can be omitted from "certain structures." Thus, in the following sentence, Ø represents an omitted relative pronoun:

Sally saw a new film by the Taiwanese director Ø Tom raves about.

   a. For each of the following sentences, identify the grammatical relation of the relativized NP within its clause, using S for subject, DO for direct object, and Obl for oblique.
      1. I lost the book [that you gave me]. _____
      2. He rented the video [that frightened you]. _____
      3. I bumped into the teacher [who taught me solid geometry]. _____
      4. I met the poet [who(m) we read about last week]. _____
      5. I found the video [that you lost]. _____
      6. I saw the oak tree [that you slept under]. _____
      7. The new teacher [that Lou liked] just quite. _____
      8. The new teacher [who liked jazz] just quit. _____
      9. I picked an apple from the tree [that you planted]. _____
     10. I like those new lyrics [that you complained about]. _____

   b. Which sentences would permit the relative pronoun to be omitted?
   c. Which would not permit the relative pronoun to be omitted?
   d. Which grammatical relations permit the relative pronoun to be omitted?
   e. Which grammatical relations do not permit the relative pronoun to be omitted?
   f. Rewrite sentences 4, 6, and 10, fronting the preposition with the relative pronoun.
   g. Can the relative pronoun be omitted from the rewritten versions of 4, 6, and 10?
   h. What generalization can you make about when a relative pronoun can be omitted from its clause?

5-10. Grammarians distinguish between *restrictive* and *nonrestrictive* relative clauses. Restrictive relative clauses provide essential information about the identity of the head noun, as in (1). Nonrestrictive relative clauses provide incidental information about the head noun, as in (2). In (1), the hearer must have the information the relative clause provides in order to understand which potion the speaker is referring to; in (2), this is not the case.

(1) The potion *that I mixed yesterday* is in the white vessel.
(2) The potion, *which I mixed just yesterday*, should still be fresh.

Compare the following sets of restrictive and nonrestrictive relative clauses, and describe in detail the structural differences between the two types of relative clauses.

The man *who wore the blue shirt* suddenly dashed away.
The man, *who had been standing idly outside*, suddenly dashed away.

The new Bond thriller *that I saw yesterday* was terrible.
The new Bond thriller, *which I saw yesterday*, was terrible.
*The new Bond thriller, *that I saw yesterday*, was terrible.

Only those books *that I hadn't opened in years* were dusty.
Only Granny's books, *which I hadn't opened in years*, were dusty.
The jacket *I wore at the reception* cost me $250.
*The jacket, *I wore at the reception*, cost me $250.

5-11. Keeping in mind the subject-auxiliary inversion operation, analyze what has happened in the derivation of the sentences below to produce the ill-formed sentences (the starred ones). How would you formulate the subject-auxiliary inversion transformation to avoid the ungrammatical examples?

The teacher who will give that lecture is Lily's aunt.
*Will the teacher who give that lecture is Lily's aunt?
Is the teacher who will give that lecture Lily's aunt?

Parisa, which was bought from Greenalls, will convert its pubs to boutiques.
*Was Parisa, which bought from Greenalls, will convert its pubs to boutiques?
Will Parisa, which was bought from Greenalls, convert its pubs to boutiques?

Jesse, who can outsing anyone, can take my place.
*Can Jesse, who outsing anyone, can take my place?
Can Jesse, who can outsing anyone, take my place?

5-12. There are other constraints on extraction besides those that block WH-movement out of coordinate NPs and out of relative clauses. Using examples like the following, construct sentence pairs like those on pages 170–171 that illustrate further constraints on WH–extraction. Then try to characterize the kinds of clauses from which such extractions are blocked (e.g., adverbial clauses, indirect questions, and so on).

Pat would buy one *whenever <u>who</u> visited?*
Pat would ask *why you bought <u>what</u>?*

5-13. Below are six sentences that a grammar checker found objectionable, along with the comment that suggests a particular correction. In each case, the grammar checker has made an incorrect analysis, and the suggested correction would yield an ill-formed sentence. For each example, identify the word or constituent structure that the grammar checker has wrongly analyzed and explain the basis for its suggested correction.

Example: "In this sentence, each embedded clause functions as a grammatical unit in its matrix clause."

Comment: The word *each* does not agree with *functions*. Consider *function* instead of *functions*." Explanation: The grammar checker incorrectly analyzed *functions* as a plural noun (rather than a third-person singular verb) and mistakenly took *each embedded clause functions* to be a noun phrase.

(1) "It is the word order in the sentence that signals who *is* doing what to whom."
   Comment: Consider *are* instead of *is*.

(2) "Do 'George Washington' and 'the first president of the United States' mean the same thing?"
   Comment: Consider *presidents* instead of *president* or consider *means* instead of *mean*.

(3) "When a student volunteers, 'Disneyland is fun,' . . . "
   Comment: The word *a* does not agree with *volunteers*.

(4) "Linguistic semantics is the study of the systematic ways in which languages structure meaning."
   Comment: Consider *language's* or *languages'* instead of *languages*.

(5) "Sentence 2 is true because we know the word *dogs* describes entities that are also described by the word *animals*."
   Comment: Consider *describe* instead of *describes*.

(6) "Harold, who has two doctorates, gave me a fascinating overview of Warhol's art last night."
   Comment: Consider *given* instead of *gave*.

Based on Languages Other Than English

5-14. Examine the tree diagram for this Fijian sentence:

ea-biuta	na ŋone	vakaloloma	na	tamata ðaa e na basi
Past-abandon	the child	poor	the	man bad on the bus

'The bad man abandoned the poor child on the bus.'

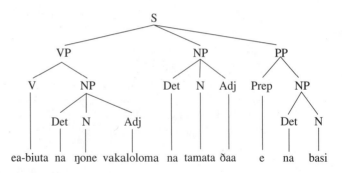

a. Provide the phrase-structure expansions that will generate this constituent-structure tree.

b. Notice that the order of certain constituents in the Fijian sentence differs from that of English. With respect to constituent order, what are the major differences between Fijian and English?

c. On the basis of the tree structure, determine which of the following sequences of words are constituents and give the name of each constituent.

vakaloloma na tamata	e na
e na basi	na ŋone
na tamata ðaa	na ŋone vakaloloma na tamata ðaa
ðaa e na basi	ŋone vakaloloma
ea-biuta	e-biuta na ŋone
ea-biuta na ŋone vakaloloma	na basi

INTERNET RESOURCES

- **LTG Helpdesk: http://www.ltg.ed.ac.uk/helpdesk/faq/index.html**
  Provides answers to frequently asked questions (FAQs) and links to a variety of language technology projects, including parsers. Among the FAQs: "Can anyone help with determining authorship through textual analysis?" "Where can I find simple phrase structure grammar rules of the form S → NP VP, NP → Det N, VP → V?" "Who has the best parser?"

- **Ergo Linguistic Technologies: http://www.ergo-ling.com/**
  This Web site will parse sample sentences that you submit and provide information about the parts of speech and phrase structures of your sentences.

SUGGESTIONS FOR FURTHER READING

- **Robert D. Borsley. 1991. *Syntactic Theory: A Unified Approach.*** (London and New York: Edward Arnold). A helpful book to read but considerably more advanced than the other two suggested readings in this section.

- **Bernard Comrie. 1989. *Language Universals and Linguistic Typology*: *Syntax and Morphology*, 2nd ed.** (Chicago: U of Chicago P). A clear, accessible discussion of syntactic universals across a wide range of languages. As a follow-up to the present chapter, the chapters on "Word Order," "Subject," "Case Marking," and "Relative Clauses" are recommended.

- **Linda Thomas. 1993.** *Beginning Syntax* (Cambridge, MA: Blackwell). With exercises and more than seventy pages of answers to those exercises, this book is a good follow-up to the discussions in LISU.

Advanced Reading

The last few decades have seen exciting developments in the study of syntax. Comprehensive and accessible treatments of syntax can be found in Aarts (1997), Cook and Newson (1996), and Radford (1997).

The volumes edited by Shopen (1985) contain a wealth of useful material; volume I, *Clause Structure,* and volume II, *Complex Constructions,* are relevant to this chapter. Probably accessible to most interested readers who have mastered the present chapter are two excellent chapters of volume I: "Parts of Speech Systems" and "Passive in the World's Languages." Volume II contains the valuable chapters "Complex Phrases and Complex Sentences," "Complementation," and "Relative Clauses."

REFERENCES

- Aarts, Bas. 1997. *English Syntax and Argumentation* (New York: St. Martin's).
- Cook, Vivian, and Mark Newson. 1996. *Chomsky's Universal Grammar: An Introduction* (Oxford: Blackwell).
- Radford, Andrew. 1997. *Syntax: A Minimalist Introduction* (Cambridge: Cambridge UP).
- Shopen, Timothy, ed. 1985. *Language Typology and Syntactic Description* (Cambridge: Cambridge UP).

CHAPTER 6

THE STUDY OF MEANING:
SEMANTICS

—

WHAT DO YOU THINK?

A friend who is studying philosophy asks whether you think "George Washington" and "the first president of the United States" mean the same thing. What response do you give?

One of your college roommates claims that no two words mean exactly the same thing. Another roommate cites fast and quick as examples of synonyms both meaning 'speedy.' The first roommate points out that a "fast talker" isn't necessarily a "quick talker" and says that such an incompatibility proves that the two words are not synonyms. What's your view?

While on spring vacation, you are asked by your grandmother whether there's a word to capture the relationship between word pairs like grandmother and granddaughter, student and teacher, doctor and patient. "They're not opposites like hot and cold," she says. "But what are they?" What do you tell her?

Your high school ESL class asks you whether bank in river bank and savings bank is the same word or different words. "Good question," you say. Then what?

At a family picnic you listen to your cousin tease his four-year-old daughter about a coloring book he has taken from her. The girl says, "That's mine." Your cousin says, "That's right, it's mine." The girl repeats, "No, it's mine." Your cousin says, "That's what I said: it's mine." "No, it's mine," the girl insists, and she grabs the coloring book. What is it about the words yours and mine that makes this kind of teasing possible?

After you tell your junior high school English class that the subject of a sentence is the "doer" of the action, you ask for exam-

> *ples. When one student volunteers "Disneyland is fun," you real-*
> *ize that "Disneyland" is the subject but not the doer of an action.*
> *To correct your explanation about what roles subjects play, what*
> *do you say?*

INTRODUCTION

—

Of the various parts of grammar to which people may refer, "semantics" is a more familiar term than phonology, morphology, or syntax. "That's just semantics" is a common claim in arguments. Even the proverbial man or woman in the street knows that semantics has to do with meaning. Linguistic semantics is the study of the systematic ways in which languages structure meaning, especially in words and sentences.

In defining linguistic semantics (which we'll call "semantics" from now on), we must invoke the word *meaning*. Just as we have many everyday notions of what semantics is, we use the words *meaning* and *to mean* in different contexts and for different purposes. For example:

> The word *perplexity means* 'the state of being puzzled.'
> *Rash* has two *meanings:* 'impetuous' and 'skin irritation.'
> In Spanish, *espejo means* 'mirror.'
> I did not *mean* that he is incompetent, just inefficient.
> The *meaning* of the cross as a symbol is complex.
> I *meant* to bring you my paper but left it at home.

WHAT IS MEANING?

Linguists also attach different interpretations to the word *meaning*. Because the goal of linguistics is to explain precisely how languages are structured and used, it is important to distinguish among the different ways of interpreting the word *meaning*.

A few examples will illustrate why we need to develop a precise way of talking about meaning. Consider these sentences:

1. I went to the store this morning.
2. All dogs are animals.

The sentences make sense – that is, have meaning – for quite different reasons. Whether sentence 1 is true depends on whether or not the speaker is in fact telling the truth; nothing about the words of the sentence makes it inherently true. By contrast, sentence 2 is true because the word *dogs* describes entities that are also described by the word *animals*. The truth of 2 does not depend on whether or not the speaker is telling the truth; it depends solely on the meaning of the words *dogs* and *animals.*

Now compare the following pairs of sentences:

3. You are too young to drink.
   You are not old enough to drink.

4. Harold spent several years in northern Tibet.
   Harold was once in northern Tibet.

The sentences of 3 basically "say the same thing" in that the first describes exactly what the second describes—no more, no less. We say they are *synonymous* sentences, or they paraphrase each other. In 4, the first sentence *implies* the second but not vice versa. If Harold spent several years in northern Tibet, then he must have set foot there at some stage in his life; but if he was once in northern Tibet, it is not necessarily the case that he spent several years there.

Next, consider the following sentences:

5. The unmarried woman is married to a bachelor.
6. My toothbrush is pregnant.

Sentences 5 and 6 are well formed syntactically, but there is something amiss with their semantics. The meanings of the words in 5 contradict each other: an unmarried woman cannot be married, and certainly not to a bachelor. Sentence 5 thus presents a *contradiction.* Sentence 6 is different: given that toothbrushes are not capable of being pregnant, its meaning is *anomalous.* To diagnose precisely what is wrong with these sentences, we need to distinguish between contradictory and anomalous sentences.

Finally, examine sentences 7 and 8:

7. I saw her duck.
8. She ate the pie.

Sentence 7 may be interpreted in two ways: *duck* may be a verb referring to the act of bending over quickly (while walking through a low doorway, for example), or it may be a noun referring to a domesticated bird. These word meanings give the sentence two distinct meanings. Because there are two possible readings of 7, it is said to be **ambiguous.** On the other hand, sentence 8 is not ambiguous, but there is an imprecise quality to it, at least when considered out of context. While we know that the subject of 8 is female, we cannot know who *she* refers to or what particular pie was eaten, although the structure of the phrase *the pie* indicates that the speaker has a particular one in mind. Taken out of context, 8 is thus *vague* in that certain details are left unspecified; but it is not ambiguous.

These observations illustrate that meaning is a multifaceted notion. A sentence may be meaningful and true because it states a fact about the world or because the speaker is telling the truth. Two sentences may be related to each other because they mean exactly the same thing or because one implies the other. Finally, when we feel that there is something wrong with the meaning of a sentence, it may be because the sentence is contradictory, anomalous, ambiguous, or merely vague. One purpose of semantics is to distinguish among these different ways in which language "means."

REFERENTIAL, SOCIAL, AND AFFECTIVE MEANING

For our purposes we can distinguish three types of meaning. **Referential meaning** is the object, notion, or state of affairs described by a word or sentence. **Social meaning** is what we rely on when we identify certain social characteristics of speakers and situations from the character of the language used. **Affective meaning** is the emotional connotation that is attached to words and utterances.

REFERENTIAL MEANING

One way of defining meaning is to say that the meaning of a word or sentence is the person, object, abstract notion, event, or state to which the word or sentence makes reference. The meaning of *John Smith,* for example, is the person who goes by that name. The phrase *Scott's dog* refers to the particular domesticated canine that belongs to Scott. That particular animal can be said to be the meaning of the linguistic expression *Scott's dog.* This type of meaning is *referential* meaning. The canine described by the expression *Scott's dog* is the **referent** of the referring expression *Scott's dog.*

Words, of course, are not the only linguistic units to carry referential meaning. Sentences also have meaning because, like words and phrases, they refer to actions, states, and events in the world around us. *Lou is sleeping on the sofa* refers to the fact that a person known as Lou is currently lying down (or sitting) on an elongated piece of furniture generally meant to be sat upon. The referent of the sentence *Lou is sleeping on the sofa* is thus Lou's state of being on the piece of furniture in question.

SOCIAL MEANING

Referential meaning is not the only type of meaning that language users communicate to each other. Consider the following sentences:

1. Then I says to him he can't do nothin' right.
2. Is it a doctor in here?
3. Y'all gonna visit over the holiday?
4. Great chow!

In addition to representing actions, states, and mental processes, these sentences convey information about the identity of the person who has uttered them. In 1, the use of the verb *says* with the first-person singular pronoun reveals something about the speaker's social class. In 2, the form *it* where some other varieties use *there* indicates a speaker of an ethnically marked variety of English (African American Vernacular English). In 3, the pronoun *y'all* identifies a particular regional dialect of American English (Southern). Finally, the choice of words in 4 indicates that the comment was made in an informal context. Social class, ethnicity, regional origin, and context are all social factors. In addition to referential meaning, therefore, every utterance also conveys social meaning, not only in the sentence as a whole but in word choice (*y'all* and *chow*) and pronunciation (*gonna* or *nothin'*).

AFFECTIVE MEANING

Besides referential and social meaning, there is a third kind of meaning. Compare the following examples:

1. Harold, who always boasts about his two doctorates, lectured me the entire evening on Warhol's art.
2. Harold, who has two doctorates, gave me a fascinating overview of Warhol's art last night.

These two sentences can be used to describe exactly the same event: they have similar referential meaning. At another level, however, the information they convey is different. Sentence 1 gives the impression that the speaker considers Harold a pretentious bore. Sentence 2, in contrast, indicates that the speaker finds Harold interesting. The "stance" of the utterances is thus quite different.

Word choice is not the only means of communicating feelings and attitudes toward utterances and contexts. A striking contrast is provided by sentences that differ only in terms of stress or intonation. This string of words can be interpreted in several ways depending on its intonation:

Harold is really smart.

The sentence can be uttered in a matter-of-fact way, without emphasizing any word in particular, in which case it will be interpreted literally as a remark acknowledging Harold's intelligence. But if the words *really* and *smart* are stressed in an exaggerated manner, the sentence may be interpreted sarcastically to mean exactly the opposite. Intonation (often accompanied by appropriate facial expressions) can be used as a device to communicate attitudes and feelings, and it can override the literal meaning of a sentence.

Consider a final example. Suppose that John Smith, happily married to Mary Smith, addresses his wife as follows:

Mary Smith, how many times have I asked you not to flip through the TV channels?

There would be reason to look beyond the words for the "meaning" of this unusual form of address. Mr. Smith may address his wife as *Mary Smith* to show his exasperation, as in this example. By addressing her as *Mary Smith* instead of the usual *Mary,* he conveys frustration and annoyance. His choice of name thus "means" that he is exasperated. Contrast the tone of that sentence with a similar one in which John Smith addressed Mary Smith as *dear.*

The level of meaning that conveys the language user's feelings, attitudes, and opinions about a particular piece of information or about the ongoing context is called *affective* meaning. Affective meaning is not an exclusive property of sentences: Words like *Alas!* and *Hurray!* obviously have affective meaning, and so can words like *funny, sweet,* and *obnoxious.* Even the most common words—like *father, democracy,* and *old*—can evoke particular emotions and feelings in us. The difference between synonymous or near-synonymous pairs of words like *vagrant* and *homeless* is essentially a difference at the affective level. In this particular pair, *vagrant* carries a negative affective meaning, while *homeless* is neutral or even positive. Little is known yet about how affective meaning works, but it is of great importance to all verbal communication.

From our discussion so far, you can see that meaning is not a simple notion but a complex combination of three aspects:

- Referential meaning: the real-world object or concept described by language
- Social meaning: the information about the social nature of the language user or of the context of utterance
- Affective meaning: what the language user feels about the content or about the ongoing context

The referential meaning of a word or sentence is frequently called its *denotation,* in contrast to the *connotation,* which includes both social and affective meaning.

This chapter focuses primarily on referential meaning, the traditional domain of semantics, but we occasionally refer to the three-way distinction. Social meaning will be investigated in detail in Chapters 10 and 11.

WORD MEANING, SENTENCE MEANING, AND UTTERANCE MEANING

—

MEANING OF WORDS AND SENTENCES

We have talked about words and sentences as the two units of language that carry meaning. **Content words**—principally nouns, verbs, prepositions, adjectives, and adverbs—have meaning in that they refer to concrete objects and abstract concepts; are marked as being characteristic of particular social, ethnic, and regional dialects and of particular contexts; and convey information about the feelings and attitudes of language users. **Function words** such as conjunctions and determiners also carry meaning, though in a different way from content words, as you will see later in this chapter. Like individual words, sentences also have social and affective connotations. The study of word meaning, however, differs from the study of sentence meaning because the units are different in kind.

In order for a sentence to have meaning, we must rely on the meaning of individual words it contains. How we accomplish the task of retrieving sentence meaning from word meaning is a complex question. One obvious hypothesis is that the meaning of a sentence is simply the sum of the meanings of its words. To see that this is *not* the case, consider the following sentences, in which the individual words (and therefore their *sum* meanings) are the same:

> The hunter bit the lion.
> The lion bit the hunter.

Obviously, the sentences refer to different events and hence have distinct referential meanings. This is conveyed by the fact that the words of the sentences are ordered differently. Thus we cannot simply say that all we need to do to retrieve the meaning of a sentence is add up the meanings of its parts. In addition, we must take into consideration the *semantic role* assigned to each word. By semantic role we mean such things as *who* did what to *whom,* with *whom,* and for *whom.* In other words, the semantic role of a word is the role that its referent plays in the action or state of being described by the sentence. Sentence semantics is concerned with semantic roles and with the relationship between words within a sentence.

Scope of Word Meaning   While it is important to distinguish between word meaning and sentence meaning, the two interact on many levels, as the following sentence indicates:

> He may leave tomorrow if he finishes his term paper.

In this sentence, the individual words *may, tomorrow,* and *if* have meanings: *may* denotes permission or possibility; *tomorrow* indicates a future time unit that begins the following midnight; and *if* indicates a condition. But the impact of these words goes beyond the phrases in which they occur and affects the meaning of the entire sentence. Indeed, if we replace *may* with *will,* the sentence takes on a completely different meaning:

> He will leave tomorrow if he finishes his term paper.

The sentence with *may* denotes permission or possibility, while the sentence with *will* is simply the description of a future event. Thus *may* affects the meaning of the *entire* sentence.

The *scope* of the meaning of the word *may* is the entire sentence. This is true also of *tomorrow* and *if.* What this example illustrates is that word meaning and sentence meaning are intimately related.

MEANING OF UTTERANCES

In addition to words and sentences, there is a third unit that also carries meaning, though we may not notice it as clearly because we take it for granted in day-to-day interactions. Consider this utterance:

I now pronounce you husband and wife.

This sentence may be uttered in very different sets of circumstances: (1) by a pastor at a ceremony, speaking to a couple getting married in the presence of their families and friends; or (2) by an actor dressed as a pastor to two actors before a congregation of Hollywood extras assembled in the same church by a director filming a soap opera. In the first instance, *I now pronounce you husband and wife* will create a marriage for the couple intending to get married. But that same utterance will have no effect on the marital status of any party on the filming location. Thus the circumstances of utterance create different meanings, although the referential meaning of the sentence remains unchanged. It is therefore necessary to know the circumstances of utterance in order to understand the effect or force of the utterance. We say that the sentence uttered in the wedding context and the sentence uttered in the film context have the same referential meaning but are different **utterances,** each with its own *utterance meaning.*

The difference between sentence meaning and utterance meaning can be further illustrated by the question *Can you shut the window?* There are at least two ways in which an addressee might react to this question. One would be to say *Yes* (meaning 'Yes, I am physically capable of shutting the window') and then do nothing about it. This is the "smart-aleck" interpretation; it is of course not the way such a question is intended in most cases. Another way in which the addressee might react would be to get up and shut the window. Obviously, these interpretations of the same question are different: the smart-aleck interpretation treats the question as a request for information; the second interpretation treats it as a request for action. To describe the difference between these interpretations, we say that they are *distinct utterances.*

Sentence semantics is not concerned with utterance meaning. (Utterances are the subject of investigation of another branch of linguistics called *pragmatics,* which is the topic of Chapters 8 and 9.) One of the premises of sentence semantics is that sentences must be divorced from the context in which they are uttered, in other words that sentences and utterances must be distinguished. To experienced language users, this stance may appear strange and counterintuitive, since so much meaning depends on context. The point is not to discard context as unimportant but to recognize that, in a fundamental sense, sentence meaning is independent of context, while utterance meaning depends crucially on the circumstances of the utterance. **Semantics** is the branch of linguistics that examines word and sentence meaning while generally ignoring context. By contrast, **pragmatics** pays less attention to the relationship of word meaning to sentence meaning and more attention to the relationship of an utterance to its context.

LEXICAL SEMANTICS

The *lexicon* can be viewed as a compendium of all the words of a language. Words are sometimes called **lexical items,** or *lexemes* (the *-eme* ending as in *phoneme* and *morpheme*). The branch of semantics that deals with word meaning is called **lexical semantics.**

Lexical semantics examines relationships among word meanings. For example, it asks what is the relationship between the words *man* and *woman* on the one hand and *human being* on the other hand. How are the adjectives *large* and *small* in the same relationship to each other as the pair *dark* and *light?* What is the difference between the meaning of words like *always* and *never* and the meaning of words like *often* and *seldom?* What do language users actually mean when they say that a dog is "a type of" mammal? Lexical semantics investigates such questions: It is the study of how the lexicon is organized and of how the meanings of lexical items are interrelated, and its principal goal is to build a model for the structure of the lexicon by categorizing the types of relationships between words.

LEXICAL FIELDS

Consider the following sets of words:

1. cup, mug, wine glass, tumbler, plastic cup, goblet
2. hammer, cloud, tractor, eyeglasses, leaf, justice

The words of set 1 all refer to concepts that can be described as 'vessels from which one drinks,' while the words of set 2 denote concepts that have nothing in common with each other. The words of set 1 constitute a **lexical field**—a set of words with an identifiable semantic affinity. The following set of words is also a lexical field, all of whose words refer to emotional states:

angry, sad, happy, exuberant, depressed, afraid

Thus we see that words can be classified into sets according to their meaning.

In a lexical field, not all lexical items necessarily have the same status. Consider the following sets, which together form the lexical field of color terms (of course there are other terms in the same field):

1. blue, red, yellow, green, black, purple
2. indigo, saffron, royal blue, aquamarine, bisque

The colors referred to by the words of set 1 are more "usual" than those described in set 2. They are said to be less **marked** members of the lexical field than those of set 2. The less marked members of a lexical field will usually be easier to learn and remember than more marked members. Children learn the term *blue* before they learn the terms *indigo, royal blue,* or *aquamarine.* Typically, a less marked word consists of only one morpheme, in contrast to more marked words (contrast *blue* and *royal blue*). The less marked member of a lexical field cannot be described by using the name of another member of the same field, whereas more marked members can be thus described (*indigo* is a kind of blue). Less marked terms also tend to be used more frequently than more marked terms; for example, *blue* occurs considerably more frequently in conversation and writing than *indigo* or *aquamarine.* (In the million-word Brown Corpus of written American English, there are 126 examples of *blue,* only one of *indigo,* and none at all of *aquamarine.*) Less marked terms are also often broader in meaning than more marked terms; *blue* describes a broader range of colors than *indigo* or *aquamarine.* Finally, less marked words are not the result of the metaphorical usage of the name of another object or concept, whereas more marked words often are; for example, *saffron* is the color of a spice that lent its name to the color.

Using our understanding of lexical field and markedness, we now turn to identifying types of relationships between words. We'll see how the words of a lexical field can have different types of relationships to each other and to other words in the lexicon, and we'll classify these relationships.

HYPONYMY

Consider again this set of unmarked color terms: *blue, red, yellow, green, black, purple.* What they have in common is that they refer to colors. We say that the terms *blue, red, yellow, green, black,* and *purple* are hyponyms of the term *color.* A **hyponym** is a subordinate, specific term whose referent is included in the referent of a superordinate term. Blue is a kind of color; red is a kind of color, and so on. They are specific colors, and *color* is the general term for them. We can illustrate the relationship by the following diagram, in which the lower terms are the hyponyms (*hypo-* means 'below'). The higher term—in this case, *color*—is called the superordinate term (technically, the *hypernym*).

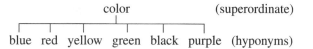

Another example is the term *mammal,* whose referent includes the referents of many other terms.

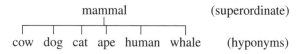

The relationship between each of the lower terms and the higher term is called *hyponymy*. It can be represented as in the triangle below:

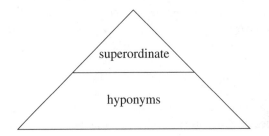

Hyponymy is not restricted to objects like mammal or abstract concepts like color—or even to nouns, for that matter. Hyponymy can be identified in many other areas of the lexicon. The verb *to cook,* for example, has many hyponyms.

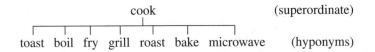

Not every set of hyponyms has a superordinate term. Consider *uncle* and *aunt.* They form a lexical field because we can identify a property that their referents share. Yet English does not have a term that refers specifically to both uncles and aunts (that is, to siblings of parents and their spouses).

By contrast, some other languages have a superordinate term for the equivalent field. In Spanish, the plural term *tios* can include both aunts and uncles, and the Spanish equivalents of the terms *uncle* and *aunt* are therefore hyponyms of *tios.*

While hyponymy is found in all languages, the concepts that have words in hyponymic relationships vary from one language to the next. In Tuvaluan (a Polynesian language), the higher term *ika* (roughly, 'fish') has as hyponyms not only all terms that refer to the animals that English speakers would recognize as fish but also terms for whales and dolphins (which speakers of English recognize as mammals) and for sea turtles (which are reptiles). Of course, we are dealing with folk classifications here, not scientific classifications.

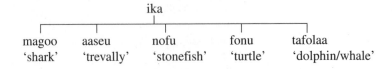

Thus there is variability across languages as to the exact nature of particular hyponymic relationships.

In a lexical field, hyponymy may exist at more than one level. A word may have both a hyponym and a superordinate term, as *blue* has in Figure 6-1. Because they refer to different "types" or "shades" of blue, the terms *turquoise, aquamarine,* and *royal blue* are hyponyms of *blue*. *Blue* in turn is a hyponym of *color*. We thus have a hierarchy of terms related to each other through hyponymic relationships. Similar hierarchies can be established for many lexical fields, almost without limit. In the "cooking" field, *fry* has hyponyms in the terms *stir-fry, saute,* and *deep-fry* and is itself a hyponym of *cook*. The lower we get in a hierarchy of hyponyms, the more marked the terms: *cook* is relatively unmarked; *stir-fry* is considerably more marked. The intermediate term *fry* is less marked than *stir-fry* but more marked than *cook*.

Examples of multiple layers of hyponymic relationships abound in the area of folk biological classification, as illustrated in Figure 6-2. Note that the term *animal* appears on two levels. English speakers use *animal* for at least two different referents: 1) animals as distinct from plants and rocks, and 2) animals (generally mammals other than humans) as distinct from humans, birds, and bugs. Cases in which a word has different meanings at different levels of a hyponymic hierarchy are not uncommon.

Hyponymy is one of several relationship types with which language users organize the lexicon. It is based on the notion of reference *inclusion:* if the referent of term A (for example, *color*) includes the referent of term B (for example, *red*), then term B (*red*) is a *hyponym* of term A (*color*). Hyponymy is important in everyday

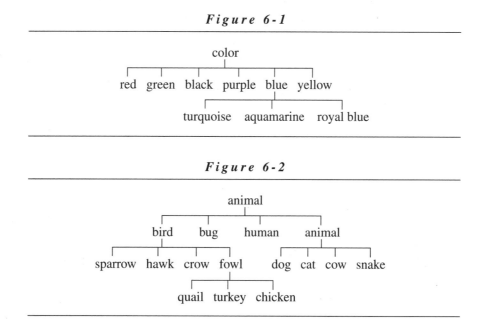

Figure 6-1

Figure 6-2

conversation—we use it whenever we say "B is a kind of A" (*red* is a kind of *color*)—and for such tasks as using a thesaurus, which is organized according to hyponymic relationships.

PART/WHOLE RELATIONSHIPS

A second important hierarchical relationship between words is the one found in pairs like *hand* and *arm* or *room* and *house*. In each pair, the referent of the first term is part of the referent of the second term. A hand, however, is not "a kind of" arm, and thus the relationship between *hand* and *arm* is not hyponymic. Instead, we call it a *part/whole relationship*. Part/whole relationships are not a property of pairs of words only: *hand, elbow, forearm, wrist,* and several other words are in a part/whole relationship with *arm*. Other important examples of part/whole relationships include words like *second* and *minute, minute* and *hour, hour* and *day, day* and *week,* none of which could be described without reference to the fact that it is a subdivision of another. Figure 6-3 illustrates the difference between a part/whole relationship and a hyponymic relationship for the word *eye*.

SYNONYMY

Synonyms

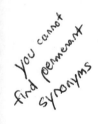

Two words are said to be **synonymous** if they mean the same thing. The terms *movie, film, flick,* and *motion picture* all have the same set of referents in the real world and are usually taken to be synonymous terms. To address the notion of synonymy more formally, we can say that term *A* is synonymous with term *B* if every referent of *A* is a referent of *B* and vice versa. For example, if every movie is a film and every film is a movie, the terms *movie* and *film* are synonymous. The "vice versa" is important: without it, we would be defining hyponymy.

You may wonder why speakers of a language bother to keep synonyms, given that they only add redundancy to the lexicon. English has many synonymous pairs like *cloudy* and *nebulous, help* and *assist, skewed* and *oblique* (the result of English having borrowed the second term of each pair from French or Latin). When we assert that two terms are synonymous, we usually base that judgment on referential meaning only. Thus, even though *movie, film, flick,* and *motion picture* have the same

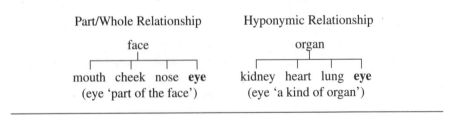

Figure 6-3

Part/Whole Relationship	Hyponymic Relationship
face	organ
mouth cheek nose **eye**	kidney heart lung **eye**
(eye 'part of the face')	(eye 'a kind of organ')

referential meaning, the terms differ in social and affective meaning. *Film* may strike you as appropriate for movie classics or art movies; it is a more highbrow term. You recognize that *flick* is used chiefly in informal contexts, while *motion picture* is somewhat traditional or industry related. Thus we can consider the terms to be synonymous if we specify that we are taking only referential meaning into account. At the social and affective levels, however, they are not synonymous.

In fact, there are very few true synonyms in the lexicon. More often than not, terms that appear to be synonymous have different social and affective connotations. Even if we restrict meaning to referential meaning, words that appear synonymous at first glance often refer to slightly different sets of concepts or are used in different situations. The adjectives *fast, quick,* and *rapid* may be used interchangeably in reference to someone's running speed, but a *fast talker* (a 'slippery or deceptive person') is different from a "quick talker"; some people lead lives in the *fast lane,* not the "rapid lane"; and *quick* is the most appropriate term to describe a mind or a glance, while *rapid* is the usual term when reference is made to a person's *strides,* especially metaphorical strides, as in learning to type or do mathematics. Under the circumstances, is it accurate to say that these adjectives are synonymous?

The fact that there are few true synonyms in the lexicon of a language reflects the general tendency of language users to make the most of what's available to them. If two terms have the same referent, the meaning of one of them is usually modified to express differences in referential, social, or affective meaning. Although true synonymy is rare, the notion is useful because it helps describe similarities between the meanings of different terms in the lexicon.

ANTONYMY

The word **antonymy** derives from the Greek root *anti-* ('opposite') and denotes opposition in meaning. In contrast to synonymy and hyponymy, antonymy is a *binary* relationship in that it can characterize a relationship between only two words at a time. Terms A and B are antonyms if, when A describes a referent, B cannot describe the same referent, and vice versa.

The prototypical antonyms are pairs of adjectives that describe opposite notions: *large* and *small, wide* and *narrow, hot* and *cold, married* and *single, alive* and *dead.* Antonymy is not restricted to adjectives, however. The nouns *male* and *female* are also antonyms because an individual cannot be described by both terms at once. *Always* and *never* form an antonymous pair of adverbs: they have mutually exclusive referents. The verbs *love* and *hate* can also be viewed as antonyms because they refer to mutually exclusive emotions. Antonymy is thus a binary relationship between terms with complementary meanings.

Intuitively, you can see a difference between the antonymous pair *large* and *small* and the antonymous pair *single* and *married.* The first pair denote notions that are relatively subjective. You would agree that humpback whales are large mammals and that mice are small mammals, but whether German shepherds are large or small dogs depends on your perspective. The owner of a Chihuahua will say that German shepherds are large, but the owner of a Great Dane may judge them to be on the small side. Furthermore, adjectives like *large* and *small* have superlative and comparative forms: humpback whales are the *largest* of all mammals; German shepherds are *larger* than Chihuahuas but *smaller* than Great Danes. Antonymous pairs that have these characteristics are called *gradable* pairs.

In contrast to *large* and *small, single* and *married* are mutually exclusive and complementary. A person cannot be single and married at the same time. With respect to marital status, a person cannot be described with a term that does not have either *single* or *married* as a hyponym; thus *single* and *married* are complementary. Furthermore, *single* and *married* generally cannot be used in a comparative or superlative sense (someone's being legally "more single" than another single person is impossible). The pair constitute an example of *nongradable* antonymy (also sometimes called *complementarity*).

There are thus two types of antonymy: gradable and nongradable. If terms *A* and *B* are *gradable* antonyms and if *A* can be used to describe a particular referent, then *B* cannot be used to describe the same referent, and vice versa. If *A* and *B* are *nongradable* antonyms, the same condition applies along with an additional condition: if *A* cannot describe a referent, then that referent must be describable by *B,* and vice versa. So *male* and *female, married* and *single, alive* and *dead* can be viewed as nongradable antonyms, while *hot* and *cold, love* and *hate, always* and *never* are gradable. Typically, for gradable antonyms, there will be words to describe intermediate stages: *sometimes, seldom, occasionally, often* are gradations between *always* and *never.*

As you recognize, the distinction between gradable and nongradable antonymy is sometimes blurred by language users. In English, for example, it is reasonable to assume that whatever is alive is not dead and that whatever is dead is not alive, and thus that the adjectives *dead* and *alive* form a nongradable pair. However, we do have expressions like *half dead, barely alive,* and *more dead than alive.* Such expressions suggest that, in some contexts, we see *alive* and *dead* as gradable antonyms. The distinction between gradable and nongradable antonymy is nevertheless useful in that it describes an important distinction between two types of word relationships.

Finally, antonymous words often do not have equal status with respect to markedness. For example, when you inquire about the weight of an object, you ask *How heavy is it?* and not *How light is it?*—unless you already know that the object is light. Notice also that the noun *weight,* which describes both relative heaviness and relative lightness, is associated with *heavy* rather than with *light* (as in the expressions *carry a lot of weight* and *throw one's weight around*). Of the antonymous pair *heavy* and *light, heavy* is more neutral than *light* and is thus less marked. In the same fashion, *tall* is less marked than *short, hot* less marked than *cold,* and *married* less marked than *single* (we say *marital status,* not "singleness status"). Although there is some variation across languages as to which word of a pair is considered less marked, there is a surprising agreement from language to language.

CONVERSENESS

Another important relationship invokes the notion of oppositeness, although it does so in a way that differs from antonymy. Consider the relationship between *wife* and *husband.* If A is the husband of B, then B is the wife of A. Thus *wife* is the converse of *husband,* and vice versa. **Converseness** characterizes a reciprocal semantic relationship between pairs of words. Other examples of converse pairs include terms denoting many other kinship relations, like *grandchild* and *grandparent* or *child* and *parent,* terms describing professional relationships, like *employer* and *employee* or *doctor* and *patient;* and terms denoting relative positions in space or time, such as *above* and *below, north of* and *south of,* or *before* and *after.*

Converse pairs can combine with other types of opposition to form complex relationships. The antonymous pair *father: mother* is in a converse relationship with the antonymous pair *son: daughter.* Generally, converse pairs denote relationships between objects or between people. Some converse relationships are a little more complex. The verb *give,* for example, requires a subject and two objects (*She gave him the book*). The converse of *give* is *receive,* except that the relationship is not a "reversal" of the subject and the direct object as it would be with *kiss* and *be kissed* (*Smith kissed Jones* versus *Jones was kissed by Smith*) or a mutual subject/possessor relation like *husband* and *wife;* rather, it is a relationship between the subject and the indirect object.

John gave Billy a present.
Billy received a present from John.

Other pairs of words with a similar relationship include *lend* and *borrow* and *buy* and *sell.* Note that *rent* is its own converse in American English.

John rents an apartment to Billy.
Billy rents an apartment from John.

When there is a possibility of confusion, the preposition *out* can be attached to *rent* in the meaning of 'lending out for money.' In British English, this sense of *rent* is described by the verb *let* (*flat to let*). In some languages, a single word is used for 'buy' and 'sell.' In Samoan, for example, the word *faʔatau* carries both meanings, while the Mandarin Chinese words *mǎi* 'buy' and *mài* 'sell' are etymologically related. These facts suggest that converseness is an intuitively recognizable relationship.

POLYSEMY AND HOMONYMY

Two additional notions that are closely related to the basic relationship types are **polysemy** and **homonymy.** In contrast to the notions discussed above, polysemy and homonymy refer to similarities rather than differences between meanings. A word is *polysemous* (or polysemic) when it has more than one meaning. The word *plain,* for example, can have several meanings, among them these:

(1) 'easy, clear' (*plain English*)
(2) 'undecorated' (*plain white shirt*)
(3) 'not good looking' (*plain Jane*)
(4) 'a level area of land' (*plains man, Plains Indian*)

Homographs have the same spelling but different meanings: *dove* 'a kind of bird' and *dove* 'past tense of *dive,'* *contact* as a verb and *contact* as a noun, where the verb has primary stress on the first syllable and the noun has it on the second syllable. *Homophones* have the same pronunciation but different meanings: *sea* and *see, so* and *sew, two* and *too, plain* and *plane, flower* and *flour, boar* and *bore, bear* and *bare,* or *eye, I,* and *aye.* Words are *homonymic* when they have the same written *or* spoken form but different meanings. A narrower definition of homonym would limit the term to word sets that are both homographic *and* homophonous, as with *bank* of a river and savings *bank* ('a financial institution') or the adjective *still* 'quiet' (*still waters*) and the adverb *still* 'yet' (*still sick*). Languages exhibit polysemy and homonymy in their lexicons to varying degrees. A language like Hawaiian, which has a restricted set of possible words because of its phonological structure, has a good deal more homonymy than English has (see Chapter 4).

A difficulty arises in distinguishing between homonymy and polysemy: How do we know when you have separate lexical items rather than a single word with different meanings? Consider *plain.* Because *plain* 'a level area of land' is a noun, it is a distinct word from *plain* in its adjectival meanings. But how would we know whether or not the three adjectival meanings ('easy,' 'undecorated,' 'not good-looking') constitute different words that happen to sound the same? Using spelling as a criterion is misleading: many sets of words are distinct but have the same spelling—as, for example, the noun *sound* 'noise' and the adjective *sound* 'healthy,' or *bank* 'financial institution' and *bank* 'shore of a river.' Yet the problem is an important one for anyone who wants to arrange or use the entries of a dictionary (in which different meanings of the same word are grouped under a single entry but each homonymous form has its own distinct entry).

There is no simple solution to the problem. If there is a clear distinction between polysemy and homonymy, it must involve several criteria, no one of which would be sufficient by itself and several of which may yield different results. We have already excluded spelling as an unreliable criterion. One modestly reliable criterion is a word's historical origin, or *etymology.* We can consider that there are two words of the form *sound* corresponding to the two meanings given above because they derive from different Anglo-Saxon roots. Likewise, the word *bank* meaning 'financial institution' is an early borrowing from French, whereas *bank* meaning 'shore of a river' has a Scandinavian origin. The various antonyms and synonyms of a word provide a different kind of criterion for distinguishing between polysemy and homonymy. *Plain* in the sense of 'easy, clear' and *plain* in the sense of 'undecorated' share a synonym in *simple* and an antonym in *complex.* This fact suggests that they are indeed two meanings of the same polysemic word. No such shared synonym or antonym can be identified for the two meanings of *sound.* Finally, we can ask whether there is any commonality between different meanings of what appears to be the same word. The first two meanings of *plain* can be characterized as 'devoid of complexity,' which suggests that they are related, but no such superordinate (or hypernymic) description exists for *bank* and *bank.* Thus *plain* in these two senses is polysemic, while the two senses of *bank* reflect homonymous lexical items. (Of course, other meanings of *plain* may or may not belong to separate words.)

While the criteria just outlined help distinguish between polysemy and homonymy, they are not foolproof. It is often difficult to decide whether a particular pair of look-alike and sound-alike word forms are separate homonymous words or simply the same polysemic word with different meanings. Though homonymy and polysemy can be distinguished as different notions, the boundary between them may not be clear-cut in particular cases.

METAPHORICAL EXTENSION

The difficulties in defining the distinction between polysemy and homonymy partly arise from the fact that language users often extend the primary meaning of words to form metaphors. A **metaphor** is an extension in the use of a word beyond its primary meaning to describe referents that bear similarities to the word's primary referent. The word *eye,* for example, can be used to describe the hole at the dull end of a needle, the bud on a potato, or the center of a storm. The similarities between these referents and the primary referent of the word *eye* are their roundish shape and their more or less central role or position in a larger form. People frequently create new metaphors, and once a metaphor becomes accepted speakers tend to view the metaphorical meaning as separate from its primary meaning—as in *booking* a flight, *tabling* a motion, *seeing* the *point, stealing* the *head*lines, *buying* time, studying a foreign *tongue.* Hence difficulty exists in determining whether one word exists with two meanings or two words exist with different but metaphorically related meanings.

All languages appear to have metaphors, and metaphors are so fundamental to human communication that small children can be observed creating them in the process of acquiring language. Very early, children extend the meaning of the words that they know to cover objects and concepts for which they do not yet know the adult word. Linguist Eve Clark reports the example of a child who first said the word *mooi* while looking at the moon. Before long, the child was using the word *mooi* to describe cakes, circles drawn on foggy windows, postmarks, and the letter *o.* Obviously, the child noticed that all these objects shared a round shape and used the word *mooi* to refer to round objects. This early process of applying a particular word to meanings that resemble the primary meaning of the word is called *overgeneralization* and can be thought of as a primitive kind of metaphor. As adults, we use metaphors not because we are unaware of the names of objects and concepts but because we find in metaphors a tool to be creative and to describe things vividly.

Metaphors occur constantly in day-to-day speaking and writing. The following examples were gleaned from the front page of a typical newspaper:

Tennis star Martina Navratilova <u>breezed</u> through the championship match.
The dollar is <u>falling sharply.</u>
His speech was the <u>catalyst</u> for a new popular upheaval.

In the first example, the verb *breeze* is of course not meant literally; it is used to give the impression that Navratilova won the championship effortlessly, as a breeze would blow over a tennis court. Similarly, the underlined words in the other two sentences are meant to be interpreted as metaphors, whose effectiveness relies on our ability to see that in some contexts words are not to be interpreted literally. (The mechanisms that we use in figuring out when a word must be interpreted metaphorically will be discussed in Chapter 9.)

Metaphors aren't formed haphazardly. Observe, for example, the following metaphors that refer to the notion of time:

I look <u>forward</u> to seeing you again this weekend.
Experts do not <u>foresee</u> an increase in inflation in the near future.
He <u>drags up</u> old grudges from his youth.
Once in a while, we need to <u>look back over our shoulders</u> at the lessons that
    history has taught us.

A pattern is apparent in these examples: in English, we construct time metaphors as if we physically moved through time in the direction of the future. Thus the future is forward in the first two examples. Metaphors that refer to the past use words that refer to what is left behind, as in the latter two examples. Metaphors that violated this pattern would sound very strange:

*I look <u>back</u> to seeing you again this weekend.
*He <u>drags down</u> old grudges from his youth.

Another principle that governs the creation of metaphors is this: "Ideas are objects that can be sensed." Thus they can be smelled, felt, and heard.

Your proposal <u>smells</u> fishy.
I failed to <u>grasp</u> what they were trying to prove.
I'd like your opinion as to whether my plan <u>sounds</u> reasonable.

Writers and critics often talk about the writing process as "cooking."

I let my manuscript <u>simmer</u> for six months.
Who knows what kind of a story he is <u>brewing</u>!
Their last book was little more than a <u>half-baked concoction</u> of earlier work.

"The heart is where emotions are experienced" is a common principle on which our metaphors for emotions are based.

> It is with a <u>heavy heart</u> that I tell you of her death.
> You shouldn't speak <u>lightheartedly</u> about this tragedy.
> The rescuers received the survivors' <u>heartfelt</u> thanks.

The construction of metaphors thus follows preset patterns.

Most of the metaphors discussed so far are relatively conventionalized—that is, they are found commonly in speech and writing because they are preset. But language lends itself to creative activities, and language users do not hesitate to create new metaphors. Even when we create our own metaphors, however, we must follow the principles that regulate conventionalized metaphors. In English, metaphors that refer to time must obey the convention of "moving through time in the direction of the future."

There is strong evidence that some metaphorical patterns are frequent across the world's languages. For example, in many languages the word for 'eye' is used metaphorically to refer to roundish objects like protuberances on a potato and the pivotally located portion of an object like the center of a storm.

But other principles of metaphorical extension vary from language to language. For example, in many languages it is not the heart that is the seat of emotions. Polynesian languages like Samoan and Tahitian treat the stomach as the metaphorical seat of emotions. It is likely that some of these principles reflect different cultures' views of the world. The exact workings of the link between culture and language are still poorly understood. Increased knowledge about metaphors in different languages should help us determine which principles are widely shared by languages, which are specific to some languages, and to what extent metaphors reflect cultural perspectives.

LEXICAL SEMANTICS: DISCOVERING RELATIONSHIPS IN THE LEXICON

Hyponymy, part/whole relationships, synonymy, gradable and nongradable antonymy, converseness, polysemy, homonymy, and metaphorical extension—lexical semantics is primarily concerned with discovering relationships in the lexicon of languages. The semantic relationships of a word are, in a sense, part of its meaning: the word *cold* can be defined as a gradable antonym of *hot,* as having the expression *sensation of heat* as a superordinate term, and as being more marked than *hot* but less marked than *chilly* and *freezing.* By knowing how the meaning of a word interacts with the meaning of other words, we can begin to understand its meaning.

Lexical semantics, of course, does not explain the difference in meaning between words that are as unlike as *gorilla* and *doubtful.* For lexical semantics to be useful, it must be applied to particular areas of the lexicon where word senses have shared characteristics. Thus the notion of lexical field becomes useful. If the word *gorilla* is placed in its appropriate lexical field, its relationship to *chimpanzee* and *great ape* can be investigated. Similarly, the word *doubtful* can be contrasted with *certain, probably,* and other words that express likelihood or certainty.

The different types of relationships described above are the most basic tools of lexical semantics. They are basic because one type cannot be characterized in terms of another type. For example, an antonymous relationship between two words cannot be explained in terms of hyponymy, part/whole relationships, synonymy, converseness, or metaphorical extension.

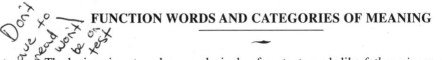

Don't have to read won't be on test

FUNCTION WORDS AND CATEGORIES OF MEANING

The lexicon is not made up exclusively of content words like *father, pigeon, stir-fry,* and *democracy,* which refer to objects, actions, or abstract concepts. It also contains function words like the conjunctions *if, however,* and *or;* the determiners *a, the,* and *these;* and the auxiliaries *may, should,* and *will.* The role of these categories is to signal grammatical relationships.

TENSE AND MODALITY

Many categories of meaning are associated with function words and function morphemes. Bound morphemes can denote several categories of meaning in English, including number (*toys*) and tense (*walked*). In other languages, the same categories are expressed not by means of bound morphemes but by separate words. In Tongan, the function word *ʔoku* denotes present tense, while *naʔe* denotes past tense.

ʔoku   ʔalu   e   fineʔeiki   ki   kolo
Present   go   the   woman   to   town
'The woman is going to town.'

naʔe   ʔalu   e   fineʔeiki   ki   kolo
Past   go   the   woman   to   town
'The woman was going to town.'

Whether tense is expressed through bound morphemes or separate lexical items is not important for semantics. What is important is that there is a semantic category *tense* that affects the meaning of sentences in both Tongan and English.

Semantic categories like tense are conveyed by function words and function morphemes, but their scope extends beyond the constituent in which they occur. The meaning of a tense morpheme affects the whole sentence because the **tense** of the verb determines the time reference of the entire clause. The category *tense* (and other semantic categories like it) thus refers to both word meaning and clause meaning.

Modality, or *mood,* is a category through which speakers can convey their attitude toward the truth or reliability of their assertions (called *epistemic modality*) or express obligation, permission, or suggestion (called *deontic modality*). The sentences in the following pairs differ as to their *epistemic* modality:

1. She has *probably* left town by now. (probability)
   She has left town by now. (assertion)

2. Harry *must've* been very tall when he was young. (conjecture)
   Harry was very tall when he was young. (assertion)

3. They *may* come to the party. (possibility)
   They are coming to the party. (assertion)

And those in the following pairs differ as to their *deontic* modality:

4. He *must* come tomorrow. (command)
   He is coming tomorrow. (statement)

5. They *may* take the dishes away. (permission)
   They are taking the dishes away. (statement)

The two types of modality are interrelated, as witnessed by the fact that the same words (*must* and *may,* for example) can denote either type, depending on the context. Modality can be expressed through auxiliary verbs such as *may, should,* or *must* (which are called *modal* auxiliaries), through *modal* verbs like *order, assume,* and *allow;* through *modal* adverbs like *possibly* or *certainly;* and in some languages through affixes attached to verbs or nouns. Such affixes are common in Native American languages, some of which can have extremely complex systems of modal affixes and particles.

REFERENCE

When a noun phrase is used in an utterance, it may or may not have a corresponding entity in the real world. **Reference** concerns the ability of linguistic expressions to refer to real-world entities. If someone says *I read a new biography of James Joyce last weekend,* the expressions *I* and *a new biography of James Joyce* refer to real-world entities. If, by contrast, someone says *I'd like to find a short biography of James Joyce,* there is in the speaker's mind a real-world entity corresponding to *I* but not to *a short biography of James Joyce.* This is not to say, of course, that a short biography of James Joyce may not exist but only that the speaker does not have in mind a real-world entity to which the expression refers.

In the examples below, note the difference in reference for different uses of a given phrase. In examples 1, 3, and 5, the underscored phrases have no referent; we say they are not referential or are nonreferential. In 2, 4, and 6, the same phrases do have referents; we say they are referential; they have referents in the real world.

1. Can you recommend <u>a good western</u> for kids? (nonreferential)
2. Last night I saw <u>a good western</u> at the Tivoli. (referential)
3. She'd buy <u>a new Ford Bronco</u> if she found one on sale. (nonreferential)
4. She test-drove <u>a new Ford Bronco</u> that she liked. (referential)
5. I'm searching for <u>the best Chinese restaurant in the city.</u> (nonreferential)
6. Tuesday I ate at <u>the best Chinese restaurant in the city.</u> (referential)

As these examples show, reference is a property not of words or phrases but of linguistic expressions as they occur in actual discourse. The same phrase can be referential in one utterance and nonreferential in another. Note, too, that reference cannot be equated with definiteness, a subject to which we return below. (Reference is investigated further in Chapter 8.)

DEIXIS

The word *deixis* comes from the Greek adjective *deiktikos* meaning 'pointing, indicative.' **Deixis** is the marking of the orientation or position of entities and events with respect to certain *points of reference.* Consider the following sentence addressed to a waiter by a restaurant customer while pointing to items on a menu:

> I want this dish, this dish, and this dish.

To interpret this utterance, the waiter must have information about who *I* refers to, about the time at which the utterance is produced, and about what the three noun phrases *this dish* refer to. We say that *I,* along with the present-tense form of the verb and the three noun phrases *this dish,* are *deictic expressions.* Our ability to interpret them enables us to interpret the sentence.

Deixis consists of three semantic notions, all related to the orientation or position of events or entities in the real world. *Personal deixis* is commonly conveyed through personal pronouns: *I* versus *you* versus *he* or *she. Spatial deixis* refers to orientation in space: *here* versus *there* and *this* versus *that. Temporal deixis* refers to orientation in time, as in present versus past, for example.

Personal Deixis Many of the utterances that we produce daily are comments or questions about ourselves or our interlocutors.

> *I* really should be going now.
> Did *you* pick up the carton of milk *I* asked *you* to?
> In this family, *we* rarely smoke or drink.

The pronouns *I, you,* and *we*—along with *she, he, it,* and *they* (and alternative forms)—are markers of personal deixis. When we use these pronouns, we orient our utterances with respect to ourselves, our interlocutors, and third parties.

Personal pronouns are of course not the only tool used to mark personal deixis. The phrase *this person* in the sentence *You may enjoy scary roller-coaster rides, but this person doesn't care for them at all* may be used to refer to the speaker if the speaker wishes to express annoyance or disdain. Similarly if you happen to be entertaining royalty, etiquette may require you to use the noun phrase *Your Highness* to refer to the addressee: *Would Your Highness like some fried oysters?* Personal deixis is thus not associated exclusively with pronouns, although pronouns are the most common way to express personal deixis. In this discussion, we will concentrate primarily on pronouns as markers of personal deixis.

The most basic opposition in personal-deixis systems is that between speaker (*I* or *me*) and addressee (*you*). This opposition in *person* is so basic that it is reflected in the pronominal systems of all languages. Pronouns that refer to the speaker (or to a group that includes the speaker) are called *first-person* pronouns, and pronouns that refer to the addressee (or to a group including the addressee) are called *second-person* pronouns.

Besides the contrast between first person and second person, pronoun systems often have separate forms for the *third person*—that is, any entity other than the speaker and the person spoken to. In English, *he, she, it,* and *they* denote third-person entities. But third-person pronouns are not found in all languages. Some languages simply do not have special forms to refer to third-person entities. In these languages, third-person entities are referred to with a demonstrative like *this* or *that,* or they remain unexpressed. In Tongan, a verb without an expressed subject is understood as having a third-person subject.

> naʔe   aʔu
> Past   arrive
> '(He/She/It) arrived.'

Tongan does have a third-person pronoun form, but it is used only for emphasis.

> naʔe   aʔu   ia
> Past   arrive   he/she
> 'He/She is the one that arrived.'

The fact that some languages lack separate third-person pronouns reflects the fact that the third person is less important than the first and second persons in personal deixis. In fact, the third person can be defined as an entity other than the first person and other than the second person. Because it can be described in terms of the other two persons, it is a less basic distinction in language in general. The singular pronoun system of English can thus be described as follows:

> speaker only   I
> hearer only   you
> *neither* speaker nor hearer   he/she/it

Some languages make finer distinctions in their pronominal systems, while others make fewer distinctions (see Chapter 8). In all languages, though, there are separate first-person and second-person pronouns.

Besides person, personal-deixis systems may mark distinctions in gender and number. In English, a gender distinction is made in the third person only: *he* for masculine and *she* for feminine referents. In other languages, gender may be marked in the other persons as well. In Hebrew, the second-person singular pronoun is *ata* for masculine referents but *at* for feminine referents. Number is marked on English pronouns in the first person (*I* versus *we*) and the third person (*he/she/it* versus *they*); the second-person pronoun *you* is used for reference to both singular and plural entities. In many languages (including French), there are separate second-person singular and plural pronouns (French *tu* and *vous*). Singular and plural are not the only number categories that can be distinguished: some languages have distinct dual forms to refer to exactly two people, and a few languages even mark a distinction between "a few" and "many" referents (see Chapter 7).

Finally, personal deixis frequently reflects the social status of referents. In French and in many other languages, the choice of a pronoun in the second person depends on the nature of the speaker's relationship to the addressee. If speaker and addressee are of roughly equal social status, the pronoun *tu* is used; to mark or create social distance or social inequality, a speaker uses the plural pronoun *vous* instead of *tu,* even when addressing one person. Considerably more complex systems are found in languages like Japanese, Thai, and Korean. Strictly speaking, the use of deictic devices to reflect facts about the social relationship of the participants is a distinct type of deixis, commonly referred to as *social deixis.*

Thus personal deixis can mark a number of overlapping distinctions: person, gender, number, and social relations. Languages combine these distinctions in different combinations, marking some and not others. The basic distinction between first person and second person, however, is found in all languages and appears to be a basic semantic category in all deictic systems.

Spatial Deixis Spatial deixis is the marking of the orientation or position in space of the referent of a linguistic expression. The categories of words most commonly used to express spatial deixis are demonstratives (*this, that*) and adverbs (*here, there*). Demonstratives and adverbs of place are by no means the only categories that have spatial deictic meaning; the directional verbs *go* and *come* also carry deictic information, as do *bring* and *take.*

Languages differ in terms of the number and meaning of demonstratives and adverbs of place. The demonstrative system of English distinguishes only between *this* (proximate—close to the speaker) and *that* (remote—relatively distant from the speaker). It is one of the simplest systems found. At the other extreme are languages like Eskimo, which has thirty demonstrative forms. In all languages, however, the demonstrative system treats the speaker as a point of reference. Thus the speaker is a basic point of reference for spatial deixis.

Many spatial-deixis systems have three terms. Three-term systems fall into two categories. In one type, the meanings of the terms are 'near the speaker,' 'a little distant from the speaker,' and 'far from the speaker.' The Spanish demonstratives *este, ese, aquel* have these three respective meanings. In another type of three-term demonstrative system, the terms have the meanings 'near the speaker,' 'near the hearer,' and 'away from both speaker and hearer.' Fijian exemplifies such a system.

na	ŋone	oⁿgo
the	child	this (near me)

'this child (near me)'

na	ŋone	oⁿgori
the	child	this (near you)

'that child (near you)'

na	ŋone	oya
the	child	that (away from you and me)

'that child (away from you and me)'

In both systems, however, the speaker is taken as either the sole point of reference or as one of two points of reference.

Spatial deixis thus represents the orientation of actions and states in space, and it is most commonly conveyed by demonstratives and by adverbs of place. Languages may have anywhere from two to thirty distinct demonstrative forms, but all demonstrative systems take the speaker as a basic point of reference.

Temporal Deixis   A third type of deixis is *temporal deixis*—the orientation or position of the referent of actions and events in time. All languages have words and phrases that are inherently marked for temporal deixis, like the English terms *before, last year, tomorrow, now,* and *this evening.* In many languages (but not all), temporal deixis can be marked through tense, encoded on the verb with affixes, or expressed in an independent morpheme. In English, you must make an obligatory choice between the past-tense and the nonpast-tense form of verbs.

I walk to school every day. (nonpast tense)
I walked to school every day. (past tense)

To express a future *time,* English has no distinct verbal inflection (it lacks a future *tense*) but uses a multi-word verb in the nonpast tense.

I will walk to school next week. (nonpast tense for future time)

Tuvaluan is like English: *e* denotes nonpast, while *ne* is a past-tense marker.

au	e	fano	ki	te	fakaala
I	Nonpast	go	to	the	feast

'I am going/will go to the feast.'

au	ne	fano	ki	te	fakaala
I	Past	go	to	the	feast

'I went to the feast.'

In some languages, the choice is between future and nonfuture (with undifferentiated present and past).

In a number of languages, temporal deixis can be marked only with optional adverbs. This Chinese sentence can be interpreted as past, present, or future, depending on the context:

> xià yǔ
> down rain
> 'It was/is/will be raining.'

When there is the possibility of ambiguity, an adverb of time ('last night,' 'right now,' 'next week') is added to the sentence.

In languages that do not mark tense on verbs, another semantic category called **aspect** is frequently obligatory. Aspect is not directly related to temporal deixis but refers to the ways in which actions and states are viewed: as continuous (*I was talking*), repetitive (*I talked (every day)*), instantaneous (*I talked*), and so on.

Tense is thus not the only marker of temporal deixis, although it is very frequently exploited by languages as the primary means of marking temporal deixis.

The most basic point of reference for tense is the moment at which the sentence is uttered. Any event that occurs before that moment may be marked as past, and any event that occurs after that moment may be marked as future.

> The train arrived. (any time before the utterance moment)
> The train is arriving. (at the moment of utterance)
> The train will arrive. (any time after the utterance moment)

When the point of reference is some point in time other than the moment of utterance, we say that tense is *relative*. Relative tense is used in many languages when speakers wish to compare the time of occurrence of two different events.

> After I had bought two, they gave me another one.
> Before I saw you yesterday, I had been sick for a week.

Languages sometimes have complex rules of *tense concord* that dictate the form of verbs in relative contexts.

Deixis as a Semantic Notion   The three types of deixis illustrate how semantic categories permeate language beyond the simple meaning of words. The deictic orientation of a sentence or part of a sentence can be conveyed through bound morphemes such as tense endings, through free morphemes and function words such as pronouns and demonstratives, or through content words such as *here* and *bring*. Deictic meaning is independent of the means used to convey it.

One of the purposes of semantics is to describe which parameters are important or essential to characterize deixis (as well as other semantic categories) in language in general. We noted, for example, that distinguishing between the speaker and the addressee is an essential function of the personal deixis system of all languages. Similarly, we found that every spatial deixis system has at least one point of reference, a location near the speaker. A spatial deixis system may also have a secondary point of reference near the hearer.

There is considerable overlap between the different types of deixis. For example, personal, spatial, and temporal deixis all share a basic point of reference: the speaker's identity and location in space and time. Many linguistic devices can also be used to mark more than one kind of deixis. The English demonstrative *this* can be used for personal deixis (*this person*), spatial deixis (*this thing*), and temporal deixis (*this morning*). Clearly, personal, spatial, and temporal deixis are closely related notions.

There is one type of deixis that we have not yet discussed. *Textual deixis* is the orientation of utterances with respect to other utterances in the string of utterances in which it occurs. Consider for example the following pair of sentences:

He started to swear at me and curse. *This* made me very angry.

The demonstrative *this* at the beginning of the second sentence refers not to a direction in space or time but rather to something previously mentioned. It marks textual deixis. Textual deixis is thus a tool that enables language users to package utterances together and indicate relationships across utterances. Because textual deixis is primarily concerned with utterances and their context, it goes beyond the scope of semantics as traditionally defined, although its importance is not to be underestimated.

SEMANTIC ROLES AND SENTENCE MEANING

We have noted that, like words, sentences must carry meaning for language speakers to understand each other at all, but that the meaning of sentences cannot be determined merely by adding up the meaning of each content word of the sentence. This fact was illustrated in the last section, where you saw that bound morphemes and function words may also carry meaning that has implication for the meaning of the entire sentence. We also noted that sentences like *The hunter bit the lion* and *The lion bit the hunter* have very different meanings, even though they contain exactly the same words. Clearly, adding together the meaning of each word will not produce the full meaning of a sentence. Such a process will not even distinguish between the two simple illustrative sentences in this paragraph. In defining what the meaning of a sentence consists of, more than just the meaning of the individual content words must be taken into consideration.

Consider the following active/passive counterparts, which, at the level of referential meaning, describe the same situation:

1. The hunter bit the lion.
2. The lion was bitten by the hunter.

These sentences differ in that 2 is a passive structure, whereas 1 is not. Since our concern here is with meaning, we ask how to account for the synonymy between 1 and 2.

Furthermore, consider the following sentences:

3. Seymour sliced the salami with a knife.
4. Seymour used a knife to slice the salami.

Here is a situation not unlike the active/passive counterparts of 1 and 2, in that the sentences have the same referential meaning. But 3 and 4 have different deep structures. Nevertheless, we need to describe how sentences 3 and 4 mean "the same thing."

The situations just presented suggest that the crucial factor in the way sentence meaning is constructed is the *role* played by each noun phrase in relation to the verb. We thus need to introduce the notion **semantic role** of a noun phrase—semantic role refers to the way in which the referent of the noun phrase contributes to the state, action, or situation described by the sentence. The semantic role of a noun phrase differs from its syntactic role (as subject, object, and so on), as illustrated by the contrast between sentences 1 and 2. In both 1 and 2, the way in which the lion is involved in the action is the same; and the way in which the hunter is involved is the same. By contrast, despite its having the same semantic role in both, *the lion* is the direct object of the verb in 1 and the grammatical subject of 2.

Semantic role is not an inherent property of a noun phrase: a given noun phrase can have different semantic roles in different sentences, as in the following:

Harold was injured by <u>a friend.</u>
Harold was injured with <u>a friend.</u>

Rather, semantic role is a way of characterizing the meaning relationship between a noun phrase and the verb of a sentence.

The first semantic roles we need to identify are *agent* (the responsible initiator of an action) and *patient* (the entity that undergoes a certain change of state). In both sentence 1 and sentence 2, above, the agent is *the hunter,* and the patient is *the lion.* That the sentences describe the same situation (and hence have the same referential meaning) can thus be explained by the fact that in both sentences each noun phrase has the same semantic role.

The role of the subject noun phrases in the following sentences is not that of agent, because Lou is not really the responsible initiator of the actions denoted by the verbs:

<u>Lou</u> likes blueberry pancakes.
<u>Lou</u> felt threatened by the lion.

In both sentences, Lou is experiencing a physical or mental sensation. The semantic role of *Lou* is *experiencer,* defined as that which receives a sensory input. In English, experiencers can be either subjects or direct objects, depending on the verb. Compare the sentences about Lou, in which the experiencer is the subject, with the following sentence, in which the experiencer is the direct object:

> Harold sometimes astounds <u>me</u> with his wit.

So far, we have identified the semantic roles of agent, patient, and experiencer. Now consider the semantic roles of the underscored noun phrases in the following sentences:

5. Harold was injured by <u>a stone</u>.
6. Harold was injured with <u>a stone.</u>

The difference between the sentences is that 6 can imply that someone used a stone to attack Harold, while 5 does not require that implication. In sentence 6, we say that *a stone* is the *instrument*—the intermediary through which an agent performs the action; note that the definition requires that there be an agent, which is consistent with our interpretation of sentence 6. In sentence 5, *a stone* could be assigned the role of instrument only if there was an agent doing the injuring. If the stone that injured Harold were part of a rockfall, *a stone* would be assigned the semantic role of *cause*—defined as any natural force that brings about a change of state. Instruments and causes can be expressed as prepositional phrases (as in the previous examples) or subjects.

> <u>The silver key</u> opens the door to the wine cellar. (instrument)
> <u>The snow</u> caved in the roof. (cause)

That the noun phrase *the silver key* is indeed an instrument and not an agent is supported by the fact that it cannot be conjoined (linked by *and*) with an agent, as the following anomalous example shows:

> *The silver key and John open the door to the cellar.

However, an instrument *can* be conjoined with another instrument, and an agent with another agent.

> <u>A push</u> and <u>a shove</u> opened the door to the cellar.
> <u>Harold</u> and <u>Hilda</u> opened the door to the cellar.

In addition to agent, patient, experiencer, instrument, and cause, a noun phrase can be a *recipient* (that which receives a physical object), a *benefactive* (that for which an action is performed), a *locative* (the location of an action or state), or a *temporal* (the time at which the action or state occurred).

> I gave <u>Hilda</u> a puppy. (recipient)
> Harold passed the message to me for <u>Hilda</u>. (benefactive)

> The Midwest is cold in winter. (locative)
> She left home the day before yesterday. (temporal)

The point of this enterprise is to characterize all possible semantic roles that noun phrases can fill in a sentence. Every noun phrase in a clause is assigned a semantic role, and, aside from coordinate NPs, the same semantic role cannot be assigned to two different noun phrases within the same clause. So, for example, a sentence like the following is ruled out as being semantically anomalous because it contains two different instrumental noun phrases, namely the two underlined noun phrases:

> *This ball broke the window with a hammer.

In addition, in most cases a single noun phrase can be assigned only one semantic role. In rare instances, a noun phrase can be assigned two different roles; in the sentence *Harold rolled down the hill,* if Harold rolled down the hill deliberately, he is both agent and patient, because he is at once the responsible initiator of the action and the entity that undergoes the change of state.

SEMANTIC ROLES AND GRAMMATICAL RELATIONS

It is important to understand the relationship between semantic roles and grammatical relations. We noted earlier that the two notions are different. In English, for example, the subject of a sentence can be an agent (as in the underlined noun phrase in sentence 1), a patient (2), an instrument (3), a cause (4), an experiencer (5), a benefactive (or recipient) (6), a locative (7), or a temporal (8), depending on the verb.

1. The janitor opened the door.
2. The door opened easily.
3. His first record greatly expanded his audience.
4. Bad weather ruined the corn crop.
5. Serge heard his father whispering.
6. The young artist won the prize.
7. Arizona attracts asthmatics.
8. The next day found us on the road to Alice Springs.

Furthermore, in certain English constructions the subject does not have any semantic role; such is the case of the so-called "dummy *it*" construction, in which the pronoun *it* fills a semantically empty subject slot.

> It became clear that the government had jailed him there.

So the notion of subject is independent of the notion of semantic role; and we could show the same thing for direct objects and other grammatical relations. Conversely, semantic roles do not appear to be constrained by grammatical relations. A locative, for example, may be expressed as a subject (as in sentence 1), a direct object (2), an indirect object (3), or an oblique (4).

1. <u>The garden</u> will look great in the spring.
2. Harold planted <u>the garden</u> with cucumbers and tomatoes.
3. The begonias give <u>the garden</u> a cheerful look.
4. The gate opens on <u>the garden</u>.

Nevertheless, there is a relationship between grammatical relations and semantic roles. Consider the following sentences, all of which have *open* as a verb:

> Harold opened the door with this key.
> The door opens easily.
> This key will open the door.
> The wind opened the door.

The grammatical subjects of the sentences above are an agent (*Harold*), a patient (*the door*), an instrument (*this key*), and a cause (*the wind*). Such extreme variety is not found with all verbs. The verb *soothe* can take an instrument or a cause as subject.

> This ointment will soothe your sunburn.
> The cold stream soothed my sore feet.

To have an experiencer as the grammatical subject of the verb *soothe,* we use a passive construction.

> I was soothed by the herbal tea.

Clearly, the verb controls the range of variation allowed in each case. Language users know the semantic roles that each verb allows as subject, direct object, and so on. In the lexicon, attached to the verb *soothe* is a tag indicating that only instruments and causes are allowed in subject position, whereas the tag attached to the verb *open* permits the subject to be agent, patient, instrument, or cause.

Semantic roles are universal features of the semantic structure of all languages, but how they interact with grammatical relations like subject and direct object differs from language to language. Equivalent verbs in different languages do not carry similar tags. The tag attached to the English verb *like,* for example, permits only experiencers as subjects.

> I like French fries.

But only patients can be the subjects of the equivalent Spanish verb *gustar.*

Las papas fritas me gustan.
the French-fries to-me like
'I like French fries.' (Literally, 'French fries to me are pleasing.')

A similar situation is found for verbs of liking and pleasing in many other languages, including Russian. In some languages, the verb 'understand' allows its subjects to be experiencers or patients, as in Samoan. The choice depends on emphasis and focus.

ʔua   maalamalama aʔu   i   le mataaʔupu.
Present-tense understand   I   Object-marker the lesson
'I understand the lesson.'

ʔua   maalamalama le mataaʔupu iate aʔu.
Present-tense understand   the lesson   to me
'I understand the lesson.' (Literally: 'The lesson understands to me.')

Some languages distinguish between agent and experiencer much more carefully than English does. For example, the verb might take a subject when the action described is intentional but take a direct object when the action is unintentional.

In addition to cross-linguistic variation with respect to specific verbs, languages vary in the degree to which different semantic roles can fit into different grammatical slots in a sentence. In English, the subject slot can be occupied by noun phrases of any semantic role—depending, of course, on the verb. Many English verbs allow different semantic roles for subject, direct object, and so on. But the situation is different in many other languages. In languages such as Russian and German, verbs do not allow nearly as much variation in semantic roles as English verbs do, and there is a much tighter bond between semantic roles and grammatical relations.

COMPUTERS, CORPORA, AND SEMANTICS

Computerized corpora are useful to dictionary makers and others in establishing patterns of language that are not apparent with mere introspection. Patterns of collocations—which words go together, for example—are much more readily understood with the help of a computerized corpus of natural-language texts. Such patterns can be very helpful in highlighting meanings, including parts of speech, and patterns of words that co-occur with some frequency.

Further, while it may appear that synonymous words can be used in place of one another, corpora can show that it is not in fact common for words to be readily substitutable. For example, *little* and *small*, *big* and *large*, and *fast* and *quick* are generally considered synonyms. But as a cursory examination of KWIC (key word in context) concordances for these pairs would show, they are not straightforwardly substitutable for one another. Table 6-1 shows a selection of KWIC entries for the word *little,* and Table 6-2 shows a selection of KWIC entries for *small.* (The samples are taken from the British National Corpus and have been concordanced with WordSmith.)

Note in Table 6-1 that quite a few of the sentences would not tolerate the substitution of *small* for *little*—for example, 2, 3, 5, 6, 9, 10, 11, 15, 16, 17, 26. Taking 3 as an example, English does not permit "not a small irritated." Of those instances where the substitution is possible, several would sound very odd or convey a different connotation—for example, 1, 4, 8. In 1, "poor little rich boy" and "poor small rich boy" carry different connotations. As the examples in Table 6-2 show, *little* is more readily substitutable for *small,* and part of the reason for that is that in its use as

an adjective *little* does in fact carry denotations and connotations much like those of most uses of *small.* But, looking back to Table 6-1, we see that the opposite is not true, and the reason is that *little* is not only an adjective meaning 'small' but also part of an adverb, as in the expressions *a little ruffled, a little dispirited,* and *a little open* (13, 20, 24), where it modifies an adjective, and *a little longer* (12), where it modifies an adverb. Yet most dictionaries will cite *little* and *small* as synonyms of one another.

At the end of this chapter you will find the address for getting a sample of sentences containing any word or expression that you are interested in examining. From such a list you can learn a great deal about the semantics of any word or phrase.

Table 6-1

LITTLE

1 n central activities like council activities and so on. The poor **little** rich boy was looked after by a second mother in the person of strict Ilse, from German

2 to be happy with a few hours of stall avoidance training and **little**, if any, spinning. Vienna Dear Fröulein Arandt, I am deeply distressed, and also not a

3 Dear Fröulein Arandt, I am deeply distressed, and also not a **little** irritated, by the direction events have taken in our correspondence. Even without the t

4 r correspondence. Even without the threat to his job, he had **little** choice. There may be little or no hope of finding those particular items, but there are n

5 thout the threat to his job, he had little choice. There may be **little** or no hope of finding those particular items, but there are many others to be collected,

6 others to be collected, some as yet unrecorded. But he had **little** reason yet to ask for a search warrant and Mr Simpson would go purple in the face an

7 onsiderable library at him if he so much as tried. But there is **little** point, for instance, in turning on an artistic, enlightened medieval king because he also

8 od on his own face and those of his friends. You noticed my **little** ploy. Current findings suggest a complex picture, where opportunity has increased, bu

9 ve chances of success between classes have changed very **little**. Objectively, he was little more attractive to the Conservatives who were hostile to Ma

10 tween classes have changed very little. Objectively, he was **little** more attractive to the Conservatives who were hostile to MacDonaldite mush than was

11 came to understand that it was necessary for him to retire a **little** from the active life in which he had previously been engaged; he told William Turner L

12 entrate his time and energy upon his real work. We talked a **little** longer, and then I bought some chocolate from her, said goodbye and went out of the

13 louse. The softness was still there, but the fur was maybe a **little** ruffled. I wish all men enjoyed their whole bodies, rather than just a little, wobbly bit of

14 I wish all men enjoyed their whole bodies, rather than just a **little**, wobbly bit of it.' There is a need, however, to look a little more at the role of Parliamen

15 t a little, wobbly bit of it.' There is a need, however, to look a **little** more at the role of Parliament. ON A SLOW pitch with little bounce, South Africa once

16 little more at the role of Parliament. ON A SLOW pitch with **little** bounce, South Africa once again were unable to set the home side a testing target, an

17 with seven wickets and seven overs to spare. Addition of a **little** silicone lubricant (vacuum grease, DOW Corning Corp., Midland, MI) to the phenol-ch

18 : phases. He was fair and quite softly-spoken and actually a **little** shy-looking, and he'd made a point of taking off his uniform cap when he talked to her

19 t and glancing, his ugly body quiet and still above them as a **little** gravestone. Once the carriage was in motion, she closed her eyes, tired now and a litt

20 arriage was in motion, she closed her eyes, tired now and a **little** dispirited. Then the front zip of her jeans yielded to his importuning hands and he ease

21 eans yielded to his importuning hands and he eased away a **little** so that his fingers could slide inside, seeking, exploring, sensitising, until shudders she

22 is increased Aboriginal access to land, an issue upon which **little** progress had been made -- with the possible exception of the sparsely populated Nort

23 t to the OECD survey, the privatization programme involved **little** change in management or improvement in efficiency. Might leave us a little open som

24 management or improvement in efficiency. Might leave us a **little** open sometimes, but with the pace we should cope, and also we are gonna score a fe

25 we are gonna score a few goals!! we reckoned we knew a **little** bit more about what makes children tick. in fact I think the lounge and the dining room

26 I think the lounge and the dining room area was probably a **little** bit smaller If you want to be happy and have a happy face and spread a little joy arour

27 you want to be happy and have a happy face and spread a **little** joy around then there is just one way.

Table 6-2

SMALL

1 ʾeaders of a myriad of papers with individual readerships too **small** for us to analyse (the Scotsman , the Glasgow Herald , and regional English papers,
2 ᵓle). Maggie burst into tears at the sight of the house and the **small** familiar crowd waiting for her outside the wooden gate of the garden. James McCloy,
3 ʾ garden. James McCloy, who lives here in town, runs a very **small** unsuccessful sort of decorating business.' Another version of the ritual dance at the f
4 ʾr version of the ritual dance at the fall of a wicket. her Milton **Small** and friends celebrate Gower's exit at Lord's in 1984. The continued unbroken trust in
5 nbroken trust in the Führer down to spring 1941 rested in no **small** measure on the lack of serious interference of the war in the conditions of ʿeveryday
6 ce of the war in the conditions of ʿeveryday life'. The Market: **Small** rise follows volatile session His clothes were too small now, pinching him at the neck
7 ırket: Small rise follows volatile session His clothes were too **small** now, pinching him at the neck, the waist and the crotch, stretched tight over the shou
8 ᵓulders, the chest and his muscled limbs. Most molluscs are **small,** a few centimetres long and some are really tiny, but a few species have attained cor
9 ʾen the samples (although of course the numbers are far too **small** for any quantitative analysis) can be summarised as follows: Still under heavy fire fro
10 vy fire from artillery and mortars, and themselves down to a **small** amount of ammunition, the remnants of the 1 st Bucks stood fast until dark. The Cap
11 ᵓod fast until dark. The Captain's white face had greyed, his **small** mouth tightening into a cruel line. As a result, the individual may retain only a very sn
12 ı cruel line. As a result, the individual may retain only a very **small** percentage of the extra income earned and, in some cases, may actually lose more t
13 lose more than the extra income earned. How could such a **small** volume produce such a colossal amount of energy? Just two of the ways in which Nc
14 nced telecommunications products are helping both big and **small** businesses in more than one hundred countries worldwide. For many years readers
15 BAILEY of Sussex longed for a pond in the garden, but with **small** children around the idea was shelved -- until now. Unions became registered, thereb
16 ᵓlishment and subsequent continuation of a large number of **small** unions and, as a secondary consequence, helped to impede amalgamation and unio
17 ıvities as possible, often near remote skerries, headlands or **small** uninhabited islands, and this necessitates the use of a boat in most cases. Also num
18 ınction with other, larger holdings, they were unavailable for **small** men, while there were not enough of the big farmers, who did occupy them, to emplo
19 ʾ, to employ more than a very limited number of servants. A **SMALL** point on your book review of Durham: Birth of a First-Class County : had Ralph De
20 lialects at the time of the Russian conquest, although only a **small** remnant of this nationality survives today. A legacy from a great-aunt had bought the
21 ı great-aunt had bought their house and provided her with a **small** income. perfect like a small velvet purse whose snout Small enough to swim under a
22 r house and provided her with a small income. perfect like a **small** velvet purse whose snout Small enough to swim under and around, large enough to :
23 small income. perfect like a small velvet purse whose snout **Small** enough to swim under and around, large enough to support a man, and big enough t
24 ʾach all of us a lesson. Right angles are often marked with a **small** step in the corner. The two Jowle brothers sat opposite Melanie and Victoria, like a m
25 ı, green tie, stabbed through, today, with a different tiepin, a **small** dagger. Also on the ground floor were a dining-room, a kitchen, a scullery, an office,
26 ᵓhen, a scullery, an office, a room for quiet meditation and a **small** library. The consequences for arbitrage risk were also generally small, and 88% of th
27 ry. The consequences for arbitrage risk were also generally **small,** and 88% of the cases fell within the range 0.1% to -0.1% (that is an extra profit or los
28 ᵓf about ú60 per contract). In doing so, she knocked down a **small** boy and immediately went down again to pull him to his feet. However, the final, as y
29 down again to pull him to his feet. However, the final, as yet, **small,** family of cell adhesion molecules bind to carbohydrates. If this can be kept in a place
30 place that is accessible to teachers, along with a monitor (a **small** black and white one would do), then it can be used for teacher viewing and for setting
31 ᵓ before a lesson. In the end they hauled the Gnomes into a **small** ante-room across the galleried landing from the Sun Chamber. Or try installing a leng
32 ı a length of the famous Shaker pegged wall-rail for hanging **small** cupboards, shelves, mirrors and even chairs. Already it had blackened on the collar ɔ
33 ıready it had blackened on the collar of his white coat and a **small** pool had separated and congealed on the Lab floor. A .22 makes only a small crack.
34 ᵓarated and congealed on the Lab floor. A .22 makes only a **small** crack. Uplands kept its wholesaling operation going for a few years after I left, but it c
35 eft, but it doesn't exist any more; I think the day of the really **small** wholesaler is gone.' The most marked contrast between the small towns and their lar
36 wholesaler is gone.' The most marked contrast between the **small** towns and their larger counterparts is the relative paucity of large public buildings, es
37 nected with amusement. Thirty years later what had been a **small** village was a big town and would have been bigger if it hadn't been for the ring of ste
38 ᵗeelworks hemming in the sprawl. With my responsibility for **small** firms, the House will not be surprised that I for one would robustly defend the exempt
39 ᵓbustly defend the exemption level and the fact that it helps **small** firms in the industry. A United States PGA official pointed out that golf crowds in Spa
40 ınted out that golf crowds in Spain and France were still too **small** to provide a meaningful income. Eve Dennis, of the Arthur Rank Centre's Church anc
41 ımpaign, believes that churchyards provide a focus and are **small** enough for a group of local enthusiasts to manage. The government confirmed on Aʃ
42 ᵖril 22 that it was pursuing a policy of devaluing the yuan in **small,** frequent steps, in an effort to boost exports and curb imports. What is global about ͱ
43 en there are so many factors specific for countries, even for **small** regions within a country and for groups of individuals? The Greek's friends at his preʾ
44 ᵖ at his previous table watched benignly; and the phalanx of **small** boys switched support. Bake at 170°C (325°F/Gas Mark 3), allowing 40 minutes for t
45 e at 170°C (325°F/Gas Mark 3), allowing 40 minutes for the **small** basins and 50 minutes for the large bowl. Between the Arch and the back of the Adm
46 ᵗween the Arch and the back of the Admiralty proper runs a **small** unnamed side-street which I must have passed a hundred times without really noticin
47 dred times without really noticing. The cosy living-room was **small** and cluttered. For example, a buyer might say ʿCompetitor X's product offers cheape
48 a salesperson might reply ʿYes, but these cost savings are **small** compared to the fuel savings you get with our machine.' Without any goodbyes he le
49 chine.' Without any goodbyes he left his house and took my **small** car to the station. It's just cos you haven't got the extra round the, round the side, but
50 ven't got the extra round the, round the side, but it just looks **small.** And of course Lewes is a small enough town that it's possible for ordinary people to
51 nd the side, but it just looks small. And of course Lewes is a **small** enough town that it's possible for ordinary people to be involved in, in central activitie

SUMMARY

- Semantics is the study of meaning in language.

- Semantics traditionally focuses on referential meaning, but languages also convey social meaning and affective meaning.

- Referential meaning is often called *denotation;* social and affective meanings are covered by the term *connotation.*

- Words, sentences, and utterances can all carry meaning, and sentence meaning and utterance meaning must be distinguished.

- The study of sentence meaning falls primarily within the scope of semantics.

- Pragmatics is the branch of linguistics that concerns itself with utterance meaning.

- Lexical semantics is the study of meaning relationships in the lexicon. The types of relationships that hold among sets of words are universal, though the particular word sets to which they apply vary from language to language.

- Lexical fields are sets of words whose referents belong together on the basis of fundamental semantic characteristics.

- The words in a lexical field can be arranged in terms of these relationships: hyponymy (a kind of), part/whole (subdivision), synonymy (similar meaning), gradable and nongradable antonymy (opposite meaning), converseness (reciprocal meaning), polysemy (multiple meanings), homonymy (same written or spoken form), and metaphorical extension (derived meaning).

- Semantic notions like deixis can be expressed by bound morphemes and function words as well as by content words.

- There are several types of deixis: personal, spatial, and temporal. All require that a point of reference be identified.

- In relation to the speaker and the moment of utterance, the here and now is highly privileged as a point of reference in all three types of deixis.

- The meaning of a sentence is not simply the sum meaning of its words.

- Sentence semantics aims to uncover the basic relationships between the noun phrases and the verb of a sentence.

- Semantic roles are not inherent properties of noun phrases but are relational notions. They are independent of the grammatical relations of the noun phrase. The verb determines which semantic role may be used in particular grammatical slots of the sentence.

- This chapter has described these semantic roles: agent, patient, experiencer, instrument, cause, benefactive (or recipient), locative, and temporal.

- While semantic roles are universal, languages differ as to how particular roles are encoded in syntax.

EXERCISES

Based on English

6-1. In the first section of the chapter we introduced the terms *synonymy, implication, contradiction, anomaly, ambiguity,* and *vagueness* to describe various sentences and sentence pairs. Determine which of these notions applies to each of the following sentences and sentence pairs:

(1) Harry's cat called me on the phone.
(2) Visiting relatives can be boring.

(3) His daughter is her brother's grandmother.

(4) My husband just returned from the store. I am a married woman.

(5) I don't like locking my car. My car's doors can be locked.

(6) The basil I will plant next weekend is growing well.

(7) She swims.

(8) I was fatally ill last year.

(9) It is still too warm to start a fire. It is not cold enough to start a fire.

(10) The wine I didn't drink tasted sour to me.

(11) My dog wants out. The canine creature that belongs to me is experiencing a desire to proceed outdoors.

(12) Pat kissed Chris, and Lou too.

6-2. The following sentences are ambiguous. Based on the discussion in this chapter and Chapter 5, describe the ambiguity.

(1) They found the peasants revolting.

(2) The car I'm getting ready to drive is a Lamborghini.

(3) There is nothing more alarming than developing nuclear power plants.

(4) Hilda does not like her husband, and neither does Gertrude.

(5) They said that they told her to come to them.

(6) Challenging wrestlers will be avoided at all costs.

(7) He met his challenger at his house.

6-3. Identify the differences in referential, social, and affective meaning among the words and phrases in each of the following sets:

(1) hoax, trickery, swindle, rip-off, ruse, stratagem

(2) delightful, pleasant, great, far-out, nice, pleasurable, bad, cool

(3) man, guy, dude, jock, imp, lad, gentleman, hunk, boy

(4) eat, wolf down, nourish oneself, devour, peck, ingest, chow down, graze, fill one's tummy

(5) tired, fatigued, pooped, weary, languorous, zonked out, exhausted, fordone, spent

(6) stupid person, idiot, nerd, ass, jerk, turkey, wimp, punk, airhead, bastard

6-4. Some of the sets of terms below form lexical fields. For each set:

a. Identify the words that do *not* belong to the same lexical field as the others in the set.

b. Identify the superordinate term of the remaining lexical field, if there is one (it may be a word in the set).

c. Determine whether some terms are less marked than others, and justify your claim.

(1) acquire, buy, collect, hoard, win, inherit, steal

(2) whisper, talk, narrate, report, tell, harangue, scribble, instruct, brief

(3) road, path, barn, way, street, freeway, avenue, thoroughfare, interstate, method

(4) stench, smell, reek, aroma, bouquet, odoriferous, perfume, fragrance, scent, olfactory

6-5. For the semantic relationships specified below, provide one or more examples of words whose referents have that relationship to the specified word, and identify the name of the semantic category that is used to cover your answer.

> *Example*: *fish* is the superordinate term (hypernym)
> Answer: *salmon, trout, ling cod, flounder, swordfish, tuna* are its hyponyms

(1) *Irish Setter, Dalmatian, Cocker Spaniel* are the hyponyms *DOG*
(2) *tabby, tom, Persian, alley* are the hyponyms *CAT*
(3) *dog, cat, goldfish, parakeet, hamster* are the hyponyms *PETS*
(4) *knife, fork, spoon* are the hyponyms *SILVERWARE*
(5) *true* is the antonym *FALSE*
(6) *inaccurate* is the antonym *ACCURATE*
(7) *sister* is the converse *BROTHER*
(8) *teacher* is the converse *STUDENT*
(9) *partner* is the converse *STRANGER - PARTNER*
(10) *toe* is the part *FOOT*
(11) *menu* is the whole *ITEM FOOD*
(12) *friend* is the synonym *BUDDY*
(13) *teacher* is the synonym *INSTRUCTOR*

6-6. Consider the following two sequences of dictionary entries, taken (slightly abbreviated) from *The American Heritage Dictionary of the English Language*, 3rd ed. (Boston: Houghton Mifflin, 1992):

Sequence 1

husk·y[1] adj. **-i·er, -i·est. 1.** Hoarse or rough in quality: *a voice husky with emotion.* **2.a.** Resembling a husk. **b.** Containing husks. [From HUSK]—**husk′i·ly** adv.
hus·ky[2] adj. **-i·er, -i·est. 1.** Strongly built; burly. **2.** Heavily built: *clothing sizes for husky boys.* —**husky** n., pl. **-ies.** A husky person. [Perhaps from HUSK]
hus·ky[3] n., pl. **-kies 1.** Often **Husky** or **Huskie**. A dog of a breed developed in Siberia for pulling sleds and having a dense, variously colored coat. Also called *Siberian husky.* **2.** A similar dog of Arctic origin. [Probably from shortening and alteration of ESKIMO.]

Sequence 2

jun·ior adj. **1.** Abbr. **jr., Jr., Jun., jun., jnr.** Used to distinguish a son from his father when they have the same given name. **2.** Intended for or including youthful persons: *junior fashions; a junior sports league.* **3.** Lower in rank or shorter in length of tenure: *a junior officer; the junior senator from Texas.* **4.** Of, for, or constituting students in the third year of a U.S. high school or college: *the junior class; the junior prom.* **5.** Lesser in scale than the usual. **-junior** n. Abbr. **jr., Jr., Jun., jun., jnr. 1.** A person who is younger than another: *a sister four years my junior.* **2.** A person lesser in rank or time of participation or service;

subordinate. **3.** A student in the third year of a U.S. high school or college. **4.** A class of clothing sizes for girls and slender women. In this sense, also called *junior miss.*

Using the terms introduced in our discussion of lexical semantics, describe in detail how these dictionary entries are organized. Include a discussion of the criteria that are used to create different entries or subentries for homonymous words.

6-7. In the following sets of sentences one or more words are used metaphorically. Provide a general statement describing the principle that underlies these sets of metaphors; then add to the set one metaphor that follows the principle.

Example:

I let my manuscript *simmer* for six months.
She *concocted* a retort that readers will appreciate.
There is no easy *recipe* for writing effective business letters.
General statement: "The writing process is viewed as cooking." Additional example: "He is the kind of writer that *whips up* another trashy novel every six months."
(1) Members of the audience besieged him with counterarguments.
   His opponents tore his arguments to pieces.
   My reasoning left them with no ammunition.
   The others will never be able to destroy this argument.
   His question betrayed a defensive stance.
(2) This heat is crushing.
   The sun is beating down on these poor laborers.
   The clouds seem to be lifting.
   The northern part of the state is under a heavy snowstorm.
   The fresh breeze cleared up the oppressive heat.
(3) She has an eye for handsome men.
   He has a palate for good Indian curry.
   My neighbor has an ear for gossip.
   I used to have an eye for good etchings.
   The French have a nose for cheese.
6-8. Determine whether the words in each of the following sets are polysemic, homonymous, or metaphorically related. In each case, state the criteria used to arrive at your conclusion. You may use a dictionary.

   (1) to run down (the stairs); to run down (an enemy); to run down (a list of names)
   (2) the seat (of one's pants); the seat (of government); the (driver's) seat (of a car)
   (3) an ear (for music); an ear (of corn); an ear (as auditory organ)
   (4) to pitch (a baseball); pitch (black); the pitch (of one's voice)
   (5) to spell (a word); (under) a spell; a (dry) spell

polysemic

(6) vision (the ability to see); (a man of) vision; vision (during a hallucination)

(7) the butt (of a rifle); the butt (of a joke); to butt (as a ram)

6-9. Identify the semantic role of each noun phrase in these sentences:

(1) In October, I gazed from the wooden bridge into the small river behind our college.

(2) I have forgotten everything that I learned in grade school.

(3) The Grand Tetons tower majestically over the valley.

(4) The snow completely buried my car during the last storm.

(5) Fifty kilos of cocaine were seized by the DEA.

(6) Lou was awarded one thousand dollars' worth of travel.

(7) The hurricane destroyed the island.

(8) Their ingenuity never ceases to amaze me.

6-10. a. Examine Table 6-1 to determine which words frequently co-occur with *little,* either preceding or following it.

b. List and name all the immediate constituents of which *little* is an element in the examples of Table 6-1. *Example* #12: a little longer—adverb phrase; #20: a little dispirited—adjective phrase

Based on English and Other Languages

6-11. A "tag" is attached to every verb in the lexicon indicating which semantic role can be assigned to each noun argument. The verb *bake,* for example, can have as its subject an agent as in sentence (1), a patient (2), a cause (3), or an instrument (4). But in subject position it does not allow locatives (5) or temporals (6).

(1) Harold baked scones.

(2) The cake is baking.

(3) The sun baked my lilies to a crisp.

(4) This oven bakes wonderful cakes.

(5) *The kitchen bakes nicely.

(6) *Tomorrow will bake nicely.

a. Determine which semantic roles these verbs allow as subject on the basis of the sentences provided: *feel, provide, absorb, thaw, taste.*

(1) His hands felt limp and moist.
I could feel the presence of an intruder in the apartment.
This room feels damp.
They all felt under the blanket to see what was there.
This semester feels very different from last semester.

(2) Gas lamps provided light for the outdoor picnic.
These fields provide enough wheat to feed a city.
Who provided these scones?
The Middle Ages provided few famous mathematicians.

The accident provided me plenty to worry about.

Your textbooks provide many illustrations of this phenomenon.

The bylaws provide for dissolution of the board in these cases.

(3) The students have absorbed so much material that they can't make sense of it anymore.

This kind of sponge does not absorb water well.

The United States absorbed the Texas Republic in 1845.

My work hours are absorbing all my free time.

The soil is absorbing the rain.

(4) If Antarctica suddenly thawed, the sea level would rise dramatically.

Chicken does not thaw well in just two hours.

The crowd thawed after Kent arrived.

Kent's arrival thawed the party.

The heat of the sun will thaw the ice in the ice chest.

Ice thaws at 0 degrees Celsius.

The peace treaty will thaw relations between the United States and China.

(5) This wine tastes like vinegar.

He's tasted every single hors d'oeuvre at the party.

I can taste the capers in the sauce.

b. Languages may differ with respect to the semantic roles that particular verbs may take. The following are semantically well-formed French sentences with the verb *goûter* 'taste':

> Il n'a   jamais goûté au caviar.
> he not-have ever   tasted the caviar
> 'He's never tasted caviar.'

> Je goûte un goût amer dans ce   café.
> I taste   a   taste bitter in   this coffee
> 'I taste a bitter taste in this coffee.'

By contrast, the following sentence is not well constructed:

> *Les cuisses de grenouille goûtent bon.
> the   thighs of frog   taste   good
> 'Frog's legs taste good.'

What is the difference between English *taste* and French *goûter* in terms of the range of semantic roles that they permit as subject?

INTERNET RESOURCES

- **British National Corpus: http://thetis.bl.uk/lookup.html**
  Here you can obtain up to fifty example sentences, chosen at random from the 100 million word resources of the British National Corpus. You may want to go

to the general information page for the BNC at http://info.ox.ac.uk:80/bnc/ and from there pursue the link to the sample search.

- **Roget's Internet Thesaurus:**
  http://www.thesaurus.com/
  At this Web site you will find access to an on-line thesaurus. With it you can explore the relationships among words, especially those in hyponymic relationships.

SUGGESTIONS FOR FURTHER READING

- **Stephen R. Anderson and Edward L. Keenan. 1985. "Deixis," in Timothy Shopen, ed.,** *Language Typology and Syntactic Description,* **vol. 3** (Cambridge: Cambridge UP), pp. 259–308. A relatively brief and comprehensive treatment of deixis.

- **Sandra Chung and Alan Timberlake. 1985. "Tense, Aspect, and Mood," in Timothy Shopen, ed.,** *Language Typology and Syntactic Description,* **vol. 3** (Cambridge: Cambridge UP), pp. 202–258. Provides a concise discussion of tense and related notions.

- **George A. Miller. 1996.** *The Science of Words* (Indianapolis: W. H. Freeman). An accessible and award-winning treatment of the psychology of lexical meaning.

Advanced Reading

The major reference work for semantics is Lyons (1977), which provides a wealth of information and critical discussion. Easier are Lyons (1996) and Leech (1981). Palmer (1981) provides a concise overview of the field. Lexical semantics is discussed in Lehrer (1974), which focuses on semantic universals (discussed in Chapter 7 of *LISU*), and in Wierzbicka (1985), in which the main concern is the meaning of the notion 'kind of.' Cruse (1986) is a good overview of lexical semantics. Hurford and Heasley (1983) is a good coursebook. Several of the papers in Holland and Quinn (1987) investigate connotation and the cultural elements in the organization of semantic fields. A basic work on metaphors is Lakoff and Johnson (1980); ideas presented in that earlier work are developed further in Lakoff (1987). Deixis is discussed in detail in Chapter 2 of Levinson (1983). A thorough discussion of mood and modality can be found in Palmer (1986). For a textbook on the areas of semantics not covered in this chapter, see Kempson (1977). The example of semantic overgeneralization in child language quoted in this chapter is from Clark (1975). Newer approaches to lexicography based on analyses of corpora are discussed in Sinclair (1991).

REFERENCES

- Clark, Eve V. 1975. "Knowledge, Context, and Strategy in the Acquisition of Meaning," in D. P. Dato, ed., *Georgetown University Roundtable in Language and Linguistics 1975* (Washington, DC: Georgetown UP), pp. 77–98.

- Cruse, D. A. 1986. *Lexical Semantics* (Cambridge: Cambridge UP).

- Holland, Dorothy, and Naomi Quinn, eds. 1987. *Cultural Models in Language and Thought* (Cambridge: Cambridge UP).

- Hurford, James R., and Brendan Heasley. 1983. *Semantics: A Coursebook* (Cambridge: Cambridge UP).

- Kempson, Ruth M. 1977. *Semantic Theory* (Cambridge: Cambridge UP).

- Lakoff, George. 1987. *Women, Fire, and Dangerous Things: What Categories Reveal about the Mind* (Chicago: U of Chicago P).

- Lakoff, George, and Mark Johnson. 1980. *Metaphors We Live By* (Chicago: U of Chicago P).

- Leech, Geoffrey. 1981. *Semantics: The Study of Meaning,* 2nd ed. (London: Penguin).

- Lehrer, Adrienne. 1974. *Semantic Fields and Lexical Structure* (Amsterdam: North-Holland).

- Levinson, Stephen C. 1983. *Pragmatics* (Cambridge: Cambridge UP).

- Lyons, John. 1977. *Semantics,* 2 vols. (Cambridge: Cambridge UP).

- Lyons, John. 1996. *Linguistic Semantics: An Introduction* (Cambridge: Cambridge UP).

- Palmer, F. R. 1981. *Semantics,* 2nd ed. (Cambridge: Cambridge UP).

- Palmer, F. R. 1986. *Mood and Modality* (Cambridge: Cambridge UP).

- Sinclair, John. 1991. *Corpus, Concordance, Collocation* (Oxford: Oxford UP).

- Wierzbicka, Anna. 1985. *Lexicography and Conceptual Analysis* (Ann Arbor, MI: Karoma).

CHAPTER 7

LANGUAGE UNIVERSALS
AND LANGUAGE TYPOLOGY

WHAT DO YOU THINK?

Your precocious third-grade daughter returns from school one day and informs you that she has learned that English has thirteen vowels. She inquires whether all languages have thirteen vowels. What do you tell her?

Several cousins are visiting you for a twenty-first birthday celebration, and you notice that a cousin from Texas says "y'all" when she addresses more than one person, while your cousin from New York City sometimes says "youse" in the same circumstances. You secretly wonder whether your own variety of English (which uses you *for both the singular and plural) might lack a useful distinction. In fact, you wonder whether it's typical for other languages to have equivalents of* y'all *and* youse *or to be like standard English. What do you conclude?*

A friend who is studying Japanese comments that Japanese word order differs from English word order and even puts its verbs at the end of the sentence instead of after the subject—"where they belong." He thinks that the English order of Subject-Verb-Object is more logical. You recall that an exchange student visiting from Japan and being tutored by you felt exactly the same—but the other way around. She thought that the English order was illogical compared to the Japanese order of Subject-Object-Verb. You claim that "Both orders are equally logical—or illogical!" What reasons can you give for your view?

SIMILARITY AND DIVERSITY ACROSS LANGUAGES

The various languages of the world are structured according to many different patterns at the level of phonology, morphology, syntax, and semantics. Some languages have very large inventories of phonemes; others have very few. In some languages, including English, French, and Italian, the basic structure of the clause is SVO: subject before verb and verb before direct object. Other languages, like Japanese and Persian, place both the subject and the direct object before the verb in an SOV pattern. You might legitimately wonder whether the world's languages have any characteristics in common.

As it happens, there are basic principles that govern the structure of *all* languages. These **language universals** determine what is possible and what is impossible in language structure. For example, while some languages have voiced and voiceless stops and others have only voiceless stops, no language has yet been encountered that has voiced stops but lacks voiceless stops. This observation can be translated into a rule expressing what is possible in the structure of a language (that is, a language can have both voiced and unvoiced stops or only voiceless stops in its phonemic inventory) and into a law that excludes a combination of phonemes that is not known to occur in any of the world's languages (that is, voiced stops without voiceless stops).

WHY UNCOVER UNIVERSALS?

The study of language universals is valuable for several reasons. First of all language universals are statements of what is possible and impossible in language. Viewed from a purely practical perspective, such principles are useful in that, if we can assume them to apply to all languages, they need not be repeated in the description of each language. Thus the study of language universals underscores the unity underlying the enormous variety of languages found in the world.

Language universals are also important to our understanding of the brain and of the principles that govern interpersonal communication in all cultures. In the course of evolution, the ability to speak is something that the human species alone has developed, thus distinguishing itself from all other animals, including other higher mammals. However, the human species has developed not a single language that is spoken and understood by everybody but about five thousand different languages, many of which are completely unrelated and each of which is as complex and sophisticated as all the others. If basic principles exist that govern all languages, they are likely to be the direct result of whatever cognitive and social skills enabled human beings to develop the ability to speak in the first place. By studying language universals and by trying to explain why they exist, we begin to understand what in the human brain and the social organization of everyday life enables people to communicate through language. The study of language universals offers a glimpse of the cognitive and social foundations of human language, about which so little is known.

When postulating language universals, researchers must exercise caution. First of all, universals are statements to the effect that some characteristics are found in all the world's languages while other characteristics are not found in any of them. When we make such statements, it is sobering to bear in mind that, of the thousands of languages spoken in the world, only relatively few have been adequately described. Furthermore, much more is known about European languages and the major non-Western languages (such as Chinese, Japanese, Hindi, and Arabic) than about the far more numerous other languages of Africa, Asia, the Americas, and Oceania. In Papua New Guinea alone, over seven hundred languages are spoken, although grammatical descriptions of only a few dozen are available; very little—and in some cases nothing at all—is known about the rest. Linguists proposing language universals must be cautious that the proposed principles are applicable to more than the familiar European languages. Language universals must be generally valid for the languages of the world, whether those languages are spoken by only a few dozen people in a small highlands village of Papua New Guinea or by millions of people in Europe, Africa, or Asia. Since little or nothing is known about the structure of hundreds of languages, universal principles can be proposed only as tentative hypotheses based on the languages for which descriptions are available. Fortunately, many linguists are now studying lesser-known languages. More often than not, first-time grammars confirm rather than disprove the language universals that have been proposed.

Caution must also be exercised in drawing inferences from language universals. As mentioned earlier, these universal principles help explain why language is species specific; but there is a big step between uncovering a language universal and explaining it in terms of the cognitive or social abilities that humans have developed through evolution. More often than not, explanations for language universals as symptoms of cognitive or social factors rely on logical arguments rather than solid empirical proof. Of course, the fact that explanations can be only tentative does not mean they should not be proposed, but it does mean that linguists must be cautious and keep in mind that languages fulfill many roles at once.

LANGUAGE TYPES

A prerequisite to the study of universals is a thorough understanding of the variety found among the world's languages. **Language typology** is a field of inquiry that focuses on classifying languages according to their structural characteristics. (*Typology* means the study of types or the classification of objects into types.) Examples of typological classifications would be "languages that have both voiced and voiceless stops in their phonemic inventories" (like English, French, and Japanese) and "languages that have only voiceless stops" (like Mandarin Chinese, Korean, and Tahitian). Remember, no language in the world has voiced stops without voiceless stops, so that type does not exist. Of course, if we look at other criteria of classification, the composition of each category will be different. For instance, if we establish a typology of languages according to whether or not they have nasal vowels in their phonemic inventory, English, Japanese, Mandarin Chinese, Korean, and Tahitian will fall into the category of languages that lack nasal vowels. In contrast, Standard French has four nasal vowels (some French dialects have only three): /ɛ̃/ as in *faim* /fɛ̃/ 'hunger'; /œ̃/ as in *brun* /bʁœ̃/ 'brown'; /ɑ̃/ as in *manger* /mɑ̃že/ 'to eat'; and /ɔ̃/ as in *maison* /mɛzɔ̃/ 'house.' Standard French thus falls into the category of languages that have nasal vowels, along with Hindi, Tibetan, and Yoruba (a language widely spoken in Nigeria). Of course, linguists can establish categories only according to specific criteria; the world's languages are so diverse in so many different ways that no overall typological classification of languages exists, even within a single level of linguistic structure such as phonology.

Typological categories have no necessary correspondence with groups of languages that have descended from the same parent language. In fact, typological categories cut across language families. In the last example just given, English, Japanese, and Tahitian are not related languages; yet they fall into the same language type with respect to the presence or absence of nasal vowels. On the other hand, French and English *are* related, but they fall into two different types. Though language types are in principle independent of language families, it is not uncommon for members of the same family to share certain typological characteristics as a result of a common heritage. Therefore linguists are always careful to include as many unrelated languages as possible in their proposed language types, so as to ensure that the similarities between languages of any category are not the result of genetic relationships.

This chapter explores both the variety found among the world's languages and the unity that underlies this variety. Uncovering language universals and classifying languages into different types are related but complementary tasks. In order to uncover universal principles, we first need to know the extent to which languages differ from one another in terms of their structure. We would not want to posit a language universal on the basis of a limited sample of languages, only to discover that the proposed universal did not work for a type of language that we had failed to consider. A universal must work for all language types and all languages.

Similarly, the way in which we go about classifying languages and describing the different types of structures is determined in large part by the search for universals. It would be possible, for example, to set up a typological category grouping all languages that have the sound /o/ in their phonemic inventory. But such a typology would tell us nothing about any universal principle underlying the structure of these languages; indeed, their structures might have little in common other than the fact that /o/ is an element of their phonemic inventory. In contrast, a typology of languages based on the presence or absence of nasal vowels reveals interesting patterns. It turns out that no language in the world has only nasal vowels. All languages must have oral vowels, whether or not they have nasal vowels. This suggests that oral vowels are in some sense more "basic" or more indispensable than nasal vowels, a fact that could be of great interest to our understanding of language structure. So this typology is a useful one in that it has helped uncover a language universal. Whether a particular typological classification is interesting or useful depends on whether it helps uncover universal principles in the structure of languages.

EXAMPLES OF LANGUAGE UNIVERSALS AND LANGUAGE TYPES

The next few sections present examples of language universals and of language types from semantics, phonology, syntax, and morphology. For each example, observe carefully the interaction of typologies with universals, and note how different kinds of language universals are stated. A number of the examples will be taken up again toward the end of the chapter, when we examine cognitive and social explanations that have been proposed to account for language universals and language types.

SEMANTIC UNIVERSALS

Semantic universals are rules that govern the composition of the vocabulary of all languages. That semantic universals should exist at all may seem surprising at first. Anyone who has studied a foreign language knows how greatly the vocabularies of two languages can differ. Some ideas that are conveniently expressed with a single word in one language may require an entire sentence in another language. The English word *privacy,* for example, does not have a simple equivalent in French. (That doesn't mean that the French lack the notion of privacy!) Similarly, English lacks an equivalent for the Hawaiian word *aloha,* which can be roughly translated as 'love,' 'compassion,' 'pity,' 'hospitality,' or 'friendliness' and is also used as a general greeting and farewell. Despite these cross-linguistic differences, however, there are some fundamental areas of the vocabulary of every language that are subject to universal rules. These areas include color terms, body part terms, animal names, and verbs of sensory perception.

Semantic universals typically deal with the less marked members of lexical fields (see Chapter 6), which are called *basic terms* in this context. As an example, consider the following terms, which all refer to shades of blue: *turquoise, royal blue,* and *blue.* Intuitively, *blue* is a more basic term than the others. *Turquoise* derives from the name of a precious stone of the same color, while *royal blue* refers to a shade of blue. The word *blue* is thus more basic than each of the other words, though for different reasons: unlike *turquoise,* the word *blue* refers primarily to a color, not an object; unlike *royal blue,* the word *blue* is a simple, unmodified term. The combination of these characteristics makes *blue* a less marked—more basic—color term than the others. *Basic terms* have three characteristics:

1. They are morphologically simple.
2. They are less specialized in meaning.
3. They are not recently borrowed from another language.

Semantic universals deal with terms like *blue* and not with terms like *turquoise* and *royal blue.*

PRONOUNS

Pronoun systems can differ greatly from language to language; yet the pronoun system of every language follows the same set of universal principles.

First, all known languages, without any exception, have pronouns for at least the speaker and the addressee: the first person (*I, me*) and the second person (*you*). But there is great variability among the world's languages in the number of distinctions that are made by pronouns. The following chart presents the English pronominal system (we limit ourselves to subject pronouns).

ENGLISH PRONOUNS

	SINGULAR	PLURAL
FIRST PERSON	I	we
SECOND PERSON	you	you
THIRD PERSON	he, she, it	they

In this chart, columns represent number: the first column "singular," the second column "plural." The rows list person: the first row shows first-person pronouns, the second row shows second-person pronouns, and the third row shows third-person pronouns. Standard American English uses the same form for both the singular and plural second-person pronoun (*you*).

The pronoun systems of other languages display other patterns. Spoken Castilian Spanish has separate forms for the singular and plural in each person; in this example, the two plural forms are the masculine and feminine pronouns. (Spanish also has "polite" pronoun forms, but we have ignored them here.)

CASTILIAN SPANISH PRONOUNS

	SINGULAR	PLURAL	
		M	F
FIRST PERSON	yo	nosotros	nosotras
SECOND PERSON	tú	vosotros	vosotras
THIRD PERSON	él, ella	ellos	ellas

Some languages make finer distinctions in number. Speakers of ancient Sanskrit made a distinction between two people and more than two people. The form for two people is called the *dual,* and the form for more than two is called the *plural.* (In the chart below, the three words for the third person are the masculine, feminine, and neuter forms.)

SANSKRIT PRONOUNS

	SINGULAR	DUAL	PLURAL
FIRST PERSON	aham	āvām	vayam
SECOND PERSON	tvam	yūvām	yūyam
THIRD PERSON	sas, tat, sā	tau, te, te	te, tāni, tās

Other languages have a single pronoun to refer simultaneously to the speaker and the addressee (and sometimes including other people) and a separate pronoun to refer to the speaker along with other people but excluding the addressee. The first of these is called a first-person *inclusive* pronoun, and the second is called a first-person *exclusive* pronoun. In English, both notions are encoded in the pronoun *we.* In contrast, Tok Pisin has separate inclusive and exclusive pronouns.

TOK PISIN PRONOUNS

	SINGULAR	PLURAL
FIRST PERSON EXCLUSIVE	mi	mipela
FIRST PERSON INCLUSIVE		yumi
SECOND PERSON	yu	yupela
THIRD PERSON	em	ol

Tok Pisin is an English-based creole (see Chapter 13) with most of its vocabulary coming from English. The English pronouns and other words that were taken by Tok Pisin speakers to form their pronoun system are easily recognizable: *mi* is from *me, yu* from *you, em* probably from *him, yumi* from *you-me, ol* from *all,* and the plural suffix *-pela* probably from *fellow.*

Fijian has one of the largest pronoun systems of any language. It has a singular form for each pronoun, a dual form for two people, a separate "trial" form that refers to about three people, and a plural form that refers to more than three people (in actual usage, trial pronouns refer to a few people and the plural refers to a multitude). In addition, in the first-person dual, trial, and plural, Fijian, like Tok Pisin, has separate inclusive and exclusive forms.

FIJIAN PRONOUNS

	SINGULAR	DUAL	TRIAL	PLURAL
FIRST PERSON EXCLUSIVE	au	keirau	keitou	keimami
FIRST PERSON INCLUSIVE		kedaru	kedatou	keda
SECOND PERSON	iko	kemudrau	kemudou	kemunii
THIRD PERSON	koya	irau	iratou	ira

Between the extremes represented by English and Fijian are many variations. Some languages have separate dual pronouns, while others do not; some systems make a distinction between inclusive and exclusive pronouns, while others do not.

All the world's languages, however, have distinct first- and second-person pronouns, and most languages have third-person pronouns, inclusive first-person pronouns, and exclusive first-person pronouns. A four-person system (inclusive first and exclusive first person, second person, and third person) is by far the most common. The four-person type of pronoun system is thus somehow more basic than a two- or three-person type. In this respect, English is atypical.

Variations in pronoun systems are governed by a set of universal rules. To discover these universals, we need to establish a typology of pronoun systems.

SOME TYPES OF PRONOUN SYSTEMS IN THE WORLD'S LANGUAGES

Systems with singular and plural forms—e.g., English, Spanish
Systems with singular, dual, and plural forms—e.g., Sanskrit
Systems with singular, dual, trial, and plural forms—e.g., Fijian
Systems lacking inclusive/exclusive distinction in first-person plural—e.g., English, Spanish
Systems with inclusive/exclusive distinction in first-person plural—e.g., Tok Pisin, Fijian

SOME TYPES OF PRONOUN SYSTEMS THAT DO *NOT* OCCUR

Systems lacking first- and second-person pronouns
Systems with singular and dual forms but no plural forms
Systems with singular, dual, and trial forms but no plural forms
Systems that make an inclusive/exclusive distinction, but not in the first person (a logical impossibility)

Based on what we do and don't find in our typology, we postulate some universal rules.

SOME UNIVERSAL RULES

1. All languages have at least first- and second-person pronouns.
2. If a language has singular and dual forms, then it will also have plural forms.
3. If a language has singular, dual, and trial forms, then it will also have plural forms.
4. If a language makes an inclusive/exclusive distinction in its pronoun system, it will make it in the first person.

Note that the converse of these rules is not true. The converse of universal rule 2, for instance, would state that if a language had separate plural forms, it would have separate dual forms. But even English proves this generalization wrong: it has separate plural forms but no dual. The implications thus go in only one direction.

It is important to note that semantic typologies and universals do not represent a measure of complexity in language or culture. The most we can infer from these differences is that some categories are more salient in some cultures than in others. Comparing the two examples of semantic universals discussed in this section, we also see that the pronoun system of English is one of the most restricted in the world, despite the fact that English has very rich scientific and color lexicons, to mention only two arenas. Thus different arenas of the lexicon exhibit different degrees of elaboration in different languages. This fact does not mean that some languages are "richer" or "better" or "more developed" than others.

PHONOLOGICAL UNIVERSALS

Vowel Systems

Another level of linguistic structure in which we can identify universal rules and classify languages into useful typological categories is phonology. In Chapter 3 we discussed the fact that languages could have very different inventories of sounds. Figure 7-1 represents the vowel system of standard American English, classified according to place of articulation. Compare this with Figure 7-2, which represents the vowel system of standard Parisian French (a conservative dialect retaining certain oppositions that have been lost in many other French dialects). The symbol /ü/ represents a high front rounded vowel as in the word /ʁü/ *rue* 'street'; /ø/ is an upper mid rounded vowel as in /fø/ *feu* 'fire'; /œ/ is a lower mid rounded vowel as in /bœʁ/ *beurre* 'butter'; and /ɛ̃/, /œ̃/, /ɔ̃/, and /ɑ̃/ are nasal vowels.

Finally, in Figure 7-3, compare the vowel systems of Quechua (spoken in Peru and Ecuador) and Hawaiian. The first thing these four examples demonstrate is that different languages may have very different sets of vowels: English has several vowels in its inventory that French does not have, and vice versa. Second, the number of vowels in a language can also vary considerably. Quechua has only three distinct vowels; along with the vowel systems of Greenlandic Eskimo and Moroccan Arabic,

Figure 7-1

VOWELS OF AMERICAN ENGLISH

i					u
	ɪ				ʊ
		e		ə	o
			ɛ	ʌ	ɔ
			æ	a	ɑ

Figure 7-2

ORAL AND NASAL VOWELS OF PARISIAN FRENCH

Oral						Nasal		
i		ü			u			
	e		ø	ə	o			
	ɛ			œ	ɔ	ɛ̃	œ̃	ɔ̃
				a				ɑ̃

Figure 7-3

VOWELS OF QUECHUA AND HAWAIIAN

i		u		i		u
					e	o
	a				a	
	Quechua				Hawaiian	

---

the Quechua vowel system is one of the smallest in the world. Hawaiian has five vowels, a very common number among the world's languages. At the other end of the spectrum, English has thirteen vowels and French has fifteen.

Underlying such diversity, however, we find universal patterns. If we charted the vowel inventories of all known languages, we would confirm that all languages have vowel systems that fall between the two extremes represented by Quechua and French. Thus every language has at least three vowel phonemes. Some have four vowels, like Malagasy, the language of Madagascar (whose vowels are /i ɛ a ʊ/), and the American Indian language Kwakiutl (which has /i a ə u/). Some have five vowels, such as Hawaiian, Mandarin Chinese, and, as shown in Figures 3-3 and 3-5, Spanish and Japanese. Others, such as Persian and Malay, have six vowels; and so on up to fifteen.

Comparing all the charts, we find that all languages include in their vowel inventory a high front unrounded vowel (/i/ or /ɪ/), a low vowel (/a/), and a high back rounded (/u/ or /ʊ/) or unrounded (/ɯ/) vowel. These vowels have allophones in some languages, particularly in languages with few vowels. In Greenlandic Eskimo, for example, /i/ has the allophones [i], [e], [ɛ], and [ə], depending on the consonants that surround it; but there are no minimal pairs that depend on these variants. Small variations also exist, but these variations do not really contradict the universal rule, which can be stated as follows: **All languages have a high front unrounded vowel, a low vowel, and a high back rounded or unrounded vowel in their phoneme inventory.** Note that this first universal rule describes what constitutes the minimal type and what is included in all other types.

The second universal rule states this: **Of the languages that have four or more vowels, all have vowels similar to /i a u/** (as indicated by the first universal rule) **plus either a high central vowel /ɨ/** (as in Russian *vɨ* 'you') **or a mid front unrounded vowel /e/ or /ɛ/.** The third universal rule we can uncover from our vowel charts is this: **Languages with a five-vowel system include a mid front unrounded vowel.** In the five-vowel system of Hawaiian, for example, /e/ has allophones [ɛ] and [e]. Other languages with five-vowel inventories include Japanese (whose inventory is /i ɛ a ɔ ɯ/) and Zulu (/i ɛ a ɔ u/). Most languages with five vowels have a mid back rounded vowel (either /ɔ/ or /o/) in their inventory, like Japanese, Hawaiian, and Zulu. A few languages with a five-vowel system lack a mid back rounded vowel, although a similar sound is often included, as with Mandarin Chinese, whose inventory (/i ü a ë u/) includes the lower-mid back unrounded vowel /ë/.

We can thus state that languages with five-vowel inventories *generally* (but not always) have a mid back rounded vowel. This observation is applicable to languages with more than five vowels as well. The fourth universal rule thus reads: **Languages with five or more vowels in their inventories generally have a mid back rounded vowel phoneme.** This rule is stated in a different way from the first three rules in that it is not absolute. But it is a useful observation because it describes a significant tendency across languages.

Languages with six-vowel inventories like Malayalam (spoken in southwestern India) include /ɔ/ in their inventory and either /ɨ/ or /e/. Malayalam has in its inventory the three "obligatory" vowels /i a u/; the vowels /e/ and /ɔ/, as predicted by the second and third universal rules; and /ɨ/. These universal rules can be summarized as in Figure 7-4.

NASAL AND ORAL VOWELS

Many more universal rules that regulate the vowel inventories of the world's languages can be uncovered, but we will mention only two more. The first states: **When a language has nasal vowels, the number of nasal vowels never exceeds the number of oral vowels.** Thus we can find examples of languages with fewer nasal vowels than oral vowels: Standard French, for example, has four nasal vowels and eleven oral vowels. We can also find examples of languages with an equal number of oral and nasal vowels: Punjabi (a language of northern India) has ten of each. But there are no languages with a greater number of nasal vowels than oral vowels.

The second universal rule of interest is not a rule in the usual sense but a description of the most common vowel system: a five-vowel system consisting of a high front unrounded vowel (/i/ or /ɪ/), a mid front unrounded vowel (/e/ or /ɛ/), a low vowel (/a/), a mid back rounded vowel (/o/ or /ɔ/), and a high back rounded vowel (/u/ or /ʊ/). Hawaiian is an example of such a system, as you can see by looking at the symmetry in the chart for Hawaiian vowels (page 234). Each vowel is maximally distant from the others, thus minimizing the possibility of two vowels

Figure 7-4

SUMMARY OF UNIVERSAL VOWEL RULES

LANGUAGE TYPE

	1	2	3	4
	i a u	ɨ ɛ	ɛ ɔ	ɔ e
NUMBER OF VOWELS	3	4	5	6
EXAMPLE	Quechua	Malagasy	Hawaiian	Malayalam

being confused. There is thus an ideal quality to such a five-vowel system, to which we will return later in this chapter.

CONSONANTS

Vowel systems are not the only area of phonology in which universal rules operate. The consonant inventories of the languages of the world also exhibit many universal properties. A few examples are presented here, though not in great detail because they do not differ in nature from universals of vowel systems.

Recall (from Chapter 3) that the sounds /p t k/ are voiceless stops. Every language has at least one of these voiceless stops as a phoneme. Some languages lack affricates or trills, but voiceless stops are found in all languages. In fact, most languages have all three of these sounds, even languages with small consonant inventories. For example, Niuean (a Polynesian language) has only three stops, three nasals, three fricatives, and an approximant, totaling ten consonants (in contrast to the twenty-four of American English). Yet the three stops are /p t k/. Put in the form of a universal, this generalization reads: **Most languages have the three stops /p t k/ in their consonant inventory.** This universal suggests that these three consonants are in some sense more basic than others.

It is clear, given our discussion, that this universal is not an absolute rule. Hawaiian (a language related to Niuean) has only /p/ and /k/. (That is why English words with the sound /t/ are borrowed into Hawaiian with a /k/, like *kikiki* 'ticket'). This universal is thus a *tendency,* rather than a statement of what is and isn't found among the world's languages.

Another important universal referring to stops has already been mentioned. Recall that the difference between the two sets of stops /p t k/ and /b d g/ is that the first set is voiceless, the second voiced. All six sounds have phonemic status in English, as is true in French, Spanish, Quechua, and many other languages. In some languages, however, we find only voiceless stops; such is the case of Hawaiian (and all other Polynesian languages), Korean, and Mandarin Chinese. Thus far, we have identified two types of languages: languages with both voiced and voiceless stops, and languages with only voiceless stops. As noted, every language has at least one voiceless stop in its inventory; consequently, there are no languages that have voiced stops but no voiceless stops and no languages that have neither voiced nor voiceless stops. This typology allows us to derive the following universal rule: **No language has voiced stops without voiceless stops.**

Note that of the universals of stop inventories explored thus far, only one rule (and it is only a tendency) says anything about *which* stops are included in the inventories of languages. But there are other universals that deal with this question. We give only one example here: **If a language lacks a stop, there is a strong tendency for that language to include in its inventory a fricative sound with the same place of articulation as the missing stop.** For instance, Standard Fijian, Amharic (the principal language of Ethiopia), and Standard Arabic all lack the phoneme /p/, which is a labial stop. As predicted by the universal rule, all these languages have a fricative whose place of articulation is similar to that of /p/—namely, /f/ or /v/. The fricative thus "fills in" for the missing stop. This rule, too, is only a tendency, as there are languages that violate it. Hawaiian, which lacks a /t/, has none of the corresponding fricatives /ð/, /θ/, /z/, or /s/. But most languages do follow the rule.

SYNTACTIC AND MORPHOLOGICAL UNIVERSALS
⟶

WORD ORDER

Speakers of English and other European languages commonly assume that the normal way of constructing a sentence is to place the subject of the sentence first, then the verb, and then the direct object (if there is one). Indeed, in English, the sentence *Mary saw John,* which follows this order, is well formed, while variations like *John Mary saw* and *saw Mary John* are not well formed.

However, normal word order in a sentence differs considerably from language to language. Consider the following Japanese sentence, in which the subject is a girl called *Akiko,* the verb is *butta* 'hit (past tense),' and the direct object is a boy named *Taro.*

> akiko ga   taroo o   butta
> Akiko Subject Taro   Object hit
> 'Akiko hit Taro.'

In Japanese, the normal word order is thus subject first, direct object second and verb last. If we changed this order (in an effort to make Japanese syntax conform to English syntax, for example), the result would be ungrammatical.

Now consider Tongan, in which the verb must come first, the subject second, and the direct object last. In the following sentence, the verb is *taaʔi* 'to hit,' the subject is a person named *Hina,* and the direct object is a person called *Vaka.*

> naʔe taaʔi   ʔe   hina ʔa   vaka
> Past hit   Subject   Hina Object Vaka
> 'Hina hit Vaka.'

Of course, not all English sentences follow the order subject-verb-direct object—SVO. To emphasize particular noun phrases, English speakers sometimes place direct objects in clause-initial position as with *whom* in *It was John whom Mary saw*; such constructions are called cleft sentences. In questions like *Who(m) did you see?*, the direct object *who(m)* is in first position. Similar word order variants are found in most languages of the world. But cleft sentences and questions derive from more basic sentences. Cleft sentences and questions are also less common than sentences that follow SVO order. Thus, even though some English constructions do not follow this order, we say that SVO order is "basic" in English, and that English is an SVO language. Examples of SVO languages include Romance languages (such as French, Spanish, and Italian), Thai, Vietnamese, and Indonesian. Japanese is an SOV language, as are Turkish, Persian, Burmese, Hindi, and the Native American languages Navajo, Hopi, and Luiseño. Tongan is a VSO language, as are most other Polynesian languages, some dialects of Arabic, Welsh, and a number of Native American languages like Salish, Squamish, Chinook, Jacaltec, and Zapotec.

There are three other logical possibilities for combining verbs, subjects, and direct objects besides VSO, SVO, and SOV. Remarkably, however, very few languages have VOS, OVS, or OSV as basic word orders. Only a handful of languages are VOS, the best known being Malagasy and Fijian. Following is a basic sentence in Fijian showing that the direct object precedes the subject.

ea   taya na ŋone na yalewa
Past hit   the child the girl
'The girl hit the child'

OVS and OSV are the basic word order of only a handful of languages of the Amazon Basin including Hixkaryana (OVS) and Nadëb (OSV). By far the most common word orders found among the world's languages are SVO, SOV, and, to a lesser extent, VSO.

What characterizes SVO, SOV, and VSO languages (the most common ones) and differentiates them from VOS, OVS, and OSV languages (the uncommon ones)? In each of the three common configurations, S *precedes* O; in the uncommon configurations, S *follows* O. We can thus make a generalized statement: **In the basic word orders of the languages of the world there is an overwhelming tendency for the subject of a sentence to precede the direct object.**

There is a great deal more to universals of syntax. Let's focus on the two extreme cases: languages in which the verb comes first in the clause (called verb-initial languages and illustrated by Tongan) and languages in which the verb comes last (called verb-final languages and illustrated by Japanese). For the sake of simplicity, we exclude VOS and OSV languages from our discussion, though they follow basically the same rules as VSO and SOV languages respectively.

POSSESSOR AND POSSESSED NOUN PHRASES

If we look at the order of other syntactic constituents in verb-initial and verb-final languages, we find strikingly regular and interesting patterns. First of all, in most verb-final languages like Japanese, possessor noun phrases precede possessed noun phrases.

taroo no imooto
Taro of sister
'Taro's sister'

In verb-initial languages the opposite order is most commonly found; in the following example from Tongan, the possessed entity is expressed first, the possessor last.

ko e tuongaʔane ʔo vaka
the sister   of Vaka
'Vaka's sister'

We have thus established the following rule: **There is a strong tendency for possessor noun phrases to *precede* possessed noun phrases in verb-final languages and to *follow* possessed noun phrases in verb-initial languages.**

PREPOSITIONS AND POSTPOSITIONS

To express position or direction, many languages use prepositions. As the word indicates, prepositions come *before* modified noun phrases. In Tongan, for example, the prepositions *ki,* which indicates direction, and *ʔi,* which denotes location, both precede the NP they modify.

ki tonga   ʔi tonga
to Tonga   in Tonga

Other languages have postpositions instead of prepositions. Postpositions fulfill the same functions as prepositions, but they follow the NP, as in this Japanese example.

tookyoo   ni
Tokyo   to
'to Tokyo'

Overwhelmingly, verb-initial languages have prepositions and verb-final languages have postpositions. The third rule can be stated as follows: **There is a strong tendency for verb-initial languages to have prepositions and for verb-final languages to have postpositions.**

RELATIVE CLAUSES

Depending on the language, relative clauses either precede or follow head nouns. In English relative clause constructions (*the book that Judith wrote*), the relative clause (*that Judith wrote*) follows its head (*the book*). The same is true in Tongan.

ko e tohi [naʔe faʔu ʔe   hina]
the   book Past write Subject Hina
'the book that Hina wrote'

In Japanese, however, the relative clause precedes its head.

[hiroo ga   kaita] hon
Hiro   Subject wrote book
'the book that Hiro wrote'

The great majority of verb-initial languages place relative clauses after the head noun, and the great majority of verb-final languages place relative clauses before the head noun. We can therefore note the following universal: **There is a strong tendency for verb-initial languages to place relative clauses after the head noun and for verb-final languages to place relative clauses before the head noun.**

OVERALL PATTERNS OF ORDERING

We have established that verb-initial languages (VSO) place possessors after possessed nouns, place relative clauses after head nouns, and have prepositions. Verb-final languages (SOV), on the other hand, place possessors before possessed nouns, place relative clauses before head nouns, and have postpositions.

In all these correlations a pattern emerges. Notice that possessors and relative clauses modify nouns; the noun is a more essential element to a noun phrase than any of the modifiers. In a similar sense, noun phrases modify prepositions or postpositions; likewise, though it is not intuitively obvious, the most important element of a prepositional phrase is the preposition itself, not the noun phrase—it is the preposition that makes it a prepositional phrase. Finally, in a verb phrase, the direct object modifies the verb. In light of these remarks, we can draw a generalization about the order of constituents in different language types: **In verb-initial languages the modifying element** *follows* **the modified element, while in verb-final languages the modifying element** *precedes* **the modified element.** This pattern is illustrated in Table 7-1.

This generalization is of course based on tendencies rather than absolute rules. At each level of the table some languages violate the correlations. Persian, for example, is an SOV language like Japanese and thus should have the properties listed in the right-hand column of the table. But in Persian possessors follow possessed nouns, prepositions are used, and relative clauses follow head nouns—all of which are properties of verb-initial languages. Such counterexamples to the correlations are rare, however.

Table 7-1

SUMMARY OF CONSTITUENT ORDERS

VERB-INITIAL LANGUAGES	VERB-FINAL LANGUAGES
(EXAMPLE: TONGAN)	(EXAMPLE: JAPANESE)
Modified—Modifier	*Modifier—Modified*
verb—direct object	direct object—verb
possessed—possessor	possessor—possessed
preposition—noun phrase	noun phrase—postposition
head noun—relative clause	relative clause—head noun

Notice that our discussion has mentioned nothing about verb-medial (SVO) languages like English. These languages appear to follow no consistent pattern. English, for example, places relative clauses after head nouns and has prepositions (both properties of verb-initial languages). With respect to the order of possessors and possessed nouns, English has both patterns (*the man's arm* and *the arm of the man*). In contrast, Mandarin Chinese, another verb-medial language, has characteristics of verb-final languages.

Word order universals are an excellent illustration of the level that linguists attempt to reach in their description of the universal properties of language. Table 7-1 implies that in the structure of virtually all verb-initial and verb-final languages, the same ordering principle is at play at the level of the noun phrase, the prepositional phrase, and the whole sentence. This fact is remarkable in that it applies to a great many languages whose speakers have never come in contact with each other. It is thus likely that underlying this ordering principle there may be some cognitive process shared by all human beings.

RELATIVIZATION HIERARCHY

Another area of syntactic structure in which striking universal principles are found is the structure of relative clauses. English can relativize the subject of a relative clause, the direct object, the indirect object, obliques, and possessor noun phrases (see Chapter 5). The following set of English examples illustrates these different possibilities.

> the teacher [*who* talked at the meeting] (subject)
> the teacher [*whom* I mentioned ——— to you] (direct object)
> the teacher [*that* I told the story to ———] (indirect object)
> the teacher [*that* I heard the story from ———] (oblique)
> the teacher [*whose* book I read] (possessor)

Other languages might not allow all these possibilities. Some languages allow relativization on only some of these categories but not others. For example, a relative clause in Malagasy is grammatical only if the relativized noun phrase is the subject of the relative clause.

> ny mpianatra   [izay nahita ny vehivavy]
> the student   who saw   the woman
> 'the student who saw the woman'

In Malagasy there is no way of directly translating a relative clause whose direct object has been relativized ('the student that the woman saw'), or the indirect object ('the student that the woman gave a book to'), or an oblique ('the student that the woman heard the news from'), or a possessor ('the student whose book the woman read'). If speakers of Malagasy need to convey what is represented by these English relative constructions, they must passivize the relative clause, so that the noun phrase that is to be relativized becomes the grammatical subject of the relative clause ('the student *who* was seen by the woman'). Alternatively, they can express their idea in two clauses—that is, instead of 'the woman saw the student who failed his exam,' they might say that 'the woman saw the student, and that same student failed his exam.'

Some languages have relative clauses in which subjects or direct objects can be relativized, but not indirect objects, obliques, or possessors. An example of such a language is Kinyarwanda, spoken in East Africa. Other languages, like Basque, have relative clauses in which the subject, the direct object, and the indirect object can be relativized, but not an oblique or a possessor. Yet another type of language adds obliques to the list of categories that can be relativized; such is the case in Catalan, spoken in northeastern Spain. Finally, languages like English and French allow all possibilities.

Table 7-2 recapitulates the types of relative clause systems found among the world's languages; the plus sign indicates a grammatical category that can be relativized, while a minus sign indicates one that cannot be relativized. Notice that a plus sign does not imply anything about the signs to the right of it—they may be plus or minus. But a plus sign impies that all other categories to its left can be relativized.

It is a remarkable fact that there are no languages in which, for example, an oblique can be relativized ('the man [that I heard the story from]') but not subjects, direct objects, and indirect objects as well. Indeed, relative clause formation in all languages is sensitive to a *hierarchy* of grammatical relations:

RELATIVE CLAUSE HIERARCHY

Subject < Direct object < Indirect object < Oblique < Possessor

---

The hierarchy predicts that if a language allows a particular category on the hierarchy to be relativized, then the grammar of that language will also allow all positions

Table 7-2

**RELATIVIZATION HIERARCHY:
TYPES OF RELATIVE CLAUSE SYSTEMS**

LANGUAGE TYPE	SUBJECT	DIRECT OBJECT	INDIRECT OBJECT	OBLIQUE	POSSESSOR	EXAMPLE
1	+	−	−	−	−	Malagasy
2	+	+	−	−	−	Kinyarwanda
3	+	+	+	−	−	Basque
4	+	+	+	+	−	Catalan
5	+	+	+	+	+	English

---

to the left to be relativized. For example, possessors in English can be relativized ('the woman [*whose* book I read]'). The hierarchy predicts that English would allow all positions to the left of possessor (namely, oblique, indirect object, direct object, and subject) to be relativized. The hierarchy also predicts that Basque, which permits indirect objects to be relativized, will allow direct objects and subjects to be relativized; Basque does *not* allow categories to the right of indirect object on the hierarchy (obliques or possessors) to be relativized. The hierarchy is thus a succinct description of the types of relative clause formation patterns found in the languages of the world.

TYPES OF LANGUAGE UNIVERSALS

In this section we draw on the universals treated in the previous sections in order to classify the different types of universals. It should be clear by now that language universals are not all alike. Some do not have any exceptions. Others hold for most languages but not all. It is important to distinguish between these two types of universals because the first type appears to be the result of an absolute constraint on language in general, while the other is the result of a tendency.

ABSOLUTE UNIVERSALS AND UNIVERSAL TENDENCIES

The first two types of universals are distinguished by whether or not they can be stated as absolute rules. The typology of vowel systems established earlier indicates that the minimum number of vowels in a language is three: /i a u/. The two universal rules that are suggested by the typology read as follows:

1. All languages have at least three vowels.
2. If a language has only three vowels, these vowels will be /i a u/.

From the descriptions of all languages studied to date, it appears that these two rules have no exceptions. The two rules are thus examples of **absolute universals**—universal rules that have no exceptions. Other examples of absolute universals include: if a language has a set of dual pronouns, it must have a set of plural pronouns; if a language has voiced stops, it must have voiceless stops.

In contrast to absolute universals, a number of universal rules have some exceptions. A good example is the rule stating that if a language has a gap in its inventory of stops, it is likely to have a fricative with the same place of articulation as the missing stop. This rule holds for most languages that have gaps in their inventory, but not all. Such rules are called **universal tendencies.** (A possible explanation for universal tendencies is that they represent the coming together of partly competing universal rules.)

Naturally, researchers must be careful when deciding that a particular rule is absolute. Until a few years ago, it would have been easy to assume that no language existed with OVS or OSV as basic word order (since none had been described) and that there was an absolute universal stating that "no language has OVS or OSV for basic word order." However, we now know of a few OVS and OSV languages, all spoken in the Amazon Basin. Thus the rule that had been stated as an absolute universal seemed absolute only because no one had come across a language that violated it.

IMPLICATIONAL AND NONIMPLICATIONAL UNIVERSALS

Independently of the contrast between absolute universals and tendencies, we can draw another important distinction—between implicational and nonimplicational universals. Some universal rules are in the form of a conditional implication, as in the following examples:

- If a language has five vowels, it generally has the vowel /o/ or /ɔ/.
- If a language is verb-final, then in that language possessors are likely to precede possessed noun phrases.

All rules of the form "if condition P is satisfied, then conclusion Q holds" are called **implicational universals.** Other universals can be stated without conditions: All languages have at least three vowels. Such universals are called *nonimplicational universals.*

There are thus four types of universals.

TYPES OF UNIVERSALS

Absolute implicational universal
    If a language has property X, it must have property Y
Implicational tendency
    If a language has property X, it will probably have property Y
Absolute nonimplicational universal
    All languages have property X
Nonimplicational tendency
    Most languages have property X

Examples of each type can be identified in the discussion of the previous section.

EXPLANATIONS FOR LANGUAGE UNIVERSALS

By any standard, it is remarkable that all languages of the world should fall into clearly defined types and be subject to universal rules, given the extreme structural diversity they otherwise exhibit. It is thus reasonable to ask why universal rules exist at all. The question is extremely complex, and no one can claim to have come up with a definitive explanation for any universal. However, for many universals, we can make empirically based hypotheses at best, and educated guesses at worst, about the reasons for their existence.

ORIGINAL LANGUAGE HYPOTHESIS

The first explanation for language universals that may come to mind is that all languages of the world derive historically from the same original language. This hypothesis is difficult to support, however. First of all, archaeological evidence strongly suggests that the ability to speak developed in our ancestors in several parts of the globe at about the same time, and it is difficult to imagine that different groups of speakers not in contact with one another would have developed exactly the same language. Secondly, even if we ignore the archaeological evidence, the existence of an original language is impossible to prove or disprove because we have no evidence for or against the hypothesis at our disposal. Thus the original language hypothesis is not a very good explanation; at best, it is so hypothetical that it does not adequately fulfill the function of an explanation.

UNIVERSALS AND PERCEPTION

A more likely explanation for language universals is the hypothesis that they are symptoms of how all humans perceive the world and conduct verbal interactions. In what follows, several such explanations will be applied to the universals established earlier in this chapter. In the discussion of vowel systems, you may have noticed that the three vowels found in all languages—/i a u/—are mutually very distant in a vowel chart. The two vowels /i/ and /u/ differ in terms of frontness and usually rounding, and /a/ differs from the other two in terms of frontness and height. From these observations, it is not difficult to hypothesize why these three vowels would be the most fundamental vowels across languages. There is no other set of three vowels that would differ from each other more dramatically.

ACQUISITION AND PROCESSING EXPLANATIONS

Some language universals have psychological explanations that have no physiological basis. The explanations that have been proposed for word order universals, for example, are based on the notion that the more regular the structure of a language, the easier it is for children to acquire it. Thus the fact that verb-initial languages have prepositions and place adjectives after nouns, possessors after possessed nouns, and relative clauses after head nouns can be summarized by the following rule: **In verb-initial languages, the modifier follows the modified element.** Languages that strictly follow this rule exhibit a great deal of regularity from one construction to the other; a single ordering principle regulates the order of verbs and direct objects, adpositions and noun phrases, nouns and adjectives, possessors and possessed nouns, and relative clauses and head nouns. Such a language would be easier to acquire as a native tongue than a language with two or more ordering principles underlying different areas of the syntax. The fact that so many languages in the world follow one overall ordering pattern (modified-modifier) or the other (modifier-modified) with such regularity thus reflects the general tendency for the structure of language to be as regular as possible so as to make it as easy as possible to acquire.

Psychological explanations have also been proposed to explain the relative clause formation hierarchy. Relative clauses in which the head functions as the subject of the relative clause ('the woman [that left]') are easier to learn and to understand than relative clauses in which the head functions as the direct object of the relative clause ('the man [that I saw]'). Small children generally acquire the first type before they begin using the second type. Further, people take less time to understand the meaning of relative clauses on subjects than on direct objects. Relative clauses on direct objects, in turn, are easier to understand than those on indirect objects, and so on down the hierarchy: Subject < Direct object < Indirect object < Oblique < Possessor. There is thus a psychological explanation for the cross-linguistic patterns in the typology of relative clause formation: a language allows a "difficult" relative clause type only if all the "easier" types are also allowed in the language.

SOCIAL EXPLANATIONS

Finally, recall that language is both a cognitive and a social phenomenon (see Chapter 1). While some language universals have a basis in cognition, others reflect the fact that language is a social tool.

Universals of pronoun systems can be explained in terms of the uses of language. Why, for example, do all languages have first- and second-person singular pronouns? Consider that the most basic type of verbal interaction is face-to-face conversation. Other contexts in which language is used to communicate (through writing, over the telephone, on the radio, and so on) are relatively recent inventions compared to the ability to carry on a conversation; they occur less frequently and perhaps less naturally than face-to-face interactions. In a face-to-face interaction, it is essential to be able to refer efficiently and concisely to the speaker and the addressee, the two most important entities involved in the interaction. An argument between two individuals who were unable to use *I* and *you,* or who had to refer to themselves and each other by name, would be notably less efficient. Obviously, first- and second-person singular pronouns are essential for ordinary efficiency of social interaction. It is thus not surprising that every language has first- and second-person singular pronoun forms, even though they may have a gap elsewhere in their pronoun systems. The universal that all languages have first- and second-person pronoun forms thus has a social motivation.

Furthermore, as noted earlier, the most frequent pronoun system has separate first-, second-, and third-person forms, and separate first-person inclusive ('you and me and perhaps other people') and exclusive ('other people and me, but not you') forms. Why would this system be so frequent and in some way more basic than other systems? Pronoun systems can be viewed as a matrix, each slot of the matrix being characterized by whether or not the speaker and the addressee are included in the reference of the pronoun.

In light of the fact that speaker and addressee are the more important elements of face-to-face interactions, it should come as no surprise that speaker and addressee

MATRIX OF PRONOUN SYSTEMS

	SPEAKER INCLUDED	SPEAKER EXCLUDED
ADDRESSEE INCLUDED	—	second person singular
	first person inclusive plural	second person plural
ADDRESSEE EXCLUDED	first person singular	third person singular
	first person exclusive plural	third person plural

inclusion or exclusion should be the crucial factor in defining each slot of the matrix. The most basic (and most common) type of pronoun system is thus the most balanced matrix, one in which each slot is filled with a separate form.

Language universals may thus stem from the way in which humans perceive the world around them, learn and process language, and organize their social interactions. Underlying the search for universals is the desire to learn more about these areas of cognition and social life.

COMPUTERS AND THE STUDY OF LANGUAGE UNIVERSALS

For more than half a century researchers have been trying to craft devices that will be able to translate between languages. Except in limited ways, however, that goal has eluded even the best attempts thus far. As everyone who has visited a foreign country knows, word-for-word translation does not do the trick. For one thing, as we've seen, languages differ in their word orders and, for another, the metaphors of one language may not translate into the relevant metaphor of another language. Countless other reasons also contribute to the failure of word-for-word translation. So even computerized bilingual dictionaries for each of the languages being translated will be insufficient.

Consider two models of translation. In the first model, one set of rules or procedures is established for translating from language A into language B and a second set for translating in reverse—that is, from B into A. The rules would have to be completely explicit, and a set of procedures in *each* direction would be needed because translation is not symmetrical. If a machine translation (abbreviated MT) device were established for even six languages, then 6 × 5 (i.e., 30) sets of procedures would be needed to translate each language into all of the other five. Such a model, referred to as a *transfer translation system,* can be represented as in the following figure.

Transfer Translation

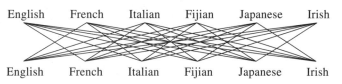

Now consider an alternative model in which the basic semantic elements of each language can be represented abstractly and then encoded into other languages. In this case, for each language a procedure would be needed to decode it into abstract semantic elements (thus forming an abstract semantic representation), along with a second procedure for encoding abstract semantic representations into the lexicon, syntax, and (for spoken texts) phonology of each target language. Such a model is called an interlingual translation system and might look like this.

Interlingual Translation

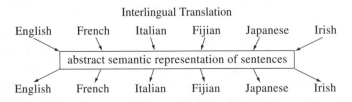

The interlingual translation model would require twelve procedures—one <u>de</u>coding procedure and one <u>en</u>coding procedure for each of the six languages. Such a model is far simpler than the transfer translation model requiring 30 procedures. Unfortunately, it isn't clear to what extent sentences can actually be decomposed into the kinds of abstract semantic representations that would be needed for an interlingual model, and especially to make the intermediate representation language neutral.

Related to translation in either model are difficulties concerning what one language encodes that another may not encode. For example, as you saw in the chart of its pronouns on page 231, Fijian has four distinct second person pronouns while English has only one. That would make it very easy to translate any second-person pronoun from Fijian into English, provided that the abstract semantic representation of the Fijian pronouns contains the element 'second person.' All such representations would be mapped onto the only second-person pronoun of English—namely, *you*. But what about translating the other way around? Would it be equally straightforward? Given an English sentence containing the pronoun *you*, no machine could determine from the form itself what its underlying semantic representation would be, other than second per-

son. In other words, English does not code the potential distinction among singular, dual, trial, and plural number in the second person. So an MT (machine translation) device could not decide which Fijian pronoun to choose if it relied solely on the form of the English pronoun *you*. We can represent the problem as in the following schema, where translating from Fijian to English would be easy.

Fijian	English

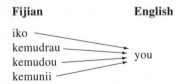

But translating English *you* into Fijian would be quite a challenge. Of course, the text or the context might make clear just how many addressees were represented by the pronoun *you*, but except in rare cases (e.g., *you two, the three of you*) it would prove difficult or impossible for an MT program to decipher that information.

As we have just seen, going from Fijian second-person pronouns to the single English second-person pronoun would be easy, but going from the English to the Fijian virtually impossible. Interestingly, the situation is reversed for third-person singular pronouns. In that case, Fijian does not distinguish masculine, feminine, and neuter singular pronouns, but English does. Thus as you saw in the chart on page 231, Fijian has only the pronoun *koya* corresponding to the three English pronouns *he, she,* and *it.*

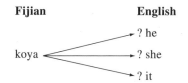

Fijian	English
koya	? he
	? she
	? it

No computational device could decide from the Fijian pronoun alone which of the English pronouns would be the correct translation. Again, the context might make it clear, but for an MT device to decipher that information would be very difficult at best.

Having noted several kinds of ways in which automatic or machine translation would be difficult or impossible, it is also important to note that considerable progress has been made in creating MT devices. The problems that we have discussed can be minimized by limiting the translation machinery to two languages and to very specialized domains of discourse within those languages. For example, if you were translating only medical texts or only technical documents from English into another language, you would be dealing with a limited subset of vocabulary and structures. Analysis of particular kinds of text may reveal that certain lexical or grammatical options rarely (or never) occur in them. In creating a list of words that appear in medical journals, for example, most informal vocabulary could be eliminated from consideration.

Similarly, to return to the pronoun problem discussed above, English medical journals would almost certainly not use the full range of potential semantic distinctions represented in Fijian, so that for projects translating medical documents, some of the possibilities of Fijian pronouns could be eliminated for all practical purposes.

The need for translation has grown urgently in recent decades with the formation of the European Union. With all the translation necessary in the EU, considerable financial resources have been made available for exploring automatic translation. In pursuit of better methods of machine translation, corpora containing more than one language have been created, and analysis of them will yield findings that will be helpful in designing automatic translation devices. Although usually containing just two languages, there is no principled reason to avoid multilingual corpora, and in fact some already exist. Some of these contain the same kinds of texts but not identical texts. One such corpus is the Aarhus Corpus of Danish, French, and English law. These texts are not translations of one another but represent a reservoir of information about the language of legislation in these three languages. Other corpora contain texts that are translations of one another, as with the Canadian Hansard Corpus, which contains parliamentary proceedings in French and English translations.

When a corpus contains translations it is possible to create what is called a "parallel aligned corpus." Such a corpus contains texts in different languages that have been aligned—sometimes automatically—so that sections correspond to one another—paragraph to paragraph or even sentence to sentence. Researchers can use these corpora to explore the mathematical properties of vocabulary and syntax in languages and pairs of languages. With knowledge of such properties in hand, automatic translation may be able in part to avoid either of the models depicted above. Instead, certain mathematical properties of languages will help determine likely translations, independently of how the human mind processes languages and makes translations.

SUMMARY

- Underlying the great diversity of the world's languages universal principles are at play at all levels of language structure—phonology, morphology, syntax, and semantics.

- The study of typology aims to catalog languages according to types, while the study of universals aims to formulate the universal principles themselves.

- In lexical semantics, the composition of pronoun systems, in which cross-linguistic variation is found, is dictated by several universal rules that regulate distinctions in number and person.

- Vowel systems and inventories of stops are two examples of universals at play in phonology.

- In syntax and morphology, universals are found regulating the basic order of constituents in sentences and phrases.

- In syntax, the relativization hierarchy is a striking example of a universal principle.

- The salient characteristic of all universals is that the most common patterns are the most regular and harmonious.

- Four types of universal rules can be distinguished, depending on whether or not they have exceptions (absolute versus tendency) and according to their logical form (implicational versus nonimplicational):

  Absolute implicational universals: Languages with property X must have property Y.

  Implicational tendencies: Languages with property X will probably have property Y.

  Absolute nonimplicational universals: All languages have property X.

  Nonimplicational tendencies: Most languages have property X.

- The ultimate goal of the study of language universals is to provide explanations for such universal principles.

- Language universals may have physiological, psychological, or social explanations:
  Physiological: Universals are often indicative of how we perceive the world around us. Thus, languages tend to highlight categories that are physiologically and perceptually salient, as with vowels.

  Psychological: Structural simplicity and consistency make languages easier to acquire and process. Thus many universals predict that the simplest and most consistent systems will be preferred.

  Social: Distinctions drawn on the expression side of language reflect important social distinctions on the content side.

EXERCISES

Based on English

7-1. Make a judgment about how usual or unusual the following features of (standard) English are in comparison with other languages discussed in this chapter. Explain your judgment in each case.

(1) a thirteen-vowel system

(2) no (phonemically distinct) nasal vowels

(3) Subject-Verb-Object word order

(4) adjectives preceding head nouns

(5) relative clauses following head nouns

(6) no dual pronoun forms

(7) no trial pronoun forms

(8) no distinct second-person plural pronouns

(9) no distinction between inclusive and exclusive pronouns

7-2. Determine whether each of the following is an absolute implicational universal, an absolute nonimplication universal, an implicational universal tendency, or a nonimplicational universal tendency.

(1) The consonant inventories of all languages include at least two different stops that differ in terms of place of articulation.

(2) Languages always have fewer nasal consonants than oral stops.

(3) In all languages, the number of front vowels of different height is greater than or equal to the number of back vowels of different height.

(4) Most VSO languages have prepositions, not postpositions.

(5) Diminutive particles and affixes tend to exhibit high vowels.

(6) If a language has separate terms for 'foot' and 'leg,' then it must also have different terms for 'hand' and 'arm.'

(7) The future tense is used to express hypothetical events in many languages, and the past tense is often used to express nonhypothetical events.

(8) Languages that have a relatively free word order tend to have inflections for case.

(9) Many verb-initial languages place relative clauses after the head of the relative clause.

Based on Languages Other Than English

7-3. In English, conditions can be expressed in two ways: by placing the conditioning clause first and the conditioned clause second, as in (1), or by placing the conditioning clause second and the conditioned clause first, as in (2). In numerous languages, however, only the first pattern is grammatical. In Mandarin Chinese, the conditioning clause must come first, as in (3); if it is placed second, as in (4), the resulting string is ungrammatical. No language allows only pattern (2)—conditioning clause second, conditioned clause first.

(1) If you cry, I'll turn off the TV.

(2) I'll turn off the TV if you cry.

(3) rúguǒ wǒ dìdi   hē   jiǔ   wǒ jiù hěn shēngqì
    If   my younger-brother drink wine I   then very angry
    'If my younger brother drinks wine, I'll be very angry.'

(4) *wǒ hěn shēngqì rúguǒ wǒ dìdi   hē   jiǔ
    I   very angry   if   my younger-brother drink wine

a. From this information, formulate descriptions of an absolute implicational universal, an absolute nonimplicational universal, and a universal tendency, all of which refer to conditional clauses.

b. Propose an explanation for the universal ordering patterns that you formulated in (a). (*Hint*: Think of the order in which the actions denoted by the conditioning and the conditioned clauses must take place.)

7-4. The composition of vowel inventories of the world's languages is predicted by the hierarchy given in Figure 7-4 (p. 235). The hierarchy predicts the composition of a vowel inventory that consists of six phonemes. Complete the next step in the hierarchy by determining the composition of seven-vowel inventories. Use the following information on the composition of the seven-vowel inventories of three languages, which you should assume are representative of possible seven-vowel inventories.

Burmese	i e ɛ a ɔ o u
Sundanese	i ɨ ɛ a o u ə
Washkuk	i ɨ e ɛ a ɔ u

7-5. Consider the following typology of pronoun systems found among the world's languages. The first column of each set represents singular pronouns, the second column dual pronouns, and the third column plural pronouns. An example of a language also is given for each type (incl. = inclusive, excl. = exclusive).

Eight-pronoun Systems

(1)
I	we-2	we	Greenlandic Eskimo
thou	you-2	you	
s/he		they	

(2)
I		we	Arabic
thou	you-2	you	
s/he	they-2	they	

(3)
I	we-2-incl	we-incl.	Southern Paiute (North America)
thou		you	
s/he		they	

Nine-pronoun Systems

(1)
I	we-2	we	Lapp (Arctic Scandinavia)
thou	you-2	you	
s/he	they-2	they	

(2)
I	we-2-incl.	we-incl.	Maya (Central America)
	we-2-excl.	we-excl.	
thou		you	
s/he		they	

(3)
I	we-2-incl.	we	Lower Kanauri (India)
	we-2-excl.		
thou	you-2	you	
s/he		they	

Ten-pronoun Systems

(1)
I	we-2-incl	we	Coos (North America)
	we-2-excl.		
thou	you-2	you	
s/he	they-2	they	

(2)
I	we-2-incl	we-incl.	Kanauri (India)
	we-2-excl.	we-excl.	
thou	you-2	you	
s/he	they-2	they	

Eleven-pronoun Systems

(1)
I	we-2-incl.	we-incl.	Hawaiian
	we-2-excl.	we-excl.	
thou	you-2	you	
s/he	they-2	they	

(2)
I	we-2-incl.	we-incl.	Ewe (West Africa)
	we-2 excl.	we-excl.	
thou	you-2	you	
s/he	they-2	they	
		he and they	

a. On the basis of these data, which you may assume to be representative, formulate a set of absolute universal principles that describe the composition
of eight-, nine-, ten-, and eleven-pronoun systems. State your principles as
generally as possible.

b. Of these systems, the most commonly found is the eleven-pronoun system
of type 1, exemplified by Hawaiian, followed by the nine-pronoun system
of type 1, exemplified by Lapp. Formulate a set of universal tendencies
that describe the preponderance of examples of these two systems.

7-6. From a logical standpoint, the possible basic ordering combinations of subject,
verb, and direct object are SOV, SVO, VSO, VOS, OVS, and OSV. We have
seen that there is great variation in the percentage of languages exhibiting each
combination as a basic word order. Linguists have recognized this fact for several decades, but there has been little agreement on the exact distribution of
these basic word order variations across the world's languages. Here are results
from five researchers who conducted cross-linguistic analyses of the distribution of basic word order possibilities. (The figures are cited from Tomlin 1986.)

RESEARCHER	LANGUAGES SAMPLED	PERCENTAGE						UNCLAS- SIFIED
		SOV	SVO	VSO	VOS	OVS	OSV	
Greenberg	30	37	43	20	0	0	0	0
Ultan	75	44	34.6	18.6	2.6	0	0	0
Ruhlen	427	51.5	35.6	10.5	2.1	0	0.2	0
Mallinson/Blake	100	41	35	9	2	1	1	11
Tomlin	402	44.8	41.8	9.2	3.0	1.2	0	0

a. In what ways do these researchers agree, and where do they disagree? Describe in detail.

b. What are the possible causes of the discrepancies in the results?

c. What lesson can typologists learn from this comparison?

7-7. Relative clauses in the world's languages can be formed in a variety of ways. In English, we "replace" the relativized element by a relative pronoun that links the relative clause to its head (type 3). Other languages do not have distinct relative pronouns but replace the relativized element by a personal pronoun (type 2). For example, in Gilbertese (spoken in the central Pacific), the position of the relativized element in the relative clause is marked with a personal pronoun.

Type 2					Type 2	
te ben	[e̲ bwaka iaon te auti]				te anene	[i nori-a̲]
the coconut	it̲ fall	on	the house	the	coconut	I saw-it̲
'the coconut	[that fell	on	the house]'		'the coconut	[that I saw]'

In other languages like Finnish, relative clauses are formed simply by deleting the relativized element from the relative clause; no relative pronoun or personal pronoun is added to the relative construction (type 1).

Type 1	Type 1
[tanssinut] poika	[näkemäni] poika
had-danced boy	I-had-seen boy
'the boy [that had danced]'	'the boy [that I had seen]'

Some languages have several types of relative clauses. Mandarin Chinese has types 1 and 2. (In Mandarin the relative clause is ordered before its head and is separated from the head by the particle *de.*)

Type 1		Type 2	
[mǎi píngguǒ de]	rén	[tā jièjie zài měiguó de]	rén
buy apples Particle	man	he̲ sister is-in America Particle	man
'the man [who bought apples]'		'the man [whose sister is in America]'	

In Mandarin Chinese, type 1 is used only when relativizing a subject or direct object, while type 2 can be used when relativizing a direct object, an indirect object, an oblique, or a possessor, as indicated in the table below. Whenever two types of relative clauses are found in a language, the pattern is the same: as we go down the relativization hierarchy (from subject to direct object to indirect object to oblique to possessor), one type can end but the other type takes over. Here are the patterns for some languages:

GRAMMATICAL RELATION RELATIVIZED

	SUBJECT	DIRECT OBJECT	INDIRECT OBJECT	OBLIQUE	POSSESSOR
Aoban (South Pacific)					
Type I	+	−	−	−	−
Type 2	−	+	+	+	+
Dutch					
Type I	+	+	−	−	−
Type 2	−	−	+	+	+
Japanese					
Type I	+	+	+	+	+
Type 2	−	−	−	−	+
Kera (Central Africa)					
Type I	+	−	−	−	−
Type 2	−	+	+	+	+
Mandarin Chinese					
Type I	+	+	−	−	−
Type 2	—	+	+	+	+
Roviana (South Pacific)					
Type I	+	+	+	−	−
Type 2	−	−	−	+	+
Tagalog (Philippines)					
Type I	+	−	−	−	−
Type 2	+	−	−	−	−
Catalan (Spain)					
Type I	+	+	+	−	−
Type 2	−	−	−	+	−

What cross-linguistic generalizations can you draw from these data on the distribution of relative clause types in each language? How can we expand the universal rules associated with the hierarchy to describe these patterns?

7-8. Below is a sentence from the program notes to *Officium,* produced by ECM Records. After that, in sections, the sentence is repeated with translations from the program notes in German and French. Comparable sections are marked typographically. After examining the English sentence and the three translations, answer the questions that follow.

The oldest pieces on this record (if one can use words like "new" and "old" in this context) are the chants, the origins of which are not known to us.

The **oldest** pieces	*on this record*
Die **ältesten** Stücke	*dieser Aufnahme*
Les morceaux **les plus anciens** figurant	*sur ce disque*
the pieces the most old	figuring on this record

(if one *can use words* like "new" and "old" in this context)
—so man in diesem Zusammenhang überhaupt von „neu" und „alt" *sprechen kann*—

if	one	in this	situation		at all		of	new	and	old	speak
can											

(si tant est que les termes «nouveau» et «ancien» conviennent à ce contexte)

if	such	it is	that	the	terms	new		and	old		suit		to this
context													

are the chants, the origins of which <u>are not known</u> **to us.**
sind Gesänge, deren Ursprung **uns** <u>nicht</u> <u>bekannt</u> <u>ist.</u>

are	chants	whose origin		to-us	not	known	is.

sont les chants, dont l'origine **nous** <u>est</u> <u>inconnue.</u>

are	the	chants	whose origin		to-us	is	unknown

a. Which of the languages have prepositions, which postpositions?
b. Each of the translations contains three clauses—the equivalents of
   i. the oldest pieces on this record are the chants
   ii. if one can use words like "new" and "old" in this context
   iii. the origins of which are not known to us

Do any of the languages use a word order other than SVO in the main clause? in the subordinate clauses? If any other word orders are represented, identify them.
c. Which languages have adjectives preceding head nouns? Which have adjectives following head nouns?
d. Neither German nor French uses a prepositional phrase to express what English expresses as *to us*. What do they do instead, and how is the meaning conveyed without a preposition?

INTERNET RESOURCE

- **The I Can Eat Glass Project: http://hcs.harvard.edu/~igp/glass.html**
  Enterprising Harvard University student Ethan Mollick has compiled a list of ways to say "I can eat glass, it doesn't hurt me" in various languages—now over 100 of them. In Mollick's words, "The project lists the language, the location in which it is spoken, how it would be written in the language (if the tongue uses the Roman alphabet), and a transliteration if available."

SUGGESTIONS FOR FURTHER READING

- **Bernard Comrie. 1989.** *Language Universals and Linguistic Typology: Syntax and Morphology,* **2nd ed.** (Chicago: U of Chicago P). The most readable basic book on the study of language universals and linguistic typology; it focuses principally on syntax and morphology.

Advanced Reading

Mallinson and Blake (1981) is a good introduction to typology. Shopen (1985) is a collection of excellent essays by distinguished authors on selected areas of syntactic typology, and it is also useful on the range of morphological and syntactic variation found among the world's languages. The first volume treats *Clause Structure,* the second *Complex Constructions,* and the third *Grammatical Categories and the Lexicon.* Some of the most influential work on language universals was conducted by Greenberg, who has edited a four-volume compendium of detailed studies of universals on specific areas of linguistic structure (1978); several papers from these volumes provided data for the exercises of this chapter. The volumes treat *Method and Theory* (I), *Phonology* (II), *Word Structure* (III), and *Syntax* (IV). Brown (1984) is an interesting investigation of universals of words for plants and animals. Lehrer (1974) is a good summary of research on semantic universals. Tomlin (1986) surveys the basic word orders of the world's languages. The relativization hierarchy was uncovered by Edward L. Keenan and Bernard Comrie, and Chapter 7 of Comrie (1989) offers a clear discussion of the topic. Butterworth et al. (1984) is a collection of papers on theoretical explanations for language universals.

REFERENCES

- Brown, Cecil H. 1984. *Language and Living Things: Uniformities in Folk Classification and Naming* (New Brunswick, NJ: Rutgers UP).

- Butterworth, Brian, Bernard Comrie, and Osten Dahl, eds. 1984. *Explanations for Language Universals* (Berlin: Mouton).

- Greenberg, Joseph H., ed. 1978. *Universals of Human Language*, 4 vols. (Stanford: Stanford UP).

- Lehrer, Adrienne. 1974. *Semantic Fields and Lexical Structure* (Amsterdam: North-Holland).

- Mallinson, George, and Barry J. Blake. 1981. *Language Typology* (Amsterdam: North-Holland)

- Shopen, Timothy, ed. 1985. *Language Typology and Syntactic Description,* 3 vols. (Cambridge: Cambridge UP).

- Tomlin, Russell S. 1986. *Basic Word Order: Functional Principles* (London: Croom Helm).

PART TWO

LANGUAGE USE

—

IN Part One you examined the structure of words, phrases, and sentences. In Part Two you'll examine how you use those structures in ordinary social interactions. You'll see that languages provide alternative ways of saying the same thing, and you'll see what those alternative ways accomplish socially and communicatively. Language exists only to be used, and our use of language distinguishes human beings from all other animals. It is language use that makes us uniquely human. By putting language to use, we accomplish things and can achieve deep social and intellectual satisfaction.

The forms of language that you use reflect your social identity and mirror the character of the situation in which you're communicating. Part Two explores *dialects*—the patterns of linguistic variation across diverse social groups—and *registers*, the patterns of linguistic variation across communicative situations. Here you will also examine writing systems and the relationships between written and spoken expression.

CHAPTER 8

INFORMATION STRUCTURE

AND PRAGMATICS

WHAT DO YOU THINK?

In answer to a question about the *and* a *asked by a student in your junior high school ESL class, you explain that the definite article* the *serves to refer to a particular person, place, or thing (as in "the Eiffel Tower" or "the Golden Gate Bridge") and the indefinite article* a *or* an *refers to* any *person, place, or thing. A student from Mexico politely notes that earlier, when you told the class about "a movie" that you recommended, you meant a particular movie. You recognize that you first referred to the movie as "a movie" you had seen and then as "it." ("You should see* it *if you can," you said. You also recall that one of your students had asked, "What's the name of* the *movie?") What revised explanation can you offer for the definite and indefinite articles?*

During a discussion of active and passive sentences with this same ESL class, a student from Malaysia asks why English needs two ways of saying what seems to be exactly the same thing:

The Florida Marlins won the World Series. *(active)*
The World Series was won by the Florida Marlins. *(passive)*

Fortunately, the bell rings and you get time to think about your answer overnight. At the next class meeting, what explanation do you give?

INTRODUCTION: ENCODING INFORMATION STRUCTURE

Syntax and semantics are not the only regulators of sentence structure. A sentence may be grammatically and semantically well formed but still exhibit problems when used in a particular context. Examine the following two versions of a local news report.

VERSION 1

At 3 A.M. last Sunday, the Santa Clara Fire Department evacuated two apartment buildings at the corner of Country Club Drive and Fifth Avenue. Oil had been discovered leaking from a furnace in the basement of one of the buildings. Firemen sprayed chemical foam over the oil for several hours. By 8 A.M., the situation was under control. Any danger of explosion or fire had been averted, and the leaky furnace was sealed. Residents of the two apartment buildings were given temporary shelter in the Country Club High School gymnasium. They regained possession of their apartments at 5 P.M.

VERSION 2

As for the Santa Clara Fire Department, it evacuated two apartment buildings at the corner of Country Club Drive and Fifth Avenue at 3 A.M. last Sunday. There was someone who had discovered a furnace in the basement of one of the buildings from which oil was leaking. What was sprayed by firemen over the oil for several hours was chemical foam. It was by 8 A.M. that the situation was under control. What someone had averted was any danger of explosion or fire, and as for the leaky furnace, it was sealed. What the residents of the two apartment buildings were given in the Country Club High School gymnasium was temporary shelter. Possession of their apartments was regained by them at 5 P.M.

Virtually the same words are used in the two versions, and every sentence in both versions is grammatically and semantically well formed. Still, there is something fundamentally odd about Version 2: it runs counter to expectations of how information should be presented in a text. Somehow, the second version emphasizes the wrong elements at the wrong time. The structures are grammatical, but they seem inappropriate.

The problem with Version 2 is the way in which different pieces of information are marked for relative significance. In any sequence of sentences, it is essential to mark elements as being more or less important or essential. Speakers and writers are responsible for highlighting certain elements and backgrounding others, just as a painter highlights some details and deemphasizes others with a judicious use of color, shape, and position.

In language texts, this highlighting and deemphasizing are called **information structure.** Unlike syntax and semantics, which are sentence-based aspects of language, information structure requires consideration of discourse—of sequences of sentences in use rather than isolated sentences. Out of context, there is nothing wrong with the first sentence of Version 2:

As for the Santa Clara Fire Department, it evacuated two apartment buildings at the corner of Country Club Drive and Fifth Avenue at 3 A.M. last Sunday.

But when this sentence serves to open a news report it is inappropriate. Thus, when we talk about information structure we must take into account the *discourse context* of a sentence—that is, the environment in which it is produced, especially what comes before it. We can describe a **discourse** as a sequence of spoken or written utterances that "go together" in a particular situation: a conversation over the family dinner table, a newspaper column, a personal letter, a radio interview, or a subpoena to appear in court. We can also say that *Oh, look!* (uttered, for example, to draw attention to a beautiful sunset) is discourse, even though it is not a sequence of utterances, because the utterance is produced within an extralinguistic environment that helps determine an appropriate information structure.

In order to mark information structure in a sentence, speakers rely on the fact that the rules of syntax permit alternative ways of shaping sentences. For example, the following sentences are alternative ways of "saying the same thing." They illustrate how broad a choice we have in expressing even simple predications.

1. The fireman discovered a leak in the basement.
2. A leak was discovered by the fireman in the basement.
3. A leak in the basement was discovered by the fireman.
4. It was the fireman who discovered a leak in the basement.
5. What the fireman discovered in the basement was a leak.
6. What the fireman discovered was a leak in the basement.
7. It was a leak that the fireman discovered in the basement.
8. What was discovered by the fireman was a leak in the basement.
9. The fireman, he discovered a leak in the basement.
10. In the basement, the fireman discovered a leak.

It is such a choice of alternatives that we exploit to mark information structure. You might ask yourself what question each of the sentences above is an appropriate answer to. This chapter will describe how that is done.

Pragmatics is the branch of linguistics that studies information structure, and the term *pragmatics* is sometimes used as an alternative to the term *information structure*. In Chapter 9, we'll discuss other aspects of language use that are also sometimes called *pragmatics*.

One of the first tasks that pragmatics must tackle is identifying the categories needed to talk about information structure. The fact that there are so many different ways to express the same thought demonstrates the need to make more subtle distinctions to describe the differences between these alternatives. A set of basic constructs must be developed to describe pragmatic differences in English and other languages.

CATEGORIES OF INFORMATION STRUCTURE

In order to describe the differences between alternative ways of "saying the same thing," we must identify the basic categories of information structure. These categories must be applicable to all languages (though the ways they are used may differ). With these categories, we want to explain how discourse is constructed in any language. Ultimately, these explanations may suggest hypotheses about how the different components of the human mind (such as memory, attention, and logic) work and interact with each other. Thus categories of information structure, like other aspects of linguistics, should be as independent of particular languages as possible.

There is an important difference between the types of syntactic constructions found in particular languages and the categories of information structure. The range of syntactic constructions available from language to language differs considerably. For example, some languages have a passive construction, but others do not. Since the categories of information structure are not language dependent, they cannot be defined in terms of particular structures.

Nevertheless, there is a close kinship between pragmatics and syntax. In all languages, one principal function of syntax is to encode pragmatic information. What differs from language to language is the way in which pragmatic structure maps onto syntax.

GIVEN INFORMATION AND NEW INFORMATION

One major category of information structure is the distinction between given and new information. **Given information** is information currently in the forefront of the hearer's mind; **new information** is information just being introduced into the discourse. Consider the following two-turn interaction:

> Alice: Who ate the custard?
> Tom: Mary ate the custard.

The noun phrase *Mary* represents new information in Tom's answer because it is just being introduced into the discourse there; *the custard,* in contrast, is given information in the reply because it can be presumed to be in the mind of Alice, who has just introduced it into the discourse in the previous turn. (We'll see shortly that given information often finds expression in condensed form—for example as *Mary ate **it*** or *Mary **did***.)

Given information need not be introduced into a discourse by a second speaker. In the following sequence of sentences, uttered by a single speaker, the underlined element represents given information because it has just been introduced in the previous sentence and can thus be assumed to be in the hearer's mind.

> A man called while you were on your break. <u>He</u> said he'd call back later.

A piece of information is sometimes taken as given because of its close association with something that has been introduced into the discourse. For example, when a noun phrase is introduced into a discourse, all the subparts of the referent can be treated as given information.

> Kent returned my car last night after borrowing it for the day. <u>One of the wheels</u> was about to fall off and <u>the dashboard</u> was missing.

> My mother went on a Caribbean cruise last year—she loved <u>the food</u>.

Because face-to-face conversation and most other kinds of discourse have at least implicit speakers and addressees, interactors always take first-person (speaker) and second-person (addressee) pronouns to be given information. These noun phrases thus do not need to be introduced into the discourse as new information.

Noun phrases carrying new information usually receive more stress than those carrying given information, and they are commonly expressed in a more elaborate fashion—for example, with a full noun phrase instead of a pronoun, and sometimes with a relative clause or adjectival modifiers. The following is typical of how new information is introduced into a discourse.

> When I entered the room, there was <u>a tall man with an old-fashioned hat on, quite elegantly dressed.</u>

In contrast, given information is commonly expressed in more attenuated ways—ways that are abbreviated or reduced. Typical attenuating devices used to encode given information include pronouns and unstressed noun phrases. Sometimes given information is simply left out of a sentence altogether. In the following interaction, the given information *is at the door* is omitted entirely from B's answer, which expresses only new information.

> A: Who's at the door?
> B: The mailman.

The contrast between given and new information is important in characterizing the function of several constructions in English and other languages, as we will show in the next section.

TOPICS

The **topic** of a sentence is its *center of attention*—what the sentence is about, its point of departure. The notion of topic is opposed to the notion of *comment,* the element of the sentence that says something about the topic. Often, given information is the sentence element about which we say something; in other words, given information is the topic. New information, on the other hand, represents what we want to say about the topic; it is the comment. Thus, if *Mary ate the custard* is offered in answer to the question *What did Mary do?,* the topic would be *Mary* (the given information) and the comment would be *ate the custard* (the new information). The topic of a sentence can sometimes be phrased as in these examples:

> <u>Speaking of Mary,</u> she ate the custard.
> <u>As for Mary,</u> she'll eat the custard.

Given information is not always the topic. In the second sentence of the following sequence, the noun phrase *her little sister* is both new information and the topic.

> Mary ate the custard. As for <u>her little sister</u>, she drank the cod-liver oil.

Similarly, given information can serve as comment, as the underlined element in the following sequence illustrates:

> Harold didn't believe anything the charlatan said. As for Hilda, she <u>believed everything he said</u>.

So the given/new contrast differs from the topic/comment contrast.

It is difficult to define precisely what a topic is. While the topic is the element of a sentence that functions as the center of attention, a sentence like *Oh, look!,* uttered to draw attention to a beautiful sunset, has an unexpressed topic ("the setting sun" or "the sky"). Thus topic is not necessarily a property of the sentence; it may be a property of the discourse context.

Topics are less central to the grammar of English than to the grammar of certain other languages. In fact, the only construction that unequivocally marks topics in English is the relatively rare *as for* construction in a sentence like the following:

> As for me, I'm gonna go to bed.

In English, marking the topic of a sentence is far less important than marking the subject.

Marking topic is considerably more important in certain other languages. Languages such as Japanese and Korean have function words whose sole purpose is to mark a noun phrase as topic (Japanese is discussed in the section Information-Structure Morphemes on p. 279). In Chinese and other languages, no special function words attach to topic noun phrases, but they are marked by word order. In these three languages, noun phrases marked in one way or another as the topic occur very frequently. Thus, despite the difficulty in defining it, the notion of topic is important and needs to be distinguished from other categories of information structure.

CONTRAST

A noun phrase is said to be **contrastive** when it occurs in opposition to another noun phrase in the discourse. Here, for example, the noun phrase *Hilda* in speaker B's answer is contrasted with the noun phrase *Matt.*

> Speaker A: Did Matt see the ghost?
> Speaker B: No, <u>Hilda</u> did.

Contrast that answer by speaker B with the following one, in which *Matt* is not contrastive.

> Speaker B: Yes, Matt saw the ghost.

Contrast is also marked in sentences that express the narrowing down of a choice from several candidates to one. In such sentences, the noun phrase that refers to the candidate thus chosen is marked contrastively.

> Of everyone present, only <u>Hilda</u> knew what was going on.

Compare that sentence with the following one, in which *Hilda* is not contrastive.

> Gerard knew what was going on, and Hilda knew what was going on.

A simple test exists for contrast: if a noun phrase can be followed by *rather than,* it is contrastive.

> Speaker A: Did Matt see the ghost?
> Speaker B: No, <u>Hilda</u>, rather than Matt, saw the ghost.

A single sentence can have several contrastive noun phrases; in speaker B's answer in the following exchange, *Hilda* contrasts with *Matt,* and *an entire cast of spirits* contrasts with *a ghost.*

> Speaker A: Did Matt see a ghost?
> Speaker B: Yes, Matt saw a ghost, but <u>Hilda</u> saw <u>an entire cast of spirits</u>.

The entity with which a noun phrase is contrasted is understood sometimes from the discourse context and sometimes from the nonlinguistic context. In the following example, *Hilda* could be marked contrastively if the sentence were part of a conversation about how the interlocutors dislike going to Maine during the winter.

> <u>Hilda</u> likes going to Maine during the winter.

In the next exchange, between an employee and one of several managers, the noun phrase *I* in the manager's reply can be made to contrast with "other managers," which is understood from the context.

> Employee: Can I leave early today?
> Manager: <u>I</u> don't mind.

The implication of the manager's answer is 'It's fine with me, but I don't know about the other managers.' The employee can readily understand the implication from knowledge of the context.

In English, contrastive noun phrases can be marked in a variety of ways, the most common of which is by pronouncing the contrastive noun phrase with strong stress.

> You may be smart, but <u>he</u>'s good-looking.

Other ways of marking contrastiveness will be investigated in the next section.

DEFINITE EXPRESSIONS

Speakers mark a noun phrase as **definite** when they assume that the listener can identify its referent; otherwise, the noun phrase is marked as **indefinite.** In this example, the definite noun phrase *the neighbor* in speaker B's answer presupposes that A can determine which neighbor speaker B is talking about.

> Speaker A: Who's at the door?
> Speaker B: It's <u>the</u> neighbor.

Speaker B's answer is appropriate if A and B have only one neighbor or have reason to expect a particular neighbor. If they have several neighbors, none of whom they know particularly well, speaker B cannot assume that speaker A will be able to identify which neighbor is at the door, and the answer to speaker A's question must be indefinite.

> Speaker B: It's <u>a</u> neighbor.

Pronouns and proper nouns are generally definite. Pronouns like *you* and *we* usually refer to particular individuals who are identifiable in the context of the discourse. And a speaker who refers to someone by the name *Hilda* or *Harry* assumes that a listener will be able to determine the referents of these names. Still, there are exceptions. Clerks in a government office may say to each other:

> I have a Susie Schmidt here who hasn't paid her taxes since 1987.

And they can do this irrespective of whether the speaker or hearer knows which particular individual goes by the name of Susie Schmidt.

Definiteness in English and many other languages is marked by the choice of articles (definite *the* versus indefinite *a*) or by demonstratives (*this* and *that,* both definite). But article choice is not always a way to mark definiteness. Some languages have only one article. In Fijian, *na,* the only article, is definite, while indefiniteness is marked with the expression *e dua* 'there is one.'

1. na   tuuraŋa   (definite)
   Article   gentleman
   'the gentleman'
2. e dua   na   tuuraŋa   (indefinite)
   there is one   Article   gentleman
   'a gentleman'

Hindi, in contrast, has only an indefinite article *ek;* a noun phrase with no article is interpreted as definite.

1. maĩ   kitaab   ḍʰũũṛʰ   rahii   tʰii   (definite)
   I   book   search   -ing   Past-tense
   'I was looking for the book.'
2. maĩ   ek   kitaab   ḍʰũũṛʰ   rahii   tʰii   (indefinite)
   I   a   book   search   -ing   Past-tense
   'I was looking for a book.'

Many languages do not have articles and must rely on other means to mark definiteness, if they mark it at all. In Mandarin Chinese, word order is used to mark definiteness. When the subject comes before the verb, as in sentence 1, it must be interpreted as definite; if it follows the verb, as in sentence 2, it is indefinite.

1. huǒchē   lái   le   (definite)
   train   arrive   New-situation
   'The train has arrived.'
2. lái   huǒchē   le   (indefinite)
   arrive   train   New-situation
   'A train has arrived.'

More exotic systems also exist. In Rotuman, spoken in the South Pacific, most words have two forms, one definite and one indefinite.

DEFINITE		INDEFINITE	
futi	'the banana'	füt	'a banana'
vaka	'the canoe'	vak	'a canoe'
rito	'the young shoot'	ryot	'a young shoot'

The indefinite form can be derived from the definite form through a set of phonological rules.

Definiteness must be distinguished from givenness because a noun phrase can be definite and given, indefinite and given, definite and new, or indefinite and new. The first and the last combinations are most common. Below, the underlined noun phrase in the first sentence is indefinite and new, and the one in the second sentence is definite and given.

> Once upon a time, there was <u>a young woman</u> who lived on a remote farm in the country. <u>The young woman</u> was named Mary.

But a noun phrase that refers to new information can also be definite. The following sentence, in which *the plumber* is definite, is acceptable whether or not the speaker has introduced a particular identifiable plumber into the previous discourse.

> The kitchen faucet is leaking; we have to call <u>the plumber</u>.

In certain circumstances, a noun phrase can be both indefinite and given, as with the underlined noun phrase in this example:

> I ate a hamburger for breakfast—<u>a hamburger</u>, I might add, that was one of the worst I've ever eaten.

Clearly, definiteness and givenness are distinct categories of information structure.

REFERENTIAL EXPRESSIONS

A noun phrase is **referential** when it refers to a particular entity. In the first example, the expression *an Italian with dark eyes* does not refer to anyone in particular and is therefore nonreferential. By contrast, in the second example, the same phrase does have a referent and is referential.

> Kate wants to marry <u>an Italian with dark eyes</u>, but she hasn't met one yet.
> Kate wants to marry <u>an Italian with dark eyes</u>; his name is Mario.

Out of context, *Kate wants to marry an Italian with dark eyes* is ambiguous because nothing in the sentence indicates whether or not a particular Italian is intended. In real-life natural discourse, sentences of this type are rarely ambiguous because of the power of context to clarify.

Referentiality and definiteness must be distinguished because a noun phrase can be:

REFERENTIAL AND DEFINITE

Where's <u>the key</u> to <u>the safe</u>?

REFERENTIAL AND INDEFINITE

She leased <u>a new Ford Bronco</u>.

NONREFERENTIAL AND DEFINITE

What's the most intelligent thing to do now?

NONREFERENTIAL AND INDEFINITE

You need to buy a new car.

While pronouns and proper nouns are usually referential, certain pronouns such as *you, it, they,* and *one* are often nonreferential.

> In this county, if *you* own a house *you* have to pay taxes.
> *It* is widely suspected that linguistics is fun to study.
> *They* have just changed the tax laws.
> *One* just doesn't know what to do in such circumstances.

None of these pronouns refers to a particular entity: they are nonreferential.

GENERIC AND SPECIFIC EXPRESSIONS

A noun phrase may be *generic* or *specific* depending on whether it refers to a category or to a particular member of a category. In the first of the following sentences, *the giraffe* is generic because it refers to the set of all giraffes; but *the giraffe* in the second sentence, which could have been uttered during a visit to a zoo, must refer to a particular animal, and is thus specific.

> The giraffe has a long neck.
> The giraffe has a sore foot.

The generic/specific contrast thus differs from definiteness and referentiality, and must be considered a separate category.

CATEGORIES OF INFORMATION STRUCTURE

Of the categories discussed in this section, givenness, topic, and contrast are not inherent properties of particular noun phrases. Like semantic roles, these categories can be defined only in relation to the discourse context in which the noun phrase occurs. For example, we can identify whether a noun phrase is contrastive or not only if we know the utterance or even the discourse in which it occurs. Givenness, topic, and contrast are thus *relational* categories of information structure.

Definiteness, referentiality, and the generic/specific contrast are *inherent* properties of the noun phrase. Given a particular noun phrase (and some information about what it refers to), we can usually decide whether it is definite or indefinite, referential or nonreferential, and generic or specific without knowing the sentence in which it occurs.

Information structure is not marked solely on noun phrases. Other parts of speech, verbs in particular, can represent given or new information and can also be contrastive. In the following exchange, the underlined verb represents contrastively marked new information.

Jerry comes to visit occasionally, but Hilda <u>moves in</u> every holiday.

Similarly, prepositions can sometimes be marked for information structure. It is not difficult to come up with examples of contrastively marked prepositions.

I said the book was *on* the table, not under it!

In this chapter, we concentrate almost exclusively on the marking of information structure on noun phrases, in part because the role of other constituents in the structure of discourse is still not well understood.

PRAGMATIC CATEGORIES AND SYNTAX

The categories of information structure can now be used to describe the functions of syntactic operations and other phenomena found in different languages. As noted earlier, every language can express the same content in a variety of ways. The differences among these various ways of expressing the same thing is frequently a pragmatic one. In this section we analyze a number of constructions, many of which are found in English, and illustrate how information structure is an important determiner of the choices we make in expressing ourselves verbally.

Languages differ in the extent to which and the ways in which pragmatic information is encoded in morphology and syntax. Some languages, like Japanese, have function words whose sole purpose is to indicate pragmatic categories. Other languages, like English, depend on syntactic structures like passives to convey pragmatic information. Intonation is also used in many languages to mark contrast. In English, intonation is an important tool in marking information structure; it is less important in languages like French and Chinese. Thus different languages use different strategies to encode pragmatic information. What follows is a sampling of some of these strategies.

FRONTING

One strategy that may be used to mark information structure is fronting. *Fronting* is a syntactic movement that operates in many languages, although its exact function varies from language to language. In English, it creates sentence 1 from the structure underlying sentence 2, which has the same meaning.

1. Lou I cannot stand.
2. I cannot stand Lou.

In English, one function of fronting is to mark givenness: a fronted noun phrase must represent given information.

> A: I heard that you really like mushrooms.
> B: <u>Mushrooms</u> I'd kill for.

A noun phrase can be fronted if its referent is part of a set that has been mentioned previously in the discourse, even though the referent itself may not have been mentioned. In the following example, *mushrooms* is a hyponym of *vegetable,* which is mentioned in the question that immediately precedes the fronted noun phrase; the result is pragmatically acceptable.

> A: What's your favorite vegetable?
> B: Mushrooms I find delicious.

Fronted noun phrases are often contrastive in English.

> A: Do you eat cauliflower?
> B: I hate cauliflower, but <u>mushrooms</u> I find delicious.

The fronted noun phrase must be the more salient element of the sentence. If this requirement is violated, the result is pragmatically ill formed (and hence starred). In speaker B's answer in the following interaction, *mushrooms* is not the most salient element in the sentence because the hearer's attention is distracted by the phrase *with butter and parsley.*

> A: What's your favorite vegetable?
> B: *Mushrooms I love to eat with butter and parsley.

(Note that in this chapter, asterisks * are not used to mark ungrammatical sentences but to mark sentences that are pragmatically ill formed—that is, sentences that do not fit well into the discourse context in which they occur.)

In other languages, fronted noun phrases do not necessarily have the same function as in English. In Mandarin Chinese, fronted noun phrases are commonly used to represent the topic of the sentence.

1. zhèi běn   shū pízi   hěn hǎo kàn
   this Classifier book cover very good-looking
   'This book, the cover is nice looking.'
2. zhèi ge   zhǎnlǎnhuì wǒ kàndào hěn duō   yóuhuàr
   this Classifier exhibition I see   very many   painting
   '(At) this exhibition, I saw many paintings.'

What is interesting about Chinese fronted noun phrases is that they do not necessarily have a semantic role in the rest of the sentence. In the following sentence, for example, *mógū* 'mushrooms' cannot be a patient because the sentence already has a patient: *zhèi ge dongxi* 'that sort of thing.' Yet the sentence is both grammatical and pragmatically acceptable.

mógū   wǒ hěn xǐhuan chī zhèi ge   dōngxi
mushroom I   very like   eat   this Classifier thing
'Mushrooms, I like to eat that sort of thing.'

Furthermore, fronted noun phrases do not need to be contrastive in Chinese, though they frequently are in English. The comparison of English and Chinese fronting illustrates an important point: a grammatical process such as a movement transformation may have comparable syntactic properties in two languages, but its pragmatic functions may differ considerably.

LEFT-DISLOCATION

Left-dislocation is an operation that derives sentences like 1 from the same underlying structures as basic sentences like 2.

1. Margaret, I can't stand her.
2. I can't stand Margaret.

Though left-dislocation is syntactically similar to fronting, there are several differences between the two. In particular, a fronted noun phrase does not leave a pronoun in the sentence, whereas a left-dislocated noun phrase does.

Margaret I can't stand. (fronting)
Margaret, I can't stand her. (left-dislocation)

Unlike fronted noun phrases, a left-dislocated noun phrase is set off from the rest of the sentence by a very short pause, represented in writing by a comma. Left-dislocation is similar in nature and function to right-dislocation, which moves the noun phrases to the right of a sentence.

I can't stand her, Margaret.

In this discussion, we will concentrate on left-dislocation.

Left-dislocation is primarily used to reintroduce given information that has not been mentioned for a while. In the following long example, the speaker lists a number of people and comments on them. Harold, mentioned early in the discourse, is reintroduced in the last sentence. Because nothing has been said about him in the previous two sentences, the speaker reintroduces *Harold* as a left-dislocated noun phrase.

I've kept in touch with lots of people from my school days. I still see Harold, who was my best friend in high school. And then there's Jim, my college roommate, and Stan and Hilda, who I met in my sophomore year at Ohio State. I really like Jim and Stan and Hilda. But *Harold,* I can't tolerate him now.

In addition to reintroducing given information, left-dislocation is contrastive. In this example, *Harold* clearly contrasts with *Jim, Stan,* and *Hilda.* As a result of its double function, left-dislocation is typically used when speakers go through lists and make comments about each individual element in the list. Some languages exploit left-dislocation considerably more frequently than English does. In spoken colloquial French, left-dislocated noun phrases are frequent, considerably more so than the equivalent basic sentences.

> Mon frère, il   s'en va en Mongolie.
> my brother he is-going to Mongolia
> 'My brother, he is leaving for Mongolia.'

Right-dislocation, illustrated by the following sentence, is equally common.

> J'sais pas, moi, c'qu'il veux.
> I know not me   what-he wants
> 'Me, I don't know what he wants.'

Left-dislocation in colloquial French has a different function from the equivalent transformation in English. In French, a left-dislocated noun phrase represents a topic. Left-dislocated noun phrases are particularly frequent when a new topic is introduced into the discourse (as in the first of the following examples) or when the speaker wishes to shift the topic of the discourse (as in the second example).

> 1. [Asking directions of a stranger in the street]
>   Pardon,   la gare,   où   est elle?
>   excuse-me the station where is it
>   'Excuse me, where is the station?'
> 2. Pierre: Moi, j'aime bien   les croissants.
>   me   I like   the croissants
>   'Me, I like croissants.'
>   Marie: Oui, mais le pain   frais, c'est bon aussi.
>   yes but the bread fresh it-is good too
>   'Yes, but fresh bread is also good.'

The pragmatic function of left-dislocation in French is thus considerably broader than its function in English.

IT CLEFTS AND **WH** CLEFTS

Clefting transformations are used in English and many other languages to mark information structure. In the following examples, sentence 1 is an *it*-cleft sentence, sentence 2 is a *WH*-cleft sentence, and sentence 3 is the basic sentence that corresponds to 1 and 2.

1. It was Harold that Stan saw at the party.   (*it*-cleft)
2. What Stan saw at the party was Harold.   (WH-cleft)
3. Stan saw Harold at the party.

It-cleft sentences are of the form *It is/was/will be . . . that,* in which what comes between the first part and the second part of the construction is the clefted noun phrase, prepositional phrase (*It was in March that she last visited*), or adverb (*It's only recently that she's learned to sing*). WH-cleft constructions can be of the form *WH-word . . . is/was/will be,* in which the WH-word is usually *what.* In WH-cleft constructions, the clefted noun phrase, prepositional phrase, or adverb is placed after the verb *be,* and the rest of the clause is placed between the two parts of the construction. Other variants of WH-cleft sentences also exist.

THE ONE THAT/WHO . . . IS/WAS/WILL BE

The one who saw Harold at the party was Stan.

. . . IS/WAS/WILL BE WHAT/WHO . . .

Harold is who John saw at the party.

Note that, besides *is, was,* and *will be,* some other forms of *be* may also occur in clefts.

Both *it*-cleft and WH-cleft constructions are used to mark givenness. In an *it*-cleft construction, the clefted phrase presents new information, and the rest of the sentence is given information. Thus the information question in 1 can be answered with 2, in which the answer to the question is clefted, but not with 3 because the clefted element is not the requested new information.

1. Who did Stan see at the party?
2. It was Harold that Stan saw at the party.
3. *It was Stan who saw Harold at the party.

That the part of the sentence following *that/who* in a cleft sentence presents given information is illustrated by the fact that it can refer to something just mentioned in the previous sentence. In the following example, the second sentence is a cleft construction in which the elements following *that* are simply repeated from the previous sentence in the discourse.

Alice told me that Stan saw someone at the party that he knew from his high school days. It turns out it was Harold *that Stan saw at the party.*

Clearly, the element following *that* in a cleft sentence represents given information.

WH-cleft constructions are similar to *it*-cleft constructions. In WH-cleft sentences, the new information comes after the verb *be,* and the rest of the clause is placed between the WH-word and the *be* verb.

1. What did Stan see at the party?
2. What Stan saw at the party was Harold dancing the rumba.

Question 1 could not be answered with either of the following clefted sentences because in neither 3 nor 4 is the clefted noun phrase the new information.

3. *The one who saw Harold dancing the rumba was Stan.
4. *Where Stan saw Harold was at the party.

The rest of a WH-clefted sentence marks given information, as in an *it*-clefted sentence. The following sentence pair, in which given information is underlined, illustrates this fact.

I liked her latest novel very much. In particular, what <u>I liked about it</u> was the way the characters' personalities are developed.

The effect of both *it*-clefting and WH-clefting is to highlight which element is new information and which element is given information.

In addition, both constructions can mark contrast. Consider the following two sequences. In both the first one (whose second sentence is an *it*-cleft construction) and the second (whose second sentence is a WH-cleft), the new information can readily be understood as contrastive. Possible implied information is provided in square brackets after each example.

1. Alice said Stan saw someone at the party that he knew from his high school days. It turns out it was Harold that Stan saw at the party. [. . . not Larry, as you might have thought.]
2. I liked her latest novel very much. In particular, what I liked about it was the way the characters' personalities are developed. [I liked the character development more than the style of writing.]

You might wonder why English should have two constructions with the same function. Languages usually exploit different structures for different purposes—and, indeed, there is a subtle difference in the uses for these two constructions. An *it*-cleft construction can be used to mark given information that the listener or reader is not necessarily thinking about. In a WH-cleft construction, though, the listener or reader must be thinking about the given information. Thus it is possible to begin a narrative with an *it*-cleft construction but not with a WH-cleft construction. Below, the first sentence, an *it*-cleft construction, would be an acceptable opening sentence for a historical narrative; but the second sentence, a WH-cleft construction, would not normally make a good beginning.

> It was to gain their independence from Britain that the colonists started the Revolution.
>
> *What the colonists started the Revolution to gain was their independence from Britain.

The first sentence is an acceptable opening because it does not necessarily assume that the reader has in mind the given information ("the colonists started the Revolution") when the narrative begins. The second sentence does assume that the given information is in the reader's mind and thus does not make a good opening sentence.

The differene between *it*-cleft and WH-cleft constructions shows that given information is not an absolute notion. There may be different types of givenness: information that the listener knows but is not necessarily thinking about at the moment and information that the listener both knows and is thinking about.

SENTENCE STRESS

In English and some other languages intonation is an important information-marking device. Generally, noun phrases representing new information receive stronger stress than noun phrases representing given information, and they are uttered on a slightly higher pitch than the rest of the sentence. This is called *new-information stress*.

> Speaker A: Whose foot marks are these on the sofa?
> Speaker B: They're *Lou's foot marks*.

English speakers also exploit stress to mark contrast.

1. Speaker A: Are these your foot marks on the sofa?
   Speaker B: No, they're not mine, they're *Lou's*.
2. They told Harold he had to put in two more years to graduate, but they gave *Hilda* an *honorary doctorate*.

Phonetically, new-information stress and contrastive stress are very similar, but functionally they differ. English uses stress in complex ways, much more so than such languages as French and Chinese.

INFORMATION STRUCTURE MORPHEMES

Some languages have grammatical morphemes whose sole function is to mark categories of information structure. In Japanese, the function word *wa,* which is placed after noun phrases, marks either givenness or contrastiveness. When a noun phrase is neither given nor contrastive, it is marked with a different function word (usually *ga* for subjects and *o* for direct objects). That *wa* is a marker of given information is illustrated by the following exchange:

> Speaker A: basu ga kimasuka
> bus Subject come-Question
> 'Is the bus coming?'
> Speaker B: basu wa kimasu
> bus Given coming-is
> 'The bus is coming.'

In speaker A's question, *basu* could not be marked with *wa* unless A and B had been talking about the bus in the previous discourse. But in speaker B's answer, *basu* is given information and must be marked with *wa*. Here's another example:

> basu ga kimasu basu wa konde-imasu
> bus Subject coming-is bus Given crowded-is
> 'The bus is coming. The bus is crowded.'

Japanese *wa* also marks contrastive information, as in the following sentence:

> basu wa kimasu demo takushi wa kimasen
> bus Contrast coming-is but taxi Contrast coming-isn't
> 'The bus is coming. But the taxi isn't (coming).'

Here, *basu wa* need not represent given information, for *wa* can simply mark the fact that the noun phrase to which it is attached is in contrast with another noun phrase also marked with *wa* (*takushi* 'taxi').

Like Japanese, many languages use function words to mark categories of information structure. This is the most transparent way of marking information structure. Unlike movement operations, such grammatical morphemes as Japanese *wa* do not affect the overall shape of a sentence. Rather, in a straightforward fashion, they point out which element of a sentence is given, which is contrastive, and so on.

PASSIVES

As with other languages that have a passive construction, the choice between an active sentence and its passive equivalent can be exploited in English to mark information structure. Compare the following sentences:

1. Bureaucrats could easily store and retrieve data about the citizenry.
2. Data about the citizenry could easily be stored and retrieved by bureaucrats.
3. Data about the citizenry could easily be stored and retrieved.

Of these three sentences, all of which can represent the same situation, sentence 1 is active, while the other two are passive structures. In sentence 2, the agent is expressed (*bureaucrats*), whereas there is no expressed agent in sentence 3. We call a passive construction like 2 an *agent passive* construction; 3 is an example of an *agentless passive.*

Agentless passives and agent passives are used in English for specific purposes. First of all, a sentence is expressed as an agentless passive if the agent is particularly unimportant in the action or state that the sentence represents. Such a situation may arise, for example, when the agent is a generic entity whose identity is irrelevant to the point of the sentence.

> A new shopping mall is being built near the interstate.
> New Christmas stamps are issued every year.

In the first sentence, the agent is likely to be some real-estate developer; in the second sentence, the postal authorities. In each case, the exact identity of the agent is either known or irrelevant to the situation represented by the sentence. In spoken language, agentless passives are often equivalent to active sentences with an indefinite and nonreferential pronoun *they.*

> They're building a new shopping mall near the interstate.
> They issue new Christmas stamps every year.

An agent passive construction is used if a noun phrase other than the agent is given information. Suppose that a news report begins as follows:

> The World Health Organization held its annual meeting last week in Geneva.

This sentence establishes the meeting as given information for the rest of the report. If the next sentence uses the noun phrase *the meeting,* it is likely that it will occur in subject position because it represents given information. If the noun phrase *the meeting* does not have the semantic role of agent in the next sentence, the sentence is likely to be expressed as a passive construction in order to allow *the meeting* to be the grammatical subject.

> The meeting was organized by health administrators from fifty countries.

This generalization is not absolute, and there is nothing fundamentally wrong with a sequence in which the second sentence is active rather than the passive predicted by the generalization, as shown below:

> The World Health Organization held its annual meeting last week in Geneva.
> Health administrators from fifty countries organized the meeting.

But the equivalent sequence with a passive second sentence seems to flow better and may be easier to understand:

The World Health Organization held its annual meeting last week in Geneva.
The meeting was organized by health administrators from fifty countries.

Clearly, in English the choice of a passive sentence over its active counterpart is regulated by information structure. Specifically, agentless passives are used when the agent is either known or not particularly significant (as in this very sentence). Agent passives (or *by* passives, as they are sometimes called) are used when a noun phrase other than the agent of the sentence is more prominent as given information than the agent itself.

Not all languages have a passive construction. Chinese and Samoan, for example, do not. Such languages have other ways of saying what English speakers express with the passive. In Samoan, when the agent of a sentence is not important, it is simply not expressed; the sentence remains an active structure.

> ʔua   ʔoteŋia le   teiŋe
> Present-tense scold   the young-woman
> 'The young woman is being scolded.'
> (Literally: 'Is scolding the young woman.')

WORD ORDER

Many languages use the sequential order of noun phrases to mark differences in information structure. English cannot use the full resources of word order for this purpose because it uses word order to mark subjects and direct objects (see Chapter 5). In the following sentence, the word order indicates who is doing the chasing and who is being chased.

> The cat is chasing the dog.

If we invert the two noun phrases, the semantics of the sentence (who is agent and who is patient) changes.

> The dog is chasing the cat.

In a language like Russian, however, we can scramble the noun phrases without changing the semantics. All the following sentences mean the same thing.

1. koška presleduet sobaku
   cat   is chasing dog
2. sobaku presleduet koška
3. presleduet koška sobaku
4. presleduet sobaku koška   'The cat is chasing the dog.'
5. koška sobaku presleduet
6. sobaku koška presleduet

In each of these sentences we know who is doing what to whom because the inflections on the noun vary with its grammatical function. The *-u* ending of *sobaku* 'dog' marks it as the direct object (if it were the subject, it would be *sobaka*), and the *-a* ending of *koška* 'cat' marks it as the subject (as direct object, it would be *košku*).

The differences among these versions of the same sentence reside in their information structure. More precisely, in Russian, word order marks givenness. The information question *Što koška presleduet?* 'What is the cat chasing?' can only be answered as follows:

> koška presleduet sobaku
> cat   is chasing dog
> 'The cat is chasing the dog.'

On the other hand, the question *Što presleduet sobaku?* 'What is chasing the dog?' must be answered as follows:

> sobaku presleduet koška
> dog   is chasing cat
> 'The cat is chasing the dog.'

Thus what comes first in the Russian sentence is not the subject but the given information, and what comes last is the new information. In answer to the question *What is the cat chasing?*, *the dog* is new information and comes at the end of the Russian sentence. In contrast, *the cat* is new information in answer to the question *What is chasing the dog?*, and it comes last in the sentence. Word order in Russian, as in many other languages, is thus used to mark givenness. Similar explanations could be offered for the other variants of the Russian sentence we have cited, but we will not develop them here. (See Exercise 8-9.)

Typically, in languages that exploit word order to encode pragmatic information, syntactic constructions like passives, *it*-clefts, and WH-clefts do not exist (or are rare). Russian has a grammatical construction that resembles the English passive, but it is rarely used. The reason is simple: given the rich inflectional system that marks grammatical relations, word order can be used to mark information structure, and there is really no need to use complex structures like passives to mark givenness. Passives are useful in languages in which word order is exploited for other purposes and thus cannot be manipulated to indicate pragmatic structure.

THE RELATIONSHIP OF SENTENCES TO DISCOURSE: PRAGMATICS

We have outlined some of the basic notions needed to describe how information is structured in discourse and have analyzed a number of constructions in terms of information structure. From the discussion in this and the previous chapter, it should be clear that the syntactic structure of any language is driven by two factors. On the one hand, syntax must encode semantic structure: the syntactic structure of a sentence must enable language users to identify who does what to whom—the agent of a sentence, the patient, and other semantic roles. On the other hand, syntax must encode information structure: which element of a noun phrase is given information, which is new information, which can be easily identified by the hearer, which cannot, and so on. Schematically, the relationship is as follows:

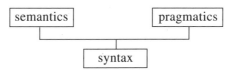

Syntax is thus used to convey two kinds of information: semantic information and pragmatic information.

COMPUTERS AND PRAGMATICS

You've seen in this chapter that a thorough acquaintance with pragmatics is needed to understand how language works. Eventually a thorough understanding of pragmatics will prove important for speech recognition and, to a lesser extent, speech synthesis. To date, however, pragmatics has not been as well explored in computational linguistics as have morphological, lexical, phonological, grammatical, and even semantic features of texts.

One reason for the relative neglect of pragmatics is that modeling the world knowledge and the discourse knowledge that speakers rely on when producing and understanding spoken and written texts is extremely challenging—far more so than creating models of structural aspects of language like morphology and syntax. A second reason is that the kinds of linguistic features by which some pragmatic categories are realized are not always expressed in texts in ways that computers can readily track.

As we saw in this chapter, speakers base several aspects of expression on their beliefs about what hearers know and what is in the forefront of their minds. This is true in marking nouns definite or indefinite, in choosing active or passive voice, in indicating contrast by intonation, and so on. These three features have some representation in a text, but others such as given and new information have little or no textual realization and would be extremely challenging or impossible for a computer to identify.

If you've ever used a grammar checker, you know that even rudimentary ones readily spot passive voice verbs (by identifying forms of the verb *be* together with—though not necessarily adjacent to—a past participle, as in *is structured, are expressed,* and *has not been explored*—all taken from paragraphs in this section). What grammar checkers cannot do is distinguish between passives that effectively serve a pragmatic function and passives that do not. As a result, a writer who uses a grammar checker may find that it flags every passive voice verb, urging the writer to consider recasting them all as actives. If a writer rewrote all passives as actives, the rewritten sentences would remain grammatical but the changes could well damage the pragmatic structure of the text. (Exercise 8-7 in this chapter asks you to consider revising the passives in a short text.)

Computer programs can identify pragmatic categories if they are marked in the text. Thus, the Japanese function word *wa* can be automatically identified as easily as an English passive. Likewise most English noun phrases can automatically be marked as definite or indefinite. But other categories—for example, topic, givenness, and referentiality—cannot be identified automatically and would have to be identified by a speaker of the language. If researchers wanted to make use of such categories in their corpora, they would have to have their texts tagged. That usually means that a program will tag each *potential* item—say, all referring expressions—as "given" and then present the human editor with a menu of alternatives that can be quickly substituted for the tentative tag and entered into the corpus, much as a spell checker does. Once such categories have been marked on the referring expressions in a corpus, researchers can explore related matters, relying on the computer's capacity for speed and accuracy.

For example, suppose a corpus contained referring expressions that had been tagged as given or new. It would then be a simple matter to calculate the number of given and new references for any group of texts in the corpus—for example for conversations or for news reportage in newspapers. It turns out that different kinds of texts differ significantly in the average number of given and new references they contain.

Figure 8-1 shows two sets of relations: those between given and new information in three kinds of text and those among the three kinds of text. For example, conversation has three times as many "given" referring expressions as "new" ones. By contrast, academic prose has about half as many given expressions as new ones. Likewise, while conversation and news reportage have approximately the same number of referring expressions in each two hundred words of text, the proportion of given and new referents is reversed in these kinds of text. Conversationalists use referring expressions that are mostly given. News reportage introduces new referents about twice as often as it refers to given information—noun phrases that have already been mentioned in the text. Now a good many referring expressions in conversation are first- and second-person pronouns, which are of course given information. (By contrast, the use of first- and second-person pronouns in news reportage is virtually limited to quoted speech.)

As Figure 8-1 shows, a second kind of information can be drawn from counts of given and new referring expressions in different kinds of text. For example, the number of new referring expressions is relatively low in conversation as compared with academic prose or news reportage. Not surprisingly, news reportage contains more than twice the number of new references as conversation; and so does academic prose.

To take another example, if in a corpus third-person pronouns have been assigned an index that matches their referent to a preceding noun phrase, then computer programs can track the distance between a third-person pronoun and its antecedent. For this purpose, a useful measure is the number of intervening noun phrases. Again, it turns out that different kinds of texts have significantly different distances intervening between third-person pronouns and their antecedents. As Figure 8-2 shows, both academic prose and news reportage have at least twice as many intervening noun phrases as conversation. In part this reflects the fact that conversation is produced

Figure 8-1

AVERAGE NUMBER OF GIVEN AND NEW REFERRING EXPRESSIONS IN THREE KINDS OF TEXTS

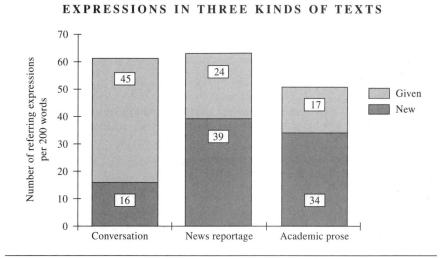

Source: D. Biber, S. Conrad, R. Reppen, *Corpus Linguistics* (Cambridge: Cambridge UP, 1998).

Figure 8-2

AVERAGE DISTANCE BETWEEN PRONOUNS AND THEIR ANTECEDENTS, MEASURED IN NUMBER OF INTERVENING REFERRING EXPRESSIONS

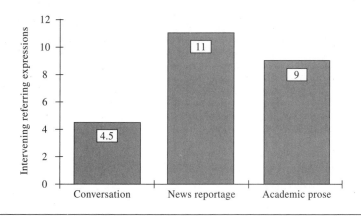

Source: D. Biber, S. Conrad, R. Reppen, *Corpus Linguistics* (Cambridge: Cambridge UP, 1998).

extemporaneously, and speakers must accommodate the need of their hearers to keep track of referents that speakers identify only by third-person pronouns.

With suitably tagged corpora, a good deal can be learned about the character of different kinds of texts. Such information will prove useful in speech recognition, machine translation, and other applications where computers and language are increasingly intertwined.

SUMMARY

- Pragmatics is concerned with the encoding of information structure—the relative significance of different elements in a clause, principally noun phrases. It treats the relationship of sentences to their discourse environment.

- Relational categories include *givenness* (whether a piece of information is new or already exists in the discourse context), *topic* (the center of attention), and *contrast* (whether or not a piece of information is contrasted with another piece).

- Nonrelational notions include *definiteness* (whether or not the referent of a noun phrase is identifiable) and *referentiality* (whether or not a noun phrase has a referent).

- Some syntactic transformations serve to mark certain elements of sentences for pragmatic categories. In English, transformations like fronting, left-dislocation, *it*-cleft, WH-cleft, and passivization have the effect of singling out particular noun phrases as sentence topics or as given or new information.

- The marking of contrast is achieved through sentence stress and is a secondary function of certain transformations like fronting.

- Many languages exploit word order and grammatical morphemes to mark information structure.

- The functions of a particular transformation or information-structure device may differ from one language to another because each language favors particular strategies over others.

- Syntax encodes two types of information: semantic information (the semantic role of a noun phrase) and pragmatic information (the relative significance of noun phrases in a discourse).

EXERCISES

Based on English

8-1. In an article called "Ellen's 'Heart Issue': A Friend's Report," actress Kathy Najimy writes as follows about her first meeting with Ellen DeGeneres. After examining the passage (sentence numbers have been added), answer the questions below:

(1) I met Ellen three or four years ago when I was a guest on her show. (2) She was funny, smart and charming, and I was moved by her vulnerability and

what she was going through in regards to her sexuality. (3) We would sit in the trailer and talk about what was happening to her personally and politically. (4) It was interesting to me because I know lots of gay people, and I know lots of famous people, but I had never known anyone who was famous and gay and struggling with what to do about it. [*Los Angeles Times,* "Calendar," December 21, 1997, page 79]

a. In 1, is the pronoun *I* given or new information? Explain the basis for your answer.
b. Identify the topic noun phrases for sentences 2, 3, and 4.
c. In 2, is *She* given or new information? Explain the basis for your answer.
d. In 3, is *We* given or new information? Explain the basis for your answer.
e. In 4, is *It* given or new information, and what constituent does *It* refer to?
f. From your answers in questions b through e, what inference can you draw about topics in this paragraph?
g. From the examples you have just examined and the other pronouns in the passage, would you say that personal pronouns generally represent given information or new information?
h. In 1, is *Ellen* given or new information? Definite or indefinite? Explain.
i. In 1, whose show does *her show* refer to? Is *her show* definite or indefinite?
j. List *all* indefinite noun phrases in the passage. (Include pronouns as noun phrases.)
k. Prior to its mention in 3, the noun phrase *the trailer* has not been mentioned, so how do you explain that it is marked definite?

8-2. Examine the passage below and answer the questions that follow:

(1) Beginning in 1999, the Rose Bowl will no longer have first shot at the top teams from the Big Ten and Pac-10 football conferences. (2) Instead, the "Bowl Alliance," which aims each year to match the top two teams in the country for the national title, will decide who goes where. (3) The alliance, a cooperative venture among six of the nation's strongest football conferences, has a seven-year deal with ABC Sports, which will televise the title game. (4) This agreement assures each conference champion and Notre Dame a berth in one of four bowl games—the Rose, Orange, Fiesta or Sugar—with the national championship game annually rotated among the four venues. [Adapted from an advertising supplement in the *Los Angeles Times* "Calendar," December 21, 1997, page M]

a. Identify two noun phrases that are referential and two that are not.
b. Identify any contrastive noun phrases in the passage.
c. In 4, *This agreement* is given information and is marked definite. What noun phrase in 3 has the same referent as *this agreement* but is indefinite? Explain why the first of these noun phrases with identical referents is indefinite and the second definite.

d. Identify an example noun phrase of each of the following kinds:
 (i) referential and definite.
 (ii) referential and indefinite
 (iii) nonreferential and definite.
 (iv) nonreferential and indefinite

8-3. Describe in detail how the following text is poorly constructed. Analyze each of the seven sentences in its context and state what is wrong with it in terms of information structure.

(1) As for the Fire Department, it evacuated two apartment buildings at the corner of Country Club Drive and Fifth Avenue at 3 A.M. last Sunday. (2) There was someone who had discovered a furnace in the basement of one of the buildings from which oil was leaking. (3) What was sprayed by firemen over the oil for several hours was chemical foam. (4) It was by 8 A.M. that the situation was under control. (5) What someone had averted was any danger of explosion or fire, and as for the leaky furnace, it was sealed. (6) What the residents of the two apartment buildings were given in the Country Club High School gymnasium was temporary shelter. (7) Possession of their apartments was regained by them at 5 P.M.

8-4. Choose a short article (approximately one newspaper column) or an excerpt of an article from the front page of a newspaper. Identify all the sentences that have undergone a syntactic operation of some kind (such as passivization or clefting). In each case, explain carefully the most likely reason for using a transformed sentence instead of the equivalent basic sentence.

8-5. In certain dialects of English there is an operation that moves a noun phrase to the beginning of its clause. This operation derives sentence (1) from the same underlying structure as the basic sentence (2):

(1) A bottle of champagne and caviar he wants.

(2) He wants a bottle of champagne and caviar.

The operation is called "Yiddish movement" because it is characteristic of the English dialect spoken by native speakers of Yiddish. Yiddish movement is syntactically similar to fronting but differs in terms of its pragmatic function. Here are three pragmatic contexts in which Yiddish movement is appropriate. On the basis of these data, describe succinctly the pragmatic function of Yiddish movement.

(a) Speaker A: What does he want?
 Speaker B: A bottle of champagne and caviar he wants!

(b) Speaker A: How's your daughter?
 Speaker B: So many worries she causes me to have!

(c) Speaker A: Are you willing to help me?
   Speaker B: A finger I would not lift for you!

Compare in particular the following interactions. In the first, the answer can undergo Yiddish movement; in the second, it cannot.

(d) Speaker A: Who is Hilda going to marry?
   Speaker B: A scoundrel Hilda is going to marry!

(e) Speaker A: Who is going to marry Hilda?
   Speaker B: *Hilda a scoundrel is going to marry!

8-6. In English, presentational constructions are sentences in which a noun phrase is preceded by *there is/was* (or any other tense variant) and followed by a relative clause. Here are two examples:

(a) Once upon a time there was a poor peasant who had three sons.

(b) There's a man who wants to talk to you; he's been waiting for more than an hour.

Presentational constructions must be distinguished from constructions with *there* that indicate location, as in *There's my lovely shawl.* Describe succinctly the pragmatic function of presentational constructions. In your discussion, you may refer to the following additional examples:

(c) There's a dog I've been looking for. It's a fawn boxer with a white chest and cropped ears.

(d) *There's a dog I've been looking for. Any dog will do.

(e) There's the new Fellini movie that's playing at the Bijou.

8-7. Examine the passage that follows and identify all the passive-voice verbs. Then note the possible pragmatic reason the writer may have had in using each passive. Next, for those clauses or sentences whose passive voice you cannot find a reason for, rewrite them using an active voice verb. Finally, consider the revised passage—containing your revised sentences—and judge whether the text is more pragmatically effective than the original. Explain your answer.

One consequence of the ideological position that individuals are the basis of society is that these individuals must be considered to be equal to each other. As will be discussed below under the topic of face systems, this egalitarianism of Utilitarian discourse is not applied to all human beings but only to "those capable of being improved by free and equal discussion" (Mill 1990:271–2). That is to say, this egalitarianism is applied only to members of the Utilitarian discourse system. [Adapted from Ron Scollon and Suzanne Wong Scollon, *Intercultural Communication* (Cambridge, MA: Blackwell, 1995, p. 110)]

Based on Languages Other Than English

8-8. As in Russian, word order in Spanish is used to encode information structure. The constituents of a sentence may be ordered in a variety of ways, as shown by the following examples from Castilian Spanish, all of which can describe the same event. (S = subject; V = verb; O = direct object)

Consuelo envió el paquete. (SVO)
Consuelo sent the package

Envió Consuelo el paquete. (VSO)
sent Consuelo the package

'Consuelo sent the package.'

Envió el paquete Consuelo. (VOS)
sent the package Consuelo

El paquete lo envió Consuelo. (OVS)
the package it sent Consuelo

Consider the following conversational exchanges, focusing on the order of constituents in the answers.

(1) Q: ¿Qué hizo Consuelo?
    what did Consuelo
    'What did Consuelo do?'
 A: Consuelo preparó la sangria.
    Consuelo prepared the sangria
    'Consuelo made the sangria.'

(2) Q: ¿Quién comió mi bocadillo?
    who ate my sandwich
    'Who ate my sandwich?'
 A: Tu bocadillo lo comió Consuelo.
    your sandwich it ate Consuelo
    'Consuelo ate your sandwich.'

(3) Q: ¿A quién dió Consuelo este regalo?
    to whom gave Consuelo this present
    'Who did Consuelo give this present to?'
 A: Este regalo lo dió Consuelo a su madre.
    this present it gave Consuelo to her mother
    'Consuelo gave this present to her mother.

(4) Q: ¿Que pasó?
    what occurred
    'What happened?'
A: Se murió Consuelo.
    died   Consuelo
    'Consuelo died.'

(5) Q: ¿Recibió Consuelo el premio?
    received Consuelo the prize
    'Did Consuelo get the prize?'
A: No, el   premio lo recibió   Paquita.
    no   the prize it received Paquita
    'No, *Paquita* got the prize.'

(6) Q: ¿Recibió Consuelo esta carta?
    received   Consuelo this letter
    'Did Consuelo get this letter?'
A: No, Consuelo recibió   este paquete.
    no Consuelo received this package
    'No, Consuelo got this *package.*'

(7) Q: Recibió Consuelo el   premio?
    received Consuelo the prize
    'Did Consuelo get the prize?'
A: Si, el   premio lo recibió   Consuelo.
    yes the prize it received Consuelo
    'Yes, Consuelo got the prize.'

a. On the basis of these data, describe how word order is used to mark information structure in Spanish statements (but not in questions). In particular, state which categories of information structure are marked through which word order possibility. Make the statement of your rules as general as possible.

b. Notice that in certain sentences the pronoun *lo* 'it' appears before the verb. What is the syntactic rule that dictates when it should and should not appear? Which rule of English does the presence of the pronoun in these sentences remind you of?

8-9. In light of the function of Russian word order, provide an information question in English to which sentences 5 and 6 on p. 281 would be pragmatically acceptable Russian answers.

8-10. Tongan has an operation that incorporates the direct object (DO) into the verb, forming a verb-noun compound. It generates a sentence like (a) from the underlying structure of the basic sentence (b):

(a) naʔa   ku inu pia   (DO incorporated)
    Past-tense I   drink beer
    'I drank beer.' (literally: 'I beer-drank.')

(b) naʔa   ku inu ʔa   e   pia   (DO not incorporated)
    Past-tense I   drink Object the beer
    'I drank the/a beer.'

Below are three more examples of object-incorporated constructions (translated loosely to highlight the meaning of the Tongan sentence):

ʔoku   nau fie kai   ika   (DO incorporated)
Present-tense they hungry-for fish
'They are fish-hungry.'

naʔa   ma   sio   faiva   (DO incorporated)
Past-tense we   see   movie
'We (went) movie-watching.'

ʔoku   ne   faʔu   hiva kakala   (DO incorporated)
Present-tense she compose   love-song
'She is love-song composing.'

An incorporated direct object cannot be followed by a restrictive relative clause but a direct object that has not been incorporated can be. Compare:

*naʔa   ku inu pia [naʔa   nau omai]   (DO incorporated)
Past-tense I   drink beer Past-tense they give-me
'I drank beer [that they gave me].'

naʔa   ku inu ʔa e pia [naʔa   nau omail] (DO not
Past-tense I   drink Object the beer Past-tense they give-me   incorporated)
'I drank the/a beer [that they gave me].'

Assuming that restrictive relative clauses have the same function in Tongan and English, describe the pragmatic function of Tongan object incorporation.

INTERNET RESOURCE

Voices Demonstration Page: http://www.att.com/aspg/odemo.html
After reading an earlier chapter, you may have tried this Web site to hear a demonstration of speech synthesis, and you may have been impressed with the synthesizer's ability to produce the consonantal and vocalic sounds of the sentence you submitted. Now it's worth returning to the site so that you can submit sentences that illustrate some of the information structure devices from this chapter—for example, left-dislocation or contrast. Judge for yourself to what extent this particular speech synthesis engine (the WATSON Flex Talk™) can capture the intonation that conveys certain pragmatic information in the sentences you submit.

SUGGESTIONS FOR FURTHER READING

- **Geoffrey N. Leech. 1983.** *Principles of Pragmatics* (London: Longman). An accessible introduction to pragmatics.

Advanced Reading

Overviews of the issues addressed in this chapter can be found in Brown and Yule (1983), Lambrecht (1994), Foley and Van Valin (1985), Givón (1979a), and Chafe (1976). The papers in Givón (1979b) and Li (1976) investigate the interaction of syntax and pragmatics in various languages. Chafe (1970) is an important study of this interaction in English. Givenness and related topics are discussed in Prince (1979), definiteness in Hawkins (1979). Japanese *wa* and other particles are discussed in Kuno (1973). The discussion of *it*-cleft and WH-cleft constructions in this chapter is based on Prince (1978) and the discussion of fronting and Yiddish movement on Prince (1981). Lambrecht (1981) analyzes left- and right-dislocation in spoken French; left-dislocation in Italian is discussed in Duranti and Ochs (1979).

English passive constructions are investigated in Thompson (1987). A concise discussion of the function of Russian word order can be found in Comrie (1979), with which Thompson's (1978) study of English word order can be usefully contrasted. For an overview of research on intonation and sentence stress and their pragmatic functions, see Bolinger (1986). Other means of marking pragmatic structure in English are discussed in Halliday and Hasan (1976). Quirk et al. (1985), an extensive description of English grammar, discusses the pragmatic functions of particular constructions.

REFERENCES

- Bolinger, Dwight L. 1986. *Intonation and Its Parts: Melody in Spoken English* (Stanford: Stanford UP).

- Brown, Gillian, and George Yule. 1983. *Discourse Analysis* (Cambridge: Cambridge UP).

- Chafe, Wallace L. 1970. *Meaning and the Structure of Language* (Chicago: U of Chicago P).

- Chafe. Wallace L. 1976. "Givenness, Contrastiveness, Definiteness, Subjects, Topics, and Point of View," in Li (1976), pp. 25–55.

- Comrie, Bernard. 1979. "Russian," in Timothy Shopen, ed., *Languages and Their Status* (Cambridge, MA: Winthrop), pp. 91–151.

- Duranti, Alessandro, and Elinor Ochs. 1979. "Left-dislocation in Italian Conversation," in Givón (1979b), pp. 377–416.

- Foley, William, and Robert Van Valin, Jr. 1985. "Information Packaging in the Clause," in Timothy Shopen, ed., *Language Typology and Syntactic Description* (Cambridge: Cambridge UP), 3, pp. 282–384.

- Givón, Talmy. 1979a. *On Understanding Grammar* (New York: Academic).

- Givón, Talmy, ed. 1979b. *Syntax and Semantics 12: Discourse and Syntax* (New York: Academic).

- Halliday, M. A. K., and Ruqaiya Hasan. 1976. *Cohesion in English* (London: Longman).

- Hawkins, John A. 1979. *Definiteness and Indefiniteness* (London: Croom Helm).

- Kuno, Susumu. 1973. *The Structure of the Japanese Language* (Cambridge, MA: MIT P).

- Lambrecht, Knud. 1981. *Topic, Antitopic, and Verb Agreement in Non-standard French* (Amsterdam: Benjamins).

- Lambrecht, Knud. 1994. *Information Structure and Sentence Form: Topic, Focus, and the Mental Representation of Discourse Referents* (Cambridge: Cambridge UP).

- Li, Charles N., ed. 1976. *Subject and Topic* (New York: Academic).

- Prince, Ellen F. 1978. "A Comparison of WH-clefts and *It*-clefts in Discourse," *Language* 54:883–906.

- Prince, Ellen F. 1979. "On the Given/New Distinction," *Papers from the Fifteenth Regional Meeting of the Chicago Linguistics Society* (Chicago: Chicago Linguistics Society), pp. 267–278.

- Prince, Ellen F. 1981. "Topicalization, Focus Movement, and Yiddish Movement: A Pragmatic Differentiation," *Proceedings of the Seventh Annual Meeting of the Berkeley Linguistics Society* (Berkeley: Berkeley Linguistics Society), pp. 249–264.

- Quirk, Randolph, Sidney Greenbaum, Geoffrey Leech, and Jan Svartvik. 1985. *A Comprehensive Grammar of the English Language* (London: Longman).

- Thompson, Sandra A. 1978. "Modern English from a Typological Point of View: Some Implications of the Function of Word Order," *Linguistische Berichte* 54:19–35.

- Thompson, Sandra A. 1987. "The Passive in English: A Discourse Perspective," in Robert Channon and Linda Shockey, eds., *In Honor of Ilse Lehiste* (Dordrecht: Foris), pp. 497–511.

CHAPTER 9

SPEECH ACTS

AND CONVERSATION

WHAT DO YOU THINK?

A friend wonders aloud one day why the very same words "I now pronounce you husband and wife" will create a marriage between two people at a wedding but not when uttered in a stage play, for example. At first you dismiss the question as silly. "No, really," she says. "What's the difference?" You try your best to explain explicitly. What's your explanation?

Your son complains to you that his friend promised to take him along the next time his family went to the beach. Asked what the friend said, your son reports that he said "Honest, I will." You ask whether he said "I promise I will." When your son says "No," you decide that his friend had not made a promise. How do you explain your conclusion to your son?

Your daughter complains that when your French friend from work phones to ask for you, she takes forever to get the to point and apologizes profusely for nothing! She wonders what's wrong with her and why she doesn't get to the point. You are aware that people from different cultures behave differently on the telephone. What explanation do you offer your daughter for your friend's telephone behavior?

LANGUAGE IN USE

—

People use language principally as a tool to *do* things: ask questions, request favors, make comments, report news, give directions, offer greetings, and perform hundreds of other ordinary verbal actions in daily life. Through language, people actually *do* things: propose marriage, declare a mistrial, swear to tell the truth, fire an employee, invite someone to dinner, and so on. These *speech acts* are part of *speech events* such as conversations, lectures, student-teacher conferences, news broadcasts, marriage ceremonies, and courtroom trials. Much of what is reported in the pages of newspapers are speech acts: arrests, claims, denials, promises, and so forth (in addition to births, deaths, hurricanes, fires, robberies, automobile accidents, and the like, which are not speech acts).

The early chapters of this book examined the structure of sentences. We now turn to the question of what people do with sentences and describe some of the ways in which sentences are used in verbal interactions. This chapter examines the nature of speech acts and how sentences are used in speech events to accomplish all that is achieved through language.

Knowing a language is not simply a matter of knowing how to encode messages and transmit them to a second party, who by decoding them understands what we intended to say. If language use were simply a matter of encoding and decoding messages—in other words, of *grammatical* competence—every sentence would have a fixed interpretation irrespective of its context of use. That is not the case, of course, as the following scenarios illustrate.

1. You are stopped by a police officer, who surprises you by informing you that you have just driven through a stop sign. "I didn't see the stop sign," you say.
2. A friend has given you directions to her new house, including the instruction to turn left at the first stop sign after the intersection of Sixth and Main. You arrive about thirty minutes late and say "I didn't see the stop sign."
3. You are driving with an aunt, who is in a hurry to get to church. You slow down and glide through a stop sign, knowing that there is seldom traffic at that intersection on Sunday mornings. As you enter the intersection, you see a car approaching and you jam on the brakes, unsettling your aunt. "I didn't see the stop sign," you say.

To the police officer, your comment ("I didn't see the stop sign") is an *explanation* for failing to stop and a *plea* not to be cited for the violation. To the friend, your utterance is an *excuse* for your tardiness and an *explanation* that it was neither intended nor entirely your fault. To your aunt, the same sentence—an untruthful one in this case—is uttered as an *apology* for having frightened her. She recognizes your intention to apologize and says "It's all right. But *please* be careful." The linguistic meaning of the sentence *I didn't see the stop sign* is the same in all three cases, but its utterance in different contexts serves quite different purposes and conveys distinct messages.

SENTENCE STRUCTURE AND THE FUNCTION OF UTTERANCES

Traditional grammar books would lead you to assume that declarative sentences make statements (*It's raining*), imperative sentences issue directives (*Close the door*), and interrogative sentences seek information (*What time is it?*). These assumptions, however, are oversimplified and misleading. Consider the sentence *Can you shut the window?* Taken literally, its interrogative structure (marked, among other ways, by the inversion of subject and auxiliary) asks about the addressee's *ability* to shut some particular window. If asked this question by a roommate trying to study while a marching band practiced nearby, you would likely interpret it not as a yes/no question about your abilities and therefore requiring a verbal response but as a request for a physical action—a request to shut the window. (A request in question form is marked in speech by the absence of voice raising and sometimes in writing by the absence of a question mark: *Would you please respond promptly.*) Conversely, the imperative structure *Tell me your name again* would normally be taken not as a directive to do something but as a request for information.

Take another case: Suppose that a knock is heard at the door, and Mary says to Alice *I wonder who's at the door.* If Mary believed that Alice knew the answer, this declarative sentence might be uttered as a request for information. More often, though, it would actually be a polite request for Alice to open the door. Finally, interrogative sentences can sometimes be used to make statements, as in Sarah's reply to Fred's question.

> Fred: Is Amy pretty easy to get along with?
> Sarah: Do hens have teeth?

Sarah's yes/no *question* communicates an emphatically negative *answer* to Fred's inquiry.

Two things are clear, then: 1) People often employ declarative, interrogative, and imperative sentences for purposes other than making statements, asking questions, and giving commands, respectively; and 2) a very important element in the interpretation of an utterance is the context in which it is uttered.

Recall that a sentence is a structured string of words that carries a certain meaning. An *utterance,* in contrast, is a sentence that is said, written, or signed *in a particular context* by someone *with a particular intention,* by means of which the "speaker" intends *to create an effect* on the addressee. Thus, as an interrogative sentence *Can you shut the window?* has the meaning of a request for *information* ('Are you able to shut the window?'); but as a contextualized utterance it would more often than not be a request for *action* ('Please shut the window.'). Drawing the requisite inferences from conversation is an essential ingredient for interpreting utterances appropriately.

To understand utterances, one must be skilled at "reading between the lines," and the skills one employs in using and interpreting the sentences that are shaped by *grammatical competence* are part of one's *communicative competence.*

SPEECH ACTS

⟶

Besides what we accomplish through physical acts such as cooking, eating, bicycling, gardening, or getting on the bus, we accomplish a great deal each day by verbal acts. In face-to-face conversation, telephone calls, job application letters, notes scribbled to a roommate, and a multitude of other speech events, we perform verbal actions of different types. In fact, language is the principal means we have to greet, compliment, and insult one another, to plead or flirt, to seek and supply information, and to accomplish hundreds of other tasks in a typical day. Actions that are carried out through language are called **speech acts.**

TYPES OF SPEECH ACTS

Various kinds of speech acts have been identified, chiefly by philosophers taking a functional approach to sentences in use. Among the various kinds of speech acts, six have received particular attention:

1. *Representatives*   These speech acts represent a state of affairs: assertions, statements, claims, hypotheses, descriptions, and suggestions. Representatives can generally be characterized as true or false.
2. *Commissives*   These speech acts commit a speaker to a course of action: promises, pledges, threats, and vows.
3. *Directives*   These speech acts are intended to get the addressee to carry out an action: commands, requests, challenges, invitations, entreaties, and dares.
4. *Declarations*   These speech acts bring about the state of affairs they name: blessings, firings, baptisms, arrests, marryings, declaring mistrials.
5. *Expressives*   These speech acts indicate the speaker's psychological state or attitude: greetings, apologies, congratulations, condolences, and thanksgivings.
6. *Verdictives*   These speech acts make assessments or judgments: ranking, assessing, appraising, condoning. Because some verdictives (such as calling a baseball player "out") combine the characteristics of declarations and representatives, these are sometimes called *representational declarations.*

LOCUTIONS AND ILLOCUTIONS

Every speech act has several principal components, two of which directly concern us here: the utterance itself and the intention of the speaker in making it. First, every utterance is represented by a sentence with a grammatical structure and a linguistic meaning; this is called the **locution** or the utterance act. Second, speakers have some intention in making an utterance, something they intend to accomplish; that intention is called an **illocution,** and every utterance consists of performing one or more illocutionary acts. (A third component of a speech act—one we will not discuss at length—is the effect of the act on the hearer; this is called the *perlocution* of the utterance, or its "uptake.")

The utterance *Can you shut the window?,* for example, can be viewed as comprising a locution and an illocution. The locution is a yes/no question about the addressee's ability to close a particular window; as such, convention would require an answer of *yes* or *no.* The illocution, let us assume, is a request for the addressee to shut the window; as such, convention would enable the addressee to recognize the structural question as a request for action and to comply or not. In discussions of speech acts, it is common for the illocutionary act itself to be called the speech act; thus promises, assertions, questions, directives, and so on would be speech acts.

DISTINGUISHING AMONG SPEECH ACTS

How do language users distinguish among different types of speech acts? How do we know whether a locution such as *Do you have the time?* is a yes/no question (*Do you have the time* [to help me]?) or a request for information about the time of day? To put the matter in more technical terms, given that a locution can serve many functions, how do addressees know the illocutionary force of a speaker's utterance? The answer of course is "context." But how do people interpret context accurately?

We begin our analysis by distinguishing between two broad types of speech acts. Compare the following two utterances:

1. I now pronounce you husband and wife.
2. It is going to be very windy today.

In an appropriate context, the first utterance creates a new relationship between two individuals; it is a declaration that effectuates a marriage. The second utterance is a simple statement or representation of a state of affairs. As any weather predictor will attest, it certainly will have no effect on the weather. As you saw earlier, utterances such as sentence 2 make assertions or state opinions and are called *representatives.* Utterances like sentence 1 change the state of things and are called *declarations;* they provide a striking illustration of how language in use is a form of action. Children exposed to fantastical declarations like "Abracadabra, I change you into a frog!" eventually learn that real-life objects are more recalcitrant than fairy-tale objects, but all speakers come to recognize a verbal power over certain aspects of life, especially with respect to social relationships.

With the utterance *I now pronounce you husband and wife,* the nature of the social relationship between two people can be profoundly altered. Similarly, the utterance *You're under arrest!* can have consequences for one's social freedom, as can *Case dismissed.* An umpire can change a baseball game with so simple a declaration as *Strike three!* or *Safe!* Typically, to be effective, declarations of this type must be uttered by a specially designated person. If called by a nondesignated individual—a fan in the stands, for example—*Out!* would be a verdictive, not a declaration. Indeed, a declaration by a single designated umpire will override a contrary call by a whole team of players and an entire stadium of fans.

APPROPRIATENESS CONDITIONS AND SUCCESSFUL DECLARATIONS

The efficacy of any declaration depends on well-established conventions. *I now pronounce you husband and wife* can bind two individuals in marriage only if a number of conditions are satisfied: the setting must be a wedding ceremony and the utterance made at the appropriate moment; the speaker must be designated to marry others (a minister, rabbi, justice of the peace) and must intend to marry the two individuals; the two individuals must be legally eligible to marry each other; and they must intend to become spouses. Finally, of course, the words themselves must be uttered. If any condition is not satisfied, the utterance of the words will be ineffectual as a performative. Made on a Hollywood movie set by an actor in the role of a pastor and addressed to two actors playing characters about to marry, the utterance will be vacuous.

The conventions that regulate the conditions under which an utterance serves as a particular speech act—as a question, marriage, promise, arrest, invitation—have been called **appropriateness conditions** by philosopher John Searle, and they can be classified into four categories. The first condition, the *propositional content condition,* requires merely that the words of the sentence be conventionally associated with the intended speech act and convey the content of the act. The locution must exhibit conventionally acceptable words for effecting the particular speech act: *Is it raining out?, I now pronounce you husband and wife, You're under arrest, I promise to . . . , I swear . . . .*

The second condition requires a conventionally recognized context in which the speech act is embedded. In a marriage, the situation must be a genuine wedding ceremony (however informal) at which two people intend to exchange vows in the presence of a witness. This condition is called the *preparatory condition.*

The third condition requires the speaker to be sincere in uttering the declaration. At a wedding, the speaker must intend that the marriage words should effectuate a marriage; otherwise, the *sincerity condition* will be violated and the speech act will not be successful.

Finally, the fourth condition requires that the involved parties all intend by this ceremony and the utterance of the words *I now pronounce you husband and wife* to create a marriage bond; this is the *essential condition.*

Successful Promises Now consider the commissive *I promise to help you with your math tonight.* In order for such an utterance to be successful, it must be recognizable as a promise; in addition, the preparatory, sincerity, and essential conditions must be met. In the propositional content condition, the speaker must state the intention of helping the addressee. The preparatory condition requires that speaker and hearer are sane and responsible, that the speaker believes she is able to help with the math, and that the addressee wishes to have help. The preparatory condition would be violated if, for example, the speaker knew that she could not be there or that she was incapable of doing the math herself, or if the participants were reading the script of a movie in which the utterance appears. If the speaker knew that the hearer did not *want* help, the promise would not succeed. For the sincerity condition to hold, the speaker must sincerely intend to help the addressee. This condition would be violated (and the promise formula abused) if the speaker had no such intention. Finally, the essential condition of a promise is that the speaker intend by the utterance to place herself under an obligation to provide some help to the hearer. These four appropriateness conditions define a successful promise.

Successful Requests and Other Speech Acts Appropriateness conditions are useful in describing not only declarations and commissives but all other types of speech acts. In a typical request (*Please pass me the salt*), the content of the utterance must identify the act requested of the hearer (passing the salt), and its form must be a conventionally recognized one for making requests. The preparatory condition includes the speaker's belief that the addressee is capable of passing the salt and that, had he not asked her to pass the salt, she would not have ventured to do so. The sincerity condition requires that the speaker genuinely desire the hearer to pass the salt. Finally the essential condition is that the speaker intend by the utterance to get the hearer to pass the salt to him.

THE COOPERATIVE PRINCIPLE
⟶

The principles that govern the interpretation of utterances are diverse and complex, and they differ somewhat from culture to culture. Even within a single culture, they are so complex that we may wonder how language succeeds at communication as well as it does. The principles that we examine in this section, however commonsensical they may seem to Western readers, are by no means universal; as you will see later, what seems common sense to one group is not necessarily common sense to all groups.

Despite occasional misinterpretations, people in most situations manage to understand utterances essentially as they were intended. The reason is that, without cause to expect otherwise, interlocutors normally trust that they and their conversational partners are honoring the same interpretive conventions. *Hearers* assume simply that speakers have honored the conventions of interpretation in constructing their utterances. *Speakers,* on the other hand, must make a twofold assumption: not only that hearers will themselves be guided by the conventions, but also that hearers will trust speakers to have honored those conventions in constructing their utterances. There is an unspoken pact that people will *cooperate* in communicating with each other, and speakers rely on this cooperation to make conversation efficient.

The **cooperative principle,** as enunciated by philosopher H. Paul Grice, is as follows:

> Make your conversational contribution such as is required, at the stage at which it occurs, by the accepted purpose or direction of the talk exchange in which you are engaged.

This pact of cooperation touches on four areas of communication, each of which can be described in a *maxim,* or general principle.

MAXIM OF QUANTITY

First, speakers are expected to give as much information as is necessary for their interlocutors to understand their utterances but to give no more information than is necessary. If you ask an acquaintance whether she has any pets and she answers, *I have two cats,* it is the *maxim of quantity* that permits you to assume that she has no other pets. The conversational implication of such a reply is 'I have two (and only two) cats (and no other pets).' Notice that *I have two cats* would be true even if the speaker has six cats or six cats, two dogs, and a llama. But if she had such other pets, you would have reason to feel deceived. While her reply was not false as far as it went, your culturally defined expectation that relevant information will not be concealed would have been violated. In most Western cultures (but not in all cultures), listeners expect speakers to abide by this maxim, and—equally important—speakers know that hearers believe them to be abiding by it. It is this unspoken cooperation that creates conversational implicatures.

To take another example, suppose you asked a man painting his house what color he had chosen for the living room, and he replied:

> The walls are going to be off-white to contrast with the black sofa and the Regency armchairs that I inherited from my great-aunt. (Bless her soul, she passed away last year after a long but distressing marriage to a man who really wasn't able to appreciate her extraordinary love of the visual and performing arts.) Then the trimmings will be peach except for the ones near the door, which Alice said should be salmon because otherwise they will clash with the yellow, black, and red Picasso print that I brought back from Spain—I vacationed in Spain in August of, let's see, 1992, and I bought it then. Or was it July? I forget, actually. Gosh! time goes fast, don't you think? Oh, never mind. And the stairway leading to the bedrooms will be a pale yellow.

In providing too much information, far more than was sought or expected, the man is as uncooperative as the woman who withheld information about her pets. The maxim of quantity provides that, in normal circumstances, speakers say just enough, that they supply no less information—and no more information—than is necessary for the purpose of the communication: *Be appropriately informative.*

Society stigmatizes individuals who habitually violate the maxim of quantity; those who give too much information are described as "never shutting up" or "always telling everyone their life story," while those who habitually fail to provide enough information are branded as sullen, secretive, or untrustworthy.

MAXIM OF RELEVANCE

The second maxim directs speakers to organize their utterances in such a way that they are relevant to the ongoing context: *Be relevant at the time of the utterance.* The following interaction illustrates a violation of this maxim.

> Speaker A: How's the weather outside?
> Speaker B: There's a great movie on TV Thursday night.

Taken literally, speaker B's utterance seems unrelated to what speaker A has said immediately before; if so, it would violate the *maxim of relevance.* Because of the maxim of relevance, when someone produces an apparently irrelevant utterance, hearers typically strive to understand how it might be relevant (as a joke, perhaps, or an indication of displeasure with the direction of the conversation). Chronic violations of this maxim are characteristic of schizophrenics, whose sense of "context" differs radically from that of healthier people.

MAXIM OF MANNER

Third, people follow a set of miscellaneous rules that are grouped under the *maxim of manner.* Summarized by the directive *Be orderly and clear,* this maxim dictates that speakers and writers avoid ambiguity and obscurity and be orderly in their utterances. In the following example, the maxim of manner is violated with respect to orderliness.

> A birthday cake should have icing; use unbleached flour and sugar in the cake; bake it for one hour; preheat the oven to 325 degrees, and beat in three fresh eggs.

This recipe is odd for the simple reason that English speakers normally follow a chronological order of events in describing a process such as baking.

Orderliness is dictated not only by the order of events: in any language there are rules that dictate a "natural" order of details in a description. Because, in American English, more general details usually precede more specific details, when a speaker violates this rule the result appears odd.

> My hometown has five shopping malls. It is the county seat. My father and my mother were both born there. My hometown is a midwestern town of 105,000 inhabitants situated at the center of the Corn Belt. I was brought up there until I was thirteen years old.

As a third example, consider the utterance *Ted died and was hit by lightning.* If it was the lightning that killed Ted, the maxim of manner has been violated here. Although in logic *and* joins clauses whose time reference is not relevant (thus, *She studied chemistry, and she studied biology* is logically equivalent to *She studied biology, and she studied chemistry*), the maxim of manner dictates that an utterance like *They had a baby and got married* has different conversational implications from those like *They got married and had a baby.* The maxim of manner in this instance would suggest that the sequence of expressions reflects the sequence of events or is irrelevant to an appropriate interpretation. Of course English and other languages provide ways around misinterpretation: *They had a baby before they got married; first they had a baby, and then they got married; they got married after they had a baby;* and so on.

MAXIM OF QUALITY

The fourth general principle governing norms of language interpretation is the maxim of quality: *Be truthful.* Speakers and writers are expected to say only what they believe to be true and to have evidence for what they say. Again, the other side of the coin is that speakers are aware of this expectation; they know that hearers expect them to honor the *maxim of quality.* Without the maxim of quality, the other maxims are of little value or interest. Whether brief or lengthy, relevant or irrelevant, orderly or disorderly, all lies are false. Still, it should be noted that the maxim of quality applies principally to assertions, and certain other representative speech acts. Expressives and directives can hardly be judged true or false in the same sense.

It is useful to reflect further on the maxim of quality. On the one hand, it is this maxim that constrains interlocutors to tell the truth and to have evidence for their statements. Ironically, however, it is this maxim that also makes lying possible. Without the maxim of quality, speakers would have no reason to expect hearers to take their utterances as true, and without the assumption that one's interlocutors assume one to be telling the truth, it would be impossible to tell a lie. Lying requires that speakers are expected to be telling the truth.

VIOLATIONS OF THE COOPERATIVE PRINCIPLE

It is no secret that people sometimes violate the maxims of the cooperative principle. Certainly not all speakers are completely truthful on all occasions; others, though truthful, have not observed that efficiency is the desired Western norm in conversational interaction. More interestingly, speakers are sometimes forced by cultural norms or other external factors to violate a maxim. For example, irrespective of your esthetic judgment, you may feel constrained to say *What a lovely painting!* to a host who is manifestly proud of some newly finished artwork. The need to adhere to social conventions of politeness sometimes invites people to violate maxims of the cooperative principle.

INDIRECT SPEECH ACTS

As mentioned earlier, interrogative structures can be used to make polite requests for action, imperative structures can be used to ask for information, and so on. Such uses of a structure with one meaning to accomplish a different task play a frequent role in ordinary interaction, as in this exchange between colleagues who have stayed at the office after dark.

> Sue: Is the boss in?
> Alan: The light's on in her office.
> Sue: Oh, thanks.

Alan's answer makes no apparent reference to the information Sue is seeking. Thus in theory it would appear to violate the maxim of relevance. Yet Sue is satisfied with the answer. Recognizing that the *literal* interpretation of Alan's reply violates the maxim of relevance but assuming that as a cooperative interlocutor Alan is being relevant, Sue seeks an *indirect* interpretation. To help her, she knows certain facts about their boss's habits: that she works in her own office, that she does not work in the dark, and that she is not in the habit of leaving the light on when out of her office. Relying on this information, Sue infers an interpretation from Alan's utterance: Alan believes the boss is in.

Alan's reply is an example of an indirect speech act. **Indirect speech acts** involve an apparent violation of the cooperative principle but are in fact indirectly cooperative. For example, an indirect speech act can be based on an apparent violation of the maxim of quality. When we describe a friend as *someone who never parts with a dime,* we don't mean it literally; we are exaggerating. By exaggerating the information, we may seem to be flouting the maxim of quality. But listeners will usually appreciate that the statement should not be interpreted literally and will make an appropriate adjustment in their interpretation. Similarly, we may exclaim in front of the World Trade Center *That's an awfully small building!* This utterance too appears to violate the maxim of quality in that we are expressing an evaluation that is manifestly false. But speakers readily spot the irony of utterances such as this and take them to be indirect speech acts intended to convey an opposite meaning.

Characteristics of Indirect Speech Acts   From these examples, we can identify four characteristics of indirect speech acts:

1. Indirect speech acts violate at least one maxim of the cooperative principle.
2. The literal meaning of the locution of an indirect speech act differs from its intended meaning.
3. Hearers and readers identify indirect speech acts by noticing that an utterance has characteristic 1 and by assuming that the interlocutor is following the cooperative principle.
4. As soon as they have identified an indirect speech act, hearers and readers identify its intended meaning with the help of knowledge of the context and of the world around them.

Thus, to interpret indirect speech acts, hearers use the maxims to sort out the discrepancy between the literal meaning of the utterance and an appropriate interpretation for the context in which it is uttered.

Indirect Speech Acts and Shared Knowledge   One prerequisite for a successful indirect speech act is that interactors share sufficient background about the context of the interaction, about each other and their society, and about the world in general. If Fred asks Ellen *Are you done with your sociology paper?* and she replies *Is Rome in Spain?,* he will certainly recognize the answer as an indirect speech act. But whether or not he can interpret it will depend on his knowledge of geography.

Using and understanding indirect speech acts requires familiarity with both language and society. To cite an example from a distant culture, when speakers of the Polynesian language Tuvaluan want to comment on the fact that a particular person is in the habit of talking about himself, they may say *koo tagi te tuli ki tena igoa* 'The plover bird is singing its own name.' The expression derives from the fact that the plover bird's cry sounds like a very sharp "tuuuuuliiiii," from which speakers of Tuvaluan have created the word *tuli* to refer to the bird itself. Thus the expression has become an indirect way of criticizing the trait of singing one's own praises. In order to interpret the utterance as an indirect speech act, one must be familiar not only with the plover bird's cry and the fact that it resembles the bird's name but also with the fact that Tuvaluans view people who talk about themselves as being similar to a bird "singing its own name." The amount of background information about language, culture, and environment needed to interpret indirect speech acts is thus considerable.

POLITENESS

Indirect speech acts appear to be a complicated way of communicating. Not only must you spot them, but you must then go through a complex reasoning process to interpret them. It would be more efficient to communicate directly, one might think. The fact is, though, that indirect speech acts have uses besides asking and answering questions, criticizing others, and so on. They sometimes add humor and sometimes show politeness. Ellen's indirect reply (*Is Rome in Spain?*) to Fred's question suggests 'Don't be ridiculous; of course I'm not done.' Questions such as *Can you shut the window?* are perceived as more polite and less intrusive and abrasive than a command such as *Shut the window!* One message that indirect speech acts convey is 'I am being polite toward you.' Indirect speech acts are thus an efficient tool of communication: they can convey two or more messages simultaneously.

Positive and Negative Politeness

There are two basic aspects to being polite. The first rests on the fact that human beings respect one another's presence, privacy, and physical space. We *avoid* intruding on other people's lives, try *not* to be overly inquisitive about their activities, and take care *not* to impose our presence on them. This is called negative politeness and involves avoidance. On the other hand, when we let people know that we enjoy their company, feel comfortable with them, like something in their personality, or are interesting in their well-being, we show *positive politeness.* While everyone expects both negative and positive politeness, the first requires us to leave people alone, while the second requires us to do the opposite. Fortunately, the needs for negative and positive politeness usually arise in different contexts. When we shut ourselves in a room or take a solitary walk on the beach, we affirm our right to negative politeness. When we attend a party, invite someone to dinner, or call friends on the telephone to check up on them, we extend positive politeness.

In conversation, interlocutors give one another messages about their needs for negative and positive politeness and acknowledge the other's needs for both types as well. The expectation that others won't ask embarrassing questions about our personal lives stems from the need for negative politeness. When you tell a friend about personal problems and expect sympathy, you are seeking positive politeness. Excusing oneself before asking a stranger for the time acknowledges the stranger's right to negative politeness (that is, privacy). When we express the hope of meeting an interlocutor at a later date (*Let's get together sometime soon!*), we acknowledge that person's need for positive politeness (that is, sociability).

SPEECH EVENTS
⌐

A political rally or debate, a public speech, a classroom lecture, a religious sermon, and a disk jockey's "Top 40 countdown" are all speech events—social activities in which language plays a particularly important role. "Speech" events need not involve speaking: personal letters, short stories, shopping lists, office memos, and birthday cards are also speech events.

Conversation provides the matrix in which native languages are acquired, and it stands out as the most frequent, most natural, and most representative of verbal interactions. A person can spend a lifetime without writing a letter, composing a poem, or debating public policy, but only in rare circumstances does anyone not have frequent conversation with friends and companions. Conversation is an everyday speech event. We engage in it for entertainment (gossiping, passing the time, affirming social bonds) and for accomplishing work (getting help with studies, renting an apartment, ordering a meal at a restaurant). Whatever its purpose, conversation is our most basic verbal interaction.

Though movie-screen lovers can conduct heart-to-heart conversations with their backs to each other, conversation usually involves individuals facing each other and taking turns at speaking, neither talking simultaneously nor letting the conversation lag. In some societies, even with several conversationalists in a single conversation, there are only tenths of a second between turns and extremely little overlap in speaking. At the beginning of a conversation, people go through certain rituals, greeting one another or commenting about the weather. Likewise, at the end of a conversation people don't simply turn their backs and walk away; they take care that all participants have finished what they wanted to say and only then utter something like "I have to run" or "Take care." Throughout the entire interaction, conversationalists maintain a certain level of orderliness—taking turns, not interrupting one another too often, and following certain other highly structured but implicit guidelines for conversation.

These guidelines can be considered norms of conduct that govern how conversationalists comport themselves. Though it is tempting to think of relaxed conversation as essentially free of rules or constraints, the fact is that many rules are operating, and the unconscious recognition of these rules helps identify particular interactions as conversations.

THE ORGANIZATION OF CONVERSATION

If it seems surprising that casual conversation should be organized by rules, the reason is that, as in most speech events, more attention is paid to content than to organization; the organization of conversations we take for granted. A conversation can be viewed as a series of speech acts—greetings, inquiries, congratulations, comments, invitations, requests, refusals, accusations, denials, promises, farewells. To accomplish the work of these speech acts, some organization is essential: we take turns at speaking, answer questions, mark the beginning and end of a conversation, and make corrections when they are needed. To accomplish such work expeditiously, interlocutors could give one another traffic directions.

> Okay, now it's your turn to speak.
> I just asked you a question; now you should answer it, and you should do so
> right away.
> If you have anything else to add before we close this conversation, do it now
> because I am leaving in a minute.

Such instructions would be inefficient, however, and would deflect attention from the content. In unusual circumstances, conversationalists do invoke the rules (*Would you please stop interrupting?* or *Well, say something!*), but such cases are avoided whenever possible because they underscore the fact that rules have been violated and thus can seem impolite. Conversations are usually organized covertly, and the organizational principles provide a discreet interactional framework.

The covert architecture of conversation must achieve the following: organize turns so that more than one person has a chance to speak and the turn taking is orderly; allow for interlocutors to anticipate what will happen next and, where there is a choice, how the selection is to be decided; provide a way to repair glitches and errors when they occur.

Turn Taking and Pausing

Participants must tacitly agree on who should speak when. Normally we take turns at holding the floor and do so without overt negotiation. A useful way to uncover the conventions of turn taking is to observe what happens when they break down. When a participant fails to take the floor despite indications that it is his turn, other speakers usually pause, and then someone else begins speaking. In this example, Alice repeats her question, assuming that Bill either did not hear or did not understand it the first time.

> Alice: Is there something you're worried about?
> [pause]
> Alice: Is there something you're worried about?
> Bill: No, but I was wondering if you could help me with a problem I'm
>   having with my brother.

Turn-taking conventions are also violated when two people attempt to speak simultaneously. In the next example, the beginning and end of the overlap are marked with brackets.

> Speaker 1: After John's party we went to Fred's house.
> Speaker 2: So you— so you— you—
>   [   ]
> Speaker 3:   What— what— time did you get there?

When such competition arises in casual conversation, a speaker may either quickly relinquish the floor or turn up the volume and continue speaking. Both silence and simultaneous speaking are serious problems in conversation, and the turn-taking norms are designed to minimize them.

Different cultures have different degrees of tolerance for silence between turns, overlaps in speaking, and competition among speakers. In some cultures, including certain Native American nations and the Eskimos, people sit comfortably together in silence. At the other extreme, in French and Argentinian cultures several conversationalists often talk simultaneously and interrupt each other more frequently than Americans typically feel comfortable doing.

However much tolerance they may have for silences and overlaps, people from all cultures appear to regulate turn taking in conversation in basically similar ways. To do this, there are two basic rules: Speakers signal when they wish to end their turn, either selecting the next speaker or leaving the choice open. The next speaker takes the floor by beginning to talk. This simple principle, which seems second nature to us, regulates conversational turn taking very efficiently.

Turn-Taking Signals   Speakers signal that their turn is about to end with verbal and nonverbal cues. As turns commonly end in a complete sentence, the completion of a sentence may signal the end of a turn. A sentence ending in a tag question (*isn't it?, are you?*) explicitly invites an interlocutor to take the floor.

> Speaker A: Pretty windy out today, isn't it?
> Speaker B: Sure is!

The end of a turn may also be signaled by sharply raising or lowering the pitch of your voice, or by drawling the last syllable of the final word of the turn. In very informal conversations, one common cue is the phrase *or something.*

> Speaker 1: So he was behaving as if he'd been hit by a truck, or something.
> Speaker 2: Really?

Other expressions that can signal the completion of a turn are *y'know, kinda, I don't know* (or *I dunno*), and a trailing *uhm.* As with *y'know,* some of these can also function within a turn for the speaker to keep the floor while thinking about what to say next. Another way to signal the completion of a turn is to pause and make no attempt to speak again.

> Speaker A: I really don't think he should've said that at the meeting,
>   particularly in front of the whole committee. It really was pretty
>   insensitive.
>   [pause]
> Speaker B: Yeah, I agree.

Of course, speakers often have to pause in the middle of a turn to think about what to say next, or to emphasize a point, or to catch a breath. To signal that a speaker has finished a turn, the pause must be long enough, but "long enough" differs from culture to culture.

Nonverbal as well as verbal signals can indicate the end of a turn. Although in speaking the principal role of gestures is to support and stress what we say, continuing our hand gestures lets our interlocutors know that we have more to say. Once we put our hands to rest, our fellow conversationalists may infer that we are yielding the floor.

In a more subtle vein, eye gaze can help control floor holding and turn taking. In mainstream American society, speakers do not ordinarily stare at their interlocutors; instead, their gaze goes back and forth between their listener and another point in space, alternating quickly and almost imperceptibly. But because listeners, on the other hand, usually fix their gaze on the speaker, a speaker reaching the end of a turn can simply return her gaze to an interlocutor and thereby signal her own turn to listen and the interlocutor's to speak. In cultures in which listeners look away while speakers stare, a speaker who wishes to stop talking simply looks away. While eye gaze plays a supportive role in allocating turns, the success of telephone conversations makes it clear that eye gaze is not essential in the allocation of turns.

Getting the Floor   In multiparty conversations, the speaker holding the floor can select who will speak next, or the next speaker can select himself. In the first instance, the floor holder may signal the choice by addressing the next speaker by name (*What've you been up to these days, Helen?*) or by turning toward the selected next speaker. If the floor holder does not select the next speaker, anyone may take the floor, often by beginning the turn at an accelerated pace so as to block other potential claims for the floor.

When the floor holder does not select the next speaker, competition can arise, as in the following example, in which overlaps are indicated with square brackets.

> Speaker 1: Who's gonna be at Jake's party Saturday night?
> [pause]
> Speaker 2: Todd to—
> [   ]
> Speaker 3: I don't kn—
> [pause]
> Speaker 2: Todd told me—
> [   ]
> Speaker 3:   I don't know who's—
> [short pause]
> Speaker 2: [to speaker 3] Go ahead!
> Speaker 3: Todd told me a lotta people would be there.
> Speaker 2: Yeah, that's what I was gonna say. I don't know who's gonna be there, but I know it'll be pretty crowded.

Friendly participants strive to resolve such competition quickly and smoothly.

Social inequality between conversationalists (boss and employee, parent and child, doctor and patient) is often reflected in how often and when participants claim the floor. In American work settings, superiors commonly initiate conversations by asking a question and letting subordinates report. Thus subordinates hold the floor for longer periods of time than superiors; subordinates perform while superiors act as spectators. In some cultures, superiors talk while subordinates listen.

ADJACENCY PAIRS

One useful mechanism in the covert organization of conversation is that certain turns have specific follow-up turns associated with them. Questions take answers. Greetings are returned by greetings, invitations by acceptances or refusals, and so on. Certain sequences of turns go together, as in these *adjacency pairs.*

QUESTION AND ANSWER

Speaker 1: Where's the milk I bought this morning?
Speaker 2: On the counter.

INVITATION AND ACCEPTANCE

Speaker 1: I'm having some people to dinner Saturday, and I'd really like you
     to come.
Speaker 2: Sure!

ASSESSMENT AND DISAGREEMENT

Speaker 1: I don't think Harold would play such a dirty trick on you.
Speaker 2: Well, you obviously don't know Harold very well.

Such **adjacency pairs** comprise two turns, one of which directly follows the other. In a question/answer adjacency pair, the question is the first part, the answer the second part. Here are other examples of adjacency pairs.

REQUEST FOR A FAVOR AND GRANTING

Guest: Can I use your phone?
Host: Sure.

APOLOGY AND ACCEPTANCE

Speaker 1: Sorry to bother you this late at night.
Speaker 2: No, that's all right. What can I do for you?

SUMMONS AND ACKNOWLEDGMENT

Mark: Bill!
Bill: Yeah?

The Structure of Adjacency Pairs   Three characteristics of adjacency pairs can be noted. First, the two parts are contiguous and are uttered by different speakers. A speaker who makes a statement before answering a question sounds strange (and can provoke anger) because the parts of the adjacency pair are not consecutive:

Speaker 1: Where's the milk I bought this morning?
Speaker 2: They said on the radio that the weather would clear up by noon. It's
     on the counter.

Second, the two parts are ordered. Except on TV game shows like "Jeopardy," the answer to a question cannot precede the question; in ordinary conversation, one cannot accept an invitation before it has been offered; and an apology cannot be accepted before uttered (except sarcastically).

Third, the first and second parts must be appropriately matched to avoid such odd exchanges as the following:

Speaker 1: Do you want more coffee?
Speaker 2: That's all right, you're not bothering me in the least!

Insertion Sequences   Occasionally, the requirement that both parts of an adjacency pair be contiguous is violated in a socially recognized way.

Ann: Where's the milk I bought this morning?
Pat: The skim milk?
Ann: Yeah.
Pat: On the counter.

In order to provide an accurate answer to Ann's question, Pat must first know the answer to another question and thus initiates an *insertion sequence*—another adjacency pair that interrupts the original adjacency pair and puts it "on hold." The interaction thus consists of one adjacency pair embedded in another one, as in the following telephone conversation.

Speaker 1: Can I speak to Mr. Higgins?
Speaker 2: May I ask who's calling?
Speaker 1: Arthur Wilcox
Speaker 2: Please hold.

main adjacency pair

insertion sequence

Preferred and Dispreferred Responses   Certain kinds of adjacency pairs are marked by a preference for a particular type of second part. For example, requests, questions, and invitations have preferred and dispreferred answers. Compare the following interactions, in which the first one has a preferred (positive) second part and the second one has a dispreferred (negative) second part.

Speaker 1: I really enjoyed the movie last night. Did you?
Speaker 2: Yeah, it was pretty good.

Speaker A: I really enjoyed the movie last night. Did you?
Speaker B: No, I thought it was pretty crummy, though I can see how you
        could've liked certain parts of it.

To an assessment also, the preferred second part is agreement.

Speaker 1: I think Ralph's a pretty good writer.
Speaker 2: I think so too.

Speaker A: I think Ralph's a pretty good writer.
Speaker B: Well, his imagery's interesting, but apart from that I don't think he
        writes well at all.

Dispreferred second parts tend to be preceded by a pause and to begin with a hesitation particle such as *well* or *uh*. Preferred second parts tend to follow the first part without a pause and to consist of structurally simple utterances.

> Speaker 1: Would you like to meet for lunch tomorrow?
> Speaker 2: Sure!

> Speaker A: Would you like to meet for lunch tomorrow?
> Speaker B: Well, hmm, let's see . . . Tomorrow's Tuesday, right? I told Harry
>   I'd have lunch with him. And I told him so long ago that I'd feel
>   bad canceling. Maybe another time, okay?

In addition, dispreferred second parts often begin with a token agreement or acceptance, or with an expression of appreciation or apology, and usually include an explanation.

> Speaker 1: Can I use your phone?
> Speaker 2: Oh, I'm sorry, but I'm expecting an important long-distance call.
>   Could you wait a bit?

OPENING SEQUENCES

Conversations are opened in socially recognized ways. Before beginning their first conversation of the day, conversationalists normally greet each other, as when two office workers meet in the morning.

> Jeff: Mornin', Stan!
> Stan: Hi. How's it goin'?
> Jeff: Oh, can't complain, I guess. Ready for the meeting this afternoon?
> Stan: Well, I don't have much choice!

Greetings exemplify opening sequences, utterances that ease people into a conversation. They convey the message "I want to talk to you."

Greetings are usually reserved for acquaintances who have not seen each other for a while, or as opening sequences for longer conversations between strangers. Some situations do not require a greeting, as with a stranger approaching in the street to ask for the time: *Excuse me, sir, do you know what time it is?* The expression *Excuse me, sir* serves as an opening sequence appropriate to the context. Thus greetings are not the only type of opening sequences.

Very few conversations do not begin with some type of opening sequence, even as commonplace as the following:

> Speaker A: Guess what.
> Speaker B: What?
> Speaker A: I broke a tooth.

Conversationalists also use opening sequences to announce that they are about to invade the personal space of their interlocutors. Here, two friends are talking on a park bench next to a stranger; at a pause in their conversation, the stranger interjects:

Stranger: Excuse me, I didn't mean to eavesdrop, but I couldn't help hearing
   that you were talking about Dayton, Ohio. I'm from Dayton.
[Conversation then goes on among the three people.]

It is not surprising that opening sequences should take the form of an apology in such situations.

Finally, opening sequences may serve as a display of one's voice to enable the interlocutor to recognize who is speaking, especially at the beginning of telephone conversations. Here, the phone has just rung in Alfred's apartment.

Alfred: Hello?
Helen: Hi!
Alfred: Oh, hi, Helen! How you doin'?

In the second turn, Helen displays her voice to enable Alfred to recognize her. In the third turn, Alfred indicates his recognition and simultaneously provides the second part of the greeting adjacency pair initiated in the previous turn.

Opening Sequences in Other Cultures   In many cultures, the opening sequence appropriate to a situation in which two people meet after not having met for a while is an inquiry about the person's health, as in the American greeting *How are you?* Such inquiries are essentially formulaic and not meant literally. Indeed, most speakers respond with a conventional upbeat formula (*I'm fine* or *Fine, thanks*) even when feeling terrible. In other cultures, the conventional greeting may take a different form. Traditionally, Mandarin Chinese conversationalists ask *Nǐ chī guo fàn le ma?* 'Have you eaten rice yet?' When two people meet on a road in Tonga, they ask *Ko hoʔo ʔalu ki fe?* 'Where is your going directed to?' These greetings are as formulaic as *How are you?*

In formal contexts, or when differences of social status exist between participants, many cultures require a lengthy and formulaic opening sequence. In Fiji, when an individual visits a village, a highly ceremonial introduction is conducted before any other interaction takes place. This event involves speeches that are regulated by a complex set of rules governing what must be said, and when, and by whom. This ceremony serves the same purpose as opening sequences in other cultures.

Functions of Opening Sequences   A final aspect of opening sequences in which cultural differences are found is the relative importance of their various functions. In American telephone conversations, opening sequences serve primarily to identify speakers and solicit the interlocutor's attention. In France, opening sequences normally apologize for invading someone's privacy.

Person called: Allo?
Caller: Allo? Je suis désolé de vous déranger. Est-ce que j'peux parler
              à Marie-France?
              ('Hello? I'm terribly sorry for disturbing you. Can I speak to
              Marie-France?')

In an American telephone conversation, such an opening sequence is not customary. Thus, in two relatively similar cultures, the role played by the opening sequence in a telephone call is different. As a result, the French can find Americans intrusive and impolite on the telephone, while Americans are puzzled by French apologetic formulas, which they find pointless and exceedingly ceremonious.

CLOSING SEQUENCES

Conversations must also be closed appropriately. A conversation can be closed only when the participants have said everything they wanted to say. Furthermore, a conversation must be closed before participants begin to feel uncomfortable about having nothing more to say. As a result, conversationalists carefully negotiate the timing of closings, seeking to give the impression of wanting neither to rush away nor to linger on. These objectives are reflected in the characteristics of the closing sequence. First of all, a closing sequence includes a conclusion to the last topic covered in the conversation. In conclusions, conversationalists often make arrangements to meet at a later time or express the hope of so meeting. These arrangements may be genuine, as in the first example here, or formulaic, as in the second.

> Speaker 1: Okay, it's nice to see you again. I guess you'll be at Kathy's party
> 　　　　　tonight.
> Speaker 2: Yeah, I'll see you there.

> Speaker A: See you later!
> Speaker B: See ya!

The first step of a closing sequence helps ensure that no one has anything further to say. This is accomplished by a simple exchange of short turns such as *okay* or *well*. Typically, such preclosing sequences are accompanied by a series of pauses between and within turns that decelerate the exchange and prepare for closing down the interaction. In the following example, speaker 2 takes the opportunity to bring up one last topic, after which speaker 1 initiates another closing sequence.

> Speaker 1: Okay, it's nice to see you again. I guess you'll be at Kathy's party
> 　　　　　tonight.
> Speaker 2: Yeah, I'll see you there.
> Speaker 1: Okay.
> Speaker 2: I hear there's gonna be lots of people there.
> Speaker 1: Apparently she invited half the town.
> Speaker 2: Should be fun.
> Speaker 1: Yeah.
> Speaker 2: Okay.
> Speaker 1: Okay. See you there.
> Speaker 2: Later!

Sometimes, after a preclosing exchange, speakers refer to the original motivation for the conversation. In a courtesy call to inquire about someone's health, the caller sometimes refers to this fact after the preclosing exchange.

Caller:　　　　Well, I just wanted to see how you were doing after your surgery.
Person called:　Well that was really nice of you.

If the purpose of a conversation was to seek a favor, this short exchange might take place:

Speaker 1: Well, listen, I really appreciate your doing this for me.
Speaker 2: Forget it. I'm glad to be of help.

Finally, conversations close with a parting expression: *bye, goodbye, see you, catch you later.*

The striking thing about closings is their deceptive simplicity. In fact, however, they are complex. Participants exercise great care not to give the impression that they are rushing away or that they want to linger on, and they try to ensure that everything on the unwritten agenda of any participant has been touched on. However informal and abbreviated, closing sequences are characterized by a great deal of negotiated activity.

CONVERSATIONAL ROUTINES

Both openings and closings are more routinized than the core parts of conversations. Core parts are relatively less predictable, and whereas children are trained not to ask certain kinds of questions, they are drilled on the proper way to open and close conversations. Because of the routinized nature of openings and closings, conversations can be begun and, equally important, ended expeditiously.

REPAIRS

A **repair** takes place in conversation when a participant feels the need to correct herself or another speaker, to edit a previous utterance, or simply to restate something, as in these examples, in which a dash indicates an abrupt cutoff.

1. Speaker:　I was going to Mary's—uh, Sue's house.
2. Speaker:　And I went to the doctor's to get a new—uh—a new whatchamacallit, a new prescription, because my old one had expired.
3. Speaker 1: Look at these daffodils, aren't they pretty?
   Speaker 2: They're pretty, but they're narcissus.

4. Speaker 1: Todd came to visit us over the spring break.
   Speaker 2: What?
   Speaker 1: I said Todd was here over the spring break.

In 2, the *trouble source* is the fact that the speaker cannot find a word. In 4, Speaker 2 initiates a repair because he has not heard or has not understood speaker 1's utterance. Conversationalists thus make repairs for a variety of reasons.

To initiate a repair is to signal that one has not understood or has misheard an utterance, that a piece of information is incorrect, or that one is having trouble finding a word. To resolve a repair, someone must repeat the misunderstood or misheard utterance, correct the inaccurate information, or supply the word. To initiate a repair, we may ask a question, as in 4; repeat part of the utterance to be repaired, as in example 5 below; abruptly stop speaking, as in example 6; or use particles and expressions like *uh, I mean,* or *that is,* as in example 1.

5. Speaker: I am sure—I am *absolutely* sure it was him that I saw last night prowling around.
6. Speaker 1: And here you have what's called the—
                [pause]
   Speaker 2: The carburetor?
   Speaker 1: Yeah, that's right, the carburetor.

Repairs can be initiated and resolved by the person who uttered the words that need to be repaired or by another conversationalist. There are thus four possibilities: repairs that are self-initiated and self-repaired; repairs that are other-initiated and self-repaired; repairs that are self-initiated and other-repaired; and repairs that are other-initiated and other-repaired. Of these possibilities, conversationalists show a strong preference for self-initiated self-repairs, which are least disruptive to the conversation and to the social relationship between the conversationalists. In general, conversationalists wait for clear signals of communicative distress before repairing an utterance made by someone else. The least preferred pattern is for repairs that are other-initiated and other-repaired. Individuals in the habit of both initiating and repairing utterances for others get branded as poor conversationalists or know-it-alls.

Found in many cultures, these preference patterns reflect a widespread but unspoken rule that all participants in a conversation among equals be given a chance to say what they want to say by themselves. Conversationalists provide assistance to others in initiating and resolving repairs only if no other option is available.

POLITENESS: AN ORGANIZATIONAL FORCE IN CONVERSATION

Violations of the turn-taking principles by interrupting or by failing to take turns are considered impolite. Turning one's back on interlocutors at the end of a conversation without going through a closing sequence is also stigmatized by the conventions of politeness. Other aspects of politeness are more subtle but nevertheless play an important role in structuring conversation.

There are also covert ways in which we communicate negative and positive politeness. When we expect interlocutors to allow us to both initiate and resolve a repair ourselves, we are expecting them to respect our right to make a contribution to the conversation without intrusion from others; that is, we are asking them to show negative politeness. Similarly, we recognize another person's need for negative politeness when, instead of ending a conversation, we initiate a preclosing exchange, affording the interlocutor a chance to say something further before closing. In contrast, when we initiate a conversation with a greeting, we convey concern about the addressee's health and well-being, thereby acknowledging the other's need for positive politeness. Many of the principles of conversational architecture can be explained in terms of politeness and the recognition of the politeness needs of others.

CROSS-CULTURAL COMMUNICATION
⟶

When people of different cultures have different norms about what type of politeness is required in a particular context, trouble can easily arise. We have described how callers in France begin telephone conversations with an apology; such apologies seldom form part of the opening sequence of an American telephone conversation. Obviously, members of the two cultures view telephone conversations differently: Americans generally see the act of calling as a sign of positive politeness, while the French tend to view it as a potential intrusion.

As a consequence of such variability, people from different cultures often misinterpret each other's signals. In the conversations of Athabaskan Indians, a pause of up to about one and a half seconds does not necessarily indicate the end of a turn, and Athabaskans often pause that long within a turn. In contrast, most European-Americans consider a pause of more than one second sufficient to signal the end of a turn (though there may be social variation). When Athabaskan Indians and European-Americans interact with each other, the latter often misinterpret the Athabaskans' midturn pauses as end-of-turn signals and feel free to claim the floor. From the Athabaskans' perspective, the European-Americans' claim of the floor at this point constitutes an interruption, and with the same situation occurring time and again in interactions between the two groups, negative stereotypes arise. Athabaskans find European-Americans rude, pushy, and uncontrollably talkative, while the European-Americans find Athabaskans conversationally uncooperative, sullen, and incapable of carrying on a coherent conversation. Carrying those stereotypes unwittingly into a classroom, white teachers may judge Indian students unresponsive or unintelligent, for their unspoken cultural expectations would have students speaking up, interacting, and being quick in their responses. While these tend to be the reactions of children in mainstream European-American culture, Athabaskan children, honoring the norms of their own culture, do not have these characteristics, at least not to the same degree. Though most people are totally unaware of such subtle cross-cultural differences, they can have profound social consequences.

COMPUTERS, SPEECH ACTS, AND CONVERSATION

As we saw in this section in the previous chapter, pragmatics has not been nearly as thoroughly explored in computational linguistics and corpora studies as have some other arenas of linguistics. As we also saw in the previous chapter, it will be necessary eventually to create models of politeness, turn taking, and the other phenomena discussed in this chapter before many of the applications of computer technology to speech will be mastered.

For various reasons, the building of corpora of written language has proceeded much faster than the compilation of spoken corpora. The reasons are fairly obvious. Especially in recent years, machine-readable texts initially prepared for book, magazine, newspaper, and other printed material are widely available. In addition, scanners can effectively transform printed materials of an earlier age into machine readable text. Spoken language is quite a different matter. First of all, it must be captured in some form or other—on tape or videocassette, for example. Then it must be transcribed—a tedious and expensive task in itself, and one dependent in great measure on the quality of the recording

and the degree of ambient noise in the original environment.

Still, for all that, one of the earliest machine-readable corpora was a transcribed version of spoken English. That corpus—called the London/Lund Corpus—has been the basis of considerable research. More recently, a good portion of the British National Corpus is based on speech. About a hundred volunteers were employed throughout Britain to carry tape recorders in the course of several days' ordinary activities, observing in a notebook the conditions surrounding the conversations and other exchanges recorded—who the participants were and their relationships to one another, the physical setting of the recorded speech, and so on. These tape recordings were then transcribed in ordinary English spelling. These conversations are now being used as the basis for research into the character of conversation, and the results are proving useful and interesting. We have already reported findings from the British National Corpus in earlier chapters of this book (for example, see the "conversation" category in Figures 8-1 and 8-2 on page 285), and we will report other findings in later chapters as well.

SUMMARY

- Utterances accomplish things like asserting, promising, pleading, and greeting. Actions accomplished through language are called speech acts.

- That language is commonly used to perform actions is most clearly illustrated by declarations such as *You're fired* or *Case dismissed!* Whether declarations or not, all speech acts can be described with four appropriateness conditions that identify aspects of or prerequisites for a successful speech act: the content, the preparatory condition, the sincerity condition, and the essential condition.

- In most normal circumstances, language users are bound by an unspoken pact that they adhere to and expect others to adhere to. This "cooperative principle" consists of four maxims—quantity, quality, relevance, and manner.

- On occasion, a speaker may flout a maxim to signal that the literal interpretation of the utterance is not the intended one.

- To encode and decode the intended meaning of indirect speech acts, people use patterns of conversational implicature based on knowledge of their language, their society, and the world around them.

- Indirect speech acts convey more than one message and are commonly used for politeness and humor.

- Respecting other people's needs for privacy demonstrates negative politeness, while showing interest and displaying sympathy expresses positive politeness.

- A speech event is a social activity in which language plays an important role.

- Speech events are structured, and appropriate verbal and nonverbal behavior characteristics of particular speech events can be described systematically.

- Conversations are organized according to certain regulatory principles.

- Turn taking is regulated by one set of norms.

- Adjacency pairs are structured by a local set of organizational principles, and many have preferred and dispreferred second parts.

- Organizational principles shape conversational openings and closings.

- The organization of repairs can be described with a set of rules that rank different repair patterns in terms of preference. Repairs that are self-initiated and made by self are favored.

- At the root of many organizational principles in conversation is the need to display positive and negative politeness to other people.

- Culture-specific norms determine when and where negative and positive politeness behaviors are appropriate.

- Because the organization of polite conversational behavior differs from culture to culture, miscommunication of intent across cultures is common.

EXERCISES

Based on English

9-1. Make a list of the headlines on the first two pages of a daily newspaper. Indicate which of the headlines report physical actions and which report speech acts.

9-2. Observe a typical lecture meeting of one of your courses and identify the characteristics that define it as a lecture (as distinct from an informal conversation, workshop, seminar, or lab meeting). Identify characterizing features in the areas listed. To what extent is there room for variability in how a lecture is conducted (depending, for example, on the personality of the participants)? When does a lecture stop being a lecture?

(1) Setting (physical setting, clothing, social identity of the participants, and so on)
(2) Nonverbal behavior of the participants (body movement, stance and position with respect to each other, and so on)
(3) Verbal behavior of the participants (turn taking, openings, closings, assignment of pair parts among participants, and so on)
(4) Topic (what is appropriate to talk about? to what extent can this be deviated from? and so on)

9-3. Make a tape recording of the first minute of a radio interview. Transcribe what is said during that first minute in as much detail as possible (indicating, for example, who talks, when pauses occur, and what hesitations occur). Label each turn as to its illocutionary force (greeting, inquiry, compliment, and so on). Then describe in detail the strategies used in opening the radio interview. Illustrate your description with specific examples taken from your transcript.

9-4. Make a tape recording of the first minute of a broadcast of the evening news on radio or television. Transcribe what is said during that minute in as much detail as possible. Then answer the following questions, citing specific illustrations from your transcript.

a. What effect do radio or television newscasters try to achieve initially?
b. How is this accomplished? Describe at least two strategies, using specific illustrations.
c. Suppose you played your tape recording to friends without identifying what was taped. Exactly what features would help them recognize it as a recording of the evening news? Cite three specific telltale characteristics other than content.
d. Which of the news items are reports of physical actions and which are reports of speech acts?

9-5. Observe the following interaction between two people who are working at nearby desks.

Anne: Ed?
Ed: Yeah?
Anne: Do you have a ruler?

Anne's first turn is an opening sequence. What does it signal, and what does Ed's response indicate? Why did Anne not merely open with *Do you have a ruler?*

9-6. The next time you talk on the telephone to a friend, observe the distinctive characteristics of talk over the telephone, and take notes immediately after you hang up. Identify several ways in which a telephone conversation differs from a face-to-face conversation. Try to recreate specific linguistic examples from your telephone conversation to illustrate your points.

9-7. Consider the following excerpts, each of which contains a repair. For each excerpt, determine whether the repair is: (a) self-initiated and self-repaired; (b) self-initiated and other-repaired; (c) other-initiated and self-repaired; or (d) other-initiated and other-repaired.

a. Jan: What's sales tax in this state?
   James: Five cents on the dollar.
   Patricia: Five cents on the dollar? You mean six cents on the dollar.
   James: Oh, yeah, six cents on the dollar.

b. Anne: There's a party at Rod's tonight. Wanna go?
   Sam: At Rod's? Rod's outta town!
   Anne: I mean Rick's.

c. Peter: And then he comes along an' tells me that he's dropping his accounting—uh, his economics class.
   Frank: Yeah, he told me the same thing the next mornin'.

d. Rick: His dog's been sick since last month an' he won't be able to go to the wedding because he's gotta take care of him.
   Alice: Well, actually, his dog's been sick for at least two months now. So it's nothin' new.

e. Samantha: Do you remember the names of all their kids? The oldest one is Daniel, the girl's Priscilla, then there's another girl—What's her name again?
   Reginald: Susie, I think.
   Samantha: Yeah, Susie, that's it.

f. Ellie: What do they charge you for car insurance?
   Ted: Two thousand bucks a year, but then there's a three-hundred-dollar deductible. Three hundred or one hundred— I can't remember.
   Ellie: Probably's one hundred, right?
   Ted: Yeah, I think you're right. One hundred sounds right.

g. Sarah: He's been cookin' all day for that dinner party.
   Anne: Actually he's been cooking for three days now.

h. Will: There wasn't much I could do for her. She needed five thousand bucks to pay for tuition and I jus' didn't have it.
   David: I thought it was four thousand.
   Will: Yeah, four thousand, but still I didn't have that much.

9-8. Consider the following excerpts, all of which are prestructures initiating conversation. Describe in detail the structure and the function of each prestructure using the terms *turn* (or *turn taking*), *signal, adjacency pair, first part, second part,* and *claiming the floor.*

a. Larry: Guess what.
   Lauren: What?
   Larry: Pat's coming tomorrow.

    b. Tom: [reading the newspaper] I can't believe this!

        Fred: What?

        Tom: Congress passed another new immigration law.

    c. Ruth: [chuckles while reading a book]

        Anne: What're you chuckling about?

        Ruth: This story, it's so off the wall!

9-9. Consider the following excerpt from a conversation among three friends.

    (1) Cindy: Heard from Jill recently? She hasn't written or called in ages.

    (2) Larry: Yeah, she sent me a postcard from England.

    (3) Barb: From England?

    (4) Larry: Oh, maybe it was from France, I can't remember.

    (5) Cindy: What's she doin—

    (6) Barb: No, I know it must've been from France 'cause she was gonna stay there all year.

    (7) Cindy: What's she doin' in France?

    (8) Larry: Why are you asking about her?

    (9) Cindy: I don't know, I've just been thinkin' about her.

   (10) Larry: She's on some sort of exchange program. Studyin' French or somethin'.

   (11) Cindy: Sounds pretty nice to me.

   (12) Larry: Yeah. Well, I don't know. She said she was tired of Europe and wants to come home.

    a. In the conversation above, how many turns does each interlocutor have?

    b. Identify an example of each of the following in the conversation above: *turn-taking signal, claiming the floor, preferred response, dispreferred response, repair, trouble source, initiation,* and *resolution.*

    c. Identify an *adjacency pair* in the conversation, giving the name of the *first part* and *second part.*

9-10. Conversations in fiction and drama and those re-created in movies or on the stage often differ from the ordinary conversations of daily living. The following is an excerpt from a conversation in Part III of Isak Dinesen's autobiographical novel *Out of Africa* (New York: Random House, 1937).

    "Do you know anything of book-keeping?" I asked him.

    "No. Nothing at all," he said, "I have always found it very difficult to add two figures together."

    "Do you know about cattle at all?" I went on. "Cows?" he asked. "No, no. I am afraid of cows."

    "Can you drive a tractor, then?" I asked. Here a faint ray of hope appeared on his face. "No," he said, "but I think I could learn that."

    "Not on my tractor though," I said, "but then tell me, Emmanuelson, what have you even been doing? What are you in life?"

Emmanuelson drew himself up straight. "What am I?" he exclaimed. "Why, I am an actor."

I thought: Thank God, it is altogether outside my capacity to assist this lost man in any practical way; the time has come for a general human conversation. "You are an actor?" I said, "that is a fine thing to be. And which were your favourite parts when you were on the stage?"

"Oh I am a tragic actor," said Emmanuelson, "my favourite parts were that of Armand in 'La Dame aux Camelias' and of Oswald in 'Ghosts'."

On the basis of this example, analyze the differences between the organization of conversations quoted in writing and the organization of actual conversations. Why do these differences exist?

RESOURCES

Video

- **John J. Gumperz, T. C. Jupp, and C. Roberts. 1979.** *Crosstalk: A Study of Cross-Cultural Communication* (London: National Centre for Industrial Language Training and BBC)

  A one-hour video illustrating and discussing miscommunication between East Indian immigrants and British bank clerks, librarians, and other institutional figures in London; a moving demonstration of the painful difficulties that can sometimes arise from differing conversational norms across cultural boundaries.

SUGGESTIONS FOR FURTHER READING

- **Deborah Tannen. 1990.** *You Just Don't Understand: Women and Men in Conversation* (New York: Ballantine). Not only accessible but popular; on the *New York Times* best seller list for several years; discusses misunderstanding between the sexes; a favorite of students; also treats the Gricean maxims in a simple, direct analysis.

- **Deborah Tannen. 1994.** *Gender and Discourse* (New York: Oxford UP). An accessible treatment of the background to Tannen's extraordinarily popular *You Just Don't Understand.*

- **Ronald Wardhaugh. 1985.** *How Conversation Works* (New York: Blackwell). A basic, well-focused book, accessible to readers of *LISU.*

Advanced Reading

The analysis of speech acts has been an enterprise chiefly of philosophers. Austin (1962) is a set of twelve readable lectures laying out the nature of locutionary acts, illocutionary acts, and perlocutionary acts. Grice (1975, 1989) formulates the cooperative principle and enumerates the conversational maxims discussed in this chapter. Searle (1976) discusses the classification of speech acts and their syntax, while Searle (1975) lays out the structure of indirect speech acts. Besides these primary sources, you can find good discussions of the work of Austin, Grice, and Searle in Levinson (1983) and Wardhaugh (1998).

Profoundly differing from the philosophical traditions in their methodological approach, the inductive studies of the conversation analysts are technical and challenging to read: turn taking was first analyzed systematically by Sacks et al. (1974), closings by Schegloff and Sacks (1973), and repairs by Schegloff et al. (1977). Atkinson and Heritage (1984) is a good collection of papers on various aspects of the organization of conversation. More accessible are these textbooks on conversation analysis and language use in various informal contexts: Levinson (1983), McLaughlin (1984), chapters 8 and 10 of Ellis and Beattie (1986), and chapters 10 and 12 of Wardhaugh (1998).

The theoretical background to the study of speech events is presented in Goffman (1974) and Hymes (1974). Goffman (1981) presents interesting and entertaining analyses of various speech events including lectures and radio talk. Kendon et al. (1975) and Goodwin (1981) describe how talk and gestures are integrated in conversation. The organization of conversation in the workplace is investigated in Boden (1988), and verbal communication (and miscommunication) between doctors and patients is analyzed in West (1984). The characterization of communication between subordinates and superordinates as spectator/performer or performer/spectator was proposed in Bateson (1972), which lays out the philosophical foundation for the study of human communication. Cross-social and cross-cultural differences in the organization of conversation are analyzed in Gumperz (1982), Gumperz (ed., 1982), Kochman (1981), and Scollon and Scollon (1981) and (1995). A few examples from Scollon and Scollon appear in this chapter. Godard (1977) is an interesting study of Franco-American differences in behavior on the telephone. Brown and Levinson (1987) and various chapters of Levinson (1983) and Wardhaugh (1998) discuss politeness. Drew and Heritage (1993) is a collection of essays discussing interaction in institutional settings.

REFERENCES

- Atkinson, J. Maxwell, and John Heritage, eds. 1984. *Structures of Social Action: Studies in Conversation Analysis* (Cambridge: Cambridge UP).

- Austin, John. 1962. *How to Do Things with Words* (New York: Oxford UP).

- Bateson, Gregory. 1972. *Steps to an Ecology of Mind* (New York: Bantam).

- Boden, Deirdre. 1988. *The Business of Talk: Organizations in Action* (Cambridge: Polity).

- Brown, Penelope, and Stephen C. Levinson. 1987. *Politeness: Some Universals in Language Usage* (Cambridge: Cambridge UP).

- Cole, Peter, and Jerry L. Morgan, eds. 1975. *Syntax and Semantics 3: Speech Acts* (New York: Academic).

- Drew, Paul, and John Heritage, eds. 1993. *Talk at Work* (Cambridge: Cambridge UP).

- Ellis, Andrew, and Geoffrey Beattie. 1986. *The Psychology of Language and Communication* (New York: Guilford).

- Godard, Daniele. 1977. "Same Setting, Different Norms: Phone Call Beginnings in France and the United States," *Language in Society* 6:209–219.

- Goffman, Erving. 1974. *Frame Analysis: An Essay on the Organization of Experience* (New York: Harper & Row).

- Goffman, Erving. 1981. *Forms of Talk* (Philadelphia: U of Pennsylvania P).

- Goodwin, Charles. 1981. *Conversational Organization: Interaction between Speakers and Hearers* (New York: Academic).

- Grice, H. Paul. 1975. "Logic and Conversation," in Cole and Morgan (1975), pp. 41–58.

- Gumperz, John J. 1982. *Discourse Strategies* (Cambridge: Cambridge UP).

- Gumperz, John J., ed. 1982. *Language and Social Identity* (Cambridge: Cambridge UP).

- Hymes, Dell. 1974. *Foundations in Sociolinguistics* (Philadelphia: U of Pennsylvania P).

- Kendon, Adam, Richard M. Harris, and Mary Ritchie Key, eds. 1975. *Organization of Behavior in Face-to-Face Interaction* (The Hague: Mouton).

- Kochman, Thomas. 1981. *Black and White Styles in Conflict* (Chicago: U of Chicago P).

- Levinson, Stephen C. 1983. *Pragmatics* (Cambridge: Cambridge UP).

- McLaughlin, Margaret L. 1984. *Conversation: How Talk Is Organized* (Beverly Hills, CA: Sage).

- Sacks, Harvey, Emanuel A. Schegloff, and Gail Jefferson. 1974. "A Simplest Systematics for the Organization of Turn-Taking in Conversation," *Language* 50:696–735.

- Schegloff, Emanuel A., Gail Jefferson, and Harvey Sacks. 1977. "The Preference for Self-Correction in the Organization of Repair in Conversation," *Language* 53:361–382.

- Schegloff, Emanuel A., and Harvey Sacks. 1973. "Opening Up Closings," *Semiotica* 7:289–327.

- Scollon, Ron, and Suzanne B. K. Scollon. 1981. *Narrative, Literacy and Face in Interethnic Communication* (Norwood, NJ: Ablex).

- Scollon, Ron, and Suzanne Wong Scollon. 1995. *Intercultural Communication.* (Oxford: Blackwell).

- Searle, John R. 1975. "Indirect Speech Acts," in Cole and Morgan (1975), pp. 59–82.

- Searle, John R. 1976. "A Classification of Illocutionary Acts," *Language in Society* 5:1–23.

- Wardhaugh, Ronald. 1998. *An Introduction to Sociolinguistics,* 3rd ed. (New York: Blackwell).

- West, Candace. 1984. *Routine Complications: Troubles in Talk between Doctors and Patients* (Bloomington: Indiana UP).

CHAPTER 10

LANGUAGE VARIATION ACROSS SITUATIONS OF USE: REGISTERS

—

WHAT DO YOU THINK?

A classmate in your linguistics course comments that she is surprised to see so many examples of contractions used in the textbook. She asks whether contractions like let's *and* here's *and* don't *aren't supposed to be limited to conversation and avoided in writing, especially formal writing such as one would expect in a textbook. You don't disagree with her, but you found that the "colloquial" contractions created a more informal, relaxed tone to the textbook, and you enjoyed them. What explanation do you offer for the difference in your views of contractions?*

Your junior high school English class asks you why teachers don't like slang or colloquialisms and what's the difference between them, anyway? What do you say?

In a conversation, a friend who is an English major comments about several novels by P. D. James she's been reading. She says the dialogue seems totally natural. You, on the other hand, had recently corrected the transcription of a deposition you had given and were struck by how much your answers to questions were incomplete sentences peppered with false starts and uhm's *and* uh's—*and practically the same thing could be said for the attorney who took the deposition. You had the impression that your transcribed conversation didn't look anything like the dialogue in novels. What do you tell your friend about your differing perceptions of what's natural and what's artificial in fictional dialogue?*

INTRODUCTION: THE CLOCKS OF BALLYHOUGH

The story is told that Ballyhough railway station on the Isle of Coll off the coast of Scotland has two clocks, which disagree by some six minutes. When a helpful traveler pointed out this fact to a porter, the porter's reply was "Faith, sir, if they was to tell the same time, why would we be having two of them?" Though the porter's logic may be faulty when applied to railway clocks, it may legitimately be applied to the many competing languages that exist throughout the world. If every language variety were to do the same work as the others, there would be no need for more than one. Each language variety serves a distinct purpose. One of the socially significant functions of a language variety is to affirm the identity and unity of its speakers; language varieties mark speakers as distinct from members of other groups. It is possible to imagine a fantasy world in which all social groups speak alike, with no dialect variations of any kind. For better or worse, this imaginary situation is not what we find in the real world. Rather, a multitude of tongues exists, each with its own regional and social dialects, all changing continuously so that each generation speaks differently from those preceding it. In the next chapter, we discuss language variation across different groups of speakers.

In this chapter we discuss language variation that is associated not with groups of language *users* but with *situations of use.* We explore the varieties of language that individuals in communities use in the course of daily living. To cite some examples, we don't talk to close friends the way we talk to our teachers, nor do we write to our parents the same way we would write to an attorney or a minister. In different circumstances, we all vary our use of language forms. In some societies, different situations call for different languages altogether; in other societies, different situations call for alternative varieties of a single language. Language varieties that are characteristic of particular situations of use are called **registers.**

LANGUAGE VARIES WITHIN A SPEECH COMMUNITY

LANGUAGE CHOICE IN MULTILINGUAL SOCIETIES

You might assume that in multilingual countries like Switzerland, Belgium, and India, different languages are spoken by different groups of people. Typically, though, each language is systematically allocated to specific social situations. In speech communities employing several languages, language choice is not arbitrary. Instead, a particular setting such as school or government may favor one language, and other languages will be appropriate to other speech situations. Where one language is appropriate, another will be inappropriate. Though there may be roughly equivalent expressions in two languages, the social meaning that attaches to use of one generally differs from that attached to use of the other. As a result, speakers must attend to the social import of language choice, however unconsciously that choice may be made.

LINGUISTIC REPERTOIRES IN BRUSSELS, TEHERAN, AND LOS ANGELES

The use of selected varieties from two languages among government workers in the capital of Belgium illustrates the nature of language choice in one European community.

> Government functionaries in Brussels who are of Flemish origin do not always speak Dutch to *each other,* even when they all know Dutch *very* well and *equally* well. Not only are there occasions when they speak French to *each other* instead of Dutch, but there are some occasions when they speak standard Dutch and others when they use one or another regional variety of Dutch with each other. Indeed, some of them also use different varieties of French with each other as well, one variety being particularly loaded with governmental officialese, another corresponding to the non-technical conversational French of highly educated and refined circles in Belgium and still another being not only a "more colloquial French" but the colloquial French of those who are Flemings. All in all, these several varieties of Dutch and of French constitute the *linguistic repertoire* of certain social networks in Brussels. (From Fishman [1972], pp. 47–48.)

The language variety that Brussels residents use is occasioned by the setting in which the talk takes place, by the topic, by the social relations among the participants, and by certain other features of the situation. In general, the use of Dutch is associated with interaction that is informal and intimate, whereas French has more official or highbrow connotations. Given these associations, the choice of French or Dutch carries an associated social meaning in addition to its referential meaning.

We use the term **linguistic repertoire** for the set of language varieties exhibited in the speaking and writing patterns of a speech community. As in Brussels, the linguistic repertoire of any speech community may consist of several languages and may include several varieties of each language. Here are two cases.

In the mid-1970s, there was considerable multilingualism in Teheran, the capital of Iran. Christian families spoke Armenian or Syriac at home and in church, Persian at school, all three in different situations while playing or shopping, and Azerbaijani Turkish at shops in the bazaar. Moslem men from northwest Iran, who were working as laborers in the booming capital, spoke a variety of Persian with their supervisors at construction sites but switched to a variety of Turkish with their fellow workers and to a local Iranian dialect when they visited their home villages on holidays; in addition, they listened daily to radio broadcasts in standard Persian and heard passages from the Koran recited in Arabic. It was not uncommon for individuals of any social standing to command as many as four or five languages and to deploy them in different situations.

To take another example, the Korean-speaking community in Los Angeles supports bilingual institutions of various sorts: banks, churches, stores, and a wide range of services from pool halls and video rental shops to hotels, construction companies, and law firms. At some banks all the tellers are bilingual, and in the course of a day's work they switch often between Korean and English. As the tellers alternate between Korean-speaking and English-speaking patrons, the language in which they conduct business alternates as well.

SWITCHING VARIETIES WITHIN A LANGUAGE

If we examine the situation in Europe, besides switching between languages we see examples of language-internal switching. Brussels residents switch not only between French and Dutch but also among varieties of French and among varieties of Dutch. In Hemnes, a village in northern Norway, residents speak two quite distinct varieties of Norwegian. Ranamål is a local dialect and serves to identify speakers of that region. Bokmål, one of two forms of standard Norwegian (the other being Nynorsk), is in use in Hemnes for education, religion, government transactions, and the mass media. All members of the community control these two varieties and regard themselves at any given time as speaking one or the other. There are differences of pronunciation, morphology, lexicon, and syntax, and speakers do not perceive themselves as mixing the two varieties in their speech. Here's an illustration with a simple sentence meaning 'Where are you from?'

Ranamål	ke du e ifrå
Bokmål	vor ær du fra

While Bokmål is the expected variety in certain well-defined situations, residents of Hemnes do not accept the use of Bokmål among themselves outside those situations. In situations in which Ranamål is customarily used, the employment of Bokmål would signal social distance and even contempt for community spirit. In Hemnes, to use Bokmål with fellow locals is to *snakkfint* or *snakk jalat* 'put on airs.' As the researchers who reported these findings note, "Although locals show an overt preference for the dialect, they tolerate and use the standard in situations where it conveys meanings of officiality, expertise, and politeness toward strangers who are clearly segregated from their personal life." [Blom and Gumperz (1972), pp. 433–434.] Regard for the social situation is thus important even in choosing varieties of the same language.

SPEECH SITUATIONS

—

As we have seen in Hemnes, Los Angeles, Brussels, and Teheran, language switching can be triggered by a change in any one of several situational factors, including the setting and purpose of the communication, the person being addressed, the social relations between the interlocutors, and the topic.

ELEMENTS OF A SPEECH SITUATION

If we define a speech situation as the coming together of various significant situational factors such as purpose, topic, and social relations, then each speech situation in a bilingual community will generally allow for only one of the two languages to be used. Table 10-1 illustrates this concept for a bilingual community in Los Angeles.

As you see from Table 10-1, in situation A a variety of Spanish is appropriate; in situation C a variety of English. Only in the relatively rare case of situation E might an individual have a genuine choice between Spanish and English without calling attention to the language chosen. In situation E, a choice is allowed because of the conflict between intimacy (which usually requires Spanish, as in situations A or B) and an academic topic (for which English is usually preferred).

Table 10-2 charts certain aspects of a speech situation that may require a change in language variety.

Related to *purpose,* the kind of activity that is involved is crucial. Are you making a purchase, giving a sermon, telling a story? The activity may have an influence on the selection of a language. Are you entertaining, reporting information, affirming a social relationship? Greeting a friend or inviting an aunt to dinner?

Table 10-1

LINGUISTIC REPERTOIRE

SITUATION	RELATION OF SPEAKERS	PLACE	TOPIC TYPE	SPANISH	ENGLISH
A	intimate	school	not academic	X	
B	intimate	home	not academic	X	
C	not intimate	school	not academic		X
D	not intimate	home	academic		X
E	intimate	school	academic	X	X

Table 10-2

ELEMENTS OF A SPEECH SITUATION

PURPOSE	SETTING	PARTICIPANTS
Activity	Topic	Speaker
Goal	Location	Addressee
	Mode	Social roles of speaker and addressee
		Character of audience

As to *setting,* you may switch from one language to another as the *topic* switches, from a topic of local interest, say, to one of national concern; or from a personal topic to one about your studies. Even the *location* can influence language choice in that you might well use one language in a university setting but a different one in church or at home for otherwise equivalent situations. The *mode*—that is, whether you are speaking or writing—can certainly influence the forms of language selected.

As to *participants,* the identity of the speaker will influence the language choice, as will the person being addressed. Speakers typically adapt their utterances to the age of an addressee. In some societies, the older the person, the higher his or her social standing; younger people must address older people more respectfully than they address their peers. In French the second-person singular pronoun 'you' has two forms: the grammatically singular form *tu* is used when addressing a social equal or as an expression of intimacy, while the plural form *vous* is reserved for a person of higher social status or to mark social distance (as well as for addressing more than one person, irrespective of status). A younger person addressing an older person is expected to use *vous,* not *tu,* unless the older person is a close relative. The French pronoun system illustrates one way in which morphology may vary according to the age of the addressee. Persian also shows many of the same patterns, and so do several European tongues.

Also with respect to participants, it is not just the social identity of speaker and addressee that is relevant but their *roles* in the particular speech situation. A judge, for example, typically speaks one variety at home—where she is mother, wife, neighbor—and another in the courtroom as judge. A parent who works as a teacher and has his child for a student may speak different varieties at home and at school, even when the topic and the addressee are the same.

The various aspects of the speech situation come together in a particular choice of language variety. In each bilingual situation—whether a general one such as home or church or a specific one such as discussing politics in a cafe with a close friend—only one variety is usually appropriate. In fact, people get so accustomed to speaking a particular language in a given setting that they often have difficulty communicating in another language in that setting, no matter how familiar the other language may be in other settings. (Exceptions to this generalization include professional translators, bilingual educators, and certain business people who are regularly engaged in negotiations with members of their own and another culture.) As a result, switching between language varieties is very common throughout the world.

REGISTERS IN MONOLINGUAL SOCIETIES

The recognition that there are settings and speech situations in multilingual societies in which one language or another is appropriate has a direct parallel in monolingual speech communities, in which varieties of a single language constitute the entire linguistic repertoire. Consider the difference between the full forms of careful speech

contraction
~~won't~~ wouldn't
I'll   ect.

REGISTERS IN MONOLINGUAL SOCIETIES — 335

and the abbreviations and reductions characteristic of fast speech that occur in face-to-face relaxed communication: not only workaday contractions like *won't* and *I'll* but reduced sentences like *Jeetyet?* [jityet] and *Wajjasay?* [wɑjǝse] for 'Did you eat yet?' and 'What did you say?'

To take a second example, you know that you do not typically use the same terms in referring to certain body parts when speaking to friends, family, and physician. The term *collarbone* might be used at home, with *clavicle* reserved for use with a physician; either could be used with friends, depending on other aspects of the speech situation. The choices that are made for certain other body parts would be more strikingly different.

The distribution of alternative terms for the same referent may seem arbitrary and without communicative benefit; indeed, in the case of body parts, all the terms may be known and used by all the parties under equivalent circumstances. A physician speaking with her own physician may use the term *clavicle;* with her family and friends, however, she will be expected to use the same terms the rest of us would use with equivalent addressees in comparable speech situations. When nonmedical people address a physician, they may use the terms appropriate to discussion of a medical situation.

Since all the terms would be equally well understood and could communicate referential meaning equally well, the choice of a socially appropriate variant is *cognitively* unhelpful. One may ask, then, why linguistic expression differs in different speech situations. The answer is that different forms for the same content can indicate your affective relationship to salient aspects of the situation (setting, addressee, topic, and so on). Such variation as has lasted for centuries in a language can be assumed to be serving a fundamental need of human communication.

Thus, just as a multilingual linguistic repertoire allocates different language varieties to different speech situations, so does a monolingual repertoire. For all speakers—monolingual and multilingual—there is marked variation in the forms of language used for different activities, addressees, topics, and settings. These marked forms of language use constitute the registers of a linguistic repertoire. By choosing among the varieties, situational variation is both created and communicated.

From a relatively young age, everyone learns to control several language varieties for use in different speech situations. No one is limited to a single variety of a single language. For some, the language varieties they control belong to one language; for others, they are drawn from more than one language. Just which speech situations—which purposes, topics, addressees—prompt a different variety depends on the norms in particular cultures. In one society, the presence of in-laws may call for a different variety (as it does in Dyirbal and several other aboriginal Australian societies). In other societies, the presence of in-laws may have no independent influence on the selection of an appropriate language variety, whereas the presence of children or members of the opposite sex may be crucial. In Western societies, adults have a mouthful of words that they avoid saying in the presence of children, and children avoid saying them in the presence of adults. Of course there are also differences associated with mode—that is, whether language is written or spoken—as you will see shortly.

MARKERS OF REGISTER

As languages and dialects differ from one another at every level, so registers can differ in vocabulary, phonology, grammar, and semantics. There may also be different interactional patterns in different speech situations—how the allocation of turns is decided in conversation, for example. In addition, there are rules governing nonlinguistic behavior such as physical proximity, face-to-face positioning, standing, and sitting that also accompany register variation; both the interactional patterns and the body language are beyond the scope of this book, and we mention them only incidentally.

When you find characteristic features of a register at one level of the grammar, you can expect to find corresponding features at other levels as well. For example, to describe the register known as legalese we must describe its characteristic lexicon, sentence structure, and semantics, as well as its characteristic terms of address, rules of interaction, and so forth.

LEXICAL MARKERS OF REGISTER

Registers vary along certain dimensions. For example, people generally speak (and write) in markedly different ways in formal and informal situations. Formality and informality can be seen as opposite poles of a situational continuum along which forms of expression may be arranged.

The four words that follow generally mean the same thing but it shouldn't be difficult for you to rank them according to degrees of formality. It would be surprising if you did not generally agree that these words could be ranked as follows, with the least formal word first: *pickled, high, drunk, intoxicated.* Think of other terms for the state that results from having consumed too much alcohol. In one context, to suggest inebriation may require the word *intoxicated,* while in another a more appropriate expression may be *drunk* or *under the influence.* The words *bombed* and *pissed* are also sometimes used, especially by younger people in situations of considerable informality. One thesaurus lists more than 125 words or phrases for 'intoxicated.' By no means are they all situationally equivalent.

Not every word that can be glossed as 'inebriated' is suitable for use on all occasions when reference to intoxication is intended. Word choice can indicate quite different attitudes toward the state, the addressees, the person being described, and so on. It can also index the speech situation in which the term is being used—as intimate or distant, formal or informal, serious or jocular, and so forth. Different expressions for 'intoxication' have different connotations, depending on the situations of use with which they are customarily associated. These affiliated situations of use add a dimension of meaning that is quite distinct from the referential meaning of a word.

Imagine the following dialogue between a judge and a defendant at an arraignment in a courtroom:

> Judge: I see that the cops say you were wasted last night and were driving an
> old jalopy down the middle of the road. True?

> Defendant: Your honor, if I might be permitted to address this baseless allegation, I should like to report that I was neither inebriated nor under the influence of an alcoholic beverage of any kind; for the record, I imbibed no booze last evening.

Of several possible observations about this exchange, we make just a few. In the first place, the judge's language seems out of place: words like *cops, wasted,* and *jalopy* strike us as inappropriate for a judge in a courtroom, perhaps even bizarre. As for the defendant's response, it too seems out of place, especially following the very informal speechways of the judge. Indeed the defendant's language might well seem too formal, even if the judge had used more elevated language. There is an incongruity in the defendant's using more formal terms than the judge. It also seems odd to have the informal word *booze* used in an utterance in which the formal words *imbibed, inebriated, beverage,* and *allegation* also occur.

Compare the judge's language in the first example with the following, which is more appropriate to the speech situation.

> Judge: You are charged with driving a 1992 blue Ford while under the influence of alcohol. How do you plead?

Thus we see that within a single language each register is appropriate to specific circumstances. Like all language varieties, registers constrain which words can be used together and which words cannot be, even though their use together would not violate the rules of syntax. These kinds of *co-occurrence restrictions* apply at all levels of grammar, as you'll see.

Terms of Address Appropriate forms of address differ from situation to situation. Judges are addressed in court as *Your Honor,* though they may be addressed by their friends and neighbors quite differently. Each of us can be addressed in several ways: by first name (*Pat*); family name (*Smith*); family name preceded by a title (*Doctor Smith, Professor Jones*); the second-person pronoun (*you*); terms showing respect (*Sir, Madam*). In the Catholic church, cardinals are addressed as *Your Eminence.* Throughout the world the Queen of England is addressed as *Your Majesty* (or *Mam*). At the opposite end of the scale are terms of disrespect such as *buster* or *you bastard.* A given individual may be addressed in different ways in the course of several speech situations. A judge's spouse does not employ *Your Honor* as a form of address, nor do parents normally address their children with a title of any sort, nor children (of any age) ordinarily address their parents with a title and name.

Slang Probably the most famous register is slang. **Slang** is the variety used in situations of extreme informality, and it often carries rebellious undertones or an intention of distancing its users from certain mainstream values. As a result, slang is particularly popular among underworld groups and among teenagers and college students in general. But by no means is its use limited to such groups, for slang has its wellsprings in specialized groups of all sorts, from physicians and computer "hacks" to police officers and stockbrokers. Many specialist terms, especially those used by occupational groups, are *argot,* not slang. **Argot** is the specialized vocabulary of various groups, often occupational or recreational groups, but argot is not limited to situations of extreme informality, and it generally lacks rebellious undertones.

It's risky providing examples of slang here because so much slang changes as quickly as clothing fashions. Still, there are dictionaries of slang, and their existence suggests that some slang expressions lead longer lives. It might be more reliable to ask student readers of this book, whose social circumstances put them within earshot of recent slang, to provide examples (and an exercise at the end of this chapter does just that). In the meanwhile, the following from the dust jacket of a recent slang dictionary may be illustrative: *Barbie Doll, bean counter, bells and whistles, cover your ass, designer drug, glitterati, kick ass, mallie, pocket pool, puzzle palace,* and *tits and zits.* If you are unacquainted with any of these terms, a classmate may be able to provide a gloss. (Alternatively, check the dictionary, identified in the "Suggestions for Further Reading" at the end of the chapter).

Slang has a legitimate place in the linguistic repertoire of speech communities. Like all registers, however, its effectiveness depends crucially on the circumstances of its use. In appropriate circumstances anyone of any socioeconomic or educational status can use slang, and usually without calling attention to its use.

The observation that the effectiveness of a particular register depends not on the socioeconomic status of the user but on the circumstances of use applies equally to all registers. Even the most formal varieties of English are not appropriate to all occasions, any more than a tuxedo is suited to all occasions. A tuxedo at the beach is as out of place as a bathing suit at a church wedding.

COLLEGE SLANG: THE TOP TWENTY

In *Slang and Sociability* Connie Eble reports the top slang expressions used by college students at the University of North Carolina between 1972 and 1993. Which of them have you used or heard used?

sweet 'excellent, superb'
chill/chill out 'relax'
slide 'easy course'
blow off 'neglect, not attend'
bag 'neglect, not attend'
killer 'excellent, exciting'
jam 'play music, dance, party'
scope 'look for partner for sex or romance'

wasted 'drunk'
clueless 'unaware'
diss 'belittle, criticize'
pig out 'eat voraciously'
bad 'good, excellent'
crash 'go to sleep'
cheezy 'unattractive, out of favor'
hook (up) 'locate a partner for sex or romance'
trip (out) 'have a bizarre experience'
dweeb 'socially inept person'
buzz/catch a buzz 'experience slight intoxication'
tool 'completely acceptable'

Just as informal clothing can extend its welcome from informal circumstances into somewhat more formal circumstances, so slang expressions often climb up the social ladder, becoming acceptable in more formal circumstances. The words *mob* and *pants* are among many that were considered slang at an earlier period of their history but can now be used in any circumstances. As words become established in more formal circumstances, they lose their status as slang, and newer slang terms replace them. (Though this climb up the social ladder is quite common, some slang expressions seem destined to remain forever consigned to the most informal circumstances. *Bones* meaning 'dice' was used by Chaucer in the fourteenth century, and *beat it* meaning 'scram' by Shakespeare in the seventeenth century. In these senses both words remain slang today—as does *scram!*)

Interesting ✳

PHONOLOGICAL MARKERS OF REGISTER

Registers are marked not only by word choice but by all other levels of grammar. For spoken registers this includes phonology. In a study of New York City speechways that we will discuss in detail in the following chapter, considerable phonological variation was uncovered among all groups of speakers in different situations of use.

Figure 10-1 presents frequencies for the pronunciation of *-ing* as /ɪŋ/ in three speech situations. We use *-ing* to represent the pronunciation of the suffix in words like *talking, running, eating,* and *watching.* The speech situations in this case consist of three kinds of interaction in the course of a sociolinguistic interview in the homes

Figure 10-1

PERCENTAGE OF PRONUNCIATION OF *-ING* AS /ɪŋ/ IN THREE SPEECH SITUATIONS AMONG FOUR SOCIAL GROUPS IN NEW YORK CITY

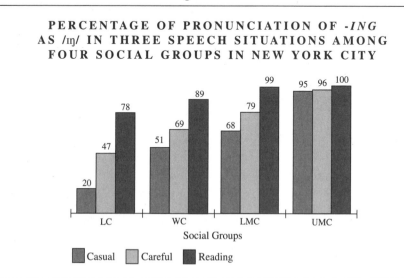

Source of data: Labov 1966

of four groups of respondents (labeled LC, WC, LMC, and UMC). The style of the interview, with its interlaced questions and answers, can be regarded as "careful" speech. In addition, respondents read a set passage aloud; this "reading" style was taken to be representative of more careful speech than that represented by interview style. At the end of the interview, in order to prompt relaxed speech, the interviewer asked respondents whether they had ever had a close call with death, and this gambit usually elicited a relaxed, unguarded variety, here called "casual" speech.

In their casual speech, LC (lower-class) respondents pronounced the -*ing* suffix as /ɪŋ/ 20 percent of the time (and as /ɪn/ the other 80 percent). In their careful speech, the occurrence of /ɪŋ/ increases to 47 percent (while /ɪn/ decreases to 53 percent). When reading a passage aloud, the same respondents pronounce /ɪŋ/ 78 percent of the time (and /ɪn/ only 22 percent). This represents a dramatic increase of /ɪŋ/ pronunciations as the speech situation changes, becoming more formal. Exactly the same overall pattern holds for the other three social groups: each one uses more /ɪŋ/ pronunciations in careful speech than in casual speech and more in reading style than in careful speech. We can generalize this finding by saying that in this speech community /ɪŋ/ indexes formality, and more frequent /ɪŋ/ pronunciations signal increased formality.

In another study, college students in Los Angeles gathered data showing that both males and females used more /ɪŋ/ pronunciations in arguments than in joking. The frequencies are given in Figure 10-2. Though men and women differ in their use of this phonological variable (a topic we return to in Chapter 11), both sexes exploit it in the same way to index different situations of use.

A study in Norwich (England) uncovered similar patterns of variation across registers. Among five different social groups, the middle middle class (the highest

---

Figure 10-2

**PERCENTAGE OF -*ING* PRONOUNCED AS /ɪŋ/
IN TWO SPEECH SITUATIONS BY MALES AND FEMALES
IN LOS ANGELES**

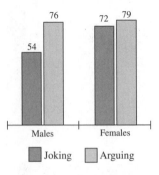

Source of data: B. Wald and T. Shopen, "A Researcher's Guide to the Sociolinguistic Variable (ING)" in Shopen and Williams (1981), p. 247.

ranking group in the study) *always* used /ɪŋ/ in the formal register of reading style, while lower working class residents *never* used it in their most casual speech. Thus, at the extremes of socioeconomic status and situational formality, the range of difference was 100 percent, but all five social groups used both pronunciations in their speech. As the frequencies in Figure 10-3 show, the pattern in Norwich is the same as in New York City: each social group uses most /ɪŋ/ in reading style and least in its casual speech, with an intermediate percentage for careful speech. It is clear that on this variable, three widely separated English-speaking communities use /ɪŋ/ to index situations of greater and lesser formality. It should be stressed that it is not the absolute percentage that indexes situations but the *relative* percentage with respect to other situations. The data indicate that this linguistic marker of situation is a continuous variable, able to indicate fine distinctions in degrees of formality across a range of speech situations.

As another example of phonological variation (or its equivalent spelling variation), we examine the distribution of ordinary contractions like *can't, won't,* and *I'll* in different situations of use, from telephone conversations between personal friends and between people who do not know one another to writing in newspapers (Press) and academic journals. Even in so straightforward a feature as contractions, speakers exhibit differential use of forms in different speech situations. The counts in Table 10-3 are based on a large corpus of written and spoken British English and represent the average number of contractions per one thousand words. Notice that in going

Figure 10-3

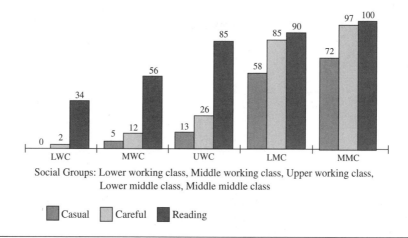

**PERCENTAGE OF PRONUNCIATION OF *-ING*
PRONOUNCED AS /ɪŋ/ IN THREE SPEECH SITUATIONS
AMONG FIVE SOCIAL GROUPS IN NORWICH**

Social Groups: Lower working class, Middle working class, Upper working class,
Lower middle class, Middle middle class

▨ Casual   ▧ Careful   ■ Reading

Source of data: Trudgill 1996

Table 10-3

NUMBER OF CONTRACTIONS PER THOUSAND WORDS OF BRITISH ENGLISH IN DIFFERENT SITUATIONS OF USE

SITUATION OF USE	CONTRACTIONS
Telephone conversation with friends	59.9
Telephone conversation with strangers	48.8
Interviews	25.4
Broadcasts	21.5
Romantic fiction	19.0
Spontaneous speeches	17.8
Prepared speeches	13.3
Science fiction	6.5
Press	1.5
Academic journals	0.1
Official documents	0.0

Source of data: Biber 1988

from telephone conversation with friends to telephone conversation with strangers to interviews to broadcasts and so on down the list there is a graded increase in formality. The increasing formality is accompanied by a decrease in the frequency of contractions.

GRAMMATICAL MARKERS OF REGISTER

Situations of use are also marked by syntactic variables. As an example, consider the occurrence of prepositions at the end of a clause or sentence. You may recall from your school days that prescriptive textbooks and some teachers sometimes frown on sentence-final prepositions, as in the sentence *That's the teacher I was telling you about*. Instead, those texts and teachers would recommend *That's the teacher about whom I was telling you*. Well, as you know, sentence-final prepositions abound in English. But they don't occur with equal frequency in all speech situations. Using the same corpus of texts used for the contractions above, the number of sentence-final prepositions per thousand prepositions for a dozen spoken and written registers is given in Table 10-4. This table does not show the same continuous incline from least formal to most formal that we saw with contractions. Instead, there is a major distinction between spoken varieties and nonfiction writing, with fiction writing (which includes fictional dialogue) having intermediate values. In the spoken registers, an average of between 33 and 56 prepositions per thousand appear in sentence-final position. In the three registers of nonfiction writing, however, final prepositions are fewer than in any of the six spoken registers. Thus there is a notable difference between speech and writing with respect to sentence-final prepositions.

Table 10-4

NUMBER OF SENTENCE-FINAL PREPOSITIONS PER THOUSAND PREPOSITIONS IN DIFFERENT SITUATIONS OF USE

SITUATION OF USE	SENTENCE-FINAL PREPOSITIONS	
Face-to-face conversation	56	
Telephone conversation with friends	50	
Interviews	50	
Spontaneous speeches	48	Speech
Broadcasts	39	
Prepared speeches	33	
Science fiction	21	
Romantic fiction	18	Fiction writing
General fiction	14	
Academic journals	8	
Press	4	Nonfiction writing
Official documents	1	

Source of data: Biber 1988

As a second example of grammatical variation across different situations of use, examine this brief passage of *legalese*—a register that is identified by name.

> Upon request of Borrower, Lender, at Lender's option prior to full reconveyance of the Property by Trustee to Borrower, may make Future Advances to Borrower. Such Future Advances, with interest thereon, shall be secured by this Deed of Trust when evidenced by promissory notes stating that said notes are secured hereby.

This passage illustrates several characteristic syntactic features of legalese:

1. Frequent use of passive structures: *shall be secured, are secured*
2. Preference for repetition of nouns in lieu of pronouns: *Lender/at Lender's option, promissory notes/said notes, Future Advances/Such Future Advances*
3. Omission of some indefinite and definite articles: *Upon request, of Borrower, to Borrower, Lender, at Lender's, by Trustee*

SEMANTIC MARKERS OF REGISTER

A given word often carries different meanings in different registers. Consider the word *notes:* As used in the legalese passage, *notes* means promissory notes, or IOUs. In its everyday meaning, however, *notes* refers to brief, informal written messages on any topic. Among words with one meaning in common everyday use but with a different meaning in legal register are the ones given below.

EXPRESSIONS CARRYING A DISTINCTIVE SENSE IN LEGALESE

to continue	hearing	sentence
to alienate	action	rider
to serve	executed	motion
save	suit	reasonable man
party	notes	consideration

Not only lawyers but also some of their clients may give specialized meanings to words. Criminal argot contains many words and expressions that are in common use but carry a different meaning when used in the context of criminal behavior. The following two lists are illustrative.

GENERAL CRIMINAL ARGOT

mob	sing	bug
hot	rat	bird cage
fence	racket	slammer
sting	a mark	joint ('prison')

DRUG WORLD ARGOT

crack	pot	downer
coke	grass	speed
snow	toot	pusher
rock	high	dealer
dime	down	joint ('marijuana cigarette')

Each of these expressions bears one meaning in everyday situations but a quite different meaning in the underworld.

SIMILARITIES AND DIFFERENCES BETWEEN SPOKEN AND WRITTEN REGISTERS

Though it is sometimes said that writing is simply speech written down—visual language as distinct from audible language—writing and speaking ordinarily serve different purposes and have distinct linguistic characteristics. Conversation is not a written register, of course, but it can be represented in novels and screenplays. Nor are legal contracts ordinarily spoken. Imagine how the words and the syntax of a handwritten last testament or will would differ from one made by a testator speaking before a videotape. Or consider the linguistic differences between a note stuck on a refrigerator door and the same basic message spoken to someone face-to-face. You'll quickly recognize that speaking and writing are not mirror images of one another.

For one thing, oral communication can exploit intonation and voice pitch to convey information. For the same purpose, face-to-face communication can also utilize gestures, posture, and physical proximity between participants. In writing, the only channels available are words and syntax, supplemented by some minor conventions of typography and punctuation. In speaking, communication is possible on additional channels simultaneously. We can criticize someone's personality in a seemingly objective manner while expressing with intonation or body language how much we greatly admire the person—or vice versa. In writing, much more must be communicated lexically and syntactically, though there are ways of achieving ironic and sarcastic tones, enabling addressees to read "between the lines."

A second difference between speech and writing lies in the amount of planning that is possible. For most written registers, more time is available for composing and for revising afterward. During a conversation, on the other hand, pausing to find just the right word can test your interlocutor's patience and risk losing the floor. The difference in the available time for planning and editing in written registers produces characteristic syntactic patterns that are difficult to achieve under the on-line processing constraints imposed in spontaneous speech. Written registers also typically show a more specific and varied vocabulary, in part because writers have time to choose their words carefully and even consult a thesaurus. Of course, not all written registers are more planned than all spoken registers. Academic lectures and job interviews reflect some of the characteristics of planned writing. On the other hand, some types of writing are produced with relatively little planning, and the language of a letter scribbled a few minutes before the mail pickup is likely to be quite speechlike.

A third distinction is that speakers and addressees often stand face-to-face, whereas writers and readers do not. In face-to-face interactions, the immediacy of the interlocutors and the contexts of interaction allow them to refer to themselves (*I think, you see*) and their own opinions and to be more personal in their interaction. By contrast, the contexts of writing limit the degree to which written expression can be personal. Again, however, we must be careful not to overgeneralize. Consider, for example, a personal letter and a face-to-face friendly conversation. People often feel that they have a right to be equally personal in both contexts. An impersonal stance is thus a feature of only some written registers, as a personal stance is a feature of only some spoken registers.

Finally, written registers tend to rely less on the context of interaction than spoken registers do. Writing is more context independent. In spoken registers, expressions of spatial deixis (such as the demonstrative pronouns *this* and *that*) and of temporal deixis (like *today* and *next Tuesday*) can be understood with reference to the here and now of the utterance. By contrast, in writing the lack of a shared environment tends to make such expressions opaque or confusing. To which day would *today* refer in an undated written text? And to what would *this* refer when found in a printed document? Like other distinctions among registers, reliance on deictic expressions does not constitute an absolute difference between speech and writing. In telephone conversations, for example, you cannot say *this thing* (referring to something in the environment of the speaker) without risking opaqueness. In contrast, you can leave a written note on the kitchen table that reads *Please don't eat this!* as long as the referent of *this* is obvious from what is near the note, and an author can reliably refer to *this page* or *this sentence.*

There are many ways in which spoken and written registers differ. But when we examine the differences (as we have just done), we find no absolute dichotomy between them. For example, not many words could occur only in speech or only in writing, even though certain words may occur more frequently in one mode or the other. Instead, written registers tend to be more formal, more informational, and less personal. Along a "personal/impersonal" continuum, for example, the type of writing found in legal documents will be at the impersonal end, while informal conversation will tend toward the personal end. But personal letters may be close to conversation in their linguistic character. Writing and speaking thus do not form a simple dichotomy, and to describe their differences we must observe which written register and which spoken register is being considered. With all language, the situation of use is the *most* influential factor in determining linguistic form.

TWO REGISTERS COMPARED

By way of illustrating the nature of register variation let's examine two brief passages of English-language text. The first passage will be immediately recognizable as legalese. While critics have remarked that legalese could be considered a foreign language because it is so different from ordinary writing and speaking, it is simply one of the many registers of English. For people not accustomed to using it, it may be more opaque than other registers but it is not a foreign tongue. This passage comes from a rider to a deed of trust. A deed of trust is a written agreement that places the title to real estate in the hands of a trustee to ensure that money borrowed with the property as collateral will be repaid; a rider is simply an addition to the basic document.

A RIDER TO A DEED OF TRUST	LINE	SENTENCE
Notwithstanding anything in the Deed of Trust to the contrary, it is	1	1
agreed that the loan secured by this Deed of Trust is made pursuant	2	
to, and shall be construed and governed by the laws of the United	3	
States and the rules and regulations promulgated thereunder,	4	
including the federal laws, rules and regulations for federal savings	5	
and loan associations. If any paragraph, clause or provision of this	6	2
Deed of Trust or the Note or other obligations secured by this Deed	7	
of Trust is construed or interpreted by a court of competent	8	
jurisdiction to be invalid or unenforceable, such decision shall	9	
affect only those paragraphs, clauses or provisions so construed	10	
or interpreted and shall not affect the remaining paragraphs,	11	
clauses and provisions of this Deed of Trust or the Note or	12	
other obligations secured by this Deed of Trust.	13	

The second passage is from a face-to-face interview of former president Harry Truman by biographer Merle Miller (*Plain Speaking* [New York: Berkley Books, 1974], p. 242).

AN INTERVIEW WITH HARRY TRUMAN	LINE	SENTENCE
Q. What do you consider the biggest mistake you made as President?	1	1
A. That damn fool from Texas that I first made Attorney General	2	2
and then put on the Supreme Court.	3	
I don't know what got into me.	4	3
He was no damn good as Attorney General, and on the Supreme	5	4
Court . . . it doesn't seem possible, but he's been even worse.	6	
He hasn't made one right decision that I can think of.	7	5
And so when you ask me what was my biggest mistake, that's it.	8	6a
Putting Tom Clark on the Supreme Court of the United States.	9	6b
I thought maybe when he got on the Court he'd improve,	10	7
but of course, that isn't what happened.	11	
I told you when we were discussing that other fellow.	12	8a
After a certain age it's hopeless to think people are going to	13	8b
change much.	14	

It's apparent at a glance how strikingly different these two passages are. The trust deed is 138 words long and comprises only two sentences. By contrast, the 135 words of the Truman interview occur in eight sentences. Average sentence length differs significantly in these samples: 69 words for the trust deed, 17 for the interview. (In transcribing Truman's words, the interviewer made nine sentences; in numbering them here, we have used the letters *a* and *b* to indicate a combining of two interviewer's sentences into single sentences so as not to exaggerate the number of separate sentences.)

You will find it instructive to examine the passages carefully to identify other linguistic features that contribute to making the registers different. Before you read the analysis that follows, try jotting down as many observations about lexicon and grammar as you can; note contrasting features as well as shared ones.

LEXICON AND GRAMMAR

One easily observed difference between the passages is in vocabulary. The deed of trust contains certain words and phrases that might seem odd if they appeared in the interview. Likewise, Truman's language contains certain earthy words that might strike you as inappropriate in a legal document.

You will also see that in the collocation of words with other words, as well as in preferred lexical categories and in syntax, there are striking differences between the passages. Such features—not in isolation but taken together—help mark passages as being particular *kinds* of text, particular language varieties suitable in particular speech situations, particular *registers*.

Vocabulary   In contrast to the short everyday words of the interview, the deed of trust uses more uncommon words, as is notoriously characteristic of legalese. Its vocabulary is more "Latinate," the words longer: *promulgated, construed, governed, regulations, obligations, decision, jurisdiction, provisions, invalid, unenforceable, pursuant, secured.* Note also the markedly legal collocation *competent jurisdiction,* in which *competent* does not carry its ordinary meaning of 'capable' but the legal meaning 'having proper authority over the matter to be decided.' Many words that are used in other registers with one meaning carry a different sense in legalese. Besides *competent,* other words in the passage have specific legal senses: *deed, trust, obligation, decision, provisions,* and *note* (as well as *rider,* which doesn't appear in the passage itself).

Nouns and Pronouns   In comparable amounts of text, the trust deed has a total of forty nouns, the interview only seventeen. On the other hand, the interview has many more pronouns than the trust deed. It uses first- and second-person pronouns frequently (a total of twelve times.) *I, me,* and *we* eight and *you* four times. (The possessive determiner *my* also occurs once.) By contrast, the trust deed has no occurrences of first- or second-person pronouns.

The interview also exhibits frequent third-person pronouns: Truman uses *he* five times in reference to Tom Clark. By contrast is the repetition of full noun phrases in the trust deed: *Deed of Trust* occurs six times, the coordinate noun phrase *rules and regulations* twice, and the triple coordinate *paragraph, clause or provision* three times (once in the singular and twice in the plural). One exceptionally long noun phrase constituent is repeated, and it contains a repetition of *Deed of Trust* within it: *this Deed of Trust or the Note or other obligations secured by this Deed of Trust.*

There are other differences in pronominal use as well. Truman uses the demonstrative pronoun *that* as a "sentence" pronoun, referring not to a noun phrase but to an entire clause, as in *that isn't what happened* (line 11). In *that's it* (line 8) *that* may refer back to *my biggest mistake* or ahead to *Putting Tom Clark on the Supreme Court of the United States.*

Prepositions and Prepositional Phrases   The trust deed has nineteen prepositions compared to only twelve in the interview. Given the need for a trust deed to be quite specific and the fact that the function of prepositional phrases is to express specific semantic roles—for example, agent (*by a court*), instrument (*by this Deed*), location (*in the Deed*)—the frequency of prepositions in the trust deed is not surprising. Registers whose purpose is in large part informational generally show a much higher proportion of prepositions than other kinds of registers precisely because prepositions provide frames for semantic information.

Note that the interview has only one instance of prepositional phrases used consecutively (*on the Supreme Court of the United States*), but the trust deed has seven, including this sequence of three: *in the deed of Trust to the contrary.* Further, the interview has an example of a sentence-final preposition (*He hasn't made one right decision that I can think of*), something that does not occur in the passage of legalese and occurs very rarely in formal writing of any kind (as Table 10-4 documents).

Verbs Taking *shall be construed and governed* as two, the number of verb groups in the trust deed is nine, about one-third the number in the Truman interview. Thus the interview is very verbal. As to particular verbs, Truman uses *think* (and *thought*), *know,* and *seem,* and his interviewer uses *consider.* Such "private" verbs represent the internal states of the speaker or writer and are appropriate in an interview and very frequent in conversation, though they would be out of place in the trust deed. Truman also employs pro–verbs of various sorts (pro–verbs take the place of other verbs, much as pronouns take the place of nouns): *do* and *happen,* which can be substituted for many verbs; *put* and *get,* which are more limited but still have far-ranging uses. In conversation, where there is pressure to find your words speedily, pro-verbs tend to occur frequently, in part because they save the time that would be needed to find a more explicit verb. In this short passage *got* appears twice, and Truman uses *put on* and *putting on* (the Supreme Court) instead of, say, *appointed to.* The verb *to be*—the most common in English—occurs as a main verb seven times, whereas in the trust deed it occurs four times as an auxiliary (*is agreed, is made, be construed,* and *is construed*) but just once as a main verb (*to be void*).

Some verbs in the trust deed are related to the topic of discussion and therefore to the register of the passage: *agree, construe, govern, promulgate, interpret,* and *affect.* Not related to topic but characteristic of legalese is the use of *shall* as an auxiliary verb. While *shall* occurs in many registers, its use is exceptionally common in legalese. *Shall* occurs as an auxiliary in both sentences of the trust deed.

The interview concerns the years of Truman's presidency, as the preponderance of past-tense verbs reflects. Among its twenty-five verb groups, fourteen are in the past tense, while the eight present-tense verbs generally make reference to the ongoing interaction between Truman and the interviewer or to Truman's own thought processes in the course of the interview: *what do you consider, when you ask, I don't know, I can think.* The one verb that refers to future time uses the construction *are going to* instead of *shall* or *will.*

Negation In the interview, four out of five negative morphemes occur as the negative adverb *not* (attached to the verb as a contraction). The fifth is the adverb *no* modifying *(damn) good.* In contrast, the trust deed incorporates elements of negation into adjectives or prepositions by the processes of derivational morphology (*invalid, unenforceable*) or compounding (*notwithstanding*); there is one isolated *not* (which occurs with reference to future time *shall not,* in contrast to a future positive *shall*). One characteristic difference between speech and writing is the much higher frequency of negation in spoken registers, where the vast majority of negative elements are separate like *not* (which is often realized as *-n't*) rather than incorporated into words like *invalid.*

Adverbs Legalese is famous for its use of compound adverbs like *thereto* and *hereinunder. Thereunder* is the only instance in our passage. In fact, besides one instance of *not,* the passage has only two other adverbs: *only* and *so.*

Truman's adverbs are quite different. They make reference to time (*first, then*) or are hedges that indicate his stance toward what he is saying: *of course, maybe.*

Passive Voice   One striking feature of the deed of trust is its frequent use of the passive voice (*is agreed, is made, shall be construed and governed, is construed or interpreted*).

Passive constructions demote an agent subject to object of a preposition, thereby permitting omission of the agent (*Lightning struck the house/The house was struck by lightning/The house was struck*). In legalese, agentless passives (those lacking the *by* phrase) and passives with *by* are both common. In marked contrast, Truman and his interviewer use *only* active voice verbs.

Questions   In using the form of a direct question (*When you ask me what was my biggest mistake*) instead of an indirect question (*When you ask me what my biggest mistake was*), Truman contributes to the impression of informality that characterizes the passage. And though it may seem too obvious to mention, the interview naturally contains a question, a syntactic structure that not only does not appear in the trust deed but would be unusual there.

Reduced Relative Clauses   Another characteristic feature of legalese is the frequency of reduced relative clauses, in which the relative pronoun and a form of the verb *be* do not appear where they might. (This feature is sometimes referred to as "whiz deletion," where *whiz* is a shortening standing for *that* or other *wh*–words and a form of *is*.) These examples show the omitted words in parentheses.

>loan (that is) secured
>rules and regulations (that are) promulgated thereunder
>paragraphs, clauses or provisions (that are) so construed or interpreted

Conjoining   The Truman interview shows frequent coordinating conjunctions, such as *and, but, and then, and so,* which serve chiefly to link clauses, as in lines 5, 6, and 8. These conjunctions are lacking in the legalese passage except for *and,* which is used to link verbs, or nouns, or adjectives, but *not* clauses.

Another feature typical of legalese is triple phrasal conjoining "X, Y conjunction Z" or "X conjunction Y conjunction Z." In legal registers, X, Y, and Z can be members of almost any lexical category, most commonly nouns (or noun phrases), adjectives, or verbs; X, Y, and Z are ordinarily members of the same lexical or phrasal category. The following exemplify the pattern:

>laws, rules and regulations (nouns)
>paragraph, clause or provision (nouns)
>deed of trust or the note or other obligation (noun phrases)
>void, invalid or unenforceable (adjectives)

Sometimes variation within the X, Y, and Z constituents produces similar but not completely parallel structures, as in these examples:

>1. is made pursuant to, and shall be construed and governed by
>2. the laws of the United States and the rules and regulations

In 1, there are two verb-phrase structures conjoined by *and,* but the second verb phrase itself contains two conjoined verbs (*construed and governed*). In 2, we might more accurately describe the structure not as "X, Y, and Z" but as "X and Y," with Y being a compound M and N; thus, "X and (M and N)."

PHONOLOGY

Since only one of the two passages originated in speech, we cannot make straightforward phonological comparisons between them. We do not have a phonetic transcription, but we can infer from the transcribed text that Truman exhibited frequent phonological abbreviation. Instead of full forms like *do not,* eight contractions occur even in this small sample: *don't, doesn't, isn't, hasn't, he's, he'd, that's,* and *it's.* In line 1, the one place in the deed of trust where a comparable form might appear, *it is* occurs, not *it's.* If we were comparing two forms of spoken English and had suitable transcriptions, we could say more about phonological similarities and differences.

COMPARING REGISTERS

In comparing and contrasting the two passages, it is not any single feature that identifies which registers they exemplify. Rather, various features occurring in combination characterize the first passage as legalese and the second as an interview. Truman's style is so informal that it suggests conversation rather than a formal interview; this may be partly the result of the interviewer's having spent several months with Truman, morning and afternoon. No doubt, as the days passed the interview came increasingly to resemble conversation between friends.

You have now seen that language features differ from one speech situation to another. Sometimes there is more of one feature in a given register than in another, occasionally a feature occurs in one register exclusively, or almost exclusively. Sometimes the same form occurs in more than one register but with different meanings or different uses.

TEXTUAL DIMENSIONS IN REGISTER VARIATION
—

The linguistic resources from which registers must draw their particular features produce consistent and coherent texts from a single grammatical system. By drawing differentially on the same grammatical resources at each level of the grammar, a writer or speaker creates texts in different registers.

Using computers and large databases, linguists have systematically identified which sets of linguistic features tend to co-occur frequently in texts. Analyzing sets of co-occurring features has contributed to our understanding of the underlying dimensions of register variation and of how sets of features co-occur in the service of common functions.

SETS OF CO-OCCURRING FEATURES

One set of linguistic features that commonly occur together in texts includes the features of set A, given below:

SET A (INVOLVEMENT FEATURES)

First- and second-person pronouns (*I, me, we, us; you*)
Omission of *that* from subordinate clauses (*She said ø he lied*)
Private verbs (*think, consider, assume, know*)
Demonstrative pronouns (*this, that, these*)
Contractions (*he's, isn't*)
Emphatics (*really, such a, so, even*)
Hedges (*kind of, more or less, maybe, about*)
Sentence relatives (*Then he lied, which bothered her a lot.*)
Clause-final prepositions (*the teacher I told you about*)
WH-questions (*What do you consider. . .?*)
Be as a main verb (*It is hopeless*)

To make some of the features of this set more concrete, it will help to reinspect the Truman interview (on page 347). First- and second-person pronouns go together because they commonly occur in face-to-face interaction, in which there is a personalized speaker/writer addressing a known addressee. In such circumstances, it may also be appropriate to express one's inner thoughts and feelings (and inquire about the addressee's), for which private verbs are useful. Emphatics (Truman's *damn* fool and *even* worse), and hedges (*maybe*) are also characteristic of such interaction. The occurrence of clause-final prepositions (*that I can think of*) marks relatively informal person-to-person speech and writing (see also Table 10-4). The use of demonstrative pronouns (*that,* as in line 8) is characteristic of a shared context between speaker and addressee, in that in many instances the addressee must be present to understand the referents of words like *that* and *these*. Virtually all the features of set A occur in the brief Truman interview, even though the determination of which features occur together was based on a much larger sample of texts, not including the two examined here.

Another set of features that commonly occur together in texts are those in set B:

SET B (INFORMATION FEATURES)

(Frequent) nouns
(Frequent) prepositions
Longer words
Lexical variety
Attributive adjectives (*federal laws*)

It is not surprising that prepositions and nouns should commonly occur together. After all, prepositional phrases include noun phrases. But why should frequent nouns and prepositions occur with longer words and with lexical variety? A moment's thought will explain this pattern. Lexical variety results from using a relatively larger number of alternative words. Given that alternative words usually have somewhat different meanings (or different connotations), lexical variety generally indicates an attempt to be exact in expressing meaning or to expand the meaning of a referent already mentioned. Contrast Truman's use of different referring expressions for Tom Clark, his Supreme Court appointee. Instead of repetition of *Tom Clark* or the pronoun *he,* the use of various referring expressions permits Truman to make additional comments that expand on his opinionated description of Clark. (In the deed of trust, the use of attributive adjectives—*federal laws* and *competent jurisdiction*—has a related function of specifying noun phrases.)

As you may have anticipated, there is a strong tendency for the linguistic features of set A to occur frequently in registers in which the features of set B are not frequent, and vice versa. That is, in texts where you find first- and second-person pronouns, *that*-omission, questions, and the other features of set A, you will typically not find many long words, much lexical variety, or frequent nouns, prepositions, or attributive adjectives—that is, the features of set B. This makes sense, for it is precisely in contexts that require lexical specificity that speakers and writers have less occasion to use personal pronouns, private verbs, and the other features of set A. And vice versa: when you are in a face-to-face interactional situation requiring the features of set A, you do not have much opportunity to choose your words carefully, and it is just such opportunity that permits us to produce lexical variety, longer words, and so on.

You can think of these two sets of features as representing opposite poles of a single dimension of linguistic variation. At one pole are texts with a heavy emphasis on interaction and personal involvement; at the other pole are texts with virtually no interaction or personal involvement but a heavy emphasis on sharing information. Each text will fall somewhere along a continuum between extremely informational and extremely involved. By calculating average values for an adequate sample of texts in various registers, average values for those registers can be determined, as you'll see below.

INVOLVED VERSUS INFORMATIONAL TEXTS

We could count the features just discussed as a way of gauging involved and informational focus in the texts of various registers. A register whose texts had higher than average frequencies for the features of set A and lower than average frequencies for the features of set B would show a high degree of personal involvement (like the interview represented in the Truman passage). A register whose texts had higher-than-average frequencies for the features of set B (and would in general then have lower-than-average frequencies for the features of set A) would show a high degree of informational focus (rather than involvement).

Based on the number of features in a wide range of registers and a large number of texts, average values for all the features discussed here have been determined for English speech and writing. In Figure 10-4, the baseline represents the average number of occurrences for the relevant features, and distances above the baseline indicate

Figure 10-4

VALUES FOR TEN REGISTERS
ON THE INVOLVED/INFORMATIONAL DIMENSION
(DEFINED BY FEATURE SETS A AND B)

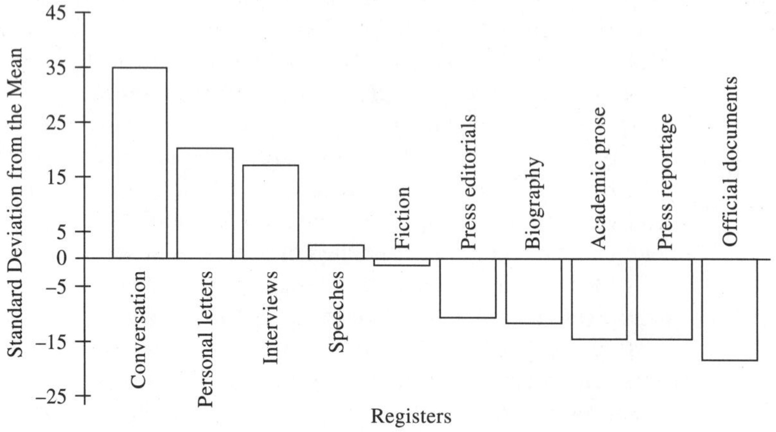

Source of data: Biber 1988

above-average frequencies for the particular features represented by that end of the dimension. The bars extending well above the baseline represent registers that show high degrees of involvement (that is, high frequencies of the features in set A); those extending well below the baseline represent registers showing high degrees of informational focus (that is, frequent occurrence of the features of set B). A register whose texts had the average number of features of set A and set B would have a value of zero in Figure 10-4, and the bar for that register would neither rise above nor fall below the baseline. (The scale of values in Figures 10-4 and 10-5 represents standard deviations from the average value for the sets of features; with the average value set at zero, a value of -1 would represent one standard deviation below the average.)

As Figure 10-4 strikingly illustrates, conversation is a register that ranks very high in involvement, while academic prose and official documents (which would be similar to documents like trust deeds) rank very low on involvement but very high on informational focus. Registers with values below the baseline are characterized by high frequencies of the information features (set B) and low frequencies of the involvement features (set A). Personal letters and interviews rank high on involvement. Recall that the Truman interview had many examples of features that contribute to the "involved" characterization. By contrast, the trust deed had higher frequencies of the features defining set B (longer words, more lexical variety, and frequent prepositions). In other words, if you calculated the values for the features of sets A and B that would be needed to place our illustrative texts on this scale, the

Truman interview would rank close to conversation and interviews, well above the baseline, while the trust deed would rank with official documents, well below the baseline.

NARRATIVE TEXTS

Two other sets of linguistic features have been shown to co-occur with great frequency in texts, and they are given below as set C and set D. The features of set C characterize texts that are very narrative or storylike, while those of set D are characteristic of nonnarrative texts.

SET C (NARRATIVE FEATURES)

Past-tense verb groups
Perfect-aspect verb groups (those that include *have* as in *have seen*)
Public verbs (*admit, say, write, explain*)
Third-person pronouns

SET D (NONNARRATIVE FEATURES)

Present-tense verb groups
Attributive adjectives (*high office*)

As with sets A and B, sets C and D also tend to be complementary. Registers marked by frequent occurrence of the features of set C typically have relatively few features of set D.

Now we turn to Figure 10-5. As with Figure 10-4, the baseline is set at zero, which represents the average values for the features in sets C and D (as determined for the same wide range and a large number of texts as for Figure 10-4). A register whose texts had the average number of features of sets C and D would have a value of zero in Figure 10-5. As you can see in Figure 10-5, the registers that rank above the baseline (those that are highly narrative) are fiction, biography, speeches, and press reportage, while official documents, academic prose, and interviews fall well below the baseline on this dimension (with below-average frequencies for the features of set C but above-average values for the features of set D). Our trust deed would also stand well below the zero line, toward the nonnarrative end of this dimension. Our trust deed passage has *no* past-tense verbs, *no* perfect-aspect verb groups, and only a single third-person pronoun—(the semantically empty *it*). By contrast, the Truman interview has fourteen verb groups in the past tense. The interview also has a relatively high number of perfect-aspect verbs, public verbs, and third-person pronouns.

If you compare particular registers on the two dimensions, you will note on Figure 10-4 that conversation ranks extremely high on involvement (indicating lots of features of set A and very few of set B), while on Figure 10-5 it ranks below the baseline on the narrative/nonnarrative dimension (indicating lower than average values for the features of set C and higher than average values for those of set D). By

Figure 10-5

VALUES FOR TEN REGISTERS
ON THE NARRATIVE/NONNARRATIVE DIMENSION
(DEFINED BY FEATURE SETS C AND D)

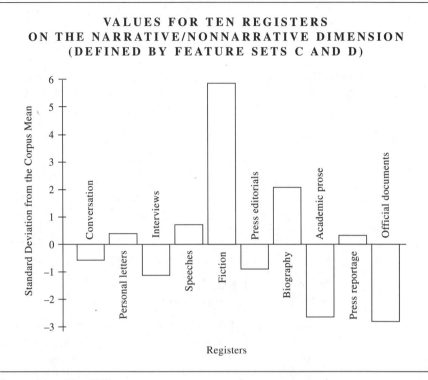

Registers

Source of data: Biber 1988

way of contrast, fiction ranks far above the baseline on the narrative dimension (Fig. 10-5) but below the baseline on the involvement dimension (Fig. 10-4), which means it has relatively more information features than involvement features. Looking at a third register, you can see that official documents rank far below the baseline on the involved/informational dimension, which indicates that they are very informational and not very involved, and they rank far below the baseline on the narrative/ nonnarrative dimension, which indicates that they are very nonnarrative.

These two dimensions can be thought of as the axes in a two-dimensional space—a plane surface on which every text can be situated. A text is situated along each dimension in accordance with the degree to which it exploits the features that define that dimension. We've seen the dimensions represented independently in Figures 10-4 and 10-5. In Figure 10-6, the two dimensions are combined to show how a few registers would align themselves in a two-dimensional space. Note that conversation ranks extremely high on the involved/informational dimension (conversations are very involved) and fairly low on the narrative/nonnarrative dimension (conversations are not very narrativelike). By contrast, fiction ranks very high on the narrative/ nonnarrative dimension but not high on the involved/informational dimension. To

Figure 10-6

DISTRIBUTION OF FIVE REGISTERS ALONG TWO DIMENSIONS OF VARIATION

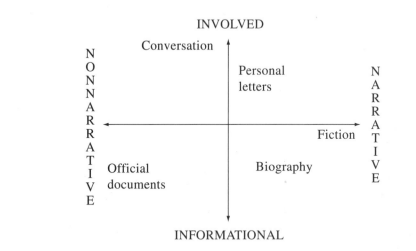

take a third example, official documents rank low on both the involved/informational dimension (they are very informational, not involved) and the narrative/nonnarrative dimension (they are very nonnarrative). Figure 10-6 also shows where personal letters and biography fall in the two-dimensional space created by the two dimensions.

ENGLISH AND OTHER LANGUAGES

It is challenging to imagine discovering other sets of co-occurring features that would represent different dimensions of textual variation. Each pair of complementary sets would constitute another dimension in a multidimensional "space" in which the full range of texts could be represented. More than two or three additional dimensions of linguistic variation would be needed to represent textual variation adequately, but analysis of other dimensions lies beyond our scope.

The distribution of features comparable to those examined here has been investigated in several languages other than English. Korean, Somali, and Nukulaelae Tuvaluan have been investigated, and dimensions of variation have been found that in some instances resemble those found in English and in other instances reflect the particular characteristics of the cultures whose languages they represent. As an example of the latter phenomenon, Korean, a language with a highly evolved set of deferential address terms and other grammatical features that show deference, has a dimension defined by complementary sets of features related to markers of deference and respect.

COMPUTERS AND THE STUDY OF REGISTER VARIATION

In the field of artificial intelligence, in expert systems, and in a number of critically important high-tech fields today, the role of registers is crucial. The reasons are complex, but you can get a feel for some of them simply by considering the different patterns of syntax and vocabulary across registers that any system would need to master—for example, information given in the form of headlines or medicalese or legalese or conversation. Think of it this way: if your corpus contained nothing but writings from newspapers but failed to distinguish among the distinctly different kinds of newspaper texts (reportage, personal ads, editorials and editorial letters, advertising, cartoons, sports commentary, business analysis, stock market and weather reports, and so on), it would have to be immeasurably more complicated than would a set of individual systems designed to handle various registers one by one.

It would be difficult to overestimate the importance of computers to the study of register and register variation. Since the beginning, compilers of corpora have been mindful of the importance of sorting texts into registers. (In effect, this means designating each text as belonging to a particular register.) Since so much study of registers has been quantitative, large-scale corpora help ensure both reliability and validity, although the design of a corpus is critically important in establishing validity for any findings within the corpus. Earlier we saw that the Brown and LOB corpora of English ran to about 1,000,000 words each. By today's standards, those are not very big corpora. Although even the British National Corpus is not the biggest corpus in the world, it has 100,106,008 words. According to information provided at the BNC Web site,

The Corpus occupies about 1.5 gigabytes of disk space—the equivalent of more than a thousand high capacity floppy diskettes. To put these numbers into perspective, the average paperback book has about 250 pages per centimetre of thickness; assuming 400 words a page, we calculate that the whole corpus printed in small type on thin paper would take up about ten metres of shelf space. Reading the whole corpus aloud at a fairly rapid 150 words a minute, eight hours a day, 365 days a year, would take just over four years.

The research findings reported throughout this chapter, with its emphasis on quantitative assessments of corpora, have relied to a notable extent on computers. Computers have assisted the researchers in numerous ways. Leaving aside the tasks of their physical creation on paper, the data in several tables and figures were generated without computers, as in Figure 10-2, which reports the frequency of *-ing* pronounced as /ɪŋ/ among males and females in Los Angeles. But for others computers were *essential,* at least in a practical sense. Most notably, this would include Figures 10-4 and 10-5. Establishing the sets of correlated features required sophisticated computer programs able to identify the features and powerful statistical tools able to sort them into co-occurring groups. As to identifying the features, some would be utterly straightforward—given a tagged corpus. In this category we can include nouns, prepositions, demonstrative pronouns, private verbs, and so on. Depending on the extent of the tagging, other categories could have been identified, such as past-tense verbs, but if the corpus weren't tagged for tense, then an algorithm would have to be specified to instruct the computer what to look for. Algorithms would also be necessary to identify such structures as sentence relatives and sentence-final prepositions. Some algorithms would prove particularly tricky to design, though once designed, computers could follow them to the letter. In this regard, you might want to think about the nature of the algorithm that would instruct a computer how to identify *that* omissions, as in *She said he lied* rather than *She said that he lied.* After all, it's one thing to write an algorithm that identifies a feature that is present, but to identify a feature that is not present is more challenging.

In all cases, counting such features within particular texts and particular registers would prove prohibitively time consuming if the work needed to be done by hand. Other aspects of the project that led to establishing the dimensions relied on sophisticated statistical programs that determined the co-occurrence patterns. In practice, these could be accomplished only with the aid of computers.

✱ SUMMARY ✱

- Three principal elements determine each speech situation: setting, purpose, and participants.

- Topic and location are part of the setting.

- Activity type and goals are part of the purpose.

- As people wear different clothing to different places and for different activities, so they generally do not speak the same way in court, at dinner, and on the soccer field.

- With respect to participants, it is not only the people themselves who influence language form but the roles they are playing at a given time.

- In multilingual communities, different situations of use call sometimes for different languages and sometimes for different varieties of the same language.

- Registers are language varieties appropriate for use in particular speech situations.

- The set of varieties used in a speech community in various speech situations is called its linguistic (or verbal) repertoire.

- In the linguistic repertoire of a monolingual community are many registers, which differ from one another in their linguistic features either in an absolute sense or (more usually) in a relative sense.

- Each register is characterized by a set of linguistic features.

- The sum total of such features (phonological, morphological, syntactic, and semantic), together with the characteristic patterns for the use of language in a particular situation, determine a register.

- By definition, all varieties within a language draw on the same grammatical system; hence the differential exploitation of that system for marking different registers must occur in an essentially relative fashion.

- Writing differs from speaking in a number of fundamental ways, but the linguistic differences between the two modes are not absolute.

- To describe the relations among registers, we invoke a series of continuous dimensions along which different registers align themselves.

- A number of feature sets frequently co-occur in natural texts and can be interpreted in functional terms.

- Every text can be positioned with respect to every other text depending on its exploitation of the features that characterize a given dimension.

- The coming together in a single text of various linguistic characteristics (and the implicit knowledge of their role in those functional dimensions) allows us to recognize texts as belonging to one register or another.

- Knowledge of the dimensions and of their functional roles enables us to use appropriate registers in different speech situations—in fact to help create those situations by marking them linguistically with appropriate lexical, phonological, syntactic, and semantic choices.

EXERCISES

Based on English

 10-1. Consider the following expressions.

> Kindly extinguish the illumination upon exiting.
> Please turn off the lights on your way out.

The content of the directive is basically the same in both cases, but the social meanings differ markedly. Identify the features that characterize the differences between the two directives; then discuss the impression that each is likely to make and under which circumstances each might be appropriate.

10-2. a. List five pairs of body part or bodily function terms like *clavicle/ collarbone* that would distinguish a conversation you were having with a physician from one with a friend on the same topic.
   b. Rank the words in each set below in order of formality:

   (1) prof, teacher, instructor, mentor, educator.
   (2) don, guru, mullah, maestro, trainer, coach

   c. Are any of these words so informal as to be slang? Explain.

 10-3. In *Slang and Sociability* Connie Eble reports the top forty slang expressions used by college students at the University of North Carolina between 1972 and 1993. The top twenty are given in the box on page 338. Below, the next twenty are listed, some with succinct definitions. Try to provide succinct definitions for the others.

grub (verb)	*hot*
geek	*slack* 'below standard, lazy'
granola	*trashed* 'drunk'
homeboy/~girl/homey	↘ *veg (out)*
not!	*word (up)* 'I agree'
ace (verb)	*awesome*
dude	*book* 'leave, hurry'
the pits	*turkey*
bagger 'fraternity member'	*fox/foxy*
flag 'fail'	*Sorority Sue/Sue/Suzi*

10-4. Tape-record about forty-five seconds of a radio news report and a television news report (if possible, use the same news item). After transcribing the passages, compare them with one another to see what effect the medium has on the choice of linguistic forms.

10-5. Here's the immediate sequel to the Truman passage quoted in this chapter; the sentences have been numbered for reference only.

Q. (1) How do you explain the fact that he's been such a bad Justice?

A. (2) The main thing is . . . well, it isn't so much that he's a *bad* man. (3) It's just that he's such a dumb son of a bitch. (4) He's about the dumbest man I think I've ever run across. (5) And lots of times that's the case. (6) Being dumb's just about the worst thing there is when it comes to holding high office, and that's especially true when it's on the Supreme Court of the United States. (7) As I say, I never will know what got into me when I made that appointment, and I'm as sorry as I can be for doing it. [*Plain Speaking,* p. 242].

a. Is it clear what *that* refers to in *that's the case* (sentence 5) and *that's especially true* (sentence 6)? If so, what type of constituent does *that* refer to in these instances?

b. What is the name of the linguistic feature that you examined in question a above? In which feature set (A, B, C, or D) does it occur?

c. What does the presence of this feature in the Truman interview indicate about how the passage is aligned on the involved/informational dimension?

d. List all other features in the sequel passage that co-occur with this feature in defining the involved/informational dimension, and give an example of each.

e. Identify all instances of *be* as a main verb? How many are there?

f. What is the function of *well* in sentence 2?

g. Wherever possible, supply a noun phrase that would have the same referent as the pronoun *it* in sentences 2, 3, 6 (two instances), 7. Explain those cases where a noun phrase could not be identified as having the same referent as *it.*

10-6. Look up the definition of *slang* in a good desk dictionary and, using it as a guideline, list as many slang words and expressions as you can for two notions each in (1) and (2) below.

(1) drunk, sexually carefree person, ungenerous with money, sloppy in appearance.

(2) sober, chaste person, generous with money, neat and tidy

a. What is it about the notions represented in (1) that makes them more susceptible to slang words and expressions than those in (2)?

b. To the extent that you could cite slang terms for the items in (2), do they have negative or positive connotations?

c. Does the dictionary definition of slang help explain the differential distribution of slang terms in (1) and (2) and the connotations associated with the slang terms in (2)? If so, explain how. If not, revise the dictionary definition so as to accommodate what you have discovered about the connotations of slang terms.

10-7. Some of the most common words of English (for example, *the, of, and, a, to, it, is, that*) appear in both the trust deed and the interview. In fact, they appear in nearly all registers of English. One register in which these words are relatively infrequent is "headlinese."

a. Identify two other registers in which you can observe a relatively infrequent use of these words.

b. Choose a sample from one of the two registers you've identified (or from newspaper headlines), and identify the lexical categories that strike you as occurring with higher frequency than in conversation; note which lexical categories, if any, occur relatively infrequently.

c. Offer a hypothesis as to why the distribution is as you found it.

d. Examine *of course* in line 11 of the Truman interview. On one level it could be analyzed as a prepositional phrase consisting of the preposition *of* and the noun *course*. If you think of it as a compound, what lexical category would it belong to? (*Hint*: Substitute single words for the compound, and decide which category the substitutes belong to.)

e. In terms of its distribution with respect to other word classes, decide which lexical category *such* belongs to in line 9 of the trust deed. Using the same criterion, what is the lexical category of *so* in line 10? What about *so* in line 8 of the Truman interview?

f. Make a list of the determiners in the deed of trust and a list of those in the Truman interview. Specify the particular word class for each determiner in your list (e.g., article, demonstrative).

g. The trust deed has one instance of *that* (line 2) and the Truman interview six—in lines 2 (twice), 7, 8, 11, 12. Identify the word class for each of these seven instances.

h. Give two arguments for categorizing *notwithstanding* (trust deed, line 1) as a preposition.

i. Bearing in mind that compounds are not always written as a single word (*notwithstanding*), identify another example of a compound preposition in the trust deed.

j. The trust deed contains several compounds (e.g., the preposition *notwithstanding* and the pronoun *anything* in line 1 and the compound noun *United States* [made up of an adjective and a noun] in lines 3–4). Identify all the compounds in the Truman interview, and note their lexical categories. What similarities and differences exist between the categories of compounds in the trust deed and the interview?

k. Examine the occurrences of *to* in the trust deed (lines 1, 3, 9) and the Truman interview (line 13). Which, if any, of these is a preposition? What are the others?

l. Assuming that the passages are typical of their registers, what generalizations can you make about the registers in terms of their exploitation of particular word classes?

10-8) Examine the following three letters. The first is a letter of recommendation for a student seeking admission to a master's degree program in linguistics, the second a letter to a magazine, and the third a personal letter from a woman to a female friend in another state. Identify the particular characteristics of each type of letter in terms of the co-occurring features on the two dimensions examined in this chapter. Then, using the features as a guide, indicate approximately where each letter might fall on the two dimensions.

Letter of Recommendation (182 words)

I have known Mr. John Smith as a student in three of my courses at State, and on the basis of that acquaintance with him, it is my recommendation that he should certainly be admitted to graduate school.

John was a student of mine in Linguistics 100, where he did exceptionally well, writing a very good paper indeed. On the basis of that paper, I encouraged him to become a linguistics major and subsequently had the good fortune to have him in two more of my classes. In one of these (historical linguistics) he led the class, obviously working more insightfully than the other seventeen students enrolled. In the other course (introduction to phonology), he did less well, perhaps because he was under some financial pressure and was forced to work twenty hours a week while carrying a full academic load. In all three courses, John worked very hard, doing much more than was required.

I recommend John Smith to you without reservation of any kind. He knows what he wants to achieve and is clearly motivated to succeed in graduate school.

Editorial Letter (91 words)

Your story on Afghanistan was in error when it stated that the Russian-backed coup of 1973 was bloodless. As a Peace Corps volunteer in Afghanistan at the time, I saw the bodies and blood and ducked the bullets. It was estimated that between 1,000 and 1,500 died, but it is hard to get an accurate count when a tank pulls up to the house of the shah's supporters and fires repeatedly into it from 30 feet away, or when whole households of people disappear in the middle of the night.

Personal Letter (142 words)

So, what's up? Not too much going on here. I'm at work now, and it's been so slow this week. We haven't done anything. I hate it when it's so slow. The week seems like it's never going to end.

Well how have you all been? Did you get the pictures and letter I sent you? We haven't heard from you in a while. Mother has your B'day present ready to send to you and Dan's too, but no tellin' when she will get around to sending it. How are the kids? Does Dan like kindergarten? Well, Al has gone off to school. I miss him so much. He left Monday to go to LLTI. It's a trade school upstate. You only have to go for two years, and he's taking air conditioning and refrigeration and then he's going to take heating.

10-9 a. Review what was said about *competent* (as in *competent jurisdiction*) in the discussion on p. 348. Then try to specify the legal senses of the following words, which are also used with specialized meanings in the trust deed: *deed, trust, obligation, decision, provisions,* and *note.* List any words used with specialized senses in the Truman interview and specify the sense.

b. List another example of a reduced relative clause ("whiz deletion") in the trust deed besides the three identified on p. 350.

c. List any examples of a reduced relative clause in the Truman passages on p. 347 and in the sequel given in Exercise 10-5 above.

10-10. Below are several personal ads (very slightly adapted) from a weekly newspaper published in Los Angeles. Examine them for their linguistic characteristics.

(1) Aquarius SWM, 33, strong build, blue eyes. You: marriage-minded, bilingual Latin Female 23–30, children ok.

(2) Busty brilliant, stunning entrepreneur, 40s (looks 30). Seeks possibly younger, tall, handsome, caring SWM, who respects individuality. Someone who lives the impossible dream, financially secure, good conversation, for relationship, n/s.

(3) SWM, 28, attractive college student, works for major US airlines, enjoys traveling. Seeks Female, 23–32, humorous and intelligent for world class romance and possibly marriage.

(4) English vegetarian. SWM, 31. Sincere, sensitive, original, thinking, untypical, amusing, shy, playful, affectionate professional. Seeking warm, witty, open-minded WF, under 29, to share my life with.

(5) Slim, young, GWM, very straight appearance, masculine, athletic, healthy, clean-shaven, discreet. Seeks similar good-looking WM, under 25, for monogamous relationship.

(6) Very romantic SBM, 24, college educated. Seeks wealthy, healthy and beautiful Lady for friendship and maybe romance. Phonies and pranksters need not apply.

(7) Hispanic DF, petite but full of life, likes sports, dancing, traveling, looking for someone with same interests, 30+, race unimportant.

(8) Evolved, positive thinking, spiritual, affectionate, honest, handsome, healthy, secure, 36, 6′, 160#, blue-eyed, unpretentious, unencumbered, professional. Seeking counterpart, soul mate, marriage, family.

a. Compared to conversation, what lexical categories are very frequent in the ads? What lexical categories are particularly rare?

b. Identify eight characteristic linguistic features of personal ads; they can be features of syntax, morphology, lexicon, abbreviatory conventions, and so on.

c. List the verbs in all the ads, and identify their grammatical person (first, second, third) and number (singular, plural) where possible. (*Hint*: Supply the pronoun that would serve as subject of each verb in order to determine person and number.)

d. Choose one of the ads and attempt to write it out fully in conversational English solely by supplying additional words; keep the same word order and word forms of the original ad.

e. On the basis of your attempt, what indication is there that the ads represent a reduced or abbreviated form of conversational English? If you judge the ads not to be reductions of the sentences of conversational English, what explanation can you offer for the form of the sentences?

f. Which linguistic features of personal ads strike you as having become conventionalized to the point of requiring previous knowledge of the customs of the register in order to write or understand the register?

10-11. Examine a current issue of your school newspaper and list as many different registers as you can identify in it (such as editorials, letters to the editor, reviews). Choose one register and list eight linguistic features that contribute by their frequency to the characterization of that register; provide an example of each feature from your passage.

10-12. Recipes, obituaries, classified ads, display ads, telegrams, birthday cards, credit applications, course descriptions in college catalogs, directions for using medicines, and essay questions are just a few of the distinctive registers you have occasion to use regularly. Choose a small textual sample from one of these registers, and provide a list of characteristic features of it, with an example of each feature from your sample.

10-13. Identify several instances of linguistic features that vary across registers in a foreign language you have studied. (Some features may be alluded to in your foreign language textbook; others may have been mentioned by your instructor.) Attempt to identify at least one phonological, one syntactic, and several lexical items. Specify for each feature the situation in which you believe it to be appropriate and another situation in which it would not be. (*Hint*: Consider gross differences of situation, such as writing versus speech, formal versus informal, deferential versus equal status, fast speech versus careful speech.)

INTERNET RESOURCE

British National Corpus: http://info.ox.ac.uk/bnc/
The home page for the British National Corpus, this one-stop supermarket provides information about and links to a myriad of other corpus pages. One link permits you to submit queries to the BNC itself and receive sample sentences containing the expression you queried. The link to "Corpora Page" leads to a host of links to other Web sites, some for corpora, some for corpus analysis tools. Well worth a visit if you are seriously interested in registers or corpora.

SUGGESTIONS FOR FURTHER READING

- **Allan Bell. 1991. *The Language of News Media*** (Cambridge, MA: Blackwell). The most accessible in-depth analysis of a single register, one that plays a prominent role in everyone's life.

- **Vijay K. Bhatia. 1993. *Analysing Genre: Language Use in Professional Settings*** (London: Longman). A qualitative approach to registers, accessible to students as a next step beyond LISU.

- **Robert L. Chapman, ed. 1986. *New Dictionary of American Slang*** (New York: Harper & Row). A handsome dictionary of slang, from whose dust jacket we have taken examples of slang for illustration in this chapter; also discusses the nature and sources of slang.

- **David Crystal and Derek Davy. 1969. *Investigating English Style*** (London: Longman). Contains accessible chapters on the language of conversation, religion, newspaper reporting, and legal documents.

- **Connie Eble. 1996. *Slang and Sociability: In-group Language among College Students*** (Chapel Hill: U of North Carolina P). Highly informative and a delightful read. Contains a glossary of over one thousand slang terms.

- **Martin Joos. 1962. *The Five Clocks*** (New York: Harcourt). A popular and entertaining introductory treatment to the notion of register, which Joos calls "style." The story of Ballyhough railway station at the top of this chapter comes from Joos's book.

- **Timothy Shopen and Joseph M. Williams, eds. 1981.** *Style and Variables in English* (Cambridge, MA: Winthrop). A collection of essays suitable for a general audience; treats discourse, literary style, and other styles.

Advanced Reading

Brown and Fraser (1979) survey the elements of speech situations that can influence language. The description of switching in Brussels comes from Fishman (1972), while Blom and Gumperz (1972) describe switching between Bokmål and Ranamål. Biber (1988) is a quantitative study of variation in a computerized corpus of spoken and written registers of English; it underlies the discussion of dimensions of textual variation in this chapter. Biber (1995) is the most thorough discussion of textual variation in English and other languages. O'Donnell and Todd (1991) treat English in the media, advertising, literature, and the classroom. Discussions of still other written registers can be found in Ghadessy (1988). Chapters in the volume edited by Biber and Finegan (1994) describe sports-coaching register, personal ads, and dinner table conversations, as well as register variation in Somali and Korean. Andersen (1990) describes register use among children. Lambert and Tucker (1976) report several social-psychological studies of address forms, principally in Canadian French, Puerto Rican Spanish, and Colombian Spanish.

REFERENCES

- Andersen, Elaine S. 1990. *Speaking with Style* (London: Routledge).

- Biber, Douglas. 1988. *Variation across Speech and Writing* (Cambridge: Cambridge UP).

- Biber, Douglas. 1995. *Dimensions of Register Variation: A Cross-Linguistic Comparison* (Cambridge: Cambridge UP).

- Biber, Douglas, and Edward Finegan, eds. 1994. *Sociolinguistic Perspectives on Register* (New York: Oxford UP).

- Blom, Jan-Petter, and John J. Gumperz. 1972. "Social Meaning in Linguistic Structure," in John J. Gumperz and Dell Hymes, eds., *Directions in Sociolinguistics* (New York: Holt), pp. 407–434.

- Brown, Penelope, and Colin Fraser. 1979. "Speech as a Marker of Situation," in Klaus Scherer and Howard Giles, eds., *Social Markers in Speech* (Cambridge: Cambridge UP), pp. 33–62.

- Fishman, Joshua A. 1972. "The Sociology of Language," in Pier Paolo Giglioli, ed., *Language and Social Context* (New York: Penguin), pp. 45–58.

- Ghadessy, Mohsen, ed. 1988. *Registers of Written English: Situational Factors and Linguistic Features* (London: Pinter).

- Labov, William. 1966. *The Social Stratification of English in New York City* (Washington, DC: Center for Applied Linguistics).

- Lambert, Wallace E., and G. Richard Tucker. 1976. Tu, Vous, Usted: *A Social-Psychological Study of Address Patterns* (Rowley, MA: Newbury House).

- O'Donnell, W. R., and Loreto Todd. 1991. *Variety in Contemporary English,* 2nd ed. (London: HarperCollins).

- Trudgill, Peter. 1996. *Sociolinguistics: An Introduction to Language and Society,* rev. ed. (New York: Penguin).

CHAPTER 11

LANGUAGE VARIATION AMONG SOCIAL GROUPS: DIALECTS

―

WHAT DO YOU THINK?

Imagine that your nine-year-old niece returns from summer camp and reports that one of the counselors "talked real funny"; he called the TV a "telly," cookies "biscuits," and trucks "lorries." What would you tell your niece about who "talks funny" and who doesn't?

Suppose you're a high school teacher in Los Angeles. Visiting from Alabama is a teacher carrying a distinct Southern accent, and he reports to your students that, like most educated Southerners, he does not speak with a Southern accent. At the time, your students smirk. Later they ask you how on earth the visitor could possibly imagine that he spoke without an accent. What explanation do you give them?

At a party one night a visitor from out of state remarks that "You don't have so strong an accent as your friends." You had previously believed that you had no accent and that you spoke like your friends, but the question helps you realize that you carry a regional accent, just like everyone else around you. What explanation could you offer your visitor for why you never realized that fact before and why you really do have an accent just like the one your friends have?

Imagine that you represent your college in a local county fair competition and have been challenged to think of a place you have visited where the language was the same as yours but the dialect differed from that of your home region. After naming the place, your challenge is to recall any five household items (frying pan, soda, wash cloth, window covering, and so on) for which the customary word in your locality differs from the name of the same object there. What is your answer?

In a discussion about the utility of American teachers knowing something about Ebonics, a college friend claims that Ebonics is "just broken English" and teachers shouldn't have to learn about it. What reasons can you give for arguing that, if Ebonics is "broken," then every variety of English is "broken" when viewed from the perspective of every other variety?

In the cafeteria, you and a group of classmates are discussing whether college women and men talk differently. One classmate claims that women generally use more prestigious speech forms than men. What do you tell her?

LANGUAGE OR DIALECT: WHICH DO YOU SPEAK?

⟶

It is an obvious fact that people of different nations tend to use different languages. Along with physical appearance and cultural characteristics, language differences are part of what distinguishes one nation from another. Of course, it isn't only across national boundaries that people speak different languages. In Canada, inhabitants of some cities have spoken different languages for centuries. In Quebec province, ethnic French-Canadians maintain a strong allegiance to the French language, while ethnic Anglos maintain a loyalty to English. In India, literally dozens of languages are spoken, some confined to small areas, others spoken regionally or nationally.

Among speakers of a single language there is considerable international variation. We can distinguish Australian, American, British, Indian, and Irish English, among others. Striking differences can be noticed between the varieties of French spoken in Montreal and in Paris, and marked distinctions exist among the varieties of Spanish in Spain, Mexico, and various Central and South American countries. In largely monolingual countries like Germany, France, England, and the United States, there is also variation from one group to another: even casual observers know that residents of different parts of the country speak regional varieties of the national language. When Americans speak of a "Boston accent," a "Southern drawl," or "Brooklynese," they reveal their perception of American English as varying from place to place and, in general, that languages have regional dialects. These linguistic markers of region serve to identify people as belonging to a particular social group, even though that group may be loosely bound together (as are most regional groups in the United States). In countries where regional affiliation may have other social correlates—of ethnicity or religion or clan—regional varieties are more important markers of social affiliation. The existence of regional varieties of a language, like the existence of different languages themselves, demonstrates that people who speak *with* one another tend to speak *like* one another and that people who view themselves as distinct from one another tend to mark that distinction in their speech, in addition to whatever other ways may mark it.

A language can be thought of as a collection of dialects that are usually related to one another historically and are similar to one another structurally and lexically; dialects are used by different social groups who *choose* to say that they are speakers of the same language.

SOCIAL BOUNDARIES AND DIALECTS

Language varies not only from region to region but also across ethnic, socioeconomic, and gender boundaries. Speakers of American English know that white Americans and black Americans tend to speak differently, even when they live in the same city. Similarly, middle-class speakers can often be distinguished from working-class speakers. You know too that women and men differ in how they use language. These variations across ethnic groups, socioeconomic classes, and gender groups also constitute social (as distinct from regional) dialects. African American and white residents of the United States speak the same language, though often somewhat differently. The American middle class and working class share the same language, though each class has distinctive speech characteristics. And though mainstream American women and men speak the same language, their speech differs in patterned ways. Throughout the world, in addition to regional dialects, there are ethnic, social class, and gender dialects.

DISTINGUISHING BETWEEN DIALECTS AND REGISTERS

The term **dialect** refers to the language varieties characteristic of regional or social groups. Partly through a dialect we recognize a person's regional, ethnic, social, and gender affiliation; thus the term *dialect* has to do with language *users,* with groups of speakers. In addition, as we saw in the preceding chapter, all dialects vary according to the situation in which they are used. The term *register* refers to language varieties characteristic of different *situations of use.* Languages, dialects, and registers are all called language **varieties.** In this chapter we deal with dialects—language varieties characteristic of particular social groups. What this means is that there is no linguistic distinction between a language and a dialect. Every dialect is a language and every language is realized in its dialects. It has been claimed that a language is a dialect with an army and a navy. The point is simply that from a linguistic point of view what is called a language and what is called a dialect are indistinguishable.

HOW DO LANGUAGES DIVERGE AND MERGE?

⟶

How is it that in the course of time certain language varieties, once similar to one another, can come to differ significantly, while other varieties remain very much alike? There is no simple answer to that question, but this much seems clear: The more people interact with one another, the more alike their language remains or becomes. The less contact two social groups have, the more likely it is that their languages will become differentiated.

Geographical separation and social distance can give rise to notable differences in speechways. From the Proto-Indo-European language spoken about six millennia ago have come most of today's European languages as well as many tongues of Central Asia and the Indian subcontinent. Not only the Romance languages but the Celtic, Greek, Baltic, Slavic, and Indo-Iranian tongues have developed from Proto-Indo-European, as have the Germanic languages including English, Norwegian, Swedish, Danish, Dutch, and German. When we consider that only some two hundred generations have lived and died during that six-thousand-year period, we can appreciate how quickly a multitude of different tongues can develop from a single parent language. Scores of mutually unintelligible languages have developed from Proto-Indo-European within the past six thousand years.

In the same vein, the Spanish varieties of the New World are developing along lines somewhat different from the Spanish of Spain. Similar contrasts can be observed between the French spoken in Paris and Montreal and among the British, American, Australian, Canadian, New Zealand, Indian, and Irish varieties of English. So physical distance can be a crucial factor in promoting dialect distinctions.

Similarly, social distance can contribute to creating and maintaining distinct dialects. Middle-class dialects differ from working-class dialects partly because of the relative lack of sustained contacts across class boundaries in American society. African-American Vernacular English remains distinct from other varieties of American English partly because of the social distance between whites and African Americans in the United States. A dialect links its users through recognition of shared linguistic characteristics, and speakers' abilities to use and understand a dialect mark them as "insiders" and allow them to identify (and exclude) "outsiders."

All languages and language varieties change and develop continuously. When two groups of people speaking a common tongue stop having sufficient social interaction to keep their language developing along the same path, the changes in the speech patterns of each group can eventually produce an inability to understand one another. That's what happened in the evolution of the many derivatives of Proto-Indo-European.

DIALECTS OR LANGUAGES?

The Romance languages arose from the regional varieties of Latin spoken in different parts of the Roman Empire. Those dialects of Latin eventually gave rise to Italian, French, Spanish, Portuguese, and Rumanian, now the distinct languages of different countries. Though these tongues share many structural features of syntax, phonology, and lexicon, the nationalistic pride taken by the Italians, French, Spaniards, Portuguese, and Rumanians contributes to the perception of the varieties as different languages rather than as dialects of a single language. The opposite situation characterizes the Chinese language. Chinese comprises several distinct dialects, including Mandarin and Cantonese. Even though not all Chinese dialects are mutually intelligible, their speakers choose to regard themselves as sharing the same language.

Thus the difference between a language and a dialect is as much a social as a linguistic question; it is strongly influenced by social and psychological factors such as nationalistic and even religious attitudes. The Hindus of northern India speak Hindi, while the Moslems there and in neighboring Pakistan speak Urdu. Opinions differ among them as to the extent to which they can understand one another. Until recently, these two varieties were regarded as a single linguistic unit and went by the name of Hindustani. The fact that linguists today write grammars of "Hindi-Urdu" reflects their professional judgment that these varieties require only a single grammatical description, despite the different language names assigned to them by their speakers. Naturally, with the passage of time, these varieties—whose different names proclaim that their speakers belong to different social, political, and religious groups—will become increasingly differentiated, as French and Spanish have done over the centuries.

Just as physical and social distance enable speakers of particular varieties to distinguish themselves from speakers of other varieties, so close contact and frequent communication foster linguistic uniformity. As dialects spoken by people in close social contact tend to become alike, so different languages spoken in a community can become similar and even tend to merge in some circumstances. The kind and degree of merger are determined by the type and degree of social integration and shared values.

LANGUAGE MERGER IN AN INDIAN VILLAGE

A fascinating case of merger occurred in Kupwar, a village in India on the border between two major language families: the Indo-European family (which includes the languages of North India) and the unrelated Dravidian family (comprising the languages of South India). Kupwar's three thousand inhabitants fall into three groups and regularly use three languages in their daily activities. The Jains speak Kannada (a Dravidian language); the Moslems speak Urdu (an Indo-European language closely related to Hindi); and the Untouchables speak Marathi (the regional Indo-European language surrounding Kupwar and the principal literary language of the area). These groups have lived in the village for centuries, and most men are bilingual or multilingual. Over the course of time, with individuals switching back and forth among at least two of these languages, the varieties used in Kupwar have come to be more and more alike. In fact, the grammatical structures of the village varieties are now so similar that a word-for-word translation is possible among the languages. This means that the word order and other structural characteristics of the three languages are now virtually identical. This merging is all the more remarkable because the varieties of these same languages that are used elsewhere are very different from one another. Indeed, they belong to two unrelated language families and certainly cannot be translated word for word into one another.

Even in Kupwar, however, where the grammars of the different languages have been merging, the vocabulary of each variety has remained quite distinct. On the one hand, the need for communication among the different groups has encouraged the grammars to converge; on the other hand, the social separation needed to maintain religious and caste differences has supported the continuation of separate vocabularies.

The need for intercommunication among the groups have had the effect of making it easy to communicate across the languages; and the fact that the groups remain distinct from one another has kept their languages from becoming so much alike that it would prove difficult to tell linguistically who belonged to which group. As things stand now, communication is relatively easy (certainly easier than speaking across different languages), while affiliation and group identification remain clear. (Americans accomplish a related thing with nearly identical grammars but distinct regional pronunciations, or accents. The result: no difficulty communicating, but little doubt about regional affiliation.) This is the linguistic equivalent of having your cake and eating it too.

In the following example sentence, the word order and morphology are relatively uniform across the three Kupwar varieties, but the vocabulary leaves no doubt as to which language is being spoken in each case.

LANGUAGE MERGER IN KUPWAR

URDU	pala	jəra	kaat	ke	le	ke	a		ya
MARATHI	pala	jəra	kap	un	gʰe	un	a	l	o
KANNADA	tapla	jəra	kʰod	i	təgond	i	bə		yn
	greens	a little	cut	having	taken	having	come	Past	I
	'I cut some greens and brought them.'								

Thus, while the three grammars have merged to a remarkable extent by combining grammatical elements from each language, social distinctions in the language have been preserved (and are partly maintained) by clear differences in vocabulary.

LANGUAGE/DIALECT CONTINUA

In contrast to the situation in Kupwar, the Romance languages, including Spanish, French, Italian, and Portuguese, have evolved distinct national varieties from the relatively uniform colloquial Latin that was spoken in their regions in Roman times. Whereas the varieties of language spoken in Kupwar have converged, the language varieties spoken where Latin was used have diverged over the centuries. The reasons in both cases are the same. First, people use language to mark their social identity. Second, people who talk with one another tend to talk *like* one another. A corollary of the second principle is that people not talking with one another tend to become linguistically differentiated.

Today the languages of Europe (in the Romance-speaking area and elsewhere) look separate and tidily compartmentalized on a map. In reality they are not so neatly distinguishable. Instead, there is a continuum of variation, and languages "blend" into one another. Near language-area borders the change is slightly more abrupt. The national border between France and Italy, for example, also serves as a dividing line between the French-speaking and the Italian-speaking area. But in practice the French spoken just over the French border shares features with the Italian spoken by Italians on the Italian side. From Paris to the Italian border, there is a continuum along which the local French varieties become more and more "Italianlike." Likewise, from Rome to the French border, Italian varieties can be viewed as becoming more "Frenchlike."

Similar situations exist all over Europe. As a result, Swedes of the far south using their local dialects can communicate better with Danish speakers in nearby Denmark than with their fellow Swedes in distant northern Sweden. The same situation exists with residents along the border between Germany and Holland. Using their own local varieties, speakers of German can communicate better with speakers of Dutch living near them than with speakers of southern German dialects. Examples of geographical dialect continua are found throughout Europe. In fact, while the standard varieties of Italian, French, Spanish, Catalan, and Portuguese are not mutually intelligible, the local varieties form a continuum from Portugal through Spain and halfway through Belgium and then through France and down to the southern tip of Italy. There is also a Scandinavian dialect continuum, a West Germanic dialect continuum, and South Slavonic and North Slavonic dialect continua.

Just as different languages may form a dialect continuum, so different dialects of a single language can constitute a continuum. This is the case in China, where several mutually unintelligible varieties constitute a single language. In the case of Kupwar, if there were no outside reference varieties against which to compare the varieties spoken in the village, we might be inclined to say that the varieties spoken there were dialects of one language; they do, after all, have basically one grammar. The residents of Kupwar, however, have found it socially valuable to continue speaking "different" languages, despite an increasing grammatical and lexical similarity. What counts most in deciding on designations for language varieties and on whether these represent dialects of a single language or separate languages is the view of native speakers.

NATIONAL VARIETIES OF ENGLISH

As we mentioned earlier, there are well-known varieties of English around the world, ranging from the most familiar British and American dialects to the somewhat less familiar varieties of Australia, New Zealand, Ireland, India and so forth. In this section we examine some of these national varieties.

AMERICAN AND BRITISH NATIONAL VARIETIES

The principal varieties of English throughout the world are customarily divided into British and American types. British English is the basis for the varieties spoken in England, Ireland, Wales, Scotland, Australia, New Zealand, India, Pakistan, Malaysia, Singapore, and South Africa. American (or North American) includes chiefly the English of Canada and the United States.

This division inevitably oversimplifies the facts. For example, despite the groupings just suggested, certain characteristics of Canadian English are closer to

British English, while certain characteristics of Irish English are closer to North American English. And there are many differences between, say, Standard British English and Standard Indian English. But we can still make a number of generalizations about British-based varieties and American-based varieties provided we keep in mind that neither group is completely homogeneous.

There are well-known spelling differences between British and American English. Red, white, and blue are *colours* in Britain and *colors* in America. The British put *tyres* on their cars and drive to the *theatre,* where they park near the *kerb.* Interestingly, Canadians usually follow British spelling rather than American spelling, a reflection of the close historical association between Canada and Britain. But these minor spelling differences do not reflect spoken differences. On the other hand, in the phonology, morphology, syntax, and lexicon of the two sets of varieties you can note some marked differences.

Speakers of most American varieties, for example, consistently pronounce the vowel of words like *can't* as [æ], while speakers of British varieties usually have the sound [ɑ:] in such words. Between two vowels the first of which is stressed, Americans and Canadians usually pronounce the stop /t/ as a flap [ɾ] so that the word *sitter* is pronounced [sɪɾer]. By contrast, speakers of British varieties do not readily pronounce /t/ as [ɾ] between vowels. Again, most American varieties have a retroflex /r/ in word-final position in words like *car, sir,* and *near,* whereas in many British varieties /r/ is dropped in these words. With respect to the last feature, speakers of Irish and Scottish English follow the American pattern rather than the British pattern, while residents of New York City and Boston, among others, follow the British pattern. This patterning illustrates the fact that British varieties can differ widely from one another, as do American varieties.

There are also some morphological and syntactic differences between British and American varieties. Many noun phrases that denote locations in time or space take an article in American English but not in British English.

AMERICAN	BRITISH
in the hospital	in hospital
to the university	to university
the next day	next day

Some collective nouns (those that refer to groups of people or institutions) are plural in British English but usually singular in American varieties. An American watching a college soccer game would say *Cornell is ahead by two,* while a British observer would say *Cornell are ahead by two.* In both varieties, a noun like *police* takes a plural verb, as in *The police are attempting to assist the neighbors.* A final illustration of the grammatical differences between the two varieties is the use of the verb *do* with auxiliaries. If asked *Have you finished the assignment?,* an American may say *Yes, I have,* while British English also allows *Yes, I have done.* Asked whether flying time to Los Angeles varies, a British flight attendant might reply *It can do* as well as *It can.*

Finally, there are differences between the word stocks of American and British varieties of English. Those given below are well known.

AMERICAN	BRITISH
elevator	lift
second floor	first floor
TV	telly
flashlight	torch
hood (of a car)	bonnet
trunk (of a car)	boot
cookies	biscuits
gas/gasoline	petrol
truck	lorry
can	tin
underwear	knickers
intermission	interval
line	queue
exit	way out
washcloth/facecloth	flannel

In general, structural differences between British varieties and American varieties are not great. But combined with social and political factors, the structural differences are sufficient to make speakers of English everywhere intensely aware of the dialect boundary that the Atlantic Ocean constitutes.

REGIONAL VARIETIES OF AMERICAN ENGLISH

Although regional differences have always been greater in Great Britain than in the United States, recent presidents have highlighted regional differences in American speech. John F. Kennedy and his successor Lyndon B. Johnson spoke markedly different dialects. George Bush and Bill Clinton, also successive occupants of the White House, articulated different policies with strikingly different speechways, the latter a reflection of their different regional origins.

Starting in the late 1940s, investigation of vocabulary patterns in the eastern United States suggested distinguishing among Northern, Midland, and Southern dialects, each with subdivisions. Midland was divided into North Midland and South Midland varieties. Boston and metropolitan New York were seen as distinct varieties of the Northern dialect. Midwestern states such as Illinois, Indiana, and Ohio, formerly thought of as representing General American, were seen as situated principally in the North Midland dialect, with a narrow strip of Northern dialect across their northernmost counties and a small strip across their southern counties belonging to the South Midland variety. The most recent research has suggested a refinement of that scheme, and the results are shown in the geographical patterns of Figure 11-1.

Figure 11-1

MAJOR DIALECT REGIONS OF THE UNITED STATES

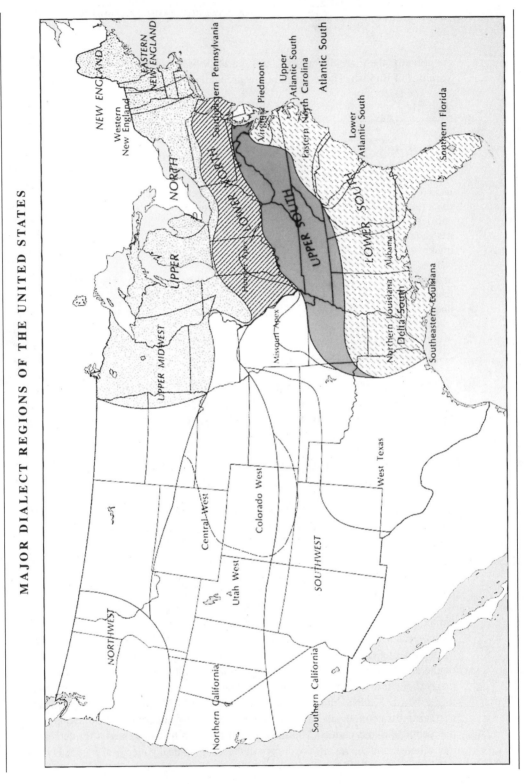

Source: Carver 1987

MAPPING DIALECTS

In order to propose a map like Figure 11-1, dialectologists investigate word usage and pronunciation as well as characteristic patterns of morphology and grammar. Typically, a researcher with a lengthy questionnaire visits a town and inquires of residents what they call certain things or how they express certain meanings.

To take an example, researchers uncovered surprising variety when they asked what word was commonly used for the large insect with transparent wings often seen hovering over water. Figure 11-2 shows that *darning needle* was most common in New England, upstate New York, metropolitan New York (including northern and eastern New Jersey and Long Island), and northern Pennsylvania. *Mosquito hawk* predominated in coastal North Carolina and Virginia, *snake doctor* occurred widely in inland Virginia, and *snake feeder* predominated along the northern Ohio River in West Virginia, Ohio, western Pennsylvania, and the upper Ohio Valley toward Pittsburgh. *Snake feeder* was concentrated in the northeastern Virginia Piedmont. Notice that not all the words were tidily limited to an area in which no other word was used. In some areas, a mixture of two or more names occurred. In other areas a single form occurred exclusively. The *O*s on the map in New England and New York indicate that *darning needle* was the only regional term found among respondents there.

As you can see in Figures 11-3 and 11-4, *mosquito hawk* was virtually the only regional response given in much of southeast Texas and portions of central Texas, as well as all of Louisiana and Florida, and much of southern Alabama, Mississippi, and Georgia. But *snake doctor* was the favored form in west, north, and northwest Texas, the western half of Tennessee, the northern parts of Alabama and Mississippi, and a part of northwestern Georgia. *Snake feeder* occurred occasionally along the Canadian and Arkansas rivers in Oklahoma and throughout eastern Tennessee. Both *mosquito hawk* and *snake doctor* were found in the southern half of Arkansas. *Darning needle,* so popular in New York and New England, occurred too infrequently even to be recorded on these maps of the South. Some respondents were unacquainted with local terms and reported using only *dragonfly.* (If you come from an area represented on the maps and find the terms indicated there unfamiliar, bear in mind that the data were often gathered in rural areas and represent not only "cultivated" speech but "folk" speech as well. Moreover, some of the data are now more than fifty years old, and in the survey a preference was given to older respondents.)

Determining Isoglosses   Once a map has been marked with symbols for various features, lines called **isoglosses** can be drawn at the boundary between regions that use different forms. From Figure 11-2, which shows the distribution of regional words for the dragonfly in the Eastern states, and from other maps (not provided here) that show the distribution of *I want off* and *Sook!* (a call to cows), dialect geographers derive Figure 11-5, on which the easternmost boundaries of the three features have been marked.

Figure 11-2

WORDS FOR 'DRAGONFLY' IN THE EASTERN STATES

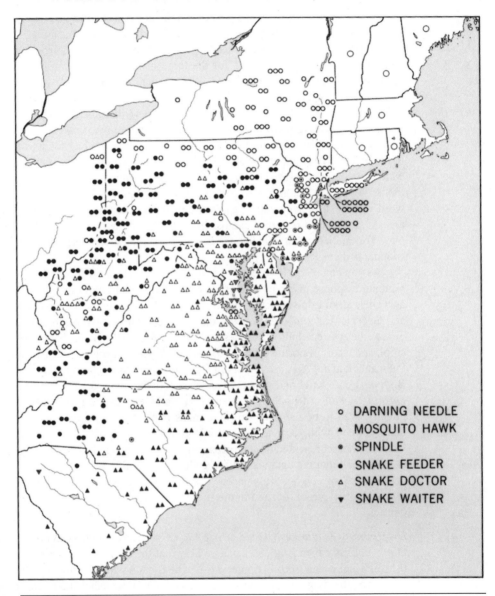

○ DARNING NEEDLE
▲ MOSQUITO HAWK
◉ SPINDLE
● SNAKE FEEDER
△ SNAKE DOCTOR
▼ SNAKE WAITER

Source: Kurath 1949

Figure 11-3

WORDS FOR 'DRAGONFLY' IN TEXAS, ARKANSAS, LOUISIANA, OKLAHOMA

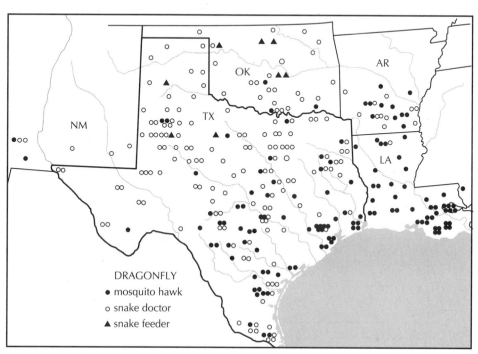

Source: Atwood 1962

Figure 11-6 shows four isoglosses traversing the three north-central states of Ohio, Indiana, and Illinois. These isoglosses represent the northernmost limits of *greasy* pronounced with a "z" as /grizi/, of *snake feeder* for 'dragonfly,' of *Sook!* as a call to cows, and of *sugar tree* meaning 'maple.'

Figure 11-7 represents seven isoglosses in the Upper Midwest. Three are the southernmost boundaries of Northern features: *humor* pronounced [hyumər]; *boulevard* referring to the grass strip between curb and sidewalk; and *come in (fresh)*, meaning 'to give birth' and usually said of a cow. Four are the northernmost boundaries of Midland features: *on* pronounced with /ɔ/ or /ɒ/ (the latter a rounded /ɑ/) instead of /ɑ/; *caterwampus* for 'askew, awry'; *roasting ears* for 'corn on the cob'; and *lightbread* for 'white bread.' You can see that each feature has a unique distribution.

Figure 11-4

WORDS FOR 'DRAGONFLY' IN THE GULF STATES

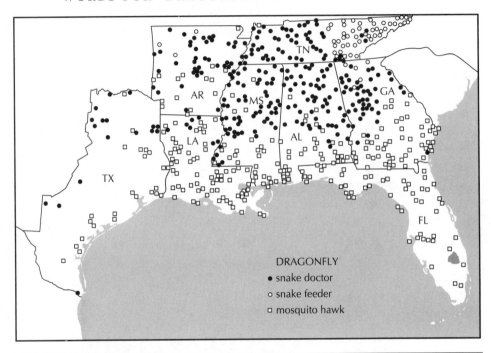

Source: Pederson 1986

DIALECT BOUNDARIES

Imagine each isogloss map drawn on a transparency and stacked one on top of the other. The result would be a map similar to that shown in Figure 11-7 and would show the extent to which the isoglosses from the different feature maps "bundle" together. The geographical limit for the use of a particular word (say, *caterwampus*) often corresponds roughly to the limit for the use of other pronunciations or words (say, *roasting ears*). Where isoglosses bundle, dialectologists draw dialect boundaries; thus, a *dialect boundary* is simply the location of a bundle of isoglosses. The map in Figure 11-1 is a distillation of dozens of maps similar to those in Figures 11-5, 11-6, and 11-7.

Speech patterns in the United States, like those elsewhere in the world, are determined partly by the geographical and physical boundaries that inhibit communication and partly by the migration routes that were followed in settling the country. Among the isoglosses of Figure 11-6, the one for /grisi/ versus /grizi/ essentially follows a line (now approximated by Interstate 70) that was the principal road for the migration of pioneers during the postcolonial settlement period.

Figure 11-5

THREE ISOGLOSSES IN THE EASTERN STATES
(EASTERN LIMITS)

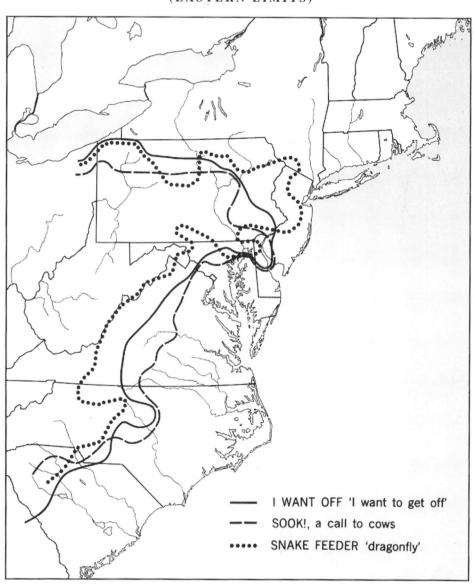

——— I WANT OFF 'I want to get off'

– – – SOOK!, a call to cows

••••• SNAKE FEEDER 'dragonfly'

Source: Kurath 1949

Figure 11-6

FOUR ISOGLOSSES IN THE NORTH-CENTRAL STATES
(NORTHERN LIMITS)

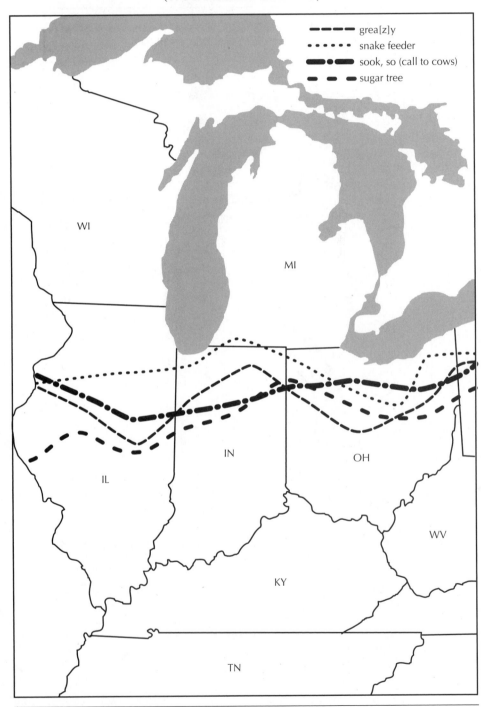

Source: Marckwardt 1957

Figure 11-7

SEVEN ISOGLOSSES IN THE UPPER MIDWEST

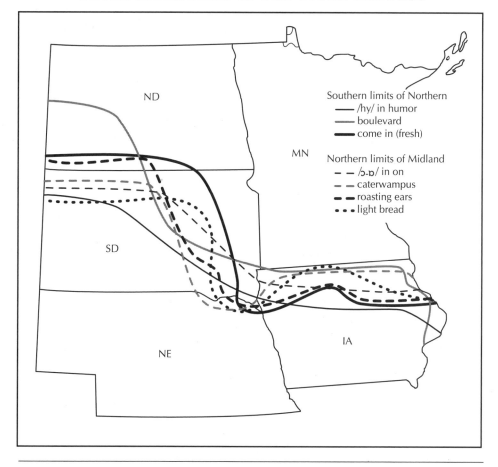

Source: Allen 1973

In the western United States, the dialect situation is more complex than in the longer established areas of the East, the South, and the Midwest. The West drew settlers speaking a range of dialects from various parts of the country. California especially continues to welcome immigrants from other parts of the country and the world, and it is a melting pot not only of races and cultures but of dialects and of languages. Such extreme heterogeneity is not conducive to the development of distinctive regional varieties of English and therefore does not lend itself so readily to the tidiness suggested by isoglosses.

An illustration of California's diversity can be seen in Figure 11-8, which shows the distribution of the words *curtains* for 'window shades,' *seed* for 'pit,' *green beans* for 'string beans,' and *took sick* for 'got sick.' The small numerals on the map represent the number of respondents (if there was more than one) using that feature in that location. Two hundred and seventy residents were interviewed in California (and thirty in Nevada): fifty-five in Los Angeles, twenty-five in San Francisco, twenty in the East Bay and five on the Peninsula (these last two locations near San Francisco), eight in San Diego, five in Sacramento, four in San Bernardino, three each in San Jose, Stockton, Fresno, Pomona, Riverside, and Bakersfield, and two each in sixty-five other communities. Looking at Figure 11-8, you can infer that most respondents used expressions other than the ones plotted; they used *shades* or *blinds* instead of *curtains; pit* or *stone* instead of *seed; string beans* instead of *green beans;* and *got sick* instead of *took sick.* You can also see that within the substantial area marked by the dialect boundary along the coast (including San Luis Obispo, Santa Barbara, Oxnard, and Oceanside) not a single respondent used any of the four mapped features. Patterns of usage in California and Nevada are not so tidy as elsewhere.

The special mixed character of California can also be heard in its pronunciations, as you can see in the map of Figure 11-9, showing locations for two pronunciations of *rodeo:* the Spanish pronunciation [rodéo] (with stress on the second syllable) and the anglicized pronunciation [ródio] (with stress on the first syllable). At least in the 1950s when the dialect survey was made, the anglicized pronunciation predominated in Nevada and was the sole pronunciation in central Nevada, as well as in the California communities along the Oregon border. The Spanish pronunciation predominated in the great bulk of California and was the *only* pronunciation in communities along the coast from Monterey to Santa Barbara and Oxnard. Even in Los Angeles, residents favored the Spanish pronunciation by almost two to one, and pronunciations in San Diego were evenly divided. The influence of Spanish thus remained strong on some pronunciations (as it continues to be in such place names as Los Angeles, San Diego, San Francisco, and Santa Barbara).

THE *DICTIONARY OF AMERICAN REGIONAL ENGLISH*

When the first volume of the *Dictionary of American Regional English* appeared in 1985, it made available more information about regional words and expressions throughout the United States than had ever been known before. *DARE* (as the project and the dictionary are called) represents the most up-to-date knowledge of American regional English.

Based on answers to almost two thousand questions (1,847, to be exact) asked by field workers who visited 1,002 communities across the country, the computer-produced maps that *DARE* uses for exhibiting its findings represent not geographical space, as most maps do, but population density. Thus the largest states on a *DARE* map are those with the largest populations. As a result, *DARE* maps appear oddly shaped.

Figure 11-10 shows the distribution of the terms *mosquito hawk* and *skeeter hawk* on a *DARE* map and on a conventional map. The word *cruller,* meaning 'a

Figure 11-8

DISTRIBUTION OF FOUR FEATURES
IN CALIFORNIA AND NEVADA

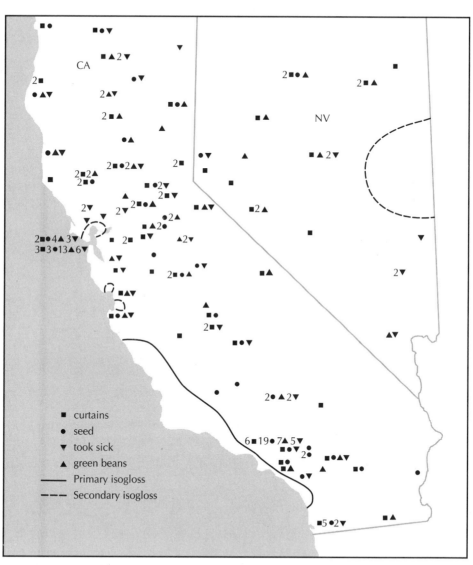

Source: Bright 1971

Figure 11-9

TWO PRONUNCIATIONS OF *RODEO*
IN CALIFORNIA AND NEVADA

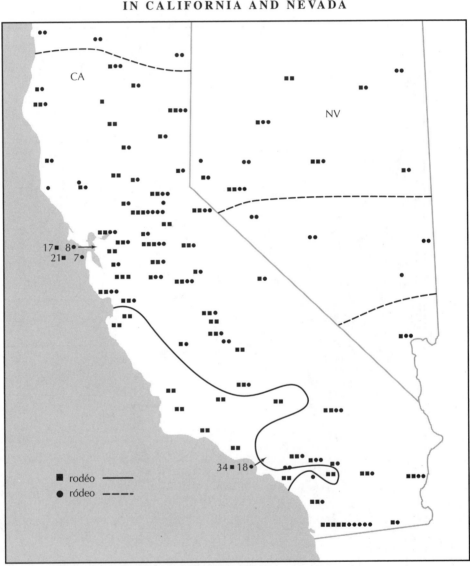

Source: Bright 1971

Figure 11-10

DISTRIBUTION OF *MOSQUITO HAWK* AND *SKEETER HAWK*
ON *DARE* MAP AND CONVENTIONAL MAP

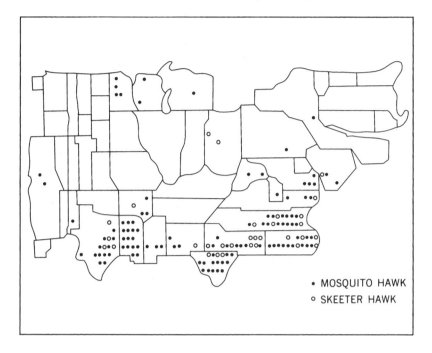

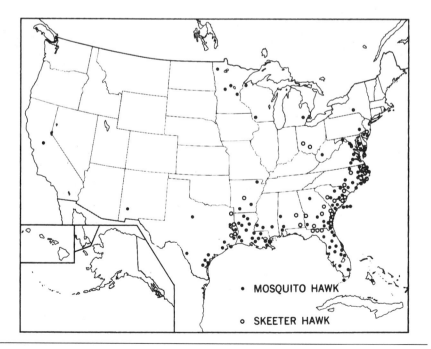

Source: Dictionary of American Regional English, 1, 1985

twisted doughnut,' has a very different distribution, as shown in the *DARE* map of Figure 11-11.

As the result of various regional dialect projects, especially *DARE,* a complex picture of American English dialects is emerging, as Figure 11-1 (page 378) shows. The darker the shading of a dialect area in that figure, the greater the number of lexical items that distinguish that dialect area from others. As you can see, the farther west you go, the fewer the peculiar linguistic characteristics of an area. The boundaries of American dialects are better established in the Eastern states than in the more recently settled Western ones.

Figure 11-11

DISTRIBUTION OF *CRULLER* ON A *DARE* MAP

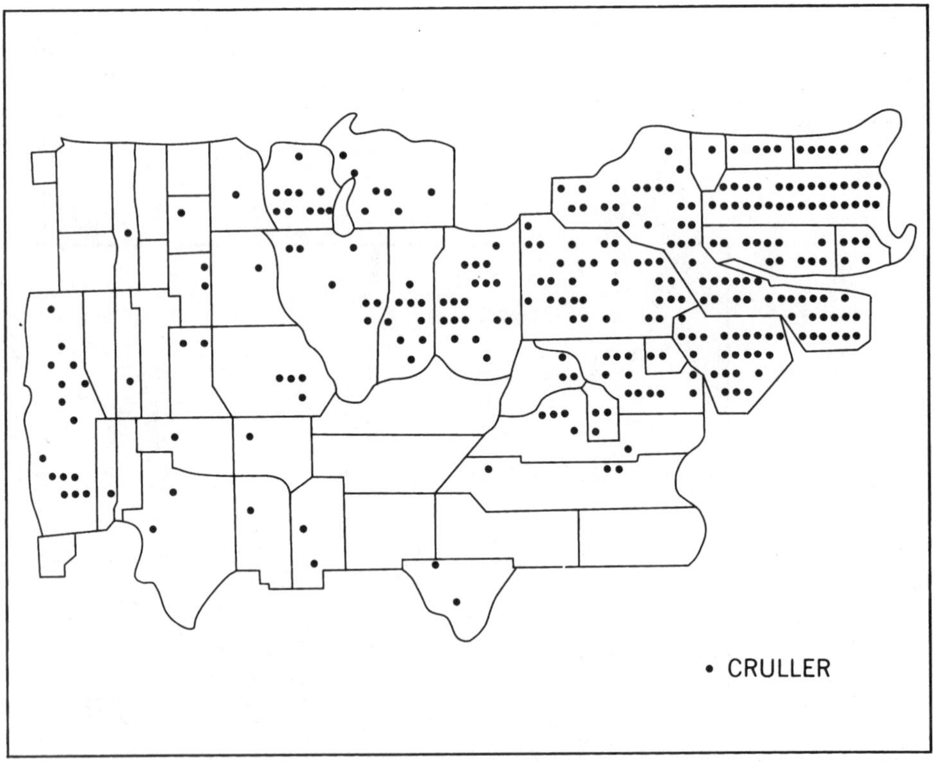

• CRULLER

Source: Dictionary of American Regional English, 1, 1985

DIALECT PATTERNS IN THE UNITED STATES

Recent research indicates that the United States has basically North and South dialects, each divided into upper and lower regions (see Figure 11-1). The Upper North contains the dialects of New England, the Upper Midwest, and the Northwest, with some lesser-marked dialect boundaries in the Central West and Northern California. The Southwest is also a dialect area, with Southern California having some distinct characteristics. The South dialect is divided into an Upper South and Lower South, and each of those also has subdialects.

COMPARING AMERICAN AND BRITISH REGIONAL DISTRIBUTIONS

Because not much information is available about the patterns of English in seventeenth- and eighteenth-century America, it is not easy to trace particular patterns of American English to their British sources. But the maps in Figures 11-12 and 11-13, showing distributions for the regional forms of past tense *see* (as in standard *He saw me*), are suggestive.

Because the map in Figure 11-12 represents three forms other than *saw,* the blank spaces indicate that *saw* is universal only in central Massachusetts, metropolitan New York City, and southeastern New York state. Throughout the rest of New England, *see* (*He see me*) predominates (by five to one: hence the large black circles). *Seen* (*He seen me*) occurs all over the map and is strongly favored in Pennsylvania except along its northern border, in most of New Jersey and West Virginia, and in much of Delaware, Maryland, and the Shenandoah Valley of Virginia. *Seed* has a single occurrence in western Massachusetts but otherwise is limited to the area south of the Pennsylvania/Maryland border, particularly North Carolina and inland South Carolina; in parts of the Carolinas, *seed* is the only regional form used (other than the standard form *saw*).

England too has sharply marked regional distribution of these same forms. The blank portions in Figure 11-13 indicate that *saw* is favored in rural speech only in the counties bordering Scotland and in parts of the northeast Midlands. Most of the southwest Midlands and Kent favor *seen,* with a narrow band of *seen* linking the two. *Seed* predominates in southwest England, most of the northwest Midlands, and the north.

From Figure 11-13 it is clear that England has its own regional patterns, and dialect geographers hope one day to be able to trace the vocabulary, pronunciations, and other linguistic features from one region to another and from one country to another. With additional information, a good deal may be learned about the diffusion of linguistic and cultural patterns.

Figure 11-12

DISTRIBUTION OF PAST TENSE OF *SEE*
IN EASTERN STATES

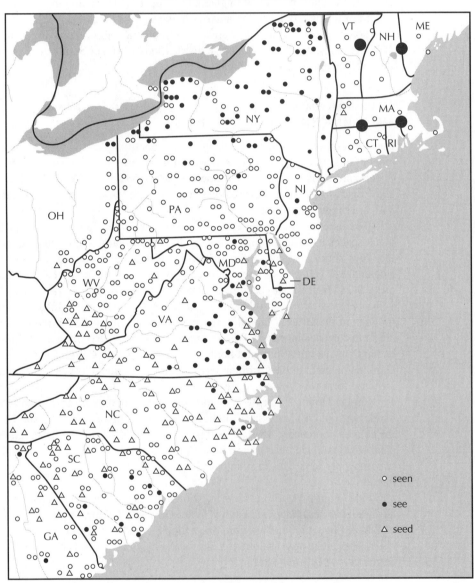

Source: Atwood 1953

Figure 11-13

DISTRIBUTION OF PAST TENSE OF *SEE* IN ENGLAND

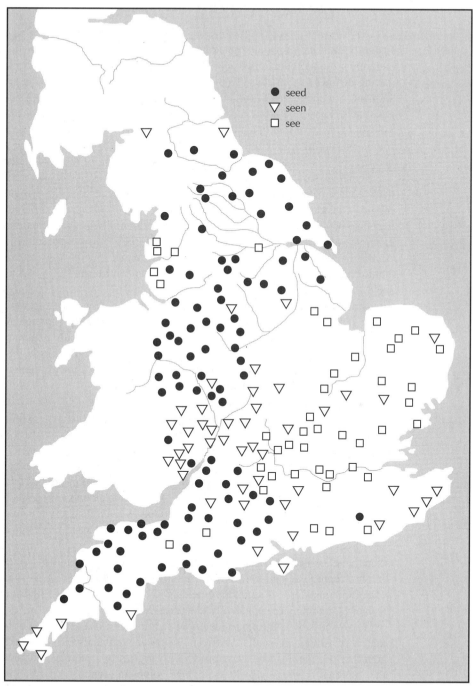

Source: Francis 1961

ETHNIC VARIETIES OF AMERICAN ENGLISH

⚊

Just as oceans and mountains separate people and lead eventually to distinct speech patterns, so social boundaries also separate people and can be instrumental in promoting distinct speechways. To the extent that such technology as the automobile, jet plane, telephone, radio, and television have reduced the effect of physical boundaries and distances between communities, physical separation has become a less significant barrier to communication. Still, social barriers continue to play an important role in promoting and maintaining characteristic speech patterns among groups of people, and it is just as valid to speak of social dialects as of regional dialects.

Social groups that claim particular social dialects as their own may identify themselves as separate classes or separate ethnic groups or, as we have seen, separate religions. In addition, cutting across all other social boundaries are differences in the ways women and men speak. In this and the following sections we explore several examples of how language varies across social boundaries, especially in America. As will be evident, society can be subdivided in a multiplicity of ways: by religion, ethnic background, social-class affiliation, and gender, to name a few. As a mirror of society, language varies across all these boundaries.

Americans commonly believe that American society is essentially homogeneous. If language is any indicator, this belief is a myth. Even though Americans may be less class-conscious than, say, the British, social-group affiliation still remains very important. In fact, the language of each American marks him or her as a member of particular social groups, and as we grow up we unconsciously learn to identify and react to other social groups.

The most notable social dialects of American English are *ethnic varieties.* Ethnicity is sometimes racial and sometimes not. For example, differences in the speech of Jewish and Italian New Yorkers have been noted, and bookstores carry books describing "Yinglish," the variety of English influenced by Yiddish speakers who have settled in America. But the social separation that leads to ethnic varieties of language is particularly noticeable in the characteristic speech patterns of urban African Americans. In some cities, the speech of African American residents is becoming increasingly distinct from the speech of white residents. Such a distinction between social groups is also noticeable in the characteristic speech patterns of other ethnic groups. Spanish-speaking immigrants in Los Angeles, New York, Chicago, Miami, and elsewhere have learned English as a second language, and their English is marked by a foreign accent. The children of these immigrants acquire English as a native language (and many are bilingual to some degree), but the variety of English that many Hispanic Americans speak natively identifies them as being of Latin ancestry.

The discussion that follows identifies certain major characteristics of two ethnic dialects of American English: African American Vernacular English and Chicano English. Both these dialects are bona fide varieties of American English like any other regional or social variety. Both have complete grammatical systems overlapping to a great degree with other varieties of English. And, like Standard American

English, both Chicano English and African American Vernacular English have a spectrum of registers. That is, speakers of African American Vernacular English and Chicano English do not speak the same way in all circumstances. While both social dialects share many characteristics with Standard American English, they also exhibit certain distinctive features.

To think of African American Vernacular English or Chicano English as an inferior variety of English or as ill formed would be erroneous. Like all other social dialects, these ethnic varieties have rules that determine what can and cannot be said. As in Standard English, a construction can be ungrammatical in African American Vernacular English or in Chicano English. Rules govern the structures and use of all dialects throughout the world, and no dialect exists without phonological, morphological, and syntactic rules, among others.

African American English

Probably the most widespread and most familiar ethnic variety of American English is African American Vernacular English (formerly called Black English or Black English Vernacular and now called Ebonics by some). Not all African Americans are fluent speakers of African American Vernacular English, and not all speakers of African American Vernacular English are African Americans. After all, people grow up speaking the language variety around them. As you could have grown up speaking Japanese, Swahili, or Arabic had you been born into a Japanese-, Swahili-, or Arabic-speaking family, children growing up among speakers of different regional and social varieties speak the variety that surrounds them. In an ethnically diverse city like Los Angeles, you can meet teenage speakers of African American Vernacular English whose foreign-born parents speak Chinese or Vietnamese. The variety of English spoken by these Asian Americans reflects the characteristic speechways of their friends and of the neighborhoods where they acquired English. To underscore an obvious but often misunderstood fact, the acquisition of a particular language or dialect is as independent of a person's skin color as it is of his or her height or weight.

The history of African American Vernacular English in the United States is not completely understood, and there are competing theories about its origins and subsequent development. But there is no disagreement concerning its structure and functioning. African American Vernacular English has characteristic phonological, morphological, and syntactic features, as well as certain vocabulary of its own. Like all other social groups, speakers of African American Vernacular English also share characteristic ways of interacting. In this section we examine some of the phonological and syntactic features of African American Vernacular English; we will not discuss lexical or interactional characteristics.

Phonological Characteristics   One of the most prominent phonological features of African American Vernacular English is the frequent simplification of consonant clusters, as in "des" /dɛs/ for *desk,* "pass" /pæs/ for *passed,* and "wile" /wayl/ for *wild.* The same feature also occurs in several regional varieties of American English, though to a lesser degree. Among speakers of Standard English, the consonant clusters <sk> in *desk* and <ld> in *wild* are also commonly simplified, as in "asthem" /æsðəm/ for *ask them* and "tole" /tol/ for *told*. But consonant cluster simplification occurs more frequently and to a greater extent in African American Vernacular English than in other varieties.

Another salient characteristic concerns the final stop consonants, such as /d/, in words like *side* and *borrowed*. Speakers of African American Vernacular English frequently delete some word-final stops, pronouncing *side* like *sigh* and *borrowed* like *borrow*. This deletion rule is influenced in systematic ways by the linguistic circumstances of the utterance. When a word-final stop consonant represents a separate morpheme (as it does in the words *followed* and *tried*), the final [d] is preserved much more frequently than when it is part of the word stem (as in the words *side* and *rapid*) and doesn't represent a separate morpheme. Another factor influencing the deletion of word-final stops is whether they occur in a syllable that is strongly stressed (*tried*) or weakly stressed (*rapid*)—note that the second syllable of *rapid* is less strongly stressed than the first syllable. Strongly stressed syllables tend to preserve final stops more than weakly stressed syllables do. A third factor is whether a vowel follows the stop (as it would in *side angle* and *tried it*) or a consonant follows it (as in *tried hard* and *side street*). A following vowel helps to preserve the stop and, in fact, appears to be the most significant factor in determining whether a final stop is deleted in African American Vernacular English.

Grammatical Characteristics African American Vernacular English distinguishes itself not only at the phonological level but also in its grammar. One prominent syntactic feature is a characteristic use of the verb *be*. Compare the uses of this verb in African American Vernacular English and Standard American English:

AFRICAN AMERICAN VERNACULAR	STANDARD AMERICAN
1. That my bike.	That's my bike.
2. The coffee cold.	The coffee's cold.
3. The coffee be cold there.	The coffee's (always) cold there.

As sentences 1 and 2 illustrate, African American Vernacular English permits *copula deletion*—omitting the verb *be* in the present tense in precisely those environments where Standard English permits a contracted form of it. As example 3 shows, speakers of African American Vernacular English express recurring or repeated action by using the form *be*. It may seem that *be* is equivalent to Standard American English *is*, but in fact *be* in sentences like 3 is equivalent to a verb expressing a habitual or continuous state of affairs. As African American linguist Geneva Smitherman wrote about sentences like 2 and 3, "If you the cook and *the coffee cold*, you might only just get talked about that day, but if *The coffee bees cold*, pretty soon you ain't gon have no job!"

Thus, in African American Vernacular English, the verb *be* (or its inflected variant *bees*) is used to indicate continuous, repeated, or habitual action. The following examples further illustrate this function.

AFRICAN AMERICAN VERNACULAR	STANDARD AMERICAN
Do they be playing all day?	Do they play all day?
Yeah, the boys do be messin' around a lot.	Yeah, the boys do mess around a lot.
I see her when I bees on my way to school.	I see her when I'm on my way to school.

Another feature of African American Vernacular English is its use of the expression *it is* where Standard American English uses *there is*.

AFRICAN AMERICAN VERNACULAR	STANDARD AMERICAN
Is it a Miss Jones in this office?	Is there a Miss Jones in this office?
She's been a wonderful wife and it's nothin' too good for her.	She's been a wonderful wife and there's nothing too good for her.

A final illustration of the distinctiveness of this ethnic variety is provided by these examples:

AFRICAN AMERICAN VERNACULAR	STANDARD AMERICAN
Don't nobody never help me do my work.	Nobody ever helps me do my work.
He *don't never* go *nowhere.*	He *never* goes anywhere.

The African American Vernacular English sentences contain more than one word marked for negation. In African American Vernacular English, multiple-negative constructions are well formed, as they are in several other varieties of American English. The fact that these constructions are not appropriate in Standard English has no effect on their grammaticality or appropriateness in other varieties.

CHICANO ENGLISH

Another important set of ethnic dialects of American English are the varieties of Latino or Hispanic English. Latino English appears in several closely related varieties in the United States. The most widespread and best known variety is Chicano English, which is spoken by many people of Mexican descent in the major urban areas of the country and in rural areas of the Southwest.

Chicano English and other varieties of Latino English have not yet been studied as thoroughly as African American Vernacular English, and so our knowledge of them is somewhat tentative. As with African American Vernacular English—and all other varieties of English—certain features of Chicano English occur in other varieties of English. In the case of Chicano English there are similarities to other varieties of Hispanic English, such as those spoken in the Cuban community of Miami and the Puerto Rican community of New York City. Chicano English—like the language used by any social group—is not a single variety but comprises many registers, which are used in different situations of use. Some characteristics of Chicano English doubtless result from the persistence of Spanish as one of the language varieties of the Hispanic American community, but it is important to recognize that Chicano English has become a distinct variety of American English and cannot be regarded as English spoken with a foreign accent. The reason is simple: Chicano English is acquired as a first language by many children and is the native language of hundreds of thousands of adults. It is a stable variety of American English, with characteristic patterns of grammar and pronunciation.

Among other well-known phonological characteristics of Chicano English is the substitution of *ch* [č] for *sh* [š], as in saying [či] instead of *she* [ši], [čuz] (homophonous with *choose*) for *shoes* [šuz], and [ɛspɛčəli] for *especially*. This feature is so distinctive that it has become a stereotype for Mexican Americans. There is also substitution of *sh* for *ch*, as in "preash" for *preach* and "shek" [šɛk], for *check* [čɛk], though this phenomenon seems not to be stereotyped. Other phonological characteristics of Chicano English are consonant cluster simplification, as in [ɪs] for *it's*, "kine" for *kind*, "ole" for *old*, "bes" for *best*, "un-erstan" [ʌnərstæn] for *understand*. Much of this can be represented in the phrase "It's kind of hard," which is pronounced [ɪs kɑnə hɑr] in Chicano English. Another major characteristic of the phonological system of Chicano English is the devoicing of /z/, especially in word-final position. Because of the widespread occurrence of /z/ in the inflectional morphology of English (plural and possessive nouns and third-person singular present-tense verbs), this salient characteristic is also stereotypical. Chicano English pronunciation is also characterized by the substitution of stops for the standard fricatives represented in spelling by *th*: [t] for [θ] and [d] for [ð], as in [tɪk] for *thick* and [dɛn] for *then*. Still another notable characteristic is the pronunciation of the morpheme *-ing* as [in] ("een") rather than as /ɪn/ ([ən]) or /ɪŋ/. Finally, perhaps the most prominent feature distinguishing Chicano English is its use of certain intonation patterns that often strike speakers of other dialects of American English as uncertain or hesitant.

Chicano English also has characteristic syntactic and lexical patterns. It often lacks the past-tense marker on verbs ending in the alveolars /t/, /d/, or /n/; thus "wan" for *wanted* and "wait" for *waited*. At least in Los Angeles, *either . . . or either* instead of *either . . . or*, as in *Either I will go buy one, or either Terry will* is sometimes heard. Another feature is the use of prepositions such as *out from* for *away from*, as in *They dance to get out from their problems*. As with African American Vernacular English and other varieties, Chicano English permits multiple negation (*Us little people don't get nothin'*).

It is important to reemphasize that some of the customary structures of Chicano English and African American Vernacular English are also characteristic of varieties of "mainstream" American English (including in some cases the standard varieties), as with consonant cluster simplification and multiple negation. What makes any variety salient is not a single characteristic feature but many characteristic features, some of which may also occur in other varieties. It is worth stressing that both African American Vernacular English and Chicano English occur in a number of varieties along a continuum of greater and lesser similarity to varieties of Standard American English.

SOCIOECONOMIC STATUS VARIETIES: ENGLISH, FRENCH, AND SPANISH

Less striking than regional and ethnic varieties, but equally significant, are the remarkable patterns of speech that characterize different socioeconomic status groups. In the discussion below, we describe some of the patterns that have been uncovered for the English spoken in New York City and in Norwich, England, as well as the French of Montreal and the Spanish of Argentina.

NEW YORK CITY

To illustrate the point, we report a well-researched example. New Yorkers sometimes pronounce /r/ and sometimes drop it in words like *car, fourth,* and *beer* (where /r/ follows a vowel and appears either at the end of a word or preceding another consonant). The presence or absence of this postvocalic /r/ does not change a word's referential meaning. The price of a "beer" and of a "beeah" in a given tavern is the same. A "cah pahked" in a red zone is ticketed as surely as a similarly "parked car." Taxi drivers with day-old "beards" and day-old "beahds" are equally in need of shaves. And whether you live in New York or "New Yoahk," you still have the same mayor (or "maya"). No difference in referential meaning is conveyed by pronunciations with or without /r/.

Still, the occurrence of /r/ in these words is anything but random and anything but meaningless. With a keen ear for variation, linguist William Labov hypothesized that /r/ pronunciations depended on social-class affiliation in New York and that any two socially ranked groups of New Yorkers would differ in their pronunciation of /r/. He predicted that members of higher socioeconomic status groups would pronounce /r/ more frequently than would individuals from lower socioeconomic classes.

To test his hypothesis, Labov investigated the speech of employees in three Manhattan department stores of different social rank: Saks Fifth Avenue, an expensive, upper-middle-class store; Macy's, a medium-priced, middle-class store; and S. Klein, a discount store patronized principally by working-class New Yorkers. He asked supervisors, sales clerks, and stock boys the whereabouts of merchandise he knew to be displayed on the fourth floor of their store. In answer to a question like "Where can I find the lamps?" he elicited a response of *fourth floor.* Then, pretending not to have caught the answer, he said, "Excuse me?" This elicited a repeated—and presumably more careful—utterance of *fourth floor.* Each employee thus had an opportunity to pronounce postvocalic /r/ four times (twice each in *fourth* and *floor*) in a natural and realistic setting in which language itself was *not* the focus of attention.

Employees at Saks, the highest-ranked store, pronounced /r/ more often than those at S. Klein, the lowest-ranked store. At Macy's, the middle-ranked store, employees pronounced an intermediate number of /r/s in *fourth floor.* Figure 11-14 presents the results of Labov's survey. The darker sections represent the percentage of employees who pronounced /r/ four times; the lighter sections above the darker area represent the percentage who pronounced /r/ one, two, or three times (but not four); employees who did not pronounce /r/ at all are not directly represented in the bar graph. As can be seen, 30 percent of the Saks employees pronounced all /r/, and an additional 32 percent pronounced some /r/. At Macy's, 20 percent pronounced /r/ four times, and an additional 31 percent pronounced some. At S. Klein, only 4 percent of the employees pronounced all /r/, with an additional 17 percent pronouncing one, two, or three /r/s. Labov's hypothesis about the social stratification of postvocalic /r/ seemed strikingly confirmed.

If you think about it, you may be able to propose other possible explanations for Labov's findings because factors other than socioeconomic status might have influenced the results of his survey, as Labov recognized. For example, if he spoke to more men than women in one store or to more stock boys than sales clerks, or more African Americans than whites, the difference in pronunciation of /r/ could have been the result of gender, job, or ethnic differences. To rule out the possibility that

Figure 11-14

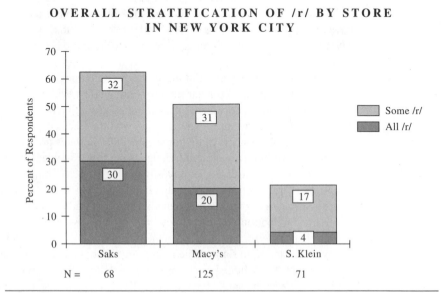

OVERALL STRATIFICATION OF /r/ BY STORE IN NEW YORK CITY

Source: Labov 1966

his findings reflected job, gender, or ethnicity, Labov examined pronunciation among the largest homogeneous group of respondents in his sample. As it happened, there were more white female sales clerks than any other single group, and looking at their pronunciations apart from those of everyone else would eliminate the possibility of findings skewed by gender, job, or ethnicity. The results, given in Figure 11-15, reveal an overall pattern of distribution similar to that for the whole sample of respondents. The white female sales clerks at Saks pronounced more /r/ than those at Macy's, who in turn pronounced more than those at S. Klein. Thus Labov ruled out the possibility that his findings reflected ethnic, gender, or in-store job differences.

In a third shuffling of the data, Labov sought to determine whether his hypothesis would hold in an even narrower range of social ranking than that across department stores. This time he examined the pronunciation of /r/ across the three occupational groups working in a single store. (He chose Macy's because it provided his largest sample.) Using the same hypothesis that predicted the ranking across the department stores, Labov predicted that he would find the highest percentage of /r/ pronunciation among the floorwalkers, least among stock boys, with an intermediate percentage among sales clerks. As Figure 11-16 shows, that is exactly what he found, and he concluded that postvocalic /r/ pronunciation is indeed socially stratified in New York City—that higher-ranking social groups pronounce more postvocalic /r/ than lower-ranking groups do.

Figure 11-15

STRATIFICATION OF /r/ BY STORE
FOR NEW YORK CITY WHITE FEMALE SALESCLERKS

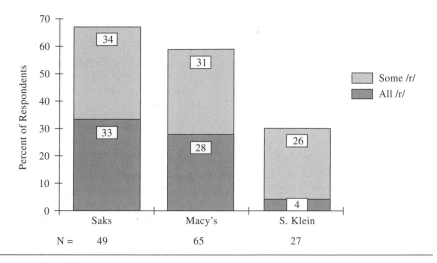

Source: Labov 1966

Figure 11-16

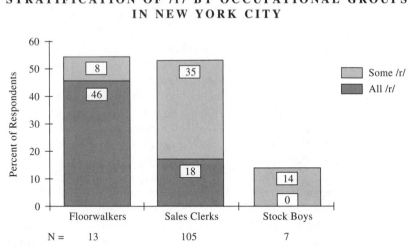

STRATIFICATION OF /r/ BY OCCUPATIONAL GROUPS IN NEW YORK CITY

Source: Labov 1966

Using his department store survey as a springboard, Labov undertook a very different kind of investigation. This time, equipped with detailed sociological descriptions of individual residents of Manhattan's Lower East Side, he spent several hours with each of about a hundred respondents there. As these New Yorkers discussed various topics, Labov tape-recorded the conversations. Labov's interviewing techniques prompted his respondents to use speech samples characteristic of different speech situations, a topic that we addressed in Chapter 10.

Besides postvocalic /r/, Labov examined *th* in words like *thirty, through,* and *with* (New Yorkers sometimes say *thirty* with /θ/ and sometimes "tirty" with /t/); and the *th* of words like *this, them,* and *breathe* (the infamous "dis," "dat," "dem," and "dose" words, which have the variants /d/ and /ð/). Labov also examined the alternate pronunciation of *-ing* words like *running* versus *runnin'* and *talking* versus *talkin',* which have /ɪŋ/ and /ɪn/ variants. (This alternation is often referred to as "dropping the g." But as you know from your study of phonetics in Chapter 3, the alternation is actually between an alveolar nasal /n/ and a velar nasal /ŋ/; there is no "g" to be dropped except in the spelling.) In addition, Labov examined the pronunciation of the vowels in the two word classes *coffee, soft, caught* and *bad, care, sag.*

In his interviews on the Lower East Side of Manhattan, Labov spoke with women and men, parents and children, African Americans and whites, Jews and Italians—a representative sample of Lower East Side residents. On the basis of extensive information available to him about their education, income, and occupation, he was able to assign each respondent to a socioeconomic status group. Using the education of the respondent, the income of the respondent's household, and the occupation of the principal household breadwinner as criteria, he placed individuals into one of four socioeconomic status categories, which he called lower class, working class, lower middle class, and upper middle class (see Figure 11-17). His findings reveal how pronunciation differences reflect aspects of American society in one major city. Such studies can provide the basis for generalizations that can help explain the social basis for linguistic variation.

As expected, upper-middle-class respondents exhibited more /r/ than lower-middle-class respondents, who in turn exhibited more than working-class respondents, who used more than lower-class respondents. Each group also pronounced more /r/ as attention paid to speech was increased in various styles. Through several graded speech registers—casual style, interview style, and reading styles—respondents in all socioeconomic groups increased the percentage of /r/ pronounced (much as you saw in Chapter 10 for the -*ing* variable).

Remarkably, Labov found that all the variables were socially stratified. The higher the socioeconomic status of an individual, the more likely that individual was

Figure 11-17

PERCENT OF -*ING* SUFFIX PRONOUNCED AS /ɪŋ/ BY FOUR SOCIOECONOMIC GROUPS IN NEW YORK CITY

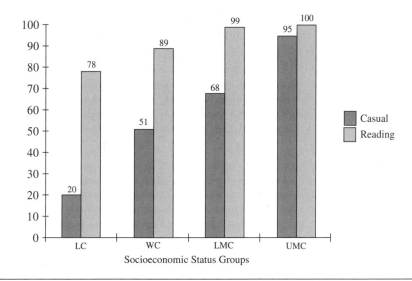

Socioeconomic Status Groups

Source of data: Labov 1966

to pronounce /r/. Each socioeconomic status group had characteristic patterns of pronunciation, and the percentage of pronunciation of the variants was ranked in the same way as the groups themselves. The upper middle class pronounced most /θ/ for *th* (as in *thing*), most /ð/ for *th* (as in *then*), most /ŋ/ (as in *running*), and most /r/ (as in *car*). The lower-class respondents pronounced fewest of these variants, while the lower middle class and working class fell in between, with the lower middle class pronouncing more than the working class. Such regular patterns of variation are remarkable, for they suggest that even subtle differences in social stratification can be reflected in language use. While it was common knowledge that differences existed in the language patterns of different social classes, no one had imagined such marked quantitative differences among very closely ranked socioeconomic groups.

The vowels were stratified in a similar way. The predicted difference in the use of vowels had to do with how high they were pronounced in the mouth. New Yorkers have several pronunciations of the first vowel in *coffee:* it ranges from the high back tense vowel [u] through the mid back vowel [ɔ] down to the low back vowel [ɑ]. (The last is more characteristic of the speech of much of the western and midwestern United States.) The vowel of words in the *bad* class also varies—from low front lax [æ] to high front tense [iᵊ] with an **offglide.** Higher socioeconomic status groups favored lower vowels in both cases.

Labov sorted the pronunciations into several discrete values depending on vowel height. (Needless to say, this required a very good ear, whose reliability was checked with acoustic phonetic equipment.)

NORWICH, ENGLAND

Curious about how widespread the kind of linguistic differentiation that Labov had found in New York might be among socially stratified groups, British linguist Peter Trudgill investigated the speech patterns of residents of Norwich, England. He found patterns strikingly similar to those of New York. In Norwich, variation in syntactic as well as phonological expression was correlated with the socioeconomic status of speakers. Trudgill divided his subjects into five groups: middle middle class (MMC), lower middle class (LMC), upper working class (UWC), middle working class (MWC), and lower working class (LWC). Figure 11-18 illustrates the distribution of one phonological feature, the alternation between final /n/ and /ŋ/ in the suffix *-ing*.

Data from both the New York City study (Figure 11-17) and the Norwich study (Figure 11-18) are given, as the comparison between the two cities is revealing. The patterns of distribution for socioeconomic status are strikingly parallel in the two cities. Each successively higher socioeconomic status group pronounces more /ŋ/ than the group immediately below it in status. To put it most generally, the higher the socioeconomic status of a group, the less frequently it pronounces *-ing* as /ɪn/ and the more frequently as /ɪŋ/.

The patterns of variation shown above are not limited to English-speaking communities. Similar variation across socioeconomic status groups is known to exist for speakers of Continental and Canadian French, Latin American Spanish, Brazilian

Figure 11-18

PERCENT OF *-ING* SUFFIX PRONOUNCED AS /ɪŋ/ BY FIVE SOCIOECONOMIC GROUPS IN NORWICH, ENGLAND

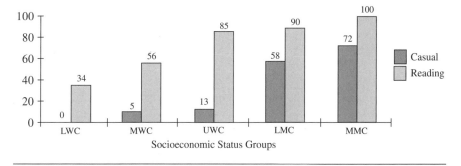

Source of data: Trudgill 1996

Portuguese and several other languages. We provide illustrations from a French-speaking and a Spanish-speaking community.

MONTREAL, CANADA

In Montreal, French speakers vary the pronunciation of pronouns and definite articles. Except in the word *le,* /l/ is sometimes pronounced and sometimes omitted in personal pronouns such as *il* 'he' and *elle* 'she' and articles (and pronouns) like *les* 'the (plural),' and *la* 'the (feminine).' (See Table 2-11, p. 60.) In the usage of two occupational groups, professionals and laborers, the laborers consistently omitted /l/ more frequently than the professionals did, as shown in Figure 11-19 for four such words.

ARGENTINA

Spanish speakers show similar patterns of phonological variation. In Argentina, to cite one example, speakers sometimes delete /s/ before pauses (as in English, /s/ is a common word-final sound, occurring on plural nouns and on several verb forms). In a study of six Argentinian occupational groups, the percentage of /s/-deletion was greatest in the lowest-status occupations and least in the higher-status occupations, as shown in Figure 11-20, where the lowest ranking group is I and the highest VI.

On the basis of evidence from these and other studies, parallel patterns of distribution may be expected for phonological variables wherever comparable social structures are found. Morphological and syntactic variation also exist, though evidence about variation at these levels of the grammar is scanty. What holds true of variation in English, French, and Spanish doubtless holds true of communities speaking other languages as well, although here too evidence is scanty.

Figure 11-19

PERCENT OF /l/-DELETION IN MONTREAL FRENCH FOR TWO OCCUPATIONAL GROUPS

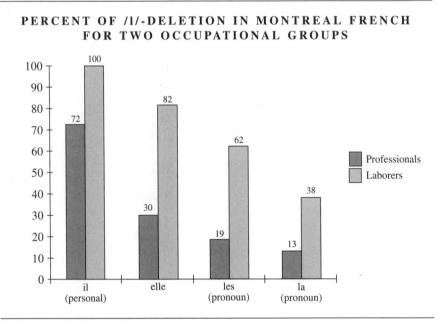

Source of data: Sankoff and Cedergren 1971

Figure 11-20

PERCENT OF PREPAUSAL /s/-DELETION IN ARGENTINE SPANISH FOR SIX OCCUPATIONAL GROUPS

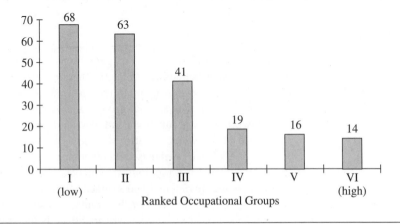

Source of data: Terrell 1981

THE LANGUAGE VARIETIES OF WOMEN AND MEN

It is well known that for many languages, in many speech communities, women and men don't speak identically. In American speech communities, for example, certain words that are closely associated with women may "sound" feminine as a result of that association. Adjectives like *lovely, darling,* and *cute* may carry feminine associations, as do words that describe precise shades of color like *mauve* and *chartreuse.* Likewise (though decreasingly so these days), certain four-letter words may surprise some people when uttered by a woman. Comedians Joan Rivers and Mo'Nique have capitalized on some of these gender differences, shocking audiences by their use of taboo words generally associated with male rather than female speakers.

In some languages, the differences between women's and men's speech are more dramatic than in English. In Japanese, even the first-person pronoun meaning 'I' differs for female and male speakers in informal situations: women use *atasi,* men *boku.* In French, *je* is the first-person pronoun for men and women alike, but because adjectives are marked for gender agreement, *Je suis heureux* 'I am happy' identifies a male speaker, while *Je suis heureuse* identifies a female speaker.

Among the Koasati Indians of Louisiana, women and men use different forms of certain indicative and imperative verbs. For example, men use /s/ instead of the nasalization characteristic of women in some verbs, as in (1) and (2) below; and men sometimes add /s/ where the women's form ends in a vowel plus consonant, as in (3) and (4).

GENDER DIFFERENCES IN KOASATI

	WOMEN	MEN	
1	lakawwã	lakawwás	'he will lift it'
2	kã	kás	'he is saying'
3	lakáw	lakáws	'he is lifting it'
4	íp	íps	'he is eating it'
5	ót	óč	'he is building a fire'

In some cases, the forms used by women are more conservative than those used by men, reflecting older forms of Koasati usage. When the research reported here was conducted sixty years ago, only middle-aged and elderly women used women's forms. (A more recent study of Koasati suggests that socially prominent women also use "male" speech forms—see Kimball [1987].) Younger women were using forms identical to those of men. (One older man reported that the forms of the older women sounded better to him!) In Koasati culture, both men and women are familiar with the forms used by the other; when stories are told the characters in the stories speak the forms characteristic of men or women as appropriate, no matter who is telling the story. Moreover, when Koasati parents correct the speech of their children, fathers may correct daughters and mothers may correct sons. Thus there is no taboo on men using women's forms or women using men's forms. Similar striking differences between the language of men and women occur in Creek and Hitchiti (other languages of the Muskogean family), Yana (a California Indian language), Siouan, and certain Eskimo languages, as well as in Carib and other South American Indian languages.

Outside the Americas, reports of striking differences between gender varieties have been made for Chukchee (spoken in Siberia) and for Thai. In polite Thai conversation between men and women of equal rank, women say *diĉʰàn* while men say *pʰŏm* for the first-person singular pronoun. Thai also has a set of particles used differently by men and women, especially in formulaic questions and responses such as 'thank you' and 'excuse me.' The polite particle used by men is *kʰráp,* while women use *kʰá* or *kʰâ*. Because these politeness particles occur frequently in daily interaction, speech differences between men and women can be quite marked in Thai, despite the fact that very few words are so differentiated.

There are also more subtle differences between men's and women's speech, the kinds of quantitative variation between the sexes that we saw between other social groups. For example, in Montreal, where professionals delete /l/ from articles and pronouns less frequently than laborers, there is a systematic difference between men and women in the pronunciation of these same words. As illustrated in Figure 11-21, men delete /l/ more frequently than women. This is true for *il* (personal, as in *il chante* 'he sings'), *elle,* and the pronouns *les* and *la*.

Figure 11-21

PERCENT OF /l/-DELETION IN MONTREAL FRENCH FOR WOMEN AND MEN

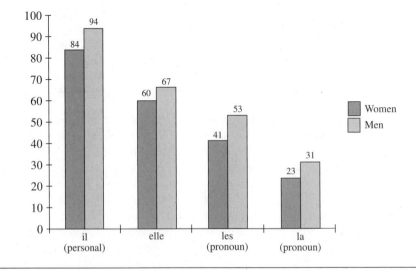

Source of data: Sankoff and Cedergren 1971

Patterns where women delete sounds less than men appear also in New York City and Norwich. In these cities, when higher social classes behave linguistically in one way to a greater extent than lower social classes, women tend to behave like the higher social classes to a greater extent than men do.

In English, besides the lexical differences between the sexes, there are more subtle differences, which can go largely unnoticed. One study by Fischer examined the pronunciation of the -*ing* suffix in words like *running* and *talking*. In a semirural New England village, the speech patterns of a dozen boys and a dozen girls between the ages of three and ten were studied. Even in such young children, all but three kids used both alveolar [n] and velar [ŋ] pronunciations of -*ing*. Interestingly, twice as many girls as boys showed a preference for the /ɪŋ/ forms. The figures are given in the table.

PRONUNCIATION OF -*ING* BY 12 BOYS AND 12 GIRLS IN A NEW ENGLAND VILLAGE

	PREFERENCE FOR /ɪŋ/	NO PREFERENCE FOR /ɪŋ/
GIRLS	10	2
BOYS	5	7

The finding that girls and boys differ in this way may seem surprising, since girls and boys in this New England village (as generally in Western societies) are in frequent face-to-face contact with each other. The separation in the communication channels suggested earlier as the important motivating factor in the differentiation of speech patterns does not appear to be the right explanation in this case. What then is the explanation for such differences between the speech of boys and girls? One hypothesis suggested by a number of researchers is the "toughness" characteristic associated with working-class life styles combined with the "masculinity" characteristic associated with the /ɪn/ forms. In other words, an association between masculinity and alveolar pronunciations /ɪn/ may outweigh the associations with prestige and higher socioeconomic status that otherwise accompany the /ɪŋ/ variant. What this analysis shows is that gender differences in language have little to do with (biological) sex and a lot to do with (social) roles.

MASCULINITY AND THE TOUGHNESS FACTOR

There's evidence for the prestige of *running* and *talking* pronunciations over pronunciations that "drop the g." Here are two facts: 1. English speakers who use both variants (that's virtually all of us) "pronounce the g" more often when we're in situations of greater formality; 2. social groups with higher socioeconomic status pronounce it more than lower status groups. Interestingly, girls and women use the *-ing* pronunciation more than boys and men do. One explanation for that may be that women are more status conscious than men—sociologists have found that to be the case in other arenas, so it wouldn't be surprising. But linguists suggest an additional reason. Think of it as the "Toughness Factor." Boys and men may associate pronunciations like *runnin'* and *talkin'* with working-class "toughness"—and that connection apparently outweighs any link to prestige. You could say that preferring the less prestigious pronunciation marks "masculinity." Now, you might object that using the term "masculinity" to explain the linguistic behavior of boys and men seems to beg the question. After all, what's gained by calling a pronunciation "masculine" just because men use it more than women? Well, masculinity and femininity are not the same thing as male

and female. Sex differences (male and female) are biological, and language differences don't reflect biology. Instead, they reflect the sociocultural phenomena of *gender*—what it *means* to be male or female. You're aware of gender differences marked by clothing, hair length, body decoration, and such things as jewelry use. ("Wear some earrings, for God's sake," Emma Thompson's character in "The Winter Guest" is told by her mother after she's cut her hair short. "Let folks know you're a woman!") So you shouldn't be surprised that language also reflects the important social identity of gender roles. It will be interesting keeping an eye and ear out for how much the ongoing efforts to equalize gender roles in Western societies also mute differences between masculine and feminine pronunciations and other patterns of speech!

WHY DO STIGMATIZED VARIETIES PERSIST?

It is no secret that some language varieties carry prestige, while others are stigmatized. Whereas the degree of stigma depends on the group making the judgment, norms of evaluation are often shared throughout a speech community, and one wonders why stigmatized varieties don't die out. Why don't speakers give them up for more prestigious varieties?

The explanation seems to lie in the fact that one's identity—as a woman or man, as an American or Australian, as a member of a particular ethnic or socioeconomic group—is tied into the speech patterns of that group. Americans talk like other Americans; Australians like Australians; men like men; and women like women. While one's sex is not a matter of choice, one's gender is, at least to some extent. What is considered masculine and feminine is a cultural, not a biological, matter, and one can choose to behave in more or less masculine or feminine ways irrespective of one's sex. To change the way you speak is to signal changes in who you are or how you want to be perceived. For a New Yorker transplanted to California to start speaking like a Californian is to relinquish some identity as a New Yorker. To give up speaking African American Vernacular English is to relinquish some identity as an

African American. To give up working-class speech patterns acquired in childhood is to take on a new identity. In short, to take on new speech patterns is to reform oneself and present oneself anew.

Language is perhaps the major symbol of our social identity, and we have seen how remarkably fine tuned to that identity it can be. Language is not set apart from social identity and social alliances. If you wish to identify with "nonnative" regional, socioeconomic, or ethnic groups and have sufficient contact with them, your speech will come to resemble theirs. In fact, socially mobile individuals have been shown to exhibit pronunciation patterns more like the group toward which they are heading than like the group of current affiliation; this is true not only of individuals moving up the socioeconomic scale but also of those whose paths are pointing lower.

We can illustrate with a telling investigation of linguistic and social identity on Martha's Vineyard. On this island off the coast of Massachusetts, the vowels /ay/ and /aw/ have two principal variants, with the first element of each diphthong alternating between [a] and [ə]. Words like *night* and *why* are sometimes pronounced with [ay] and sometimes with a more centralized [əy], while words like *shout* and *how* are pronounced with [aw] or the more centralized [əw]. These phonological variants are not typical dialect features; they do not reflect gender, ethnicity, or socioeconomic status. Rather, on Martha's Vineyard, vowel centralization represents identity with traditional island values—with the island and its life. The up-island residents have more centralization than do the residents in sections catering to summer visitors. Most interestingly, young men intending to leave the island and lead their lives on the mainland have the least centralization, while the greatest centralization was shown by a young man who had moved to the mainland but returned to Martha's Vineyard. Thus the centralized diphthongs represent a rejection of mainland values and a positive view of the values of island life.

The important symbolic value of one's language variety cannot be overestimated. In evaluating oral arguments in Britain, speakers of regional varieties rated the quality of an argument higher when presented in standard accent, but found the same argument more persuasive when it was made using a regional accent.

It is easy for one group of speakers higher on the socioeconomic ladder to ask about a group of speakers lower on the ladder, "Why don't they start talking like us?" The answer is simple: their social identity is different, and they do not necessarily share the values of the higher socioeconomic groups. Some insight can be gained by thinking about gender dialects, in which the situation is less complicated. Though there have been stirrings of neutrality recently, most people still agree that everyone is entitled to a gender dialect. It is perfectly acceptable for women to speak like women and men to speak like men. Imagine men asking women to speak like them in order to get ahead in "a man's world." Imagine a woman head of a company asking her truck drivers to speak more like women to get ahead in "a woman's world." These are patently unacceptable (though not unimaginable) scenarios. Women's and men's speech patterns are equally acceptable. Rough equality of status is granted to most regional varieties. Imagine a Bostonian moving to Atlanta and being told by the boss to "lose" the New England accent in order to succeed. The employee might rightly infer that the Boston origin, not the Boston accent, was at issue.

When it comes to ethnic and social-class varieties, perceptions are quite different. The widely held view is that African American Vernacular English and Chicano English and the dialects of lower socioeconomic status groups cannot be employed at schools or in the professional workplace. These views reflect language attitudes; as such, they are social, not linguistic, biases, and they are partly based on attitudes toward speakers, not speech!

In study after study, language has been shown to be a central factor in a person's identity. Asking people (asking *you*) to change their (change *your*) customary language patterns is not like asking them (asking *you*) to try on different sweaters; it is asking people to take on a new identity and to espouse the values associated with speakers of a different dialect. One principal reason that nonstandard varieties are so robust, so resistant to the urgings of education, is that all vernacular language varieties are deeply entwined with the social identities of their speakers and with the values of the social groups speaking them.

COMPUTERS AND THE STUDY OF DIALECT

 Given the mass of both quantitative and qualitative data represented in our discussion of dialects, it should be no surprise that computers are being used increasingly to help dialectologists accomplish their goals. Researchers are digitizing the kinds of data that in the past have been manually represented as on most of the maps in this chapter. For example, researchers for the Linguistic Atlas of the Middle and South Atlantic States (LAMSAS) have used a program called MapInfo to plot longitude and latitude coordinates for the residences of all 1,162 LAMSAS informants. That will enable maps of various sizes and degrees of detail to represent features that were elicited from the informants. You have also seen in Figures 11-10 and 11-11 the use of computers in generating nontraditional maps for dialectology.

In addition to a wide variety of tasks that have enlisted computers for activities related to maps, the kinds of resources that corpora make available to researchers interested in language variation across social groups are beginning to revolutionize the study of all types of dialects, especially national, regional, social, and gender dialects. A huge project called the International Corpus of English ("ICE"), begun in 1990, aims to provide texts totaling about one million words of written and spoken English of the 1990s from each of twenty centers around the world representing the English spoken in the Caribbean, Fiji, Ghana, Hong Kong, India, Kenya, Nigeria, the Philippines, and Singapore, to mention only some. The texts of these corpora will be tagged and annotated, making their use in dialect comparisons extremely valuable. The first of the ICE corpora to be made available—the one for Great Britain—was released in 1998.

In earlier chapters we described the LOB Corpus of British writing published in 1961 and the Brown Corpus of American writing published in 1961. A number of studies have examined the vocabulary in these matched corpora (as well as in corpora of spoken British and American English). Based on the linguistic features defining the involved/informational dimension (described in Chapter 10, page 352) and represented in Figure 10-4, written American English is more "involved" than the corresponding British registers. That means that on average written American English contains a greater frequency of certain features (those of set A on page 352—first- and second-person pronouns, *that* omission from subordinate clauses, contractions, and so on) while British writing shows more frequent use of other features (those of set B on page 352—nouns, prepositions, longer words, lexical variety, and so on). Studies have also compared the English of Australia and New Zealand. No doubt a good many more such comparative studies will be undertaken when the resources of ICE are fully developed and accessible.

In this chapter in our discussions of phonological variation across dialects we have focused chiefly on consonants, but vowels too vary, as even a glance at a transcription of Southern American English makes clear (as in Exercise 11-5b of this chapter, for example). Well, in at least one case, vowels proved useful in keeping an innocent person out of jail. Computers were used to help analyze the quality of vowel characteristics in tape recordings that contained illegal speech acts—in this case, threatening. A caller had telephoned a major airline with a serious threat of violence. Workers who heard the call thought they recognized the voice as that of a disgruntled former fellow employee. A computer analysis of the vowel quality of the caller showed that his dialect was not the same as that of the former employee.

SUMMARY

- When separated physically or socially, people who otherwise would share speechways come to speak differently. Given sufficient time and separation, distinct languages can arise.

- Conversely, the speech of people talking as members of the same community can develop in unison, even tending to merge in some situations.

- There are important linguistic differences among social groups of speakers within every speech community.

- Linguistic forms can vary greatly from one social group to the next, and social groups may be defined in a number of ways besides regionally.

- A social group may differ from the rest of the community in ethnicity or in socioeconomic status.

- Females and males may also be thought of as belonging to different social groups, called gender groups.

- If we combine these different group distinctions, we obtain a complex picture of the composition of society: within a particular ethnic group, we find socioeconomic classes whose members are male or female. Dialect differences support such social identities.

- Whatever the social group, its language variety will typically exhibit characteristics that distinguish it from the language varieties of other social groups.

- The linguistic markers that characterize social varieties may also serve as markers (or symbols) of group membership.

- When an African American man wants to stress his membership in his ethnic group, he may exaggerate the African American Vernacular English features in his speech.

- If a woman wants to appear particularly feminine, she may choose to exhibit features associated with women's speech and avoid "masculine-sounding" expressions.

- Individuals can take advantage of socially marked language characteristics for their own purposes.

EXERCISES

Based on English

11-1. Distinguish between an accent and a dialect, and between a dialect and a language. What is meant by a "language variety"? Does it make any sense to say of a language variety that "it isn't a language, but *only* a dialect"?

11-2. Examine a copy of a newspaper or magazine published in Britain (one or more of the following should be available in your library's periodicals room: *The Times, The Economist, Punch, The Spectator, The Listener*) and list as many examples of differences between American and British English as you can notice on two pages. Include examples of words, syntax, spelling, and punctuation. Can you identify any examples of discourse differences?

11-3. Which of the following words are you familiar with? Make two lists: one consisting of those words you normally use and the other consisting of words you don't use but have heard others use. With what regional or national group do you associate the words you have heard others use but don't use yourself? Compare your judgments with those of your classmates.

dragonfly   darning needle, mosquito hawk, spindle, snake feeder, snake doctor
pancake   fritter, hotcake, flannel cake, batter cake
cottage cheese   curds, curd cheese, clabber cheese, dutch cheese, pot cheese
string beans   green beans, snap beans
earthworm   night crawler, fishing worm, angle worm, rain worm, red worm, mud worm
lightning bug   firefly, fire bug
baby carriage   baby buggy, baby coach, baby cab, pram

11-4. The following questions are part of the questionnaire used in gathering data for *DARE*. After you answer each question, compare your answers with those of your classmates. Do you and your classmates agree on the regions in which the particular variants are used? (Volume I of *DARE* provides maps for answers to each of the questions.)

a. What names are used around here for:
(1) the part of the house below the ground floor?
(2) a container for coal to use in a stove?
(3) a small stream of water not big enough to be a river?
(4) a round cake of dough, cooked in deep fat, with a hole in the center?

(5) an oblong cake cooked in deep fat?

(6) a piece of cloth that a woman folds over her head and ties under her chin?

(7) the common worm used as bait?

(8) vehicles for a baby or small child, the kind it can lie down in?

b. What expressions do you have around here for:

(1) someone who is confused or mixed up, as in "So many things were going on at the same time that he got completely__"?

(2) someone who seems to be very stupid—"He doesn't know__"?

(3) a very skilled or expert person (for example at woodworking)—"He's a__"?

How do the answers of your classmates to the last question in group a compare with Figure 11-22, a map from *DARE* for *baby buggy?*

Figure 11-22

DARE MAP FOR *BABY BUGGY*

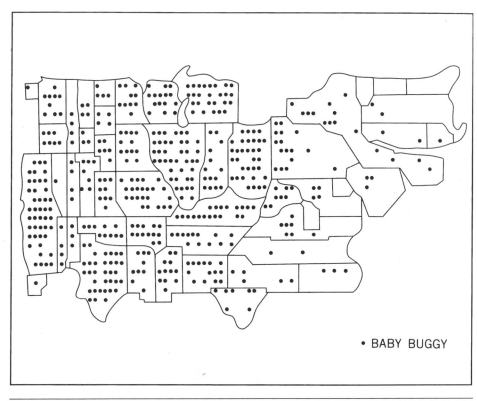

• BABY BUGGY

Source: Dictionary of American Regional English, vol. I, 1985

11-5. a. Below are the opening words of a presentation by a college teacher to a group of Southern teachers at a professional meeting. (You might wish to imagine it spoken with marked Southern pronunciations, as the teacher was born in the South and clearly wished to play upon those affiliations.)

"Years ago, during my first week in Wisconsin, I was asked by a fellow teacher, 'Do you mean they let *you* teach English?' The speaker was a Canadian with what I thought a very peculiar accent. Soon after that, a woman working on a degree in speech asked me with all the kindness and gentleness of which she was capable whether I would let her teach me how to talk right. If I had had her zeal and patience and kindness, I might very well have made the offer first, for I thought her speech highly unsatisfactory."

Provide answers to these six questions, most of which the teacher posed to her audience:

(1) Who should teach whom?
(2) What is the standard pronunciation in American English?
(3) Should education aim to make everybody sound like everybody else?
(4) Could training make everybody sound like everybody else?
(5) How then would everybody sound?
(6) Assuming uniformity could be achieved, how long could it last?

b. The same teacher reports that another southern teacher told her this:

[a: hæv dɪlɪbərɪtlɪ wəkt tu gɛt rɪd av ɪnɪ tresɪz av æksɪnt æz a: θɪŋk ɔwl ɛȷ̌əkɛtɪd pipəl šʊd du a: prad masɛf ðæt a: hæv nat wən hwɪt av ɪnɪ tresəbəl æksɪnt ɪn ma spič]

And a southern physician reported this to her:

[mɪnɪ av ma pəyšəns θɪŋk a: æm fram ðə nɔəθ bɪkɔwz æz ən eȷ̌əkɛtɪd pəsən a: don av kɔəs hæv ə səðən æksɪnt]

(1) Read the transcribed utterances of the teacher and physician aloud, and write them down using standard orthography.
(2) Make a list of six pronunciation features in these utterances that are characteristic of Southern American speech.
(3) Give the standard orthography for these words as pronounced in the same dialect:

[mɔwnɪn], [kaəd], [kent], [hɛp], [spikɪn], [həyd], [mɪnɪ], [bɪnɪfɪt].

c. Now answer these questions:

(1) Why do many people believe that they speak *without* an accent?
(2) What would it mean to speak without an accent? (Think globally as well as nationally: what would it mean to speak without an American or British or Australian accent?)

(3) Provide a list of four regional features of *your own* pronunciation that others perhaps have called to your attention.

[Slightly adapted from Jane Appleby, "Is Southern English Good English?" In David L. Shores and Carol P. Hines, eds., *Papers in Language Variation* (University: U of Alabama P, 1977), p. 225.]

11-6. What was Labov's hypothesis about the distribution of /r/ in New York City department stores? In your city or town, are there three socially ranked stores that could be similarly investigated? Which two or three phonological features do you expect to be socially differentiated in your stores? Design a question for each feature that would uncover the data needed to test your hypothesis. (Make the question a natural one for the kind of store you have in mind.) Would you ask your respondents to repeat their answers as Labov did? Explain why or why not.

11-7. "William Labov . . . once said about the use of black English, 'It is the goal of most black Americans to acquire full control of the standard language without giving up their own culture.' . . . I wonder if the good doctor might also consider the goals of those black Americans who have full control of standard English but who are every now and then troubled by that colorful, grammar-to-the-winds patois that is black English. Case in point—me."

So wrote a twenty-one-year-old African American college sophomore in *Newsweek* (Dec. 27, 1982, p. 7). The student cites several features of African American Vernacular English such as those described in this chapter.

a. Look up the meaning of *patois* in your desk dictionary and note the connotations it carries in referring to particular language varieties. Would you characterize those connotations as positive or negative? What does the phrase "grammar-to-the-winds" suggest about the writer's attitude toward the grammaticality of African American Vernacular English?

b. What features of African American Vernacular English do you think the writer means in calling it a "grammar-to-the-winds patois"?

c. What would be the implications for communication if any speech variety were indeed "grammarless"? Give two reasons why African American Vernacular English cannot accurately be called a "grammar-to-the-winds" dialect.

d. What would you assume to be the reason for the writer's judgments about and attitudes toward African American Vernacular English? What might you explain to the student about patterns of language in every variety and about the status of particular varieties *in terms of their linguistic features?*

11-8. Comment on the validity of the quotation that follows, and explain your view: "If there were as many oil barons coming up from Mexico as there are farm laborers, the accents of Pancho Villa might sound more musical to American ears." [William F. Mackey in Cobarrubias and Fishman (1983), p. 186]

11-9. Describe two ways in which the speech of women and men differs in greetings, threats, swearing, and promises. What do you think accounts for these differences? Do you think the differences are increasing or decreasing? Explain the bases for your answers.

11-10. In order to indicate a direct quotation, writers typically use quotation marks. In imitation of those visible marks, speakers sometimes gesture with their hands. Sometimes, too, speakers say *quote unquote* as a form of voiced quotation marks. Among many functions of the word *like* in English, it is used by certain speakers to mark the beginning of a direct quotation. Here are two examples of this so-called quotative *like:*

And then she's like, "I don't want to go."
So he's like, "But you promised!"

To complete this exercise, you will need natural data from the speech of your acquaintances. Collect twenty or more naturally occurring examples of quotative *like* from the speech of at least five people. As soon as you can after hearing them, write down the examples exactly as they were spoken, taking care not to call attention to the speech of your acquaintances or the fact that you are observing their language use. Relying on five-year ranges (15–19, 20–24, and so on), note the approximate age of every speaker you set out to observe (whether or not they actually use quotative *like*). Once you've collected your data, answer the questions:

(1) In both examples above, quotative *like* is preceded by the verb *be*. In your collected examples, which other verbs, if any, precede *like?*

(2) Some researchers call this feature "quotative *be like*" because their data indicate that this use of *like* generally occurs with the verb *be,* as in the examples above. Explain whether or not your data would lend support to using the alternative name.

(3) Identify the tense (past or nonpast) of the verbs that precede quotative *like* in your data. Identify the time (present, past, or future) that the verbs refer to. (Keep in mind that tense and time are not the same phenomena.)

(4) In both the examples given above, the verb form has been contracted to *'s*. What fraction of your examples show a similar contraction?

(5) In both the examples above, the subject of *be* in the quotative *like* clauses are pronouns (*he, she*). What categories are the subjects in your examples?

(6) Grouping your speakers into five-year age ranges, identify which age groups use this feature and which do not. Then make a hypothesis about whether use of this feature is age related.

(7) Compare your findings about use and age with the findings of some classmates, and reconsider your hypothesis in light of the pooled data.

(8) Do you think younger users will continue using quotative *like* as they get older (that would make it an example of language change in progress) or

that they will not continue using it beyond a certain age (that would make it an age-graded feature)?

(9) When collecting your data, did you note any examples that you now recognize as representing uses of *like* other than the quotative, leaving aside its use as a preposition (*He looks like his dad*), subordinating conjunction (*Winstons taste good like a cigarette should*), or verb? If so, analyze those uses and try characterizing them; what name(s) might suit them?

(10) What other expressions have you heard that function like quotative *like?*

INTERNET AND OTHER RESOURCES

- **American Dialect Society: http://www.et.byu.edu/~lilliek/ads/index.htm**
  This Web site contains information about the century-old ADS, including a special page for student members. It also provides links to pages for *DARE*—the *Dictionary of American Regional English*—and for the various Linguistic Atlas projects sponsored by the American Dialect Society. As of September 1997, some of the Atlas pages were not completed, but there is plenty at this Web site to keep a student of American dialects enjoyably busy for hours.

- **The Empirical Linguistics and Linguistic Atlas Page:**
  http://hyde.park.uga.edu/
  An ambitious Web site that aims to provide information about the nine Linguistic Atlas projects in the United States. As of the date of publication, however, the only Atlas project well represented is LAMSAS—the Linguistic Atlas of the Middle and South Atlantic States (ranging from New York to northern Florida and including West Virginia and Pennsylvania). Information about the other Atlas projects was still under construction at the time of this book's publication, but there is plenty about the LAMSAS project to make a visit to the Web site worthwhile.

- **The Organization of Dialect Diversity in America:**
  http://www.ling.upenn.edu/phono_atlas/ICSLP4.html
  This site presents a paper by William Labov, a leading analyst of American English dialects. The paper contains—and the site reproduces—maps from The Phonological Atlas of North America, which reflect patterns of linguistic dialect change.

- **Linguist List's Topic Page on Ebonics:**
  http://linguist.emich.edu/topics/ebonics/
  The Linguist List is the major discussion list among linguists for issues of general interest. Ebonics was such a popular topic in 1996 and 1997 that the list managers decided to collect all the information it has on the topic at one site.

- **Phonological Atlas of North America:**
  http://babel.ling.upenn.edu/phono_atlas/home.html
  This page reflects the latest research into phonological change in the dialects of North America. The Phonological Atlas of North America is a creation of the Telsur Project at the Linguistics Laboratory at the University of Pennsylvania. Telsur

is a telephone survey of the major urban areas of the United States and Canada. The page offers very interesting maps treating change in progress and the urban dialect areas of the United States based on an acoustic analysis of vowel systems.

- **Ebonics Information Page: http://www.cal.org/ebonics/**
  Maintained by the Center for Applied Linguistics, this is a rich page, full of valuable discussion and analysis of African American Vernacular English and issues related to Ebonics.

- **Survey of English Usage: http://www.ucl.ac.uk/english-usage/**
  At this site you can find information about the International Corpus of English, especially the million-word British contribution.

Video and Audio Recordings

The videos listed below are informative and well worth viewing. Some are readily available in libraries and video rental outlets. All of them can be purchased through one of several educational video suppliers, such as Insight Media (http://www.insight-media.com). Though now dated, Linn and Zuber (1984) offers a handy discography of language recordings.

- **American Tongues** This award-winning video treats regional accents from Boston to Texas, with a focus on the speech of some very engaging teenagers. Entertaining and informative.

- **Communities of Speech** In this video Walt Wolfram and Deborah Tannen debate issues as they examine the concept of standard American English and other American dialects.

- **Black on White** From the BBC's *Story of English* series narrated by Robert MacNeil; explores the origins and spread of African American Vernacular English.

SUGGESTIONS FOR FURTHER READING

- **John Baugh. 1985.** *Black Street Speech: Its History, Structure, and Survival* (Austin: U of Texas P). This accessible book offers excellent treatment of various features of African American Vernacular English. The chapters are organized by level of grammar: phonology, morphology, syntax, and so on.

- **Craig M. Carver. 1987.** *American Regional Dialects: A Word Geography* (Ann Arbor: U of Michigan P). This handsome book is an up-to-date overview of American English dialects, emphasizing their cultural and historical origins; contains good maps and accessible discussion.

- **Frederick Cassidy, ed. 1985—.** *Dictionary of American Regional English* (Cambridge, MA: Belknap P). The most comprehensive treatment of American regional vocabulary. Three of a projected four volumes have been published.

- **W. Nelson Francis. 1983.** *Dialectology: An Introduction* (New York: Longman). An excellent introductory treatment. Contains maps of the United States and United Kingdom and relates American dialect features to their British origins.

- **Arthur Hughes and Peter Trudgill. 1996.** *English Accents and Dialects: An Introduction to Social and Regional Varieties of English in the British Isles.* 3rd ed. (London: Arnold). As the title indicates, this book is particularly good on pronunciation and pays little attention to features of lexicon or grammar. Includes discussion of the English of Belfast, Dublin, and Edinburgh. A cassette containing edited interviews with speakers from twelve regions of Britain is available, and those edited interviews are transcribed in the book.

- **Rosina Lippi-Green. 1997.** *English with an Accent: Language, Ideology, and Discrimination in the United States* (New York: Routledge). An excellent introduction to the facts and myths surrounding the discussion of accent and other aspects of dialect in the United States.

- **Salikoko S. Mufwene, John R. Rickford, Guy Bailey and John Baugh, eds. 1998.** *African American English: Structure, History and Use* (New York: Routledge). Ten excellent chapters by the editors and other distinguished researchers analyze the structure and use of African American English. Chapters treat phonology, lexicon, grammar, and discourse, as well as the history and use of African American English. Here you can find out what linguists and anthropologists think of Ebonics, the Oakland school district resolution, obscenity, hip-hop and Ice-T.

- **Joyce Penfield and Jacob L. Ornstein-Galicia. 1985.** *Chicano English: An Ethnic Contact Dialect* (Amsterdam: Benjamins). One of a very few treatments of Chicano English, this book is reasonably accessible to interested beginners.

- **K. M. Petyt. 1980.** *The Study of Dialect: An Introduction to Dialectology* (London: Andre Deutsch). With an emphasis on British dialects and other dialects of Europe, this book complements the treatment in this chapter.

- **Deborah Tannen. 1994.** *Gender and Discourse* (New York: Oxford UP). Discusses differences between the sexes in conversational practices and includes a chapter on ethnic style in male-female conversation.

- **Peter Trudgill. 1990.** *The Dialects of England* (Cambridge, MA: Blackwell). An up-to-date treatment of traditional and modern dialects in England; contains thirty-four maps.

- **Peter Trudgill. 1996.** *Sociolinguistics: An Introduction to Language and Society,* rev. ed. (New York: Penguin). A very basic and accessible short treatment.

- **Peter Trudgill and J. K. Chambers, eds. 1991.** *Dialects of English: Studies in Grammatical Variation* (New York: Longman). Contains twenty-two treatments of grammar in various dialects of America, Australia, Canada, Scotland, and especially England.

- **Walt Wolfram. 1991.** *Dialects and American English* (Englewood Cliffs, NJ: Prentice-Hall). The best introduction to dialects of the USA.

Advanced Reading

Hudson (1996), Wardhaugh (1998), and Fasold (1984, 1990) discuss dialects generally. Scherer and Giles (1979) is a collection of essays that treat the linguistic marking of social categories such as gender, social class, and ethnicity. The data and discussion of convergence in Kupwar reported in this chapter are based on Gumperz and Wilson (1971). Labov (1972a) is a frequently cited description of African American Vernacular English. Other treatments of African American Vernacular English include Smitherman (1977), from which some of the examples in the chapter are taken. From Labov (1966, 1972b) come the New York City and Martha's Vineyard data, from Trudgill (1996) the Norwich data, from Sankoff and Cedergren (1971) the Montreal French data, from Terrell (1981) the Spanish data, from Biber (1987) the observations on British/American differences. On the sociolinguistics of French, see Ager (1990) and Sanders (1993); on German, Barbour and Stevenson (1990) and Clyne (1984).

Ferguson and Heath (1981) is a collection of essays describing language use among Native and other Americans: Filipinos, Puerto Ricans, Jews, Italian Americans, French Americans, German Americans, African Americans, and others. Kurath (1972) is a thorough analysis of the methods and some of the findings of dialect geography, with emphasis on American English (and its roots in England) but with attention to Romance and Germanic languages as well. A brief introduction to American English dialects can be found in Reed (1977), with a number of maps, mostly of the Great Lakes states and the Northwest. The principal findings of American dialect geographers on the East Coast can be found in Kurath (1949), Atwood (1953), and Kurath and McDavid (1961). See Allen (1973–1976) for the Upper Midwest, Pederson (1986–1991) for the Gulf states, Bright (1971) for California and Nevada, Atwood (1962) for Texas. Recent work that takes advantage of computers is illustrated and discussed in Kretzschmar et al. (1993) for the Middle and South Atlantic states and more generally in Kretzschmar and Schneider (1996).

The relationship between language and the sexes is treated in Smith (1985); Thorne, Kramarae, and Henley (1983) provide an overview of research on this topic in the preceding decade, a number of individual studies, and a lengthy annotated bibliography. The data in this chapter on gender differences in Koasati and Thai come from Haas (1940), who also discusses Chukchee. Fischer (1958) reports the New England *-ing* data cited in this chapter. Philips et al. (1987) is a collection of essays examining women's and men's speech in a cross-cultural perspective and looking at gender differences in the language of children. Coates and Cameron (1988) is a collection of provocative perspectives on language and gender; Johnson and Meinhof (1997) is a collection of thoughtful essays on masculine sociolinguistics that address power, conversation, gossip, expletives, and other topics. Holmes (1995) asks whether women are more polite than men and answers the question thoroughly and interestingly. Ochs (1992) relates language and gender through social activities, social stances, and social acts. The relationship between language and social identity is treated in Edwards (1985). Routledge publishes a series of accessible "practical introductions to the sociolinguistics" of various languages: for French, see Ball (1997); for Spanish, Mar-Molinero (1997); for German, Stevenson (1997).

REFERENCES

- Ager, Dennis. 1990. *Sociolinguistics and Contemporary French* (Cambridge: Cambridge UP).

- Allen, Harold B. 1973–1976. *The Linguistic Atlas of the Upper Midwest,* 3 vols. (Minneapolis: U of Minnesota P).

- Atwood, E. Bagby. 1953. *A Survey of Verb Forms in the Eastern United States* (Ann Arbor: U of Michigan P).

- Atwood, E. Bagby. 1962. *The Regional Vocabulary of Texas* (Austin: U of Texas P).

- Ball, Rodney. 1997. *The French-Speaking World: A Practical Introduction to Sociolinguistic Issues* (New York: Routledge).

- Barbour, Stephen, and Patrick Stevenson. 1990. *Variation in German* (Cambridge: Cambridge UP).

- Biber, Douglas. 1987. "A Textual Comparison of British and American Writing." *American Speech* 62:99–119.

- Bright, Elizabeth S. 1971. *A Word Geography of California and Nevada* (Berkeley: U of California P).

- Chambers, J. K., and Peter Trudgill. 1980. *Dialectology* (Cambridge: Cambridge UP).

- Clyne, Michael. 1984. *Language and Society in the German-Speaking Countries* (Cambridge: Cambridge UP).

- Coates, Jennifer, and Deborah Cameron, eds. 1988. *Women in Their Speech Communities* (London: Longman).

- Cobarrubias, Juan, and Joshua A. Fishman, eds. 1983. *Progress in Language Planning: International Perspectives* (Berlin: Mouton).

- Edwards, John. 1985. *Language, Society and Identity* (New York: Blackwell).

- Fasold, Ralph W. 1984. *The Sociolinguistics of Society* (New York: Blackwell).

- Fasold, Ralph W. 1990. *The Sociolinguistics of Language* (Cambridge, MA: Blackwell).

- Ferguson, Charles A., and Shirley Brice Heath, eds. 1981. *Language in the USA* (Cambridge: Cambridge UP).

- Fischer, John L. 1958. "Social Influences on the Choice of a Linguistic Variable," *Word* 14:47–56; repr. in Hymes 1964, pp. 483–488.

- Francis, W. Nelson. 1961. "Some Dialectal Verb Forms in England," *Orbis* 10:1–14; repr. in Juanita V. Williamson and Virginia M. Burke, eds., *A Various Language: Perspectives on American Dialects* (New York: Holt), pp. 108–120.

- Gumperz, John J., and Robert Wilson. 1971. "Convergence and Creolization: A Case from the Indo-Aryan/Dravidian Border in India," in Dell Hymes, ed., *Pidginization and Creolization of Languages* (Cambridge: Cambridge UP), pp. 151–167.

- Haas, Mary R. 1940. "Men's and Women's Speech in Koasati," *Language* 20:142–149; repr. in Hymes 1964, pp. 228–233.

- Holmes, Janet. 1995. *Women, Men and Politeness* (London: Longman).

- Hudson, R. A. 1996. *Sociolinguistics,* 2nd ed. (Cambridge: Cambridge UP).

- Hymes, Dell, ed. 1964. *Language in Culture and Society* (New York: Harper & Row).

- Johnson, Sally, and Ulrike Hanna Meinhof, eds. 1997. *Language and Masculinity* (Oxford: Blackwell).

- Kimball, Geoffrey. 1987. "Men's and Women's Speech in Koasati: A Reappraisal," *International Journal of American Linguistics* 53:30–38.

- Kretzschmar, William A., Jr., Virginia G. McDavid, Theodore K. Lerud, and Ellen Johnson, eds. 1993. *Handbook of the Linguistic Atlas of the Middle and South Atlantic States* (Chicago: U of Chicago P).

- Kretzschmar, William A., Jr., and Edgar W. Schneider. 1996. *Introduction to Quantitative Analysis of Linguistic Survey Data: An Atlas by the Numbers* (Thousand Oaks, CA: Sage).

- Kurath, Hans. 1949. *A Word Geography of the Eastern United States* (Ann Arbor: U of Michigan P).

- Kurath, Hans. 1972. *Studies in Area Linguistics* (Bloomington: Indiana UP).

- Kurath, Hans, and Raven I. McDavid, Jr. 1961. *The Pronunciation of English in the Atlantic States* (Ann Arbor: U of Michigan P).

- Labov, William. 1966. *The Social Stratification of English in New York City* (Washington, DC: Center for Applied Linguistics).

- Labov, William. 1972a. *Language in the Inner City* (Philadelphia: U of Pennsylvania P).

- Labov, William. 1972b. *Sociolinguistic Patterns* (Philadelphia: U of Pennsylvania P).

- Linn, Michael D., and Maarit-Hannele Zuber. 1984. *The Sound of English* (Urbana, IL: National Council of Teachers of English).

- Marckwardt, Albert H. 1957. "Principal and Subsidiary Dialect Areas in the North-Central States." *Publications of the American Dialect Society* 27.

- Mar-Molinero, Clare. 1997. *The Spanish-Speaking World: A Practical Introduction to Sociolinguistic Issues* (New York: Routledge).

- Ochs, Elinor. 1992. "Indexing Gender," in Alessandro Duranti and Charles Goodwin, eds., *Rethinking Context* (Cambridge: Cambridge UP), pp. 335–358.

- Pederson, Lee. 1986–1991. *Linguistic Atlas of the Gulf States*, 7 vols. (Athens: U of Georgia P).

- Philips, Susan U., Susan Steele, and Christine Tanz, eds. 1987. *Language, Gender, and Sex in Comparative Perspective* (Cambridge: Cambridge UP).

- Reed, Carroll E. 1977. *Dialects of American English,* rev. ed. (Amherst: U of Massachusetts P).

- Sanders, Carol, ed. 1993. *French Today: Language in its Social Context* (Cambridge: Cambridge UP).

- Sankoff, Gillian, and Henrietta Cedergren. 1971. "Some Results of a Sociolinguistic Study of Montreal French," in R. Darnell, ed., *Linguistic Diversity in Canadian Society* (Edmonton: Linguistic Research), pp. 61–87.

- Scherer, Klaus R., and Howard Giles, eds. 1979. *Social Markers in Speech* (Cambridge: Cambridge UP).

- Smith, Philip M. 1985. *Language, the Sexes and Society* (Oxford: Blackwell).

- Smitherman, Geneva. 1977. *Talkin and Testifyin: The Language of Black America* (Boston: Houghton Mifflin).

- Stevenson, Patrick. 1947. *The German-Speaking World: A Practical Introduction to Sociolinguistic Issues* (New York: Routledge).

- Terrell, Tracy D. 1981. "Diachronic Reconstruction by Dialect Comparison of Variable Constraints," in David Sankoff and Henrietta Cedergren, eds., *Variation Omnibus* (Edmonton: Linguistic Research), pp. 115–124.

- Thorne, Barrie, Cheris Kramarae, and Nancy Henley, eds. 1983. *Language, Gender and Society* (Rowley, MA: Newbury House).

- Wardhaugh, Ronald. 1998. *An Introduction to Sociolinguistics,* 3rd ed. (New York: Blackwell).

CHAPTER 12

WRITING

—

INTRODUCTION

—

"Writing is the single most important sign system ever invented on our planet," a linguist has recently claimed. Whereas the ability to speak arose hundreds of thousands of years ago as part of our intellectual developments during evolution, writing was invented quite recently. Humans have been able to represent language in written form for a mere five or six thousand years. Though language underlies both spoken and written communication, the two modes are fundamentally different in nature. For one thing, speaking developed in human beings naturally, but writing had to be invented. For another, speaking has been with us for hundreds of millennia, writing for only a few. In every society, every ordinarily healthy human being knows how to speak; writing, on the other hand, is an advanced technology, even a luxury, and it is not a luxury possessed by everyone.

Writing has become second nature to most members of literate societies, so much so that it colors much of our thinking about language itself. Elementary school students, asked how many vowels there are, will commonly respond "five," and cite <a>, <e>, <i>, <o>, <u>—and, some will add, sometimes <y>. In terms of speech, this reply misses the mark, but it demonstrates that when some people talk of *vowels* it is almost second nature to think of *letters* of the alphabet. Commonly, in literate societies people ostensibly speaking of "language" say things that are appropriate only to writing but not to speech. This is perhaps not surprising in most Western societies, where language is first discussed objectively in schools, whose primary linguistic goal is to teach children literacy—to teach them to master the *written* word. Because the spoken word often plays only an incidental role in education, from an early age it is writing that comes to be the salient focus of our linguistic analysis.

In Chapter 10 we examined certain grammatical relationships between spoken and written registers. In this chapter we examine the history of writing and the development of different types of writing. As will become apparent, our knowledge about the history of writing is uneven. We have a reasonably good understanding of how writing has evolved over the centuries, but just how it was invented, and how many times, remains unclear. While we understand how spoken language and written language differ, just how such differences arise is open to discussion. Such unanswered questions, however, do not prevent us from marveling at the extraordinary human achievement that writing represents. More than being the single most important *sign system* ever invented on our planet, there are those who would claim that writing is the single most important invention in human history.

THE HISTORICAL EVOLUTION OF WRITING

—

Long before we developed writing, humans were producing graphic representations of the objects that surrounded us. The prehistoric records in the extraordinary cave paintings of Spain, France, and the Sahara Desert, which are between twelve thousand and forty thousand years old, bear witness to an age-old fascination with animals, hunters, and deities. In that they represent concepts rather than words, these paintings differ from writing. They are representations of real-life objects and not of the *words* that represent those objects. Writing, by contrast, is a system of visual symbols representing audible symbols.

Of course the drawings and paintings produced by prehistoric people contained the seeds of writing. At first, people would communicate by using drawings. In time, certain stylized representations of objects like the sun came to be associated with the *words* for those objects. Thus, to imagine an example, the drawing ☀, which originally represented the sun as an object or concept, could have come to be associated with the sound of the word *sun*—with [sʌn]. This association—between ☀ and the sound [sʌn]—was the first symptom of the birth of a writing system, in which a visual representation did not directly evoke a concept but evoked the *spoken word* for the concept. The stage was set for using such a visual symbol to represent other words that *sounded* the same. If we think of English, the symbol ☀ as a representation of the sun could be extended to represent the word *son* or the first part of *Sunday*. From a picture of an object, a written symbol of a *sound* is born.

THE LEAP FROM PICTURES TO WRITING

To use a *written* symbol to represent a sound is an extraordinary achievement. It is comparable to using a spoken symbol to represent a concept. To use a *symbol* to represent another *symbol* required a stunning leap of the imagination.

For all that, writing appears to have been invented several times in the course of human history. Still, it is not surprising that not all the world's great civilizations made the leap. For example, the Aztecs, technological geniuses of pre-Columbian Central America, developed intricate systems of drawings and symbols for calendars, genealogies, and history. An illustration of their **pictograms** is provided in Figure 12-1. (*Pictogram* comes from the Latin root *pictus* 'painted' and the Greek root *graphein* 'to write.') But the Aztecs may not have thought of using these pictograms to represent the sounds of spoken language. In any case, Aztec pictograms did not evolve into writing.

Today, the same impetus that gave rise to the first writing systems recurs so commonly that it is difficult to appreciate the breathtaking magnitude of that original imaginative leap that used a visual mark—a written symbol—not to represent an object itself but to represent another symbol, an oral symbol of the object. Writing thus involved a leap from primary to secondary symbolization.

A modest modern example of creative secondary symbolization occurs when automobile owners design their own license plates. The space limitations of license plates invite such secondary symbolization as "GR8" and "GR8FUL," "SK8ING" and "4GET IT," along with such inventive items as "C-SIDE," "7T YRS," and "PLEN-T," some of which have arisen because the traditional spellings of the words are too long or have been preempted by other license plates. A similar ingenuity now expressed in license plates (and in advertising) originally sparked what is arguably

Figure 12-1

AZTEC INSCRIPTION

Source: Gelb 1963 (from Eduard Seler, *Gesammelte Abhandlungen zur amerikanischen Sprach- und Alterthums-kunde*)

humanity's greatest invention, for once a visual symbol like <8> came to stand for an auditory symbol (the sound [et]), and not for the notion 'eight,' an alphabetic writing system was coming to life.

In what may have been the first instance, the leap of imagination that gave rise to writing took place around 3500 B.C. in Mesopotamia between the Tigris and Euphrates rivers in what is modern-day Iraq. Sometimes referred to as "the cradle of Western civilization," Mesopotamia (meaning 'between the rivers') was inhabited at the time by the Sumerians and the Akkadians. These peoples were city dwellers with a sophisticated economic system based on agriculture, cattle, and commerce. Exactly how the Sumerians and Akkadians invented writing will never be known, but we can surmise that the potential for secondary symbolization was discovered fortuitously as someone struggled to formulate a visible message for which no agreed-upon visual symbols existed.

As early as 3000 B.C. the Egyptians had developed a writing system of their own, and writing also appeared in the valley of the Indus (now in Pakistan and India) around 2500 B.C. Around 2000 B.C. the Chinese began using pictograms as symbols for words rather than concepts. By 1500 B.C. several of the world's most technologically complex civilizations had developed systems to commit spoken language to visual representation.

The most ancient inscribed stone tablets that have been found talk of cattle, sales, and exchanges. Thus the most extraordinary invention in human history may have arisen in response to the mundane task of recording commercial transactions. Gradually, over the centuries, our ancestors began exploring the world of possibilities opened by the invention of writing. Writing could be used to record important events in a way that was less likely to be forgotten or distorted than oral accounts. Dwellers of the ancient world also found that writing could be exploited to communicate across distances: you could write a letter and entrust it to a messenger, who would deliver it to its addressee. Letters were more confidential and secure than oral messages sent by messenger because they often could not be read by the messenger, and they could be sealed. The use of literacy as a recording tool and as a means to communicate at a distance could also be combined to build and maintain large states ruled by a central government, as the Mesopotamians and the ancient Chinese discovered. Laws could be recorded by those in command; orders could be transmitted to lower-echelon executives in faraway provinces; data on the citizenry could be stored and retrieved whenever needed. In short, a literate bureaucracy could function with an efficiency that could never be attained in a preliterate culture.

Of course, it took centuries for early societies to explore the avenues opened by the invention of writing. The ability to read and write does not automatically make a society more technologically developed, better equipped to become a bureaucratic state, or otherwise superior to a preliterate society. As recently as the Middle Ages, for example, the English had a basic suspicion of written land-sale contracts (because they could be tampered with), and the courts gave more credence to oral testimony if a land dispute arose. It took centuries for Europeans to discover that sentence boundaries could be marked with punctuation to ease reading and that book pages could be numbered to ease the task of retrieving information. Obviously, the fact that a particular society is literate does not necessarily mean that its members will exploit all the possibilities literacy offers. Sometimes strong social pressures prohibit writing down certain materials. For example, the Warm Springs Indians of Oregon regard any attempt to make written records of their traditional religious songs and prayers as offensive. For them, writing down these texts would violate their sacredness. Literacy opens novel ways of communicating and recording language, but whether or not these possibilities will be exploited depends in large part on a society's norms.

WRITING SYSTEMS

The writing systems that developed in ancient Mesopotamia, India, and China were fundamentally different from the writing system now used in Western societies. Ours is an *alphabetic* system based on the premise that one graphic symbol (a letter) should correspond to one significant sound in the language (a phoneme). The writing systems originally developed in the Middle East and Asia were based on a relationship not between graphs and individual sounds but between graphs and words or graphs and syllables. Though they developed at different times in history, all three types of writing—alphabetic, syllabic, and word writing—are still in use today.

SYLLABIC WRITING

When the dwellers of the ancient Middle East and Asia began developing their writing systems, they had at their disposal the earlier pictograms, which were symbols for objects and concepts. Rather than create an entirely new system of symbols, the inventors of writing modified these pictograms and used them to develop writing systems. The pictograms were not modified overnight, of course; their shapes gradually became more and more stylized in the process of becoming written symbols. Figure 12-2 illustrates the evolution of a number of symbols over time. Its left-hand column shows the original pictograms, which become more like writing as we proceed to the right. After many centuries of gradual evolution, the symbols illustrated in the right-hand column had become so stylized that they no longer bore any resemblance to the pictograms from which they originated.

The written symbols that the Sumerians and Akkadians had developed at that stage are called **cuneiform** symbols. *Cuneiform* means 'in the shape of a wedge' and

Figure 12-2

EVOLUTION OF CUNEIFORM WRITING FROM PICTOGRAMS

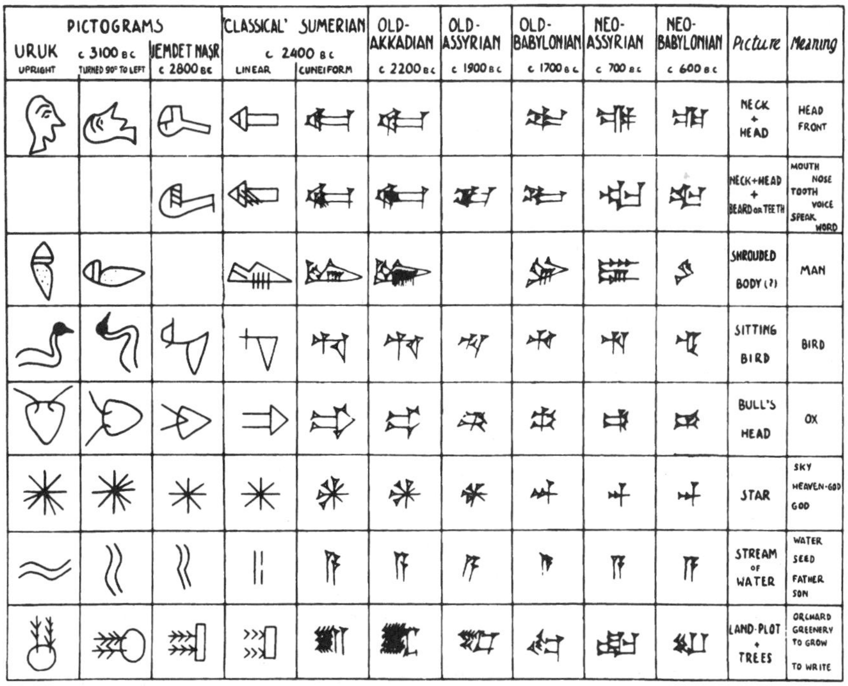

Source: Gaur 1984

refers to the peculiar form the symbols took. The ancient Mesopotamians were not familiar with paper, but clay from the Tigris-Euphrates river basin was readily available as a writing material. From the beginning, writing consisted of engraving marks pressed into soft clay tablets with a hard, sharp, pointed object called a stylus, typically a cut reed. Since it is difficult to draw curved strokes on clay with a stylus, the first written symbols consisted of various combinations of straight strokes.

Not only the shape but also the meaning of cuneiforms evolved from early pictograms. The pictogram that represented an arrow evolved into this cuneiform symbol for the Sumerian word /ši/ 'arrow.'

Sumerian scribes had difficulty finding appropriate symbols for more abstract notions. There was no modified pictogram for the word 'life,' for example. But the word for 'life' happened to be homophonous with the word for 'arrow,' much as the *bank* of a river and a financial *bank* are homophonous in English. Since finding a symbol for the concept 'life' was not an easy task, why not use the symbol for 'arrow'—seeing that 'arrow' and 'life' are both pronounced /ši/? It was through this extension of a symbol's representing a thing to its representing a sound that writing as we know it was invented.

Having solved that problem, the Sumerians recognized that the same symbol could also be used to represent the *syllable* /ši/ whenever it occurred in a word. For example, they started using it to represent the first syllable of the word /šibira/ 'blacksmith.' In due course, the cuneiform symbol lost its original association with the concept 'arrow' and became a symbol for the syllable /ši/ wherever that syllable occurred. Cuneiform writing is thus a **syllabic writing** system, in which graphic symbols represent whole syllables, not individual sounds as in an alphabet.

The process through which early pictograms evolved from being graphic symbols for concepts to being graphic symbols for syllables was a long and arduous one. Archaeological remains found in Mesopotamia indicate that for many centuries the Sumerians and the Akkadians used an extremely complex system in which some symbols were "ideograms," representing objects and concepts, while others were true writing, representing syllables. Even when all graphic symbols had come to represent syllables, the system was imperfect, because some graphs could represent different syllables depending on the word in which they were used, and several different graphs might represent the same syllable. Despite its imperfections, this system appears to have been used for centuries.

The Mesopotamian syllabic system may have been the model for several other systems. The ancient Egyptians, who had their own ideographic system, may have borrowed from the Sumerians and Akkadians the idea of representing spoken syllables with graphic symbols; in any case, around 3000 B.C. they began using their ideograms to represent different sound combinations. These Egyptian written symbols are the famous *hieroglyphics* (see Figure 12-3). Like cuneiform writing, hieroglyphic writing

Figure 12-3

EGYPTIAN HIEROGLYPHICS

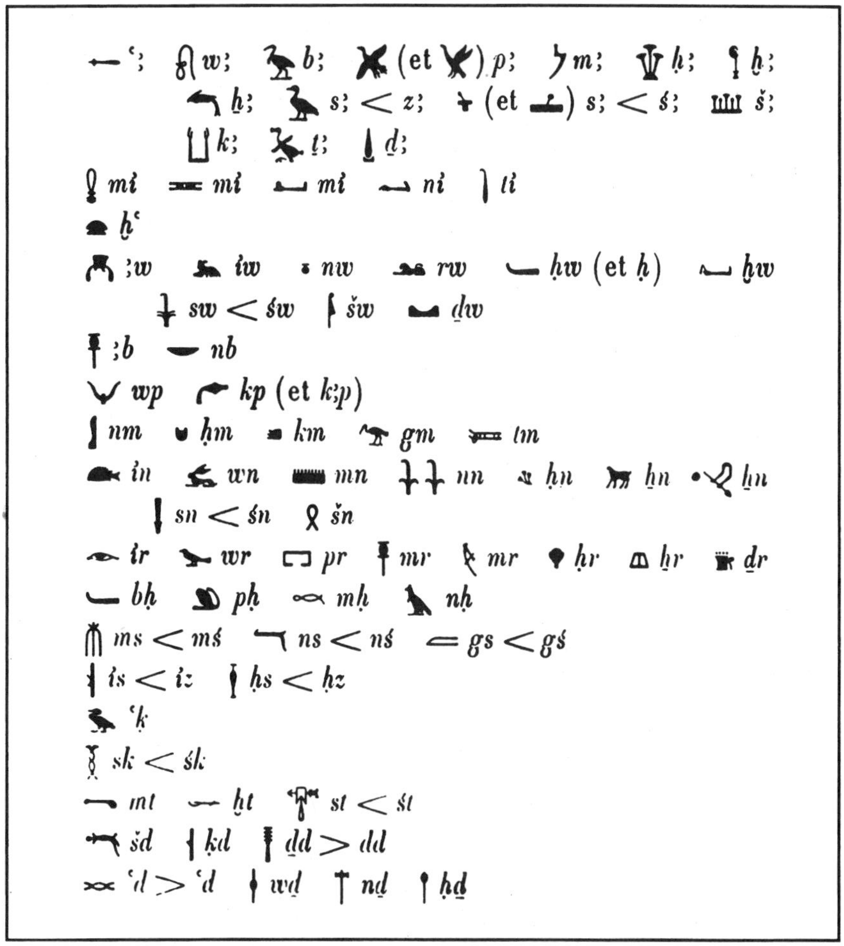

⏤ ʾ; 𒀳 w; ᴥ b; ✖ (et ✖) p; ⟩ m; ♕ h; ❘ ḫ;
🦆 ḥ; 🦅 s; < z; ✚ (et ⚊) s; < š; ⨎ š;
⊔ k; 🦅 ṭ; ❙ ḏ;

❘ mi ▭ mi ⏝ mi ⏤ ni ❘ ti
● ḥʿ

🦅 ʾw ▬ iw · nw ◆ rw ⏝ ḥw (et ḥ) ⏝ ḫw
✚ sw < šw ❘ šw ⏝ ḏw

❘ ʾb ⏝ nb

∨ wp ☛ kp (et kʾp)

❘ nm ● ḥm ▬ km ◆ gm ▭ tm

◄ in ◄ wn ▬ mn ♓ nn ◄ ḥn 🐖 ḫn ◆ hn
❘ sn < šn ꝯ šn

◄ ir ⟩ wr ▭ pr ❙ mr ◆ mr ● ḥr ▢ ḫr ▨ dr

⏝ bḥ ◆ pḥ ◆ mḥ 🦅 nḥ

⩜ ms < mš ⟩ ns < nš ⊏ gs < gš

❙ is < iz ❙ ḥs < ḥz

🦅 ʿk

🦅 sk < sk

⏤ mt ⏤ ḫt ♕ st < št

◄ šd ❙ ḳd ❙ ḏd > dd

✕ ʿḏ > ʿd ❙ wḏ ❙ nḏ ❙ ḥḏ

Source: Gelb 1963 (Because this figure comes originally from a French language source, the French word *et* [and] appears in several lines.)

was basically syllabic, and it had the same complexity and shortcomings as cuneiforms. Thus the hieroglyph for 'house' ▭ (third sign from the left in the thirteenth line of Figure 12-3) stood for several syllables in which the consonants /p/ and /r/ were coupled with any permitted vowel such as /per/ and /par/.

There is nothing inherently cumbersome in syllabic systems of writing. The difficulties of the Mesopotamian and Egyptian systems can be attributed to the fact that they continued to bear traces of their ideographic origins. Much later in history, an efficient syllabic system was devised by a Cherokee Indian named Sequoya. Its eighty-four symbols, shown in Figure 12-4, are based on the Latin alphabet, and they were used in the early part of the nineteenth century by both missionaries and Cherokee for writing the Cherokee language.

Another syllabic system devised around the same time by the Vai, an ethnic group of about twelve thousand people in western Liberia, is still in use. The Vai system has one graph for each of the approximately two hundred syllables in the language. This system is particularly well adapted to the Vai language, which has relatively few possible syllables. The Vai syllabary is given in Figure 12-5.

Syllabic writing is also used to represent various languages of India. Tamil, spoken in the southern tip of the subcontinent, is written with a syllabic system of 246 graphic symbols, given in Figure 12-6. The Tamil syllabic system is highly regular.

Figure 12-4

THE CHEROKEE SYLLABARY

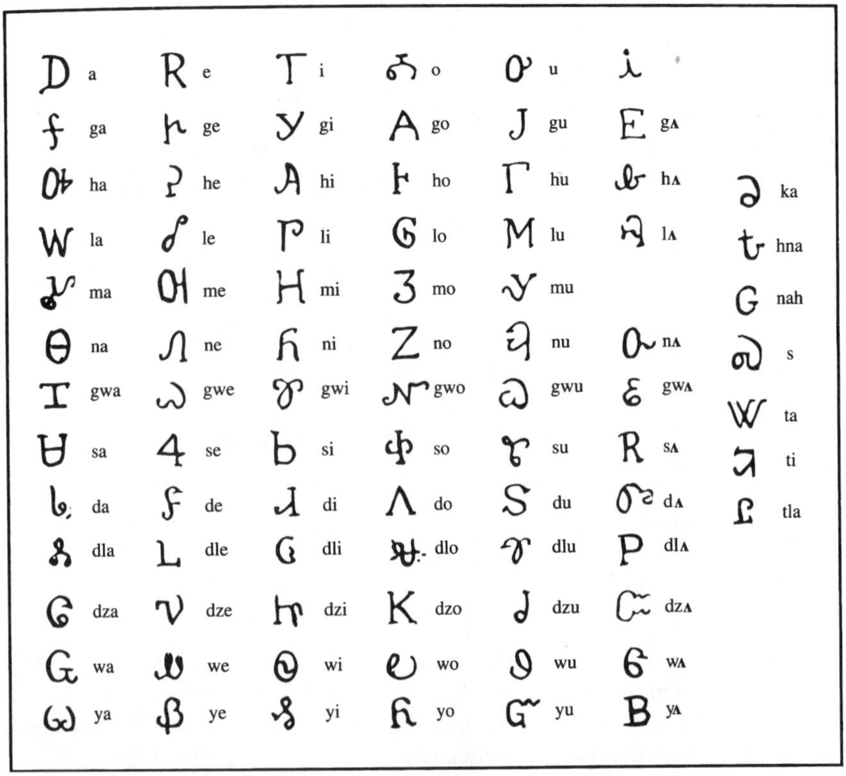

Source: H. A. Gleason. 1961. *An Introduction to Descriptive Linguistics*, rev. ed. (New York: Holt, Rinehart and Winston)

Figure 12-5

THE VAI SYLLABARY

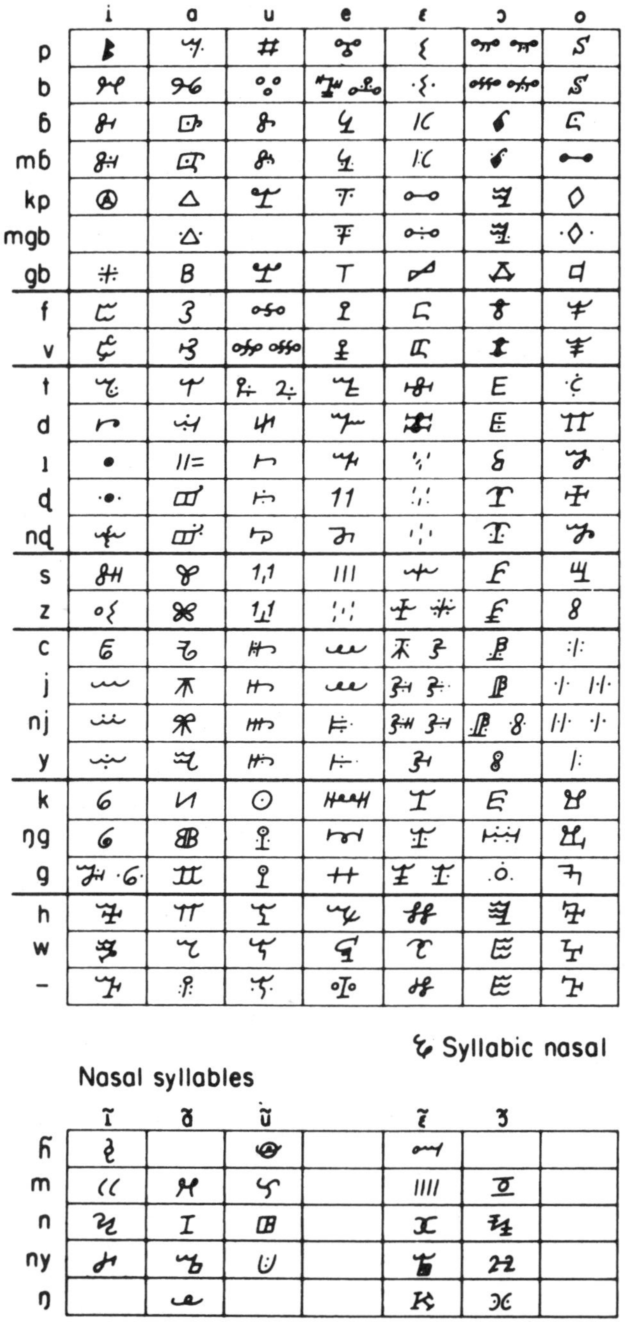

	i	a	u	e	ɛ	ɔ	o
p							
b							
ɓ							
mɓ							
kp							
mgb							
gb							
f							
v							
t							
d							
l							
ɖ							
nɖ							
s							
z							
c							
j							
nj							
y							
k							
ŋg							
g							
h							
w							
–							

ϟ Syllabic nasal

Nasal syllables

	ĩ	ã	ũ	ɛ̃	ɔ̃
ɦ					
m					
n					
ny					
ŋ					

Source: Sylvia Scribner and Michael Cole. 1981. *The Psychology of Literacy* (Cambridge: Harvard U P)

Figure 12-6

THE TAMIL SYLLABARY*

		அ a	ஆ a:	இ i	ஈ i:	உ u	ஊ u:
க்	k	க ka	கா	கி	கீ	கு	கூ
ங்	ŋ	ங ŋa	ஙா	ஙி	ஙீ	ஙு	ஙூ
ச்	ç	ச ça	சா	சி	சீ	சு	சூ
ஞ்	ɲ	ஞ ɲa	ஞா	ஞி	ஞீ	ஞு	ஞூ
ட்	ḍ	ட ḍa	டா	டி	டீ	டு	டூ
ண்	ṇ	ண ṇa	ணா	ணி	ணீ	ணு	ணூ
த்	t	த ta	தா	தி	தீ	து	தூ
ந்	n	ந na	நா	நி	நீ	நு	நூ
ப்	p	ப pa	பா	பி	பீ	பு	பூ
ம்	m	ம ma	மா	மி	மீ	மு	மூ
ய்	y	ய ya	யா	யி	யீ	யு	யூ
ர்	r	ர ra	ரா	ரி	ரீ	ரு	ரூ
ல்	l	ல la	லா	லி	லீ	லு	லூ
வ்	v	வ va	வா	வி	வீ	வு	வூ
ழ்	ṛ	ழ ṛa	ழா	ழி	ழீ	ழு	ழூ
ள்	ḷ	ள ḷa	ளா	ளி	ளீ	ளு	ளூ
ற்	r	ற ra	றா	றி	றீ	று	றூ
ன்	n	ன na	னா	னி	னீ	னு	னூ

*A dot beneath the phonetic representation indicates a retroflex sound (one in which the tip of the tongue is curled up and back, just behind the alveolar ridge). Note that there are two graphic symbols for /r/ and two for /n/.

Each vowel has two graphic representations in the syllabary. One is an independent graph used at the beginning of a word; the other is used when the vowel combines with a consonant elsewhere in a word. Thus, in initial position, /a:/ is represented by ஆ , but appears as ா when it combines with consonants as in /ka:/ கா , /ḍa:/ டா , /ta:/ தா . To represent a consonant sound alone, the graph used to represent that consonant as it appears with /a:/ is used, but a dot is placed above the symbol to mute the vowel. Thus, except for the dots, the graphs of the first column are identical to those of the second column. In the first row across the top of the syllabary are the written vowel symbols and their phonemic value; next to each graph of the first column is its

Figure 12-6 (Continued)

எ e	ஏ e:	ஐ ai	ஒ o	ஓ o:	ஒள au
கெ	கே	கை	கொ	கோ	கௌ
ஙெ	ஙே	ஙை	ஙொ	ஙோ	ஙௌ
செ	சே	சை	சொ	சோ	சௌ
ஞெ	ஞே	ஞை	ஞொ	ஞோ	ஞௌ
டெ	டே	டை	டொ	டோ	டௌ
ணெ	ணே	ணை	ணொ	ணோ	ணௌ
தெ	தே	தை	தொ	தோ	தௌ
நெ	நே	நை	நொ	நோ	நௌ
பெ	பே	பை	பொ	போ	பௌ
மெ	மே	மை	மொ	மோ	மௌ
யெ	யே	யை	யொ	யோ	யௌ
ரெ	ரே	ரை	ரொ	ரோ	ரௌ
லெ	லே	லை	லொ	லோ	லௌ
வெ	வே	வை	வொ	வோ	வௌ
ழெ	ழே	ழை	ழொ	ழோ	ழௌ
ளெ	ளே	ளை	ளொ	ளோ	ளௌ
றெ	றே	றை	றொ	றோ	றௌ
னெ	னே	னை	னொ	னோ	னௌ

phonemic value. You can readily see that one part of the symbol represents the consonant, the other part the vowel. Learning this system thus amounts to learning the different parts of symbols and the possible combinations between these different parts. One attractive feature of the Tamil system is its simplicity and regularity, which make it easy to learn.

Syllabic systems thus have the potential of being highly regular, with a one-to-one correspondence between syllables and graphs. Furthermore, the shape of the graphic symbols can be such that their pronunciation is retrievable from a decomposition of the graph into different parts. A regular syllabary like the Vai or Tamil systems is easily learned and simple to handle. Such a writing system is best adapted to languages that have a limited number of possible syllables. Syllabic systems can be economical, needing only as many symbols in a word as there are syllables.

LOGOGRAPHIC WRITING

Around four thousand years ago in China, a new writing system was developed that used symbols to represent *words,* not *syllables.* Such a **logographic writing** system differed fundamentally from the Sumerian-Akkadian syllabic system. Partly for this reason, it is believed that the Chinese did not borrow the idea of writing from the Mesopotamians but developed it on their own.

Like the ancient Middle Eastern syllabic writing, the Chinese logographic system originated in ideograms. From archaeological records, we know that ideograms like those in Figure 12-7 were used to represent objects and ideas such as 'cow,' 'river,' and 'below.'

Toward the end of the Bronze Age (around 1700 to 500 B.C.), these ideograms came to represent not concepts but words. Today, in the three characters (or logographic symbols) that denote the Modern Chinese words *niú* 'cow,' *chuān* 'river,' and *xià* 'below' (see Figure 12-8), we can recognize the ideograms that originally represented these three notions.

From a very early stage, ideograms were combined to represent abstract ideas and other notions that are difficult to represent graphically. Figure 12-9 (a), for example, is made up of two ideograms placed one on top of the other. The lower part represents a type of dish used in divination ceremonies; the upper part represents a tree upon which the divination dish was suspended. This complex ideogram was modified over the centuries to become a character that in Modern Chinese represents the word *gào,* which means 'to announce, to proclaim.' As Figure 12-9 (b) shows, the modern character with this meaning bears a striking resemblance to the ideogram from which it originates. Such similarities between modern-day characters and

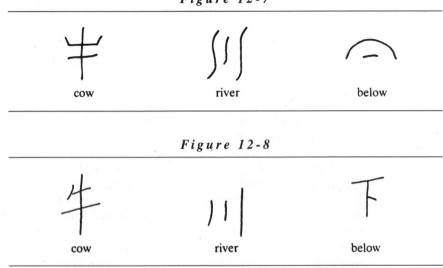

Figure 12-7

| cow | river | below |

Figure 12-8

| cow | river | below |

Figure 12-9

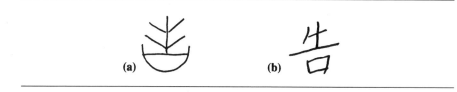

(a) (b)

ancient ideographs are few and far between. The shapes of most modern Chinese characters have lost all traces of the original ideograms from which they originated some three or four thousand years ago.

Modern Chinese Characters   In an ideal logographic system each word of the spoken language would be represented by a different graphic symbol. To a certain extent, the Modern Chinese system has this characteristic, in that a portion of its vocabulary is represented by individual characters, as illustrated by Figure 12-10.

Most modern Chinese characters can be decomposed into two elements. One is called the *radical* (or *signific*) and can sometimes hint at meaning. The other, of which there are many types, can sometimes give a clue to pronunciation and is known as the *phonetic*. Most radicals can also be used alone as characters, and some dictionaries are organized according to radicals, of which there are 214. The signific that traditionally corresponds to the character for the word *wéi* 'enclosure' occurs as the radical of many characters, some of which have a meaning related to 'enclosure' and some of which have little to do with the meaning of the radical (see Figure 12-11). In Modern Chinese, the radical for 'enclosure' is not used as an independent

character and has been replaced by the more complex character 圍 —which has the same meaning and pronunciation.

It is difficult to know exactly how many different characters the Chinese logographic system contains, just as it is virtually impossible to know how many words are in the lexicon of any language. It is estimated that you must be able to recognize about five thousand characters (and have a good command of spoken Chinese) in

Figure 12-10

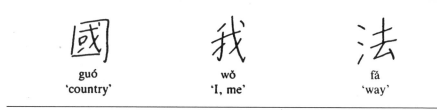

國	我	法
guó	wǒ	fǎ
'country'	'I, me'	'way'

Figure 12-11

囗	國	圖	園	固
wéi	guó	tú	yüán	gù
'enclosure'	'country'	'map'	'garden'	'obstinate'

order to read a Chinese newspaper. To read a learned piece of literature, you would need to be familiar with up to thirty thousand characters. Compared to the number of words needed for similar tasks in English, these numbers are relatively modest. The reason can be found in the morphological structure of Chinese. In Chinese, morphemes (which are always one syllable long) can combine with each other to form compounds that together denote a new idea whose meaning is more or less clearly related to the meaning of the parts. Of course, this is reflected by corresponding compounds in writing. The word for 'bicycle,' for example, is made up of three morphemes that together mean 'self-propelled vehicle'; the three characters corresponding to these three morphemes are used to represent 'bicycle' in writing. Similarly, the word for 'grammar' is a compound that means 'language rule' (see Figure 12-12).

Though compounding greatly reduces the number of characters needed in common use, learning to read and write the Chinese logographic system is still a formidable task, considerably more difficult and time consuming than learning the Vai or Tamil syllabary or the English alphabet. Bear in mind that since modern characters provide a reader little information as to the pronunciation or meaning of the words they represent, learning to read and write Chinese involves learning the shape of characters as well as their meaning and pronunciation. Though several transcription systems have been devised for Chinese (some of which use the Roman alphabet, others a type of syllabary), the logographic system continues to survive after nearly four thousand years.

Figure 12-12

自行車	語法
zi xíng chē	yǔ fǎ
'bicycle'	'grammar'

Why would such a seemingly impractical and complex system endure for so long, you might wonder. Well, not surprisingly, the Chinese logographic system has a number of important advantages. The first stems from the fact that though there are many homophonous words in Chinese, they usually have different written representations—as illustrated by the five characters in Figure 12-13, each of which represents a word that is pronounced [jīn]. Thus the Chinese character system provides a way of distinguishing in writing among different words that a syllabic system or an alphabet could not provide. (Compare the unusual distinction in English of homophones like *cite, site,* and *sight* or *read* and *reed* with the more common orthographic confusion between a river *bank* and a savings *bank*). A logographic system enables writers to compensate for homophony. This feature is especially advantageous for a language with as many homophonous words as Chinese.

The second major advantage of the Chinese logographic system is peculiar to the Chinese situation. The language that is called Chinese is a set of numerous spoken dialects, some of which are mutually intelligible, some not. Fortunately, for written communication all these dialects use the same set of characters. A character may be pronounced one way in one region of China and another way in another region, making spoken communication complicated, but the *meaning* of the character remains the same throughout that vast country. For example, the character 我 is read [wǒ] in the Beijing dialect, [gòa] in the Taiwan dialect, [wà] in the Minnan dialect (spoken in south China), [ŋə́] in the northwestern dialect of Shanxi, [ŋō] in the southern dialect of Hunan, and [ŋú] in the Shanghai dialect. In all dialects, it means 'I' or 'me.' Furthermore, since the syntax of most Chinese dialects is similar, any dialect can be more or less understood *in writing* (though not in speech) by speakers of a wide variety of dialects. The character system thus has a unifying force for a nation that comprises many ethnicities speaking so many different language varieties.

The Chinese logographic system thus meets two important objectives: the need to distinguish between homophones and the need to communicate across dialect boundaries. It is a system well equipped for the situation it serves, despite the difficulties involved in learning it and in managing the enormous variety of characters in arenas like computer processing and telegraphic communication.

Figure 12-13

斤	金	津	筋	襟
'hatchet'	'gold'	'ford'	'tendon'	'lapel'

In the course of history, many nations of the Far East have borrowed the Chinese logographic system. The Vietnamese modified certain Chinese characters to create their own writing system, which was essentially logographic as well. (Today the Vietnamese no longer use this system.) The Koreans and the Japanese borrowed the Chinese character system very early, and in time each developed several subsidiary systems. Koreans now write their language with the help of an alphabet and the original Chinese characters. Similarly, several systems are combined for use in modern Japan: two syllabic systems known as *hiragana* and *katakana* are used alongside Chinese characters, called *kanji* (a word borrowed from the Chinese compound *hànzì* 'character'). Both written Korean and written Japanese are curious in that symbols from different systems can appear within the same sentence and even within the same word. Today the Chinese remain the only people to make exclusive use of a logographic system.

ALPHABETIC WRITING AND ORTHOGRAPHY

An **alphabet** is a set of graphic symbols each of which represents a distinctive sound. Alphabetic writing thus differs from syllabic writing (whose graphs represent syllables) and from logographic writing (whose graphs represent words). In the view of some scholars, the first true alphabet was developed by the ancient Greeks from a North Semitic writing system that they had borrowed, probably from the Phoenicians, probably about 900 B.C. The claim that credits the Greeks with inventing the first true alphabet rests on one interpretation of how to evaluate the so-called consonantal scripts, which came into use in about 1700 B.C. Consonantal scripts are writing systems that represent only the consonants, not the vowels, of a language, and it was just such a script that the Greeks borrowed from the Phoenicians.

It is not surprising that a consonantal script should have been developed to represent Semitic languages. Recall from Chapter 2 that Semitic morphology builds upon tri-consonantal roots such as Arabic /k-t-b/. In languages like Arabic and Hebrew, vowels are interdigitated with tri-consonantal roots to produce words such as *kitaːb* 'book,' *kutub* 'books,' *kaːtib* 'writer,' and *kitaːba* 'writing'—all of which contain the same tri-consonantal root. The paramount role of consonants in such a system led, perhaps inevitably, to a consonantal script. The graphs used for writing Semitic languages can be viewed in one of two ways: as representing *only* the consonants (which would be a kind of alphabet, though lacking in vowel graphs) or as representing the consonants plus any vowel (which would be a kind of syllabary, albeit an unusual one). In the first view, a graph would represent a single consonant, say /k/; in the second view, the same graph would represent /k/ plus any permissible vowel: /ka/, /ki/, /ku/, and so on. The first view of consonantal writing would incline one to credit a Semitic origin of the alphabet. The second view would incline one to credit a Greek origin, for it was the Greeks then who viewed graphs as representing a single sound and therefore assigned specific symbols (those not needed to represent Greek consonants) for representing vowels. Whatever interpretation one is inclined to, it is clear that the Greeks definitely had a true alphabet and that around

600 B.C. the Romans borrowed it (via the Etruscans) and developed the basis of today's familiar Roman alphabet.

The Roman alphabet is not the only alphabet currently in use. The Greeks still use an alphabet of their own, as do the Russians, Ukrainians, Bulgarians, and Serbs. These alphabets are based on the same principles as the Roman alphabet, differing only in the shape of certain letters. The alphabet currently in use for Russian, called Cyrillic in honor of Saint Cyril, who devised it in the ninth century, is partly given in Table 12-1.

An alphabet is matched as closely as possible to the sound system of the language it must represent. The system used to achieve this match is the **orthography,** or spelling system. In an ideal orthography, each phoneme of the spoken language would be represented by a different graph, and each graph would represent only one phoneme. Spanish orthography comes close to this ideal: there is a virtual one-to-one correspondence between letters of the Roman alphabet and the phonemes of the language, and it is this match that students of Spanish have in mind when they say that in Spanish "every letter is pronounced." In contrast, English and French do not have anything close to a perfect match. As you saw in Chapter 4, the number of distinctive sounds in English includes twenty-four consonants and between fourteen

Table 12-1

THE CYRILLIC ALPHABET
AS USED IN MODERN RUSSIAN
(ONLY PRINTED LOWERCASE LETTERS SHOWN)

CYRILLIC LETTER	RUSSIAN PHONEME REPRESENTED	CYRILLIC LETTER	RUSSIAN PHONEME REPRESENTED
а	a	п	p
б	b	р	r
в	v	с	s
г	g	т	t
д	d	у	u
е	ye	ф	f
ё	yo	х	x
ж	ž	ц	ts
з	z	ч	č
и	i	ш	š
й	y	щ	šč
к	k	ы	ɨ
л	l	ь	(y)
м	m	э	є
н	n	ю	yu
о	o	я	ya

and sixteen vowels and diphthongs. With only twenty-six letters of the alphabet, English orthography falls short of an ideal one-sound/one-graph model. Because there are not enough letters to provide a symbol for each phoneme, some phonemes must be represented by a combination of letters (for example, the phoneme /i/ is represented by a double <e> in *meet*; the phoneme /θ/ is represented by the two letters <th> as in *thin*.) In addition, English pronunciation and orthography have not kept pace with one another over time, so that some words contain letters that no longer represent any sounds (like <k> and <gh> in *knight*). On the other side of the coin, a particular sequence of letters can represent a diverse spectrum of sounds, as <ough> does in the words *cough, tough, through, trough, though, thorough, bough,* and *hiccough.*

A common response to the chaos of the English orthography is to call for spelling reform, as George Bernard Shaw did early in the twentieth century. But for an international lingua franca like English, an orthography that genuinely attempted to represent pronunciation would have to sacrifice the uniformity that exists across national varieties. Spelling reform would raise other serious problems as well, having to do with the considerable morphophonemic variation of the language (which was treated at the end of Chapter 4). Recall that a word such as *photograph* in its normal phonological contexts has different stress patterns: [ˈforəgræf] versus [fəˈtʰɑgrəfər]. Compare the three vowels in *photograph* [o ə æ] with the first three in *photographer* [ə ɑ ə]. An orthography that attempted to represent actual sounds would be forced to represent the vowels of *photograph* and *photographer* differently, perhaps as "photagraeph" and "phataagraphar."

Because English has such complex morphophonemic alternations, the differences in the pronunciation of a given morpheme can be considerable, as with *photograph* and *photographer.* If an orthography were devised in which sounds and symbols were closely matched, the task of reading would be greatly complicated. While English does have a few words whose morphophonemic variants are represented orthographically (the [f]/[v] sounds of *wife* and *wives* are distinguished orthographically, but the contrast between [θ]/[ð] in *breath* and *breathe* is not), we'd have many more pairs and trios in which the spelling system would better represent pronunciations. Given their different pronunciations, we would even have to spell the plural inflection of *dogs* and *cats* differently, perhaps as <dogz> and <kats>, obscuring the fact that <z> and <s> represent the same morpheme. (Notice, of course, that English doesn't ignore the difference between /z/ and /s/ in general.) Similarly, the morpheme MUSIC would sometimes be spelled <muzak> (as in *musical*) and sometimes <muzish> (as in *musician*). By the same token, all homophonous words would be spelled alike, so that *wood/would, balm/bomb, sea/see, to/too/two,* and *quaffed/coifed,* could not be distinguished.

Advocates of English spelling reform thus tend to overlook the advantages of the current spelling system, which places a premium on morphological resemblance. Just as the Chinese logographic system is well adapted to the situation in which it functions, the Roman alphabet and English orthography are remarkably well adapted to English and its worldwide use.

DEVELOPING WRITING SYSTEMS
IN NEWLY LITERATE SOCIETIES

The twentieth century witnessed an astonishing increase in communications among regions, countries, and continents. Oceans and mountains, challenging obstacles only a hundred years ago, are now easily overflown. There is probably not a single inhabited area of the world that has had no contact with the outside. This is a remarkable fact, given that as recently as the 1950s large inhabited areas of Papua New Guinea, Amazonia, and the Philippines remained completely isolated from the rest of the world.

The consequence of this communications boom is that many people who had never seen writing a few decades ago are now literate. When a language is written down for the first time, a number of important questions arise: What kind of writing system should be used? How should the system be modified or adapted to fit the shape of the language and the needs of its speakers? Who makes these decisions?

Literacy has often been introduced to a people along with a new religion. For example, literacy was first imported into Tibet from India in the seventh century, the same time the Tibetans converted to Buddhism. Today literacy is commonly introduced to preliterate societies by Christian missionaries. What links religion and literacy is the fact that the reading of religious texts is an important doctrinal element of many religions. Because literacy is commonly introduced by missionaries, their foreign writing system is usually adopted by the incipiently literate society to write its language. Today, newly literate societies commonly adopt the Roman alphabet because English-speaking and other Western missionaries are the most active promoters of literacy in many regions of the world.

At times a society will change from one writing system to another. Vietnam, for example, was colonized by the Chinese around 200 B.C. and remained colonized for about twelve centuries. During that time, Chinese was used for writing, while Vietnamese remained unwritten. After the end of Chinese domination, the Vietnamese began to use a syllabic writing system adapted from Chinese logographic writing for their own language. Then, at the beginning of the seventeenth century, Jesuit missionaries devised an alphabetic system for Vietnamese, which the Vietnamese gradually adopted, partly under pressure from the French colonial government. Today the system devised by the Jesuits is the only one in use for Vietnamese.

One thorny problem that newly literate societies face is developing a standard orthography that everyone will agree to use. Ideally, an orthography must be regular, so that native writers will be able to spell a word that they have never before seen in writing. The orthography must also be easy to learn and to use. Finally, it must be well adapted to the phonological and morphological structure of the language. As we saw in our discussion of English orthography, satisfying all these requirements can be challenging. A system that looks complex at first blush can have hidden advantages. Devising a standard orthography can be such a difficult task that a few Western nations (including Norway) have not yet done so, even after centuries of literacy.

Language-related concerns are not the only factors involved in devising orthographies. An important factor is social acceptance. An orthography that, for one reason or another, rubs users the wrong way will never be successful. If the orthography is imposed by an outside political or religious body, it may carry negative associations and never succeed. For several decades, the United States Bureau of Indian Affairs hired linguists and anthropologists to devise orthographies for Native American languages, but because the Indians viewed the bureau and its activities with suspicion they never really accepted its orthographies.

Likewise, at the end of the last century Methodist and Catholic missionaries devised different orthographies to transcribe Rotuman, the language of the South Pacific island of Rotuma. Since then, because relations between Methodist Rotumans and Catholic Rotumans have been strained, both orthographies have survived, and there is no prospect of either group adopting the other's orthography. Similar situations can involve not only orthographies but writing systems. In Serbia and Croatia, a single language is used, but the Serbs use a Cyrillic alphabet similar to that used for Russian, while Croats use the Roman alphabet. Even when they were united in a single country, both groups adamantly kept their alphabet as a symbol of social identity. Social acceptance is thus extremely important to the development of a standard orthography.

COMPUTERS AND WRITING

In connection with writing, computers have mostly served highly technical functions—some of them related, quite surprisingly, even to space travel and the most advanced space-age technologies. For example, using software developed by the Jet Propulsion Laboratory (JPL) in Pasadena, California, computers have been used to help enhance the images of the writing in the Dead Sea Scrolls. Computers have also been used to retrieve writing that had been erased from manuscripts and even written over. Perhaps the most familiar use of computers in connection with writing is to enable images to be transmitted over the Internet, including writing systems strikingly different from the Roman alphabet. You may not be familiar with all the writing systems available on the Internet, but some of your classmates may read newspapers written in Chinese logographs or Japanese kanji or any of several other scripts. Ask a volunteer to show you how it works.

A few words about the Dead Sea Scrolls. In 1947 a twelve-year old shepherd in Palestine discovered a number of leather scrolls in a cave in Qumran near Jerusalem. These scrolls were composed in the period overlapping Old and New Testament times and are of extraordinary interest and importance to Christians, Jews, and Moslems, who have given the discovery and the linguistic recovery of the texts worldwide attention. Written in Hebrew, Aramaic, and Greek, the scrolls have provided substantial additions to the corpus of Jewish texts and genres from around the time of Christ.

Now the computer connection. The Web site for the Jet Propulsion Laboratory reports that the previously invisible lettering of certain scrolls was made distinguishable by advanced "multispectral" imaging techniques originally developed at JPL for remote sensing and planetary probes. Researchers were able to view the Dead Sea Scrolls in wavelengths beyond the sensitivity even of infrared film. (Other technologies originally devised by JPL's team of image analysts to help read images sent from the Hubble Space Telescope and the Galileo planetary probe have been used by the National Archives to monitor deterioration in documents like the original U. S. Constitution, the Bill of Rights, and the Declaration of Independence.)

SUMMARY

- Writing is a relatively recent invention that developed from pictograms, which became writing when they began representing sounds rather than objects and concepts.

- There are several types of writing systems in use today: syllabic, logographic, and alphabetic.

- In syllabic writing, symbols represent syllables.

- In logographic writing, symbols represent morphemes or words.

- In alphabetic writing, symbols represent phonemes.

- The system that dictates how the letters of the alphabet are used to represent the phonemes of a language is called its orthography.

- The writing system used for English utilizes the Roman alphabet, and English orthography is strongly influenced by morphological considerations.

- Devising orthographies for hitherto unwritten languages is a difficult task that must take into account both linguistic and social factors.

EXERCISES

12-1. a. Identify two invented sign systems besides writing, and briefly evaluate their importance relative to writing.
   b. Identify what you judge to be two of the most important human inventions of all time, and evaluate their importance in comparison to writing.
   c. Specify two or three of the central criteria you used in evaluating "importance" in a and b above.

12-2. Discuss the relative merits and disadvantages of logographic, syllabic, and alphabetic writing systems. In your discussion of each type of system, address the following questions:

   a. How easy is it to learn the system?
   b. How easy is it to write the individual graphs?
   c. How efficiently can one read the graphs?
   d. What kinds of problems does the system present for printing?
   e. How adaptable is it to computer technology such as word processing?

f. How easy is it to represent foreign names and new borrowings from other languages?

g. What sociological and historical factors might interact with the preceding questions in evaluating the appropriateness of each system to particular situations? (Be concrete by considering a particular situation you are familiar with.)

12-3. English is often said to have a phonemic orthography (approximating one graph for each distinct sound). To some extent this is true in that English orthography distinguishes between, say, <b> and <p> but not among [p], [pʰ] and [pˈ]. In light of this claim, examine the following typical sets of words and compare their orthographic representation with their pronunciation: *cats/dogs/judges; history/historical; knife/knives.*

a. Is English orthography phonemic? Explain.

b. In what sense would it be more accurate to describe the English orthographic system as morphophonemic?

c. To what extent would it be fair to say that English is logographic in representing such sets of homonyms as the following: *meet/meat/mete; leaf/lief; seize/sees/seas?*

d. What is the nature of such graphic symbols as <&>, <301>, <$>, and <%>? Can they be called logographic? Explain.

12-4. a. Using the Tamil syllabic symbols given in Figure 12-6 (pp. 436–437) transcribe the following Tamil words into Roman script:

தொழில்	'work'	ஏழு	'seven'
மூக்கு	'nose'	புலி	'tiger'
அவன்	'he'	ஆடு	'goat'
வாழைப்பழம்	'banana'	மரம்	'tree'

b. Briefly describe the general patterns that are used in forming syllabic characters in this script. For example, how is the symbol for /ke/ formed from the symbols for /k/ and /e/? How are word-final consonants and word-initial vowels represented?

12-5. The following table (adapted from Sampson 1985) is a partial representation of the inventory of graphs used in writing Korean consonants. "Tense" means (in part) that the sound is held for a longer period of time than normal, and "lax" means that the sound is held for the normal duration. (The tenseness is represented in phonetic symbols with an apostrophe as in [p'].)

a. What principles govern the shape of graphs in this system?

b. What are the advantages of such a system over an alphabetic system like the Roman system in which the shape of graphs is completely arbitrary?

	Bilabial	*Dental*	*Palatal*	*Velar*
Lax nasals	ㅁ m	ㄴ n		
Lax fricatives		ㅅ s		
Lax stops/affricate	ㅂ p	ㄷ t	ㅈ c	ㄱ k
Tense aspirated stops/affricate	ㅍ p^h	ㅌ t^h	ㅊ c^h	ㅋ k^h
Tense fricative		ㅆ s		
Tense unaspirated stops/affricate	ㅃ p'	ㄸ t'	ㅉ c'	ㄲ k'

12-6. Suppose you were devising a syllabic writing system for English. What steps would you take to make such a system as simple to learn as possible? To what extent does the phonological and morphological structure of English present problems for syllabic writing?

12-7. Hebrew and Arabic are written from right to left, using a type of phonetic writing called "consonantal." Here is an example of a Classical Hebrew sentence from the Old Testament (adapted from Comrie [1987]).

ואינם מכירים לדבר יהודית

Transliteration: W?YNM MKYRYM LDBR YHWDYT
Pronunciation: wə?ē^{y}n'ẳm makkī^{y}r'ī^{y}m ləðabb'er yəhū^{w}ð'ī^{y}θ
[*Note:* ẳ represents a low round back vowel]
'And they do not know how to speak Judean.'

a. On the basis of this sample, describe precisely how consonantal writing differs from straightforward alphabetic writing.

b. Write out an English sentence in Roman script using the principle of consonantal writing; then ask a couple of people to figure out what you have written. In light of which syllable structures your readers found easy and which syllables they found tough to decipher, assess how practical such a system would be for use with the English language.

c. Review what you read about the morphological structure of Hebrew and Arabic in Chapter 2. What makes consonantal writing better adapted to these languages than to English?

INTERNET RESOURCES

- **Decryption of the Rosetta Stone:**
  http://www.cs.oberlin.edu/classes/cs115/lect29n.html
  If you are interested in decryption or hieroglyphics, this Web site takes you through the process of decipherment of the Rosetta Stone clearly, simply, and in just a few minutes. It also discusses its importance.
- **Images of the Dead Sea Scrolls: http://www.flash.net/~royal/scroll3.html or**
  http://sunsite.unc.edu/expo/deadsea.scrolls.exhibit/Library
  /library.html#scrolls
  At either of these sites you can view a dozen Dead Sea Scroll fragments and read a description of them. (At the english.harbrace.com/ling/ Web site you will find links to images of the caves where the Dead Sea Scrolls were discovered.)

SUGGESTIONS FOR FURTHER READING

- **Albertine Gaur. 1984.** *The Story of Writing* (London: The British Library). A readable and lavishly illustrated history of writing.
- **J. T. Hooker, ed. 1990.** *Reading the Past: Ancient Writing from Cuneiform to the Alphabet* (Berkeley: U of California P/British Museum). Six excellent booklets, each by a distinguished author, have been gathered into this book and introduced by the editor. Among other topics, it treats cuneiform, Egyptian hieroglyphs, and the early alphabet.
- **Roger Woodard. 1996. "Writing Systems."** In *The Atlas of Languages,* B. Comrie, S. Matthews, and M. Polinsky, eds. (New York: Facts on File), pp. 162–209. In a lavishly illustrated book, this is a singularly accessible chapter-length source of scholarly information about the development of writing.

Advanced Reading

Gelb (1963) is a classic study of the development of different writing systems in antiquity. Linguistically oriented surveys of writing systems can be found in Sampson (1985) and Coulmas (1989); the quotation at the opening of our chapter is from Coulmas. The story of the decipherment of ancient scripts is told in Gordon (1982). Diringer (1968) discusses the discovery and development of alphabetic writing through the centuries. Comrie (1987) provides illustration and discussion of orthography for some of the world's major languages. Interesting hypotheses about the influence of literacy on thinking and on culture are advanced in Goody (1977) and in Ong (1982). These hypotheses are constructively criticized by Street (1983).

REFERENCES

- Comrie, Bernard, ed. 1987. *The World's Major Languages* (New York: Oxford UP).

- Coulmas, Florian. 1989. *The Writing Systems of the World* (Cambridge, MA: Blackwell).

- Diringer, David. 1968. *The Alphabet* (London: Hutchinson).

- Gelb, I. J. 1963. *A Study of Writing.* 2nd ed. (Chicago: U of Chicago P).

- Goody, Jack. 1977. *The Domestication of the Savage Mind* (Cambridge: Cambridge UP).

- Gordon, Cyrus H. 1982. *Forgotten Scripts: Their Ongoing Discovery and Evolution,* 2nd ed. (New York: Basic Books).

- Ong, Walter. 1982. *Orality and Literacy* (London: Methuen).

- Sampson, Geoffrey. 1985. *Writing: A Linguistic Introduction* (Stanford: Stanford UP).

- Street, Brian V. 1983. *Literacy in Theory and Practice* (Cambridge: Cambridge UP).

PART THREE

LANGUAGE CHANGE AND

LANGUAGE DEVELOPMENT

⟶

P ART Three combines Part One's focus on language structure with Part Two's emphasis on language use. Here you'll examine three topics that are perennial favorites:

how languages change over time
how languages are related to one another
how kids and adults learn languages

Everyone knows that French and Spanish are related languages and that Shakespeare's English differs from today's. In this section you'll learn how languages change and develop and which languages are related to one another. You'll also investigate language acquisition. For children acquiring a first language and for anyone interacting with them during that process, the mysteries surrounding language acquisition prompt wonder and tickle the imagination. By contrast with the frolicsome time children spend mastering a native tongue, adolescents and adults often exert strenuous efforts learning a foreign language. For kids, success with a native language is guaranteed; for adults, learning a second language can be a challenge. You'll see why.

CHAPTER 13

LANGUAGE CHANGE OVER TIME: HISTORICAL LINGUISTICS

WHAT DO YOU THINK?

Your niece is studying Latin in high school and reports to you that English must have come from Latin because English contains so many Latin words. What do you tell her about the relationship between Latin and English?

On a field trip to Chinatown in Los Angeles with your seventh-grade class, a colleague from Taiwan accompanies you. When your colleague tries to buy some inexpensive pieces of jade from a street vendor, both seem to be speaking Chinese, but it becomes apparent that they cannot understand one another, and they enlist help from a translator. Your students are perplexed that two Chinese speakers should be unable to understand one another. Afterwards your colleague explains that she speaks only the Mandarin dialect of Chinese, while the vendor spoke only Cantonese. Your students claim that if speakers of Mandarin and Cantonese cannot understand one another, they must be speaking different languages. What reasons do you give your students for considering Cantonese and Mandarin dialects of a single language?

Your junior high school geography students are examining an atlas of the Middle East and notice that many cities in Saudi Arabia have names beginning with "Al" (Al Jawf, Al Khunn, Al Kahfah, Al Kharj, Al Khurmah) but that the cities in nearby Iran don't have such names. By contrast, many cities in Iran have two-part names that are linked by "e" (Dasht-e Kavir, Posht-e Badam, Torbat-e Jam, Naft-e Safid), while none of the Saudi Arabian names have that form. They are surprised because they thought that Persian, the language spoken in Iran, was related to Arabic, and they offer as evidence the fact, that the writing systems are alike and that both countries are Islamic. What do you tell them about the relationship between Persian and Arabic? About the relationship between speech and writing? Between writing and culture?

On another occasion in that same geography class, students are examining the names of places in Oklahoma and note two distinct kinds—those represented by transparent names like Sweetwater, Stillwater, Sand Springs, Willow, Granite, Beaver, Oakwood, Commerce, Mountain View, Antelope Hills, and Grove and those represented by Okmulgee, Oktaha, Chickasha, Comanche, Chattanooga, Manitou, Cherokee, Arapaho, Wapanucka, Waurika, Wichita, Muskogee, Wetumka, Nashoba, Tuskahoma, Tonkawa, Pocasset, Apache, Osage, Wyandotte, and Wynona, which don't have independent meanings in English. They recognize this last set as containing Native American names, and they ask you whether they are also English words and, if so, why they appear so different from the words of the first set. What do you tell them about languages coming into contact with one another and how place names come to be?

DO LIVING LANGUAGES ALWAYS CHANGE?

⎯

It's no secret that languages change over the years. Sometimes, especially in times of social and political upheaval, they may change dramatically. Usually, though, the changes are more subtle. Still, all of us can recognize different speech patterns between one generation and the next. There are probably notable differences between the speech patterns of your parents and your friends and even greater ones between your grandparents and your friends. The most noticeable differences between one generation and another are in vocabulary. What one generation calls *icebox, record player* (or *hi-fi*), *car phone,* and *studious young man* a younger generation calls *fridge, stereo, cell phone,* and (in some instances) *nerd.* Your grandparents had not heard of *doublespeak, tank tops, six packs, sitcoms,* or *cyberspace* in their youth, nor did they refer to certain verbal actions as *bad-mouthing, dissin,* or *dumping on* someone.

Pronunciation changes too. A change is currently under way for the word *nuclear,* which a couple of decades ago was more commonly pronounced [nukliər] but today is increasingly pronounced [nukyələr]. In the same vein, the word *realtor,* formerly pronounced [riəltər], is increasingly pronounced [rilətər]. Regional accents and dialects change: the /r/ in words like *car* and *beard,* which is pronounced in most of the United States, is coming to be pronounced more and more in New York City where it has been missing for a couple of centuries. Southerners and Yankees raised in an age of national television programming sound more alike than their parents do. And throughout the United States is an increasing tendency not to differentiate the vowel sounds in words pairs like *knot* and *nought* or *cot* and *caught.*

The meaning of a term can also change. About a thousand years ago, the English verb *starve* (Old English *steorfan*) meant simply 'die (by any cause)'; today, *starve* refers principally to deprivation and death by hunger (or, by metaphorical extension, 'deprive of affection'). Similarly, the Old English verb *berēafian* meant 'to deprive of, take away, rob'; today, the much narrower principal meaning of *bereave* is 'to deprive of life or hope.' Until recently, the adjective *natural,* which is over seven hundred years old, did not have the meaning 'without chemical preservatives' that it now commonly has, as in *all-natural ice cream.* And the meanings of *joint, bust, fix, high, hit,* and many other words have been extended by their use in the world of drugs.

There can also be grammatical differences in the speech of different generations. *Goes the king hence today?* is what Shakespeare wrote in *Macbeth.* Today, the same inquiry would have a form more like *Is the king going out today?* because certain grammatical features of seventeenth-century English are no longer in use.

Linguistic alterations often prompt comment, especially from people who believe that language change reflects corruption. For some people, the best language forms are those that have stood the test of time. Though generalizing from one's own linguistic experience can be risky, it is safe to say that the common experience of noticing linguistic differences between one generation and another reflects the simple fact that languages do not stand still but are always in the process of changing.

In this chapter, we explore language change: what kinds of change occur, how languages are related to one another historically, and how language families are established. We also describe the linguistic and cultural prehistory of the Polynesians as a way of illustrating how some challenges of historical linguistics are met.

LANGUAGE FAMILIES AND THE INDO-EUROPEAN FAMILY

One result of the ongoing changes that affect a language is that a single language can develop into several languages. The early stages of such development are apparent in the differences among Australian, American, Canadian, Indian, and Irish English dialects, all of which have sprung from the English spoken in the United Kingdom. In order for different dialects to develop into separate languages, groups of speakers must remain relatively isolated from one another, separated either by physical barriers such as impassable mountains and great bodies of water, or by social and political barriers such as those drawn along tribal, religious, racial, or national boundaries.

You have probably heard it said that French, Spanish, and Italian come from Latin. That statement is true, provided that by "Latin" one understands the different dialects spoken throughout the Roman Empire, not the written variety of classical Latin studied in school. The "Vulgar Latin" spoken throughout the Roman Empire lives on in today's French, Italian, Spanish, and Portuguese as well as in Rumanian, Catalan, and Provençal, all of which are its direct descendants. On the other hand, the classical Latin of Cicero, Virgil, Caesar, and other Roman writers is "dead," and the written varieties of French, Spanish, and Italian are based on the modern spoken languages, not the classical written language.

You may also have heard it claimed that English comes from Latin. That claim is false. English and Latin are indeed related, but Latin is not an ancestor of English. Both English and Latin come from a common ancestor, but they traveled along different paths. Then, during the Renaissance, English borrowed thousands of words from Latin and thereby created striking lexical parallels, especially in the sciences and humanities. But by no stretch of the imagination is English a daughter of Latin in the sense that Spanish, French, Italian, and Portuguese are. English is descended from Proto-Germanic, a language that was spoken about the time of classical Latin and a few centuries earlier and that ultimately gave rise not only to English but to German, Dutch, Norwegian, Danish, and Swedish (among others). Thus, as Latin is the parent language of French and Spanish, so Proto-Germanic is the parent language of English and German.

Except for a few carved *runic* inscriptions from the third century A.D., Proto-Germanic (unlike Latin) has left no written records. Modern knowledge of Proto-Germanic—and it is considerable—has been inferred from the character of its daughter languages through *comparative reconstruction,* a technique explained in this chapter. Proto-Germanic and Latin are themselves daughters of Proto-Indo-European, another *unattested* (unrecorded) language. In a simplified manner, we can represent the situation by the family tree in Figure 13-1, which has two *branches.*

While the notion that languages change and give rise to new languages is familiar to modern readers, it is a notion that was postulated clearly only two centuries ago. In 1786, while he was serving as a judge in Calcutta, Sir William Jones addressed the Royal Asiatic Society of Bengal about his linguistic experience.

> The Sanskrit language, whatever be its antiquity, is of a wonderful structure; more perfect than the Greek, more copious than the Latin, and more exquisitely refined than either, yet bearing to both of them a stronger affinity, both in the roots of verbs and in the forms of grammar, than could possibly have been produced by accident; so strong indeed, that no philologer could examine them all three, without believing them to have sprung from some common source, which, perhaps, no longer exists: there is a similar reason, though not quite so forcible, for supposing that both the Gothic and the Celtic, though blended with a very different idiom, had the same origin with the Sanskrit; and the old Persian might be added to the same family. . . .

Today linguists would shy away from such judgmental statements as Sanskrit having a "more perfect" structure than Greek and being "more exquisitely refined" than Latin, but Jones clearly recognized that languages give rise to other languages. Indeed, we now know that Sanskrit, Latin, Greek, Celtic, Gothic, and Persian *did* spring from a "common source" that "no longer exists." Jones had made

Figure 13-1

GERMANIC AND ROMANCE BRANCHES OF THE INDO-EUROPEAN FAMILY

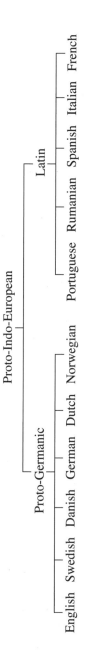

an important discovery. The common source of Latin, Greek, Sanskrit, Celtic, Gothic, Persian, and many other languages (including English and its Germanic relatives, and French and Spanish and their Romance relatives) is Proto-Indo-European. A parent language and the daughter languages that have developed from it are collectively referred to as a **language family**, and the family that Jones discovered is called the **Indo-European** family. While there are no written records of Proto-Indo-European itself, a rich vein of inferences about its words and structures can be mined from the linguistic characteristics of its daughter languages. Exercising certain well-defined precautions, scholars can confidently reconstruct a parent language from the shared characteristics of its daughters.

The working assumption of historical linguists is this: a feature that occurs widely in daughter languages and whose presence cannot be explained by reference to language typology, language universals, or borrowing from another tongue is likely to have been inherited from the parent language.

HOW TO RECONSTRUCT THE LINGUISTIC PAST

The past century has witnessed great migrations from one end of the globe to another—from Europe to the Americas and Australia, from the Far East to North America and Southeast Asia. There is evidence of massive migrations from Central Asia to Europe in about 4000 B.C. by a people who probably spoke Proto-Indo-European. There are no written records to document these earlier migrations, but archaeologists have found buried remains from the daily life of people who inhabited particular parts of the globe. Combined with what we can reconstruct of ancestral languages, archaeological records enable researchers to make educated guesses about where our ancestors came from and where they migrated to, as well as how they lived and died.

When scholars reconstruct an ancestral language, they also implicitly reconstruct an ancestral society and culture. Every culture lives on the lips of its speakers so that words ascribed to a prehistoric group represent artifacts in their culture and facets of their daily social and physical activities. In this chapter, we concentrate not on Indo-European culture and the Indo-European homeland (which are discussed in other accessible sources) but on the Polynesians, whose linguistic development presents another interesting case of reconstruction of a protolanguage and the culture of its speakers.

POLYNESIAN AND PACIFIC BACKGROUND

On land, the only physical obstacles to sustained contacts between people are insurmountable mountains and wide rivers, which are in fact not very common. As a result, boundaries between different languages and cultures are often blurred. In contrast, once people settle on an isolated island, contact with inhabitants of other islands is difficult and limited, and languages and cultures develop in relative isolation. Islands thus offer an opportunity to study what happens when a protolanguage evolves into distinct daughter languages. Because the South Pacific region consists of small islands and island groups quite isolated from one another, it provides an almost ideal "laboratory" for researchers interested in the past.

The South Pacific is home to three different cultural areas—Polynesia ('many islands'), Melanesia ('black islands'), and Micronesia ('small islands')—whose approximate boundaries are shown in Figure 13-2. Among other things, each area is distinguished by the physical appearance of its inhabitants: Polynesians are generally large, with olive complexions and straight or wavy hair; Melanesians typically are dark skinned, with smaller frames and curlier hair; and Micronesians are slight of frame, with light brown complexions and straight hair. We will concentrate on Polynesians and ask what we can learn about their origins and their early life in Polynesia from the languages they speak today.

The islands of Polynesia vary greatly in size and structure. The main island of Hawaii and the islands of Samoa and Tahiti are comparatively large land masses formed through volcanic eruptions. Other islands are tiny atolls, little more than sand banks and coral reefs that barely reach the surface of the ocean; typically, one can walk (or wade) around an atoll in a few hours. Atolls are found in Tuvalu, the Tuamotu Archipelago, and the northern Cook Islands. Some coral islands in Tonga and elsewhere have been raised by underground volcanic activities and are medium sized and often hilly—in contrast to atolls, which are utterly flat.

There are no written records to aid in tracing the Polynesians' cultural and linguistic development because they had no system of writing before literacy was introduced by Westerners. But the modern languages and the archaeological record provide useful tools for reconstruction.

There is every indication that all the islands of Polynesia were settled by a people who shared a common language, a common culture, and a common way of dealing with the environment. We know that they traveled by sea from west to east, settling islands on their way, because the languages of Polynesia are clearly related to languages spoken to the west in Melanesia but have no connection with languages spoken to the east in South America. In addition, Polynesian cultures have many affinities with Melanesian cultures but virtually none with those of South America. Finally, the human bones, artifacts, and other archaeological remains found on the western islands of Polynesia are older than those found on the eastern islands. The obvious conclusion that western Polynesia was settled prior to eastern Polynesia contradicts the theory, popularized by Norwegian explorer Thor Heyerdahl, that the Polynesians originated in South America.

The oldest archaeological records in Polynesia were found in western Polynesia: in Tonga, Samoa, Uvea, and Futuna (see Figure 13-2). Consisting mostly of pottery fragments similar to those found farther west in Melanesia, these records date to between 1500 and 1200 B.C. This implies that people moved from somewhere outside Polynesia and settled on these western islands about thirty-five hundred years ago. No pottery has been found in eastern Polynesia (the Cook Islands, Tahiti and the Society Islands, the Marquesas Islands, and the Tuamotu Archipelago), but other archaeological remains indicate that these eastern islands were settled around the first century A.D. The most recent remains are found in Hawaii and New Zealand.

Figure 13-2

CULTURAL AREAS IN THE PACIFIC

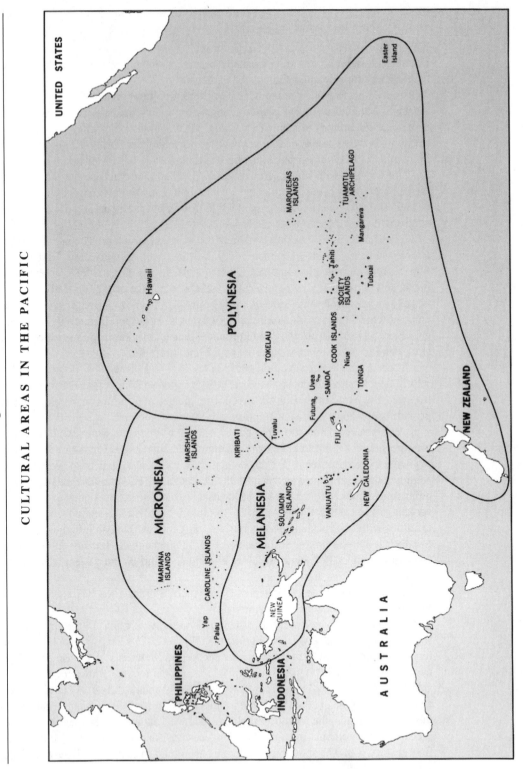

That these two island groups were settled last is not surprising, given that they are the most remote from other islands of the region. The earliest artifacts found on these islands suggest that the ancient Hawaiians and the ancestors of the New Zealand Maoris first arrived on their respective island homes between the seventh and eleventh centuries A.D.

POLYNESIAN LANGUAGES AND THEIR HISTORY

We said earlier that all of Polynesia was settled by the same people or by groups of closely related people from a single region. Linguistic evidence can help us determine the original homeland of the Polynesians. In Table 13-1 you can see some striking similarities among words in five Polynesian languages. These and other widespread similarities of expression for equivalent content demonstrate that the languages of Polynesia are manifestly related. Not finding similar close correspondences in vocabulary between the languages of Polynesia and any other language, we can safely say that Polynesian languages form a language family. In other words, all the Polynesian languages are daughter languages of a single parent language, the ancestor of the thirty or so Polynesian languages and of no other existing language. Known as Proto-Polynesian, the parent language was spoken by the people who first settled western Polynesia between 1500 and 1200 B.C.

In Table 13-1, the word *manu* 'bird' is exactly the same—in form and content—in all five languages. The other words have the same vowel correspondences (where one has /a/, all have /a/) and differ slightly from one another in some of the consonants. The Polynesian words in each line of the table are **cognates**—words that have developed from a single, historically earlier word. In examining other words, you'll find the consonant correspondences between the different languages to be strikingly regular. On the basis of many words such as those in Table 13-1, it can be seen that

Table 13-1

COMMON WORDS IN FIVE POLYNESIAN LANGUAGES

TONGAN	SAMOAN	TAHITIAN	MAORI	HAWAIIAN	
manu	manu	manu	manu	manu	'bird'
ika	iʔa	iʔa	ika	iʔa	'fish'
kai	ʔai	ʔai	kai	ʔai	'to eat'
tapu	tapu	tapu	tapu	kapu	'forbidden'
vaka	vaʔa	vaʔa	waka	waʔa	'canoe'
fohe	foe	hoe	hoe	hoe	'oar'
mata	mata	mata	mata	maka	'eye'
ʔuta	uta	uta	uta	uka	'bush'
toto	toto	toto	toto	koko	'blood'

in words where the phonemes /m/ and /n/ (as in *manu*) occur in one Polynesian language, they tend to occur in all. On the other hand, Tongan, Samoan, Tahitian, and Maori /t/ corresponds to /k/ in Hawaiian (as in the words for 'forbidden' and 'eye'). We can represent these *sound correspondences* as in Table 13-3 on page 463.

If we examine still other words, these sound correspondences are maintained, and additional **correspondence sets** can be established. As the words in Table 13-2 reveal, Tongan and Maori /k/ corresponds to a glottal stop /ʔ/ in Samoan, Tahitian, and Hawaiian, while Tongan, Samoan, and Maori /ŋ/ corresponds to Tahitian /ʔ/ and Hawaiian /n/. We can thus establish regular sound correspondences among modern-day Polynesian languages.

In comparative reconstruction, it is important to exclude all borrowed words because the only words that can profitably provide sounds for use in a correspondence set are those that have descended directly from the ancestor language. For example, because Proto-Polynesian *s became /h/ in Tongan (but remained /s/ in some daughter languages), Tongan has very few words with /s/—among them *sikaleti,* meaning 'cigarette.' While *sikaleti* was obviously borrowed from a language outside the Polynesian family, words borrowed from other languages within the same family may not be so easy to spot.

COMPARATIVE RECONSTRUCTION

The method just illustrated is known as **comparative reconstruction.** It aims to reconstruct an ancestor language from the evidence that remains in daughter languages. Its premise is that, borrowing aside, similar forms with similar meanings across related languages are *reflexes* of a single form with a related meaning in the parent language. This commonsense approach is at the foundation of the comparative method and, indeed, of historical linguistics.

When we examine *correspondence sets* such as m-m-m-m-m and t-t-t-t-k in Table 13-3, it seems reasonable to assume that *m and *t existed in the parent language and

Table 13-2

COGNATES IN FIVE POLYNESIAN LANGUAGES I

TONGAN	SOMOAN	TAHITIAN	MAORI	HAWAIIAN	
toki	toʔi	toʔi	toki	koʔi	'axe'
taŋi	taŋi	taʔi	taŋi	kani	'to cry'
taŋata	taŋata	taʔata	taŋata	kanaka	'man'
kafa	ʔafa	ʔaha	kaha	ʔaha	'rope'
kutu	ʔutu	ʔutu	kutu	ʔuku	'louse'
kata	ʔata	ʔata	kata	ʔaka	'to laugh'
moko	moʔo	moʔo	moko	moʔo	'lizard'

Table 13-3

SOUND CORRESPONDENCES
IN FIVE POLYNESIAN LANGUAGES

TONGAN	SAMOAN	TAHITIAN	MAORI	HAWAIIAN
m	m	m	m	m
n	n	n	n	n
ŋ	ŋ	ʔ	ŋ	n
p	p	p	p	p
t	t	t	t	k
k	ʔ	ʔ	k	ʔ

that /m/ was retained in each of the daughter languages, while /t/ was retained except in Hawaiian, where it became /k/. Such assumptions are the everyday fare of historical linguistics. When we assume the existence of a sound (or other structure) in a language for which we have no evidence except what can be inferred from daughter languages, that sound (or structure) is said to be *reconstructed.* Reconstructed forms are "starred" to indicate that they are unattested. We can represent the reconstructions from correspondence sets this way:

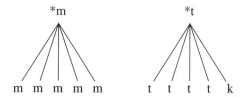

In describing the development of Hawaiian from Proto-Polynesian, we would postulate a historical rule of the form: *t > k. (A shaftless arrow indicates that one form developed into another form over time.)

Instead of *t, we could have reconstructed a *k in Proto-Polynesian. We would then say that *k was retained in Hawaiian and became /t/ in *all* the other languages. But we posit *t because experience with many languages has led historical linguists to prefer reconstructions that assume the *least* change consistent with the facts, unless there is good reason to do otherwise. In this instance, reconstructing *t assumes fewer subsequent changes than would a reconstruction of *k. You can think of this as the majority rule.

Now let's inspect the reconstruction of *m more closely. To postulate that *m existed in the protolanguage and was retained in all the daughter languages is the simplest hypothesis but not the only logical one. You could hypothesize some other sound in the protolanguage that independently became /m/ in each daughter language.

Both the *bilabial* *b and the *nasal* *n would be likely candidates for this reconstruction because they share phonetic features with the *bilabial nasal* /m/. However, since Polynesian languages generally lack the phoneme /b/, it seems more reasonable to assume that the parent language also lacked *b. Alternatively, you could reconstruct an *n that changed to /m/ in all the daughter languages independently of one another. But this hypothesis must be rejected for two reasons. First, it is not a minimal assumption, and second, the daughter languages have an /n/ that also requires a source in the parent language. We thus postulate Proto-Polynesian *m and *n, which were retained unchanged in all the daughter languages.

Let's examine one other correspondence set: ŋ-ŋ-ʔ-ŋ-n. We have just postulated Proto-Polynesian *n as the reconstructed earlier form (technically, the **etymon**), of the correspondence set n-n-n-n-n. It is interesting to compare this reconstruction with one for the correspondence set ŋ-ŋ-ʔ-ŋ-n, for which the most likely reconstruction is *ŋ.

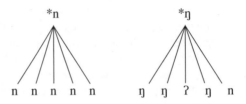

Given these reconstructions *ŋ was retained in Tongan, Samoan, and Maori but became /ʔ/ in Tahitian and /n/ in Hawaiian. As a result, the distinction between *n and *ŋ that existed in Proto-Polynesian and is maintained in Tongan, Samoan, and Maori does not exist in Hawaiian, where *n and *ŋ have merged in /n/. Hawaiian /n/ therefore has two historical sources. We can represent the historical merger in rules (*n > n; *ŋ > n) or schematically.

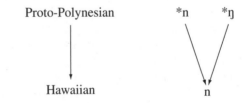

Subgroups On the basis of lexical and structural characteristics, it is apparent that some Polynesian languages are more closely linked than others. As shown in Table 13-4, Tongan differs from other Polynesian languages in at least two respects: it has initial /h/ where other languages do not have anything; and it has nothing where other languages have either /l/ or /r/. Niuean, another Polynesian language, shares these and certain other characteristics with Tongan. On the basis of such evidence, Tongan and Niuean can be seen to form a **subgroup**, or *branch*, of Polynesian. This implies that Tongan and Niuean were at one time a single language distinct from

Table 13-4

COGNATES IN FIVE POLYNESIAN LANGUAGES II

TONGAN	SAMOAN	TAHITIAN	MAORI	HAWAIIAN	
hama	ama	ama	ama	ama	'outrigger'
hiŋoa	iŋoa	iʔoa	iŋoa	inoa	'name'
mohe	moe	moe	moe	moe	'to sleep'
hake	aʔe	aʔe	ake	aʔe	'up'
ua	lua	rua	rua	lua	'two'
ama	lama	rama	rama	lama	'torch'
tui	tuli	turi	turi	kuli	'knee'

Proto-Polynesian and that Proto-Tongic, as that language is called, developed certain features before splitting into Tongan and Niuean. The retention in both languages of these features (those that developed after Proto-Tongic split from Proto-Polynesian but before Tongan and Niuean split into separate languages) constitutes the characteristic shared features of the Proto-Tongic branch of the Polynesian family.

In the meantime, the other branch of Proto-Polynesian also evolved independently after its speakers lost contact with speakers of Proto-Tongic. As this second branch, called Proto-Nuclear-Polynesian, developed its distinctive characteristics, it emerged as a separate language that gave rise to still other languages. Except for Tongan and Niuean, all modern Polynesian languages share certain features inherited from Proto-Nuclear-Polynesian. In turn, Proto-Nuclear-Polynesian has two main subgroups: Samoic-Outlier and Eastern Polynesian. The evolution of Polynesian languages can be represented in the *family tree* shown in Figure 13-3. Such family trees usefully represent the general genetic relationships in a family of languages,

Figure 13-3

POLYNESIAN LANGUAGES

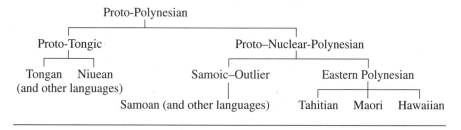

but they inevitably oversimplify the complex facts of history, especially by excluding borrowing and other influences that languages can exert on one another.

RECONSTRUCTING THE PROTO-POLYNESIAN VOCABULARY

On the basis of the evidence provided by modern-day Polynesian languages, we can reconstruct the sound system and vocabulary of Proto-Polynesian (and make educated guesses about its grammatical structure). In turn, reconstructed linguistic information can tell us a good deal about the people who first settled Polynesia more than three thousand years ago.

A word can be reconstructed for Proto-Polynesian if we find **reflexes** of it—that is, cognates—in at least one language of each major subgroup (Tongic, Samoic-Outlier, and Eastern Polynesian) and are confident that the cognates are not borrowed words. (If we reconstructed a lexical item for Proto-Polynesian based simply on evidence from Tongan and, say, Samoan, we would run the risk of having found a word that existed originally only in Tongan—after Tongan became a separate language—and was borrowed by the early Samoans. You can see from Figure 13-2 that Tonga and Samoa are close enough to have had contacts in prehistoric times.)

For example, since cognate words for 'bird,' 'fish,' and 'man' are found in all major subgroups of the Polynesian family (as shown in Tables 13-1 and 13-2), we can reconstruct a Proto-Polynesian form for each. According to regular sound correspondences and the most plausible reconstructed sounds, these words are *manu, *taŋata,* and *ika.* In contrast, the word for a 'night of full moon,' which in Maori and Tahitian is *hotu* and in Hawaiian *hoku,* cannot be reconstructed for Proto-Polynesian because there is no cognate in any Tongic or Samoic-Outlier language. Similarly, an etymon for the Tongan and Niuean word *kookoo* 'windpipe' cannot be reconstructed for Proto-Polynesian because there is no reflex in any Samoic-Outlier or Eastern Polynesian language.

Using the comparative method of historical reconstruction just outlined, the lexical items in Table 13-5, all referring to the physical environment, can be reconstructed for Proto-Polynesian.

Table 13-5

RECONSTRUCTED TERMS IN PROTO-POLYNESIAN I

*awa	'channel'	*hafu	'waterfall'
*hakau	'coral reef'	*lanu	'fresh water'
*kilikili	'gravel'	*lolo	'flood'
*peau	'wave'	*mato	'precipice'
*sou	'rough ocean'	*maʔuŋa	'mountain'
*tahi	'sea'	*rano	'lake'
*ʔone	'sand'	*waitafe	'stream'

From Table 13-5, you can see that the Proto-Polynesain people had words for ocean-related notions (the left-hand column) and for topographic features typically found on large volcanic islands (the right-hand column). As it happens, there are no waterfalls, mountains, precipices, or lakes on coral atolls, and only rarely are they found on raised coral islands.

In interpreting such results, linguists make the commonsense assumption that the presence of a word for a particular object in a language usually indicates the presence of that object in the speakers' environment. (There are exceptions to this rule, as we will see, but they are few and far between.) In particular, complete land-lubbers will not normally have an elaborate native vocabulary for the sea and for seafaring activities (barring the possibility of a recent move inland from a coastal area). We thus surmise that the early Polynesians inhabited a high island or a chain of high islands but lived close enough to the ocean to be familiar with the landscape and phenomena of the sea.

In Table 13-6, we reconstruct still other Proto-Polynesian names for animals and make the assumption that the ancient Polynesians were familiar with them. Names of many other reef and deepwater fish and other sea creatures can be reconstructed besides those listed in the left-hand column. In contrast, we can reconstruct only a handful of names for land animals: a few domesticated animals (dog, pig, chicken) and a few birds and reptiles. We surmise that the Polynesians' original habitat was rich in sea life but probably relatively poor in land fauna—that the Polynesians originally inhabited coastal regions and not island interiors.

The character of the land fauna offers pointed information about the Proto-Polynesian homeland. Since the Proto-Polynesian terms *peka* 'bat' and *lulu* 'owl' can be reconstructed, we can exclude as possible homelands Tahiti, Easter Island, and the Marquesas, where these animals are not found.

Table 13-6

RECONSTRUCTED TERMS IN PROTO-POLYNESIAN II

*maŋoo	'shark'		*kulii	'dog'
*kanahe	'mullet'		*puaka	'pig'
*sakulaa	'swordfish'		*moko	'lizard'
*ʔatu	'bonito'		*kumaa	'rat'
*ʔono	'barracuda'		*ŋata	'snake'
*ʔume	'leatherjacket'		*fonu	'turtle'
*manini	'sturgeon'		*peka	'bat'
*nofu	'stonefish'		*namu	'mosquito'
*fai	'stingray'		*lulu	'owl'
*kaloama	'goatfish'		*matuku	'reef heron'
*palani	'surgeonfish'		*akiaki	'tern'
*toke	'eel'		*moa	'chicken'

Furthermore, snakes are found only east of Samoa. Though we find reflexes of Proto-Polynesian *ŋata 'snake' in many languages, we find no snakes west of Samoa. Had the Proto-Polynesians inhabited an island west of Samoa, they would very likely have lost the term *ŋata over the centuries. Similarly, we know that pigs (for which the word *puaka can be reconstructed) are not native to Polynesia, but Europeans first arriving between the sixteenth and nineteenth centuries found them everywhere except on Niue, Easter Island, and New Zealand. These three regions are thus unlikely homelands.

Words for some animals have undergone interesting changes in certain Polynesian languages. For example, New Zealand is much colder than the rest of Polynesia, and its native animals are very different from those found on the tropical islands to the north. Upon arrival in New Zealand, the ancient Maoris encountered many new species to which they gave the names of animals they had left behind in tropical Polynesia; thus the following correspondences exist.

PROTO-POLYNESIAN		MAORI	
*pule	'cowrie shell'	pure	'bivalve mollusk'
*ŋata	'snake'	ŋata	'snail'
*ali	'flounder'	ari	'small shark'

Other animal names were dropped from the Maori vocabulary or applied to things commonly associated with the animal.

PROTO-POLYNESIAN		MAORI	
*ane	'termite'	ane	'rotten'
*lupe	'pigeon'	rupe	'mythical'

Other changes are more complex. The word *lulu* (or *ruru*) refers to owls in languages such as Tongan, Samoan, and Maori, which are spoken in areas where owls are found. On some islands like the Marquesas and Tahiti, owls do not exist, and the reflex of Proto-Polynesian *lulu 'owl' has either disappeared from the language, as in Marquesan, or been applied to another species, as in Tahitian. Owls inhabit Hawaii, but the Proto-Polynesian term *lulu has been replaced by the word *pueo* there.

Why would the early Hawaiians replace one word with the other? In the Marquesas, as we noted, there are no owls, and the language spoken there has no reflex of *lulu. Apparently the ancient Polynesians settled the Marquesas and stayed there for several centuries, during which they lost the word *lulu for lack of anything to apply it to. When they subsequently traveled north and settled Hawaii, they encountered owls, but by that time the word *lulu* had long been forgotten, and a new word had to be found.

The linguistic evidence argues that the ancestors of the Polynesians were fishermen and cultivators. Here are a few of the many terms that refer to fishing and horticulture.

*mataʔu 'fishhook'	*too 'to plant'
*rama 'to torch fish'	*faki 'to pick'
*paa 'fish lure'	*lohu 'picking pole'
*kupeŋa 'fishnet'	*hua 'spade'
*afo 'fishing line'	*maʔala 'garden'
*faaŋota 'to fish'	*palpula 'seedling'

In contrast to this rich vocabulary, hunting terms are limited, with three words apparently exhausting all possible reconstructions for verbs related to hunting: *fana 'to shoot with a bow,' *welo 'to spear,' and *seu 'to snare with a net.' It is probably safe to infer that the major source of food for the ancient Polynesians was not the bush but sea and garden.

One field with a notable array of vocabulary is canoe navigation, with the following reconstructions: *folau 'to travel by sea,' *ʔuli 'to steer,' *fohe 'paddle,' *fana 'mast,' *laa 'sail,' *kiato 'outrigger boom,' *hama 'outrigger.' That the speakers of Proto-Polynesian were expert seafarers comes as no surprise, given that they traveled enormous distances between islands (two thousand miles stretch between Hawaii and the closest inhabited island).

HISTORICAL LINGUISTICS AND PREHISTORY

The linguistic evidence combined with evidence from archaeology leads to the following hypotheses:

1. The speakers of Proto-Polynesian inhabited the coastal region of a high island or group of high islands.
2. This homeland is likely to have been in the region between Samoa and Fiji, including the islands of Tonga, Uvea, and Futuna.
3. The ancient Polynesians were fishermen, cultivators, and seafarers.
4. Around the first century A.D., the ancient Polynesians traveled eastward from their homeland, settling eastern Polynesia: Tahiti, the Cook Islands, the Marquesas, the Tuamotu, and the neighboring island groups.
5. Then, between the fourth and sixth centuries, Easter Island, Hawaii, and New Zealand were settled from eastern Polynesia.

The history of Polynesian settlement and migrations is summarized in Figure 13-4.

Our discussion has focused on Polynesian origins and migrations. By judiciously combining linguistic evidence with evidence from other disciplines, we constructed a probable picture of an ancient people, the environment they lived in, and the skills they developed for survival. Linguists have applied the same methods to other peoples, including the Indo-Europeans and the Algonquian Indians.

Figure 13-4

THE SETTLEMENT OF POLYNESIA

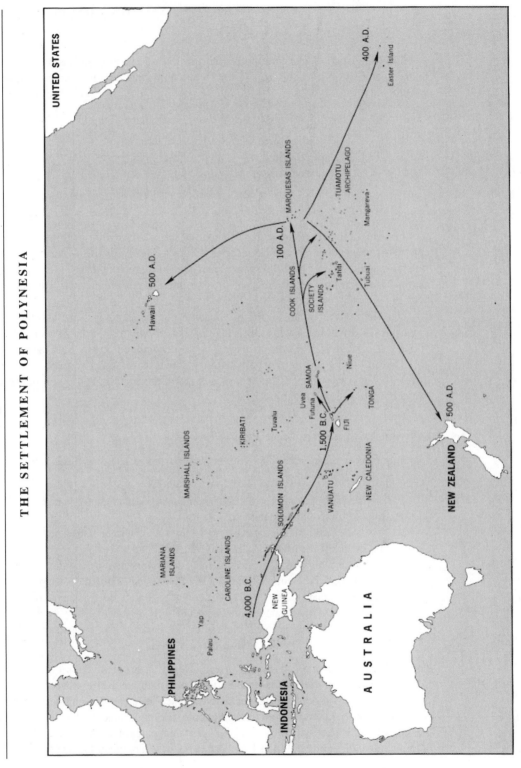

WHAT ARE THE LANGUAGE FAMILIES OF THE WORLD?

The same comparative method used to trace the historical development of languages can be applied to determine which languages are related within families. In this section we survey the major language families of the world, paying particular attention to those families with the greatest number of speakers and those that include most languages.

COUNTING SPEAKERS AND LANGUAGES

It is not easy to determine with certainty how many people speak languages like English, Chinese, and Arabic. Nevertheless, these and a few others stand out for the sheer number of people that claim them as a native language. Of the world's several thousand languages, almost a dozen are spoken natively by 100 million individuals or more. In the following table, numbers have been rounded off to the nearest 50 million.

Chinese	1 billion
English	350 million
Spanish	250 million
Bengali	200 million
Hindi	200 million
Portuguese	150 million
Indonesian-Malay	150 million
Russian	150 million
Arabic	150 million
Japanese	100 million
German	100 million

Five of these languages—Chinese, English, Spanish, Russian, Arabic—and French are the working languages of the United Nations.

Equally difficult to estimate is the number of languages currently spoken in the world. The figure commonly cited is 4,000 to 5,000, while a more conservative estimate would be about 2,000. It is difficult to determine, in many cases, whether particular communities speak different dialects of the same language or different languages. Furthermore, little is known about many of the world's languages. In Papua New Guinea, a nation of only 3 million people, as many as 800 languages (about one fifth of the world's total) are spoken, although we have descriptions of a mere handful. Many Papuan languages are spoken in remote communities by only a few hundred speakers, or even a few dozen.

The discussion below is arranged by language family, beginning with Indo-European, Sino-Tibetan, Austronesian, and Afroasiatic, which together are the four most important families in terms of numbers of both speakers and numbers of languages. The three major language families of sub-Saharan Africa are then discussed together, followed by other language families of Europe and Asia, including important isolated languages like Japanese. Finally, we discuss the native languages of the Americas, Australia, and central Papua New Guinea. Pidgins and creoles will be discussed at the end after a brief discussion of the proposed Nostratic macrofamily.

THE INDO-EUROPEAN FAMILY

To the Indo-European language family belong most languages of Europe (which are now spoken natively in the Americas and Oceania and play prominent roles in Africa and Asia) as well as most languages of Iran, Afghanistan, Pakistan, Bangladesh, and most of India. Of the 11 languages with more than 100 million native speakers, 7 belong to the Indo-European family. Yet Indo-European languages number only about 150, a small fraction of the world's languages. The extensive spread of Indo-European languages is shown in Figure 13-5.

The Indo-European family is divided into several groups, which we discuss briefly. Figure 13-6 is a family tree showing a few languages for each group.

Germanic Group   Modern-day Germanic languages include English, German, Yiddish, Norwegian, Swedish, Danish, Dutch (and its derivative Afrikaans), and a few other languages like Icelandic, Faroese, and Frisian. Frisian, spoken in the northern Netherlands, is the closest relative to English. As Table 13-7 illustrates, Germanic languages bear striking similarities to one another in vocabulary, and similarities in phonology and syntax are also numerous. Some Germanic languages are mutually intelligible, and all bear the imprint of a common ancestor.

Swedish, Danish, Norwegian, Icelandic, and Faroese—the North Germanic group—are more closely related to each other than to the other languages of the Germanic group. They descended from Proto-North-Germanic, which evolved as a single language for a longer period of time than the West Germanic subgroup that includes English, Frisian, Dutch, and German. We also have written records of Gothic, which was spoken in central Europe but which disappeared around the eighth century. Gothic alone forms the East Germanic subgroup. Figure 13-7 is the family tree for the Germanic group (Gothic is in parentheses because it is extinct).

With about 350 million speakers, English is native to the inhabitants of the British Isles, the United States, most of Canada, the Caribbean, Australia, New Zealand, and South Africa. In addition, there are numerous bilinguals of English and another language on the Indian subcontinent, in eastern and southern Africa, and in Oceania. To these we must add the countless speakers of English as a second language scattered around the globe. English is the second most populous spoken language in the world after Chinese, but it is unrivaled in terms of its geographical spread and popularity as a second language. German, which has not spread as much as English, is still one of the world's most widely spoken languages. It claims about 100 million native speakers, mostly in central Europe.

Figure 13-5

LOCATION OF THE MAJOR INDO-EUROPEAN, DRAVIDIAN, CAUCASIAN, URALIC, AND TURKIC LANGUAGES

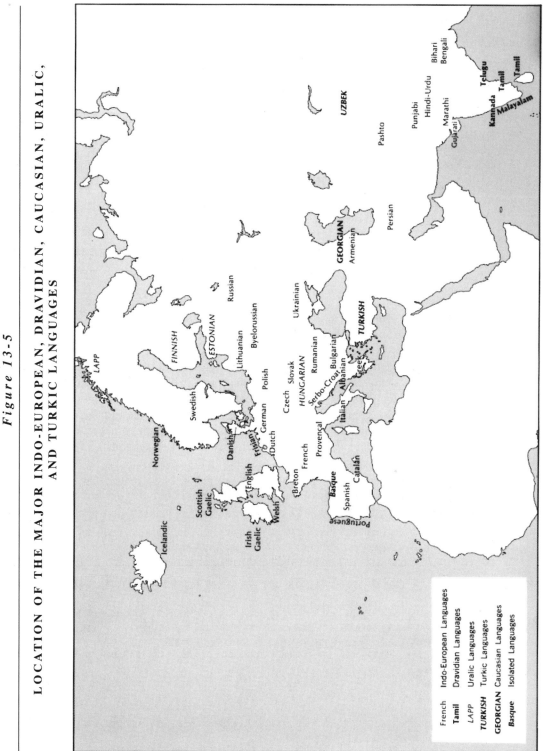

French	Indo-European Languages
Tamil	Dravidian Languages
LAPP	Uralic Languages
TURKISH	Turkic Languages
GEORGIAN	Caucasian Languages
Basque	Isolated Languages

Figure 13-6

PARTIAL TREE OF THE INDO-EUROPEAN LANGUAGE FAMILY

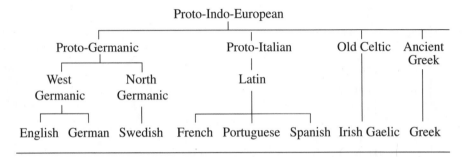

Italic Group and Romance Subgroup   The Romance languages include French, Spanish, Italian, Portuguese, and Rumanian, as well as Provençal (spoken in the south of France), Catalan (spoken in northern Spain), and Romansch (spoken in Switzerland). The Romance languages are closely related to each other, as witnessed by the sample of vocabulary correspondences in Table 13-8. The Rumanian words for 'mother,' 'father,' 'foot,' and 'month,' which are not derived from the same roots as those in the other Romance languages, illustrate the type of historical change that hinders communication between speakers of closely related languages. Such examples are particularly common in Rumanian, which is geographically isolated from other Romance languages.

The languages of the Romance family are descendants of Vulgar Latin. Because the Romance languages have remained in close contact over the centuries, subgroups

Table 13-7

COMMON WORDS IN SEVEN GERMANIC LANGUAGES

ENGLISH	GERMAN	DUTCH	SWEDISH	DANISH	NORWEGIAN	ICELANDIC
mother	Mutter	moeder	moder	moder	moder	móðir
father	Vater	vader	fader	fader	fader	faðir
eye	Auge	oog	öga	øje	øye	auga
foot	Fuss	voet	fot	fod	fot	fótur
one	ein	een	en	en	en	einn
three	drei	drie	tre	tre	tre	þrír
month	Monat	maand	månad	måned	måned	mánaður

Figure 13-6 (Continued)

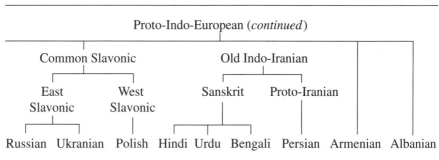

Proto-Indo-European (*continued*)

Figure 13-7

GERMANIC LANGUAGES

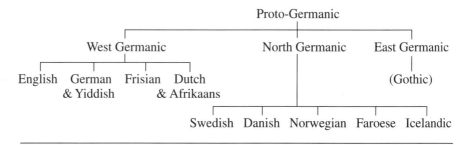

Table 13-8

COMMON WORDS IN SIX ROMANCE LANGUAGES

FRENCH	ITALIAN	SPANISH	RUMANIAN	CATALAN	PORTUGUESE	
mère	madre	madre	mamă	mare	mãe	'mother'
père	padre	padre	tată	pare	pai	'father'
oeil	occhio	ojo	ochiu	ull	ôlho	'eye'
pied	piede	pie	picior	peu	pé	'foot'
un	uno	uno	un	un	um	'one'
trois	tre	tres	trei	tres	três	'three'
mois	mese	mes	lŭna	mes	mês	'month'

are more difficult to identify than for Germanic languages. Latin is one descendant of Proto-Italic. Oscan and Umbrian, the other principal descendants, were once spoken in southern Italy but are now extinct. While written records abound for Latin, little is known about Oscan and Umbrian. The tree for Italic and Romance languages is shown in Figure 13-8.

Spanish, with approximately 250 million native speakers in Spain and the Americas, is the third most populous language. Portuguese is spoken by nearly 150 million people, principally in Portugal and Brazil. French has almost 100 million native speakers in France, Canada, and the United States, as well as many second-language speakers, particularly in North Africa and West Africa.

Slavonic Group Slavonic languages are spoken in eastern Europe and the former Soviet Union. The Slavonic group can be divided into three subgroups: East Slavonic, which includes Russian, Ukrainian, and Byelorussian (spoken in the westernmost part of the former USSR); South Slavonic, which includes Bulgarian and Serbo-Croat; and West Slavonic, which groups together Polish, Czech, Slovak, and a few minor languages. All are derived from Common Slavonic (see Figure 13-9). Even more so than the Germanic and Romance languages, Slavonic languages are remarkably similar to each other, especially in their vocabulary (see Table 13-9).

Figure 13-8

ITALIC LANGUAGES

French   Italian   Catalan   Spanish   Provençal   Portuguese   Rumanian

Proto-Italic / Latin / Osco-Umbrian / (Oscan) (Umbrian)

Figure 13-9

SLAVONIC LANGUAGES

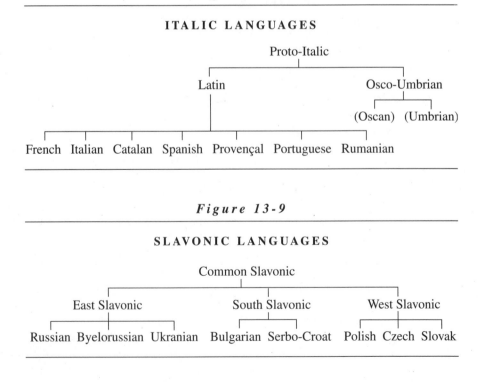

Common Slavonic

East Slavonic — South Slavonic — West Slavonic

Russian Byelorussian Ukranian   Bulgarian Serbo-Croat   Polish Czech Slovak

Table 13-9

COMMON WORDS IN SIX SLAVONIC LANGUAGES

RUSSIAN	UKRAINIAN	POLISH	CZECH	SERBO-CROAT	BULGARIAN	
mat'	mati	matka	matka	mati	mayka	'mother'
otec	otec'	ojciec	otec	otac	bašča	'father'
oko*	oko	oko	oko	oko	oko	'eye'
noga	noga	noga	noha	noga	krak	'foot'
odin	odin	jeden	jeden	jedan	edin	'one'
tri	tri	trzy	tři	tri	tri	'three'
mesyac	misyac'	miesiac	mešíc	mjesec	mesec	'month'

*Russian *oko* 'eye' is archaic; the more modern word is *glaz.*

By far the most widely spoken Slavonic language is Russian, which is spoken natively by 150 million people and as a foreign language by an additional 65 million. Ukrainian has 50 million speakers, Polish 35 million, Serbo-Croat 17 million, Czech 10 million, and Byelorussian 10 million.

Indo-Iranian Group   At the other geographical extreme of the Indo-European family we find the Indo-Iranian group, which is subdivided into Iranian and Indic (see Figure 13-10). The two most important Iranian languages are Persian (also called Farsi), with 35 million speakers in Iran, and Pashto, with 11 million speakers in Afghanistan and northern Pakistan. Indic languages include Hindi-Urdu, spoken by about 200 million people in India (where it is called Hindi and is written in Devanāgarī script) and Pakistan (where it is called Urdu and uses the Arabic script); Bengali, spoken in India and Bangladesh by 200 million people; Bihari, spoken in northeastern India by 25 million; Punjabi, with 40 million speakers in northern India and Pakistan; Marathi, spoken in central India by 65 million people; and Gujarati, spoken in western India by 44 million. Many of these languages are also spoken by

Figure 13-10

INDO-IRANIAN LANGUAGES

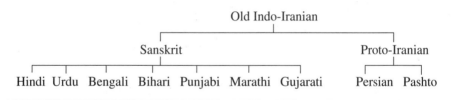

ethnic Indian populations in Southeast Asia, Africa, the Americas, Great Britain, and Oceania. The parent language of the modern Indic languages is Sanskrit, the ancient language of India immortalized in the Vedas and other classical texts.

Table 13-10 presents sample vocabulary correspondences among a few Indo-Iranian languages. Not all the words with one meaning are cognates because some have sources other than a common parent language.

Hellenic Group The sole member of the Hellenic group is Greek. Certain languages, while belonging to a major language family, were isolated early enough that they do not bear any particularly close affiliations to other languages of the family. Such is the case with Greek, which evolved through the centuries in relative isolation. Greek stands out from other isolated Indo-European languages because of its relatively large number of speakers (10 million) and its historical importance in Indo-European linguistics owing to the fact that early written records of Ancient Greek have survived.

Other Indo-European Language Groups Of the other Indo-European groups, Celtic includes Irish Gaelic, Scottish Gaelic, Breton, and Welsh, which together are spoken by no more than 1 million people today; Baltic includes Lithuanian, with 3 million speakers, and Latvian. Tocharian and Anatolian (including Hittite) are now extinct. Armenian and Albanian, each with more than 5 million speakers, form two additional language groups.

THE SINO-TIBETAN FAMILY

Included in the Sino-Tibetan family are about 300 East Asian languages, many of which remain relatively unexplored. This family is divided into a Sinitic group and a Tibeto-Burman group.

The Sinitic group includes a dozen named varieties (Mandarin, Cantonese, and so on). Most of them are structurally similar and are regarded by their speakers as

Table 13-10

COMMON WORDS IN SIX INDIC LANGUAGES

HINDI	BENGALI	MARATHI	GUJARATI	PERSIAN	PASHTO	
mã:	ma	ma:	ma:	madær	mo:r	'mother'
ba:p	ba:p	baba:	ba:p	pedær	pla:r	'father'
ã:kʰ	cókʰ	dola	a:nkʰ	čæšm	starga	'eye'
pã:w	pa:	pa:	pa:g	pa	xpa	'foot'
ek	ak	ek	e:k	yek	yau	'one'
ti:n	ti:n	ti:n	tra:n	se	dre:	'three'
mahi:na:	mas	mahi:na:	mahi:no	mah	mia:sht	'month'

dialects of a single language. With more than 1 billion speakers, this language is the world's most populous language; it is of course Chinese. Five dialect groups can be identified. The Mandarin group includes the Bĕijīng (Peking) dialect, which serves as the official language of the People's Republic of China; the Yuè dialects include the dialect of Guǎngzhōu (Canton), which is spoken by the greatest number of overseas Chinese, now scattered throughout the world.

By comparison, the Tibeto-Burman group includes many different languages, each with relatively few speakers. The only members of this group that have more than a million speakers are Burmese (22 million) and Tibetan (1 million). Figure 13-11 maps the major Sino-Tibetan languages.

Figure 13-11

LOCATION OF THE MAJOR SINO-TIBETAN, MON-KHMER, AND TAI LANGUAGES, AND OF THE MAJOR ISOLATED LANGUAGES OF ASIA

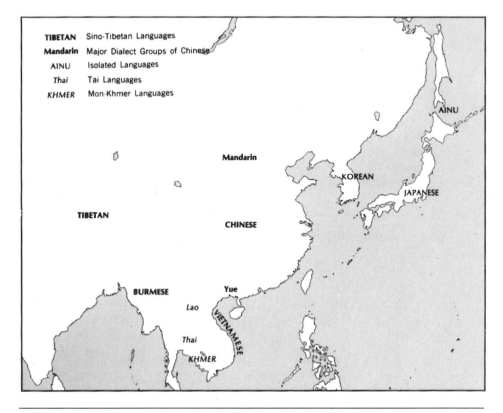

THE AUSTRONESIAN FAMILY

The Austronesian family has up to 1,000 different languages scattered over one-third of the Southern Hemisphere. It includes Indonesian-Malay, spoken by about 150 million people in Indonesia and Malaysia; Javanese, with 75 million speakers on the island of Java in Indonesia; Tagalog or Pilipino, the official language of the Philippines, with 15 million speakers; Cebuano, another language of the Philippines (15 million speakers); and Malagasy, the principal language of Madagascar (10 million speakers). Most other Austronesian languages have fewer than 1 million speakers each, and many of them are spoken by only a few hundred people.

The Austronesian family contains several groups. The most ancient division is between three groups of minor Formosan languages spoken in the hills of Taiwan and all other Austronesian languages; the latter group is called Malayo-Polynesian. The most important split divides Western Malayo-Polynesian (languages spoken in Indonesia, Malaysia, Madagascar, the Philippines, and Guam) from Oceanic or Eastern Malayo-Polynesian, (extending from the coastal areas of Papua New Guinea into the islands of the Pacific). Fijian and the Polynesian languages are Oceanic languages. Table 13-11 gives a sample of vocabulary correspondences between representative Austronesian languages. Figure 13-13 is a simplified tree of the family, and the distribution of Austronesian languages is illustrated in Figure 13-12.

THE AFROASIATIC FAMILY

The Afroasiatic family comprises about 250 languages scattered across the northern part of Africa and western Asia. It includes Arabic, dialects of which are spoken across the entire northern part of Africa and the Middle East; Hebrew, the traditional language of the Jewish nation and revived in this century as the national language of Israel; Egyptian, the now extinct language of the ancient Egyptian civilization; and

Table 13-11

COMMON WORDS IN SIX AUSTRONESIAN LANGUAGES

MALAY	MALAGASY	TAGALOG	MOTU	FIJIAN	SAMOAN	
ibu	ineny	inâ	sina	tina	tinaa	'mother'
bapa	ikaky	amá	tama	tama	tamaa	'father'
mata	maso	mata	mata	mata	mata	'eye'
satu	isa	isa	ta	dua	tasi	'one'
tiga	telo	tatló	toi	tolu	tolu	'three'
batu	vato	bato	nadi	vatu	fatu*	'stone'
kutu	hao	kuto	utu	kutu	ʔutu	'louse'

*Samoan *fatu* actually means 'fruit pit,' a meaning closely related to 'stone.'

Figure 13-12

MAP OF AUSTRONESIAN LANGUAGES

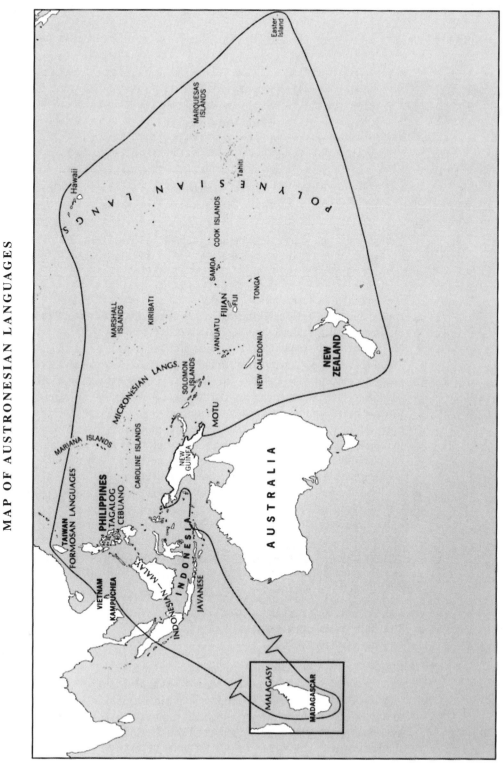

Figure 13-13

TREE OF AUSTRONESIAN LANGUAGES

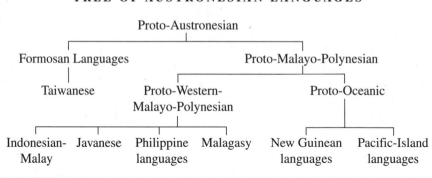

Hausa, one of Africa's major languages, spoken natively by about 22 million people in Chad, Nigeria, and neighboring nations (see Figure 13-14).

Hebrew and Arabic form the Semitic group within the Afroasiatic family. To this group also belong Amharic, the official language of Ethiopia, and Akkadian, a language of ancient Mesopotamia (modern Iraq), now extinct. Akkadian appears to have been the first language ever written, but it was replaced largely by Aramaic, which is also Semitic. Aramaic comprises a group of dialects. These include Palestinian Aramaic, the language Jesus spoke, and Modern Syriac, spoken by Christians in Iran, Iraq, and Soviet Georgia. A distinctive property of Semitic languages is their morphological system; noun and verb roots consist of a series of consonants in which vowels are interdigitated to represent inflection (see Chapter 2).

Somali, the principal language of Somalia, is one of 40 languages of the Cushitic group. Kabyl and other languages that belong to the Berber group (with 10 million speakers) are scattered across North Africa. Hausa and about 130 other languages form the Chadic group, all of which have developed tone systems. Ancient Egyptian forms a separate Afroasiatic group. Table 13-12 is a comparative vocabulary for representative members of the Afroasiatic family. ([ħ] is the symbol for a voiceless pharyngeal fricative and [ʕ] for its voiced counterpart.)

THE THREE MAJOR LANGUAGE FAMILIES OF SUB-SAHARAN AFRICA

Besides the Afroasiatic family spoken north of the Sahara Desert, Africa is home to three other language families: the Niger-Kordofanian family, with several hundred languages spoken by about 150 million people in a region that stretches from Senegal to Kenya to South Africa; the Nilo-Saharan family, with about 100 languages spoken by 10 million people in and around Chad and the Sudan; and the Khoisan family in southern Africa, with 50 languages spoken by fewer than 75,000 people altogether.

Figure 13-14

THE LANGUAGE FAMILIES OF AFRICA

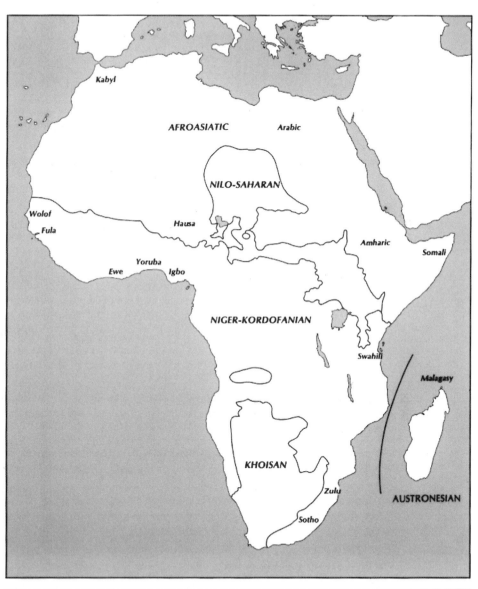

Source: Adapted from Gregersen 1977

Table 13-12

COMMON WORDS IN SIX AFROASIATIC LANGUAGES

ARABIC	HEBREW	AMHARIC	KABYL	HAUSA	SOMALI	
um	ɛm	annat	yemma	inna	hooyyo	'mother'
ab	av	abbat	baba	baba	aabe	'father'
ʕain	ayin	ayn	allen	ido	il	'eye'
ʔežer	regɛl	agar	aḍaṛ	k'afa	ʕag	'foot'
waḥad	ɛxad	and	waḥed	'daya	hal	'one'
talaṭa	šloša	sost	tlata	uku	saddeh	'three'
šaher	xodɛš	wár	eccher	wata	bil	'month'

The Khoisan family, traditionally associated with the Bushmen of the Kalahari Desert, is the only language family in the world that has click sounds (discussed in Chapter 3). The boundaries between these language families are shown in Figure 13-14.

Most of the better-known languages of sub-Saharan Africa belong to the Niger-Kordofanian family. These include Fula, spoken by 2 million speakers in Guinea and Senegal; Wolof, with 2 million speakers in Senegal, Gambia, Mali, and Guinea; Yoruba, spoken in Nigeria by almost 19 million; Ewe, spoken by 1 million in Togo, Benin, and Ghana; Igbo, with 17 million speakers in Nigeria; Swahili, with approximately 30 million first- and second-language speakers in East Africa; and other Bantu languages of southern Africa like Zulu (9 million speakers) and Sotho (4 million).

OTHER LANGUAGE FAMILIES OF ASIA AND EUROPE

Scattered throughout Asia and Europe are a few smaller language families and a few languages that seem not to be genetically related to any other language family, so far as linguists can determine, and are therefore called *isolates*.

The Dravidian Family Languages of the Dravidian family are spoken principally in southern India (see Figure 13-5). The four major Dravidian languages are Tamil (60 million speakers), Malayalam (34 million speakers), Kannada (33 million speakers), and Telugu (73 million speakers), all of which have been written for many centuries. All Dravidian languages have been somewhat influenced by the Indic languages spoken to their north. In Table 13-13, the Indic influence is evident in the Tamil and Kannada words for 'month,' which are of Indo-European origin and were borrowed into these languages.

The Mon-Khmer Family The Mon-Khmer family includes about 100 languages spoken in Southeast Asia (Vietnam, Laos, Kampuchea, Thailand, and Burma). The most important of these is Cambodian or Khmer, the official language of Cambodia, spoken by nearly 8 million people (see Figure 13-11). The Mon-Khmer languages may be related to other minor families of the same region.

Table 13-13

COMMON WORDS IN FOUR DRAVIDIAN LANGUAGES

TAMIL	MALAYALAM	KANNADA	TELUGU	
amma:	amma	awwa	amma	'mother'
appa:	a:chchan	tande	na:nna	'father'
kaṇṇu	kaṇṇu	kaṇṇu	kannu	'eye'
ka:lu	ka:l	ka:lu	ka:lu	'foot'
onru	oru	ondu	okaṭi	'one'
mu:nru	mu:nnu	mu:ru	mu:ḍu	'three'
ma:sam	nela	tingaḷu	tinglu	'month'

The Tai Family   The best-known languages of the Tai family are Thai (20 million speakers) and Lao (3 million speakers), the official languages of Thailand and Laos respectively (shown in Figure 13-11). There are about 50 other members of the Tai family scattered throughout Thailand, Laos Vietnam, Myanmar, eastern India, and southern China, where they intertwine with Sino-Tibetan languages, Mon-Khmer languages, and Vietnamese. Tai languages may be related to a number of languages spoken in Vietnam, with which they may form a Kam-Tai family. It has also been suggested that Tai languages may be related to Austronesian, but the evidence supporting that hypothesis is scanty.

The Caucasian Family   With about 30 languages, the Caucasian family is confined to the mountainous region between the Black Sea and the Caspian Sea, which is part of the former Soviet Union, Turkey, and Iran. Spoken by about 5 million people altogether, Caucasian languages typically have complex phonological and morphological systems. The best-known Caucasian language is Georgian (see Figure 13-5).

The Turkic Family   This family comprises about 60 languages, all of which are quite similar. The better-known members are Turkish, spoken by 59 million people, and Uzbek, with 18 million speakers in Uzbekistan. Most Turkic languages are spoken in Turkey and central Asia (see Figure 13-5). Some scholars include Turkic in a larger Altaic family.

The Uralic Family   With about 30 members, the Uralic family is thought by some to be related to the Turkic family, though this link is tenuous. The better-known Uralic languages are Finnish (6 million speakers) and Hungarian (15 million speakers); also included are Estonian and Lapp (see Figure 13-5).

Japanese   Japanese, with more than 125 million speakers, does not have any universally agreed upon relatives, although many scholars regard it and Korean as belonging to an Altaic family, along with Turkic. Ryūkyūan, spoken in Okinawa, is a dialect of Japanese, and Ainu, spoken by about 15,000 people in the north of Japan, may also be related. Japanese has absorbed considerable influence from Chinese, to which it is *not* related (see Figure 13-11).

Korean   Korean is spoken by about 75 million people. Many scholars regard Korean and Japanese as related members of the Altaic family, but this hypothesis remains unproven. Like Japanese, Korean has been greatly influenced by Chinese over the centuries (see Figure 13-11).

Vietnamese   Vietnamese, the language of the 65 million inhabitants of Vietnam and neighboring areas, does not have any clear genetic relationships, although it may be a distant relative of Mon-Khmer languages (see Figure 13-11).

Other Isolated Languages of Asia and Europe   Of the remaining isolated languages of Eurasia, Basque is the best known. It is spoken by almost 600,000 inhabitants in an area that straddles the Spanish-French border on the Atlantic coast (see Figure 13-5).

NATIVE AMERICAN LANGUAGES

Compared to the Old World, the linguistic situation in the New World is bewildering, with numerous American Indian language families in North and South America. While proposals for the genetic integration of these languages have been made, solid evidence for a pan-American link is lacking. Below are listed a few of those families and some of their members. You can see the approximate locations of some of these languages in Figure 13-15.

Eskimo-Aleut   In North America, we distinguish the Eskimo-Aleut family (whose speakers are not genetically related to Amerindians) from other language families. Inuit has 21,500 speakers across northern Canada and Alaska, and Yupik has about 16,000 speakers in Alaska and several hundred in Siberia.

Algonquian   Among the Algonquian languages are Cree (with 67,000 speakers in Canada and Montana) and Ojibwa (with more than 50,000 speakers living in Ontario, Manitoba, Michigan, Minnesota, and North Dakota). Represented by fewer speakers are Arapaho (1,000 in Wyoming), Blackfoot (9,000 in Montana and Canada), Cheyenne (1,700 in Montana and Oklahoma), Kikapoo (850 in Kansas, Oklahoma, and Coahuila, Mexico), Malecite-Passamaquoddy (1,500 in Maine and New Brunswick), Micmac (with 6,000 in Maritime Canada and 2,000 in Boston), Potawatomi (300 spread across Wisconsin, Michigan, Kansas, Oklahoma, and Ontario), and Shawnee (with 200 in Oklahoma). Related to the Algonquian languages are the Muskogean languages, discussed next.

Muskogean   The largest Muskogean language is Choctaw-Chicasaw, with 9,200 speakers in Oklahoma, Mississippi, and Louisiana. Also Muskogean are Koasati (300 speakers in Louisiana and Texas) and Alabama (250 in Texas).

Figure 13-15

NATIVE AMERICAN LANGUAGES

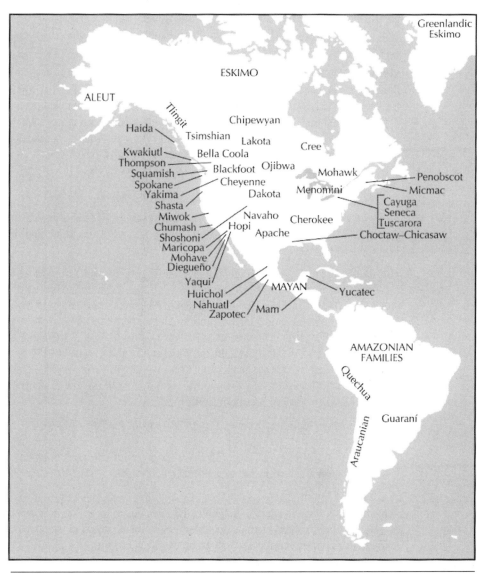

Athabaskan   In the Athabaskan family, some varieties of Apache are becoming extinct, but Western Apache has 11,000 speakers in Arizona, and Mescalero-Chiricahua Apache has 1,800 speakers chiefly in New Mexico. Navaho has 150,000 speakers in Arizona, Utah, and New Mexico. Chipewyan has 4,000 speakers in Alberta, Saskatchewan, Manitoba, and the Northwest Territories. Often included with the

Athabaskan languages in a group called Na-Dene are Tlingit and possibly Haida, both spoken in Alaska and British Columbia.

Iroquoian   Excepting principally Cherokee (with 22,500 speakers in Oklahoma and North Carolina), the Iroquoian languages are spoken mainly in Ontario and Quebec, as well as in upstate New York. The other Iroquoian languages include Cayuga, with 370 speakers; Mohawk, with 3,000; Oneida; with 250; and Seneca, with 200.

Siouan   The Siouan family, located mainly in the upper midwest of the United States and in Canada, includes Dakota, with 19,000 speakers in Manitoba and Saskatchewan, as well as Minnesota, Montana, Nebraska, and the Dakotas. Crow has 5,500 speakers in Montana, and Lakota has 6,000 in Manitoba and Saskatchewan, as well as Nebraska, Minnesota, Montana, and the Dakotas. Omaha has 1,500 speakers in Nebraska, while Winnebago has 1,500 in Nebraska and Wisconsin.

Penutian   The Penutian family includes Tsimshian (with 300 speakers in Canada), Yakima (with 3,000 in Washington), and Walla Walla (with 100 speakers in Oregon).

Salishan   Among the languages of the Salishan family are Shuswap (with 500 speakers in British Columbia), Spokane (with 50 in Washington), and Thompson (with 500 in British Columbia).

Uto-Aztecan   The Uto-Aztecan language family remains robust. Varieties of Nahuatl are spoken by about 1 million people in central and southern Mexico. On a much smaller scale, Huichol has 12,500 speakers in Nayarit and Jalisco, and Papago-Pima has 15,000 in Arizona and Mexico. Hopi is spoken by 5,000 speakers in Arizona and Yaqui by 17,000 near Phoenix and Tucson and in Mexico. Shoshoni has 3,000 speakers in California, Nevada, Idaho, Wyoming, and Utah, while Ute–Southern Paiute is spoken by 2,500 speakers in Colorado, Utah, Arizona, and Nevada. Comanche has 500 speakers in Oklahoma. Also Uto-Aztecan are Cahuilla (50) and Luiseño (100), spoken in Southern California.

Hokan   Hokan includes Diegueño (with 350 to 400 speakers in Baja California and Southern California), Havasupai-Walapai-Yavapai (with 1,200 in Arizona), Karok (with 100 in northwestern California), Maricopa (with 150 near Phoenix), Mohave (with 700 on the California-Arizona border), and Washo (with 100 on the California-Nevada border).

Mayan   The largest Mayan language is Yucatec, whose 940,000 speakers live mostly in the Yucatán Peninsula. Mam has about 400,000 speakers, most in Guatemala. The Mayan family also embraces Kekchi (with perhaps 365,000 speakers), Quiché (with perhaps 600,000), Cakchiquel (with perhaps 400,000), and about two dozen other languages.

Quechua   Quechua was the language of the ancient Incan Empire. It still has 6 million speakers in the Andes and is the most popular indigenous South American language; its genetic affiliation is unclear.

Tupi   The Tupi family includes Guaraní, with about 4 million speakers in Paraguay (where it is an official language) and in southwestern Brazil.

Oto-Manguean   Members of the Oto-Manguean family include Zapotec (with almost half a million speakers), Mixtec (with about 250,000), and Otomi (with 100,000), all spoken in central and southern Mexico.

Totonacan   Totonacan includes Totonaco, with about 250,000 speakers in Mexico.

Extinct and Dying Amerindian Languages   Scores of indigenous languages of the Americas have fallen silent over the past few decades. Red Thunder Cloud, the last speaker of the Siouan language Catawba died in 1996 in Worcester, Massachusetts. The last speaker of Tillamook, a Salishan language, died in 1970, eight years after the last speaker of Wiyot, related to the Algonquian languages. Algonquian has also lost Miami, spoken in Indiana and Oklahoma, and Massachusett (also called Natick and Wampanoag). Also now extinct are Huron (or Wyandot) of the Iroquoian family, and the Hokan languages Chumash, spoken around Santa Barbara, California, but extinct since 1965, and Salinan, spoken on the central coast of California. Other extinct Amerindian languages include Chinook, of Washington and Oregon; Natchez and Tonkawa, both of Oklahoma; and Mohegan-Montauk-Narrangansett, heard earlier in Wisconsin and from Long Island to Connecticut and Rhode Island.

Amerindian languages are disappearing in the face of mounting pressure for younger speakers to adopt English, Spanish, or Portuguese, and many native languages are known only to a few older speakers. Among languages with fewer than fifty speakers are Abnaki-Penobscot (spoken in Maine and Canada); several varieties of Apache; the Salishan languages Coeur d'Alene (in Idaho) and Squamish (near Vancouver); Cupeño (of the Uto-Aztecan family in Southern California); Delaware and Menomini (Algonquian languages, the latter spoken in Wisconsin); Iowa and Osage (Siouan); Wichita (of the Caddoan family, spoken in Oklahoma); Miwok and Yokuts (Penutian languages spoken in California); Coos (also Penutian, spoken in Oregon); Pomo and Shasta (both Hokan); and Tuscarora (an Iroquoian language formerly of North Carolina and now spoken near Niagara Falls, New York, and in Ontario, Canada).

LANGUAGES OF ABORIGINAL AUSTRALIA

Before settlement by Europeans in the eighteenth century, Australia had been inhabited by Aborigines for up to fifty millennia. It is estimated that at the time of first contact with Europeans about two hundred to three hundred Aboriginal languages were spoken. Today many of these languages have disappeared, along with their speakers, decimated by imported diseases and sometimes (as on the island of Tasmania) by genocide. Today, only about a hundred Aboriginal languages survive, most spoken by tiny populations of older survivors.

Virtually all Australian languages fall into a single family with two groups: the large Pama-Nyungan group, which covers most of the continent and includes most Aboriginal languages, and the Non–Pama-Nyungan group, which includes about fifty languages in northern Australia.

PAPUAN LANGUAGES

Papuan languages are spoken on the large island of New Guinea, which is divided politically between the nation of Papua New Guinea and the Indonesian-controlled section called Irian Jaya. While the inhabitants of coastal areas of the island speak Austronesian languages, about eight hundred of the languages are not Austronesian languages. Referred to as Papuan languages, most are not in any danger of extinction, though many are spoken by small populations. They fall into more than sixty different families, with no established genetic link among them. Little is known about most of these languages.

NOSTRATIC MACROFAMILY

Recent years have seen renewed focus on linking certain language families within larger "macrofamilies." One proposed macrofamily that has received attention even in the popular press is the Nostratic macrofamily. Some scholars, especially in the former Soviet Union and the United States, have proposed that several language families that are generally regarded as distinct should be viewed as having a common source farther back in time. The languages hypothesized to belong to Nostratic differ slightly from scholar to scholar, but most scholars espousing this theory include Indo-European, Afroasiatic, Uralic, Altaic, Dravidian, and Eskimo-Aleut. Assuming that detailed comparative reconstruction confirmed this hypothesis, the Nostratic macrofamily would then make distant cousins of English (Indo-European); Hebrew, Arabic, Somali, and Hausa (Afroasiatic); Finnish and Hungarian (Uralic); perhaps Korean and Turkish (Altaic); Tamil (Dravidian); and Inuktitut.

Although the links among these far-flung languages are not widely accepted among scholars, the hypothesis is provocative in an important way. As demonstrated in this chapter, the principal method for establishing genetic relations among languages is by comparative reconstruction, whereby the forms of a parent language are hypothesized and the forms of the various daughter languages are derived by regular rules. Before any comparative reconstruction can be attempted, there must be hypotheses about which languages are and are not related. Without such hypotheses, just which languages would constitute the bases for establishing the sound correspondences (and other correspondences not emphasized in this chapter) that make the stuff of comparative reconstruction? With the Nostratic hypothesis in mind, you may find it thought provoking to reexamine the tables of common words for those Nostratic languages illustrated in this chapter: tables 13-7 through 13-10 for four Indo-European groups, 13-12 for Afroasiatic, and 13-13 for Dravidian. Bear in mind that the sound correspondences among these languages would not be between the sounds of the daughter languages directly but between the sounds of the reconstructed parent languages, so any immediate correspondences that you might spy may be deceptive.

LANGUAGES IN CONTACT

At no other time in history have there been such intensive contacts between language communities as in the last few centuries. As a result of the exploratory and colonizing enterprises of the English, French, Dutch, Spanish, and Portuguese, European languages have come into contact with languages of Africa, Native America, Asia, and the Pacific. These colonizing efforts put members of different speech communities in contact with each other. For example, the importing of slaves from Africa to the Americas forced speakers of different African languages to live side by side. Several language contact phenomena can take place when speakers of different languages interact.

MULTILINGUALISM

Bilingualism   The first of these phenomena is **bilingualism** or multilingualism, in which members of a community acquire more than one language natively. In a multilingual community, children grow up speaking several languages. In many multilingual communities, use of each language is compartmentalized, as when one language is used at home and another at school or at work. Multilingualism is such a natural solution to the problem of language contact that it is extremely widespread throughout the world. In this respect, industrialized societies like the United States and Japan, in which bilingualism is not widespread, are exceptional. In the United States bilingualism is mostly relegated to immigrant communities, whose members are expected to learn English upon arrival. The adaptation is one-sided in contrast to what is found in most other areas of the globe, where neighboring communities learn each other's languages with little ado. In central Africa, India, and Papua New Guinea, it is commonplace for small children to grow up speaking four or five languages. In Papua New Guinea, multilingualism is a highly valued attribute that enhances a person's status in the community.

Nativization   A possible side effect of multilingualism is **nativization,** which takes place when a community adopts a new language (in addition to its native language) and modifies the structure of that new language, thus developing a dialect that becomes characteristic of the community. That is precisely what has happened with English in India, where Indian English is recognized as a separate dialect of English with its own structural characteristics. Indeed, it has become one of India's two national languages (along with Hindi, the most widely spoken indigenous language) and is used in education, government, and communications within India and with the rest of the world.

Pidgins   Another process that may take place in language contact situations is pidginization. Though probably derived from the word *business*, the origin of the word **pidgin** is unclear, but it is used to refer to a contact language that develops where groups are in a dominant/subordinate situation, often in the context of colonization.

Pidgins arise when members of a politically or economically dominant group do not learn the native language of the people they interact with as political or economic subordinates. To communicate, members of the subordinate community create a simplified variety of the language of the dominant group as their own second language. Pidgins then become the language of interaction between the colonizer and the colonized. Pidgins are thus defined in terms of sociological and linguistic characteristics: They are based on the language of the dominant group but are structurally simpler. They have no native speakers and are typically used for a restricted range of purposes.

Pidgins have arisen in many areas of the world, including West Africa, the Caribbean, the Far East, and the Pacific. Many pidgins have been based on English and French, the languages of the two most active colonial powers in the eighteenth and nineteenth centuries. Other languages that have served as a base for the development of pidgins include Portuguese, Spanish, Dutch, Swedish, German, Arabic, and Russian.

From Pidgin to Creole   Today, most pidgins have given way to creole languages. At some point, a pidgin may begin to fulfill a greater number of roles in social life; instead of using the pidgin language only in the workplace to communicate with traders or colonizers, speakers of a pidgin may begin to use the language at home or among themselves. Such situations frequently arise when the colonized population is linguistically diversified. Members of that community may find it convenient to adopt the new language as a **lingua franca**—a means to communicate across language boundaries. As a result, small children begin to grow up speaking the new language, and as greater demands are put onto that language its structure becomes more complex in a process called creolization. A **creole** language is thus a former pidgin that has "acquired" native speakers. Creoles are structurally complex, eventually as complex as any other language, and they differ from pidgins in that they exhibit less variability from speaker to speaker than pidgins do.

The boundary between pidgin and creole is often difficult to establish. Creolization is a gradual process, and in many situations pidgins are undergoing creolization. In such situations, there will be much variability from speaker to speaker and from situation to situation. For some speakers and in some contexts, the language will clearly be at the pidgin stage; for speakers whose language is more advanced in the creolization process, or in contexts that call for a more elaborated variety, the language will be structurally more complex. Furthermore, as a creole gains wider usage and becomes structurally more complex, it often comes to resemble the language on which it is based. For example, in the Caribbean and in Hawaii, English-based creoles are very similar to standard English for many speakers. Typically in such situations we find a continuum from speaker to speaker and from situation to situation—from a nonstandard dialect of the parent language to a very basic pidgin.

Figure 13-16 shows the location of the more important creoles in the world. Note that in common parlance many creoles are called pidgins. Such is the case with Hawaiian Pidgin and Papua New Guinea Tok Pisin (from 'talk Pidgin'), both of which are actually creoles.

Figure 13-16

LOCATION OF MAJOR PIDGIN AND CREOLE LANGUAGES

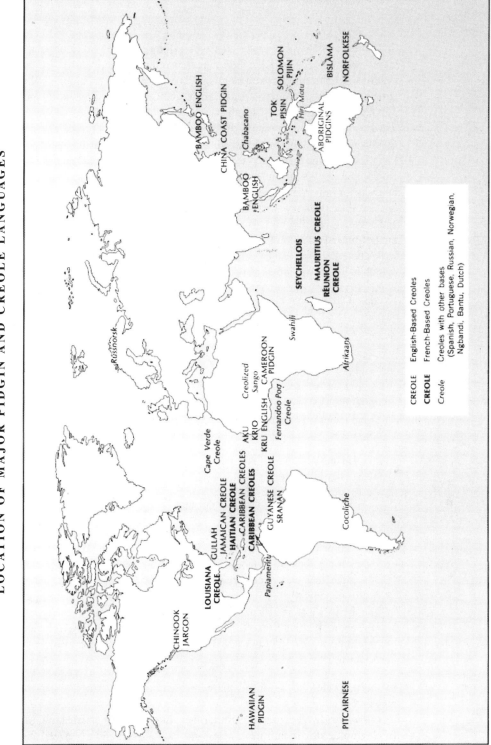

CREOLE   English-Based Creoles

CREOLE   French-Based Creoles

Creole   Creoles with other bases
(Spanish, Portuguese, Russian, Norwegian,
Ngbandi, Bantu, Dutch)

Some creoles have low status where they are spoken. Such is the case with Hawaiian creole, or Da Kine Talk, which is often referred to as a "bastardized" version of English or as "broken English." The fact is that Hawaiian creole has its own structure, different from that of English, and one cannot pretend to speak Da Kine Talk by speaking "broken" English.

In contrast, in many areas of the world creoles have become national languages used in government proceedings, education, and the media. In Papua New Guinea, Tok Pisin is one of the three national languages (along with English and Kiri Motu, also a creole) and has become a symbol of national identity. Some creoles have become the language of important bodies of literature, particularly in West Africa. Elsewhere, creoles are used in newspapers and on the radio for various purposes, including cartoons and commercials. Figure 13-17 is a publicity cartoon in Papua New Guinea Tok Pisin; the English translation of the captions is given underneath. Tok Pisin is even used to write about linguistics, as illustrated by the following discussion of relative clause formation in Tok Pisin; it begins with three example sentences.

1. Ol ikilim pik bipo.
2. Na pik bai ikamap olosem draipela ston.
3. Na pik *ia* [ol ikilim bipo *ia*] bai ikamap olosem draipela ston.

Sapos yumi tingting gut long dispela tripela tok, yumi ken klia long tupela samting. Nambawan samting, sapos pik istap long (1) em inarapela pik, na pik istap long (2) em inarapela, orait, yumi no ken wokim (3). Tasol sapos wanpela pik tasol istap long (1) na (2), em orait long wokim (3). Na tu, tingting istap long (1) ia, mi bin banisim insait long tupela banis long (3), long wonem, em bilong kliaim yumi long wonem pik Elena itok en.

[Translation]
1. They killed the pig.
2. The pig looks like a big rock.
3. The pig [that they killed] looks like a big rock.

If we think carefully about these three sentences, we can obtain two interpretations. First, if the pig of sentence (1) is one pig, and the pig of sentence (2) is another pig, then we cannot construct (3). However, if the pig in (1) and (2) is the same, then we can construct (3). Thus, I have bracketed in (3) the meaning corresponding to (1) with two brackets, because it has the purpose of identifying for us which pig Elena [the speaker who produced these sentences] is talking about. [Gillian Sankoff, "Sampela Nupela lo Ikamap Long Tok Pisin," in McElhanon, ed., *Tok Pisin i Go We?* (Ukarumpa: Linguistic Society of New Guinea, 1975).]

In short, creoles can fulfill all the demands that are commonly imposed on a language.

The worldwide structural similarities among creoles are striking. Many creoles, for example, lack indefinite articles and lack a distinction between the future and

Figure 13-17

PUBLICITY CARTOON IN TOK PISIN

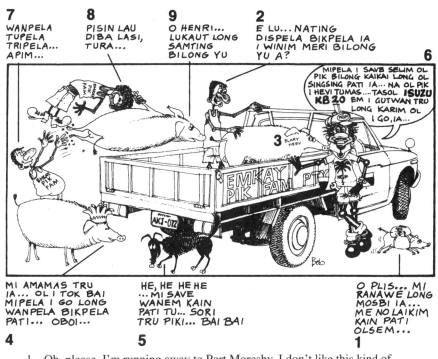

7
WANPELA
TUPELA
TRIPELA...
APIM...

8
PISIN LAU
DIBA LASI,
TURA...

9
O HENRI...
LUKAUT LONG
SAMTING
BILONG YU

2
E LU... NATING
DISPELA BIKPELA IA
I WINIM MERI BILONG
YU A?

6
MIPELA I SAVE SELIM OL
PIK BILONG KAIKAI LONG OL
SINGSING PATI IA... NA OL PIK
I HEVI TUMAS....TASOL **ISUZU**
KB 20 EM I GUTWAN TRU
LONG KARIM OL
I GO, IA...

3 BLARY
NERV

4
MI AMAMAS TRU
IA... OL I TOK BAI
MIPELA I GO LONG
WANPELA BIKPELA
PATI... OBOI...

5
HE, HE HE HE
... MI SAVE
WANEM KAIN
PATI TU... SORI
TRU PIKI... BAI BAI

1
O PLIS... MI
RANAWE LONG
MOSBI IA...
ME NO LAIKIM
KAIN PATI
OLSEM...

1. Oh, please. I'm running away to Port Moresby. I don't like this kind of party.
2. Hey, Lu! It's not for nothing that this big fat one beats your wife (in size).
3. The bloody nerve!
4. I am so happy. They all say that we are going to a big party. Oh, boy.
5. Hee, hee, hee, hee. I know what kind of party too. Very sorry, Piggy. Bye bye.
6. We frequently sell pigs for eating at dance parties. But pigs are very heavy so Isuzu KB20s are excellent to carry them all away.
7. One, two, three, up . . .
8. (speaking in Hiri Motu) Friend, I don't speak Tok Pisin.
9. Hey, Henry! Watch out for your things.

other tenses, and many have preposition stranding (like the English *the house I live in*). These and other similarities have led some researchers to propose that the development of pidgins and creoles follows a "program" that is genetically innate in humans. There are, however, many differences among the world's creoles, in which the imprint of various native languages is clear. In many South Pacific creoles, for example, a distinction is made in the pronoun system between dual and plural and between inclusive first-person dual and plural and exclusive first-person dual and plural (see Chapter 7, page 231 where the Tok Pisin pronoun system is given). These distinctions are not found in West African creoles, and their presence in South Pacific creoles reflects the fact that many languages spoken in the South Pacific make these distinctions. In Nigerian creole, on the other hand, we find honorific terms of address (*Mom* and *Dad*) that are used when addressing high-status individuals. These honorifics are not found in any other creole; again, they are transferred from local languages. Thus there is both homogeneity and heterogeneity among the creoles of the world.

COMPUTERS AND THE HISTORY OF LANGUAGES

In the study of historical linguistics and language change, computers have been particularly helpful in their ability to manipulate large quantities of data accurately and efficiently. Several major historical corpora have been compiled over the past couple of decades, and their ability to aid researchers in tracing lexical, morphological, semantic, and syntactic change in language has proven impressive and interesting.

Among the influential historical corpora is the Helsinki Corpus of English Texts: Diachronic and Dialectal (called the Helsinki Corpus for short). Here we concentrate on the historical (diachronic) part. Compiled by researchers at the University of Helsinki, this corpus contains (among other things) texts of English from the Old English period (starting at about A.D. 800) and continuing through the early eighteenth century in the period known as Early Modern English. Unlike the LOB and Brown corpora, which contain 2,000-word extracts of texts, the Helsinki Corpus contains texts varying in length from 2,500 to almost 20,000 words. Altogether, there are 242 text files totaling about 1.5 million words of running text. Like many corpora, for each of its texts the Helsinki Corpus includes information about the author's name, sex, education, origin, and social status, as well as information about the date of composition and the genre of the text (which is related to what we have been calling register). Using the Helsinki Corpus, researchers have been able to investigate patterns of development with certain genres across time, across genres within a given period of time, between men and women writers, and between British and American English, to mention just some of the dimensions along which it is possible to explore.

Another corpus, known as ARCHER—A Representative Corpus of Historical English Registers—includes ten registers over the centuries from 1650 to 1990, broken into periods of half a century each. For the periods 1750 to 1799, 1850 to 1899, and 1950 to 1990, ARCHER contains parallel British and American texts; for the other periods, only British texts. The ten registers include both written (such as fiction, legal opinions) and speech-based registers (fictional conversation, drama, sermons). All told, ARCHER contains over 1,000 texts and about 1.7 million words. In the next chapter, you will see some of the findings that researchers have established by mining the riches of ARCHER.

SUMMARY

- Languages are always changing.

- All levels of the grammar change: phonology, morphology, lexicon, syntax, semantics, and pragmatics.

- From one language many other languages can develop in the course of time if groups of speakers remain physically or socially separated from one another.

- The method of comparative reconstruction enables linguists to make educated guesses about the structure and vocabulary of prehistoric peoples and to infer a good deal about their cultures from the nature of the reconstructed lexicon.

- The thousands of languages in the world can be grouped for the most part into language families whose branches represent languages that are genealogically closer to one another than other languages of the family.

- When speakers of different languages come into contact, bilingualism may develop, with speakers commanding two or more languages.

- In some circumstances—usually when a dominant and a subordinate group are in contact—a pidgin may spring up for very limited use, usually in trade. If in time the pidgin comes to be used for other purposes and children learn it at home as a first language, the process of creolization starts.

- Creolization is a process of expansion in terms of both uses and structures.

EXERCISES

Based on Languages Other Than English

The Amara data used here are taken from an unpublished Amara lexicon by Bil Thurston; the Hiw, Sowa, Mota, and Raɣa data, from Darrell Tryon, *New Hebrides Languages* (Pacific Linguistics, series C, vol. 50, 1976); the Waskia data, from Malcolm Ross and John Natu Paol, *A Waskia Grammar Sketch and Vocabulary* (Pacific Linguistics, series B, vol. 56, 1978); the Lusi and Bariai data, from Rick Goulden, "A Comparative Study of Lusi and Bariai" (McMaster University M.A. thesis, 1982).

13-1. The following is a comparative word list from seven languages spoken in the South Pacific. (β represents a voiced bilabial fricative and ɣ a voiced velar fricative.)

Hiw	Waskia	Motu	Amara	Sowa	Mota	Raɣa	
yoŋ	utuwura	lai	akauliŋ	laiŋ	laŋ	laŋi	'wind'
en	laŋ	miri	olov	on	one	one	'sand'
βət	maŋa	nadi	epeiouŋo	βət	βət	fatu	'stone'
yə	didu	matabudi	opon	tariβanaβi	uwə	afua	'turtle'
eɣə	wal	gwarume	ouŋa	ek	iɣa	iɣa	'fish'
noɣa	kasim	namo	ovinkin	tapken	nam	namu	'mosquito'

Hiw	Waskia	Motu	Amara	Sowa	Mota	Raɣa	
yo	nup	lada	serio	se	sasa	iha	'name'
moɣoɣe	kulak	natu	emim	dozo	natu	nitu	'child'
suɣe	buruk	boroma	esnei	bo	kpwoe	poe	'pig'
tø	kemak	tohu	elgo	ze	tou	toi	'sugarcane'

a. Identify which languages are likely to be related and which are not, and justify your claims.

b. Of the languages that appear to be part of the same family, which are more closely related? Justify your answer.

13-2. The following is a comparative word list from Lusi and Bariai, closely related languages spoken on the island of New Britain in Papua New Guinea.

Lusi	Bariai		Lusi	Bariai	
βaza	bada	'to fetch'	βua	bua	'Areca nut'
kalo	kalo	'frog'	niu	niu	'coconut'
ɣali	gal	'to spear'	uβu	ubu	'hip'
ahe	ae	'foot'	rai	rai	'trade wind'
zaŋa	daŋa	'thing'	oaɣa	oaga	'canoe'
tazi	tad	'sea'	mata	mata	'eye'
tupi	tup	'to peek'	zoɣi	dog	a type of plant
tori	tol	'to dance'	hani	an	'food'
ŋiŋi	ŋiŋ	'to laugh'	aŋari	aŋal	a type of bird

a. List the consonant correspondences between Lusi and Bariai.

b. Identify which vowel is lost in Bariai and give a rule that states the environment in which it is lost.

13-3. Table 13-3 (p. 463) provides some correspondence sets among five Polynesian languages. We noted that Tongan had lost a phoneme /r/ from its inventory, which was kept as /r/ or became /l/ in the other four languages. Furthermore, Tongan has kept a phoneme /h/ in certain words, which has been lost in all other Polynesian languages. The following cognates illustrate these two changes.

Tongan	Samoan	Tahitian	Maori	Hawaiian	
hama	ama	ama	ama	ama	'outrigger'
ama	lama	rama	rama	lama	'torch'

a. On the basis of this information and the following words, complete the table of consonant correspondences for Tongan, Samoan, Tahitian, Maori, and Hawaiian.

Tongan	Samoan	Tahitian	Maori	Hawaiian	
leʔo	leo	reo	reo	leo	'voice'
ʔuha	ua	ua	ua	ua	'rain'
lili	lili	riri	riri	lili	'angry'

Tongan	Samoan	Tahitian	Maori	Hawaiian	
hae	sae	hae	hae	hae	'to tear'
hihi	isi	ihi	ihi	ihi	'strip'
huu	ulu	uru	uru	ulu	'to enter'
fue	fue	hue	hue	hue	type of vine
afo	afo	aho	aho	aho	'fishing line'
vela	vela	vera	wera	wela	'hot'
hiva	iva	iva	iwa	iwa	'nine'

b. Using your table of consonant correspondences and, assuming that vowels have not undergone any change in any Polynesian language, complete the following comparative table by filling in the missing words.

Tongan	Samoan	Tahitian	Maori	Hawaiian	
kaukau					'to bathe'
	mata				'eye'
		tafe		kahe	'to flow'
laʔe					'forehead'
laŋo					'fly'

c. Reconstruct the Proto-Polynesian consonant system on the basis of the information you now have; take into account the genetic classification of Polynesian languages discussed in this chapter. (*Hint:* The protosystem has to be full enough to account for all the possible correspondences found in the daughter languages. No daughter language has innovated new phonemes, but all have lost one or more from the protosystem.)

d. Reconstruct the Proto-Polynesian words for 'outrigger,' 'rain,' 'to enter,' 'strip,' and 'nine.'

13-4. Following is a list of Modern French words in phonetic transcription with the Vulgar Latin words from which they derive. (Notice that word-initial /k/ in Latin becomes /k/, /š/, or /s/ in Modern French, depending on its environment.)

Modern French	Vulgar Latin	
koʁd	korda	'rope'
šɑ̃	kampus	'field'
sedʁ	kedrus	'cedar'
kʁaše	krakkaːre	'to spit'
šamo	kameːlus	'camel'
seʁkl	kirkulus	'circle'
kuʁiʁ	kurrere	'to run'
šaʁ	karrus	'carriage'
kle	klavis	'key'
siteʁn	kisterna	'tank'
kɔlɔ̃b	kolomba	'dove'
ša	kattus	'cat'
ku	kollum	'neck'

a. Provide a rule that predicts which of the three French phonemes will appear where Latin had /k/. (Consider only the first phoneme of words.)

b. Consider the additional data below.

Modern French	Vulgar Latin	
šov	kalvus	'bald'
šɛn	katena	'chain'
šo	kalidum	'hot'
šɛʁ	karo	'flesh'

At first glance, these forms are problematic for the rule that you stated in (a). Note, however, that in Modern French these four words are spelled *chauve, chaine, chaud,* and *chair,* respectively. Given the fact that French orthography often reflects an earlier pronunciation of the language, explain in detail what has happened to the four words in the history of the language.

13-5. Consider the following Proto-Indo-European reconstructions. Conspicuously, no word for 'sea' can be reconstructed for Proto-Indo-European.

*rtko	'bear'		*peisk	'fish'
*laks	'salmon'		*sper	'sparrow'
*or	'eagle'		*trozdo	'thrush'
*gʷou	'cow/bull'		*suː	'pig'
*kwon	'dog'		*agwʰno	'lamb'
*mori	'lake'		*sneigʷʰ	'snow'
*bʰerəg	'birch'		*grano	'grain'
*yewo	'wheat'		*medʰu	'honey'
*weik	'village'		*sel	'fortification'
*seː	'to sow'		*kerp	'to collect (food)'
*yeug	'to yoke'		*webʰ	'to weave'
*sneː	'to spin'		*arə	'to plow'
*ayes	'metal'		*agro	'field'

a. Describe in detail what these reconstructions (or lack of reconstruction) tell us about the activities and environment of the Proto-Indo-Europeans.

b. Based on these reconstructions and on what you know about the current distribution of Indo-European languages, which area or areas of the world would be the best candidates as the homeland of the Proto-Indo-Europeans? Defend your claim.

13-6. The following is a list of Proto-Indo-European reconstructions. Cite a Modern English word that contains a reflex for each one of them; ignore the question as to whether the Modern English word is itself a borrowing or not.

*akwaː	'water'		*agro	'field'
*kwetwer	'four'		*bʰugo	'ram, goat'
*bʰreu	'to boil'		*carcer	'prison'
*pel	'skin'		*genə	'to give birth'
*reg	'to rule'		*gel	'to freeze'

*wen	'to strive for'	*g^{h}ans	'goose'
*med	'to measure'	*yeug	'to join together'
*macula	'blemish'	*ped	'foot'

INTERNET AND OTHER RESOURCES

- **Ethnologue: Languages of the World: http://www.sil.org/ethnologue/search**
  The *Ethnologue* is a huge catalog of the world's languages. It is an extraordinary source of information about all languages—where they are spoken, by how many people, and to what family they belong. Much of the data about speakers and locations presented in the present chapter comes from the *Ethnologue*. This Web site, which is maintained by the Summer Institute of Linguistics, provides an electronic version of the *Ethnologue*. It includes a Language Name Index and a Language Family Index. It excludes the language maps of the original printed volumes. A typical entry is given below:
  UTE-SOUTHERN PAIUTE [UTE]1,984 speakers including 20 monolinguals (1990 census), out of 5,000 population (1977 SIL), including 3 Chemehuevi (1990 census). Ute in southwestern Colorado and southeastern and northeastern Utah; Southern Paiute in southwestern Utah, northern Arizona, and southern Nevada; Chemehuevi on lower Colorado River, California. Uto-Aztecan, Northern Uto-Aztecan, Numic, Southern. Dialects: SOUTHERN PAIUTE, UTE, CHEMEHUEVI. Most adults speak the language but most younger ones do not, 75% to 100% literate. Work in progress.
- **Sample of Spoken Navaho:**
  http://www.teleport.com/~napoleon/navaho/sample.html
  At this Web site you can find a sample of spoken Navaho.
- **Alphabetical Language Index:**
  http://www.teleport.com/~napoleon/alphabetical.html
  Contains links to sites for dozens of languages, many of which provide a substantial spoken sample, including Basque, Frisian, Italian, Korean, Maori, Tamil, and even the artificial language Esperanto.

Video

- **In Search of the First Language**
  In the NOVA video series, this fascinating exploration was first broadcast in 1997. It includes discussion by prominent linguists—including William Labov and Joseph Greenberg—of a wide range of topics related to language change and language families, including the controversial Nostratic hypothesis. (To order this video, visit Nova's Web site at http://www.pbs.org/, where you can also find leads to a transcript of the broadcast.)

SUGGESTIONS FOR FURTHER READING

- **Jean Aitchison. 1991.** *Language Change: Progress or Decay?,* 2nd ed. (Cambridge: Cambridge UP). Combines traditional historical analysis with sociolinguistic insights.

- **Anthony Arlotto. 1972.** *Introduction to Historical Linguistics* (Lanham, MD: UP of America). A good next step after the present chapter; the treatment focuses on Indo-European.
- **Calvert Watkins. 1992. "Indo-European and the Indo-Europeans."** *The American Heritage Dictionary of the English Language,* 3rd ed. (Boston: Houghton Mifflin). Conveniently appended to the dictionary, this article describes Indo-European and the cultural inferences that can be drawn from the reconstructed lexicon. The article provides an introduction to a dictionary of Indo-European Roots, with cognates in several languages.

Advanced Reading

There are many good textbooks treating historical linguistics, among them McMahon (1994) and Bynon (1977); the latter combines traditional historical analysis with sociolinguistic insights. Lehmann (1967) provides many of the original documents of historical work from the nineteenth century, including the speech of Sir William Jones quoted on page 456. Bellwood (1979; 1987) and Jennings (1979) survey research on Polynesian and Austronesian migrations; all include extensive discussions of language history. Pawley and Green (1971) discuss the linguistic evidence for the location of the Proto-Polynesian homeland. Bomhard (1992) and Kaiser and Shevoroshkin (1988) discuss the Nostratic macrofamily.

A convenient reference work treating about a dozen language families and forty of the world's major languages is Comrie (1987), with a list of references for each family and language. In addition, there is the Cambridge Language Survey Series on language areas and language families, including volumes on lesser known areas and language families like Comrie (1981), Dixon (1980), Foley (1986), and Suárez (1983), and on major languages like Shibatani (1990). Outside this series, African languages are succinctly surveyed in Gregersen (1977), the languages of China in Ramsey (1987), North American Indian languages in Campbell and Mithun (1979), Amazonian languages in Derbyshire and Pullum (1986), and South American languages in Manelis Klein and Stark (1985). A proposal that all Amerindian languages can be classified into three families appears in Greenberg (1987). Using a method like that used to determine the Proto-Polynesian homeland, Siebert (1967) discusses the original home of the Proto-Algonquian people. Buck (1949) is a compilation of Indo-European roots with the reflexes in various languages. Baldi (1983) is a useful overview of the Indo-European language family.

Nativization is discussed in Kachru (1982). Good recent surveys of the structure and use of pidgins and creoles include Mühlhäusler (1986) and Romaine (1988). The papers in Hymes (1971) also touch on aspects of pidgins and creoles worldwide. An interesting hypothesis about pidginization as an innate program is advanced by Bickerton (1981).

Ruhlen (1986) lists the languages of the world and their genetic affiliation. Additional problems of comparative reconstruction are provided in Cowan (1971) and in Chapter 5 of Langacker (1972); the latter contains some solutions as well.

REFERENCES

- Baldi, Philip. 1983. *An Introduction to the Indo-European Languages* (Carbondale: Southern Illinois UP).

- Bellwood, Peter. 1979. *Man's Conquest of the Pacific: The Prehistory of Southeast Asia and Oceania* (New York: Oxford UP).

- Bellwood, Peter. 1987. *The Polynesians. Prehistory of an Island People,* rev. ed. (London: Thames and Hudson).

- Bickerton, Derek. 1981. *Roots of Language* (Ann Arbor: Karoma).

- Bomhard, Allan R. 1992. "The Nostratic Macrofamily (with Special Reference to Indo-European)" *Word* 43:61–83.

- Buck, Carl D. 1949. *A Dictionary of Selected Synonyms in the Principal Indo-European Languages* (Chicago: U of Chicago P).

- Bynon, Theodora. 1977. *Historical Linguistics* (Cambridge: Cambridge UP).

- Campbell, Lyle, and Marianne Mithun, eds. 1979. *The Languages of Native America: Historical and Comparative Assessment* (Austin: U of Texas P).

- Comrie, Bernard. 1981. *The Languages of the Soviet Union* (Cambridge: Cambridge UP).

- Comrie, Bernard, ed. 1987. *The World's Major Languages* (New York: Oxford UP).

- Cowan, William. 1971. *Workbook in Comparative Reconstruction* (New York: Holt).

- Derbyshire, Desmond C., and Geoffrey K. Pullum, eds. 1986. *Handbook of Amazonian Languages,* 3 vols. (New York: Mouton).

- Dixon, R. M. W. 1980. *The Languages of Australia* (Cambridge: Cambridge UP).

- Foley, William A. 1986. *The Papuan Languages of New Guinea* (Cambridge: Cambridge UP).

- Greenberg, Joseph H. 1987. *Language in the Americas* (Stanford: Stanford UP).

- Gregersen, Edgar A. 1977. *Language in Africa: An Introductory Survey* (New York: Gordon & Breach).

- Hock, Hans Henrich. 1986. *Principles of Historical Linguistics* (New York: Mouton de Gruyter).

- Hymes, Dell, ed. 1971. *Pidginization and Creolization of Languages* (Cambridge: Cambridge UP).

- Jennings, Jesse D., ed. 1979. *The Prehistory of Polynesia* (Cambridge: Harvard UP).

- Kachru, Braj, ed. 1982. *The Other Tongue: English Across Cultures* (Urbana: U of Illinois P).

- Kaiser, M., and V. Shevoroshkin. 1988. "Nostratic," *Annual Review of Anthropology* 17:309–329.

- Langacker, Ronald W. 1972. *Fundamentals of Linguistic Analysis* (New York: Harcourt).

- Lehmann, Winfred, ed. 1967. *A Reader in Nineteenth-Century Historical Linguistics* (Bloomington: Indiana UP).

- Manelis Klein, Harriet E., and Louisa R. Stark, eds. 1985. *South American Indian Languages: Retrospect and Prospect* (Austin: U of Texas P).

- McElhanon, K. A., ed. 1975. *Tok Pisin i Go We?* (Ukarumpa: Linguistic Society of New Guinea).

- McMahon, April M. S. 1994. *Understanding Language Change* (Cambridge: Cambridge UP).

- Mülhäusler, Peter. 1986. *Pidgin and Creole Linguistics* (Oxford: Blackwell).

- Pawley, Andrew, and Kaye Green. 1971. "Lexical Evidence for the Proto-Polynesian Homeland," *Te Reo* 14:1–35.

- Romaine, Suzanne. 1988. *Pidgin and Creole Languages* (London: Longman).

- Ramsey, S. Robert. 1987. *The Languages of China* (Princeton, NJ: Princeton UP).

- Ruhlen, Merritt. 1986. *A Guide to the World's Languages* (Stanford: Stanford UP).

- Sankoff, Gillian. 1975. "Sampele Nupela lo Ikamap Long Tok Pisin." In McElhanon, ed. *Tok Pisin i Go We?* Ukarumpa: Linguistic Society of New Guinea).

- Shibatani, Masayoshi. 1990. *The Languages of Japan* (Cambridge: Cambridge UP).

- Siebert, Frank T. 1967. "The Original Home of the Proto-Algonquian People," *Bulletin No. 214* (Ottawa: National Museum of Canada), pp. 13–47.

- Suárez, Jorge A. 1983. *The Mesoamerican Indian Languages* (Cambridge: Cambridge UP).

CHAPTER 14

HISTORICAL DEVELOPMENT

IN ENGLISH

—

WHAT DO YOU THINK?

You visit Ye Olde Coffee Shoppe with a friend, who reads on the back of the menu that the "ye" in the shopname is not related to the pronoun "you" and should not be pronounced "yee." According to the menu, it's related to "the" and is historically "the old coffee shop." Your friend scoffs and says that would be awfully dull—and that it's hogwash. What's your response?

In looking at maps of the United States, your sixth-grade geography class notices that many cities in California and the Southwest have names like San Diego and Santa Monica that include the words "San" or "Santa" and they ask why those names don't occur elsewhere in the United States. What do you tell them?

A nephew returns from a traditional church service and asks about the difference between the words "thee" and "thou" and why people don't use them anymore except sometimes in church. What do you say?

A fellow secondary school teacher of German asks you why English has so few noun inflections, while its close relative German has so many. What answer do you give?

An international student, a roommate of a friend of yours, asks why some English nouns like "sheep" and "deer" do not have ordinary plural forms like most English nouns. Besides the fact that they are "irregular," what explanation do you give?

After you answer the previous question, your friend figures you're a treasure trove of information. She asks why in some English phrases a singular form is used where a plural would be right. She mentions phrases like "a ten-foot pole" and "a twenty-six-mile race." How do you reply?

A THOUSAND YEARS OF CHANGE

Nearly every secondary school student in the English-speaking world has studied the writings of William Shakespeare and Geoffrey Chaucer, two of the greatest writers ever to use English (or any language) as a poetic vehicle. You may recall that when you read Shakespeare's plays, some of his lines were opaque, as with the opening lines of *I Henry IV:*

> So shaken as we are, so wan with care
> Find we a time for frighted peace to pant
> And breathe short-winded accents of new broils
> To be commenced in stronds afar remote.

The fact that some of Shakespeare's lines are opaque has a straightforward explanation (besides the fact that they are poetry): the English spoken in and around London four centuries ago is often subtly and sometimes strikingly different from the English spoken today. Still, much of it is altogether accessible, and very little of it is so foreign that it eludes us completely. Many of the words in the brief passage just cited are familiar enough, though some are used in ways that strike the modern reader as peculiar. While the words of the opening line are mostly familiar to us and can be sorted out syntactically as poetic English, line two is a bit tougher, even though all the words (except *frighted*) exist in Modern English in exactly the same forms. (The line means 'Let us find a time for frightened peace to catch its breath.')

As the many worldwide Shakespearean productions testify to, reciting Shakespeare's plays with their sixteenth-century lexicon and syntax but with a modern pronunciation enables today's audiences to follow his plays with little difficulty. With the support of costumed actors interacting with props on a rich visual set, there is not much in *Romeo and Juliet, Henry IV,* or *King Lear* that modern audiences fail to grasp.

Far more difficult to understand than Shakespeare's English is Middle English, the language of Chaucer, who lived in London two centuries earlier. Chaucer's *Canterbury Tales,* whose opening lines follow, was the first major book to be printed in England. William Caxton published it in 1476, almost a century after it was written and long after Chaucer's death in 1400.

> Whan that Aprill with his shoures soote
> The droghte of March hath perced to the roote,
> And bathed every veyne in swich licour,
> Of which vertu engendred is the flour; . . .
> Thanne longen folk to goon on pilgrimages.

Though their pronunciation differs dramatically from ours, quite a few of Chaucer's fourteenth-century words have the same written form now as they did then: *that, with, his, the, of, bathed, every, folk, pilgrimages,* along with seven or eight others. Several others can easily be recognized, though their Modern English counterparts differ: *droghte* 'drought,' *perced* 'pierced,' *veyne* 'vein,' *vertu* 'virtue, strength,' and *flour* 'flower.' Of course, some are more opaque: *soote* 'sweet,' *swich* 'such,' *thanne* 'then,' and the verbs *longen* 'to long' and *goon* 'to go.' As a whole, the Chaucer passage is harder to grasp than the Shakespeare one. Thus, in the two centuries between Chaucer (1340–1400) and Shakespeare (1564–1616), English changed—as languages always do. Chaucer understood language change and the arbitrariness of linguistic form for accomplishing the ends of language, as we learn in these lines from his *Troilus and Criseyde* (II, 22–26), with a modern version on the right.

Ye knowe ek, that in forme of speche is chaunge	You know also that in speech's form (there) is change
Withinne a thousand yeer, and wordes tho	Within a thousand years, and words then
That hadden pris, now wonder nyce and straunge	That had value, now wondrously foolish and strange
Us thinketh hem, and yet thei spake hem so,	To us seem them, and yet they spoke them so,
And spedde as wel in love as men now do.	And fared as well in love as men now do.

The English spoken in Chaucer's time is far enough removed from today's English that students often study the *Canterbury Tales* in "translation"—from fourteenth-century English into twentieth-century English. Though we are not yet so estranged from Shakespeare's language to require a translation, editions of his plays have glosses and footnotes aplenty.

If we now examine the language of the epic poem *Beowulf,* written down almost four centuries before Chaucer lived, we are struck by the utterly foreign appearance of Old English. Indeed, speakers of Modern English cannot recognize *Beowulf* as English; it is as far removed as Dutch and German seem. The *Beowulf* poet, whose identity is lost to history, composed his grim epic in the first half of the eighth century, about six hundred years before Chaucer, who surely would have found its language about as unintelligible as modern readers do. Here are the first three lines from a *Beowulf* manuscript transcribed around the year A.D. 1000, with a rough word-for-word translation on the right:

Hwæt wē Gār–Dena in geārdagum	What! We of Spear-Danes in yore-days
þēodcyninga þrym gefrūnon,	People's-kings glory have heard,
hū ðā æþelingas ellen fremedon.	How the nobles heroic-deeds did.

A more colloquial rendering would be: 'Yes, we have heard of the might of the kings of the Spear-Danes in days of yore, how the chieftains carried out deeds of valor.'

No one needs to be persuaded that Old English is a "foreign" language. Scarcely a word in the passage seems familiar (though when you have finished reading this chapter, a few may not seem quite so strange). Even some of the letters, or graphs, are different: Modern English no longer uses <æ>, <þ>, or <ð>. Still, an imaginative inspection may reveal that some function words remain in present-day English (*wē*

= *we, in* = *in,* and *hū* = *how*). Perhaps you also suspected *ðā* as Modern English *the* and *hwæt* as *what,* but it is not easy to recognize *geārdagum* as *yore* plus *days* or *cyninga* as *kings.* Even knowing these words, however, you would find the passage far from transparent. You would need to know the meaning of the nouns *þēod, þrym,* and *æþelingas* (none of which survives in Modern English), the verbs *gefrūnon* and *fremedon,* and the adjective *ellen* (here used as a noun). And given all that lexical information, the syntax of Old English would still be elusive. About a thousand years old, Old English is indeed a long way from Modern English.

WHERE DOES ENGLISH COME FROM?

⤙

Where did English come from, and how long has it been spoken in England? What are its principal ancestors and its closest relatives?

Before the beginning of the modern era, Britain was inhabited by Celtic-speaking peoples, ancestors of today's Irish, Scots, and Welsh. In 55 B.C., Britain was invaded by Julius Caesar, but that attempt to colonize it failed, and the Romans conquered Britain only in A.D., 43. When the Roman legions withdrew in A.D. 410, the Celts, who had long been accustomed to their protection, were at the mercy of the Picts and the Scots from the north of Britain. In a profoundly important development for the English language, Vortigern, king of the Romanized Celts in Britain, sought help from three Germanic tribes. In A.D. 449 these tribes set sail from what is today northern Germany and southern Denmark, and when they landed in Britain they decided to settle, leaving the Celts only the remote corners—today's Scotland, Wales, and Cornwall.

The invaders spoke closely related varieties of West Germanic—the dialects that were to become English. The word *England* derives from the name of one of the tribes, the Angles: thus England, originally *Englaland,* is the 'land of the Angles.' The Old English language used by the early Germanic inhabitants of England and their offspring up to about A.D. 1100 is often called Anglo-Saxon, after two of the tribes (the Jutes were the third tribe). Early Anglo-Saxon has left no written records. The oldest surviving English-language materials come from the end of the seventh century, and there is an increasing quantity after that, giving rise to abundant and impressive literature, including *Beowulf.*

Once the Anglo-Saxon peoples had settled in Britain, there were additional onslaughts from other Germanic groups starting in A.D. 787. In the year 850, a fleet of 350 Danish ships arrived. In 867, Vikings captured York. Danes and Norwegians settled in much of eastern and northern England and from there launched attacks into the kingdom of Wessex in the southwest. In 878, after losing a major battle to King Alfred the Great of Wessex, the Danes agreed by the Treaty of Wedmore to become Christian and to remain outside Wessex in a very large section of eastern and northern England that became known as the Danelaw because it was subject to Danish law. After the treaty, Danes and Norwegians were assimilated to Anglo-Saxon life, so much so that fourteen hundred English place names are Scandinavian, including all those ending in *-by* 'farm, town' (*Derby, Rugby*), *-thorp* 'village' (*Althorp*), *thwaite* 'isolated piece of land' (*Applethwaite*), and *-toft* 'piece of ground' (*Brimtoft, Eastoft*).

Attacks from the Scandinavians continued throughout the Viking Age (roughly 750–1050), until finally King Svein of Denmark was crowned king of England and was succeeded almost immediately by his son Cnut in 1016. England was then ruled by Danish kings until 1042, when Edward the Confessor regained the throne his father, Aethelred, had lost to the Danes. The intermingling between the Anglo-Saxon invaders and the subsequent Scandinavian settlers created a mix of Germanic dialects in England that molded the particular character of the English language and distinguishes it markedly from its cousins. (You may wish to visit the Anglo-Saxon map of England at http://www.georgetown.edu/cball/oe/oe-map.html.)

ENGLISH IS A GERMANIC LANGUAGE

We noted in Chapter 13 that West Germanic is distinguished from two other branches of the Germanic group of Indo-European languages: North Germanic (which includes Swedish, Danish, and Norwegian) and East Germanic (including only Gothic, which has since died out).

During the first millennium B.C., before Germanic had split into three branches but after it had split from the other branches of Indo-European, Common (or Proto-) Germanic developed certain characteristic features that continue in its daughter languages, setting them apart as a group from all other Indo-European varieties. Among these characteristics are features belonging to every level of grammar: phonology, lexicon, morphology, and syntax.

Germanic Sounds   The most striking phonological characteristic of the Germanic languages is a set of consonant correspondences found in none of the other Indo-European languages. It was Jacob Grimm, one of the Brothers Grimm of fairy-tale fame, who in 1822 formulated these correspondences in what is now called "Grimm's Law." Grimm described the sound shifts that had occurred within three natural classes of sounds in developing from Indo-European into Germanic.

> **GRIMM'S LAW**
> 1. Voiceless stops became voiceless fricatives:
> $p > f$ $t > \theta$ $k > h$
> 2. Voiced stops became voiceless stops:
> $b > p$ $d > t$ $g > k$
> 3. Voiced aspirated stops became voiced unaspirated stops:
> $b^h > b$ $d^h > d$ $g^h > g$

The impact of these changes can be seen in Figure 14-1 by examining the shift of voiceless stops in Indo-European to voiceless fricatives in Germanic. We illustrate this shift by citing English words that have inherited the sounds /f θ h/ from Germanic and by contrasting them with corresponding words in Romance languages,

Figure 14-1

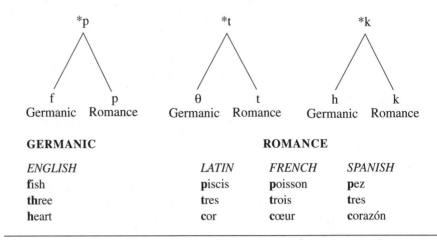

REFLEXES OF INDO-EUROPEAN VOICELESS STOPS IN GERMANIC AND ROMANCE

	GERMANIC		**ROMANCE**	
	ENGLISH	*LATIN*	*FRENCH*	*SPANISH*
	fish	piscis	poisson	pez
	three	tres	trois	tres
	heart	cor	cœur	corazón

which (like all the other branches of Indo-European) did not undergo these sound shifts.

Another important phonological development of Common Germanic was a shifting of stress patterns. Indo-European had variable stress on its words, so that a morpheme could be stressed on a particular syllable in the context of a given word and elsewhere in a different word, much like Modern English *'photograph* and *pho'tographer.* But in Common Germanic, stress shifted systematically to a word's first or root syllable. Compare Modern English *'father, 'fatherly, un'fatherly,* and *'fatherless,* all having stress on the root syllable in the Germanic fashion, with the Greek borrowings *'photograph, pho'tographer,* and *photo'graphic,* which have variable stress in the Indo-European fashion.

Germanic Vocabulary   The pattern of sound shifting described by Grimm's Law set apart the pronunciation of the Germanic vocabulary from that of other Indo-European languages (as seen in the Romance examples in Figure 14-1). In addition, the Germanic languages have a set of words found nowhere else in Indo-European. Once the Germanic tribes separated from the rest of the Indo-European peoples, any words innovated or borrowed from speakers of a non-Indo-European tongue would be distinctively Germanic within Indo-European. Among the English words found in other Germanic languages but not in any other Indo-European languages are the nouns *arm, blood, earth, finger, hand, sea,* and *wife;* the verbs *bring, drink, drive, leap,* and *run;* and the adjectives *evil, little,* and *sick.* Here are the strictly Germanic nouns from English and German (to illustrate the similarity among Germanic tongues) and from French (to illustrate the striking contrast between Germanic and Romance languages).

ENGLISH	GERMAN	FRENCH
arm	Arm	bras
blood	Blut	sang
earth	Erd	terre
finger	Finger	doigt
hand	Hand	main
sea	See	mer
wife	Weib	femme

It is conceivable that these Germanic words could have existed in Indo-European and were lost in all daughter languages except Germanic, but it is hardly likely. Hence we can assume they were not inherited from Indo-European but were innovated or borrowed during the Common Germanic period.

MORPHOLOGY AND SYNTAX IN INDO-EUROPEAN

Indo-European—at least at some stages—was certainly a highly inflected language. In fact, Sanskrit, one of the oldest attested Indo-European languages, had eight case inflections on nouns, so it is possible that Indo-European itself had eight cases (though, alternatively, case distinctions absent from Proto-Indo-European could have arisen in the Indic branch to which Sanskrit belongs). If we assume that the rich inflectional morphology of Sanskrit reflects the complexity of Indo-European, then Indo-European nouns would have had eight *cases,* three *numbers* (singular, dual, and plural), and three *genders* (masculine, feminine, and neuter). Verbs were also highly inflected, probably for two *voices* (active and a kind of passive), four *moods* (indicative, imperative, subjunctive, and optative), and three *tenses* (present, past, and future). In addition, verbs carried markers for *person* and *number.*

The Indo-European system of indicating verb tenses was principally word internal (as in English *sing/sang/sung*). While this internal sound *gradation* (sometimes called *ablaut*) is typical of Indo-European languages, the typical English inflection, pronounced [-t] (*kissed*) or [-d] (*judged*) for the past tenses, is characteristically Germanic. Thus the two-tense system, with past tense marked by a dental or alveolar suffix, sets the Germanic group apart from all its Indo-European cousins.

PERIODS IN THE HISTORY OF ENGLISH

Because languages change continuously, any division into historical stages or periods must be somewhat arbitrary. Nevertheless, scholars have divided the history of English into three main periods representing very different stages of the language. We now refer to the language spoken in England from the end of the seventh century to the end of the eleventh century (700–1100) as Old English (or Anglo-Saxon). The

English spoken since 1450 or 1500 is called Modern English. The language spoken in between—roughly from 1100 to 1450 or 1500—is known as Middle English. Thus *Beowulf* is written in Old English, the *Canterbury Tales* in Middle English, and *Henry IV* in (early) Modern English.

OLD ENGLISH: 700–1100

When the Angles, Saxons, and Jutes began to invade England in 449, they settled in different parts of the island, and four principal dialects of Old English sprang up: Northumbrian in the north (north of the Humber River); Mercian in the Midlands; Kentish in the southeast; and West Saxon in the southwest (see Figure 14-2). Because Wessex was the seat of the powerful King Alfred, its dialect, West Saxon, achieved a certain status; it forms the basis of most surviving Old English literature and of the study of Old English today.

Like the classical Latin of Roman times and like today's German and Russian, Old English was a highly inflected language. It had an elaborate system of inflectional suffixes on nouns, pronouns, verbs, adjectives, and even determiners. Only traces of these inflectional forms of Old English survive in Modern English.

OLD ENGLISH SCRIPT

Only a few Old English letters differ from those of Modern English, but they occurred in some of the most frequently used words, giving Old English an exaggerated air of strangeness. Among the graphs no longer used in English are <þ> (called thorn), ð (eth), <ƿ> (wynn), and <æ> (ash). Modern day editors usually let the graphs <þ>, <ð>, and <æ> stand in modern texts, but they almost invariably substitute <w> for wynn.

Both <þ> and <ð> (and their capitals <Þ> and <Ð>) were alternative spellings for two sounds; each graph represented the sounds [θ] or [ð], which were allophones of a single phoneme in Old English. Old English scribes did not assign one graph to the sound [θ] and the other to [ð] because the two sounds were not perceived as different: they were allophones of a single phoneme. Old English speakers were no more aware of the difference between [θ] and [ð] than Modern English speakers are aware that they are pronouncing different /p/ sounds in *pot* and *spot.* Besides, alphabetic systems ideally assign different symbols *not* to different sounds (allophones) but to different *distinctive* sounds (phonemes).

The graph <æ>, rarely used in Modern English, represented a pronunciation in Old English much like the one it represents in the phonetic alphabet used today (the vowel of *hat*). The Old English vowel combinations <ēo> and <ēa> represented the diphthongs [eːɔ] and [ɛːə] respectively. The letter sequence <sc> (as in *Englisce*) is equivalent to Modern English <sh> [š]. The letter <c> represented two sounds: [k] as in *cȳpmenn* or [č] as in *æðellīce.* The letter <g> represented three sounds: it was pronounced as [y] word-initially when it preceded a front vowel (as in *gelamp* and *gȳt*) and word-finally when it followed one (as in *Rōmānabyrig*); elsewhere it was pro-

Figure 14-2

THE OLD ENGLISH DIALECTS

nounced as [g] or [ɣ]. The letter <y> was always the vowel [ü]. The letters <j> and
<q> were not used in Old English, and <k> was rare (hence *folc* 'folk'), though the
sounds they represent today did exist (compare *cwēn* 'queen' and *cēpan* 'keep'). The
letter <x> was an alternative spelling of <cs>, pronounced [ks], as in *axode* [ɑksɔdɛ]
'asked.' Finally, we might mention that <⁊> 'and' was the customary representation
in original manuscripts of the Old English equivalent of an ampersand sign <&>.

OLD ENGLISH SOUNDS

A good deal could be said about the Old English sound system. We'll make only a few
observations about some patterns that have implications for the development of Modern English. Old English had long and short vowels and diphthongs, though in late Old
English the diphthongs tended to become simplified. (A similar simplification occurs
today in American dialects of the South, in which words like *time* /taym/ tend to be
pronounced [tʰam]; throughout the United States the pronounciation of *I* is simplified

from [ay] to [a] in a phrase like *I'm gonna . . .* [amgʊnə].) Over the centuries the short vowels have remained relatively constant so that many words are pronounced today much as they were pronounced in Old English: *fisc* 'fish,' *æt* 'at,' *þorn* 'thorn,' *benc* 'bench,' and *him* 'him.' By contrast, the long vowels have undergone marked changes. Suffice it to say that Old English long vowels had their "continental" values, as in the following words: *stān* [staːn] 'stone'; *sēon* [seːɔn] 'see'; *sōðlice* [soːðliːče] 'truly'; *būton* [buːtɔn] 'without, except'; and *swīðe* [swiːðe] 'very.'

As to consonants, Old English permitted certain word-initial combinations that Modern English does not permit: /hl/, /hr/, and /kn/. Three pairs of sounds whose members are distinct phonemes in Modern English were allophones of single phonemes in Old English: [f] and [v]; [θ] and [ð]; and [s] and [z]. The voiceless allophones [f θ s] occurred at the beginning and end of words and when adjacent to voiceless sounds within words; between voiced sounds, however, the voiced allophones occurred. Thus in the nominative case of the word *wīf* [wiːf], <f> represented the allophone [f], but in the genitive case it represented the allophone [v]: *wifes* [wiːvɛs] (note the final [s] too). The phonemes /s/ and /θ/ figure prominently in the history of English because so many inflections and so many function words contain them.

OLD ENGLISH VOCABULARY AND MORPHOLOGY

Compounds Old English writers were fond of compounding. The three lines of *Beowulf* cited earlier contain three compounds: *Gār-Dena* meaning 'spear Danes,' *geārdagum* meaning 'yore days' (that is, 'days of yore'), and *þēodcyninga* meaning 'nation kings.'

Noun Inflections Old English had several inflections for noun phrases, depending on their grammatical and semantic role in a sentence. Four principal cases could be distinguished: *nominative* (usually for subjects), *genitive* (for possessives and certain other functions), *dative* (for indirect objects and certain other functions), and *accusative* (for direct objects and objects of certain prepositions). Each noun carried a grammatical gender, which occasionally reflected natural gender; *guma* 'man' and *brōðor* 'brother' were masculine, while *brȳd* 'bride' and *sweostor* 'sister' were feminine. But usually gender had little to do with the natural sex of a noun's referent. For example, the nouns *mīl* 'mile,' *wist* 'feast,' and *lēaf* 'permission' were feminine; *hund* 'dog,' *hungor* 'hunger,' *wīfmann* 'woman,' and *wīngeard* 'vineyard' were masculine; and *wīf* 'woman, wife,' *manncynn* 'mankind' and *scip* 'ship' were neuter. Thus grammatical gender is simply a grammatical category that determined the way each noun was inflected and also determined the inflections on adjectives and other agreeing constituents of the noun phrase.

Table 14-1 shows the paradigms for the nouns *fox* 'fox,' *lār* 'learning, lore,' *dēor* 'animal,' and *fōt* 'foot.' From the Old English *fox* declension (declension is the name for a noun paradigm) come the only productive Modern English noun inflections: the genitive singular in *-s* and all plurals in *-s*. The *dēor declension* survives in uninflected modern plurals like *deer* (whose meaning has been narrowed from 'animal') and *sheep,* but new words never follow this pattern. The *fōt* declension has

Table 14-1

FOUR OLD ENGLISH NOUN DECLENSIONS

	MASCULINE 'FOX'	FEMININE 'LEARNING'	NEUTER 'ANIMAL'	MASCULINE 'FOOT'
SINGULAR				
Nominative	fox	lār	dēor	fōt
Accusative	fox	lār-e	dēor	fōt
Genitive	fox-es	lār-e	dēor-es	fōt-es
Dative	fox-e	lār-e	dēor-e	fēt
PLURAL				
Nom./Acc.	fox-as	lār-a	dēor	fēt
Genitive	fox-a	lār-a	dēor-a	fōt-a
Dative	fox-um	lār-um	dēor-um	fōt-um

yielded a few nouns (like *food, goose, tooth, louse, mouse,* and *man*) whose plurals are signaled by an internal vowel change rather than by the common -*s* suffix. Modern English phrases like *a ten-foot pole* are relics of the Old English genitive plural ('a pole of ten feet'), whose form *fōta* has given rise to *foot*. Over the centuries, most nouns that had previously been inflected according to other declensions have come to conform to the *fox* paradigm, and new nouns (with the exception of a few borrowings from other languages) are also inflected like it. Irregular forms of words tend to be relics that have been inherited from earlier regularities.

Articles   The Modern English definite article is simple in form. It has a single orthographic shape *the* with two standard pronunciations, [ði] before vowels and [ðə] elsewhere. In sharp contrast, the Old English demonstratives—forerunners of today's definite article—were inflected for five cases and three genders in the singular and for three cases without gender distinction in the plural (see Table 14-2). A fifth case, the instrumental, was used either with or without a preposition to indicate such semantic roles as accompaniment or instrument ('with the chieftains,' 'by an arrow'). It may be instructive to compare the Old English demonstrative as represented in Table 14-2 with the Modern German definite article represented in Table 2-10 (p. 60). The similarities are striking.

As with Modern English indefinite plural noun phrases, Old English indefinite noun phrases frequently lacked an explicit marker of indefiniteness (*She writes books*). But sometimes in the singular *sum* 'a certain' and *ān* 'one' occurred for emphasis, and they were inflected like adjectives.

Adjective Inflections   The Old English adjective system owes its complexity to innovations that had arisen in Common Germanic and consequently do not appear in other Indo-European languages; they also have not survived into Modern English.

Table 14-2

OLD ENGLISH DECLENSION
OF DEMONSTRATIVE 'THAT'

	SINGULAR			PLURAL
	MASCULINE	FEMININE	NEUTER	ALL GENDERS
Nominative	sē	sēo	þæt	þā
Accusative	þone	þā	þæt	þā
Genitive	þæs	þære	þæs	þāra
Dative	þǣm	þære	þæm	þǣm
Instrumental	þȳ	þære	þȳ	þǣm

Old English adjectives were inflected for gender, number, and case to agree with their head noun. There were two distinct kinds of adjective declensions. When a noun phrase had as one of its constituents a highly inflected possessive pronoun or demonstrative, adjectives were declined with one set of inflections—the so-called "weak" (or *definite*) declension. In other instances, such as predicative usage (*It is tall*), when indicators of grammatical relations were few or nonexistent, the more varied forms of the strong (or *indefinite*) declension were required. Table 14-3 gives

Table 14-3

OLD ENGLISH DECLENSIONS
OF THE ADJECTIVE 'GOOD'

	SINGULAR			PLURAL		
	MASC.	FEM.	NEUT.	MASC.	FEM.	NEUT.
INDEFINITE						
Nom.	gōd	gōd	gōd	gōd-e	gōd	gōd
Acc.	gōd-ne	gōd-e	gōd	gōd-e	gōd	gōd
Gen.	gōd-es	gōd-re	gōd-es	gōd-ra	gōd-ra	gōd-ra
Dat.	gōd-um	gōd-re	gōd-um	gōd-um	gōd-um	gōd-um
Ins.	gōd-e	gōd-re	gōd-e	gōd-um	gōd-um	gōd-um
DEFINITE				*All genders*		
Nom.	gōd-a	gōd-e	gōd-e	gōd-an		
Acc.	gōd-an	gōd-an	gōd-e	gōd-an		
Gen.	gōd-an	gōd-an	gōd-an	gōd-ra (gōd-ena)		
Dat.	gōd-an	gōd-an	gōd-an	gōd-um		

the indefinite and definite adjective paradigms for *gōd* 'good.' Notice that Old English has ten different forms as compared to a single form in Modern English.

Nothing remains of the Old English inflectional system for adjectives. Today all adjectives occur in a single shape such as *tall, old,* and *beautiful* (except for the comparative and superlative inflections, as in *taller* and *tallest*). For any gender, number, or case of the modified noun, and for both attributive functions (*the tall ships*) and predicative functions (*the ship is tall*), the form of a Modern English adjective remains invariant.

Personal Pronouns   The Modern English personal pronouns preserve more of their earlier complexity than any other word class. The Old English paradigms for personal pronouns are given in Table 14-4, alongside their Modern English counterparts. As you can see, besides singulars and plurals Old English had a dual number in the first and second persons to refer to exactly two people ('we two' and 'you two'). The dual was already weakening in late Old English and eventually disappeared from English, as did the distinct number and case forms of the second-person pronoun (*þū* 'thou'/*þē* 'thee' and *gē* 'ye'/*ēow* 'you' are all now *you*); the distinct dative case form the third-person singular neuter pronoun has also disappeared.

Table 14-4

OLD ENGLISH AND MODERN ENGLISH PRONOUNS

	OLD ENGLISH					MODERN ENGLISH				
	FIRST	SECOND	THIRD PERSON			FIRST	SECOND	THIRD PERSON		
			MASC.	FEM.	NEUT.			MASC.	FEM.	NEUT.
SINGULAR										
Nom.	ic	þū	hē	hēo	hit	I	you	he	she	it
Acc.	mē	þē	hine	hie	hit	me	you	him	her	it
Gen.	mīn	þīn	his	hiere	his	mine	yours	his	hers	its
Dat.	mē	þē	him	hiere	him	me	you	him	her	it
DUAL										
Nom.	wit	git								
Acc.	unc	inc								
Gen.	uncer	incer								
Dat.	unc	inc								
			All Genders					*All Genders*		
PLURAL										
Nom.	wē	gē	hīe			we	you	they		
Acc.	ūs	ēow	hīe			us	you	them		
Gen.	ūre	ēower	hiera			ours	yours	theirs		
Dat.	ūs	ēow	him			us	you	them		

Relative Pronouns In Old English, an invariant particle þe or ðe marked the introduction of relative clauses, though þe was often compounded with the demonstrative sē, sēo, þæt, as in sē þe (for masculine reference) and sēo þe (for feminine reference) 'who, that.' The forms of the demonstrative sē, sēo, þæt also occurred alone as relatives:

ānne aðeling sē   wæs Cyneheard hāten
a   prince Rel was Cyneheard called
'a prince who was called Cyneheard'

Old English relative clauses were also sometimes introduced by þe and a form of the personal pronoun; as in this example with þe and *him.*

Nis   nū cwicra nān   þe ic him mōdsefan mīnne durre āsecgan.
(there) isn't now alive no one Rel I him mind   my   dare speak
'There is no one alive now to whom I dare speak my mind.'

As this example shows, Old English relativized indirect objects. Therefore, according to the universals examined in Chapter 7, we would assume that it also relativized direct objects and subjects—which in fact it did.

Verbs and Verb Inflections Like other Germanic languages, Old English exhibits two types of verbs. The characteristically Germanic verbs have a [d] or [t] suffix in the past tense (and are called "weak"). The traditional Indo-European "strong" type show a vowel alternation (as in *sing/sang/sung*). Old English had seven patterns of "strong" verbs. Table 14-5 lists the principal parts (the forms from which all other inflected forms can be derived) of the seven Old English verb classes. These illustrative strong verbs survive as irregular verbs in Modern English, but quite a few Old English strong verbs have developed into Modern English *regular* verbs in the course of time. The Modern English past-tense forms of *shove, melt, wash,* and *step,* for instance, followed strong (irregular) patterns in Old English.

Table 14-5

SEVEN CLASSES OF OLD ENGLISH STRONG VERBS

INFINITIVE	PAST SINGULAR	PAST PLURAL	PAST PARTICIPLE	
1. rīdan	rād	ridon	geriden	'ride'
2. frēosan	frēas	fruron	gefroren	'freeze'
3. drincan	dranc	druncon	gedruncen	'drink'
4. beran	bær	bǣron	geboren	'bear'
5. licgan	læg	lǣgon	gelegen	'lie'
6. standan	stōd	stōdon	gestanden	'stand'
7. feallan	fēoll	fēollon	gefeallen	'fall'

Two tenses (present and past) and two moods (indicative and subjunctive) could be formed from a verb's principal parts. Table 14-6 gives a typical Old English regular verb conjugation for *dēman* 'judge, deem.' (*Conjugation* is the name for a verb paradigm.) Note that the present-tense indicative had three singular forms and one plural, but the present-tense subjunctive had only one singular and one plural form. Compared to the twelve distinct forms of an Old English weak verb paradigm, the Modern English regular paradigm has only four distinct forms (*judge, judges, judged,* and *judging*), and it does not include any distinctly subjunctive forms.

Compared to its elaborate Indo-European ancestors and some of its even more elaborate cousins, Old English had a simple verbal system. Old English verbs were inflected for person, number, and tense in the indicative mood and for number and tense in the subjunctive mood; the subjunctive mood was used far more frequently in Old English than it is in Modern English. By way of contrast, Latin was inflected for active and passive *voice;* for perfective and imperfective *aspect;* and for present, past, and future *tenses;* as well as for three *moods.*

INFLECTIONS AND WORD ORDER IN OLD ENGLISH

Having a rich inflectional system, Old English could rely on its morphological distinctions to indicate the grammatical relations (subject, object) of nouns (and, to a lesser extent, their semantic roles). Noun phrases had agreement in gender, number,

Table 14-6

CONJUGATION OF 'JUDGE, DEEM' IN OLD ENGLISH

	INDICATIVE MOOD	SUBJUNCTIVE MOOD
PRESENT TENSE		
Singular		
first person	dēm-e	
second person	dēm-st (or dēm-est)	dēm-e
third person	dēm-þ (or dēm-eþ)	
Plural		
first, second, and third	dēm-aþ	dēm-en
PAST TENSE		
Singular		
first person	dēm-d-e	
second person	dēm-d-est	dēm-d-e
third person	dēm-d-e	
Plural		
first, second, and third	dēm-d-on	dēm-d-en
GERUND	tō dēm-enne (or dēm-anne)	
PRESENT PARTICIPLE	dēm-ende	
PAST PARTICIPLE	dēm-ed	

and case among the demonstrative/definite article, the adjective, and the head noun; adjectives were declined, either definite or indefinite, as already described. Using some of the declensions provided in Tables 14-1, 14-2, and 14-3, and two other adjectives, we can form the following Old English noun phrases. Note that in each instance the adjective and demonstrative article *agree* with the noun (that is, they must have inflections that match the noun in gender, case, and number).

sē gōda fox	'the good fox' (masc. nom. sg.)
gōd dēor	'good animals' (neuter nom./acc. pl.)
þā gōdan fēt	'the good feet' (masc. nom./acc.pl.)
langra fōta	'of long feet' (masc. genitive pl.)
þǣre micelan lāre	'of/for the great learning' (fem. genitive/dative sg.)

The rich inflectional system operating within Old English noun phrases could indicate grammatical relations and certain semantic roles without having to rely on word order the way Modern English does. Word order was therefore more flexible in Old English than in Modern English. Still, by late Old English, word order patterns were already similar in many respects to those of Modern English. Both Old English and Modern English show a preference for SVO order (*subject* preceding *verb* preceding *object*) in main clauses. Modern English prefers SVO in subordinate clauses as well. Old English (like Modern German) preferred verb-final word order (SOV) in subordinate clauses.

As in Modern English, the order of elements in Old English noun phrases was usually determiner-adjective-noun: *sē gōda mann* 'the good man.' Far more frequently than in Modern English, genitives preceded nouns, as in the following:

folces weard 'people's protector'

mǣres līfes mann 'a man of splendid life'
(literally 'splendid life's man')

fōtes trym 'the space of a foot'
(literally 'foot's space')

We saw in Chapter 2 that adpositions can either follow or precede their nouns. Old English generally had prepositions, though with pronouns prepositions often occurred in postposition (that is, after the pronoun), as shown in this example:

sē hālga Andreas him tō cwæþ . . .
the holy Andrew him to said . . .
'St. Andrew said to him . . .'

Like Modern English adjectives, Old English adjectives almost uniformly preceded their head nouns (*sē foresprecena here* 'the aforesaid army'), though they could sometimes follow them:

wadu weallendu
waters surging
'surging waters'

As they do in Modern English, relative clauses generally followed their head nouns.

ðā cyningas ðe   ðone onwald hæfdon
the kings   who the   power had
'the kings who had the power'

COMPANIONS OF ANGELS: A NARRATIVE IN OLD ENGLISH

The Old English passage in Figure 14-3 originates in Bede's *Ecclesiastical History of the English People* completed in A.D. 731 and subsequently translated from Latin into English, perhaps by Alfred the Great during his reign as king of Wessex (871–899). The version given here is a slightly edited version of a later translation by the English abbot Ælfric (about 955–1020). Written in the plain style that Ælfric sometimes used, the story tells how Gregory the Great, who reigned as pope between 590 and 604, first learned of the English people as he walked through a marketplace in Rome and saw boys being sold as slaves. The passage seems as foreign as any language written in the Roman alphabet and more so than some, given its unfamiliar letters.

VOCABULARY IN THE NARRATIVE

There is greater difference between Old English and Modern English in nouns, verbs, and adjectives than in function words.

Function Words Focusing on prepositions, demonstratives, and pronouns, you'll see some notable similarities between the Old English passage and Modern English: in the prepositions *æt* 'at,' *tō* 'to,' *betwux* 'between, among,' *of* 'of, from'; in the conjunction <⅂> 'and,' which occurs more than half a dozen times in the passage; in the conjunction *þā* 'then,' used frequently to introduce sentences. The subordinator *þæt* (lines 8 and 17) was used just as it is in Modern English. Some of the personal pronouns functioned exactly as they do in Modern English: *hit* 'it,' *he* 'he,' *hi* 'they,' *him* 'him.' (Note that some of the demonstratives in the passage differ slightly in spelling from those in Table 14-2, as with the dative plural *þām* in lines 3 and 4 as compared to *þǣm*.)

Content Words Some of the unfamiliarity of nouns, verbs, and adjectives is due to inflections (*mannum*, the dative plural of 'man') and much of it to spelling differences or pronunciation rather than to loss or gain of words themselves. Thus you can see in *Englisce, strǣt, ðing, menn,* and *nama*, earlier forms of the nouns *English, street, thing, men,* and *name.* In *brōhton, behēold, sǣde,* and *wǣre* are the etymons

Figure 14-3

(OLD ENGLISH) NARRATIVE
WRITTEN AROUND THE YEAR 1000

1 Ðā gelamp hit æt sumum sæle, swā swā gyt for oft dēð,

Then happened it at a certain time as yet very oft does,

2 þæt Englisce cȳpmenn brōhton heora ware tō Rōmānabyrig,

that English traders brought their wares to Rome

3 ⁊ Grēgōrius ēode be þǣre strǣt tō ðām Engliscum mannum,

and Gregory went through the street to the English men,

heora ðing scēawigende.

their things looking at.

4 Ðā geseah hē betwux ðām warum cȳpecnihtas gesette,

Then saw he among the wares slaves seated

5 þā wǣron hwītes līchaman ⁊ fægeres andwlitan menn, ⁊ æðelīce gefexode.

who were of white body and of fair countenance men, and nobly haired.

6 Grēgōrius ðā behēold þǣra cnapena wlite,

Gregory then saw the boys' countenances.

7 ⁊ befrān of hwilcere þēode hī gebrōhte wǣron.

and asked from which people they brought were.

8 Ðā sǣde him man þæt hī of Englalande wǣron,

Then said to him someone that they from England were,

9 ⁊ þæt ðǣre ðēode mennisc swā wlitig wǣre.

and that that nation's people so handsome were.

10 Eft ðā Grēgōrius befrān, hwæðer þæs

Again then Gregory asked, whether that

11 landes folc crīsten wǣre ðe hǣðen.

land's people Christian were or heathen.

12 Him man sǣde þæt hī hǣðene wǣron. . . .

Him someone told that they heathen were. . . .

13 Eft hē āxode, hū ðǣre ðēode nama wǣre þe hī of cōmon.

Later he asked, how the people's name was that they from came.

14 Him wæs geandswarod, þæt hī Angle genemnode wǣron.

To him was answered that they Angles named were.

15 Hwaet, ðā Grēgōrius gamenode mid his wordum tō ðām naman ⁊ cwæð,

Well, then Gregory played with his words on the name and said,

16 "Rihtlīce hī sind Angle gehātene, for ðan ðe hī engla wlite habbað,

"Rightly they are Angles called, because they angels' countenances have.

17 ⁊ swilcum gedafenað þæt hī on heofonum engla gefēran bēon.

and for such it is right that they in heaven angels' companions be.

of the modern verbs *brought, beheld, said,* and *were.* You can see in the verb *to be* the singular past-tense inflection *-e* (*wǣre*) and the plural past-tense inflection *-on* (*wǣron*). Among other words that still exist today are *hwæðer* 'whether,' *hū* 'how,' *crīsten* 'Christian,' and *hǣðen* 'heathen.' Not quite so transparent are a few others that can trigger a flash of recognition once the link is pointed out: *rihtlīce* 'rightly,' *cwæð* 'quoted,' *heofonum* 'heaven,' *engla* 'angel.'

GRAMMAR: SYNTAX AND MORPHOLOGY IN THE NARRATIVE

Given its highly inflected morphology, Old English had considerable freedom of word order. While there was a preference for SVO in main clauses and for SOV in subordinate clauses, other orders also occurred. Note, though, that the verb appeared in second position after an introductory adverb such as *þā* (*þā gesēah he,* line 4; note also lines 1 and 8). Otherwise, the verb tended to occur in final position in subordinate clauses (*þæt hī hǣðene wǣron,* line 12, and 1, 7, 9, 13, 14, and 17). As in Modern English, noun phrases had the order adjective-noun (*sumum sǣle* 'a certain time') or article-noun (*þǣre strǣt* 'the street'), and prepositional phrases had the order preposition-(article)-(adjective)-noun (*æt sumum sǣle, be þǣre strǣt*).

TEXT STRUCTURE OF THE NARRATIVE

One striking characteristic of Old English writing was the strong preference for linking sentences together with < ⅂ > 'and' and *þā* 'then,' much as is done in Modern English oral narratives. Subordinators that made explicit the relation between one clause and another (*because, since, until, when*) existed in Old English but their frequent use in writing was a later development. More typically in Old English writing (as in Modern English conversation) clauses are introduced with 'and' or 'then' as in lines 1, 3, 4, 8, and 17. In addition to relative clauses the passage contains a few examples of subordination: *swā swā* 'as' in line 1, *hwæðer* 'whether' in line 10 and *for ðan ðe* 'because' in line 16.

MIDDLE ENGLISH: 1100–1500
⟶

Middle English is a term used to refer to period of great variation and instability in the history of English.

THE NORMAN INVASION

In the year 1066, William, Duke of Normandy, sailed across the Channel to claim the English throne. After winning the Battle of Hastings, William was crowned king of England in Westminster Abbey on Christmas Day, and with that coronation Anglo-Saxon England passed into history. Thus was established a Norman kingdom in England, and for generations the king of England and the duke of Normandy would be one person. The Norman invasion would not only reshape England's institutions but exercise a profound effect on its language.

The Norman French spoken by the invaders quickly became the language of England's ruling class, while the lower classes retained English as their language. Following the invasion, English had a recess from many duties it had previously performed. In particular, it was relieved of many of its functions in the affairs of government, the court, the church, and education; all these important activities were conducted in French. Indeed, for two centuries after the conquest, the kings of England could not speak the language of many of their subjects, and English-speaking subjects could not understand their king. The most famous king of this period, Richard the Lion-Hearted, was in every way French: during his ten-year reign (1189–1199), he visited England only twice (both times to raise money), staying a total of less than ten months. Eventually the middle classes became bilingual, speaking to peasants in English and to the ruling classes in French.

After 1200 the situation began to change, when King John lost Normandy to King Philip of France. On both sides of the Channel, decrees were issued commanding that no one could own land in both England and France. Cut off from its Norman origins, the force that had sustained the use of French in Britain began to collapse.

MIDDLE ENGLISH VOCABULARY

A hundred years later, at the beginning of the fourteenth century, English came to be known again by all inhabitants of England. Not surprisingly, however, the language that emerged was strikingly different from the Old English used prior to the Norman invasion, at least as that Old English is reflected in the surviving written documents. The vocabulary of Middle English was heavily spiced by Norman French. The English word stock was swollen by the addition of thousands of French words because speakers learning English used French words to refer to things whose English labels they no longer knew. Based on calculations by the Danish scholar Otto Jespersen, it has been estimated that approximately ten thousand French words came into English during the Middle English period, and most of them remain in use today! Especially plentiful were words pertaining to religion, government, the courts, and the army and navy, though many borrowings relate to food, fashion, and education—those arenas in which the invaders and their successors had wielded great influence in England.

Once English had been reestablished as the language of the law, the residents of England found themselves without sufficient English terminology to carry on the activities that had been conducted for centuries in French. Hence a good many French legal terms were borrowed, including even the words *justice* and *court* (the word *law* itself, however, derives from Old English *lagu*). To discuss events in a courtroom today, the following words—all borrowed from French during the Middle English period—are used: *judgment, plea, verdict, evidence, proof, prison,* and *jail.* The actors in a courtroom now have French names: *bailiff, plaintiff, defendant, attorney, jury, juror,* and *judge.* The names of certain crimes are French, including *felony, assault, arson, larceny, fraud, libel, slander,* and *perjury,* as is the word *crime* itself. We have cited examples only from the law, and by no means all of them; extensive lists of French borrowings could also be provided for the other arenas in which the French were socially and culturally influential.

MIDDLE ENGLISH SOUNDS

There was considerable change in some vowels and consonant patterns between Old English and Middle English.

Vowels   Most long vowels of Old English remained unchanged in Middle English. But the Old English long vowel /ɑː/ in words like *bān, stān,* and *bāt* became in Middle English long /ɔː/ (and in Modern English /o/) as in *boon* 'bone,' *stoon* 'stone,' and *boot* 'boat.' Many diphthongs were simplified in late Old English and early Middle English. Thus the vowels of the words *sēon* 'see' and *bēon* 'be' were leveled to long /eː/, a sound that went on to become [i] in Modern English.

Short vowels in unstressed syllables, which had been kept distinct at least in early West Saxon, tended to merge in schwa [ə], usually written <e>.

Consonants and Consonant Clusters   The Old English initial consonant clusters /hl-/, /hn-/, /hr-/, and /kn-/ were simplified to /l/, /n/, and /r/, all losing their initial /h/ or /k/: *hlāf* 'loaf,' *hlot* 'lot,' *hnecca* 'neck,' *hnacod* 'naked,' *hrōf* 'roof,' *hræfn* 'raven,' *hring* 'ring,' *cnīf* 'knife,' *cnoll* 'knoll,' *cniht* 'boy, knight.' A phonological change of considerable consequence was the merging of word-final /-m/ and /-n/ in a single sound (/-n/) when they occurred in unstressed syllables (*foxum > foxun*). Significantly, unstressed syllables included *all* the inflections on nouns, adjectives, and verbs. By the end of the Middle English period even this /-n/ was dropped altogether (*foxun > foxen > foxe*), and the final -*e* was also eventually dropped.

MIDDLE ENGLISH INFLECTIONS

Three of the phonological changes just mentioned had a profound effect on the morphology of Middle English.

1. -m > -n
2. -n > Ø
3. a, o, u, e > e [ə] (when not stressed)

Figure 14-4 shows how, as a consequence of these sound changes, certain sets of Old English inflections merged, becoming indistinguishable in Middle English and being further reduced or dropped altogether in early Modern English. As a result of these mergers, the Old English noun and adjective paradigms became greatly simplified in Middle English, and grammatical gender disappeared (see Table 14-7).

Nouns   The frequently used subject and object noun phrase forms (nominative and accusative cases) established the nominative and accusative plural form *foxes* (and the -*es* inflection for other nouns in general) throughout the plural; they also

Figure 14-4

THE HISTORICAL REDUCTION OF ENGLISH INFLECTIONS

Old English   Middle English   Early Modern English

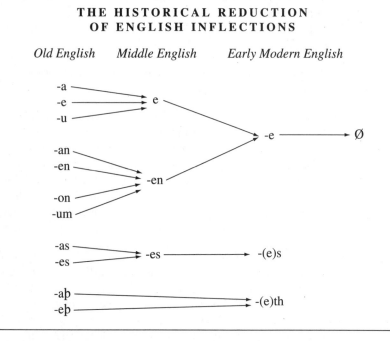

established the nominative and accusative singular throughout the singular except that the genitive in *-s* was maintained. Thus the Middle English paradigm for a noun like *fox* came to be what it is in Modern English: *fox* and *foxes* (the latter now spelled *fox's*) in the singular and *foxes* throughout the plural (possessive *foxes'*).

In some of the other noun paradigms, the damage to the morphological distinctions caused by the merging of unstressed vowels was even greater. Old English

Table 14-7

FOUR MIDDLE ENGLISH NOUN DECLENSIONS

	'FOX'	'LORE'	'ANIMAL'	'FOOT'
SINGULAR				
Nom./Acc.	fox	loor	deer	foot
Genitive	foxes	loor(e)	deeres	footes
Dative	fox(e)	loor(e)	deer(e)	foot
PLURAL				
Nom./Acc.	foxes	loor(e)	deer	feet
Genitive/Dative	foxes	loor(e)	deer(e)	foot(e)

dēor was reduced to three forms (*deer/deeres/deere*), while *lār* was reduced to two (*loor* and *loore*), a distinction that was in turn lost when final inflected *-e* vanished about 1500.

We have the Modern English forms of the word *deer* (*deer* and *deer's*) from the nominative and accusative singular inflection, which were extended throughout the singular (except that the ending in *-s* has been kept in the genitive). The parallel nominative and accusative plural form extended throughout the plural (except that by analogy with all other nouns the genitive plural is formed by adding *-s* to the form of the nominative plural). From the *foot* declension, the origin of the Modern English forms are clear: Middle English nominative and accusative *foot* was extended throughout the singular, with the *-s* of the genitive form *footes* maintained; the nominative and accusative plural *feet* was extended throughout the plural (and, as usual, the inflected genitive is formed by adding *-s* to the nominative). Modern English expressions like *a ten-foot pole* 'a pole of ten feet' and *a three-day weekend* 'a weekend of three days' are simply relics of the Old English constructions with genitive plurals (for example, *fōta*), whose final *-a* became *-e* in Middle English and then was dropped.

Adjectives   The same merging of distinct inflections that collapsed the noun declensions also had a devastating effect on adjectives. The only indefinite forms to survive the phonological change from Old English were *goodne* (masculine accusative singular), *goodes* (masculine and neuter genitive singular), and *goodre* (feminine genitive, dative, and instrumental singular, and genitive plural). Then *good* became the universal form for the singular. In the plural, the nominative, accusative, and dative forms for all genders became *good,* and the genitive plural also became *good* by analogy. That left only a single form in the singular and plural, namely *good,* which yielded Modern English *good* as the invariable form of the adjective (comparative and superlative forms aside).

In the definite declension, the only two forms surviving were *good* and *goodre.* Then *goodre* was re-formed by analogy (whereby one form takes on the shape of other forms in the same or another paradigm) to *good,* thus leaving only a single definite adjective form, which was the same as the indefinite. Thus a few seemingly simple phonological changes (and some analogical adaptations) reduced the complex forms of Old English adjectives to the striking simplicity of today's single forms.

MIDDLE ENGLISH WORD ORDER

Much could be said about Middle English syntax, but the language changed so thoroughly during the four centuries of this period that a good deal of provision would have to be made for intermediate stages. Since we have described Old English and Modern English syntax at some length, suffice it to say that Middle English was a transitional period, especially with respect to the change from a reliance on inflection to a reliance on word order for a considerable amount of information about grammatical relations. As the inflections of Old English disappeared, the word order of Middle English became increasingly fixed. The communicative work that had previously been done for nouns by inflectional morphology still needed doing, and it fell principally to prepositions and word order to perform these tasks. We have already said that Old English preferred SVO word order in main clauses but often had SOV word order in subordinate clauses. The exclusive use of the SVO pattern emerged in the twelfth century and has remained part of English ever since.

WHERE MEN AND WOMEN GO ALL NAKED: A MIDDLE ENGLISH TRAVEL FABLE

—

You can now see how some of these features of morphology and syntax came together in Middle English prose. Figure 14-5 is passage from *The Travels of John Mandeville*. It's a translation made from Mandeville's French work by an unknown English writer in the early fifteenth century (about the time of Chaucer's death in 1400). These travel fables were extremely popular and survive in several hundred manuscripts. In the passage quoted here, Mandeville describes a fabulous place called Lamary.

We analyze this passage with a view to how English of the early fifteenth century differs from today's. First of all, the passage is quite intelligible, though you can note a few marked differences (and some subtle ones) between it and today's English.

VOCABULARY IN THE FABLE

Not a single word in the passage will be unknown to readers today, though a few (such as *lond* 'land,' *hete* 'heat,' *ʒeer* 'year,' *byʒen* 'buy,' and *hem* 'them') might not be instantly recognizable. (The graph <ʒ>, called *yogh*, was pronounced like [y].) Not all the words borrowed from French during the Middle English period immediately took their current form, but most are nevertheless transparent: *custom, strange, clothed, nature, comoun, clos, contradiccioun, contree, habundant, marchauntes.*

MORPHOLOGY IN THE FABLE

In the fable, only a few inflections remain from Old English that have not survived in Modern English. For example, third-person singular present-tense verbs end in -*(e)th: holdeth, hath, lyketh, taketh* (but compare past tense *made*); and plural present-tense verbs end in -*n* or -*en: gon, scornen, seyn, ben, eten, bryngen, byʒen,* and others. This -*n* or -*en* is not the direct reflex of the Old English plural form -*aþ* but has apparently been introduced from the subjunctive plural so as to maintain a distinction between the singular and the plural, which otherwise would have been lost when the unstressed vowels of the singular -*eþ* and the plural -*aþ* merged to give Middle English -*eth* for both forms. As shown in Figure 14-15, Mandeville's translator alternates between the two spellings *þei* and *thei* for the third-person plural subject pronoun, but the *þ/th* forms of the objective case do not yet appear in this passage, which instead shows the objective form *hem* (lines 19, 20, and 21). Otherwise, several of the Modern English

Figure 14-5

A TRAVEL FABLE WRITTEN IN MIDDLE ENGLISH AROUND THE YEAR 1400

1 In þat lond is full gret hete,
  In that land is very great heat,

2 and the custom þere is such þat men and wommen gon all naked.
  and the custom there is such that men and women go all naked.

3 And þei scornen, whan thei seen ony strange folk goynge clothed.
  And they scorn, when they see any strange folk going clothed.

4 And þei seyn, þat god made Adam and Eue all naked
  And they say, that God made Adam and Eve all naked

5 and þat no man scholde schame him to schewen him such as god made him;
  and that no man should shame himself to show himself such as God made him;

6 for no thing is foul þat is of kyndely nature . . .
  for no thing is foul that is of natural nature . . .

7 And also all the lond is comoun; for all þat a man
  And also all the land is common; for all that a man

8 holdeth o ȝeer, another man hath it anoþer ȝeer,
  keeps one year, another man has it another year,

9 and euery man taketh what part þat him lyketh.
  and every man takes what part that him pleases.

10 And also all the godes of the lond ben comoun, cornes and all oþer þinges;
  And also all the goods of the land are common, grains and all other things;

11 for no þing þere is kept in clos, ne no þing þere is vndur lok,
  for no thing there is kept in a closet nor no thing there is under lock,

12 and euery man þere taketh what he wole, withouten ony contradiccioun.
  and every man there takes what he wants, without any contradiction.

13 And als riche is o man þere as is another.
  And as rich is one man there as is another.

14 But in þat contree þere is a cursed custom:
  But in that country there is a cursed custom:

15 for þei eten more gladly mannes flesch þan ony oþer flesch.
  for they eat more gladly man's flesh than any other flesh.

16 And ȝit is þat contree habundant of flesch, of fissch,
  And yet is that country abundant with flesh, with fish,

17 of cornes, of gold and syluer, and of all oþer godes.
  with grains, with gold and silver, and with all other goods.

18 Þider gon marchauntes and bryngen with hem children,
  Thither go merchants and bring with them children,

19 to selle to hem of the contree; and þei byȝen hem.
  to sell to them of the country; and they buy them.

20 And ȝif þei ben fatte, þei eten hem anon; and ȝif þei ben lene,
  And if they are fat, they eat them at once; and if they are lean,

21 þei feden hem till þei ben fatte, and þanne þei eten hem.
  they feed them until they are fat, and then they eat them.

22 And þei seyn, þat it is the best flesch and the swettest of all the world.
  And they say, that it is the best flesh and the sweetest of all the world.

inflections have their current form (after some slight spelling adjustments): *goynge* 'going,' *clothed, godes* 'goods,' *þinges* 'things,' *marchauntes* 'merchants,' and *swettest* 'sweetest.' Even certain words that had kept their exceptional forms from Old English are the same or nearly the same in 1400 and today: *men, wommen, folk, children,* and *best.* Being among the more common words of the language they were more likely to maintain their unusual forms than were words used less frequently.

Syntax in the Fable

One notable difference in syntax occurs in the first line. Where Modern English requires a "dummy subject" (a subject without a referent), Middle English did not: *In þat lond is. . . .* But note the dummy *þere* in line 14: *But in þat contree þere is. . . .* Another striking difference is the double negative *ne no þing* 'nor nothing' in line 11.

There are marked word order differences. Compare in line 13 this word-for-word equivalent with its current English version (which follows the slash): *And as rich is one man there as is another/And one man there is as rich as another.* Note too that the adverbial phrase *more gladly* (line 15) follows its verb instead of preceding it as it would in Modern English. Finally, note the relic of Old English verb-second word order in line 18 (*Thither go merchants*) and the prepositional phrase *with hem* in the same line, which in current English would follow the direct object *children.*

Among some of the subtler syntactic differences are the intransitive use of *scorn* (that is, without a direct object) in line 3. Modern English would require a direct object: you must scorn something or someone. Note, too, the use of the nonreflexive pronoun *him* where current English would reflexivize (line 5). One final interesting difference occurs in line 9, where *him* is an object form that complements the verb *lyketh* (in a benefactive semantic role); *him lyketh* literally translates *to him (it) likes* 'it pleases him.' Since Old English times, this "impersonal" construction had not required a subject but had required a dative (or, later, objective) case form of the pronoun. It resembles the French *s'il vous plait* 'if it you pleases,' which may have influenced the now archaic formulation *if it please you* or *if it please my lord.*

We may overlook some of the syntactic differences between this passage and current English because we are accustomed to finding relatively conservative syntax in such places as the King James Bible and certain formal prose styles such as legalese. Still, it is fair to say that this Middle English passage, now six centuries old, is obviously English and almost completely transparent to modern readers.

MODERN ENGLISH: 1500–PRESENT

—

Chapters 2 through 6 of this book examined the structure of twentieth-century English in detail, and there is no need to recapitulate that material here. This section focuses instead on what changes occurred in the earliest stages of Modern English to move the language from the forms of Middle English to those we know today.

EARLY AND LATE MODERN ENGLISH

As our analysis of Mandeville's travel fable shows, by the beginning of the fifteenth century Middle English had developed many of the principal syntactic patterns we know today. The complex inflectional system of Old English had been simplified ("destroyed" may be a more accurate description); and today's system, with fewer than ten inflections, had emerged. Most nouns that had been inflected in Old English according to various patterns now conformed to the *fox* pattern. By the time of Shakespeare, third-person plural pronouns with *th-* instead of *h-* (*they, their,* and *them*) were in general use and had been for a century; Chaucer and the Mandeville translator had used *they,* but both still used the older possessive form *her* (*their*) and objective form *hem* (*them*). In addition, word order had become more fixed, essentially as it is in Modern English.

The language of the late 1400s is in most ways Modern English—though we should be mindful that the principal phonological development of English vowels took place sometime between 1450 and 1650, when all the long vowels changed their quality very markedly, as we'll see. If that phonological change is not apparent, it is simply because the modern spelling of English vowels had essentially been established by the time of William Caxton, who founded his printing press in the vicinity of Westminster Abbey in 1476—before the phonological change had progressed very far at all. Caxton's spellings thus disguise the fundamental alteration that has occurred in the system of English vowels, throwing it out of harmony with the representations that these same written vowels have in the continental languages.

PHONOLOGY: THE ENGLISH VOWEL SHIFT

In the Mandeville travel passage, certain words are easily recognized by their similar spellings to Modern English. In particular, the words *gret, hete, schame,* and *foul* are similar to their modern counterparts. The written similarity, however, disguises the fact that the words as *pronounced* in Chaucer's time are not likely to be recognizable by a modern listener. Sometime during the two centuries between 1450 and 1650, all the long vowels of Middle English underwent a systematic shift. Each long front vowel was raised and became pronounced like another vowel higher in the system. The same thing occurred with back vowels: each long vowel was raised to be pronounced like the vowel next higher in the vowel chart. Thus /ɔː/ came to be pronounced /oː/, /eː/ came to be pronounced /iː/, and so on. The two highest long vowels, high front /iː/ and high back /uː/, could not be raised any farther and instead were diphthongized to /ay/ and /aw/ respectively. Thus Middle English *I* /iː/ became /ay/, *hous* /huːs/ became /haws/ 'house,' and so on. We can represent the situation as in Figure 14-6.

MODERN ENGLISH MORPHOLOGY

Verbs Of the hundreds of strong (irregular) verbs in Old English, relatively few survive in Modern English. Of those that do, many came to be inflected like the weak (regular) verbs, with an alveolar stop suffix rather than a vowel gradation. One

Figure 14-6

THE ENGLISH VOWEL SHIFT

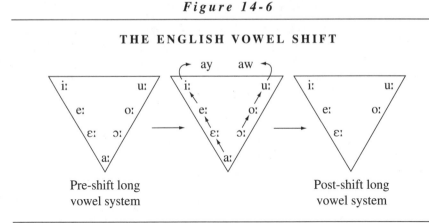

Pre-shift long
vowel system

Post-shift long
vowel system

Source: Adapted from Theodora Bynon. *Historical Linguistics* (Cambridge: Cambridge UP, 1977), p. 82.

tally suggests that of the 333 strong verbs of Old English, only 68 continue as irregular verbs in Modern English. Among those that have become regular over the centuries are *burn, brew, climb, flow, help,* and *walk.* By contrast, slightly more than a dozen weak verbs have become irregular in the history of English, including *dive,* which has developed a past-tense form *dove* alongside the historical form *dived.* You may also have heard *drug* for *dragged,* as its use seems to be increasing as well. Among other verbs that are now irregular but were formerly regular are *wear, spit,* and *dig.*

Definite Article   The initial consonant of *sē* and *sēo,* the Old English masculine and feminine nominative singular demonstrative, differed from all other forms, which began with [θ] (orthographic <þ>). *Sē* was apparently reshaped by analogy with forms having initial [θ]. By Middle English, *þe* had become the invariant definite article in the north of England, and its use soon spread to the other dialects. Chaucer uses only *the,* pronounced [θə]. The voicing of the initial consonant as you know it today occurred because the customary lack of stress on *the* encouraged assimilation to the vowel nucleus, which of course is voiced. Such a history is somewhat surprising for what is by far the most commonly used word in Modern English.

Indefinite Article   The history of the indefinite article *a/an* is also remarkable, for while Old English did not use an indefinite article, today *a/an* is among the top ten most common words in English, written and spoken, British and American.

Personal Pronouns   Though the personal pronouns retain more of their Old English diversity than any other part of speech, our earlier comparison of Old and Modern English pronouns (Table 14-4) indicates that the dual number was lost entirely (starting even at the beginning of the Middle English period). During the early Mod-

Ye Olde Booke Shoppe

In the early fourteenth century some English writers merged the runic letter <þ> and the Roman letter <y> in their manuscripts, thereby setting the stage for readers to confuse the two graphs. In the fifteenth century, the use of <þ> decreased, but even Chaucer, who died in 1400, generally used <th> where earlier writers had used <þ>. Some writers and printers of the time used y^e, y^t, y^{ei}, y^m, y^u to represent the words *the, that, they, them,* and *thou,* and such abbreviations (or *compendia,* as they are called) continued in manuscripts into the eighteenth century. In books printed as late as the sixteenth century you can find y^e for *the* (sometimes with <e> superscripted directly above <y>) and y^t for *that* (also sometimes with <t> appearing directly above <y>). Among the citations listed in the *Oxford English Dictionary* are these from eighteenth-century letters: "I am to inform you yt ye Duchess continues as well as can be, and ye Babe too" and "He told y^m yt ye French was landing in the Marsh." Certain of these shorthand forms continued into nineteenth-century correspondence as well. As for current use of <y> for <th>, the *OED* characterizes it as pseudoarchaic and gives as examples Lewis Carroll's 'Ye Carpette Knighte' and shop signs like Ye Olde Booke Shoppe.

ern English period, the distinction between the second-person singular and plural forms—between singular *thou* and *thee* (Old English *þū* and *þē*) and plural *ye* and *you* (Old English *gē* and *ēow*)—disintegrated.

Under the apparent influence of French, speakers of English began using the plural forms *ye, your,* and *you* as a sign of respect or formality, much as happens with the French pronoun *vous,* which is grammatically plural but can be used to show respect and deference when addressing a single stranger, elder, or social superior. Among the upper social classes in England, the historical plural form *you* came to be used as a mutual sign of respect even in informal conversation between equals. In time, the singular forms all but disappeared along with the distinction between the plural subject and plural object forms *ye* and *you.* Thus, from the sixfold distinction found in Old English and much of Middle English, Modern English has only a twofold distinction—between *you* and *yours.*

The loss of a singular/plural distinction for *you* is an accident of history, and many Modern English speakers find it difficult to get along without a distinctive second-person plural pronoun. In fact, certain varieties of Modern English have created distinct plural forms, although these are regionally marked (*y'all* in the American South) or socially stigmatized (*youse,* pronounced [yuz], [yɪz], or [yəz] in New York City and parts of Ireland and England, and *y'uns,* pronounced [yənz] in western Pennsylvania and the Ohio valley). Standard English has no way to mark the second-person pronoun for plurality, though of course one can say such things as *you two* or *you all.*

MODERN ENGLISH WORD ORDER

Deprived of the richness of its earlier inflectional signposts to meaning, Modern English has become an analytical language—more like Chinese than Latin and the other early offshoots of Proto-Indo-European. With nouns inflected only for the possessive case (and for number, of course), word order is now the chief signal of grammatical relations like subject and object. Even the more differentiated pronouns are subordinate to the grammatical relations that word order signals, so that *Him and me saw her at the party,* though not standard, is nevertheless not confusing in any way as to subject and object.

Why English advanced farther than its Germanic cousins along the path to becoming an analytical language (rather than remaining an inflected language) is not altogether clear. Possible explanations may be found in the thoroughgoing contact between the Danes and the English after the ninth century, in the French ascendance over English for numerous secular and religious purposes in the early Middle English period, and in the preservation of the vernacular chiefly in folk speech and therefore without the conservationist brake of writing for several generations in the eleventh and twelfth centuries. The influence of the Danes is particularly important. When they invaded England in the eighth and ninth centuries, the Danes spoke varieties of Germanic that must have been quite similar to the dialects spoken in England but with different inflections. It is easy to imagine that children exposed to parents using different inflectional suffixes and to friends whose inflectional suffixes were not uniform might readily look for other means to signal the differences formerly indicated by inflections.

In any case, decades before the Norman Conquest, those inflectional reductions started that became apparent when English reemerged; doubtless they had advanced farther in speech than the written texts of the day indicate. Thus phonological reductions undermined the inflectional morphology, and, as inflection grew less able to signal grammatical relations and semantic roles, word order and the deployment of prepositions came to bear those communicative tasks less redundantly. Gradually, the freer word order of Old English yielded to the relatively fixed order of Modern English, whose linear arrangements are the chief carrier of grammatical functions.

Spurred by an almost total absence of inflections on nouns, Modern English syntax has evolved to permit unusually free interplay among grammatical relations and semantic roles. With nouns marked only for possessive case, and pronouns marked for possessive and objective cases, Modern English exercises minimal inflectional constraint on subject noun phrases, which are consequently free to represent an exceptionally wide range of semantic roles (as illustrated in Chapter 6, p. 212).

MODERN ENGLISH VOCABULARY

As in the course of the Middle English period, when English supplanted French and borrowed thousands of French words, so in the course of early Modern English, as English came to be used for functions Latin had previously served, a great many words were borrowed from Latin (and through Latin from Greek). The words borrowed from Latin are not common words like the courtroom terminology from French. Instead, they're learned words, reflecting the arenas in which Latin had been used. Even with these borrowings, English found itself in need of a great many more words as it spread from principally literary and personal uses into every sphere of activity. The *Oxford English Dictionary* records words from about fifty different languages borrowed into English during the first century and a half of Modern English (1500–1650), the period during which the vernacular came to replace Latin in nearly every learned arena.

Among the Latin borrowings of this early Modern English period are the following: *allusion, anachronism, antipathy, antithesis, appendix, atmosphere, autograph,* and *axis* among the nouns (to stick to those beginning with <a>); *abject, agile,* and *appropriate* among the adjectives; and *adapt, alienate,* and *assassinate* among the verbs. Some of these words, though introduced to English from Latin, came originally from Greek. During the Renaissance, words were borrowed directly from Greek as well. These include *acme, anonymous, catastrophe, criterion* (and its plural, *criteria*), *idiosyncrasy, lexicon, ostracize, polemic, tantalize,* and *tonic.* Not everyone appreciated borrowed words, and many writers who used these thenstrange terms were criticized for their "inkhorn" words. Not every borrowed term was successful; many failed to survive.

HOW COMPUTERS TRACK CHANGE IN ENGLISH

A project of major importance for the study of the history of English is the digitizing of the *Oxford English Dictionary.* The *OED* is a mammoth multivolume set of dictionaries recording every word that has appeared in English printed materials since the Old English period. (Parenthetically, we might add that the *OED* was compiled during Victorian times and not *every* word of English found its way onto its Victorian pages. You won't be surprised that among the words you can't find in the original *OED* are the infamous four-letter "Anglo-Saxonisms" familiar to everyone.) The *OED* took roughly half a century to complete, and by time the final volume was published in 1928, a good deal more had been learned about the words at the beginning of the alphabet, which had appeared in the earliest volumes. That required a large supplement. Again, in the 1970s a further supplement was needed, and it ballooned into four very large volumes, so much had the language changed since the previous supplement in 1933. Subsequently, in 1989, the original twelve volumes were digitized with the five supplements incorporated, thereby creating a second edition. The second edition was published in book form (twenty large volumes weighing 137 pounds and taking up nearly four feet of shelf space). More to the point, it was made available as a compact disc, not only much smaller and far less expensive, but much easier to use in many respects—and certainly more efficient. Now, if you have access to the CD-ROM you can readily search through a thousand years of English language history, finding citations for any word that interests you, along with information about the author, date, and source for each citation. You can determine the date of a word's first recorded use; you can limit your search to any time period or author. The CD-ROM makes it possible to discover all the words that entered the language in a specified time period or all the words borrowed from a particular language–say, Japanese or French or Hindi.

Several major historical corpora of English have been compiled in recent years. In the previous chapter, we discussed the Helsinki Corpus, which covers the period from Old English through 1710, and ARCHER, which covers the period from 1650 through 1990. Corpora like these have made possible a considerable amount of previously unknown information about the history of English. Ready accessibility to some of these corpora has given students an opportunity to explore the history of particular structures or words for

themselves, and some college and university courses are based on working with such corpora.

We can illustrate the utility of corpora with one simple finding here. This finding would not have been practical without computers. Using ARCHER, researchers discovered a general movement in the texts of some registers from relatively "informational" to relatively "involved," as measured by the features that define the involved/informational dimension discussed in Chapter 10. As you recall from Chapter 10, the features of the involved/informational dimension capture an underlying textual purpose of showing involvement or conveying information (and these are polar opposites), and the dimension is defined by the complementary feature sets A and B (given on page 352).

Figure 14-7 traces the dimension scores for drama, diaries, letters, and fiction over

Figure 14-7

CHANGE IN FOUR SPEECH-RELATED REGISTERS ALONG THE INVOLVED/INFORMATIONAL DIMENSION FROM THE SEVENTEENTH TO THE TWENTIETH CENTURIES

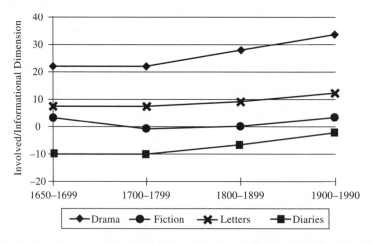

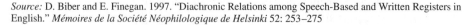

Source: D. Biber and E. Finegan. 1997. "Diachronic Relations among Speech-Based and Written Registers in English." *Mémoires de la Société Néophilologique de Helsinki* 52: 253–275

four centuries. These four registers are speech based (as in the case of drama) or nonexpository written prose (as in the case of fiction). A glance at Figure 14-7 shows a clear overall historical pattern for registers of this kind: a general tendency toward increasing *involvement* and away from *informational* textual characteristics. This finding doesn't mean that the texts contain less information but that they have decreasingly exploited the linguistic features (nouns, prepositions, longer words, and so on) that are associated typically with texts intended to be informational. At the same

time these registers have become increasingly involved—that is, over time they have shown a more frequent use of the linguistic features (first- and second-person pronouns, contractions, emphatics, WH-questions, and so on) that are typically associated with texts whose principal purpose is to express involvement.

Strikingly different from the patterns for these four registers are the patterns for four others—medical writing, scientific writing, legal writing, and news writing. As Figure 14-8 shows, these specialist written registers have shown a steady decrease in the features

Figure 14-8

CHANGE IN FOUR WRITTEN REGISTERS ALONG THE INVOLVED/INFORMATIONAL DIMENSION FROM THE SEVENTEENTH TO THE TWENTIETH CENTURIES

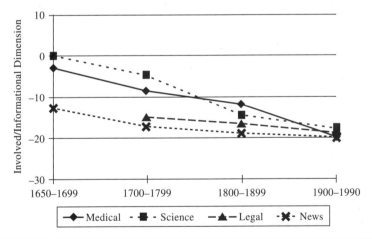

Source: D. Biber and E. Finegan. 1997. "Diachronic Relations among Speech-Based and Written Registers in English." *Mémoires de la Société Néophilologique de Helsinki* 52: 253–275

of involvement (Set A, page 352) and a greater use of the features that characterize texts with an informational purpose (Set B, page 352). It will be no surprise to you that legal writing and medical writing are strongly "informational" and not very "involved." Before the availability of suitable corpora, how-

ever, no one could have been certain to what extent and in which registers the movement toward informational characteristics in texts had occurred.

Unlike most earlier historical linguistics studies, the kind of research represented in figures 14-7 and 14-8 reports change in *quantitative* exploitation of linguistic features. More typically, until recently at least, studies have tended to focus on *qualitative* changes, such as that Indo-European /p/ became Germanic /f/. The analyses that are possible with the Helsinki Corpus, ARCHER, and other corpora now under development will enable researchers to trace quantitative as well as qualitative changes in the development of languages and to explore the introduction of change into particular registers and its spread from register to register.

SUMMARY

- English belongs to the West Germanic group of the Germanic branch of the Indo-European language family. It is *not* descended from Latin, but both Latin and English are members of the Indo-European language family and are descended from Proto-Indo-European.

- Among major languages, the closest relatives of English are German and Dutch.

- In the course of its history, English has been greatly enriched by thousands of words borrowed from more than a hundred languages—most notably from French, as the descendants of the Norman invaders started using English in the thirteenth century, and from Latin, when the vernacular came to be used during the Renaissance in arenas previously reserved for the classical language.

- *Beowulf* is an epic poem of the Old English period (700–1100). Chaucer (1340–1400) wrote during the Middle English period (1100–1500). Shakespeare (1564–1616) wrote early in the Modern English period (1500–present).

- Old English was a highly inflected language, but sound changes eroded most of the inflectional morphology in Middle English.

- As a result of the erosion of inflections, Modern English is an analytical language, relying principally on word order to express grammatical relations formerly marked by inflections.

EXERCISES

14-1. Modern English words that were borrowed from Latin or Greek do not show the influence of Grimm's Law (which affected only the Germanic branch of Indo-European). For many such borrowed words, English also has a related word that it inherited directly from Indo-European through Germanic. Any such inherited word would not have undergone the consonant shifts described by Grimm. For each borrowed word given below, cite an English word that is related in meaning and whose pronunciation shows the result of the consonant shift. For this exercise, focus only on the initial consonant of each word. For example, given *pedal,* you would seek a word like *foot* that has a related meaning and begins with [f] (because Indo-European [p] became [f] in Germanic).

cardiac   paternal   plenitude
dual   pentagon   dentist

capital	piscatorial	triangle
cordial	canine	decade

14-2. This exercise is like the preceding one, except that here you will find English words that have undergone the Germanic consonant shift and must provide another English word that is likely to have been borrowed because it has a closely related meaning but does not show the results of Grimm's Law. Bear in mind that most Latin and Greek borrowings tend to be more learned and technical than the related ones inherited directly from Indo-European. Focus only on the boldfaced consonant. For example, given *foot,* you would cite a word that begins with p such as *podiatrist* 'foot doctor.'

*t*ooth	li*p*	*f*ire
*t*en	*h*ound	ea*t*

14-3. You know that, by the effects of Grimm's Law, Indo-European *[bʰ] became [b] and Indo-European *[gʰ] became [g] in Germanic. Not being a Germanic language, Latin did not undergo these consonant shifts. Instead, Indo-European *[bʰ] became [f] in Latin, and Indo-European *[gʰ] became [h] in Latin. We represent these facts in the following correspondences:

Indo-European

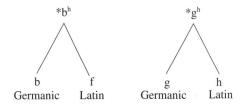

b	f	g	h
Germanic	Latin	Germanic	Latin

With this information, you may be able to provide an English word inherited directly from Indo-European for each of the following words, which are all borrowed from Latin. Focus on the initial consonant, and bear in mind that other changes may have affected the remainder of the word so that the resemblance is distant.

fraternity	flame
fundamental	hospitable
fragile	fracture

14-4. Indicate which allophone of /f/, /θ/, or /s/ was pronounced in each of the following Old English words (use the description of the allophonic distribution given on p. 514 to help you determine the correct answer): *þæt, sēo, his, ūs, wæs, æðeling* 'prince,' *frēosan* 'freeze,' *dēmst* 'judge,' *līfes* 'of life,' *þā* 'then,' *drīfan* 'drive,' *wulfas* 'wolves,' *hræfn* 'raven,' *bosm* 'bosom,' *seofon* 'seven,' *bæþ* 'bath,' *sceaft* 'shaft.'

14-5. a. Identify the grammatical gender of the following Old English nouns, and then write out the full declension (all cases, singular and plural) for each of the noun phrases in which they appear; use the paradigms given in this chapter as models.

sē stān   'the stone'
þæt word   'the word'
sēo wund   'the wound'

b. For each of these Old English noun phrases, provide the Old English pronoun that would be used in the space given.

Sē stān, _____ is gōd.   'The stone, it is good.'
Ðæt word, _____ is gōd.   'The word, it is good.'
Sēo wund, _____ nis gōd.   'The wound, it isn't good.'

14-6. Compare the Old English passage on p. 522 with the Middle English passage on p. 529 and identify ways in which Middle English differs from Old English in orthography, vocabulary, morphology, and word order. Provide an example from the passages to illustrate each point.

14-7. You have seen several words in this chapter whose meaning has changed from Old English to Modern English. One example is the word *dēor*, which meant 'animal' in Old English but has narrowed its meaning to 'deer' in Modern English. Among several other ways, words can change their meaning by becoming more specialized, as with *deer*, or becoming more generalized. Examine the Old English words and meanings that follow and note what each word has become in Modern English. State whether the word's meaning has become more specialized or more generalized in the course of its development from Old English into Modern English.

Old English	*Modern English*
steorfan 'die'	starve
berēafian 'deprive of'	bereave
hlāf 'bread'	loaf
spēdan 'prosper'	speed
spellian 'speak'	spell
hund 'dog'	hound
mete 'food'	meat
wīf 'woman'	wife
dōm 'judgment'	doom
sellan 'give'	sell
tīd 'time'	tide

14-8. Nearly all of the words listed below were borrowed into English from other languages. Keeping in mind the character of the words and what they signify, make an educated guess as to the likely source language for each word and the approximate date of borrowing. Then, for each word, look up its origin in a good dictionary, noting for borrowed words the actual source language and the date of borrowing. For which words has no source been identified? (While the source language will be identified in most good dictionaries, the date of borrowing may not be. *Webster's Ninth New Collegiate Dictionary* and *Merriam-Webster's Collegiate Dictionary,* tenth edition, do supply dates. It may be useful for different students or student groups to tackle different columns of words and then to compare their findings.)

barf	duffel	hummus	tandoori
zilch	mai tai	tortilla	ginseng
kibble	moped	nosh	glitch
bummer	jeans	ginger	schlock
dinosaur	disco	giraffe	kvetch
leviathan	dude	ciao	glasnost
tae kwon do	sphere	karate	kayak
piña colada	taffy	kimono	shtick
kerchief	dim sum	kung fu	moussaka
teriyaki	cadaver	paparazzi	whiskey
catsup	denim	taffeta	karma
hunk	algebra	falafel	caucus
honcho	alarm	mutton	caddie
macho	a la mode	klutz	goober

14-9. Go to a Web site at which you can find an image of the beginning of the *Beowulf* poem (one site is identified as "Hwæt we Gar-Dena" in the "Internet and Other Resources" section that follows). Carefully compare the beginning of the manuscript version with the transcription given in this chapter on page 507. Then, on the basis of the correspondences between the Old English orthography and the Modern English transcriptions, provide transcriptions for another three lines.

INTERNET AND OTHER RESOURCES

- **Old English Pages: http://www.georgetown.edu/cball/oe/old_english.html**
  An award-winning Web site, not to be missed. Supplies easily accessible information about Old English and links to other fascinating views of the period. Includes a link to the British Museum, where artifacts from the Sutton Hoo Burial Ship can be found. Provides access to electronic texts, translations, manuscript images, art, history, and the language itself. Also contains useful references to Old English fonts, sound files, CD-ROMs and cassettes, instructional software, and—for those with wondrous ambition—access to a forum for composition in Old English. There is also a linked audio page at http://www.georgetown.edu/cball/oe/oe-audio.html; it will lead you to recordings of portions of "The Battle of

Brunanburh," *Beowulf,* "The Funeral of Scyld Scefing," "The Lord's Prayer," "Cædmon's Hymn," and "Deor."

- **Hwæt we Gar-Dena:**
  ftp://beowulf.engl.uky.edu/pub/beowulf/129rcol.nu.jpg
  To see an Old English manuscript containing the words from Beowulf given on page 507, visit this site. For an enlargement—and for Exercise 14-9, visit ftp:// beowulf.engl.uky.edu/pub/beowulf/129r.jpg. (*Note:* Both these addresses begin with *ftp,* not *http.*)
- **The Oxford English Dictionary Online:**
  http://www.oed.com/dictsframe.html
  At the time of writing, the *OED* is not available online, but this Web site promises that it soon will be. When it becomes available, it will be a great boon to anyone interested in the development of English.

Video and Audio Recordings

- *The Story of English*
  A popular video series hosted by Robert MacNeil. Two videos treat the development of English—"The Mother Tongue" and "A Muse of Fire." Readily available in libraries and video rental outlets. Highly recommended.
- **The Chaucer Studio**
  Perhaps the best source for audiocassettes of Old and Middle English. See the Web page at http://english.byu.edu/factftt-z/thomasp/chaucer/index.htm. You can hear spoken samples from the General Prologue of the *Canterbury Tales,* the Knight's, Summoner's, and Nun's Priest's tales, and some of *Gawain and the Green Knight* at:
  http://www.millersv.edu/~english/homepage/duncan/chaucer/audio.html.

SUGGESTION FOR FURTHER READING

- **Tim William Machan and Charles T. Scott, eds. 1992. English in its Social Contexts: Essays in Historical Sociolinguistics** (New York: Oxford UP). Accessible essays aiming to contextualize changes in English within the social contexts of their times. Also contains chapters on current British, American, and Australian English, and on the spread of English around the globe.

Advanced Reading

There are several excellent general histories of the English language. Baugh and Cable (1993)—from which our examples of French borrowings in Middle English, Latin and Greek borrowings in early Modern English, and regular and irregular verbs are taken—is superb on the external history of the language. Pyles and Algeo (1993), from which we have borrowed a few examples, is balanced between internal and external history and complements Baugh and Cable (1993) by being stronger on the internal history. Millward (1990) and Bolton (1982) are also very good. Smith (1996) is a refreshingly different approach, integrating internal and external history in systematically explanatory ways. Algeo (1993) is a workbook for the history of English. A useful and easy-to-use Old English reference grammar is Quirk and Wrenn (1957), from which several of our examples are taken. Especially valuable for Old English syntax and reliable as a pedagogical grammar is Mitchell and Robinson (1986). Burrow and Turville-Petre (1992) provides Middle English texts and discussion. For the early Modern English period, Barber (1976) is good on language structure, on attitudes toward borrowing and correctness, and on semantic change in the lexicon. Görlach (1991) is also useful, especially on writing and spelling. Denison (1993) is a corpus-based treatment of historical syntax, somewhat advanced. Dillard (1992) treats American English.

Background information about Indo-European is conveniently found in Philip Baldi's "Indo-European Languages," in Comrie (1987), and information about Germanic in "Germanic Languages," by John A. Hawkins, is in the same volume. Two excellent books about life in Anglo-Saxon Britain are Campbell, John, and Wormald (1982) and Wood (1986), which have photographs of artifacts, ruins, and manuscripts; Wood's book was written to accompany a BBC television series. The lavishly illustrated Evans (1986) describes the treasures evacuated at the site of a burial ship for a seventh-century king of an Anglo-Saxon kingdom. Also very readable is Laing (1982), with a bias toward the archaeological.

The Cambridge History of the English Language is a multivolume reference work that aims to synthesize what is known about the history of English to date. Designed for an educated general audience rather than a professional one, some *CHEL* chapters are nevertheless written above the level easily accessed by students whose principal exposure to the history of English is *LISU.* But other *CHEL* chapters are accessible, and instructors will find *CHEL* useful in providing additional insight into most matters related to historical English. Volume 1 treats "The Beginnings to 1066," Volume 2 "1066–1476," Volume 3 "1476–1776," Volume 4 "1776–present day," Volume 5 "English in Britain and Overseas," and Volume 6 "English in North America." For *CHEL,* see Hogg (1992–) below.

REFERENCES

- Algeo, John. 1993. *Problems in the Origins and Development of the English Language,* 4th ed. (Fort Worth: Harcourt Brace Jovanovich).

- Barber, Charles. 1976. *Early Modern English* (London: Andre Deutsch).

- Baugh, Albert C., and Thomas Cable. 1993. *A History of the English Language,* 4th ed. (Englewood Cliffs, NJ: Prentice-Hall).

- Bolton, W. F. 1982. *A Living Language: The History and Structure of English* (New York: Random House).

- Burrow, J., and T. Turville-Petre, eds. 1992. *A Book of Middle English* (Oxford: Blackwell).

- Campbell, James, Eric John, and Patrick Wormald. 1982. *The Anglo-Saxons* (Oxford: Phaidon).

- Comrie, Bernard, ed. 1987. *The World's Major Languages* (New York: Oxford UP).

- Denison, David. 1993. *English Historical Syntax: Verbal Constructions* (London: Longman).

- Dillard, J. L. 1992. *A History of American English* (London: Longman).

- Evans, Angela Care. 1986. *The Sutton Hoo Ship Burial* (London: British Museum Publications).

- Görlach, Manfred. 1991. *Introduction to Early Modern English* (Cambridge: Cambridge UP).

- Hogg, Richard M. 1992– . *The Cambridge History of the English Language,* 6 vols. (Cambridge: Cambridge UP).

- Laing, Lloyd and Jennifer. 1982. *Anglo-Saxon England* (London: Paladin).

- Millward, C. M. 1990. *A Biography of the English Language* (Fort Worth: Holt, Rinehart and Winston).

- Mitchell, Bruce, and Fred C. Robinson. 1986. *A Guide to Old English: Revised with Prose and Verse Texts and Glossary* (New York: Blackwell).

- Pyles, Thomas, and John Algeo. 1993. *The Origins and Development of the English Language,* 4th ed. (Fort Worth: Harcourt Brace Jovanovich).

- Quirk, Randolph, and C. L. Wrenn. (1957). *An Old English Grammar* (New York: Holt).

- Smith, Jeremy. 1996. *An Historical Study of English: Function, Form and Change* (New York: Routledge).

- Wood, Michael. 1986. *Domesday: A Search for the Roots of England* (London: BBC Books).

CHAPTER 15

ACQUIRING FIRST
AND SECOND LANGUAGES

INTRODUCTION

The language of children, even very young ones, is remarkably rich. Early in life children reveal mastery of the phonological, syntactic, and semantic systems described in earlier chapters, as well as a high degree of communicative competence in the appropriate use of language. As early as age five, children playing with hand puppets demonstrate productive control over a range of registers, including aspects of the characteristic talk between doctors and patients and doctors and nurses. Language acquisition seems so natural and effortless that parents, elated with the addition of each successive word, take it for granted that children will acquire their native language without a hitch. It seems obvious to everyone who has interacted with children that the process of acquiring a first language is relatively automatic, although it is subject to certain predictable missteps. Still, if the apparent ease with which a child accomplishes this magnificent achievement titillates parents, it baffles researchers. In this chapter you'll see why language acquisition intrigues and puzzles linguists and psychologists and why not everyone agrees about the nature of a child's task.

Earlier in the twentieth century, it was widely believed that, like other learned behavior, language learning was essentially a process of induction. A child would generalize about linguistic patterns from the language samples it heard in its interactions with parents, siblings, and other caretakers. Rather than resembling such bodily systems as digestion and respiration (which manifestly do *not* require learning), language was thought to be different. Because languages vary from culture to culture, it was thought that children must *induce* the rules and patterns of their language from the speech of those around them. In this respect, language learning appeared to resemble other forms of cultural behavior—like brushing your teeth, tying your shoelaces, or doing addition and subtraction.

In a dramatic shift of perceptions, the view of first-language learning as similar to other forms of learning is now regarded as implausible, and language acquisition is widely viewed as an inductive process only in limited respects. Indeed, rather than focusing on differences in languages, some linguists and psychologists focus on the similarities across languages (the linguistic universals of Chapter 7) and explain their universality as innate structures of the human mind that do not require learning. Other linguists and psychologists view the similarities across languages as the result not so much of uniform mental *structures* as of uniform mental *strategies* or dispositions for analyzing and acquiring language. In either case, there is now intense interest in characterizing what psycholinguists often call the *language-making capacity* and grammarians prefer to call the *language acquisition device.*

Researchers have recently uncovered a good deal about patterns of acquisition in diverse languages, and our understanding of how these patterns can differ from culture to culture while remaining strikingly similar continues to grow. In this chapter we explore certain basic findings about first-language acquisition in children and second-language acquisition among adults. We then briefly examine some animal communication studies.

ACQUIRING A FIRST LANGUAGE

You now know that acquiring a language entails far more than learning the meaning of various expressions. A child acquiring a language must learn a system that can generate countless sentences (relatively few of which have been heard before) and deploy them appropriately in conversations, stories, inquiries, and the other social interactions of everyday life. Language acquisition also entails ability to understand both the new and the familiar utterances of those around us and to interpret them appropriately in their social contexts.

Besides the words of their language and a range of meanings for virtually every word, children must master all the morphological, phonological, syntactic, semantic, and pragmatic rules of their language. Every child must know when to speak and when to listen, when and how to interrupt, when and how to greet, when to tease and how to recognize teasing from its contextualization cues, and so on. All children must learn how to make utterances achieve their intended objective and how to understand under what circumstances a particular utterance serves different functions—to offer food to someone (*Do you like chocolate?, Have you ever tasted a kumquat?*) or request information (*Do you like chocolate?, Have you ever tasted a kumquat?*). In other words, every child must learn the grammar of its language and the effective and culturally appropriate use of grammatical rules in diverse social situations. Put tersely, acquiring a language entails mastery of the full range of grammatical and communicative competence.

There is evidence to suggest that at least some (and perhaps a good deal) of what children know about language structure could not have been learned from the data surrounding them. To the extent that certain language structures cannot be inferred from the data available to children, it is reasonable to hypothesize that the human language capacity provides those structures at birth or through natural development. The issue can be framed in terms of "nature" versus "nurture," what is inborn versus what must be learned, what is prewired into the brain at birth ("hardware") versus what must be programmed by interaction with adult language ("software"). The challenge is to determine the nature and degree of the contributions made by biology and by socialization.

Alternatively, some psychologists and linguists suspect not so much that children share particular language structures as that they share strategies for analyzing language. In Chapter 4, for instance, we discussed how difficult it would be for a child to sort out the continuous string of sound that constitutes adult speech into the distinct sounds that constitute the phonological inventory of its language. There is now widespread agreement that children arrive at the task of language learning already in possession of the "knowledge" that language consists of distinct sounds. They are "preprogrammed" to analyze a continuous string of vocal sounds for its individual phonological segments. In the same way, then, children are thought to be naturally endowed with certain strategies for analyzing other aspects of language, and it is this set of *operating principles* for analyzing language that would contribute to the similarity of acquisition patterns across languages. As illustrations of such operating principles, children are thought to pay attention to the order of words in utterances, pay attention to the order of morphemes in words, pay attention particularly to the ends of words (where inflections are found), focus on consistent relationships between form and content, and look for generalizations.

OPERATING PRINCIPLES IN FIRST-LANGUAGE ACQUISITION
Pay attention to the order of words in utterances.
Pay attention to the order of morphemes in words.
Pay particular attention to word endings (inflections).
Focus on consistent relationships between expression and content.
Look for generalizations.

Many linguists and psychologists are convinced that language is not acquired by imitation—certainly not solely by imitation and probably not principally—although exposure to a particular language is, obviously, an essential ingredient in the process of acquiring it. Still, children have an undeniable capacity to be creative with language and certainly don't need to hear a particular sentence before saying it. They often utter sentences they are unlikely to have heard before, and they know intuitively which sentences are possible and which are not, although all children go through periods when they make predictable mistakes. They may say *He eated my candy* or *Oh! Hurt meself* or *Where did you found it?* but not "Mine is candy that" or "Candy my eated he" or countless other conceivable but nonoccurring sentences. In fact, the errors that children make are of a very limited sort. English-speaking children can be heard overgeneralizing that the past tense of all verbs is formed by adding an *-ed* ending and making the other mistakes noted previously. Because adults don't say *eated* or *did you found* and because even children who lack contact with other children do say such things, errors like these cannot arise from mimicry. Whatever is involved in language acquisition, it is certainly a robust process that goes beyond inducing the correct generalizations on the basis of forms that have been heard.

PRINCIPLES OF LANGUAGE ACQUISITION

Two aspects of general maturation are crucial to a child's ability to acquire a language: *the ability to symbolize* and *the ability to use tools.*

Maturation and Symbolization As a system of symbols, language is an arbitrary representation of other things—other entities, experiences, feelings, thoughts, and so on. In order to acquire language, a child must first be able to hold in mind a symbolic realization of something else. Even if it is no more than a mental picture of an absent object, such symbolization is a prerequisite to language acquisition.

Using Tools The second ability—wider ranging than its application to language—is the ability to use tools to accomplish goals. Language is a tool made up entirely of symbols, and among other characterizations it can be seen as a system of symbols that gets work done. From an early age, children routinely use language to get fed, changed, handed a toy, and the many other things they cannot do for themselves. Such purposeful activity is called tool use, and language is a most effective tool for accomplishing work of almost any sort. Given their extremely limited ability to achieve their goals physically, the motivation to develop this powerful symbolic tool must be extraordinarily strong in children (and may be influential in the evolution of the human species).

All Languages Are Equally Challenging Every child who is capable of acquiring a particular human language is capable of acquiring any human language. There is no biological basis—in the lips or the brain—that disposes some children to learn a particular language. Children find all languages about equally simple to acquire, although particular features of one language may be more difficult to acquire than equivalent aspects of a different language. For example, as you saw in Chapter 2 (see Table 2-10, page 60), German definite articles have several different forms representing three genders, two numbers, and four cases. Children acquiring German need more time to master its definite articles than English-speaking children need to learn the single form *the* that English uses for any gender, number, and case. (English speakers use *the* in the phrases *the boy,* for *the daughter,* and *to the lions,* where the German definite article would have different forms in those phrases: *der, dem,* and *den,* respectively). On balance, though, when considered in their entirety, all languages are about equally easy (or equally challenging) for a child to learn.

Barring severe mental or physical impairments, children the world over have acquired most of what they need to know to speak their language fluently by the age of six. By the time a child arrives in school, perhaps 80 percent of the structures of its language and more than 90 percent of the sound system have been acquired. "Doubtless the greatest intellectual feat any one of us is ever required to perform," Leonard Bloomfield remarked of language acquisition earlier in this century. Fortunately, it is a feat that all human beings are gifted at. This universal success has convinced linguists and psycholinguists that infants come to the task of acquiring a language with a genetic predisposition to do so and with certain analytical advantages that facilitate the process of acquisition. There is little doubt that, at the very least, children are born with certain mechanisms or cognitive strategies that help in the task of language acquisition, and it may well be that certain structures, or kinds of structure, are innate as well.

ADULT INPUT IN LANGUAGE ACQUISITION

Stating that language acquisition is not a process of imitation doesn't diminish the crucial importance of exposure to linguistic input in acquiring a language. Acquisition requires interaction with speakers of the language being acquired. As witness to the necessity of adult input, there is the case of Genie, a child who was not exposed to any language while she was growing up. Genie's parents locked her away in an attic for the first thirteen years of her life and seldom spoke to her. When Genie was discovered in 1970, she was unable to speak, and linguist Susan Curtiss tried teaching her English, but the attempts were not very successful. Deprived of linguistic input in the first few years of life, Genie's capacity for language acquisition had become impaired.

On the other hand, parents do not generally teach language to young children directly. Instead, children spontaneously acquire language on the basis of the input they receive. Conscious attempts to teach correct linguistic forms to children lead nowhere, for children simply ignore instruction and go on acquiring a native tongue at their own pace. In ordinary settings, parents rarely correct young children's grammatical mistakes, although they do correct utterances that are inaccurate or misleading. A child who says *Kitty's hands are pink* may be told *No. Kitty doesn't have hands: Kitty has PAWS.* But if a child asks *Where Kitty go?* (for 'Where did Kitty go?'), adults are not likely to correct the utterance. To a very great extent, then, children acquire the grammatical rules of their language without direct instruction from adults.

Of course, certain aspects of language use *are* deliberately taught to children. In cultures around the world, children are engaged in conversation with adults almost from the start. In Western cultures, mothers often treat baby noises (and not only vocal ones!) as openings to conversations. From their first few months children are socialized into interactional routines of turn taking, where even their burps, hiccups, and sneezes are regarded as opening turns to which mothers respond as though they were weighty proclamations. Children are socialized so effectively that the turn-taking patterns of school-age children have been pretty much established since age one. Later, when young children go trick-or-treating at Halloween (to take the example of a context in which politeness becomes a salient aspect of interaction), they may not produce the appropriate utterances unless prompted (*Say "thank you"! What do you say?*). So children need to learn certain rules of language use consciously, and adults typically provide instruction for these politeness rules.

Baby Talk: How Adults Talk to Children   Even when adults are not explicitly teaching children the rules of language use, they frequently modify their speech, adapting it to what they think children will readily understand and acquire. You have probably witnessed parents and siblings using *baby talk* (some people call it "motherese" or "infant-directed speech") in addressing babies.

- Ooohh, what a biiig smiile! Is Baby smiling at Mommy?
- Baby is smiling at her Mommy? Yeess!
- Is Baby happy to see Mommy?
- Is Baby hungry? Yeess? Oopen wiiide . . .
- Hmmmm! Baby likes soup. Yeess!
- Wheere's the soup? All gone!

This example, uttered slowly and with exaggerated intonation, is typical of the kind of linguistic input that English-speaking mothers and other caregivers provide to young children.

Baby talk differs from talk between adults in characteristic ways. When addressing babies, adults' voices frequently assume a higher pitch than usual. Adults also exaggerate their intonation and speak slowly and clearly. Repetitions and partial repetitions (*Is Baby smiling at Mommy? Baby is smiling at her Mommy?*) are frequent in baby talk. Sentences are short and simple, with few subordinate clauses and few modifiers. Personal names like *Baby* and *Mommy* are preferred over pronouns like *you* and *I*. Compared to adult talk to other adults, baby talk has more frequent content words (nouns, verbs, and adjectives) and fewer function words (subordinators, determiners). Utterances addressed to very young children frequently include special baby-talk vocabulary—words like *doggie, horsie, tummy,* and *din-din* that are more easily perceived or pronounced but do not normally occur in adult talk—and the choice of baby-talk words is more restricted than in ordinary speech. Baby talk is typically concrete and refers to items and actions in the child's immediate environment and experience. It also includes a high proportion of questions, particularly for young children (*Is Baby hungry?*), and of imperatives (*Oopen wiiide*). These modifications may serve to hold a child's attention or to simplify the linguistic input that it hears, possibly making it easier to perceive or analyze. Especially in repetitions and shorter expressions addressed to young children, adults chunk their speech by constituent structure, a practice that could provide useful syntactic insight to learners. Baby talk features are summarized in the table below.

CHARACTERISTICS OF TALK TO BABIES

Higher than usual pitch	Concrete, immediate referents
Frequent questions	Exaggerated intonation contours
Frequent repetitions	Slow and clear enunciations
Frequent imperatives	Baby-talk words (*doggie, tummy*)
Few modifiers	Frequent content words (nouns, verbs)
Few function words	Personal names instead of pronouns (*Mommy,* not *I*)
Few subordinate clauses	Chunking by constituent structure

At a somewhat more advanced stage, when children start producing utterances, mothers and other caretakers have been observed to echo those utterances in a fuller form than the child offered. Sometimes the intonation of the caretaker's expansions confirms what the child has said; sometimes a questioning intonation seems to be seeking clarification. The following examples are illustrative.

ADULT EXPANSIONS OF CHILDREN'S UTTERANCES

CHILD	ADULT
Baby highchair	Baby is in the highchair.
Mommy eggnog	Mommy had her eggnog.
Eve lunch	Eve is having lunch.
Throw Daddy	Throw it to Daddy.

Expansions occur far less frequently when mothers (and other caretakers) are alone with children than when other adults are present (including researchers), and such expansions may be intended as "translations" of the baby's speech, more for the aid of the observer than for the benefit of the child.

Features of baby talk are found in cultures far and wide. When the Berbers of North Africa address babies, they simplify their language in some of the same ways that Americans do, and the same is true of the Japanese. Not all cultures modify speech to children, but modification is widespread. Children themselves acquire baby talk very early in life, and four-year-olds can be heard using features of this register when addressing younger children, while even two-year-olds use it with younger siblings.

The extent to which baby talk helps children in acquiring language is difficult to assess, but in cultures where baby talk is absent (as it is in Samoa, certain parts of Papua New Guinea, and among the Kipsigis of Kenya, for example) children acquire their native language at the same rate as children exposed to baby talk. So we must conclude that baby talk is not essential to successful language acquisition.

Still, baby talk does serve some functions. First, it exposes small children to simple language, and simple language may be helpful in the task of unraveling constituent structures and certain rules of grammar. Since children have to figure out so many different grammatical features, selective input (fewer words, fewer complex sentences, and repetitions) facilitate their task. In addition, considering English, the unusually high percentage of questions that caregivers address to infants has the effect of exposing them to a greater number of auxiliaries (*Did Baby fall?*) than would the use of declarative sentences (*Baby fell*). Baby talk may also inculcate certain rules of language use, the rules of conversation in particular (see Chapter 9). By asking many questions of small children, adults help socialize them into the question-answer sequences and into the alternating turn-taking patterns of conversation. From the earliest stages, adults alternate their utterances with a baby's babblings, and the implicit message is to alternate your utterances with your interlocutor's. Interactional patterns between caregivers and children can thus provide a framework within which utterances can be situated and acquisition of grammar take place.

STAGES OF LANGUAGE ACQUISITION

Babbling   Whatever the nature of the input they receive, children go through several stages in the process of acquiring their native language. At the babbling stage, which starts at about six months of age, children first utter a series of identical syllables such as *ba-ba-ba* or *ma-ma-ma*. A couple of months later, as the vocal apparatus matures, this reduplicated babbling blossoms into a wider range of syllable types such as *bab-bab* and *ab-ab*. These early babblings are similar the world over and occur with or without others present. When some babbled sounds stabilize for a child and are linked to a consistent referent or appear to be used with a consistent purpose (for example to be handed something), they are called *vocables* or protowords. A child may use a vocable like *baba* to indicate it does not want something while *mama* serves to indicate it does want something.

One-Word Stage   Starting around a year old, when children take their first steps, they are also heard uttering words like *mama, dada,* and *up.* These early words are of simple structure and typically refer to familiar people (mother and father), toys and pets (teddy bear and kitty), food and drink (cookie and juice), and social interaction (as in *bye-bye*). By this stage children already use vocal noises to get and hold attention socially and to achieve other objectives.

Often, the same word is used to refer to things that have a similar appearance, as when a child learns the word *doggie* for the family dog and then extends it to all dogs. Children are thus inclined to generalize word meanings and even to overgeneralize, as when *doggie* is applied to cats as well as dogs, or even to all animals.

Observation of utterances at the one-word stage suggests that children are not rehearsing simple words but expressing single words to convey whole propositions. A child uses the word *dada,* for example, to mean different things in different contexts: 'Here comes Daddy' (upon hearing a key in the door at the end of the day); 'This is for Daddy' (when handing Daddy a toy); 'That is where Daddy usually sits' (when looking at Daddy's empty chair at the kitchen table); or 'This shoe is Daddy's' (when touching a shoe belonging to Daddy).

ONE-WORD STAGE

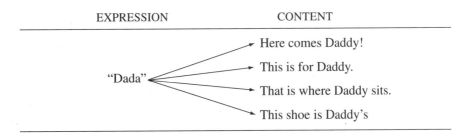

In different contexts, a child may give the same word different intonations. Holding a shoe and uttering *Dada,* a child is not merely naming the object of its focus but is using a relatively simple expression to communicate relatively complex content.

Two-Word Stage   From the one-word-utterance stage, children move on to utterances like *Daddy come, Shoe mine,* and *Apple me.* The transition from the one-word stage to the two-word stage occurs at about twenty months of age, when the child has a vocabulary of about 50 words. At this stage, utterances show a preference for combining a nounlike element with a predicatelike element, and children tend to verbalize in propositions—to name something and then say something about it: *Daddy, [he is] com[ing], Shoe, [it's] mine; Apple, [give it to] me.* Other forms also occur, as in *More juice* and *There Daddy,* in which the predicatelike element precedes the noun. One striking fact about the two-word-utterance stage is that children from different cultures appear to express basically similar things in their propositions at this stage.

TWO-WORD STAGE

EXPRESSION	CONTENT
"Daddy come"	Daddy, he is coming.
"Shoe mine"	The shoe, it's mine.
"Apple me"	The apple, give it to me.
"More juice"	I want more juice.
"There Daddy"	There is Daddy.

We don't know whether the disposition to verbalize in propositions is a tendency of the language process itself or is tied to aspects of perception. But from the start children seem to be trying to convey propositions, even when the expression is a mere word. If this interpretation is correct, children at the two-word stage are not attempting to communicate more content by using two words instead of one but to *express* more of the content than at the one-word stage. In terms of the ideal languages described in the first chapter of this book, the child is progressing on a journey from the "uh" ideal in which a single expression would represent any and all content (we called this language Quikish) toward the one-to-one ideal, where each expression would represent unique content (we called this language Uneekish). As the child masters its language system, it will learn to balance *expression* and *context* so as to communicate *content* efficiently and effectively.

Beyond Two Words   Beyond the two-word stage, distinct three-word and four-word stages are not recognized. Instead, progress is typically measured by the average number of morphemes (or sometimes words) in a child's utterances. Between about two years (2;0) and two and a half years (2;6) of age, a child's expressions become considerably more complex. Utterances contain several words representing single clauses.

Consider these single-clause utterances from a boy of two years, five months:

1. Mimo hurt me. [about a past action by his brother]
2. Yeah, that money Neina. ('Yeah, that money is Neina's.')
3. Me put it back. ('I'll put it back.')
4. No do that again! [to an adult whispering in his ear]
5. Oh! hurt meself. [upon bumping his arm into a door]
6. That's mine, Uncle Ed. [showing a toy to an uncle]

Consider what the child must already know in order to make such utterances. Obviously, he knows some English words: *money, mine, that's.* That entails knowing what sounds they contain and in what order. That the words are used in appropriate contexts indicates that he also knows what the words refer to and in what situations they are appropriate. He knows the lexical categories (the parts of speech) of these words and how to combine them with other categories both morphologically (*me, meself, mine*) and syntactically (*Mimo hurt me* and *Me put it back*). Possibly he knows which form of the copula BE agrees with the demonstrative subject *that* and how to contract *is* to *'s* and attach it to *that,* although *that's* may be an unanalyzed unit for him at this stage. The child has also mastered basic SVO word order, as in *Mimo hurt me* and *Me put it back* (although pronominal subjects are not yet obligatory, as a comparison between *Me put it back* and *Hurt meself* shows). He also shows knowledge of declarative and imperative sentence structures and of negative imperatives.

The phrase *that money* indicates knowledge that *money* belongs to the category of nouns—the category that takes determiners like *that* and *the.* Given the contexts in which the utterances occur, it is also apparent that the child is uttering propositions, although some are incompletely encoded or differ from adult formulations of the same propositions. More noteworthy than the matches between some of these utterances and those of an adult grammar, as with 1 and 6, is the fact that the child is using language in a systematic fashion. The structured utterances are governed by rules of grammar that stay constant from utterance to utterance: subjects precede verbs; verbs precede objects and other complements; and adverbs (*back* and *again*) follow objects.

Of course, there are many other forms of the adult grammar that the child has not yet fully mastered, and these include syntactic and morphological matters. Syntactically, no subject is expressed in 5, no verb in 2, and no auxiliary in 3, all of which would be required in well-formed adult utterances. Morphologically, the possessive marker is not fully mastered: it appears in *mine* but is lacking in *Neina;* the adult subject form of the first-person pronoun *I* and the adult reflexive form *myself* have not yet been acquired.

By around three years of age, utterances containing multiple clauses appear, at first coordinating two clauses as in *There's his face and he's Mister George Happy.* Later, children subordinate one clause to another with subordinators like *'cause, so,* and *if* in the early stages and then *why* and *what: Me don't know where box is now. Why did you give to her when her been flu?*

How Children Acquire Morphology and Grammar

Interestingly, the morphemes and grammatical structures of language are generally acquired by children in a set order, with variation from child to child usually slight. This pattern suggests that there is an internally regulated sequence for grammatical acquisition. Psychologist Roger Brown examined the order in which fourteen morphological and grammatical morphemes were acquired by three English-speaking children and found that they were acquired in the order given below:

ACQUISITION ORDER FOR ENGLISH MORPHEMES
1. Present progressive verb (with or without auxiliary): (*is*) *playing,* (*was*) *singing*
2–3. Prepositions *in* and *on*
4. Regular noun plural: *toys, cats, dishes*
5. Irregular past-tense verbs: *came, fell, saw, hurt*

6. Possessive noun: *Daddy's, doggie's*
7. Uncontractible copula: *Here I am, Who is it?*
8. Articles: *a* and *the*
9. Regular past-tense verbs: *played, washed, wanted*
10. Regular third-person singular present-tense verbs: *sees, wants, washes*
11. Irregular third-person singular present-tense verbs: *does, has*
12. Uncontractible auxiliary: *She isn't crying, He was eating*
13. Contractible copula: *That's mine, What's that?*
14. Contractible auxiliary: *He's crying*

Although the children acquired these forms basically in the same *order,* they did not acquire them *at the same speed.* Between acquisition of the present progressive (the earliest acquired) and the contractible auxiliary (the last), anywhere from six to fourteen months elapsed. One child acquired the contractible auxiliary by 2;3, while another took until 3;6.

The order tracked among Brown's young "consultants" basically replicated the order other linguists and psychologists had tracked with different children, and the slight variations reported probably have to do with the criteria used for judging "acquisition." For example, Brown judged a feature to be acquired only when a child used it correctly in 90 percent of the required cases in three successive sampling sessions. Other researchers used different criteria, such as the first time that a correct use was observed.

What Determines Acquisition Order? As to what determines the order of acquisition, it would seem reasonable to suppose that the frequency with which a child hears a form from the adults around it will influence the order of acquisition. In fact, however, Brown was unable to correlate frequency of parental use with the order of acquisition. The most frequent of the fourteen morphemes in the parents' speech was the articles, which appeared eighth in the order of child acquisition. The prepositions, on the other hand, were acquired second by children, although they were used relatively little by parents. In determining the order of acquisition, what seems more influential than frequency is relative complexity. Morphemes that encode several semantic notions and those that are syntactically more complex tend to be acquired later than those that encode a single semantic notion and are syntactically simpler.

Exceptions and Overgeneralizations No doubt you have observed that children tend to overgeneralize the patterns of inflectional morphology. You've heard them say things like "eated" for *ate* and "foots" for *feet.* There are some sixty-odd irregular verbs in English, and among those that get overgeneralized are the ones listed below.

OVERGENERALIZATION OF PAST-TENSE VERBS

eated	ate	doed	did
maked	made	speaked	spoke

finded	found	breaked	broke
hitted	hit	goed	went
falled	fell	runned	ran

English has far fewer common nouns like *foot* that form their plurals irregularly; among those that children overgeneralize are the ones listed below.

OVERGENERALIZATION OF NOUN PLURALS

foots	feet	mans	men
tooths	teeth	mouses	mice
childs	children	peoples	people

Evidence from several languages suggests that children tend naturally to overgeneralize or "overregularize" the morphological rules that they acquire.

Sentence Structure   The sentences of the twenty-nine-month-old (2;5) boy (given on page 554) contain single clauses only. Before that boy was five years old, negative sentences were under control, as in *That isn't yours* and *That doesn't belong to you,* and sentences incorporating more than one clause were commonplace, including imperatives (*Guess who's visiting me*) and interrogatives (*Do you know what I did at school today?*). Even at age five, though, relative clauses were not fully acquired, although certain kinds of relatives are understood by children even at three years of age. When children first produce relative clauses, they attach them to object noun phrases, as in *You broke the one that I found.* Attaching relative clauses to subjects (as in *The one that I found is red*) represents a later stage of acquisition, and attaching them to other grammatical relations comes later still.

Negation   Every language has ways of expressing negation. At first, children express negation by the simple utterance *no,* either alone or preceding other expressions: *No. No want. No that. No do that.* At a somewhat later stage, by three years of age, more complex expressions incorporate negations, as in these: *Can't get it off. Don't know. It doesn't go that way. That not go in there.*

Questions   As with negations, every language has ways of asking questions. Some do so simply by adding a question word to the end of a statement. English has a relatively complex way of forming questions, and mastery of its question-formation rules takes time. In the early stages, interrogative utterances have the same syntax as declaratives, as in *That mine;* sometimes, though not always, the intonation of questions differs from that of statements. By three years of age, children have mastered most aspects of question formation, as in these questions from a three-year old girl named Sophie:

INFORMATION QUESTIONS	**YES/NO QUESTIONS**
What is he called?	Is this a box?
What goes in this hole?	Do it go this side?

INFORMATION QUESTIONS	YES/NO QUESTIONS
Why didn't me get flu?	Can me put it in like that?
Why's he so small?	
Where are you Mummy?	

HOW FAST DO CHILDREN ACQUIRE VOCABULARY?

At the start of the two-word stage, around twenty months (1;8) of age, a child knows approximately 50 words. Mostly they are nouns referring to concrete, familiar objects (*shoe, clock, apple, baby, milk, nose*) or expressions for salient notions in the child's environment (*more, no, bye-bye, oh, walk, what's that*). By age five, the child's vocabulary is increasing by about 15 or 20 words a day. Estimates of the number of basic words known by schoolchildren of age six run about 7,800, even counting a word set like *cat, cats, cat's, cats'* or *walk, walks, walked, walking* as a single word. If you count derived forms like *dollhouse* as a third word besides *doll* and *house,* then 13,000 words would be a reliable figure. Astonishingly, two years later, by age eight, a child's vocabulary has increased to 17,600 basic words (or 28,300 words including derived forms). This represents an average increase of more than 13 basic words (or 21 words and derived forms) *each day.* Of course, a word isn't acquired in its semantic fullness on a single occasion; rather, a full range of meanings for any word is generally acquired only by stages over a period of time. Indeed, this phenomenon, like the acquisition of vocabulary itself, continues well into adulthood, though at a drastically reduced rate.

HOW DO CHILDREN ACQUIRE THE SOUNDS OF LANGUAGE?

You have probably listened to a child uttering words and expressions that you could understand within their context even though the pronunciations did not match your own. "Neina" /nena/ for *Zeina* /zena/ in the speech from the boy of two years, five months is one illustration. Other examples might be "poon" or "bude" for *spoon,* "du" for *juice,* and "dis" or "di" [dɪ] for *this.* Such pronunciations suggest that a child masters certain aspects of a word before others. In these cases, the context indicates that the child knows the word's lexical category and certain semantic information (such as its referent); the child also knows some of its phonological content although mastery of the pronunciation is manifestly incomplete. Here we examine certain patterns of phonological acquisition among English-speaking children and draw some cross-linguistic comparisons.

From as early as two months, infants react differently to different speech sounds, and they can recognize individual voices—their mother's for example. (We know this from changes in the rate of sucking when voices alternate.) Prior to their production of recognizable utterances at about twelve months of age, infants go through a lengthy babbling stage, during which they appear to be rehearsing a wide range of sounds, extending beyond the sounds spoken around them and therefore beyond the phonological inventory needed for their own language.

Early babbling consists of simple syllablelike sequences of a consonant followed by a vowel: *ba-ba-ba*. Repetitions of CV syllables are then followed by sequences that juxtapose different CV syllables (*bamama*), first yielding CVCV patterns and then CVC patterns (such as *bam* and *mam,* which lack the vowel of the second CVCV syllable). These early babblings reveal a preference for voiced stops and nasals [b d g m n] and a dispreference for fricatives [f v θ ð s z] and liquids [l r]. Not surprisingly, sounds that are relatively rare among the world's languages tend to be acquired later than sounds that are common among languages. By eight or nine months of age children are able to mimic adult intonation patterns to a striking degree, and unlike the sounds of babbling these intonation patterns differ from language to language.

CONSONANT SOUNDS OF BABBLING

PREFERRED			DISPREFERRED		
b	d	g	v	ð	z
m	n		f	θ	s
			l/r		

Before the first recognizable words are produced around age one, the list of speech sounds actually shrinks (and a few children even go through a silent period), after which the inventory of sounds belonging to the adult language is gradually and systematically acquired. Full phonological development takes several years, and the last sounds may not be acquired before age six or so.

Between twelve months and eighteen months of age, a child learns to produce about 50 words (which is only about a fourth of those it can recognize). The range of sounds and of syllable types needed to give voice to so small a lexicon is relatively limited (5 vowels and 10 consonants would generate 50 monosyllabic words of CV type). At about eighteen months of age, however, children typically experience a "word spurt," and for this larger lexicon the previous inventory of sounds and syllables is inadequate, and an expansion of the system is necessary.

Around twenty-four months (2;0) of age, an English-speaking child typically has acquired the following consonant sounds, although not all of them can be produced in every position in which adults produce them:

INVENTORY OF ENGLISH CONSONANTS AT AGE TWO

NASALS	m		n	
STOPS	b		d	g
	p		t	k
FRICATIVES		f	s	h
GLIDES	w			

A year later, at about thirty-six months (3;0), the child has added /y/ and /ŋ/ to its inventory, although [b], [d], [g], and [k] still remain elusive in word-final position.

Consonant clusters (as in *spilled* [spɪld], *stopped* [stɑpt], and *asked* [æskt]) present children with particular challenges. In fact, of the wide range of clusters that adults use, the three-year-old may have mastered only final /ŋk/ as in *pink* and *sink*.

By around four years of age, the inventory of consonants has expanded significantly and stands approximately as given here.

INVENTORY OF ENGLISH CONSONANTS AT AGE FOUR

NASALS	m		n	ŋ
STOPS	b		d	g
	p		t	k
FRICATIVES		f	s	š	h
		v	z		
AFFRICATES				č	
				ǰ	
GLIDES	w	l/r		y	

At this stage the voiced fricatives /v/ and /z/ may be present only in medial position (as in *over* and *dizzy*), but the child may not yet be able to produce them in word-final or word-initial position. Recall that the twenty-nine-month-old (2;5) boy whose utterances we analyzed earlier substituted the nasal [n] for initial [z] in the name *Zeina,* presumably influenced by anticipation of the [n] to follow, as commonly happens with children. The interdental fricative sounds /θ/ and /ð/ (as in *thin* and *then*) have yet to be added to the four-year old's inventory in any position, as has the relatively rare /ž/ (as in *measure*). Thus, between the ages of four and six years old, an English-speaking child may still lack /ž/, /v/, /θ/, /ð/, and /z/, at least in some positions. And still ahead lies mastery of the morphophonemic rules that account for variation between underlying forms and surface forms (as in the [t]/[ɾ] alternation of *late* [let] and *later* [leɾər] or the [d]/[ɾ] alternation of *dad* and *daddy*). Mastery of the more complex syllable structures and consonant clusters also lies ahead.

Substituting and Omitting Sounds   One could imagine that until a child mastered the phonological inventory of its language, the sounds not yet learned would be skipped, producing pronunciations like *oo* [u] for *shoe* and *juice.* Of course, that isn't what happens. Instead, children generally attempt to pronounce all the sounds of words, although they do this by various simplifications. The principal simplifications in the early pronunciations of children involve substituting easier sounds for harder ones, as in the following processes:

Stopping: fricatives and affricates pronounced as stops
Devoicing: final obstruents devoiced
Voicing: initial obstruents voiced before vowels
Fronting: velars and alveopalatals pronounced as alveolars
Gliding: liquids pronounced as glides
Vocalization: liquids replaced by vowels
Denasalization: nasals replaced by oral stops

PROCESSES OF SUBSTITUTION IN CHILD LANGUAGE

STOPPING	v → b	van	→ [bæn]
	ð → d, n	that	→ [dæt], there → [nɛr]
	ǰ → d	Jack	→ [dæk], jam → [dæb]
	č → d	check	→ [dɛk]
DEVOICING	b → p	knob	→ [nɑp]
	-d → t	bad	→ [bæt]
	-g → t	dog	→ [dɑt]
	-v → f	stove	→ [duf]
VOICING	p- → b	pot	→ [bɑt]
	t- → d	toe	→ [do]
	k- → d	kiss	→ [dɪ]
FRONTING	k → t	duck	→ [dɑt]
	g → d	gate	→ [det]
	θ → f	thumb	→ [fʌm]
	š → z	shoes	→ [zus]
	ž → z	rouge	→ [wuːz]
	č → ts	match	→ [mæts]
	ǰ → dz	cabbage	→ [tæːbədz]
GLIDING	r → w	rock	→ [wɑt], sorry → [sɑwɑ]
VOCALIZATION	l → u	table	→ [dubu]
DENASALIZATION	m → p, b	lamb	→ [bæp], broom → [bub], jam → [dæb]

(After Ingram, 1989, pp. 371–72)

Actually, besides the substitution processes described above, some omission also takes place. For example, as illustrated below, young children typically delete unstressed syllables from trisyllabic words (as in *nana* for *banana*) and sometimes the unstressed syllable of a disyllabic word; they sometimes omit final consonants; and they often reduce consonant clusters.

PROCESSES OF OMISSION IN CHILD LANGUAGE

DELETION OF SYLLABLE	banana → [nænɑ], kitchen → [kɪč], pocket → [bɑt]
DELETION OF FINAL CONSONANT	doll → [dɑ], far → [fɑ]
REDUCTION OF CONSONANT CLUSTERS	
stop + liquid → stop	glass → [dæs], bread → [but]
s- + stop → stop	star → [dɑ]
s- + nasal → nasal	snake → [nek]
nasal + voiced stop → nasal	hand → [hæn]

Determinants of Acquisition Order   It isn't entirely clear what determines the order in which sounds are acquired. If it would seem reasonable to assume that the more frequently a child heard a particular sound, the sooner that sound would be acquired, the facts point elsewhere. Consider that the most frequent English consonant sounds are the fricatives [s], [d], [z], and [v]. Either [s] or [z] occurs in the plural forms of most nouns, the possessive form of every noun, the third-person singular present-tense form of all verbs (*eats, does, is*), certain common pronouns and possessive determiners (*his, hers, yours*), and some other common words (*was* and *some*). In light of such frequency, it is not surprising that [s] is acquired relatively early (by about twenty-four months). But, perplexingly, [z] is not acquired until four years of age and then usually only in medial position. Consider also that [ð], though it occurs in extremely frequent words like *this, that,* and *the,* is acquired very late, while [v], even at four years of age, is produced in medial position but not initially or finally, where it is common in such words as *very, have,* and *of.* Clearly, frequency of occurrence in adult speech cannot be the sole determinant in the order of acquisition.

Of greater influence than frequency is the functional importance of a sound within its phonological system. A sound is said to have a high *functional load* if it serves to differentiate many words (or words that are very frequent), and high functional load seems to promote early acquisition. Thus /č/ is acquired much later by children learning English than by Guatemalan children learning the Mayan language Quiché. The reason appears to be that in Quiché /č/ contrasts with other sounds in many more words than it does in English, and the high functional load of the /č/ sound in Quiché fosters early acquisition. By contrast, the low functional importance of /č/ in English tends to bump it towards the end of the acquisition line.

Phonological Idioms   Before acquiring all the sounds in the inventory of its language, a child may be able to produce some sounds as part of fixed phrases or phonological "idioms." In much the same way that adults have semantic idioms (*kick the bucket*) and syntactic idioms (*the sooner the better*), so children may produce unanalyzed words containing sounds that they have not yet added as separate units of their phonological inventory. They have learned to pronounce the word as a whole but haven't mastered all the individual sounds as such. The child can thus make a lexical contrast without yet having the contrasting sounds in its phonological inventory.

HOW DO RESEARCHERS STUDY LANGUAGE ACQUISITION?

Studies of child language and language acquisition have most commonly been observational studies. Researchers have tape recorded ordinary interactions between adults and children or among children at regular intervals and transcribed those results for analysis. There have also been diary studies (carried out by parents who were themselves linguists or psychologists) that record a child's utterances, the age at which they occur, and the situational context surrounding them. Depending on the focus and goals of the observer, diary studies represent different degrees of detail, from ordinary orthography to a narrow phonetic transcription. Quite naturally, then, observational studies of child language have focused on the *production* of words and sentences.

RECEPTIVE COMPETENCE AND PRODUCTIVE COMPETENCE

So far we haven't said much about a child's *receptive* mastery, or understanding, nor have we drawn a distinction between what a child's grammatical competence might allow but its production apparatus be unable to utter. After all, a child could have the grammatical competence to generate adult pronunciations as far as the phonological processes of the internalized grammar are concerned but remain unable to utter them because of physiological immaturity in the vocal apparatus.

"FIS" Phenomenon An oft-repeated story tells of a child who pronounced *fish* as *fis* [fɪs] but objected to an adult imitating the *fis* pronunciation. "This is your *fis?*" the adult asked. "No," said the child: "my *fis.*" When the adult repeated the question, the child again rejected the *fis* pronunciation. When the adult eventually said, "Your *fish?*" the child concurred: "Yes, my *fis*"! The child could hear the distinction between *fish* and *fis* and recognized *fis* as an incorrect pronunciation. But in attempting to say *fish* the child produced a word that replicated the *fis* it knew to be wrong. We should be careful interpreting such data, however. It may seem that the child knows and recognizes the difference between [fɪš] and [fɪs] while being unable to pronounce [fɪš] because of limitations in the vocal apparatus, but there are other possible explanations. Consider the case of the child who consistently pronounced *puddle* as *puggle:* the obvious hypothesis that the vocal apparatus was not yet capable of pronouncing /d/ intervocalically was belied by the fact that the child systematically pronounced *puzzle* as *puddle.*

Big Bigs In saying a word like *pig* or *tug,* the voicing required in pronouncing the *vowels* is anticipated by adults in such a fashion that /p/ and /t/, though they begin without voicing, become voiced just preceding the onset of the vowel. It is almost as if the pronunciation were [pbɪg] and [tdʌg]. The key to an adult's distinguishing initial /p/ and /b/ before vowels is *how long* the voicing is delayed, not whether it is present or absent. A child may be perceived as failing to distinguish voiced from voiceless initial stops, pronouncing *tug* and *Doug* alike as [dʌg] or *pig* and *big* alike as [bɪg]. But laboratory analyses indicate that some children systematically distinguish initial /t/ from /d/ and initial /p/ from /b/ by delaying the voicing onset time for the voiceless stops (/t/ and /p/) for a longer period than they delay voicing for the voiced stops (/d/ and /b/). The delayed voicing is detectable by laboratory instruments but cannot be detected by the human ear. This would indicate that the child has heard the voiceless and voiced stops and internalized the difference between them in its lexicon but has not yet learned to delay the onset of voicing long enough to be detected by adults.

There is general agreement that receptive mastery of language outpaces production, but it is not clear that this is so at all stages of language development and in all respects. Still, children generally seem able to understand more than they can produce—that is, their lexical and syntactic repertoire is greater than their production reveals. At about eighteen months of age, as we mentioned above, a child understands about 200 words although only about 50 appear in its speech. In an attempt, then, to analyze the language competence of children, naturalistic observation alone may offer an incomplete picture, so researchers have had to invent ingenious ways to get at receptive competence.

WUGS AND OTHER EXPERIMENTAL TECHNIQUES

One experimental technique elicits utterances that children would not otherwise have occasion to say. In one study, children were shown drawings of an imaginary bird or animal and told, for example, "This is a wug." The next drawing would depict two such birds or animals, and the child would be suitably prompted to offer a plural form: "Now there is another one. There are two of them. There are two _____?" (See Figure 15-1.) This technique can uncover how much morphophonemic variation of the plural morpheme the child has mastered. Alternatively, pictures of people carrying out novel actions such as "ricking" can be used to elicit past tenses and progressive forms of verbs. With another technique, children using hand puppets speak in the voices of their puppets to another puppet that is given voice by the researcher. In a third technique, children are asked simply to repeat words or sentences (to display their progress for repetition of sounds, syllable structures, and grammatical

---

Figure 15-1

A TEST FOR PLURAL ALLOMORPHS

THIS IS A WUG.

NOW THERE IS ANOTHER ONE.
THERE ARE TWO OF THEM.
THERE ARE TWO _____ .

Source: Jean Berko (Gleason). 1958. "The Child's Learning of English Morphology," *Word,* 14:154.

forms). In a fourth technique, designed to gauge understanding, children playing with dolls are asked to act out such sentences as "The horse pushed the cow" and "The horse was pushed by the cow."

Although child language and first-language acquisition are important to many aspects of linguistic theory, a great deal about the processes of acquisition remains unclear or uninvestigated. The interaction between physiological and mental limitations, on the one hand, and the nature of the internalized grammar, on the other, makes interpreting child language data challenging. Given the complexities of interpreting child language data, the most reliable findings and theories will be those that emerge from using a variety of investigative methodologies.

ACQUIRING A SECOND LANGUAGE
—

Besides their first language, most readers of this book have probably acquired at least the rudiments of a second language, perhaps Russian, Spanish, German, French, Japanese—or English. The term *first language* refers to the language one acquires in infancy. A second language is *any* language that is acquired after one's first language—it may well be a third or fourth "second language." When we speak of second languages in this chapter, we focus on those acquired as adults.

FIRST AND SECOND LANGUAGES

There are two common situations in which adults learn a second language. The one familiar to most of you occurs when someone studies a foreign language in school or college. As with English taught abroad, such situations often provide relatively little opportunity for experience with the spoken language outside the classroom. In this sense, the study of French in the United States could be called "French as a foreign language," paralleling the "English as a foreign language" studied in Jiddah, Tokyo, Taipei, and elsewhere. Indeed, we talk of foreign-language requirements for graduation from college, and it is useful to bear in mind that studying a foreign language typically involves activities that differ significantly from those surrounding first-language acquisition and the acquisition of a second language in a community where it is spoken natively and widely. When people acquire a language in a community in which it is spoken natively, they can participate in a range of communicative activities in the target language.

When populations of Poles, Italians, Germans, Norwegians, and others migrated to America in the nineteenth and early twentieth centuries, they settled in a land that was largely English speaking, though many immigrants initially lived in neighborhoods where their first language could be used with neighbors and shopkeepers as well as at home. The migrations of the present day, for example from Asia and Latin America, represent a similar situation although the communities in which immigrants now settle often have large enough immigrant populations to maintain the "foreign" language in newspapers and in radio and television broadcasting, as well as in shops, churches, and homes. In some metropolitan areas, dozens of locally broadcast "foreign" languages can be heard on the radio every day, and cable networks broadcast news and entertainment in languages other than English throughout the day. In Los Angeles, television news in broadcast in Korean, Mandarin, and Spanish every day, and there are soap operas and variety shows in these languages and several others. Daily newspapers are also published locally in several languages and sold at newsstands side by side with English-language dailies. During presidential elections in the 1990s, the sample ballot in Los Angeles included a full-page notice informing registered voters: "Under federal law, voter information and sample ballots are available in the following languages." Five brief paragraphs followed, each in a different language, giving telephone numbers for obtaining alternative-language ballots in Chinese, Japanese, Vietnamese, Tagalog, and Spanish.

Staff members at many bank branches in Los Angeles are bilingual in English and another language spoken in the neighborhood, and many other commercial and professional establishments routinely provide bilingual service. As a result of such interwoven linguistic networks in some North American communities, and in communities around the globe, the distinction between second language and "foreign" language is not altogether tidy.

COMPARING FIRST- AND SECOND-LANGUAGE ACQUISITION

Typically there are significant differences between first- and second-language learning. To begin with (and by definition), first-language acquisition involves an initial linguistic experience, while a second language is mastered only by someone who already speaks another language. However blank the language slate may be at birth, it is certainly not so after first-language acquisition is completed.

Second, a first language is usually acquired in a home environment by an infant in the care of parents and other caretakers, with many activities—linguistic and otherwise—jointly focused on the child. In such circumstances, language use is closely tied to the immediate surroundings, to the context of language use. Caretakers use language in reference to objects in the immediate environment (objects that can be seen or heard by the infant), and language content reflects ongoing activity in which child and caretaker are participating as actors (as with eating or bathing) or as observers (of activities within sight or earshot). In contrast, second-language learning is seldom so context bound. Ordinarily an adult speaking a second language as in a classroom is using it to discuss imaginary or decontextualized events removed from the learning situation.

A third difference has to do with the adaptability and malleability of learners as a consequence of age and of social identity. Infants have not yet developed strong social identities as to gender, ethnicity, or social status—factors that can be an important part of the social identity and self-awareness of adolescents and adults. Since language use reflects (and helps create) social identity, as you saw in Chapter 11, the social-psychological experiences of first- and second-language acquisition can differ greatly. For many second-language learners, the language variety being studied is emblematic of a different social status or different ethnicity from that represented by their first language, and for nearly all learners it represents new and different cultural values. For infants, this is not the case, of course, so such factors do not come into play in first-language acquisition. Ordinarily, acquisition of a first language and of a social identity go hand in hand and are inseparable.

A fourth difference is that second-language learners ordinarily have linguistic meta-knowledge that is lacking at least in the early stages of a first language. That is, with a second language, speakers may already possess a vocabulary for referring to language structures and language uses. They will certainly be aware that words and sounds differ from language to language, that some sounds are more difficult to make than others, that languages differ grammatically, and that speakers can be recognized as native or nonnative by their speech patterns. Naturally, such meta-knowledge is lacking for the first-language acquirer, who plays with language spontaneously and unself-consciously.

Even when second-language learners haven't been exposed to such terms as *noun, verb,* and *sentence,* they are aware of certain linguistic phenomena—the existence of words, the notions of regional, social, and foreign accent, the existence of well-formed and ill-formed sentences, and so on. For many other second-language learners, phonological terms like *consonant* and *vowel* and grammatical terms like *verb* and *subject* are familiar. Just what influence knowledge of such categories may have on second-language acquisition is not known. Some investigators believe that conscious knowledge of grammar can facilitate acquisition for some learners, but to what degree and in what ways is not well understood.

MOTIVATION'S ROLE IN SECOND-LANGUAGE LEARNING

Among the things that do clearly affect mastery of a second language is the kind of motivation that a learner has. People learn another language for many reasons, from vacationing abroad where you may need to seek directions in the local language to taking up permanent residence in a locale where it is the sole means of communication. For some American students the principal reason for second-language study is to meet a graduation requirement. Motivations for second-language learning can be grouped under the headings of instrumental and integrative.

Instrumental Motivation An **instrumental motivation** is one a learner has because knowledge of the target language will help achieve some other goal: reading scientific works, singing or understanding opera, graduation. For such uses, only a narrow range of registers (or even a single register) is necessary, and little or no social integration of the learner into a community using the language is desired.

Integrative Motivation Integrative motivation is fundamentally different from instrumental motivation. When you take up residence in a community that uses the target language in its social interactions, **integrative motivation** encourages you to learn the new language as a way to integrate yourself socially into the community and become one of its members. Integrative motivation typically underlies successful acquisition of a wide range of registers and a nativelike pronunciation, achievements that usually elude learners with instrumental motivation.

TEACHING AND LEARNING FOREIGN LANGUAGES

Of the several methods of foreign-language instruction in use, you are probably familiar with pattern drills, translation, composition, listening comprehension, and a few others. Some methods are grounded in the behaviorist assumption that language mastery is a matter of inducing the right habits, much as first-language acquisition was assumed to be earlier in this century. Other methods, aiming to be more "naturalistic," attempt to emulate the kinds of language experience children have when acquiring a first language. With naturalistic methods the emphasis is on interactional use, especially conversation, focused on matters close at hand; noninteractional use aims to provide abundant input that is nearly fully comprehensible to the learner because of its familiarity.

Contrastive Analysis   For many decades learning a second language was viewed as a matter of knowing and practicing the well-formed utterances of the target language. Learning a second language was approached as a matter of drilling grammatical patterns, and drill focused on patterns that differ from those of the first language. To prepare teaching materials, researchers carried out a **contrastive analysis** of the phonological and grammatical structures of the native and target languages, producing a list of morphological, grammatical, and phonological features that could be expected to prove difficult for learners because they differed from those of the first language.

For various reasons, teaching materials based on contrastive analysis have not proven very effective. A number of problems have been uncovered, among them the recognition of an asymmetry between learners acquiring one another's language. Contrastive analysis predicts that when two languages contrast, the difference between them should prove equally challenging for speakers of both languages. In fact, however, difficulties typically prove asymmetrical. Rather than English and Chinese speakers having equivalent difficulties learning one another's language, there are great differences in various parts of the grammar. A distinction such as English (and other European languages) makes between masculine and feminine singular pronouns (*he* versus *she*) proves difficult to master for speakers of Chinese, which makes no such distinction, whereas it is easy for English speakers to ignore the distinction. Similarly, Chinese doesn't express the copula BE in many places where English requires it. It is relatively easy for English speakers to omit BE in such sentences but very challenging for Chinese speakers to express it where it is required in English. Likewise, English speakers find it tough to learn the Chinese tone system, while Chinese speakers find it easy to adapt to the absence of a tone system in English. Contrastive analysis also suggests that certain differences in structure should warrant considerable attention, whereas in practice learners avoid the structure altogether, substituting alternative means of expression in the target language.

Interlanguage   Some researchers view second-language learners as developing a series of interlanguages in their progression towards mastery of the target language. An **interlanguage** is that form of the target language that a learner has internalized, and the interlanguage grammar underlies the spontaneous utterances of a learner in the target language. The grammar of an interlanguage can differ from the grammar of the target language in various ways: by containing rules borrowed from the native language, by containing overgeneralizations, by lacking certain sounds of the target language, by inappropriately marking certain verbs in the lexicon as requiring (or not requiring) a preposition, by lacking certain rules altogether, and so on. A language learner can be viewed as progressing from one interlanguage to another, each one approximating more closely the target language.

Fossilizing   For various reasons, often related to the kind of motivation a learner has, the language-learning process typically slows down or ceases at some point, and the existing interlanguage stabilizes, with further acquisition negligible (leaving aside new vocabulary). When such stabilization occurs, the interlanguage may contain rules or other features that differ from those of the target language. This **fossilization** underlies the nonnative speech characteristics of someone who may have spoken the target language for some time but has stopped the process of learning. In other words, many second-language learners fossilize at a stage of acquisition that falls short of nativelike speech. Fossilization then is at the root of a foreign accent when, for instance, certain sounds have not been acquired or their allophonic distribution in the fossilized interlanguage does not match that of native speakers of the target language. The pronunciation of English *thin* and *then* as *sin* and *zen* by native speakers of French may reflect fossilization at a stage before the English sounds /θ/ and /ð/ (which do not occur in the French inventory) have been acquired. Likewise, the English speaker who pronounces the French words *pain* 'bread' and *Pierre* with the aspirated [pʰ] that English has in word-initial position (instead of the unaspirated [p] of French) may have fossilized before the distribution of the French allophones was mastered.

Grammatical fossilization is manifest in expressions like those below, which come from a native speaker of Mandarin.

1. I want to see what can I buy.
2. Where I can buy them?
3. What you gonna do on Tuesday?
4. I will cold.
5. Where did you found it?
6. Why you buy it?
7. How you pronounce this word?
8. Oh! Look this.

Such sentences reflect the speakers' current interlanguage grammar; for a speaker whose acquisition of English has ceased to develop, the utterances would represent fossilization.

The Role of Attitudes
in Second-Language Learning

Language attitudes can have a profound effect on your ability to acquire a second language, especially beyond adolescence. *Studying* a foreign language is parallel to learning math or history; a body of information must be mastered, certainly including much vocabulary and perhaps including terms such as case, tense, (subjunctive) mood, and (subordinate) clause. This kind of foreign-language learning differs not only from first-language acquisition but also from second-language acquisition in immersion situations in which you can acquire a language in a fashion approximating (however inadequately) the environment normally surrounding first-language acquisition. Because the language variety you acquire becomes part of your social identity, the acquisition of a second language must be seen not just as an intellectual exercise but as an enterprise that affects or alters one's social identity.

Your attitude toward the second language and your motivation can have a profound effect on the success of acquisition. In acquiring a foreign language, your efforts are mediated by what linguist Stephen Krashen has called an affective filter—a psychological disposition that facilitates or inhibits your natural language-acquisition capacities. Krashen maintains that if there is sufficient comprehensible language use surrounding a learner, the acquisition of a second language, even by an adult, can proceed as effortlessly and efficiently as first-language acquisition, provided that the affective filter is not blocking the operation of these capacities.

The learning of a second language in school is increasingly viewed not as an intellectual or educational phenomenon but as a social-psychological phenomenon. One social psychologist describes this perspective as follows:

> In the acquisition of a second language, the student is faced with the task
> not simply of learning new information . . . which is part of his *own* culture
> but rather of *acquiring* symbolic elements of a different ethnolinguistic
> community. The new words are not simply new words for old concepts,
> the new grammar is not simply a new way of ordering words, the new pro-
> nunciations are not merely 'different' ways of saying things. They are charac-
> teristics of another ethnolinguistic community. Furthermore, the student is not
> being asked to learn about them; he is being asked to acquire them, to make
> them part of his own language reservoir. This involves imposing elements of
> another culture into one's own lifespace. As a result, the student's harmony
> with his own cultural community and his willingness or ability to identify
> with other cultural communities become important considerations in the
> process of second language acquisition. [R. C. Gardner, "Social Psychologi-
> cal Aspects of Second Language Acquisition," in Howard Giles and Robert
> St. Clair, eds., *Language and Social Psychology* (Oxford: Blackwell, 1979),
> pp. 193–194.]

DO ANIMALS AND HUMANS COMMUNICATE ALIKE?

When you observe animals in groups, it doesn't take long to realize that they too interact: dogs display their fangs to communicate displeasure or aggression; bees appear to tell each other where they have found flowers; male frogs croak in order to attract female frogs. It is only natural to ask, How do the forms of communication used by animals differ from human language?

People sometimes speak of porpoises, chimpanzees, gorillas, dolphins, whales, bees, and other animals as though they had language systems similar to those of humans. Almost any week, television programs show people trying to communicate through music with apes, alligators, or turkeys (turkeys gobble when a particular note is played on a wind instrument). There is no doubt that most, and presumably all, species of animals have developed systems of communication with which they can signal such things as danger and fear, hunger and the whereabouts of food, rutting instincts and sexual access. We now know a good deal about what, why, and how bees communicate. More recently, chimpanzees, with their extremely limited vocal apparatus, have been raised as human infants and taught sign language so as to skirt the difficulties or impossibility of their vocalizing.

How Animals Communicate
in Their Natural Environment

People had wondered for a long time how bees were able to communicate to one another the exact location of a nectar source, and there was speculation about a "language" that bees must possess. After years of careful observation and hypothesizing, Karl von Frisch claimed that honeybees have an elaborate system of dancing by which they communicate the whereabouts of a honey supply. Various aspects of the dance of a bee returning to a hive indicate the distance and the direction of a nectar source. The quality of the source can be gauged by sniffing the discovering bee. Although some of his interpretations have been questioned, Von Frisch's careful analysis demonstrated that the kind of creativity characteristic of a child's speech is lacking in the bee's dance. Bees do not use their communicative system to convey anything beyond a limited range of meanings (such as 'There is a pretty good source of nectar in this direction'). Analogies between bee dancing and child language are therefore far-fetched and misleading.

The same lack of creativity characterizes the communication that takes place between other animals. Beyond a limited repertoire of meanings, even intelligent mammals like dogs do not have the mental capacity to be communicatively creative.

Furthermore, much of the communication that occurs between animals relies on nonarbitrary signs. When gazelles sense potential danger, they flee and thereby signal to other gazelles in the vicinity that danger is lurking. The communicative function of the act is incidental to its more pressing survival function. Similarly, a dog signals the possibility that it might bite by displaying its fangs. These acts are not arbitrary symbols but nonarbitrary signs that accompany desires and possibilities.

Vocalizations that might be construed as symbols of various sorts in different animals are usually accompanied by gestures. One study found that only 3 percent of the vocalizations among rhesus monkeys were not accompanied by gestures. Whatever animals express through sounds seems to reflect not a logical sequence of thoughts but a sequence accompanying a series of emotional states. Animals' communicative activities thus differ from human language in that they do not consist essentially of arbitrary signs.

CAN CHIMPANZEES LEARN A HUMAN LANGUAGE?

The situation with chimpanzees is more complicated and more interesting. In the wild, chimps use a limited nonlinguistic communicative system similar to that of other mammals, though more sophisticated. However, because the intelligence of chimps comes closest to that of humans, there have been several attempts to teach chimps human language in laboratory settings. There is disagreement among researchers as to whether and to what degree chimps can achieve humanlike linguistic competence.

The earliest chimp to gain some notoriety for her communicative prowess was named Vicki. After being raised for about seven years by psychologists Keith and Catherine Hayes, Vicki could utter only four words—*mama, papa, up,* and *cup*—and she managed these only with considerable physical strain. Chimps are simply not equipped with suitable mouth and throat organs to enable them to speak.

Though chimps do not have the *physiological* capacity to speak, the question remains, Do they have the *mental* capacity to learn language? After viewing a film of Vicki trying to vocalize human language with her limited vocal apparatus, psychologists Allan and Beatrice Gardner began their own research on chimp language. In 1966 they gave a home to ten-month-old Washoe, a chimpanzee whom they raised as a human child in as many ways as possible. Eventually, Washoe came to eat with a fork and spoon, to sit at a table and drink from a cup, and even to wash dishes after a fashion. She wore diapers and became toilet trained; she played with dolls and showed affection toward them. Like human children of her age, Washoe was fond of picture books and enjoyed having her human friends tell her stories about the pictures in them.

Ingeniously, the Gardners arranged to conduct all communication with Washoe in American Sign Language (also known as ASL or Ameslan), which they also used to communicate between themselves and with members of their research team whenever Washoe was present. ASL consists of both representational and arbitrary gestural signs that can be combined in accordance with rules that resemble the grammar rules of ordinary spoken language.

The Gardners were keen observers of the kinds of simplified communication that human parents commonly provide for children, and, like parents talking to human babies, they used repetition and simplified signing in talking with Washoe.

The results? In the first seven months in her very human environment, Washoe learned 4 signs. In the next fourteen months, she mastered an additional 30 signs. After fifty-one months, Washoe had acquired 132 signs that describe objects and thoughts, and she understood about three times that many. Washoe used the signs not only for particular objects but also for classes of objects. She used the sign for 'shoe' to mean shoes in general; she used the 'flower' sign for flowers in general, and even for aromas like the smell of tobacco. Washoe signed to everyone, even to dogs and trees. She asked questions about the world of objects and events around her. After mastering the use of only 8 signs, Washoe started combining signs to make complex utterances: YOU ME HIDE; YOU ME GO OUT HURRY LISTEN DOG (when a dog barked); BABY MINE (referring to her doll); and so on. After just ten months in her foster home, Washoe made scores of combinations of 3 or more signs, such as ROGER WASHOE TICKLE and YOU TICKLE ME WASHOE.

In subsequent work with four other chimps (Moja, Pili, Tatu, and Dar) who arrived at the Gardners' laboratory within days of birth, the Gardners demonstrated that chimps who are cross-fostered by human adults replicate many of the basic aspects of language acquisition characteristic of hearing and hearing-impaired human children, including the use of signs to refer to natural language categories such as DOG, FLOWER, and SHOE. Remarkably, when these chimps subsequently took up residence in another laboratory, an infant chimp named Loulis acquired at least 47 signs that had no other source than the signing of his fellow chimps.

In cross-fostering Washoe and her chimpanzee playmates, the Gardners had made the simple but crucial assumptions that human language is acquired by children in a rich social and intellectual environment and that such richness contributes to the cognitive and linguistic life of a child. The Gardners are convinced—and have convinced some other observers by their research with cross-fostered chimpanzees—that there is no absolute difference between human language and the communicative system that chimps can learn. They believe there is a continuum between human and nonhuman communication, albeit a continuum about which a great deal remains to be learned.

The language activities of other celebrity chimps were neither vocal like Vicki's nor gestural like Washoe's, but visual. Sarah used plastic chips as symbols for words and showed considerable ability to put them in sequence. Lana used an appropriately marked computer terminal to create series of symbols similar to the plastic ones used by Sarah.

DID PROJECT NIM FAIL?

Certain psychologists have voiced skepticism about the various projects to teach chimps human-style language. Some critics believe that the individual words that the chimps select in the various modes could have been triggered in some instances by inadvertent clues from the researchers. As a result, they claim, the sequences of strings produced by chimps are not productive sentences parallel to those that human children create. Other critics doubt that chimps have the ability to use language to make comments, ask questions, and express feelings as humans do.

In an attempt to provide more control on the effort to teach language to a chimp, a rigorous experiment sought to avoid many of the objections to previous research (though, inevitably, it introduced new problems of its own). The chimp in this instance was named Nim Chimpsky, after the well-known linguist Noam Chomsky, a proponent of the hypothesis that the nature of human language is very different from that of animal communication. In the course of his education Nim had several linguistic accomplishments, in part reflecting repetitions of the achievements of his predecessors. However, after five years of work with Nim, psychologist Herbert Terrace concluded that chimpanzees are incapable of learning language as children do. Even with elaborate training, Nim produced very few longer utterances and displayed little creativity and spontaneity in his use of signs. Unlike Washoe, Nim would sign only when researchers prompted him and would never initiate interactions. These characteristics, Terrace contends, clearly distinguish between what Nim was able to learn and what children can do with language.

Critics of Project Nim note that Terrace employed some sixty-odd research assistants over the five years and believe that fact may have contributed importantly to the limitations in Nim's linguistic achievements. Moreover, the assistants were instructed to treat Nim not like a human baby but in a detached fashion. They were forbidden, for example, to comfort Nim even if he cried during the night. The question arises as to how similar Nim's learning environment was to the environment in which a normal human child acquires language. Critics maintain that the research conditions of Project Nim had a crippling impact on Nim's emotional and linguistic education.

CONCLUSIONS AND IMPLICATIONS

What sense can we make of the seemingly contradictory conclusions of these researchers? What is clear is that chimps can learn to symbolize and to use such symbolization as a tool for achieving other ends. It is also clear that chimpanzees are more intelligent than had previously been suspected and that their intelligence may be only quantitatively different from that of human children. With respect to chimps' acquisition of language, it would appear that the exceptional success of the Gardners' cross-fostering may be due in large part to their efforts to encourage the acquisition of signing in heavily contextualized circumstances approximating those ordinarily provided for infant children. The Gardners have in fact been critical of researchers who attempt to teach language to chimps in essentially laboratory training sessions. Similar exercises and drills have proved woefully inadequate in teaching foreign languages to human beings in schools and colleges and would presumably also fail to foster first-language acquisition in children in the absence of a rich, natural, and socially and emotionally interactive home life.

We have described several attempts to teach language to chimps, thought to be the most likely candidates to demonstrate that animals could acquire something akin to human language. Research with porpoises and monkeys has rather consistently failed to provide convincing evidence that animals could develop anything closely resembling human language, although some success with a gorilla named Koko has aroused renewed interest in this perennial question. The consensus of opinion at present seems to be that animal expression is usually tied directly to the animal's emotional state at the time of utterance, but that the evidence produced by the Gardners and other psychologists working with chimpanzees raises serious questions about the extent of this generalization. Many observers believe that Washoe and her chimpanzee companions learned to communicate in ASL about as well linguistically as human children two to three years old. Others remain skeptical. Research in the future will unravel the mysteries of child language acquisition and of animal communication. Probably some readers of this book, perhaps you, will be among the contributors to this enterprise.

COMPUTERS AND LANGUAGE LEARNING

In recent years, computers have been playing increasingly important roles in the study of first-language acquisition. The question of nature versus nurture—addressing the likelihood that language is either partly innate or entirely learned—has invited researchers to create models of how language would be acquired given one set of assumptions or another. Computers have proven essential to such complicated modeling as language acquisition entails, and while no agreement exists about what the facts of acquisition are, computational modeling is a strong ally in answering the question.

On another front, data collection and analysis have been the bedrock foundation of many of the best studies of child language acquisition, so it is not surprising that corpora of children's language have been compiled. As you can imagine, collecting copious data of children's language is technically challenging and time consuming, as well as difficult and expensive to transcribe for research purposes. In order to pool resources and make available to a wide spectrum of researchers the data that have been collected, researchers at Carnegie Mellon University have spearheaded an impressive project that goes by the name of CHILDES (Child Language Data Exchange System). CHILDES makes its database and software programs available via the Internet to scholars worldwide. The collection of child language data gathered and transcribed to agreed-upon standards by researchers around the globe is accompanied by a set of software programs nicknamed CLAN. With CLAN, researchers have explored the vast resources of the CHILDES database and have made a major impact on the ways in which research into first-language acquisition is carried out. (For more information about CHILDES or for access to the files, see the CHILDES Web site, cited in the "Internet and Other Resources" section at the end of this chapter.)

Besides first-language corpora like those in the CHILDES project, corpora of second-language learners are now being compiled. They too give promise of providing researchers with previously unimagined access to high-quality data in great abundance. For example, the compilers of the *Longman Active Study Dictionary of English* relied on the "Longman Learner's Corpus of Students' English" to write over 250 new usage notes.

Computers have for some decades been used in language laboratories to help students studying foreign languages. An entire field has sprung up that goes by the nickname of CALL, which is an acronym for computer assisted language learning. Although you may not be familiar with the acronym, you are almost certainly familiar with some of the language teaching methods that have been facilitated by CALL. Among the most familiar ways in which computers have assisted language learners are by making CD-ROMs available for listening to language lessons. Of course, in some sense CD-ROMs have simply replaced audiocassette recordings, but more importantly they enable much freer interaction with the foreign-language materials. They also enable multimedia language lessons, including not only audio but visual presentations. Programs that one can find on CD-ROM are sometimes accompanied by interactive teaching and testing.

Other uses of the computer are even more innovative, though not everyone is convinced of their efficacy. In one interesting application, CD-ROM audio programs are accompanied by voiceprints of native speakers and a microphone for use by the learner. Using the microphone and a relatively advanced speech recognition technology, learners of Spanish, German, French, and English, for example, can practice their pronunciation until it matches the pronunciations of the native speaker voice. (If you're interested in finding out more about these programs, you can search the Internet for "globalink," a company that already has such products in shops.)

There is no doubt that computers will enable researchers to test their hypotheses more efficiently and more definitively than has been possible before. There is also no doubt that microcomputer technologies are revolutionizing the way that learners can tackle a foreign language. What the future holds in these respects can hardly be imagined.

SUMMARY

- Children do not acquire their native language through instruction by adults or through mere imitation of what they hear adults say.

- While a child must receive some linguistic input in order to acquire language, input is not the sole factor and may not be the chief factor that accounts for the development of grammatical competence and the ability to produce and understand language.

- There is considerable evidence that children are born with the mental capacity to acquire language, probably with a disposition to acquire certain kinds of structures, and perhaps with additional specifications as to the kinds of grammar that are eligible for acquisition.

- Various stages of language acquisition can be identified, distinguished by the amount of content a child is able to express in an utterance vis-à-vis an adult's expression in equivalent circumstances.

- Even before children utter their first interpretable words, they use language socially, for example by engaging in turn-taking expressions with caregivers.

- Adopting a second-language variety—whether a standard variety of one's first language or a foreign language—is not merely an intellectual exercise but an experience fraught with emotional overtones.

- The study of a foreign language cannot be equated with the study of history or math because, more than understanding, it involves adapting to certain customs of a different social group.

- Human language is primarily a system of arbitrary signs rather than nonarbitrary signs, and this fact distinguishes human language from the communicative systems that animals use in their natural environment.

- Animal communication is more akin to a system of nonarbitrary signs.

- Humans are the only species that has evolved an innate ability to use language, but it is unclear to what extent animals (chimpanzees in particular) are able to learn human language in experimental settings.

- Some researchers claim that chimps are capable of learning and using sophisticated systems of arbitrary signs, but others conclude that language is the exclusive property of human beings.

EXERCISES

15-1. Provide a list of baby talk vocabulary in your language. Identify the kinds of referents baby talk vocabulary has, the lexical categories most frequently represented, and the phonological form of such vocabulary. If there are different first languages represented in your class, compare the characteristics of baby talk terms cross-linguistically as to kinds of referents, lexical categories, and phonological form.

15-2. a. Explain in what ways the use of personal names like *Baby* and *Mommy* could be easier for a young child to perceive and analyze than personal pronouns like *I* and *you.*
   b. Explain in what ways the use of content words (nouns, verbs, adjectives) could make baby talk easier for a child to analyze and understand than function words such as conjunctions and articles.

15-3. Tape-record a brief passage of talk between an adult or older child and a young child. Transcribe forty-five seconds of the recorded talk and identify an example of each feature of baby talk discussed in this chapter; organize your list into features of phonology, lexicon, syntax, and discourse. (*Hint:* Television shows for children may provide the readiest access to such samples.)

15-4. On the basis of what you know about overgeneralizations of morphological rules, what forms might you predict children to use for each of the adult words below? In each case identify the rule that is being overgeneralized.

Verbs				*Nouns*	*Adjectives*	*Pronouns*
threw	told	took	hurt	geese	better	I
ate	came	bled	broke	sheep (pl.)	beautiful	myself

15-5. The utterances below (taken, slightly adapted, from Fletcher [1985]) were spoken by an English child named Sophie on three separate days over the course of about a year. Examine them closely and characterize the progress of Sophie's language acquisition across the three occasions with respect to the following features:

possessive determiners (*my, your*)	yes-no questions
the copula BE (*is, are*)	prepositions
adverbs (*down, there*)	interrogative word order
declarative word order	negative sentences
clauses per utterance	information questions
auxiliary DO	auxiliaries other than DO
contractible copula	regular noun plurals

Example: Personal pronouns. Based on this sample, Sophie, at 2;4, displays second-person *you* and first-person singular *me; me* is used for both subject and oblique grammatical relations. At 3;0 *her* is used for subject and oblique relations. At 3;5, the adult forms *I, you,* and *we* occur as subjects, *me* as object, and *it* as subject and object, but *her* appears as the subject form instead of *she.*

Age Two Years, Four Months

(1) Me want your tea.
(2) Where's the doll house?
(3) Mary come me.
(4) Me want Daddy come down.
(5) That your turn.
(6) That's a mess.
(7) You play "Snakes and Ladders" me?

Age Three Years

(8) Shall me sit mon my legs?
(9) Can me put it in like that?
(10) That not go in there.
(11) Why did Hester be fast asleep?
(12) What this one called?
(13) What did her have wrong with her?
(14) What is that one called?
(15) Daddy didn't give me two in the end.

Age Three Years, Five Months

(16) This isn't a piano book.
(17) I don't know what to do.
(18) Where my corder?
(19) Can you take off my shoes?
(20) How did that broke?
(21) You won't let me play a guitar.

(22) If you do it like this, it won't come down.

(23) While Hester at school we can buy some sweets.

(24) When her's at school I'll buy some sweeties.

(25) I want to ring up somebody and her won't be there tomorrow.

15-6. List four reasons that make it more difficult to gather language data from preschoolers than from adults, and identify several technological advances (such as the tape recorder) that can help overcome those difficulties and increase the data on which first-language acquisition research can be carried out.

15-7. Compare the nonnative adult English sentences on page 569 with the native English sentences of the child Sophie given in Exercise 15-5 above. List as many features as you can that are shared by both sets of data; list as many features as you can that belong only to one set or the other. Which features seem easier for the young Sophie to learn than for the adult nonnative speaker, and which seem easier for the nonnative speaker than for Sophie? What explanation can you offer for why certain features might be harder for Sophie or harder for the nonnative speaker to learn?

15-8. Most linguists would claim that animal languages are fundamentally different from human languages. Identify three significant ways in which animal language and human language differ, and give an argument for each that supports (or denies) its status as a fundamental difference.

INTERNET AND OTHER RESOURCES

- **CHILDES: http://poppy.psy.cmu.edu/childes/index.html**
  A rich source of information about research in child language acquisition, this Web site also offers data and software.
- **LTG Helpdesk: http://www.ltg.ed.ac.uk/helpdesk/faq/index.html**
  A useful Web site providing a series of frequently asked questions (FAQ) and answers as well as many links to a variety of language technology projects. Among the FAQs: Does anyone know of a corpus containing data on second-language learning? Can you tell me where to find Arabic texts? Persian texts? Do you have any information on automatic translation software? What Web-based resources are there for learning of natural languages?
- **The Sensory Basis of the Honeybee's Dance Language: http://www.sciam.com/0694issue/0694kirchner.html**
  An interesting Scientific American Web site offering the latest information about the language of honeybees.

Video Recordings

- **"Acquiring the Human Language: 'Playing the Language Game' "**
  One of four videos in *The Human Language Series,* an award-winning set of videos originally broadcast on PBS in 1995. This fifty-five-minute video explores

how children seem to acquire language spontaneously and without instruction. It asks, "Do people imitate those around them or is grammar inherited?" (Available for rent or purchase from Transit Media, 22-D Hollywood Avenue, Ho-Ho-Kus, NJ 07423/Tel. (800) 343-5540.)

- **"The Human Language Evolves: 'With and without Words' "**
  Part of the same series as the previous entry, an excellent fifty-five-minute video that explores the reasons human beings acquired language while chimpanzees and other species did not; includes fascinating discussion of animal and human gestures. (Available for rent or purchase from Transit Media, as above.)

- **"Baby Talk"**
  An interesting and informative video about first-language acquisition beginning even in the womb, produced by NOVA for public television and first broadcast in 1985; available for rent in video stores.

- **"Secret of the Wild Child"**
  An Emmy-winning video in the NOVA series; explores the troubled history of Genie. You can get NOVA videos from many video rental stores. For information about purchasing NOVA videos, contact WGBH:NOVA Videos/P.O. Box 2284/South Burlington, VT 05407-2284/Tel. (800) 255-WGBH. Or visit WGBH's Web site at http://www.pbs.org/wgbh/nova/novastore.html. To read an online transcript of this video, visit http://www.pbs.org/plweb-cgi/fastweb?search and click on "Secret of the Wild Child."

- **"English-Speaking World"**
  From *The Story of English* series with host Robert MacNeil, this video discusses English around the world and offers insight into instrumental motivations for second-language acquisition.

- **"Signs of the Apes, Songs of the Whales"**
  Part of the NOVA Video Library, this WGBH-BBC coproduction looks at the chimpanzee Washoe and her use of American Sign Language, as well as other apes, and dolphins, sea lions, and whales. (Released by Time-Life Video in 1984.)

SUGGESTIONS FOR FURTHER READING

- **Gerry T. M. Altmann. 1997.** *The Ascent of Babel: An Exploration of Language, Mind, and Understanding* (Oxford: Oxford UP). Written by a psychologist, this wide-ranging treatment of the cognitive aspects of first-language acquisition, though written in nontechnical language, requires some effort but is worth it.

- **Roger Brown. 1973.** *A First Language: The Early Stages* (Cambridge, MA: Harvard UP). An accessible classic, now available in paperback. Our examples of adult expansions of children's utterances and the list of fourteen morphemes ordered by sequence of acquisition come from this book.

- **Jean Berko Gleason, ed. 1989.** *The Development of Language,* 2nd ed. (Columbus: Merrill). A good next step after the present chapter, with separate chapters on phonology, syntax, semantics, and pragmatics, among others.

- **Alison J. Elliot. 1981.** *Child Language*   (Cambridge: Cambridge UP). Another good follow-up to the present chapter; highly accessible.

- **Rod Ellis. 1986.** *Understanding Second Language Acquisition* (Oxford: Oxford UP). An accessible and comprehensive textbook about how second languages are acquired.

- **Wolfgang Klein. 1986.** *Second Language Acquisition* (Cambridge: Cambridge UP). An accessible and comprehensive treatment of second-language acquisition.

- **Philip Lieberman. 1998.** *Eve Spoke: Human Language and Human Evolution* (New York: W. W. Norton). A brief, accessible introduction to the relationship between evolution and language.

- **Robert E. Owens, Jr. 1996.** *Language Development: An Introduction.* 4th ed. (Boston: Allyn and Bacon). A detailed, accessible treatment attending to both social and psychological concerns.

Advanced Reading

The most comprehensive treatment of first-language acquisition is in the set of articles in Fletcher and MacWhinney (1995). In some instances, these chapters may rely on more background than students who have read only *LISU* will possess, but they are useful overviews for instructors. Chapter 4 of Slobin (1979) is highly accessible. Goodluck (1991) provides a clear introduction to aspects of child language acquisition that bear closely on current grammatical theory.

Curtiss (1977) recounts the story of Genie, the child who received virtually no language input. Schieffelin and Ochs (1986) contains fascinating descriptions of socialization into linguistic and social roles in diverse cultures, including those of Samoa, Papua New Guinea, Lesotho (in southern Africa), and Japan. Andersen (1990) describes preschoolers' mastery over the registers associated with social roles such as father, mother, and child in middle-class American homes, as well as teacher and doctor. The socialization of children into gender roles is explored in Swann (1992). Gleason (1980) describes observations of adults teaching children politeness rules for Halloween trick-or-treating, an example of consciously prescriptive input. Slobin (1985) provides a wealth of information on language acquisition around the globe. Peters (1983) investigates the strategies that children use to analyze linguistic input and ways in which baby talk may help that process.

Wanner and Gleitman (1982) lays out the state of knowledge in language acquisition from diverse vantage points; we have relied for some of our discussion on the overview chapter by the editors and on Slobin's chapter, "Universal and Particular in the Acquisition of Language." Ingram (1989), on which we have relied for the stages of phonological acquisition, offers detailed discussion of the research on first-language acquisition. Fletcher (1985) contains four samples of Sophie's language at six-month intervals between 2;6 and 4;0; we have borrowed quite a few examples from these transcriptions. Our discussion of vocabulary acquisition follows M. C. Templin's *Certain Language Skills,* as reported in Miller (1977).

For second-language acquisition, Krashen and Terrell (1983) presents an integrated approach emphasizing naturalistic ways of experiencing comprehensible input. Ryan and Giles (1982) discuss the empirical study of language attitudes and address the role of attitudes in second-language acquisition. Gardner and Lambert (1972) discuss attitudes and motivation in second-language acquisition.

Ranging from the popular to the technical, sources on animal communication abound. A useful survey can be found in Premack (1985), in which the chimpanzee Sarah is discussed. Von Frisch (1967) reports his findings on the dance language of bees. The Gardners (1971; 1974; 1978) compare Washoe's acquisition patterns to those of children. Vicki's attempts to speak are described in Hayes and Hayes (1952), while Terrace (1979) gives an account of the Nim Chimpsky project. Relevant to the study of animal language are Lieberman (1975; 1984), which offer fascinating hypotheses about how humans evolved the ability to speak; Chapter 10 ("Apes and Children") of the 1984 work provides a good summary of research on chimpanzees to that time.

REFERENCES

Andersen, Elaine Slosberg. 1990. *Speaking with Style: The Sociolinguistic Skills of Children* (London: Routledge).

Curtiss, Susan. 1977. *Genie: A Psycholinguistic Study of a Modern-day "Wild Child"* (New York: Academic).

Fletcher, Paul. 1985. *A Child's Learning of English* (London: Blackwell).

Fletcher, Paul, and Brian MacWhinney. 1995. *The Handbook of Child Language* (Cambridge, MA: Blackwell).

Gardner, Beatrice T., and R. Allan Gardner. 1971. "Two-Way Communication with an Infant Chimpanzee," in A. M. Shrier and F. Stollnitz, eds., *Behavior of Nonhuman Primates,* vol. 4 (New York: Academic).

Gardner, Beatrice T., and R. Allan Gardner. 1974. "Comparing the Early Utterances of Child and Chimpanzee," in Anne D. Pick, ed., *Minnesota Symposia on Child Language* (Minneapolis: U of Minnesota P), pp. 3–23.

Gardner, R. Allan, and Beatrice T. Gardner. 1978. "Comparative Psychology and Language Acquisition," *Annals of the New York Academy of Science,* 309: 37–76.

Gardner, Robert C., and Wallace E. Lambert. 1972. *Attitudes and Motivation in Second-Language Learning* (Rowley, MA: Newbury House).

Gleason, Jean Berko. 1980. "The Acquisition of Social Speech: Routines and Politeness Formulas," in Howard Giles, W. Peter Robinson, and Philip M. Smith, eds., *Language: Social Psychological Perspectives* (New York: Academic).

Goodluck, Helen. 1991. *Language Acquisition: A Linguistic Introduction* (Oxford: Blackwell).

Hayes, Keith, and Catherine Hayes. 1952. "Imitation in a Home-Raised Chimpanzee," *Journal of Comparative and Physiological Psychology,* 45: 450–459.

Ingram, David. 1989. *First Language Acquisition: Method, Description, and Explanation* (Cambridge: Cambridge UP).

Krashen, Stephen D., and Tracy D. Terrell. 1983. *The Natural Approach: Language Acquisition in the Classroom* (Hayward, CA: Alemany).

Lieberman, Philip. 1975. *On the Origins of Language: An Introduction to the Evolution of Human Speech* (New York: Macmillan).

Lieberman, Philip. 1984. *The Biology and Evolution of Language* (Cambridge, MA: Harvard UP).

Miller, George A. 1977. *Spontaneous Apprentices: Children and Language* (New York: Seabury).

Peters, Ann M. 1983. *The Units of Language Acquisition* (Cambridge: Cambridge UP).

Premack, David. 1985. *Gavagai! On the Future History of the Animal Language Controversy* (Cambridge, MA: MIT P).

Ryan, Ellen Bouchard, and Howard Giles, eds. 1982. *Attitudes towards Language Variation: Social and Applied Contexts* (London: Edward Arnold).

Schieffelin, Bambi B., and Elinor Ochs, eds. 1986. *Language Socialization across Cultures* (Cambridge: Cambridge UP).

Slobin, Dan I. 1979. *Psycholinguistics,* 2nd ed. (Glenview, IL: Scott Foresman).

Slobin, Dan I., ed. 1985. *The Crosslinguistic Study of Language Acquisition.* 2 vols. (Hillsdale, NJ: Erlbaum).

Swann, Joan. 1992. *Girls, Boys and Language* (Oxford: Blackwell).

Terrace, Herbert S. 1979. *Nim: A Chimpanzee Who Learned Sign Language* (The Hague: Mouton).

Von Frisch, Karl. 1967. *The Dance Language and Orientation of Bees,* trans. Leigh E. Chadwick (Cambridge, MA: Harvard UP).

Wanner, Eric, and Lila R. Gleitman, eds. 1982. *Language Acquisition: The State of the Art* (Cambridge: Cambridge UP).

GLOSSARY

⌐

This Glossary characterizes important terms used in this book. When first discussed in the text, such terms are printed in **boldface** to indicate their importance. Within the Glossary, *italicized* terms with an asterisk have their own entry. For further discussion of a term, consult the index on pages 597–607.

Absolute universal   A linguistic pattern at play in all languages of the world without exception. Example: "Any language with voiced stops also has voiceless stops."

Accent   The pronunciation features of any spoken *variety*.

Acronym   An abbreviation formed by combining the initials of an expression into a pronounceable word. Examples: *NATO, radar, yuppy, scuba* (but not *USA, UK, EU, UN, PC, A.M., ABC, BBC, ATM,* whose pronunciations merely voice the names of the letters, as in B-B-C).

Adjacency pair   A set of two consecutive, ordered turns that "go together" in a conversation, such as question/answer sequences and greeting/greeting exchanges.

Adjective   A lexical category of words that serve semantically to specify the attributes of nouns (as in *tall* ships) and that can represent degrees of comparison morphologically (*taller*) or syntactically (*most beautiful*); adjectives can have *attributive* function (*those tall* ships) or *predicative* function (*those ships are tall*).

Adposition   A cover term for *prepositions* and *postpositions*.

Adverb   A lexical class with wide-ranging functions and no inflections. Many English adverbs are derived from adjectives with the *derivational morpheme* -LY (as in *suddenly, quickly* from *sudden, quick*), but the most common adverbs have no distinguishing marks (*soon, very, today*).

Affective meaning   Information conveyed about the attitudes and emotions of the language users toward the content or context of their expression; together with *social meaning*, affective meaning is sometimes called *connotation*.

Affix   A *bound morpheme* that attaches to a root or stem *morpheme* (called the *root* or *stem*). *Prefixes* and *suffixes* are the most common types of affixes in the world's languages; less common are *infixes* and *circumfixes*.

Affricate   A sound produced when air is built up by a complete closure of the oral tract at some *place of articulation* and then released and continued like a *fricative*; also called a *stop fricative*. Examples: English [č] (IPA [tʃ]), as in *chin*; English [ǰ] (IPA [dʒ]) as in *gin*; German [ts] as in *Zeit* 'time.'

Agreement   The marking of a word (as with an *affix*) to indicate its grammatical relationship to another word in the sentence. Thus, a verb that *agrees* with its *subject* in *person* and *number* has a form that indicates that relationship; an adjective may agree with a noun in *gender*, *number*, and *case*.

Allomorph An alternant realization (i.e., phonological form) of a morpheme in a particular linguistic environment. For example, the English 'PLURAL' morpheme has three allomorphs: [əz] (as in *buses*), [z] (*twigs*), and [s] (*cats*).

Allophone A phonetic realization (i.e., a pronunciation) of a *phoneme in a particular phonological environment. Example: in English, unaspirated [p] and *aspirated [pʰ] are allophones of the phoneme /p/, and they occur in *complementary distribution.

Alphabet A writing system in which, ideally, each graphic sign represents a distinctive sound (i.e., a *phoneme) of the language.

Alveolar A sound articulated at the alveolar ridge, the bony ridge just behind and above the upper teeth.

Alveo-palatal A *place of articulation in the oral cavity between the alveolar ridge and the palate. Example: The English sound [š] (IPA [ʃ]) represented by <sh> in *shoe* is articulated in the alveo-palatal region.

Ambiguous A term used to characterize an expression that can be interpreted in more than one way as a consequence of having more than one *constituent structure (*John or Jack and Bill*) or more than one *referential meaning (river <u>bank</u>, savings <u>bank</u>).

Antonymy A term used in *lexical semantics to denote opposite meanings; word pairs with opposite meanings are said to be *antonymous*, as with *wet* and *dry*.

Appropriateness conditions Conventions that regulate the interpretation under which an *utterance serves as a particular *speech act, such as a question, promise, or invitation.

Approximant A sound produced when one articulator approaches another but the vocal tract is not sufficiently narrowed to create the audible friction that typically characterizes a *consonant. Examples: [w], [y], [r], [l].

Argot The specialized vocabulary of a group, often an occupational or recreational group; unlike *slang, argot is not limited to situations of extreme informality.

Argument A noun phrase occurring with a verb as part of a proposition. For example, in *Alice washed the car* the verb *wash* has two arguments, a *subject (*Alice*) and a *direct object (*the car*). (Some analysts do not treat subjects as arguments.)

Aspect A grammatical category of verbs, marking the way in which a situation described by the verb takes place in time, for example as continuous, repetitive, or instantaneous.

Aspirated A term for sounds produced with an accompanying puff of air; represented in phonetic transcription by a following raised [ʰ].

Assimilation A phonological process whereby a sound becomes phonetically similar (or identical) to a neighboring sound. Examples: In Korean, underlying /p/ is pronounced as [b] between vowels; that is, /p/ assimilates to the voicing of the neighboring vowels.

Attributive adjective An adjective that is syntactically part of the noun phrase whose head it modifies (*a <u>spooky</u> house*); distinguished from a *predicative adjective (*The house is <u>spooky</u>*).

Auxiliary verb A verb used with (or instead of) the main verb to carry certain kinds of grammatical information, such as *tense and *aspect. In English, the auxiliary verb is inverted with the *subject in yes/no questions (<u>Can</u> *Lou fail?*) and carries the negative element in contractions (*Lou <u>can't</u> sing*).

Bilabial A *place of articulation involving both lips; a sound produced there.

Bilingualism The state of having *competence in more than one language.

Bound morpheme A *morpheme that cannot stand alone as a word. Examples: -MENT (as in *establishment*), -ER (*painter*), and 'PLURAL' (*zebras*). See *free morpheme.

Case A grammatical category associated with nouns and pronouns, indicating their grammatical relationship to other elements in the clause, often the verb. Example: The pronoun *I* is marked for common case, *me* for objective case, while *book* is said to be unmarked or to be marked for common case. In some languages, adjectives agree in case with nouns.

Circumfix A discontinuous morpheme that combines a *prefix and *suffix in a single *morpheme* occurring on both ends of a root or stem.

Clause A constituent unit of syntax consisting of a verb with its *argument noun phrases; a clause can stand alone as a simple sentence or function as a *constituent of another clause.

Click A *stop *consonant defined by its *manner of articulation and pronounced at various *places of articulation; clicks such as the alveolar click used in English to express disapproval as in *tsk-tsk* or *tut-tut* function as phonemes in some Bantu languages, such as Zulu and Xhosa.

Cognates Words or *morphemes that have developed from a single, historically earlier source. Example: English *father*, German *Vater*, Spanish *padre*, and Gothic *fadar* are cognates because all of them have developed from the same reconstructed Proto-Indo-European word (*pǝter*). The term *cognates* is also used of languages that have a common historical ancestor, as with English, Russian, German, Persian, and the other *Indo-European* languages.

Collocation Word pairs or sets that habitually co-occur (i.e., occur near one another) in *texts.

Communicative competence See *competence.

Comparative reconstruction A method used in historical linguistics to uncover vocabulary and structures of an ancestor language by drawing inferences from the evidence remaining in several daughter languages. See also *cognates and *correspondence set.

Competence The ability to produce and assign meaning to grammatical sentences is called *grammatical competence*; the ability to produce and interpret utterances appropriate to their context of use is called *communicative competence*.

Complementary distribution A pattern of distribution of two or more sounds that do not occur in the same position within words in a given language. Example: In English, [pʰ] does not occur where [p] occurs (and vice versa).

Complex sentence A sentence consisting of a matrix *clause and at least one embedded (i.e., subordinate) clause.

Conjugation See *paradigm.

Conjunction A closed class of words that serve to link clauses or phrases; coordinating conjunctions conjoin expressions of the same status, as with clauses (*She went <u>but</u> he stayed*) or noun phrases (*Alice <u>and</u> I*); subordinating conjunctions embed one clause into another (*Leave <u>when</u> you're ready*).

Consonant A speech sound produced by partial or complete closure of part of the vocal tract, thus obstructing the airflow and creating audible friction. Consonants are described in terms of *voicing, *place of articulation, and *manner of articulation. Abbreviated C.

Constituent A syntactic unit that functions as part of a larger unit within a sentence; typical constituent types are verb phrase, noun phrase, prepositional phrase, and *clause.

Constituent structure The linear and hierarchical organization of the words of a sentence into syntactic units.

Content Information conveyed or communicated by linguistic *expression as interpreted in a particular *context.

Content word A word whose primary function is to describe entities, ideas, qualities, and states of being in the world; *nouns, *verbs, *adjectives, and *adverbs are content words; content words are contrasted with *function words.

Context One of three main elements (context, *expression, *meaning) in a speech situation. Context typically refers to those aspects of a speech situation that affect the expression and enable an interpretation of the context.

Contractions Spoken or written expressions that represent a fusion of two or more words in a single word. Examples: *can't/cannot; she'll/she will; could've/could have; wanna/want to; gonna/going to.*

Contrastive A term used in *semantics of a noun phrase that is marked as being in opposition to another noun phrase in the same *discourse.

Contrastive analysis A method of analyzing languages for instructional purposes whereby a native language and target language are compared with a view to establishing points of difference likely to cause difficulties for learners.

Converseness The term for a reciprocal relationship between two words, as in *husband* and *wife* or *buy* and *sell*.

Cooperative principle Four maxims that describe how language users cooperate in producing and understanding utterances in context: *quantity, quality, relevance, orderliness.*

Coordinate sentence A sentence that contains at least two *clauses, neither of which functions as a *constituent of the other. Example: *John went to England, and Mary went to France.*

Coordinating conjunction A category of *function words that serve to conjoin expressions of the same status, such as *clause (*He spoke and I wept*), *adverb (*slowly but surely*), or noun (*Thelma and Louise*).

Corpus A representative collection of texts, usually in machine-readable form and including information about the situation in which each text originated, such as the speaker or author, addressee, or audience.

Corpus linguistics The activities involved in compiling and using a *corpus to investigate natural language use.

Correspondence set A set of sounds in different languages, all of which derive from a single sound in a historically earlier language.

Creole A contact language, a former *pidgin, that has "acquired" native speakers.

Cuneiform A written sign developed by the Sumerians and Akkadians in the Middle East around 3000 B.C.; characterized by the wedgelike shape that results from its being written on wet clay with a stylus.

Declension The term used for a noun *paradigm.

Deep structure See *underlying structure.

Definite A noun phrase that is marked to indicate that the speaker believes the addressee can identify its referent; contrast with *indefinite*. In English, definiteness and indefiniteness can be marked by the choice of determiner (e.g., *the* versus *a*).

Degree A grammatical category associated with the extent of comparison for *adjectives and *adverbs; positive degree (as in *speedy*); comparative degree (*speedier* or *more speedy*); superlative degree (*speediest* or *most speedy*).

Deixis The marking of the orientation or position of entities and situations with respect to certain points of reference such as the place (*here/there*) and time (*now/then*) of utterance.

Derivation   In morphology designates a process whereby one lexical item is transformed into another one with a related meaning but belonging to a different lexical class. Example: the adverb *slowly* is derived from *slow* (an adjective) by suffixing the *derivational morpheme* -LY.

Derivational morpheme   A *morpheme* that serves to derive a word of one class or meaning from a word of another class or meaning. Examples: -MENT (as in *establishment*) derives the noun from the verb *establish*; RE- (*repaint*) changes the meaning of the verb *paint* to 'paint again.'

Dialect   A language variety characteristic of a particular social group; dialects can be characteristic of regional, ethnic, socioeconomic, or gender groups.

Diphthong   A vowel sound whose production requires the tongue to start in one place and move to another. Examples: the vowels in *lied*, *loud*, and *Lloyd*. See also *glide*.

Direct object   A kind of grammatical relation; one of two kinds of objects; the noun phrase in a *clause* that, together with the verb, usually forms the verb phrase *constituent*; the object NP is immediately dominated by the VP. Example: *She drove <u>a truck</u>*. See also *indirect object*.

Discourse   Spoken or written language use in particular social situations; discourse is a broader term than *text* in that it includes context and the intended and actual interpretations.

Etymon   The linguistic form from which a word or *morpheme* is historically derived.

Expression   Any bit of spoken, written, or signed language; the audible or visible aspect of language use that conveys particular *content* in a given *context*.

Family   See *language family*.

Flap   A *manner of articulation* produced by quickly flapping the tip of the tongue against some *place of articulation* on the upper surface of the vocal tract, commonly the *alveolar ridge*, as for <t> in the American pronunciation of *metal* [mɛɾəl].

Fossilization   A term used to refer to a final form of *interlanguage* that falls short of the target language; the stage of second-language acquisition where a learner has ceased making substantial progress toward the target language.

Free morpheme   A *morpheme* that can stand alone as a word. Examples: ZEBRA, PAINT, PRETTY, VERY. See *bound morpheme*.

Free variation   A term used to characterize *allophones* of a given *phoneme* that can occur in the same position in a word without altering the word's meaning, as in the final sound of the English word *step*, which can be released [p] or unreleased [p˺].

Fricative   A consonant sound made by passing a continuous stream of air through a narrowed passage in the vocal tract thereby causing turbulence, such as that created between the lower lip and the upper teeth in the production of [f] and [v].

Function words   Words such as determiners and *conjunctions* whose primary role is to mark grammatical relationships between *content words* or structures such as *phrases* and *clauses*.

Gender   A system in which all the nouns of a language fall into distinct classes. Example: German has a gender system of three noun classes (masculine, feminine, and neuter) whose inflections and associated determiners and *adjectives* vary in form for *number* and *case* in *agreement* with the gender class of the noun.

Given information   *Context* already introduced into a *discourse* and therefore presumed to be at the forefront of a hearer's mind; also called old information.

Glottis   A narrow aperture between two folds of muscle (the vocal cords) in the *larynx*.

Glide   A transition from a vowel of one quality to the vowel of another quality. In [iᵊ], the superscript schwa represents a glide from the high front position of [i] to the mid central position of [ə]. Glides can be offglides, with the peak on the first element (as in [iᵊ]), or onglides, with the peak on the second element (as in certain pronunciations of *spoon* [ɪᵘ]). See also *diphthong*.

Grammatical competence   See *competence*.

Grammatical relation   The syntactic role that a noun phrase plays in its *clause* (for example, as *subject* or *direct object*).

Homonymy   The term used for the state of having identical expression but different meanings (*book a flight* and *buy a book*); *homophonous* is sometimes used with the related sense of 'sounding alike' but not necessarily having the same written form (*see* and *sea*) or meaning.

Homophony   The term used in semantic analysis to refer to words that are pronounced alike but have different meanings, as in *two, to, too*; *see, sea*.

Hyponym   A term whose *referent* is included in the referent of another term. Example: *blue* is a hyponym of *color*; *sister* is a hyponym of *sibling*.

Iconic sign   See *representational sign*.

Illocution   The intention that a speaker or writer has in producing a particular utterance. Example: The illocution of the utterance *Can you pass the salt?* is a request that the salt be passed and not (as the structure would indicate) an inquiry about the addressee's *ability* to pass the salt.

Implicational universal   A universal rule of the form "If condition P is satisfied, then conclusion Q holds."

Indefinite   See *definite*.

Indirect object   One of two *grammatical relations* known as objects, the other being a *direct object*. Indirect objects usually occur in English before the direct object (*He gave the clerk a rose*).

Indirect speech act   An *utterance* whose *locution* (or literal meaning) and *illocution* (or intended meaning) are different. Example: *Can you pass the salt?* is literally a yes/no question but is usually uttered as a request or polite directive for action.

Indo-European   A *language family* all of whose members are descendants of an ancestral language called Proto-Indo-European, spoken probably in Central Asia about 5,000 years ago.

Infinitive   The basic form of a verb, expressed in English sometimes with the particle *to*, as in *to see*.

Infix   A *morpheme* that is inserted within another morpheme.

Inflectional morpheme   A *bound morpheme* that creates variant forms of a word to mark its syntactic function in a sentence. Examples: The suffix *-s* added to a *verb* (as in *paints*) marks the verb as agreeing with a third-person singular *subject*; *-er* (*taller*) marks *adjectives* for comparative *degree*.

Information structure   The level of structure at which certain elements in a sentence are highlighted or backgrounded according to their prominence in the discourse. See also *pragmatics*.

Instrumental motivation   A term used for the kind of motivation one has in acquiring a second language so as to be able to use it for any purpose other than becoming a participating member of the social community that speaks the language.

Integrative motivation   A term used for the kind of motivation one has in acquiring a second language in order to become a socially functioning member of the community speaking that language.

Interdental   A *place of articulation* between the upper and lower teeth. Also used of sounds produced at that place. Examples of the letter: <th> as in English *thin* [θ] and *then* [ð].

Interlanguage   The term used for the form of a second language that a learner has internalized at any point in the acquisition process and which therefore underlies the learner's spontaneous utterances in the target language.

Intransitive verb   A verb that does not take a *direct object*. Examples: *She smiled. Joyce died in Zurich.*

Isogloss   The geographical boundary marking the limit of the regional distribution of a particular word, pronunciation, or usage.

Language family   A group of languages that have all developed from a single ancestral language.

Larynx   The part of the windpipe that houses the vocal cords; also called the voice box or Adam's apple.

Lexical field   A set of words with an identifiable semantic affinity. Example: *angry, sad, happy, exuberant, depressed.*

Lexical item   A unit in the *lexicon*; the notion of lexical item includes all inflected forms; for example, *child, child's, children,* and *children's* constitute the lexical item CHILD.

Lexical semantics   The branch of *semantics* that deals with word meaning.

Lexical variety   An index of the number of different words in a text, usually expressed as a fraction of the number of different words divided by the number of running words. Example: *He told her he loved her* would have an index of 0.66, representing four different words in a total of six running words.

Lexicon   The list of all words and *morphemes* stored in a native speaker's memory; this internalized dictionary includes all nonpredictable information about *lexical items.*

Lingua franca   A language *variety* used for communication among groups of people who do not otherwise share a common language, as English is the lingua franca of the international scientific community.

Linguistic repertoire   The set of language *varieties* (including *registers* and *dialects*) used in the speaking and writing practices of a speech community; also called verbal repertoire.

Locution   The literal meaning of an *utterance*. Example: The locution of the utterance *Can you close the window?* is a question about the hearer's ability to close the window.

Logographic writing   Writing in which each sign represents a word. Examples: <8> 'eight' and <$> 'dollar' are logographic signs, as are Chinese characters and Japanese kanji.

Manner of articulation   How the airstream is obstructed in the vocal tract in the production of a sound.

Marked   The elements of a *lexical field* with less basic meaning. Usually, more marked elements have more precise meanings than less marked elements, can be described in terms of less marked elements, and are less frequent in natural speech. Example: *cocker spaniel* is more marked than *dog.*

Meaning   The term used to refer to the senses and referents of expressions, including words, phrases, clauses, and sentences.

Metaphor   An extension of a word's use beyond its primary meaning to include referents that bear some similarity to the word's primary referent, as in <u>*eye*</u> *of a needle*.

Minimal pair   A pair of words that differ by only a single sound in the same position. Examples: *look/took*; *spill/still*; *keep/coop*.

Modality   A grammatical category of **verbs* marking speakers' attitudes toward the status of their assertions as factual (indicative), hypothetical (subjunctive), and so on; also called *mood*. While some languages mark modality by inflection on the verb, English uses *modal* verbs (e.g., *must*, *may*, and *can*, as in *must begin*, *may arrive*, *can talk*), which lack typical morphological inflections such as *-s* and *-ing*.

Modes   Channels of linguistic expression: speaking, writing, and signing.

Mood   See **modality*.

Morpheme   The smallest unit of language that carries meaning or serves a grammatical function. A morpheme can be a word, as with *zebra* and *paint*, or part of a word, as in *zebras* and *painted*, which contain two morphemes each (ZEBRA and 'PLURAL'; PAINT and 'PAST TENSE').

Nasals   A class of sounds (including the consonants [m] and [n]) produced by lowering the velum and allowing air to pass out of the vocal tract through the nasal cavity.

Nativization   The process through which a speech community adopts another speech community's language as its own and modifies the structure of that new language, thus developing a new dialect that becomes characteristic of the adopting community.

Natural class   A set of speech sounds that can all be characterized by one or a few phonetic features and that includes all the sounds of a given language that are characterized by those phonetic features. Example: /p t k/ form the natural class of voiceless stops in English because the class includes all the voiceless stops in the language and no other sounds.

Neutralized   The localized loss of a distinction between two **phonemes* that have identical **allophones* in a certain environment. Example: In American English, /t/ in *metal* and /d/ in *medal* are neutralized in that both are pronounced [ɾ] (i.e., intervocalically following a stressed syllable).

New information   **Content* introduced into a **discourse* for the first time. See **given information*.

Noun   A lexical category of words that function syntactically as heads of noun phrases and semantically as **referring expressions*; nouns can be characterized morphologically by certain inflections and syntactically by their distribution in phrases and clauses; in traditional terms, a noun is defined semantically as the name of a person, place, or thing.

Number   A grammatical category associated with **nouns* and **pronouns* and indicating something about the quantity of referents. Example: *car* and *he* are marked for singular number, while *cars* and *they* are marked for plural number. Number can also be marked on verbs, usually in **agreement* with subjects, as in singular *He* <u>*sleeps*</u>, plural *They* <u>*sleep*</u>.

Object   See **direct object*.

Oblique   A noun phrase whose **grammatical relation* in a **clause* is other than **subject*, **direct object*, or **indirect object*; oblique usually marks semantic categories such as location or time.

Obstruent   A cover term for **stops*, **fricatives*, and **affricates*, three classes of consonant sounds that impede or obstruct the airflow by constricting the vocal passage.

Offglide   See **glide*.

Orthography   A system of spelling used to achieve a match between the sound system of a language and the alphabet representing it.

Paradigm   The set of forms constituting the inflectional variants of a particular word; see also *declension* and *conjugation*.

Participle   A term used to refer to -ING and -ED/-EN forms of the verb, as in *is walking*, *had kicked* or *had been stolen*. (It does not refer to past-tense forms as in *they walked* or *she swam*); traditional terminology calls the -ING form the present or progressive participle and the -ED/EN form the past or perfective or passive participle.

Person   A grammatical category associated principally with pronouns marking reference to the speaker (first person), the addressee (second person), a third party (third person), or a combination of these; verbs in a clause are sometimes marked for person *agreement*, usually with their *subject*.

Phoneme   A distinctive and significant structural element in the sound system of a language. A phoneme is an abstract element (defined by a set of phonetic features) that can have alternative manifestations (called *allophones*) in particular phonological environments. Example: The English phoneme /p/ has several allophones, including aspirated [pʰ], unreleased [p̚], and unaspirated [p].

Phonetics   The study of sounds made in the production of human speech.

Phonological rule   A rule that specifies the *allophones* of a *phoneme* and their distribution in a particular language.

Phonotactic constraints   Rules that specify the structure of *syllables* permitted in a particular language.

Phrase   The term used to refer to syntactic *constituents* smaller than a *clause* and, usually, larger than a word—thus noun phrase, adjective phrase, prepositional phrase.

Phrase-structure rule   A rule that describes the composition of *constituents* in *underlying structure*; also called rewrite rule. Example: S → NP VP is a phrase-structure rule stating that a sentence is made up of a noun phrase and a verb phrase in that order.

Pictogram   A symbolic drawing that represents an object or idea independently of the word that refers to that object or idea. Example: highway signs that pictorially indicate dangerous curves or merging traffic without the use of words.

Pidgin   A contact language that develops in multilingual colonial situations, in which one language (commonly that of the colonizer) forms the base for a simple and usually unstable new variety; pidgins are restricted in use and not spoken natively by anyone.

Place of articulation   The location in the mouth cavity where the airstream is obstructed in the production of a sound. Example: *Alveolar* sounds such as [t] and [s] are produced by obstructing the airstream at the alveolar ridge.

Polysemy   The term used to refer to multiple meanings for a given word or sentence; a word with more than one meaning is said to be polysemic.

Possessor   A *grammatical relation* between two nouns that are closely associated, often by virtue of having a possessive relationship. Examples: <u>Luke's</u> harp, the <u>book's</u> cover, <u>arm's</u> length.

Postposition   A category of words that serve syntactically as heads of postpositional phrases and semantically to indicate a relationship between two entities; except that they follow their complements, postpositions are like prepositions. Examples: Japanese *Taroo <u>no</u>* 'of Taro' and *hasi <u>de</u>* 'with chopsticks.'

Pragmatics   The branch of linguistics that studies language use, in particular the relationship among *syntax*, *semantics*, and interpretation in light of the context of situation.

Predication   The part of a **clause* that makes a statement about a particular entity. Example: In the clause *Lou likes ice cream*, the predication made of Lou is *likes ice cream*.

Predicative adjective   An **adjective* that serves syntactically as a complement to the verb in a **clause* and predicates something of the **subject* (*The soup is <u>cold</u>*); contrasted with **attributive* adjective (*the <u>cold</u> soup*).

Prefix   An **affix* that attaches to the front of a word stem.

Preposition   A category of words that serve syntactically as heads of prepositional phrases and semantically to indicate a relationship between two entities. Examples: *<u>to</u> school*, *<u>with</u> liberty*, *<u>in</u> the spring*. See also **postpositions*.

Pronoun   A term used for several closed categories of words. Traditionally defined as taking the place of nouns (or more accurately noun phrases), personal pronouns, such as *it*, *me*, *he*, *she*, *they*, and *you*, are the most familiar type. Other types include relative pronouns (*who*, *whose*, *which*, *that*), demonstrative pronouns (*this*, *that*, *those*), interrogative pronouns (*who*, *which*, *whose*), and indefinite pronouns (*anyone*, *someone*).

Prosody   The term used to refer to variations in the volume, pitch, rhythm, and speed of speech.

Redundancy   The term used to refer to repeated information in a linguistic expression. Example: An expression like *those books* represents the plurality of the noun phrase in both its words, as contrasted with *the books*, which represents it only on the noun.

Reference   A semantic category through which language provides information about the relationship between noun phrases and their **referents*.

Referent   The real-world entity (person, object, notion, situation) referred to by a linguistic expression.

Referential   Said of a noun phrase that refers to a particular entity; *a good piano teacher* is referential in *Tom knows a good piano teacher* but not in *Tom wants to find a good piano teacher*.

Referential meaning   The meaning that an **expression* has by virtue of its ability to refer to an entity; referential meaning is contrasted with **social meaning* and **affective meaning* and is sometimes called denotation.

Referring expression   An **expression* that refers to an entity or situation.

Reflex   A term used in historical linguistics for a linguistic form that derives from an earlier form called its **etymon*; reflexes of the same etymon are called **cognates*.

Register   A language **variety* associated with a particular situation of use. Examples: baby talk, legalese.

Relative clause   A **clause* syntactically embedded in a noun phrase and semantically serving to modify a noun. The modified noun is the head of the relative clause. Example: In *This is the book that I told you about*, the relative clause *that I told you about* modifies the head *book*.

Repair   A sequence of turns in a conversation during which a previous **utterance* is edited, corrected, or clarified.

Repertoire   See **linguistic repertoire*.

Representational sign   A sign that is basically arbitrary but nevertheless bears some resemblance to its referent or some feature of its referent. Example: *III* 'three'; *trickle*, *meow*.

Semantic role   The way in which the **referent* of a noun phrase is involved in the situation described or represented by the **clause*, for example as agent, patient, or cause.

Semantics   The study of the systematic ways in which languages structure meaning, especially in words, phrases, and sentences.

Sibilant   A member of a set of *fricative sounds made by passing a continuous stream of air through a narrowed passage in the vocal tract, thereby causing hissing, such as that created between the blade of the tongue and the back of the *alveolar ridge in the production of [s] and [š] (IPA [ʃ]).

Sign   An indicator of something else, for example of an object or event, as smoke is a sign of fire and <7> is a sign of the number 'seven.' See also *representational sign.

Simple sentence   A sentence that contains only one *clause.

Slang   A language *variety used in situations of extreme informality, often with rebellious undertones or an intention of distancing its users from certain mainstream social values; *slang* also refers to particular expressions of extreme informality.

Social dialect   A language *variety characteristic of a social group, typically socioeconomic groups, gender groups, or ethnic groups, as distinct from regional groups.

Social meaning   Information that linguistic *expressions convey about the social character- istics of their producers and of the situation in which they are produced; together with *af- fective meaning, social meaning is sometimes called *connotation*.

Sonorant   A class of *consonant sounds comprising *nasals and liquids.

Speech act   An action carried out through language, such as promising, lying, and greeting.

Standard variety   The language variety that has been recorded in dictionaries and gram- mars and serves a speech community especially in its written and public functions.

Stop   A speech sound created when air is built up at a *place of articulation in the vocal tract and suddenly released through the mouth; sometimes called *oral stops* when nasals are ex- cluded.

Subcategorization   Information about the types of clause structure that each *verb permits in the verb phrase. For example, a verb may permit one or two noun phrases, or none; as in *He burned the rice*, *She sold him the book*, and *He fell*, respectively.

Subgroup   The term used to refer to a set of languages that belong to the same *language fam- ily and developed as a single language for a period of time after other subgroups had become separate languages. Examples: Romance and Germanic are subgroups of *Indo-European*; West Germanic is the subgroup of Germanic to which English belongs; also caled *branch*.

Subject   A noun phrase immediately dominated by S in a phrase structure.

Subordinating conjunction   A word that links clauses to one another in a noncoordinate role, thus marking the boundary between an embedded clause and its matrix clause; also called a subordinator. Example: *I think that he fell*.

Suffix   An *affix that attaches to the end of a word stem.

Surface form   A word's actual pronunciation; generated by the application of the *phono- logical rules of a language to the *underlying form; sometimes also said of sentences (see *underlying structure*).

Surface structure   The *constituent structure of a sentence after all applicable *transforma- tions have applied.

Syllabic writing   Writing in which each graphic *sign represents a *syllable rather than a word or a sound.

Syllable   A phonological unit consisting of one or more sounds, including a peak (or nu- cleus) that is usually a *vowel or *diphthong; frequent syllable types are CV and CVC.

Synonymous   The term used in *semantics to refer to words or sentences that mean the same thing.

Syntax The term used to refer to the structure of sentences and to the study of sentence structure.

Tense A category of the *verb that marks time reference, for example as past (*walked*) or present (*walk*).

Text A unitary stretch of *expression created in a real-world social situation; usually but not always longer than a sentence (*Smoking Not Permitted*; *Closed*; *Gesundheit*); more commonly used of written than of spoken or signed expression but applicable to any mode; sometimes used for a piece of text rather than an entire text. Examples: a novel, a personal letter, a classified advertisement, a screenplay, a song lyric, a scholarly or scientific article, a (transcribed) conversation.

Topic The main center of attention in a sentence.

Transformation A syntactic process (or rule) that changes one *constituent structure to another in a systematic way.

Transitive verb A verb that takes a *direct object, as in She <u>found</u> the book.

Trill A *manner of articulation characterized by the rapid vibrating of an articulator caused by air passing rapidly over it (but not including vocal cord vibration).

Turn A basic term in the analysis of conversation, which comprises a series of turns among interlocutors.

Typology A field of inquiry that seeks to classify the languages of the world into different types according to particular structural characteristics.

Underlying form The form of a *morpheme that is stored in the internalized *lexicon; sometimes also said of sentences (see *underlying structure).

Underlying structure The abstract structure of a sentence before any *transformations have applied; also called deep structure.

Universal A linguistic pattern at play in most or all of the world's languages. See also *absolute universal and *universal tendency.

Universal tendency A linguistic pattern at play in most, but not all, of the world's languages. Example: most (but not all) verb-final languages place adjectives before the nouns they modify.

Utterance *Expression produced in a particular context with a particular intention.

Variety Any language, *dialect, or *register.

Velar A *consonant sound whose *place of articulation is the velum, that is, a consonant produced by the tongue approaching or touching the roof of the mouth at the velum.

Verb A category of words that syntactically determine the structure of a *clause, especially with respect to noun phrases; that semantically express the action or state of being represented by a clause; and that morphologically can be marked for certain categories (not all of which are realized in English): *tense (present: *walk*/past: *walked*), *mood, *aspect (*walk*/*walking*), *person (first: *walk*/third: *walks*), and *number (singular: *walks*/plural: *walk*).

Voicing The vibration in the *larynx caused by air from the lungs passing through the vocal cords when they are partly closed; speech sounds are said to be *voiced* or *voiceless*.

Vowels One of two major classes of sounds (the other being *consonants); vowels are articulated without complete closure in the oral cavity and without sufficient narrowing to create the friction characteristic of consonants. Abbreviated V.

INDEX

＿

Separate indexes for languages, Internet sites, and videos follow this general index. Terms followed by an asterisk (*) are defined in the Glossary, on pages 585–596. The abbreviation "ex" following a number refers to an exercise.

INDEX OF LANGUAGES

INDEX OF INTERNET SITES

⌣

INDEX OF VIDEOS

⌣

ACKNOWLEDGMENTS

—

British Library. Figure 12-2: The Evolution of Cuneiform Writing from Pictograms, by Albertine Gaur, from *A History of Writing,* © 1984. Reprinted by permission.

Cambridge University Press. Figures 13-2 and 13-4: Cultural Areas in the Pacific; and The Settlement of Polynesia by John Terrell, from *Prehistory in the Pacific Islands: A Study of Variation in Language, Customs, and Human Biology,* © 1986. Reprinted by permission.

Harcourt Brace & Company. Figure 12-4: The Cherokee Syllabary, from *An Introduction to Descriptive Linguistics,* revised edition by Henry A. Gleason, copyright 1961 by Holt, Rinehart and Winston and renewed 1989 by H. A. Gleason Jr., reproduced by permission of the publisher.

Harvard University Press. Figures 11-10, 11-11, 11-22: Four maps, reprinted by permission of the publisher from *Dictionary of American Regional English* by Frederic G. Cassidy, Cambridge, Mass.: Harvard University Press. Copyright © 1985 by the President and Fellows of Harvard College.

Harvard University Press. Table 12-5: Vai Syllabary from *The Psychology of Literacy* by Sylvia Scribner and Michael Cole, Cambridge, Mass.: Harvard University Press, Copyright © 1981 by the President and Fellows of Harvard College.

Houghton Mifflin. Entries "husky" and "junior" from *The American Dictionary of the English Language, Third Edition.* Copyright © 1996 by Houghton Mifflin Company. Reproduced by permission from *The American Heritage Dictionary of the English Language, Third Edition.*

Kay Elemetrics Corporation. Figure 4-1: Sound Spectrogram of a Casual Utterance (Type B/65 Sonogram). Reprinted by permission.

New Guinea Motors. Figure 13-17: Publicity cartoon in Tok Pisin by Bob Browne.

University of Chicago Press. Figures 12-1 and 12-3: Aztec Inscription and Egyptian Hieroglyphics from *A Study of Writing* by Gelb, © 1963.